SORT OF SUPER

SORT OF SUPER

by Eric Gapstur

COLOR BY
DEARBHLA KELLY

ALADDIN
NEW YORK LONDON TORONTO SYDNEY NEW DELHI

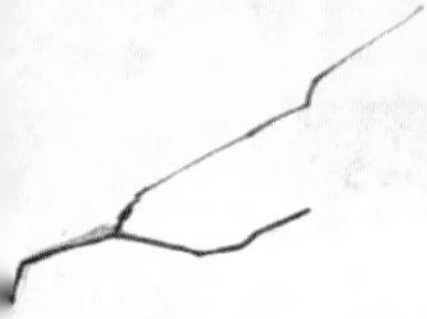

ALADDIN
An imprint of Simon & Schuster Children's Publishing Division
1230 Avenue of the Americas, New York, New York 10020
First Aladdin paperback edition March 2022
Copyright © 2022 by Eric Gapstur
Also available in an Aladdin hardcover edition.
For information about special discounts for bulk purchases, please contact
Simon & Schuster special sales at 1-866-506-1949 or business@simonandschuster.com.
The Simon & Schuster Speakers Bureau can bring authors to your live event.
For more information or to book an event contact the Simon & Schuster Speakers
Bureau at 1-866-248-3049 or visit our website at www.simonspeakers.com.
Color by Dearbhla Kelly
Book designed by Laura Lyn DiSiena and Eric Gapstur
The illustrations for this book were rendered in ink and colored digitally.
The text of this book was set in Gapstur and Gapstur Shouting.
Manufactured in China 1221 SCP
2 4 6 8 10 9 7 5 3 1
Library of Congress Control Number 2021940159
ISBN 978-1-5344-8029-2 (hc)
ISBN 978-1-5344-8028-5 (pbk)
ISBN 978-1-5344-8030-8 (ebook)

TO MICHELLE,
LIAM, AND HENRY

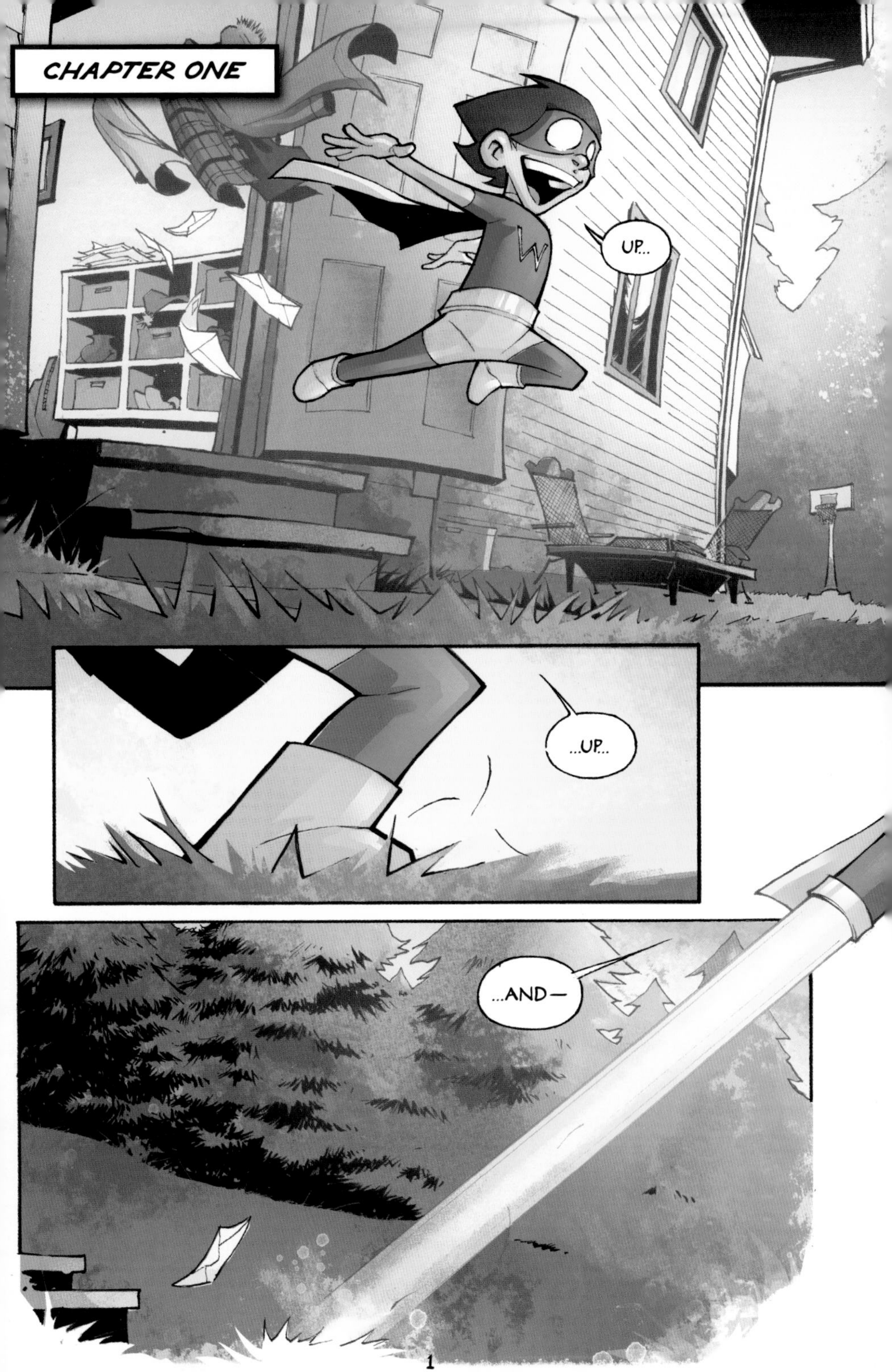
CHAPTER ONE
UP...
...UP...
...AND—

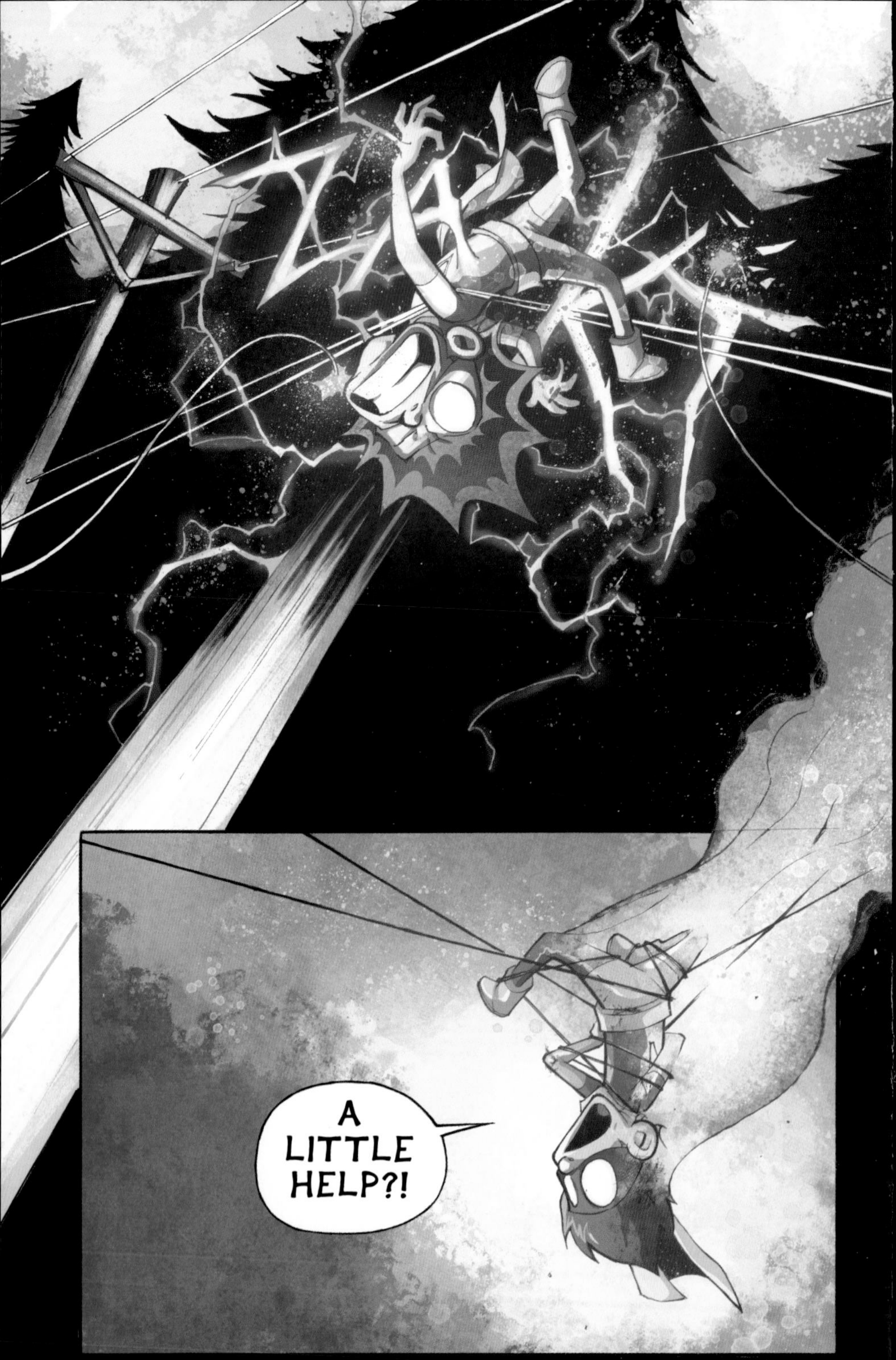
A LITTLE HELP?!

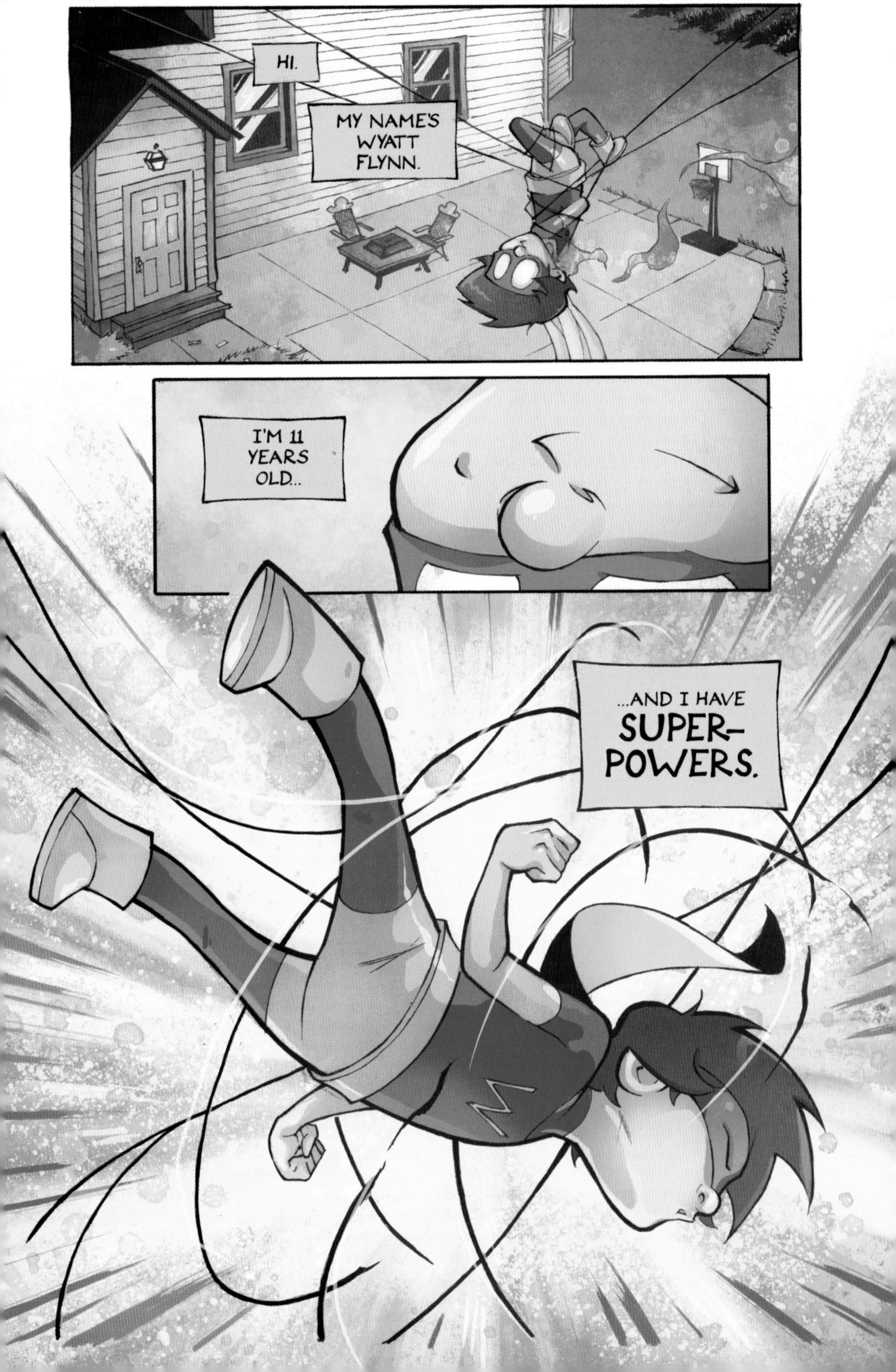

HI.
MY NAME'S WYATT FLYNN.
I'M 11 YEARS OLD...
...AND I HAVE SUPER-POWERS.

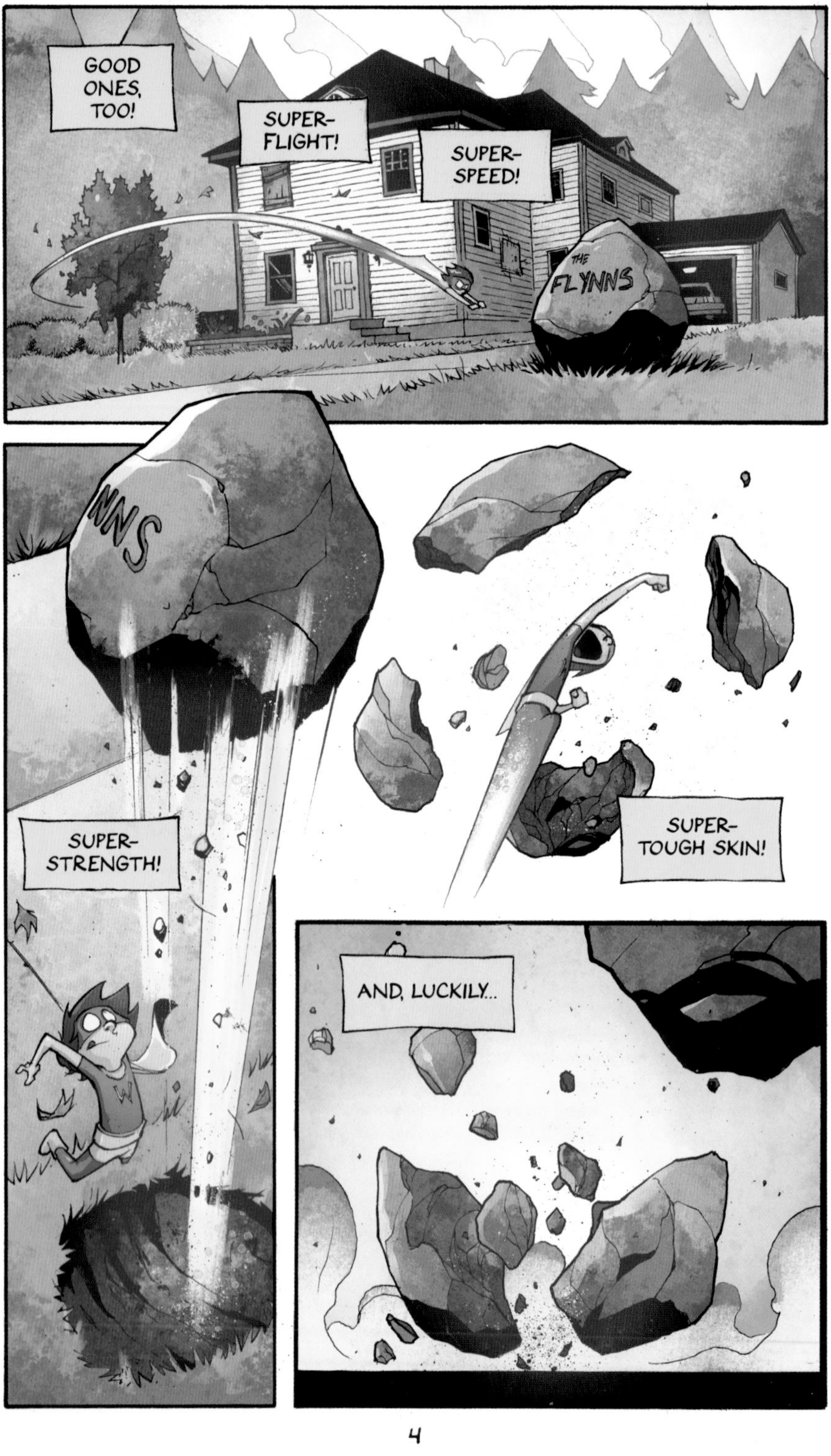
GOOD ONES, TOO!
SUPER-FLIGHT!
SUPER-SPEED!
THE FLYNNS
NNS
SUPER-STRENGTH!
SUPER-TOUGH SKIN!
AND, LUCKILY...

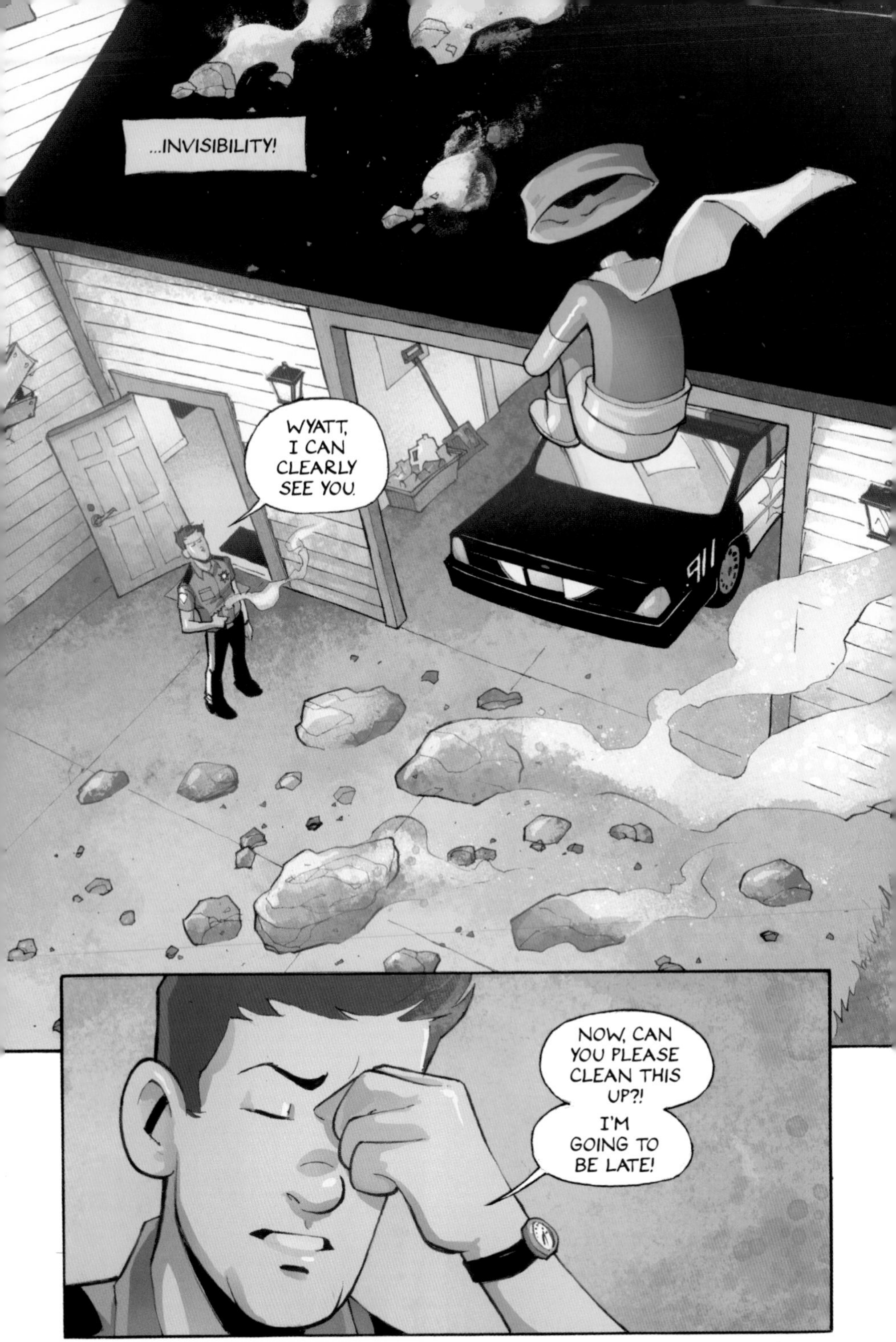
...INVISIBILITY!
WYATT, I CAN CLEARLY SEE YOU.
911
NOW, CAN YOU PLEASE CLEAN THIS UP?!
I'M GOING TO BE LATE!

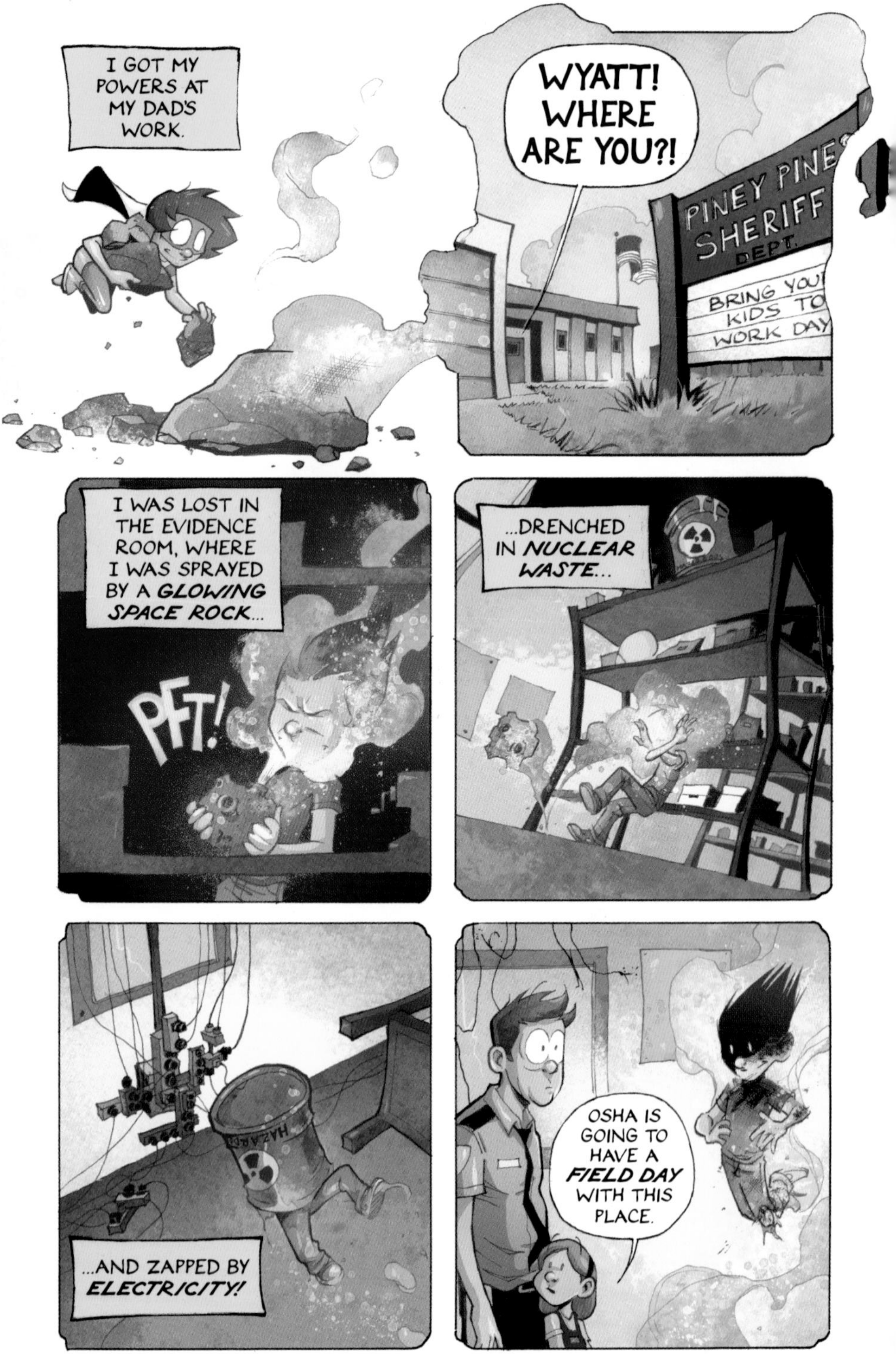
I GOT MY POWERS AT MY DAD'S WORK.
WYATT! WHERE ARE YOU?!
PINEY PINES SHERIFF DEPT.
BRING YOUR KIDS TO WORK DAY
I WAS LOST IN THE EVIDENCE ROOM, WHERE I WAS SPRAYED BY A GLOWING SPACE ROCK...
PFT!
...DRENCHED IN NUCLEAR WASTE...
HAZARD
...AND ZAPPED BY ELECTRICITY!
OSHA IS GOING TO HAVE A FIELD DAY WITH THIS PLACE.

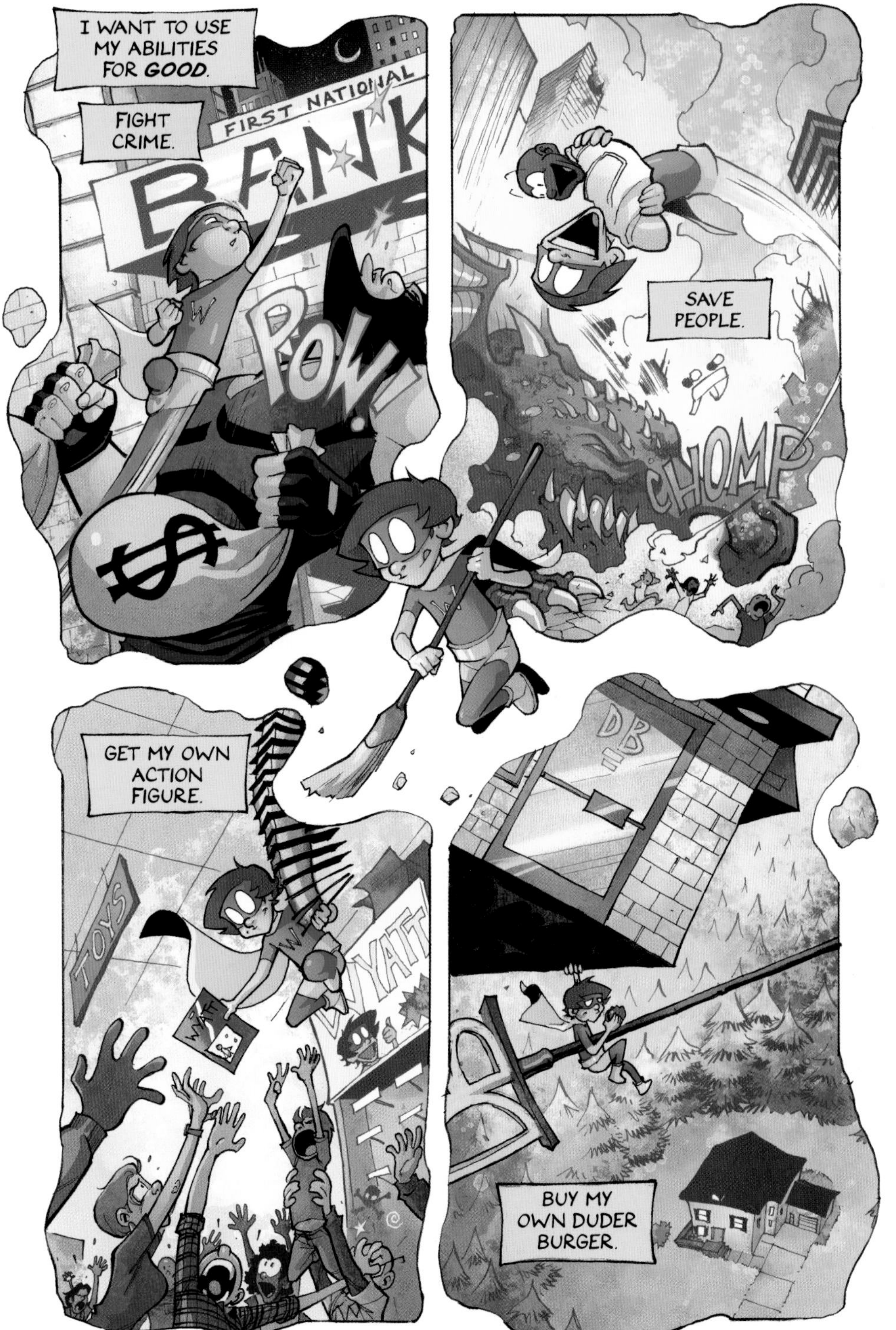
I WANT TO USE MY ABILITIES FOR **GOOD**.
FIRST NATIONAL
BANK
FIGHT CRIME.
POW!
SAVE PEOPLE.
CHOMP
GET MY OWN ACTION FIGURE.
TOYS
WYATT
DB
BUY MY OWN DUDER BURGER.

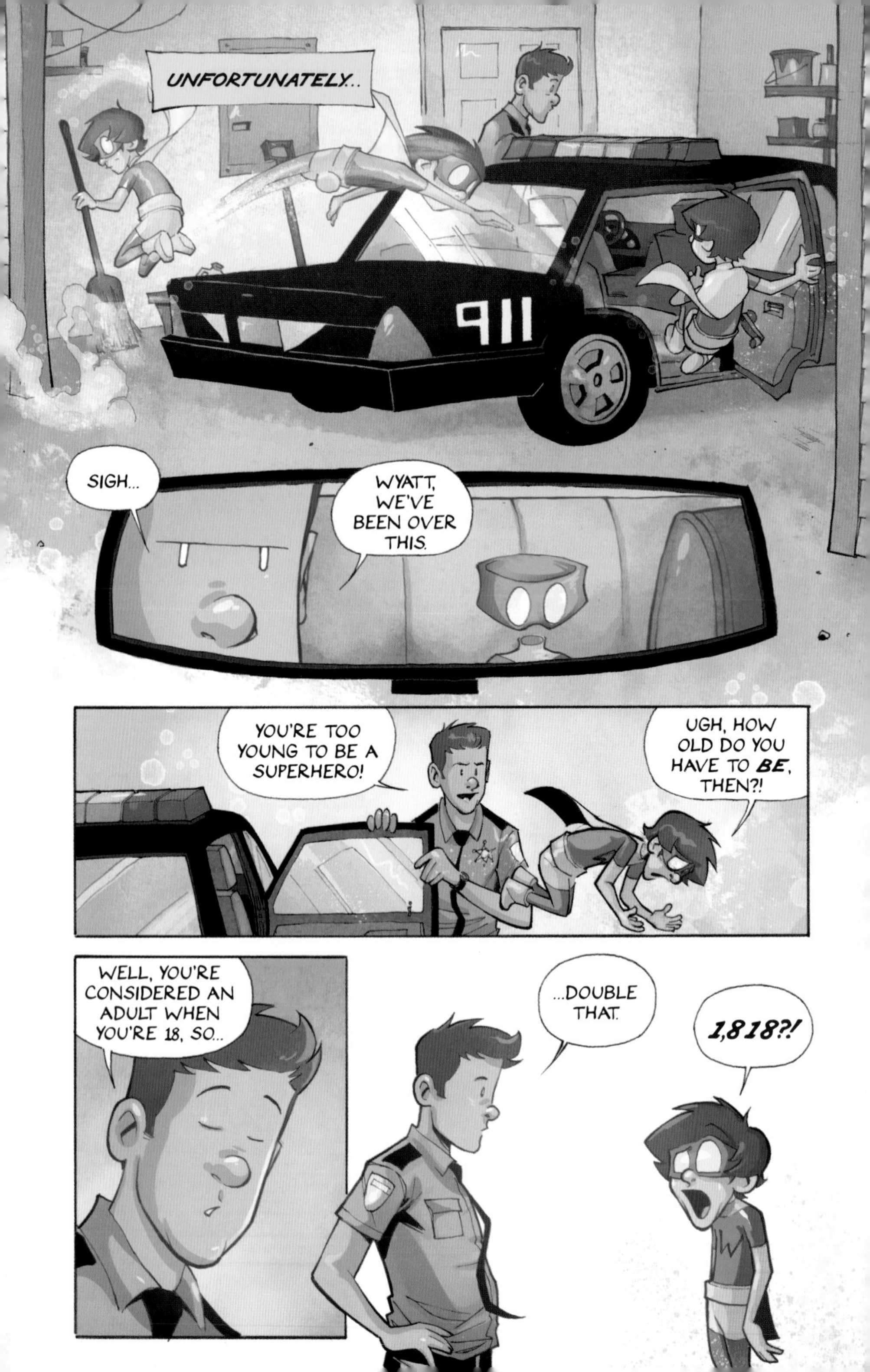
UNFORTUNATELY...
911
SIGH...
WYATT, WE'VE BEEN OVER THIS.
YOU'RE TOO YOUNG TO BE A SUPERHERO!
UGH, HOW OLD DO YOU HAVE TO *BE*, THEN?!
WELL, YOU'RE CONSIDERED AN ADULT WHEN YOU'RE 18, SO...
...DOUBLE THAT.
1,818?!

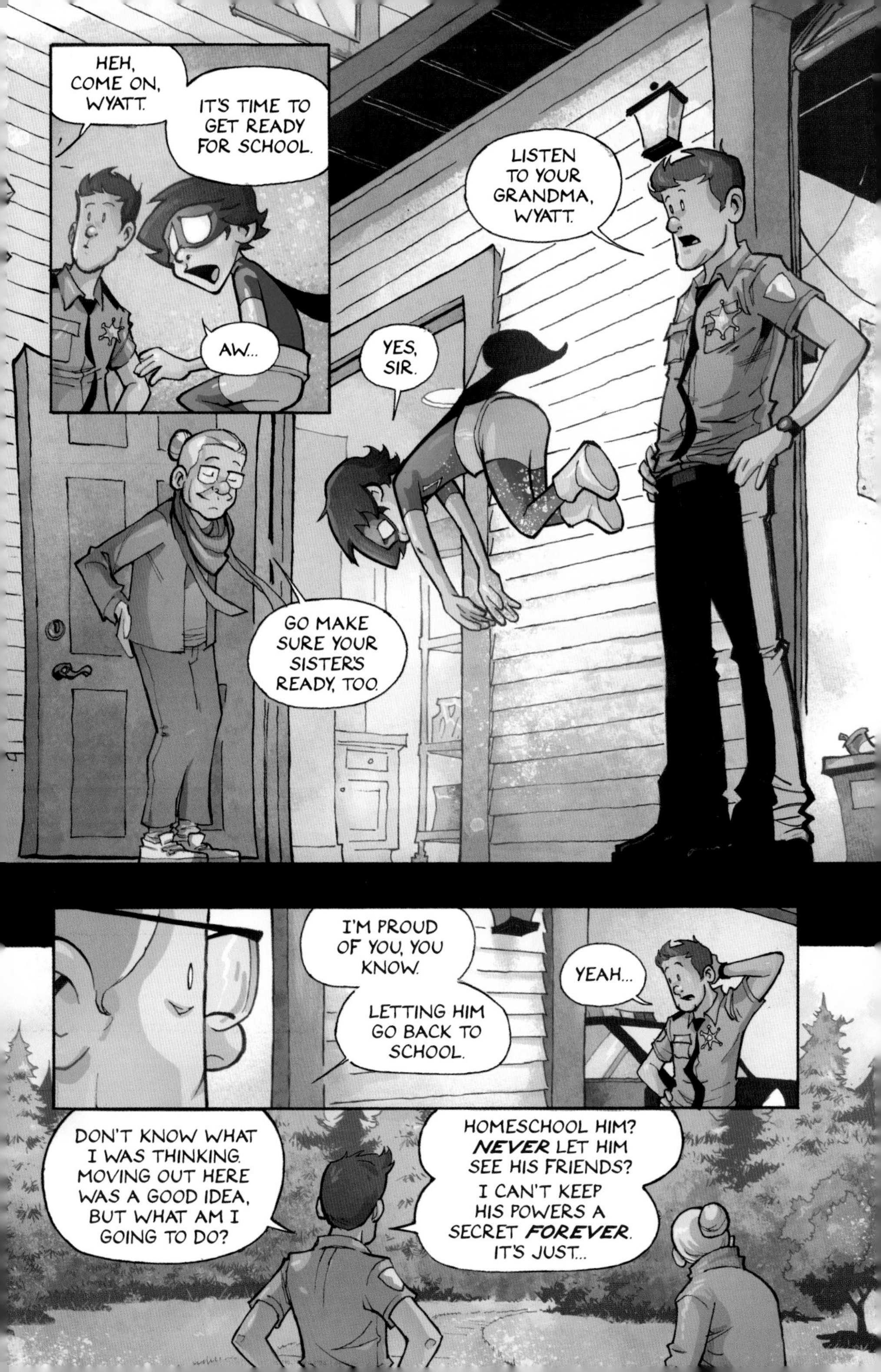
HEH, COME ON, WYATT.
IT'S TIME TO GET READY FOR SCHOOL.
AW...
LISTEN TO YOUR GRANDMA, WYATT.
YES, SIR.
GO MAKE SURE YOUR SISTER'S READY, TOO.
I'M PROUD OF YOU, YOU KNOW.
LETTING HIM GO BACK TO SCHOOL.
YEAH...
DON'T KNOW WHAT I WAS THINKING. MOVING OUT HERE WAS A GOOD IDEA, BUT WHAT AM I GOING TO DO?
HOMESCHOOL HIM? NEVER LET HIM SEE HIS FRIENDS?
I CAN'T KEEP HIS POWERS A SECRET FOREVER. IT'S JUST...

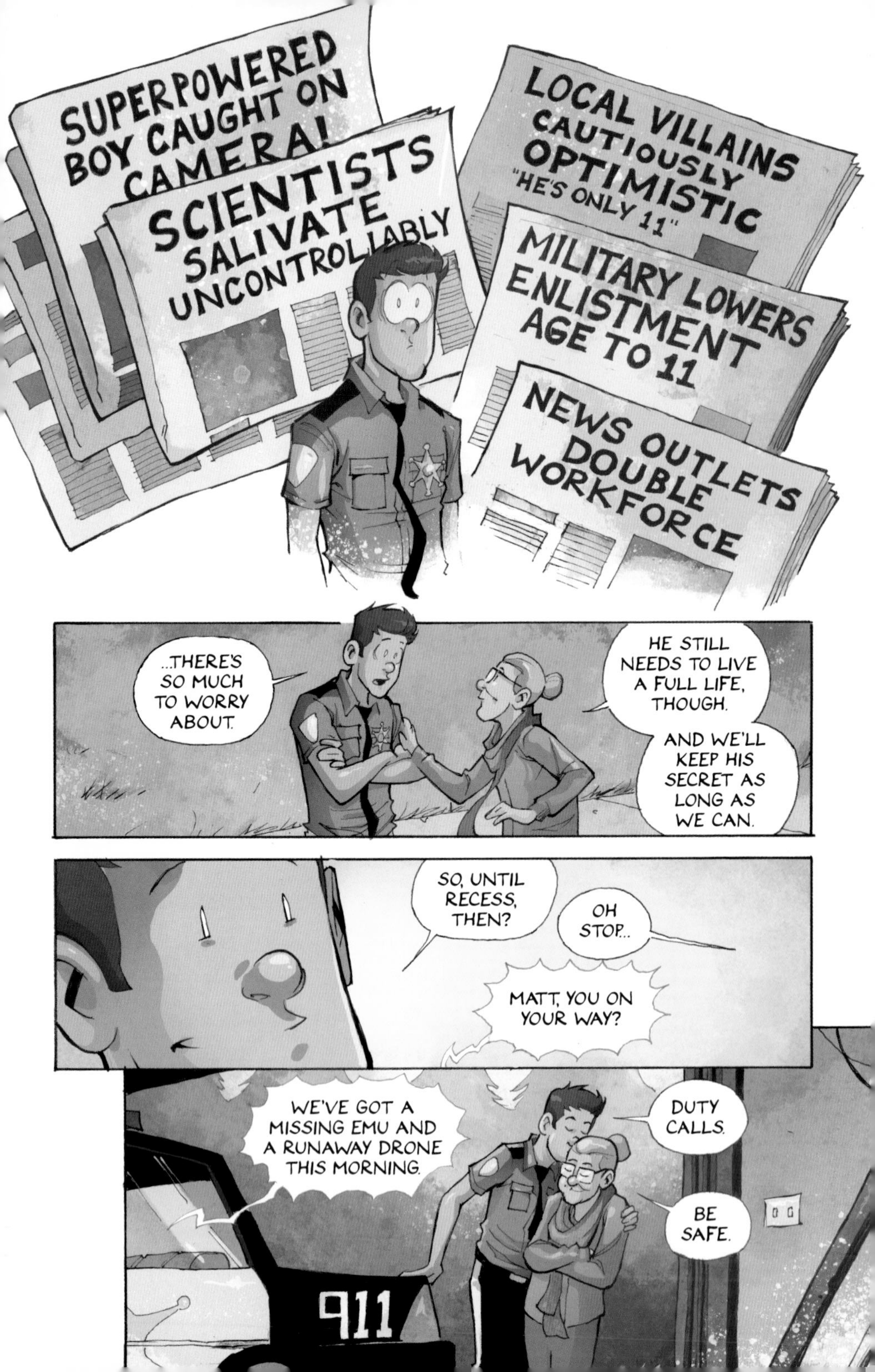
SUPERPOWERED BOY CAUGHT ON CAMERA!
SCIENTISTS SALIVATE UNCONTROLLABLY
LOCAL VILLAINS CAUTIOUSLY OPTIMISTIC "HE'S ONLY 11"
MILITARY LOWERS ENLISTMENT AGE TO 11
NEWS OUTLETS DOUBLE WORKFORCE
...THERE'S SO MUCH TO WORRY ABOUT.
HE STILL NEEDS TO LIVE A FULL LIFE, THOUGH.
AND WE'LL KEEP HIS SECRET AS LONG AS WE CAN.
SO, UNTIL RECESS, THEN?
OH STOP...
MATT, YOU ON YOUR WAY?
WE'VE GOT A MISSING EMU AND A RUNAWAY DRONE THIS MORNING.
DUTY CALLS.
BE SAFE.
911

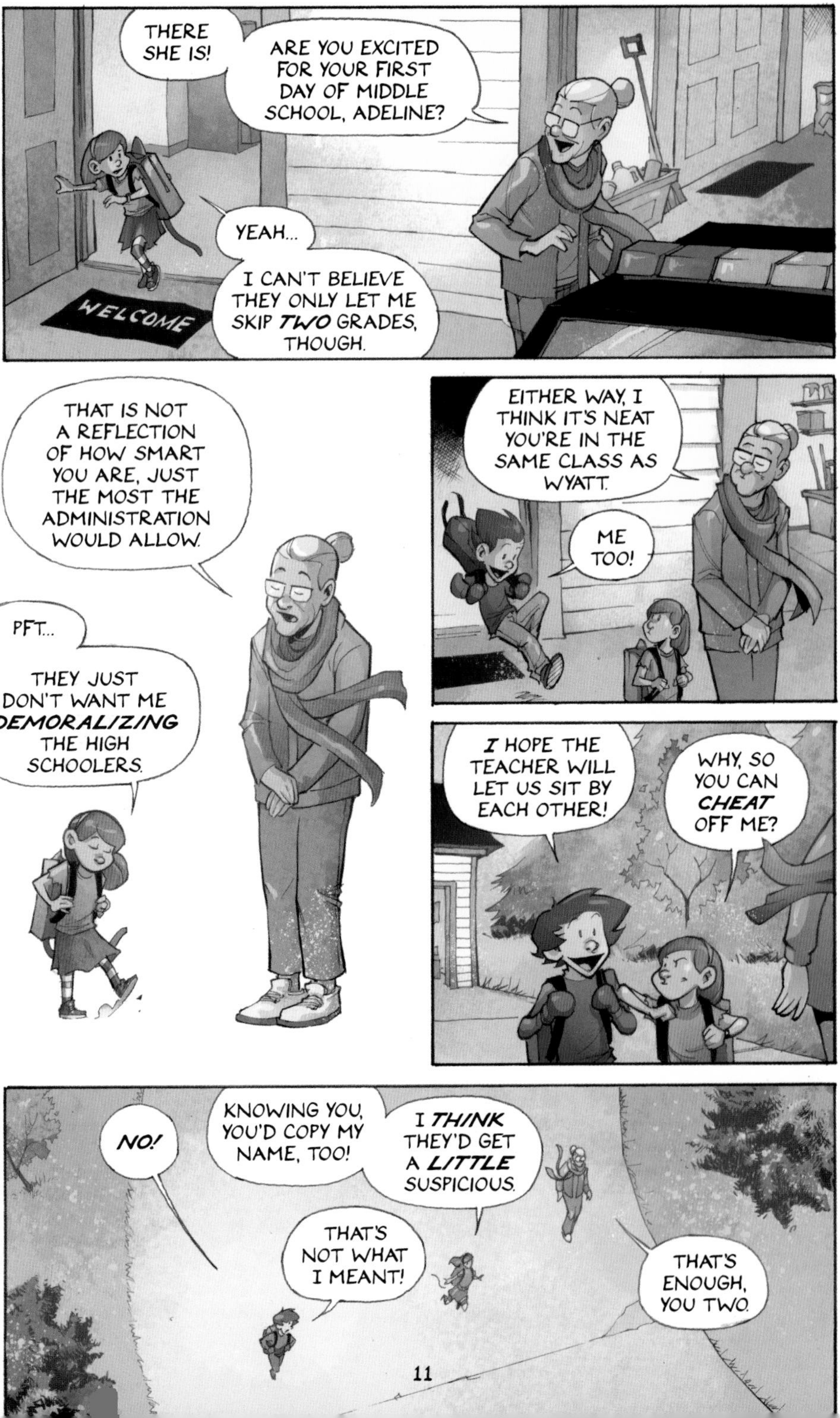

THERE SHE IS!
ARE YOU EXCITED FOR YOUR FIRST DAY OF MIDDLE SCHOOL, ADELINE?
YEAH...
I CAN'T BELIEVE THEY ONLY LET ME SKIP *TWO* GRADES, THOUGH.
WELCOME
THAT IS NOT A REFLECTION OF HOW SMART YOU ARE, JUST THE MOST THE ADMINISTRATION WOULD ALLOW.
PFT...
THEY JUST DON'T WANT ME *DEMORALIZING* THE HIGH SCHOOLERS.
EITHER WAY, I THINK IT'S NEAT YOU'RE IN THE SAME CLASS AS WYATT.
ME TOO!
I HOPE THE TEACHER WILL LET US SIT BY EACH OTHER!
WHY, SO YOU CAN *CHEAT* OFF ME?
NO!
KNOWING YOU, YOU'D COPY MY NAME, TOO!
I *THINK* THEY'D GET A *LITTLE* SUSPICIOUS.
THAT'S NOT WHAT I MEANT!
THAT'S ENOUGH, YOU TWO.

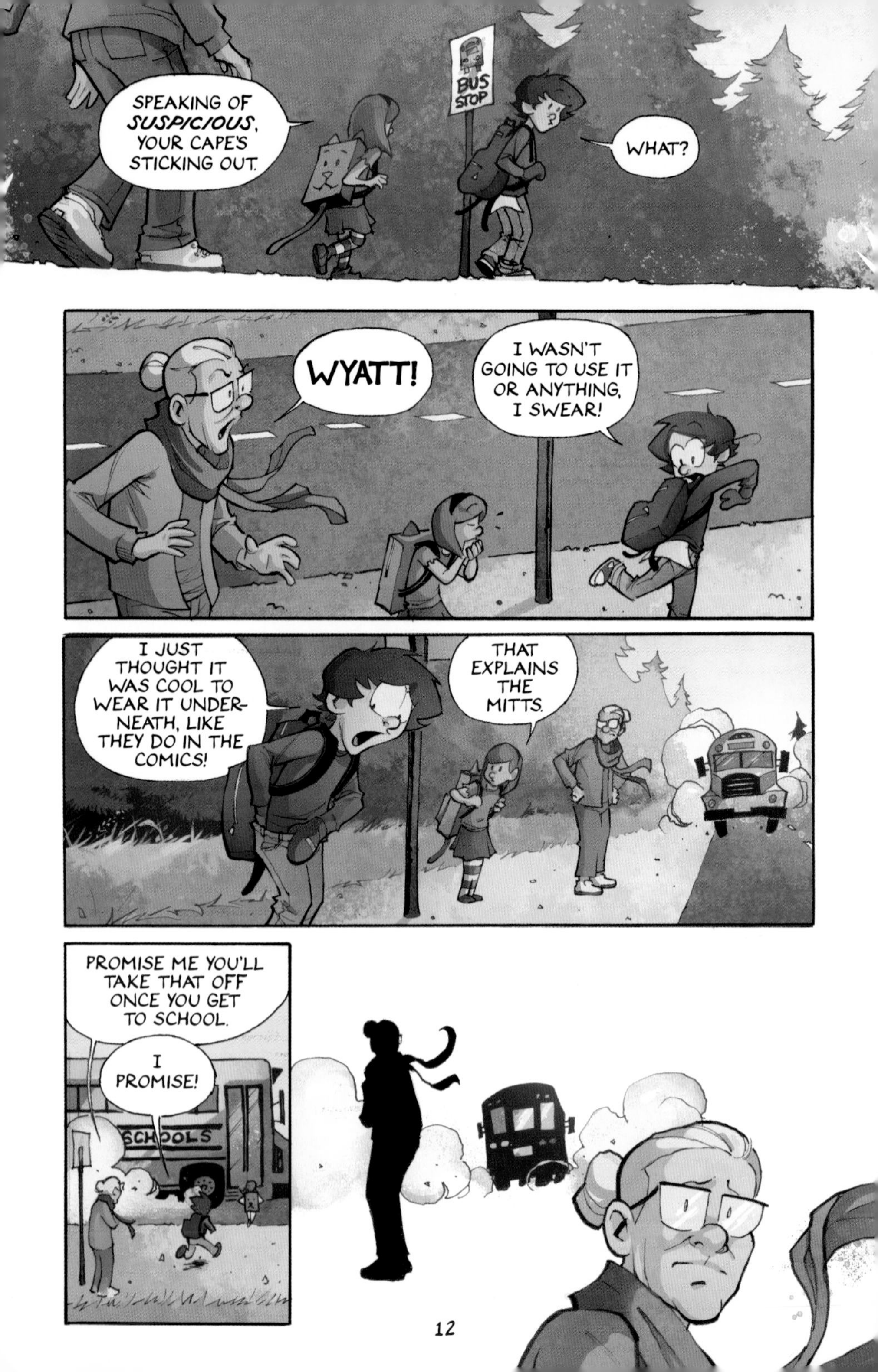
BUS STOP
SPEAKING OF SUSPICIOUS, YOUR CAPE'S STICKING OUT.
WHAT?
WYATT!
I WASN'T GOING TO USE IT OR ANYTHING, I SWEAR!
I JUST THOUGHT IT WAS COOL TO WEAR IT UNDERNEATH, LIKE THEY DO IN THE COMICS!
THAT EXPLAINS THE MITTS.
PROMISE ME YOU'LL TAKE THAT OFF ONCE YOU GET TO SCHOOL.
I PROMISE!
SCHOOLS

CHAPTER TWO

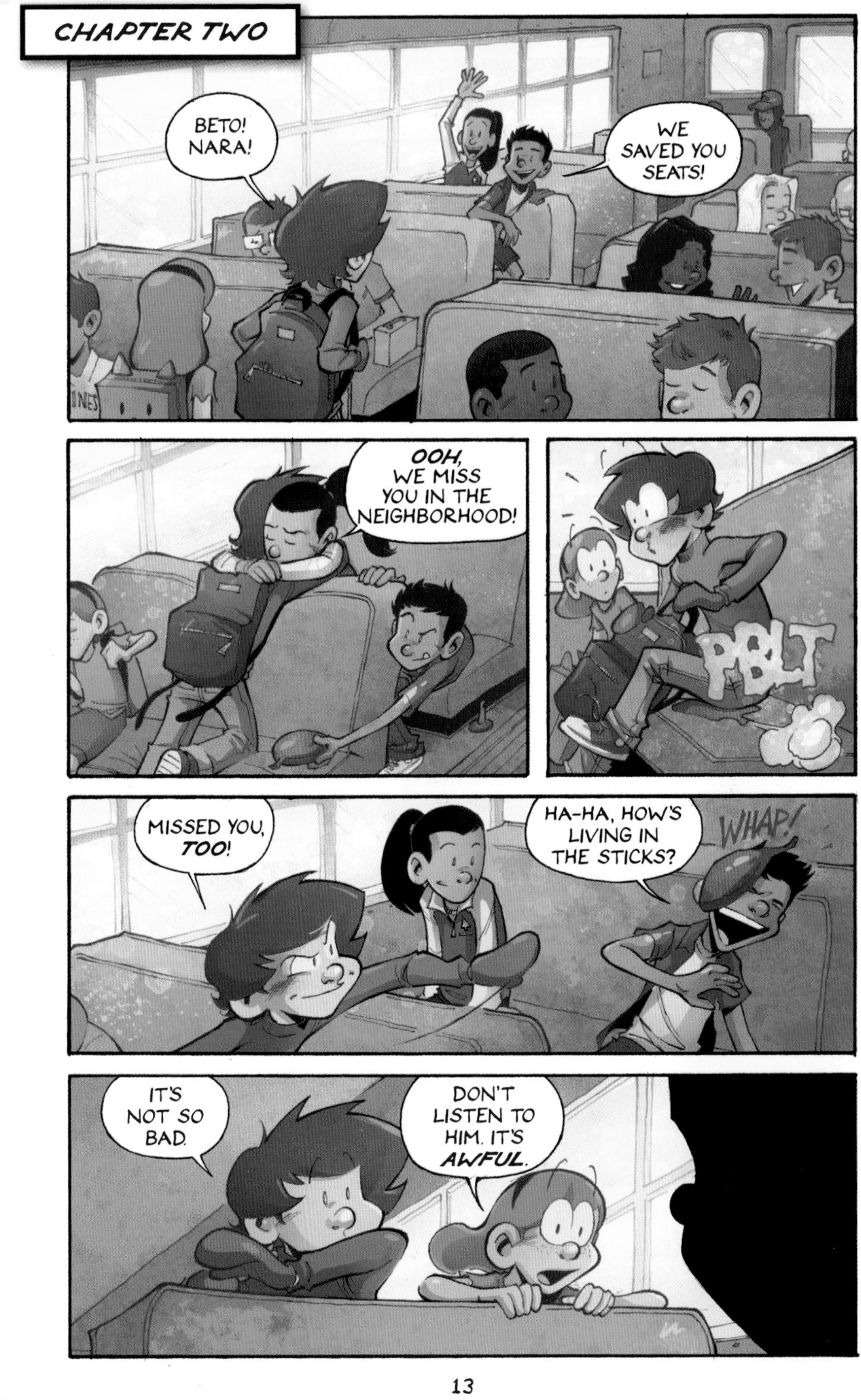
BETO! NARA!
WE SAVED YOU SEATS!
OOH, WE MISS YOU IN THE NEIGHBORHOOD!
PBLT
MISSED YOU, TOO!
HA-HA, HOW'S LIVING IN THE STICKS?
WHAP!
IT'S NOT SO BAD.
DON'T LISTEN TO HIM. IT'S AWFUL.

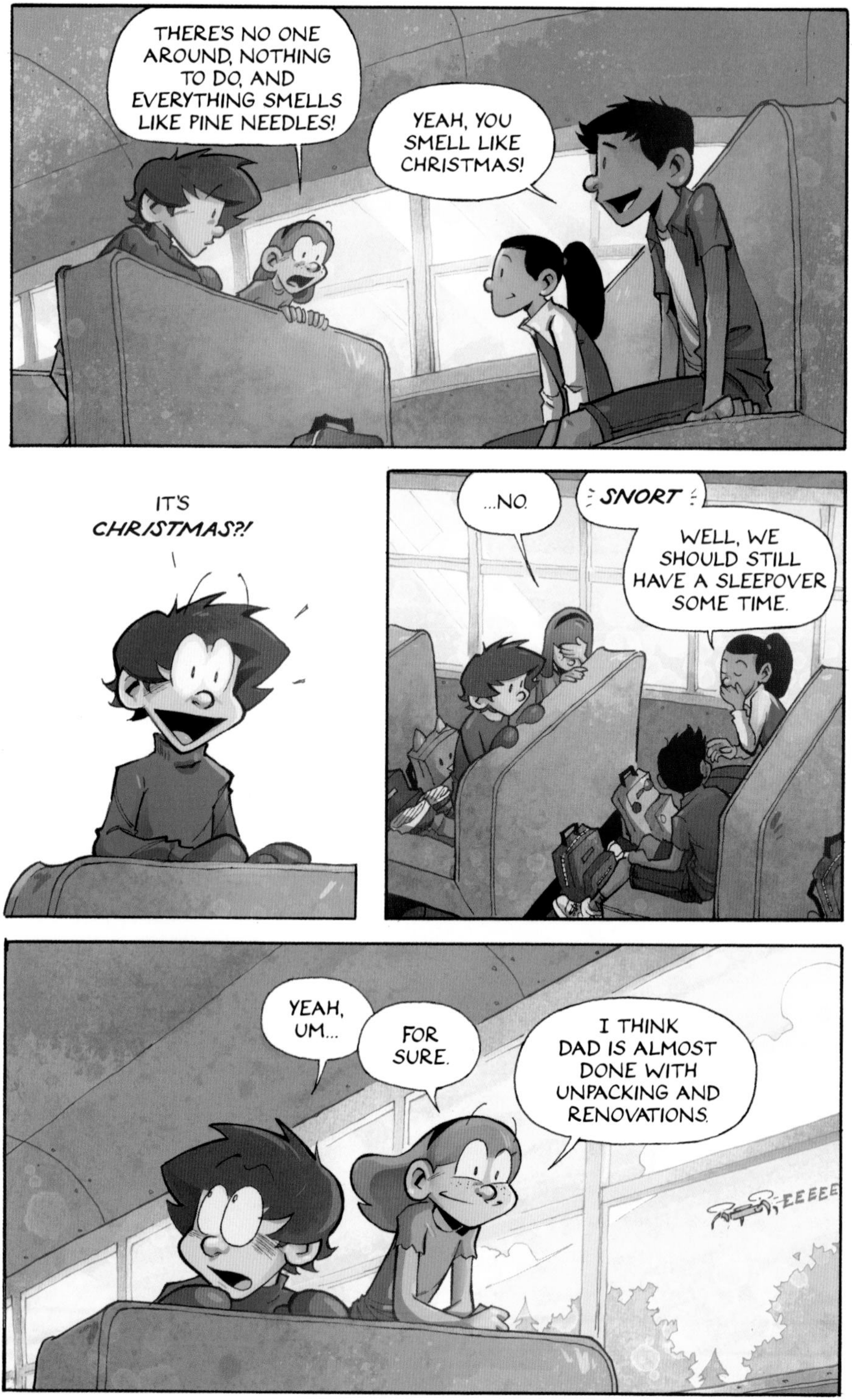
THERE'S NO ONE AROUND, NOTHING TO DO, AND EVERYTHING SMELLS LIKE PINE NEEDLES!
YEAH, YOU SMELL LIKE CHRISTMAS!
IT'S *CHRISTMAS?!*
...NO.
SNORT
WELL, WE SHOULD STILL HAVE A SLEEPOVER SOME TIME.
YEAH, UM...
FOR SURE.
I THINK DAD IS ALMOST DONE WITH UNPACKING AND RENOVATIONS.
EEEEE

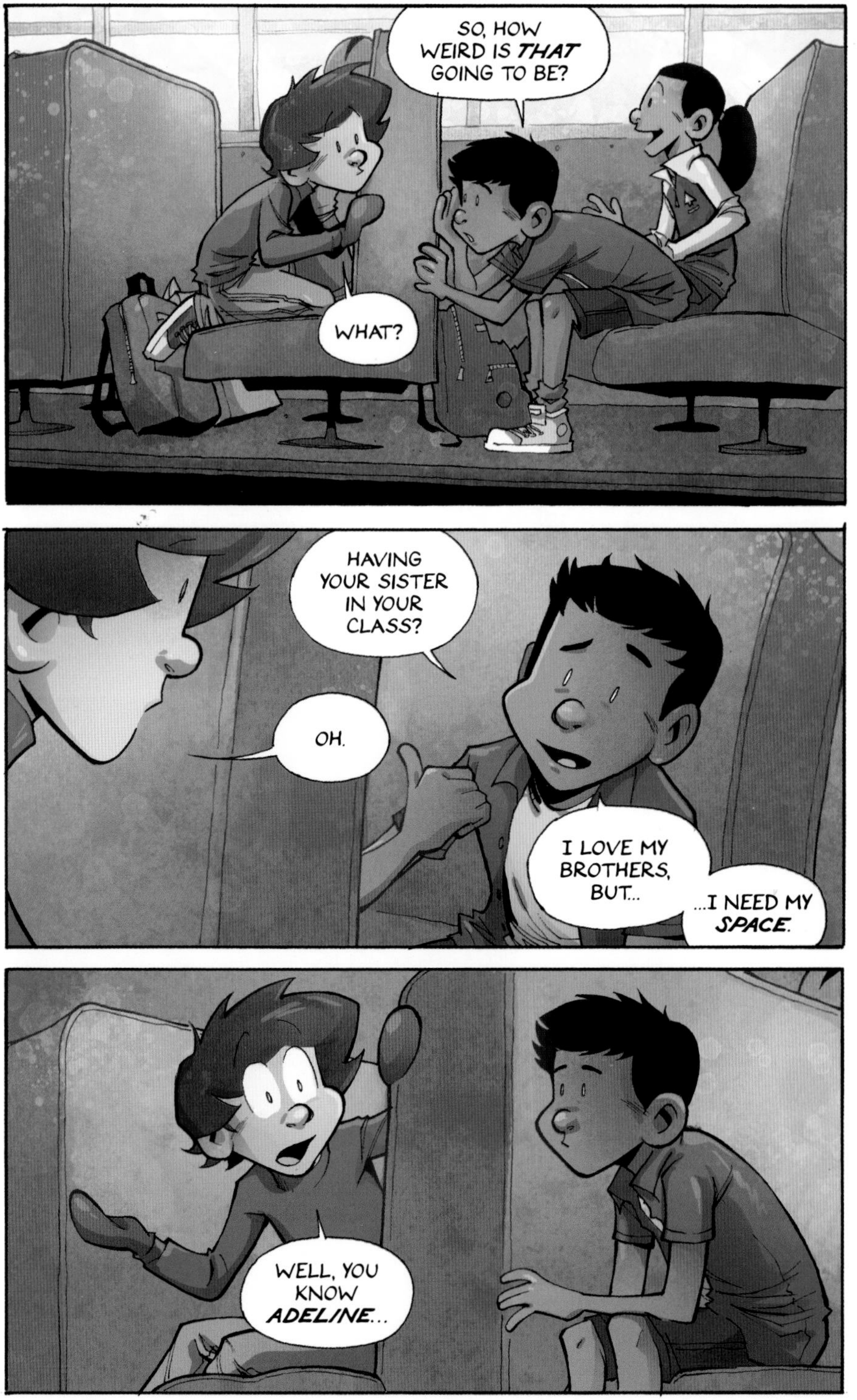
SO, HOW WEIRD IS THAT GOING TO BE?
WHAT?
HAVING YOUR SISTER IN YOUR CLASS?
OH.
I LOVE MY BROTHERS, BUT...
...I NEED MY SPACE.
WELL, YOU KNOW ADELINE...

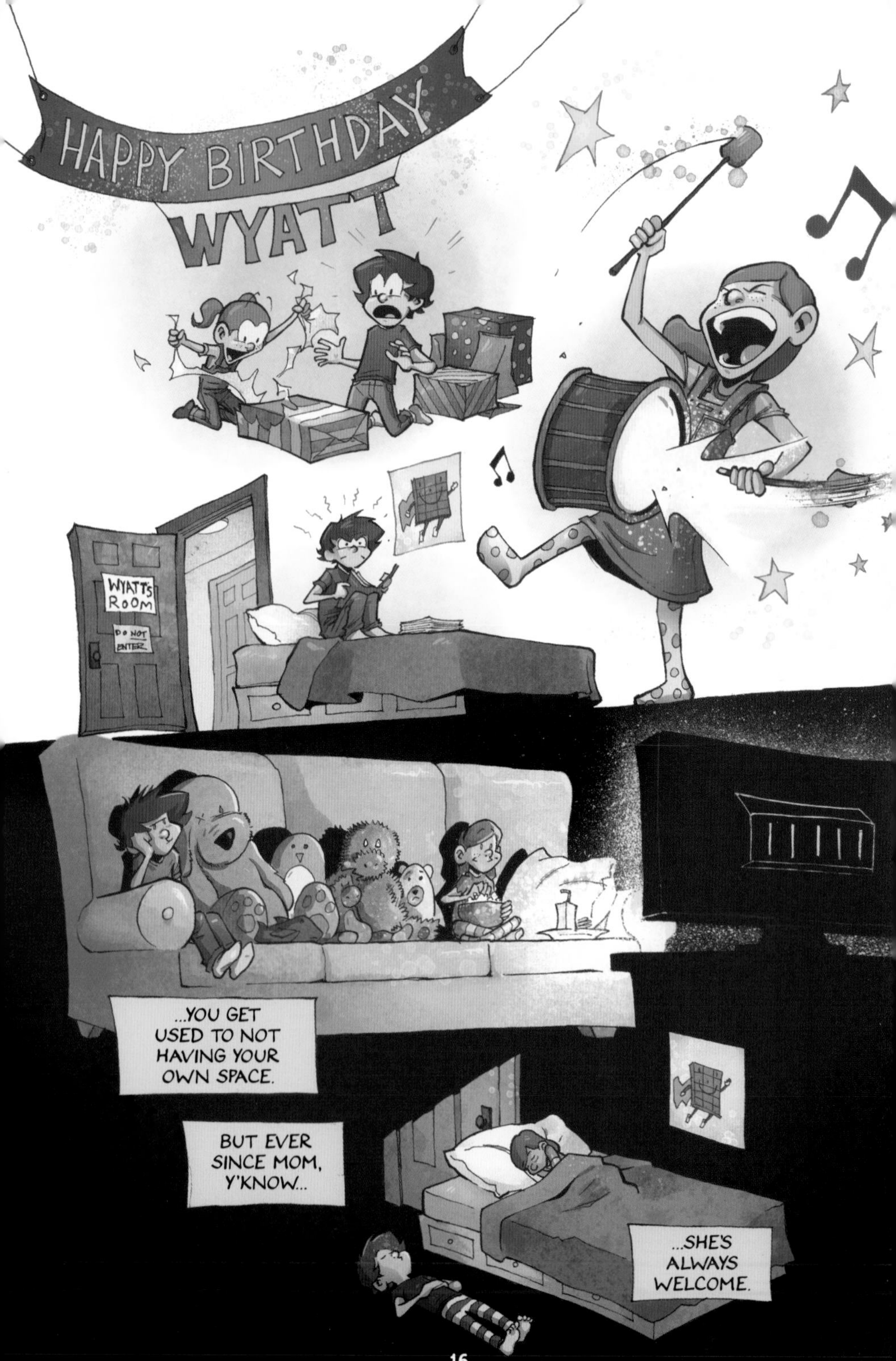

HAPPY BIRTHDAY
WYATT
WYATT'S ROOM
DO NOT ENTER
...YOU GET USED TO NOT HAVING YOUR OWN SPACE.
BUT EVER SINCE MOM, Y'KNOW...
...SHE'S ALWAYS WELCOME.

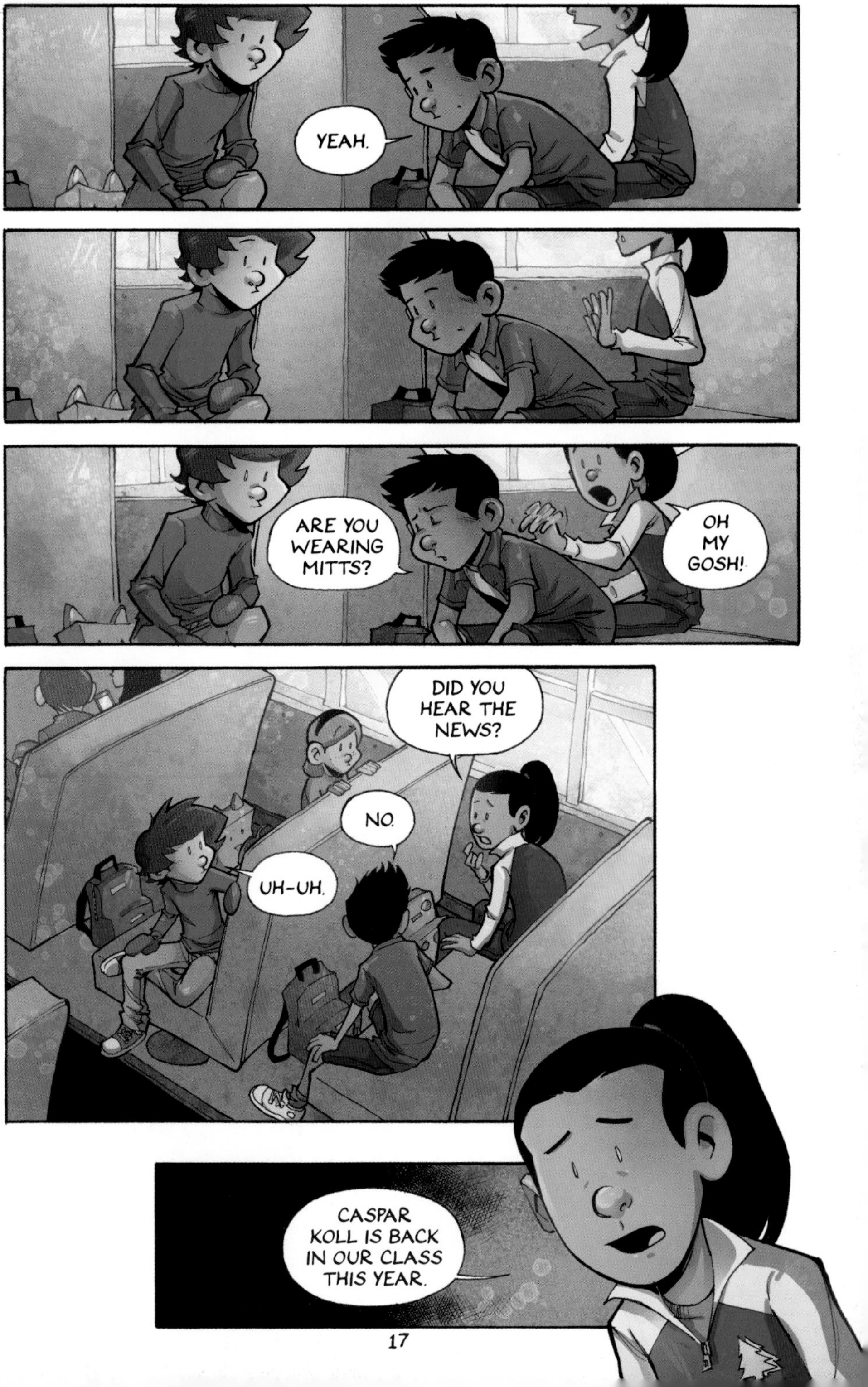
YEAH.
ARE YOU WEARING MITTS?
OH MY GOSH!
DID YOU HEAR THE NEWS?
NO.
UH-UH.
CASPAR KOLL IS BACK IN OUR CLASS THIS YEAR.

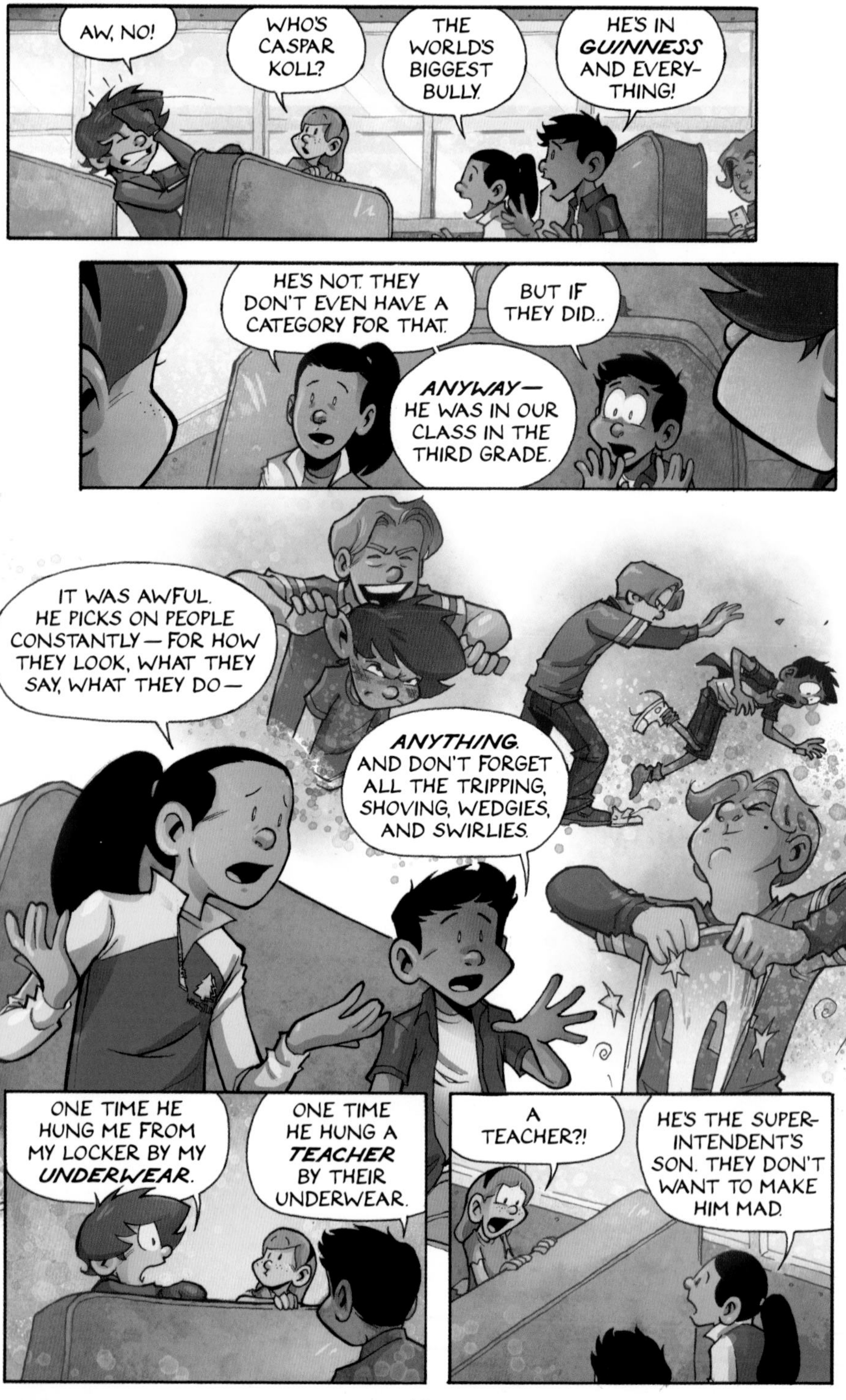
AW, NO!
WHO'S CASPAR KOLL?
THE WORLD'S BIGGEST BULLY.
HE'S IN *GUINNESS* AND EVERY-THING!
HE'S NOT. THEY DON'T EVEN HAVE A CATEGORY FOR THAT.
BUT IF THEY DID...
ANYWAY— HE WAS IN OUR CLASS IN THE THIRD GRADE.
IT WAS AWFUL. HE PICKS ON PEOPLE CONSTANTLY— FOR HOW THEY LOOK, WHAT THEY SAY, WHAT THEY DO—
ANYTHING. AND DON'T FORGET ALL THE TRIPPING, SHOVING, WEDGIES, AND SWIRLIES.
ONE TIME HE HUNG ME FROM MY LOCKER BY MY *UNDERWEAR*.
ONE TIME HE HUNG A *TEACHER* BY THEIR UNDERWEAR.
A TEACHER?!
HE'S THE SUPER-INTENDENT'S SON. THEY DON'T WANT TO MAKE HIM MAD.

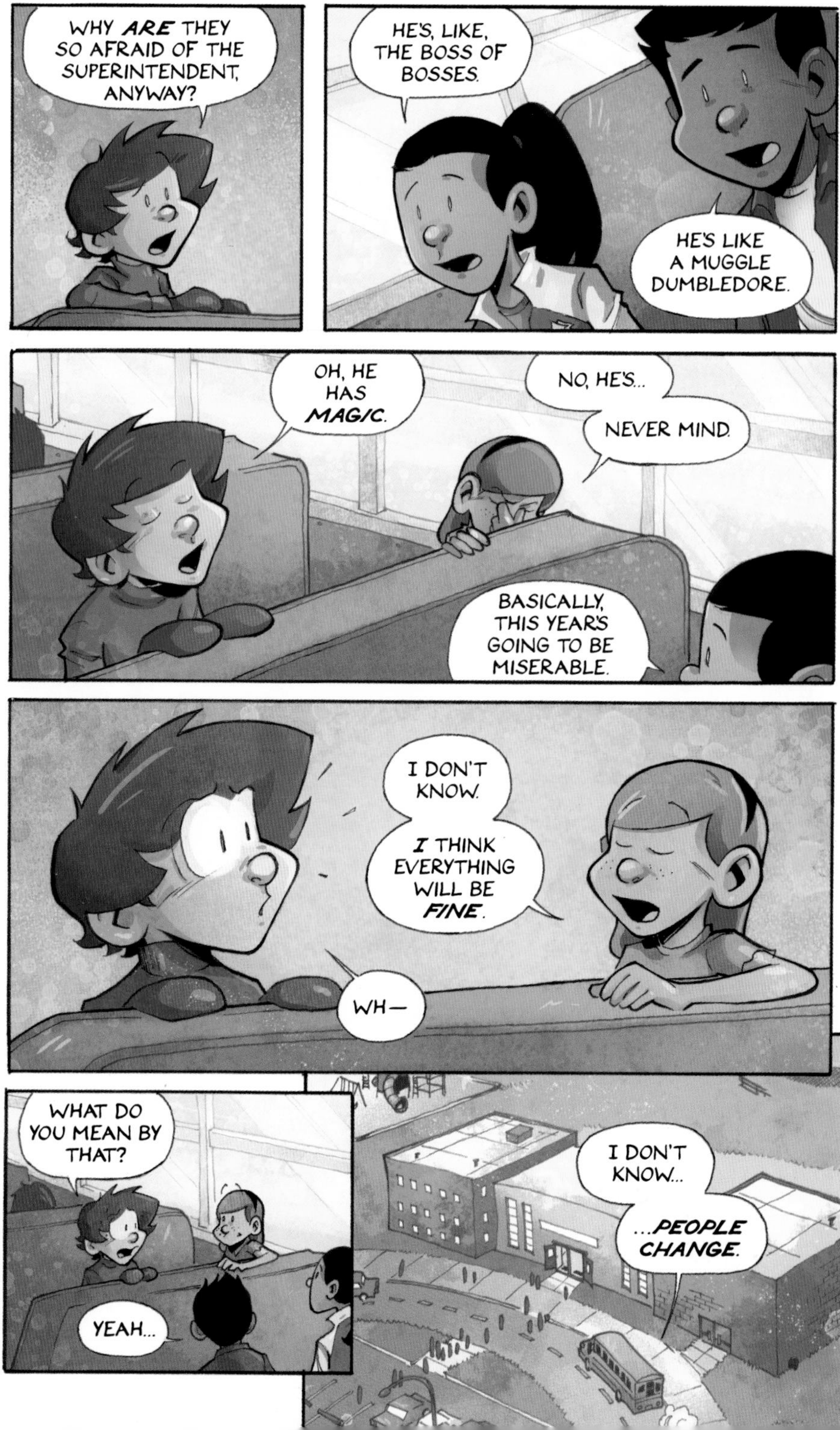
WHY *ARE* THEY SO AFRAID OF THE SUPERINTENDENT, ANYWAY?
HE'S, LIKE, THE BOSS OF BOSSES.
HE'S LIKE A MUGGLE DUMBLEDORE.
OH, HE HAS *MAGIC*.
NO, HE'S...
NEVER MIND.
BASICALLY, THIS YEAR'S GOING TO BE MISERABLE.
I DON'T KNOW.
I THINK EVERYTHING WILL BE *FINE*.
WH—
WHAT DO YOU MEAN BY THAT?
YEAH...
I DON'T KNOW...
...*PEOPLE CHANGE*.

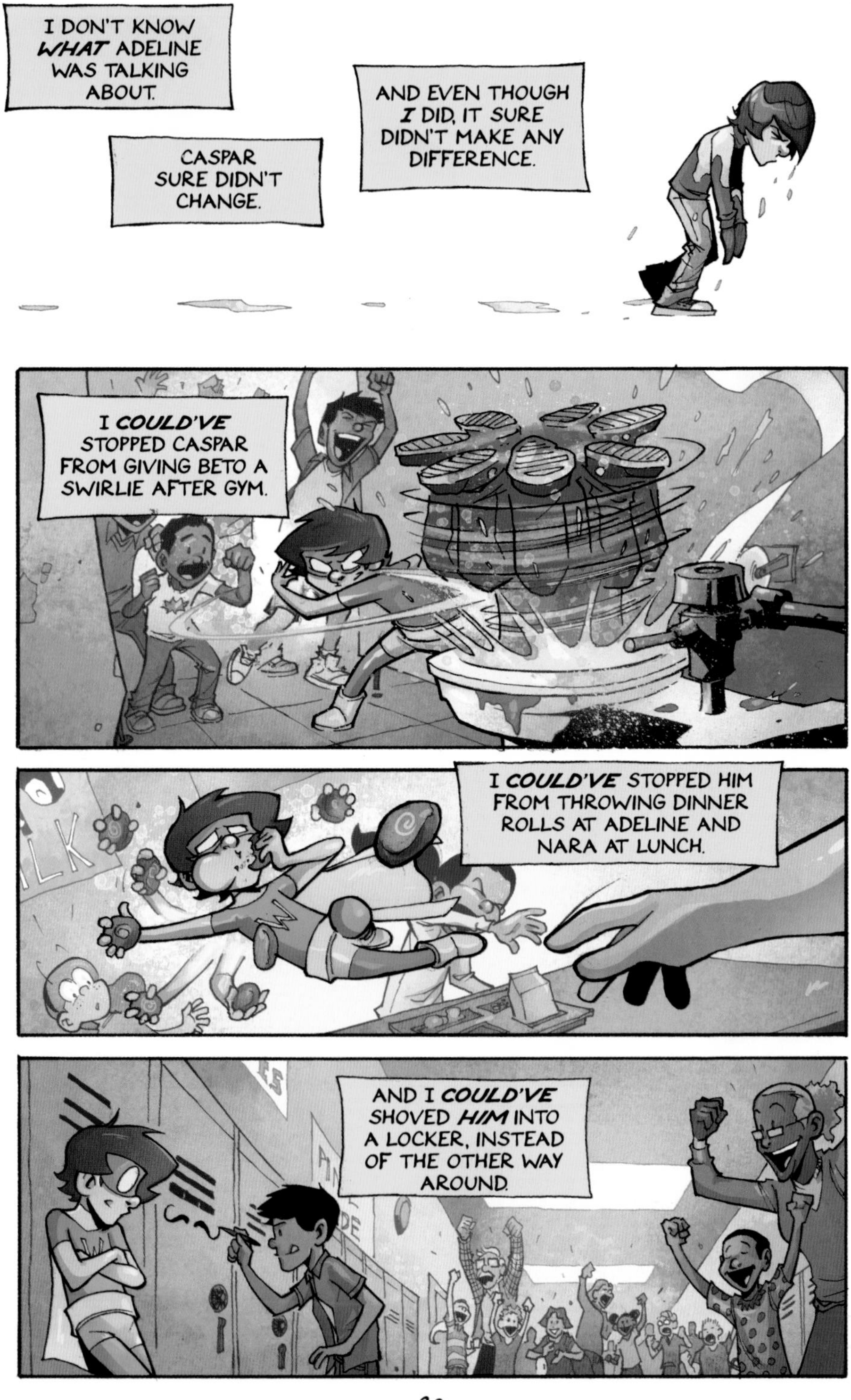
I DON'T KNOW *WHAT* ADELINE WAS TALKING ABOUT.
CASPAR SURE DIDN'T CHANGE.
AND EVEN THOUGH *I* DID, IT SURE DIDN'T MAKE ANY DIFFERENCE.
I *COULD'VE* STOPPED CASPAR FROM GIVING BETO A SWIRLIE AFTER GYM.
I *COULD'VE* STOPPED HIM FROM THROWING DINNER ROLLS AT ADELINE AND NARA AT LUNCH.
AND I *COULD'VE* SHOVED *HIM* INTO A LOCKER, INSTEAD OF THE OTHER WAY AROUND.

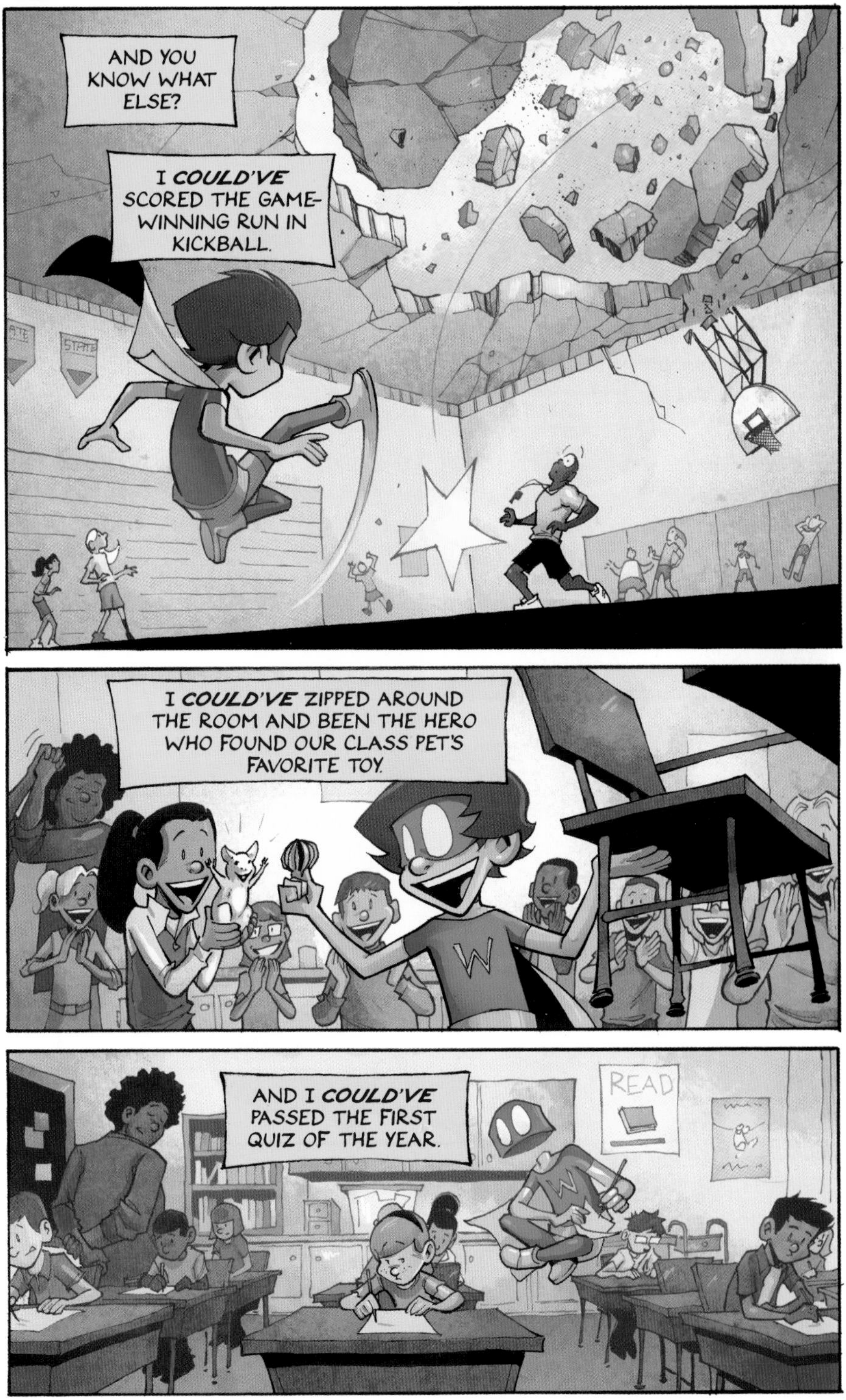
AND YOU KNOW WHAT ELSE?
I *COULD'VE* SCORED THE GAME-WINNING RUN IN KICKBALL.
STATE
I *COULD'VE* ZIPPED AROUND THE ROOM AND BEEN THE HERO WHO FOUND OUR CLASS PET'S FAVORITE TOY.
AND I *COULD'VE* PASSED THE FIRST QUIZ OF THE YEAR.
READ

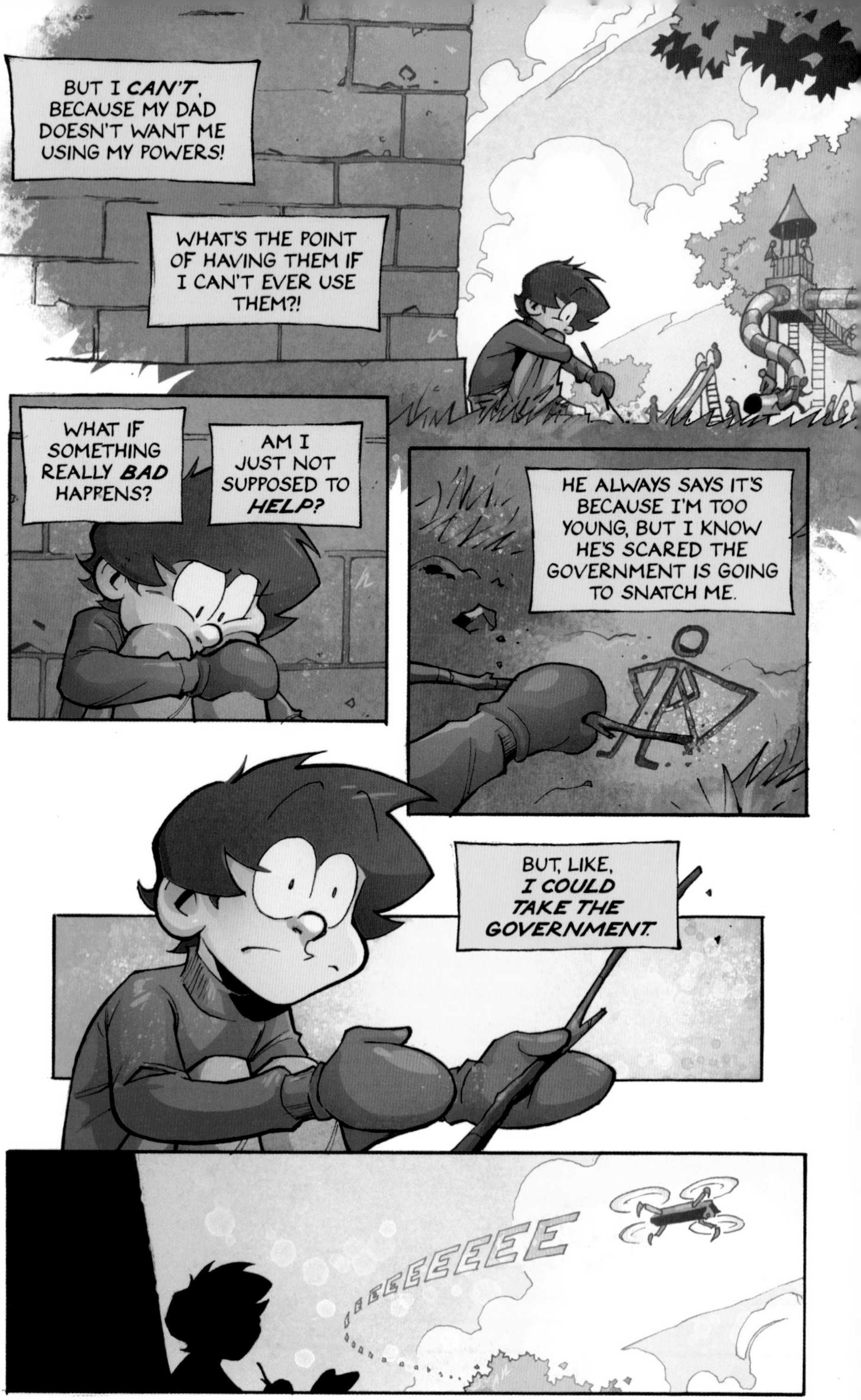

BUT I *CAN'T*, BECAUSE MY DAD DOESN'T WANT ME USING MY POWERS!
WHAT'S THE POINT OF HAVING THEM IF I CAN'T EVER USE THEM?!
WHAT IF SOMETHING REALLY *BAD* HAPPENS?
AM I JUST NOT SUPPOSED TO *HELP?*
HE ALWAYS SAYS IT'S BECAUSE I'M TOO YOUNG, BUT I KNOW HE'S SCARED THE GOVERNMENT IS GOING TO SNATCH ME.
BUT, LIKE, *I COULD TAKE THE GOVERNMENT.*
EEEEEEEEEEE

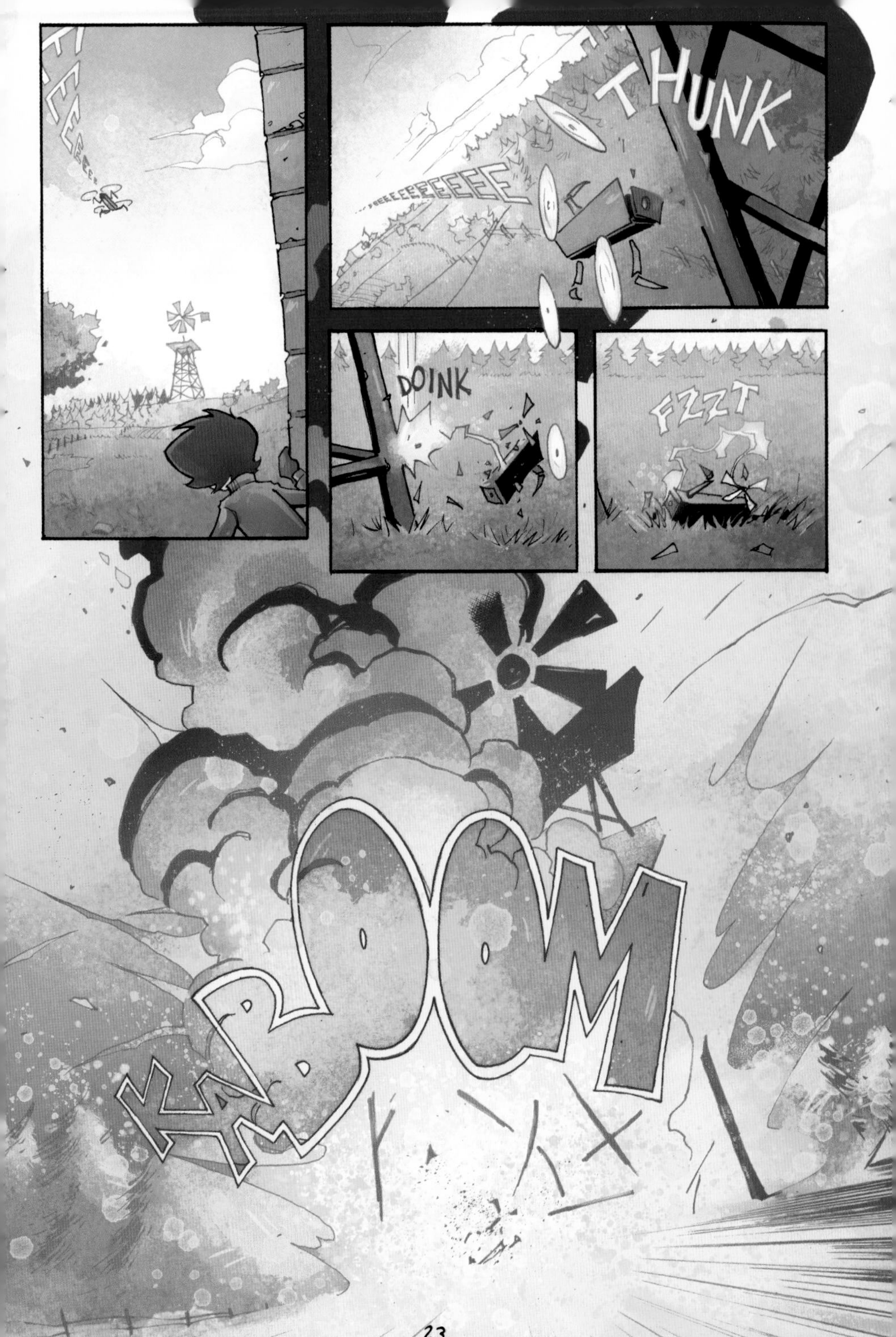
EEEE
EEEEEEEEE
THUNK
DOINK
FZZT
KABOOM

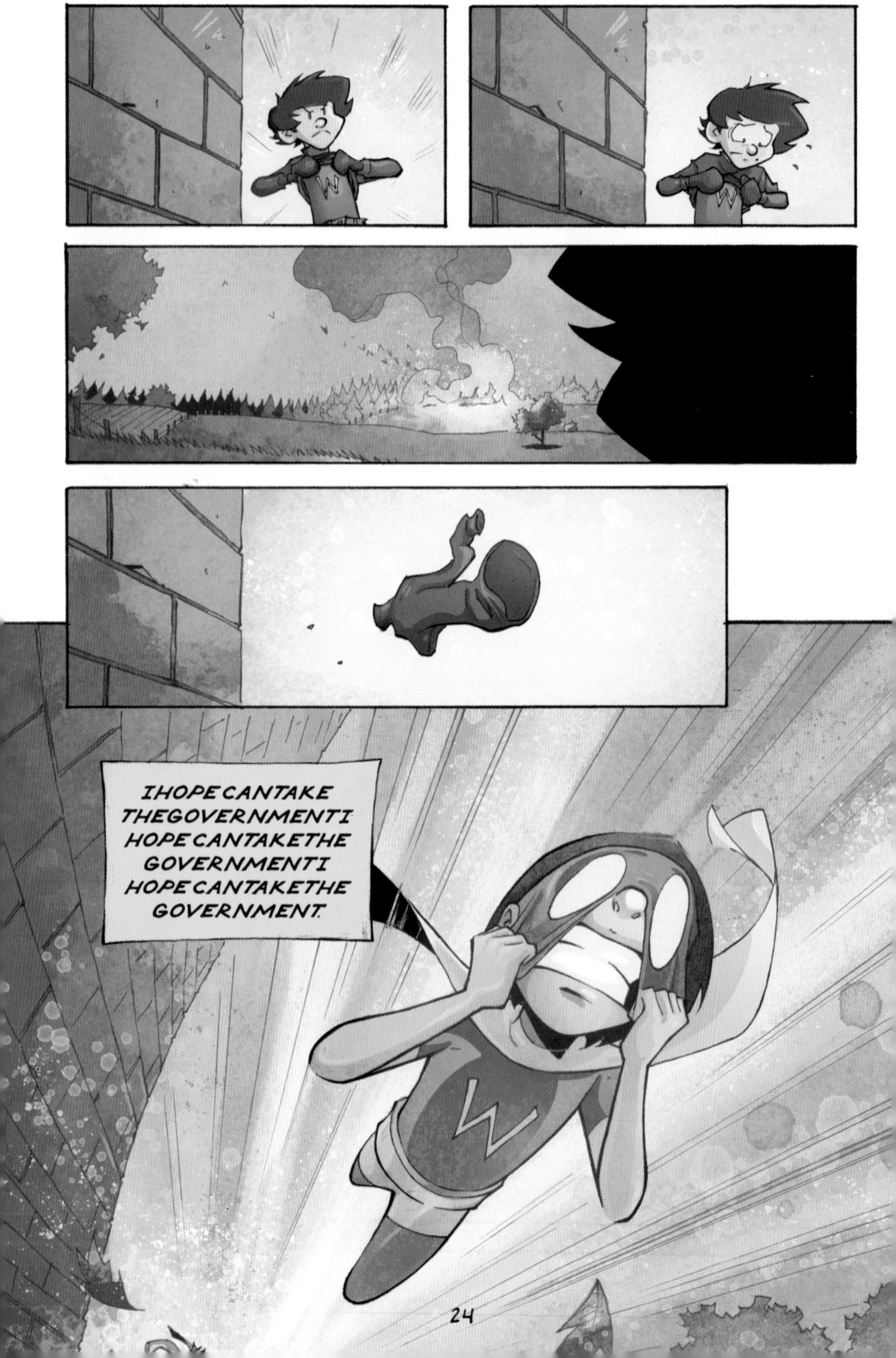
IHOPECANTAKE
THEGOVERNMENTI
HOPECANTAKETHE
GOVERNMENTI
HOPECANTAKETHE
GOVERNMENT.

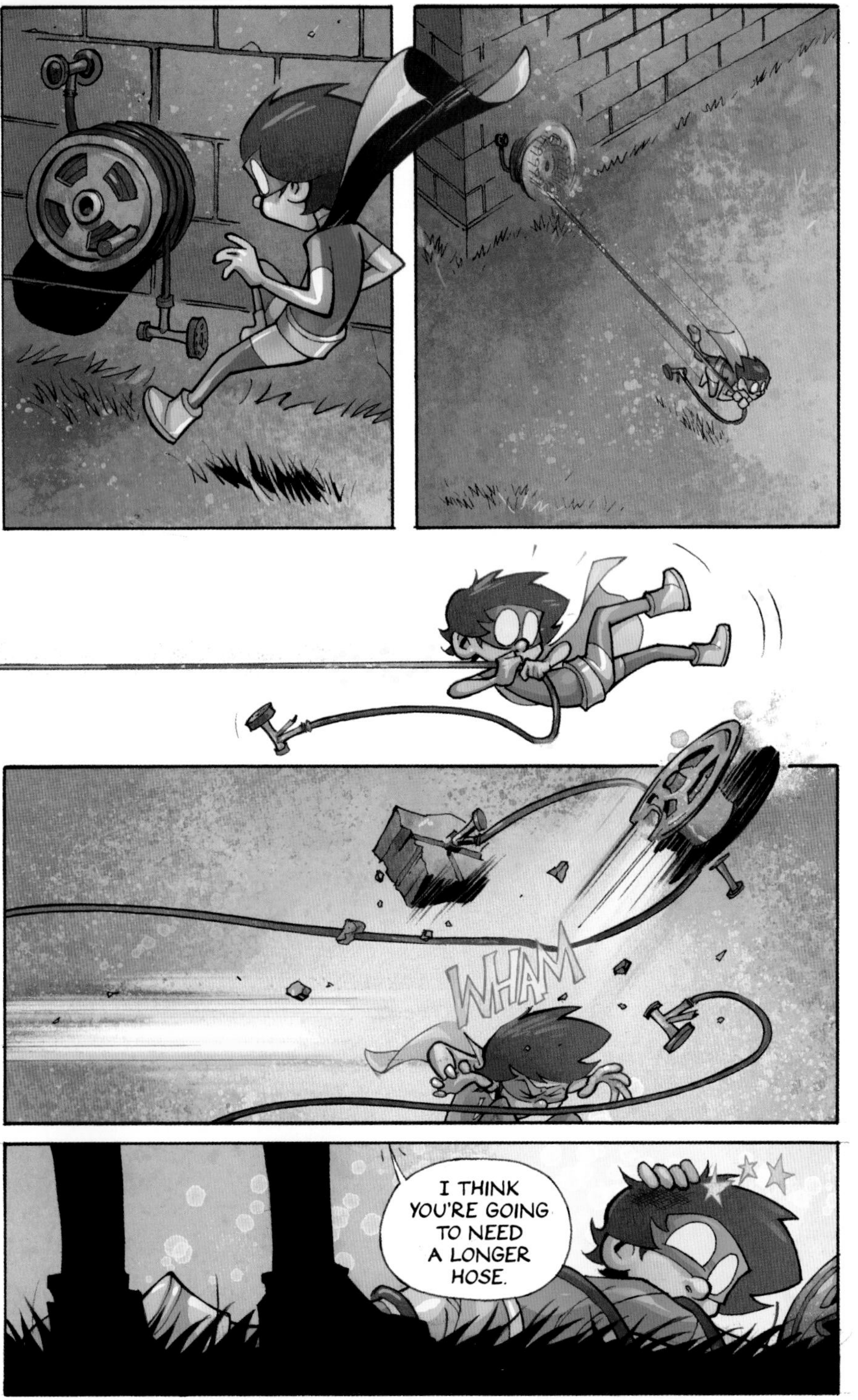
WHAM
I THINK YOU'RE GOING TO NEED A LONGER HOSE.

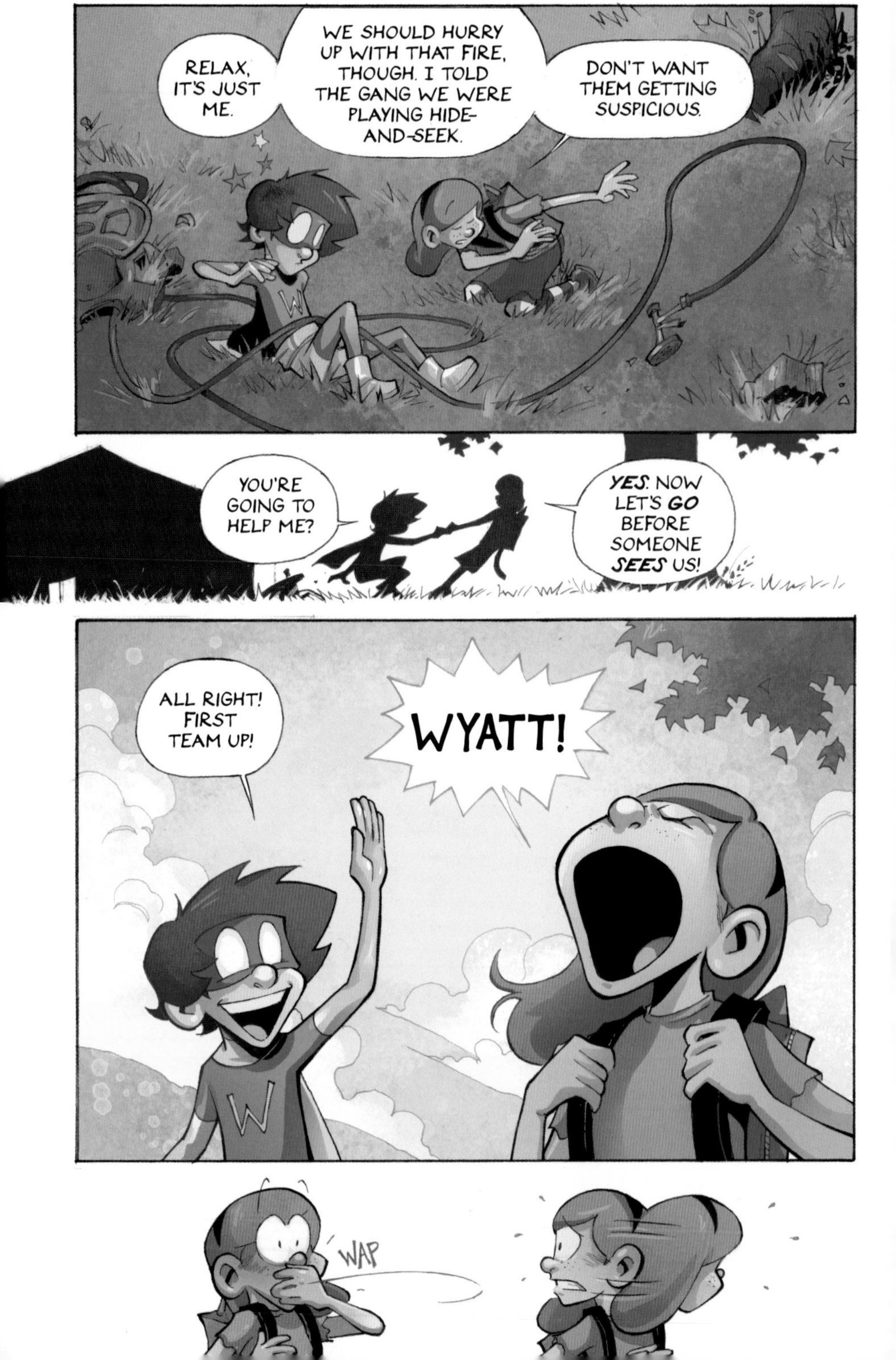
RELAX, IT'S JUST ME.
WE SHOULD HURRY UP WITH THAT FIRE, THOUGH. I TOLD THE GANG WE WERE PLAYING HIDE-AND-SEEK.
DON'T WANT THEM GETTING SUSPICIOUS.
YOU'RE GOING TO HELP ME?
YES. NOW LET'S GO BEFORE SOMEONE SEES US!
ALL RIGHT! FIRST TEAM UP!
WYATT!
WAP

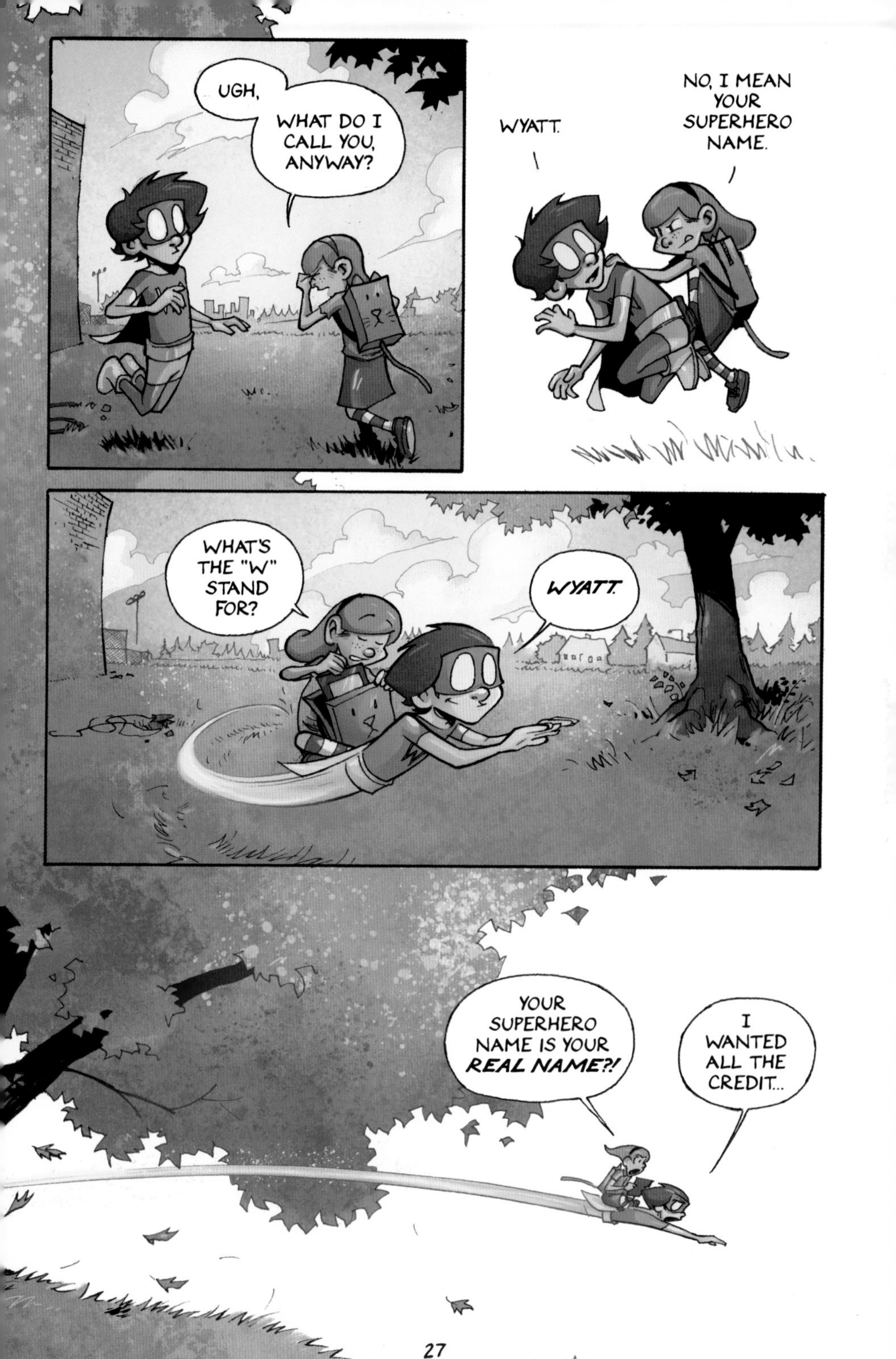
UGH,
WHAT DO I CALL YOU, ANYWAY?
WYATT.
NO, I MEAN YOUR SUPERHERO NAME.
WHAT'S THE "W" STAND FOR?
WYATT.
YOUR SUPERHERO NAME IS YOUR ***REAL NAME?!***
I WANTED ALL THE CREDIT...

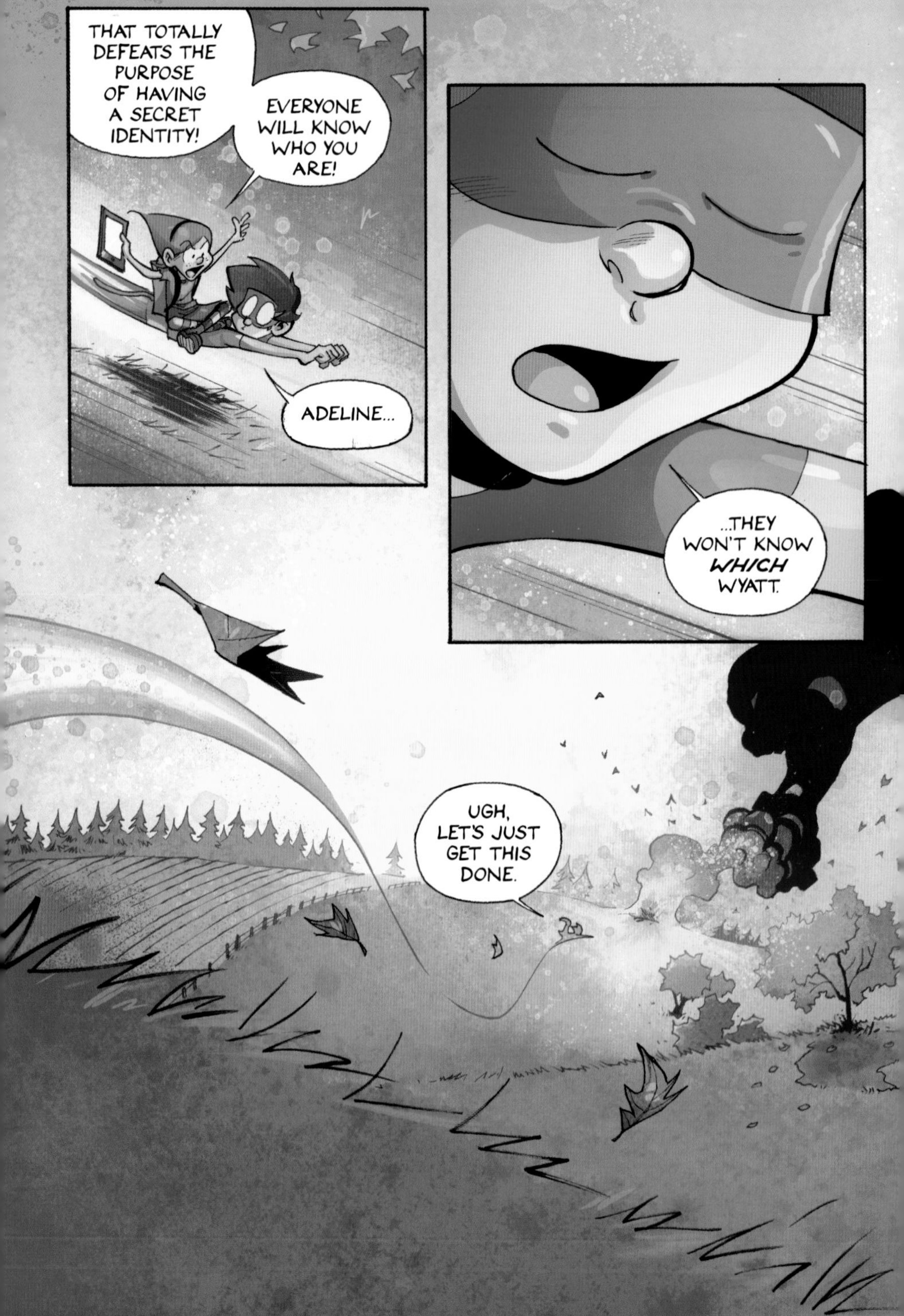
THAT TOTALLY DEFEATS THE PURPOSE OF HAVING A SECRET IDENTITY!
EVERYONE WILL KNOW WHO YOU ARE!
ADELINE...
...THEY WON'T KNOW *WHICH* WYATT.
UGH, LET'S JUST GET THIS DONE.

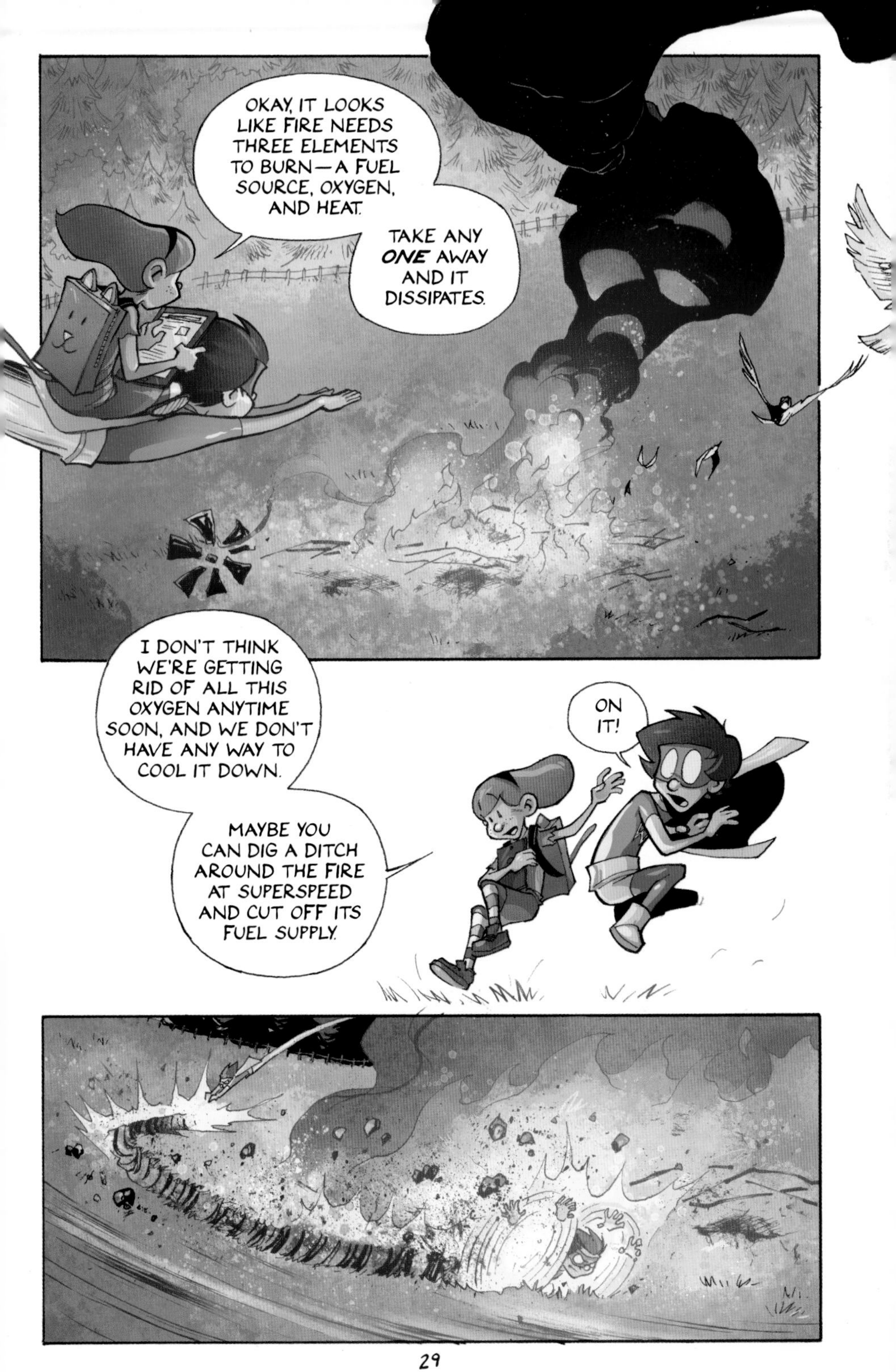
OKAY, IT LOOKS LIKE FIRE NEEDS THREE ELEMENTS TO BURN—A FUEL SOURCE, OXYGEN, AND HEAT.
TAKE ANY ONE AWAY AND IT DISSIPATES.
I DON'T THINK WE'RE GETTING RID OF ALL THIS OXYGEN ANYTIME SOON, AND WE DON'T HAVE ANY WAY TO COOL IT DOWN.
MAYBE YOU CAN DIG A DITCH AROUND THE FIRE AT SUPERSPEED AND CUT OFF ITS FUEL SUPPLY.
ON IT!

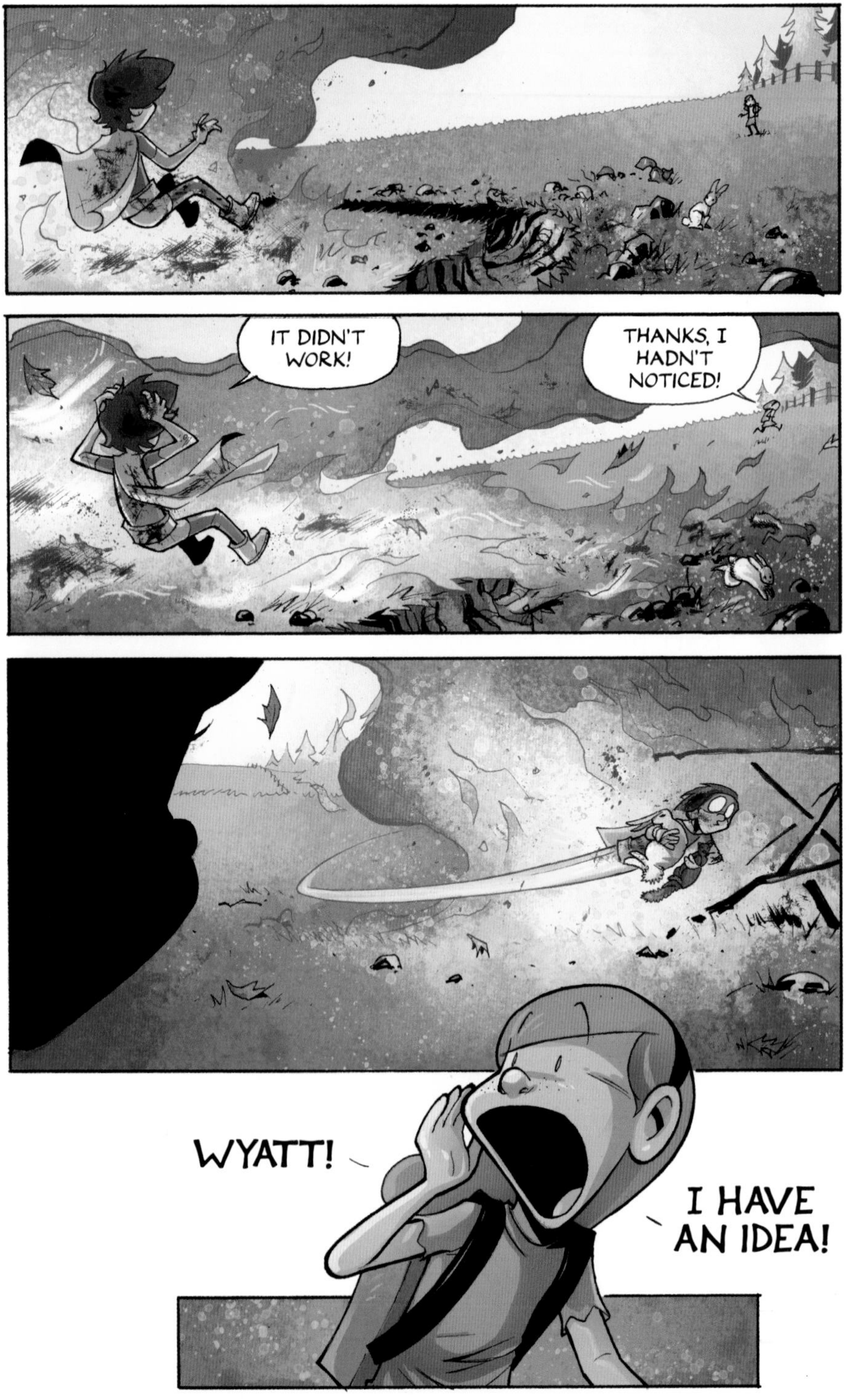
IT DIDN'T WORK!
THANKS, I HADN'T NOTICED!
WYATT!
I HAVE AN IDEA!

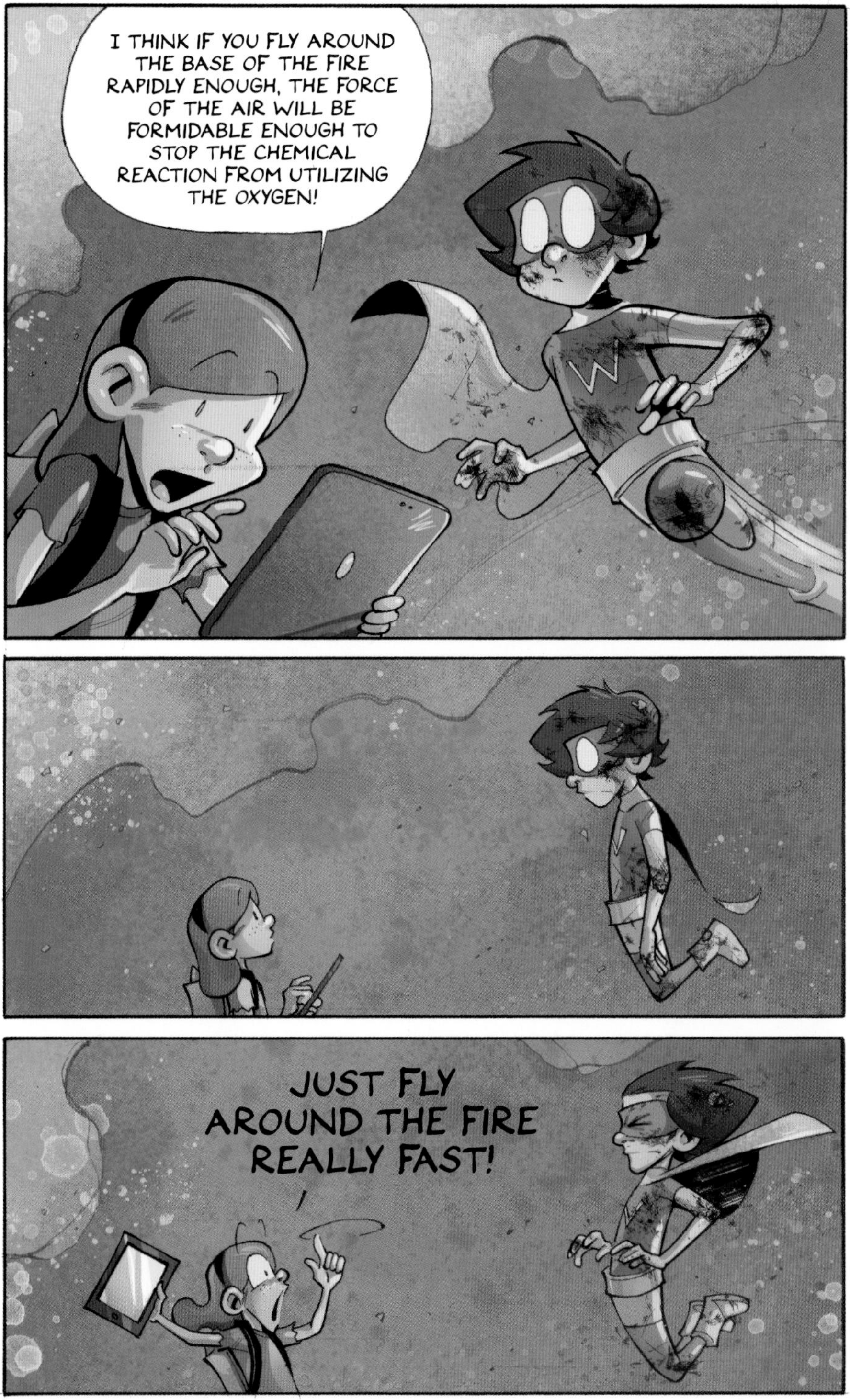
I THINK IF YOU FLY AROUND THE BASE OF THE FIRE RAPIDLY ENOUGH, THE FORCE OF THE AIR WILL BE FORMIDABLE ENOUGH TO STOP THE CHEMICAL REACTION FROM UTILIZING THE OXYGEN!
JUST FLY AROUND THE FIRE REALLY FAST!

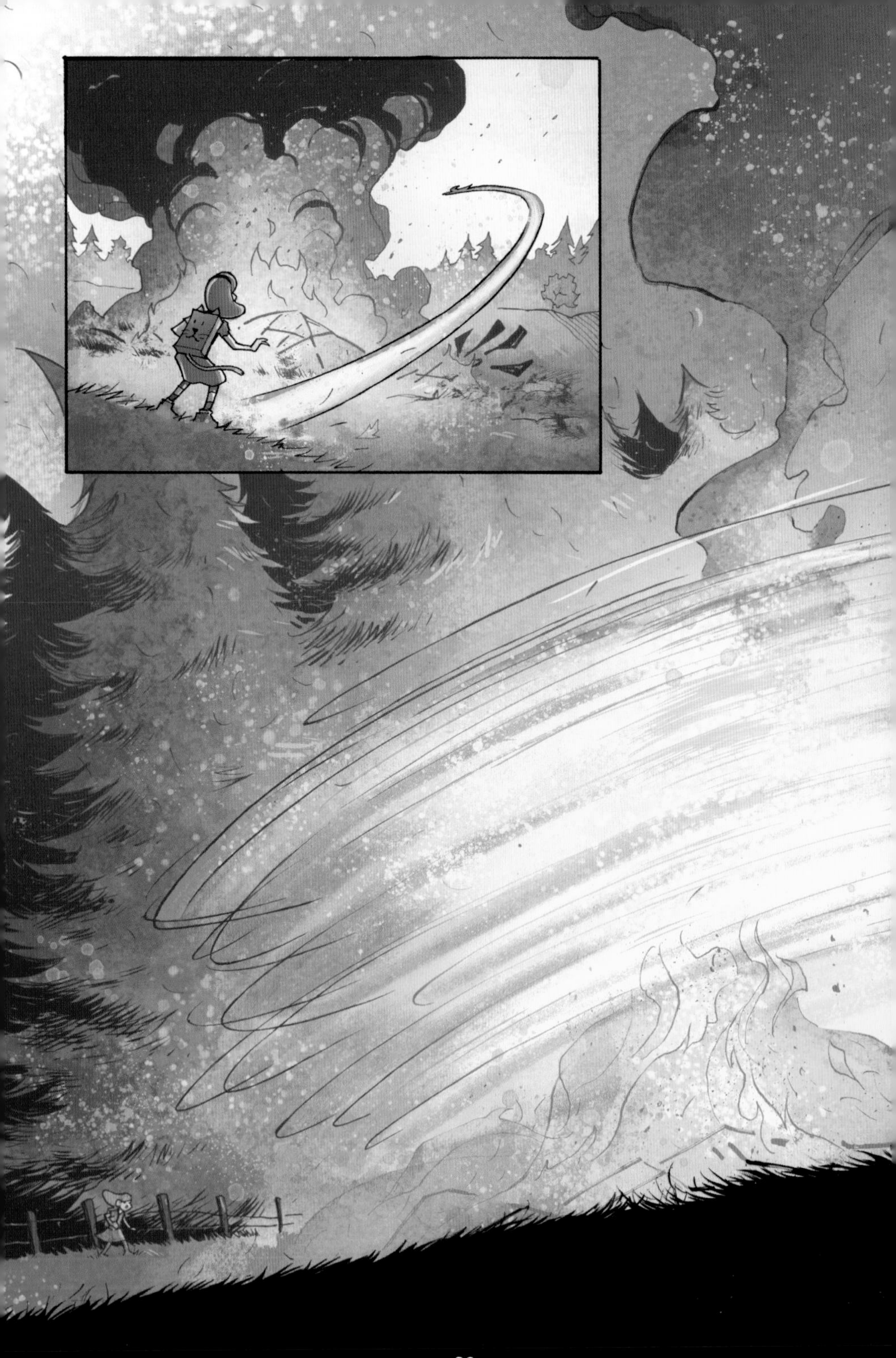

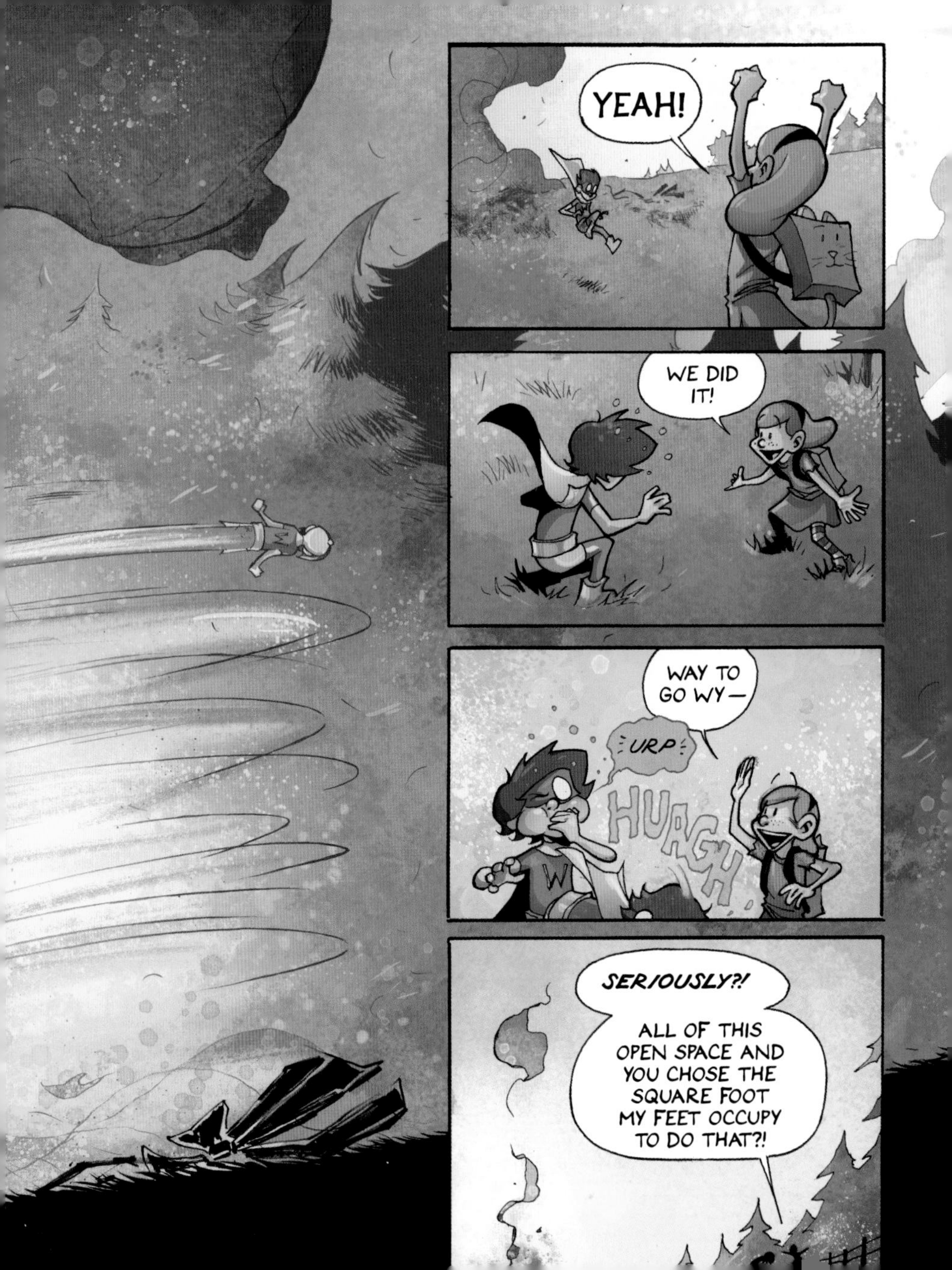
YEAH!
WE DID IT!
WAY TO GO WY—
URP
HUAGH
SERIOUSLY?!
ALL OF THIS OPEN SPACE AND YOU CHOSE THE SQUARE FOOT MY FEET OCCUPY TO DO THAT?!

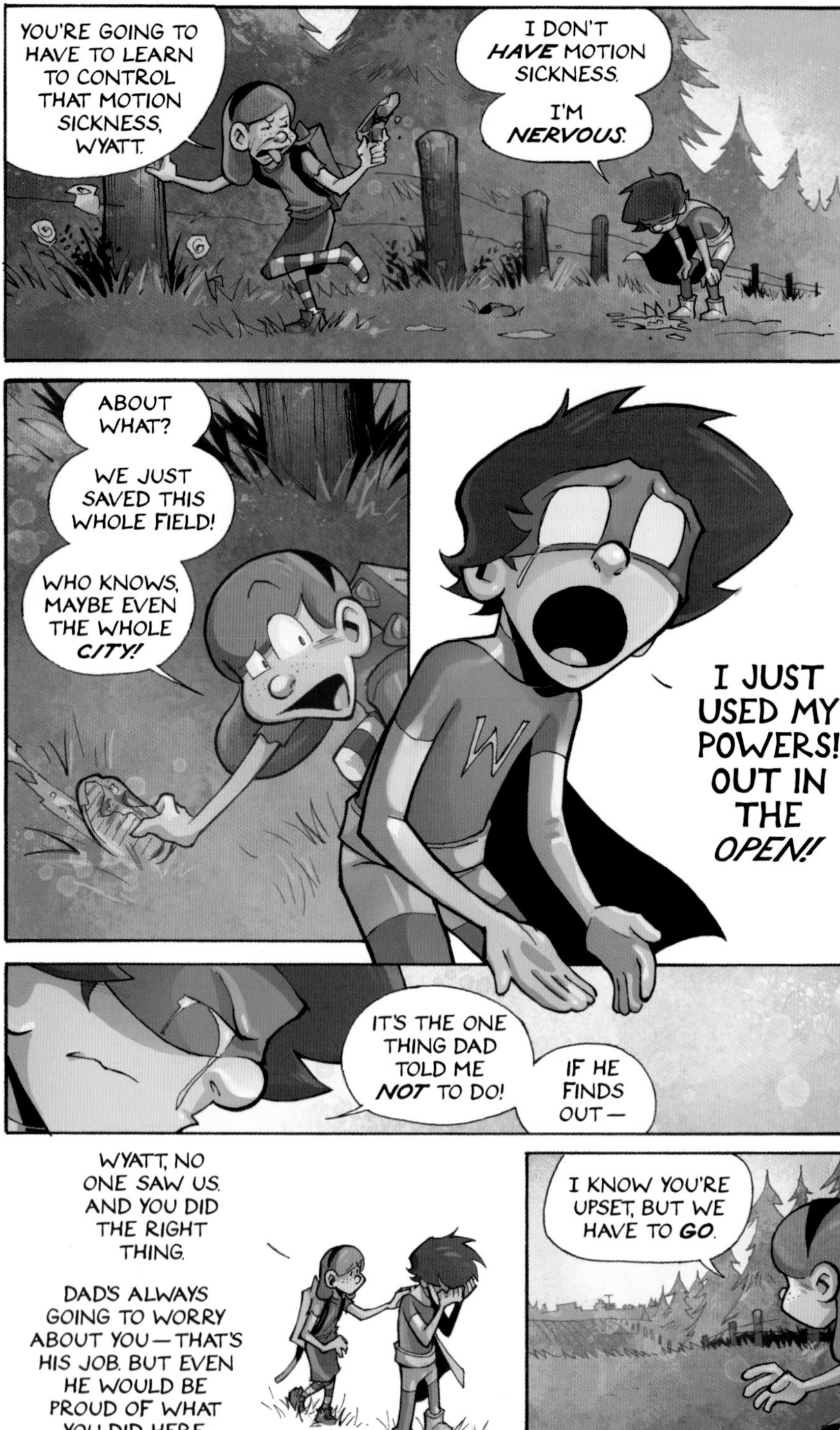
YOU'RE GOING TO HAVE TO LEARN TO CONTROL THAT MOTION SICKNESS, WYATT.
I DON'T *HAVE* MOTION SICKNESS.
I'M *NERVOUS*.
ABOUT WHAT?
WE JUST SAVED THIS WHOLE FIELD!
WHO KNOWS, MAYBE EVEN THE WHOLE *CITY!*
I JUST USED MY POWERS! OUT IN THE *OPEN!*
IT'S THE ONE THING DAD TOLD ME *NOT* TO DO!
IF HE FINDS OUT—
WYATT, NO ONE SAW US. AND YOU DID THE RIGHT THING.
DAD'S ALWAYS GOING TO WORRY ABOUT YOU—THAT'S HIS JOB. BUT EVEN HE WOULD BE PROUD OF WHAT YOU DID HERE.
I KNOW YOU'RE UPSET, BUT WE HAVE TO *GO*.

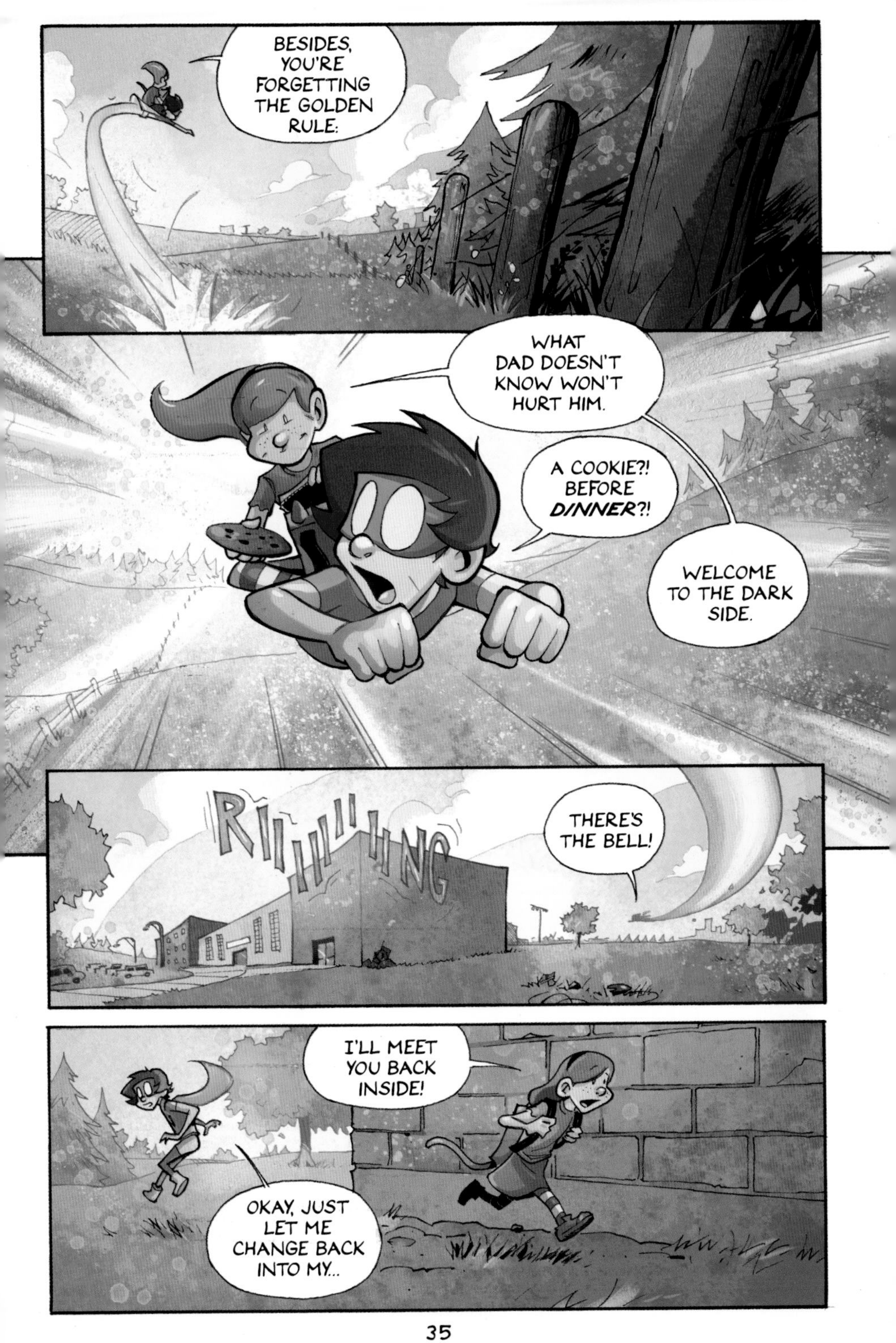
BESIDES, YOU'RE FORGETTING THE GOLDEN RULE:
WHAT DAD DOESN'T KNOW WON'T HURT HIM.
A COOKIE?! BEFORE *DINNER*?!
WELCOME TO THE DARK SIDE.
RIIIIII'' IING
THERE'S THE BELL!
I'LL MEET YOU BACK INSIDE!
OKAY, JUST LET ME CHANGE BACK INTO MY...

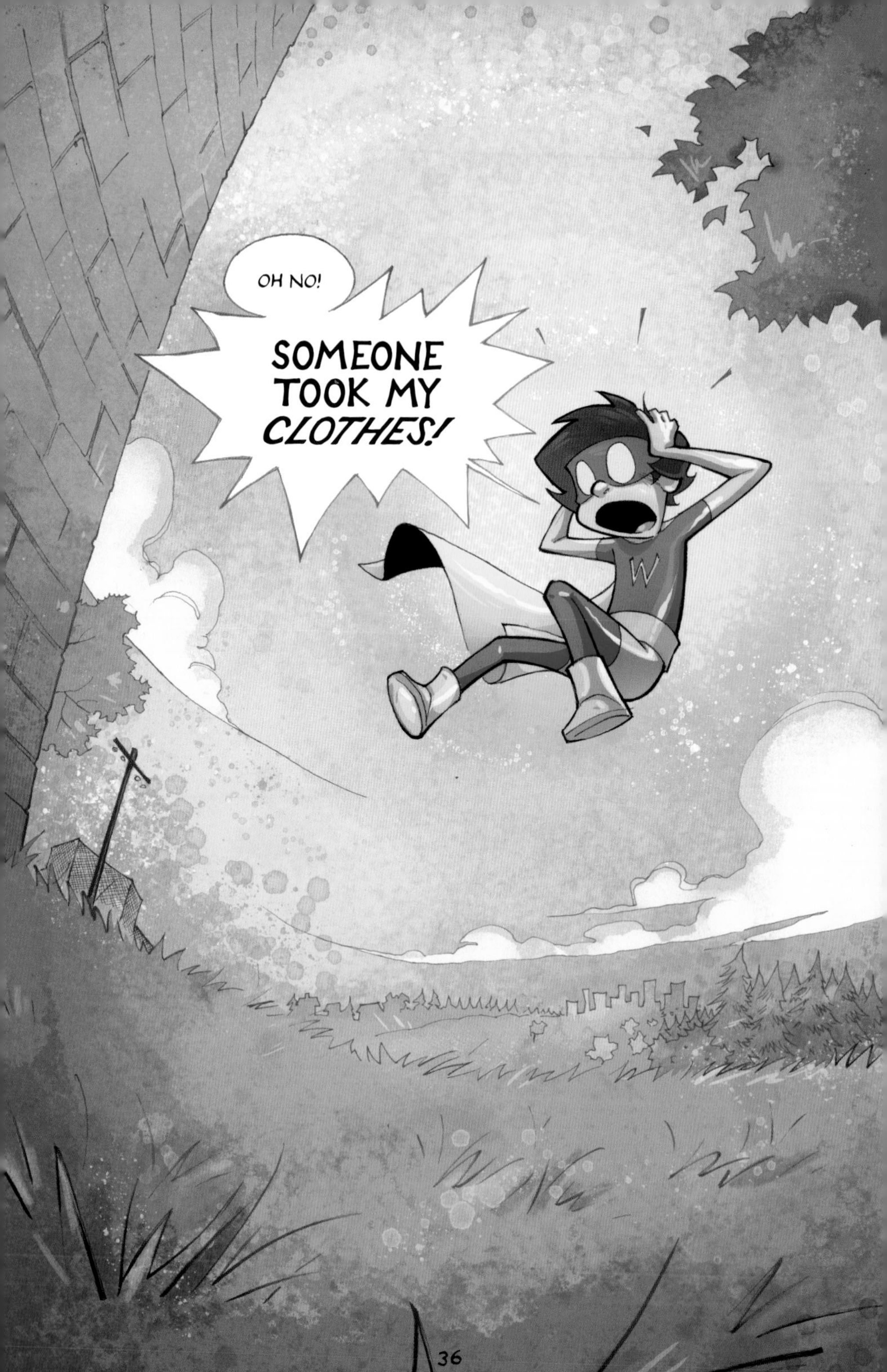
OH NO!
SOMEONE TOOK MY *CLOTHES!*

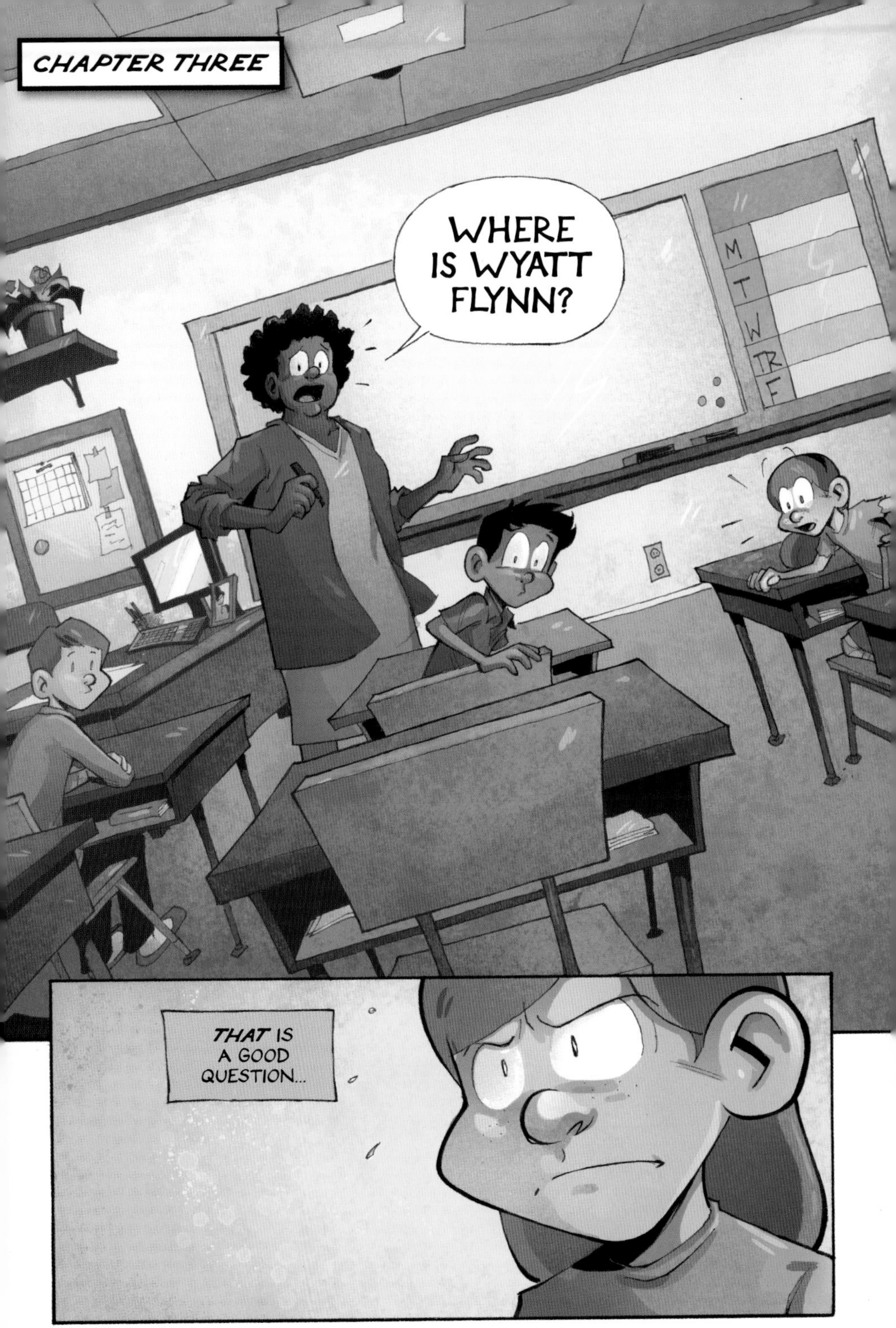
CHAPTER THREE
WHERE IS WYATT FLYNN?
M
T
W
TR
F
THAT IS A GOOD QUESTION...

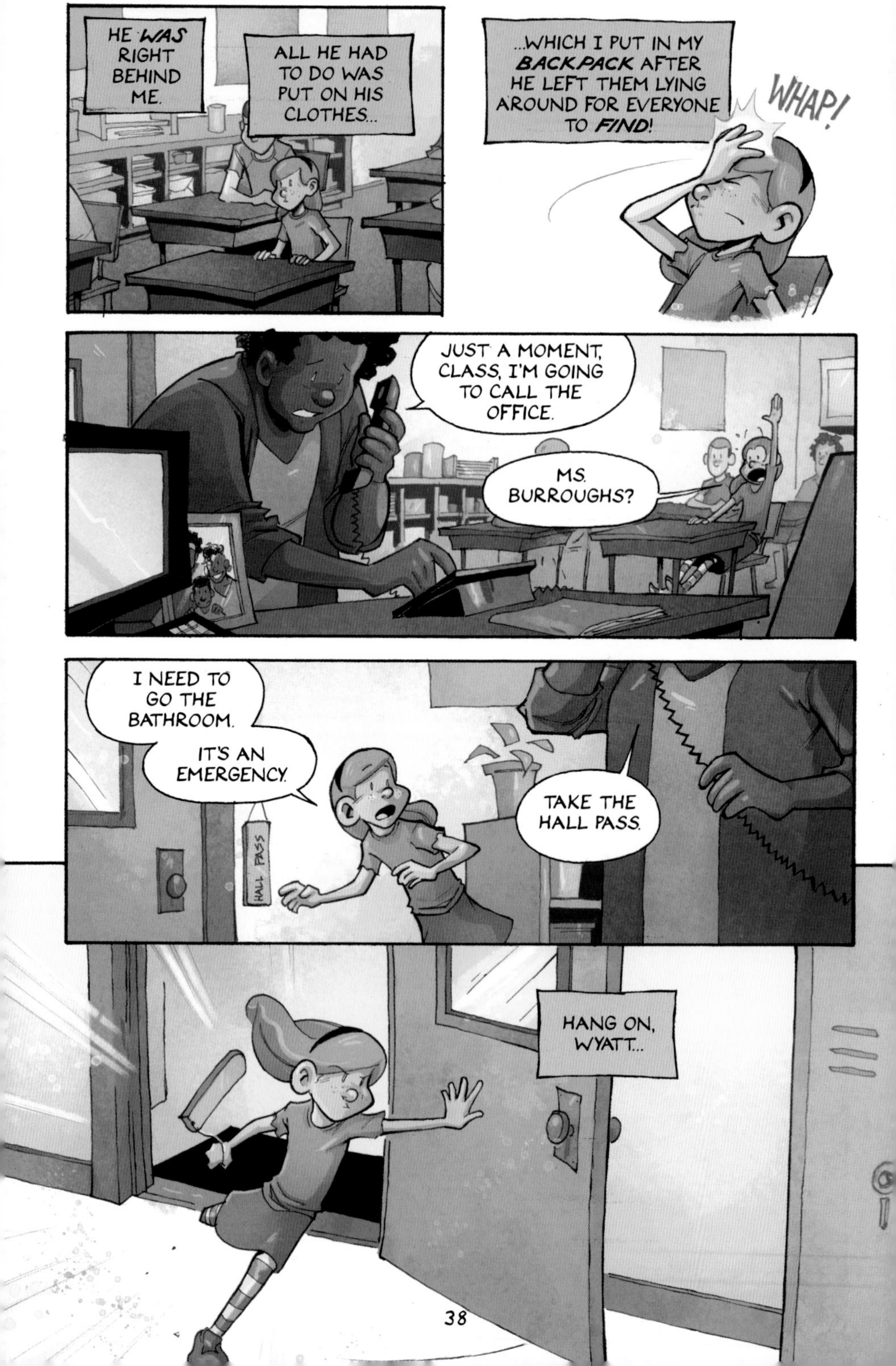
HE WAS RIGHT BEHIND ME.
ALL HE HAD TO DO WAS PUT ON HIS CLOTHES...
...WHICH I PUT IN MY BACKPACK AFTER HE LEFT THEM LYING AROUND FOR EVERYONE TO FIND!
WHAP!
JUST A MOMENT, CLASS, I'M GOING TO CALL THE OFFICE.
MS. BURROUGHS?
I NEED TO GO THE BATHROOM.
IT'S AN EMERGENCY.
HALL PASS
TAKE THE HALL PASS.
HANG ON, WYATT...

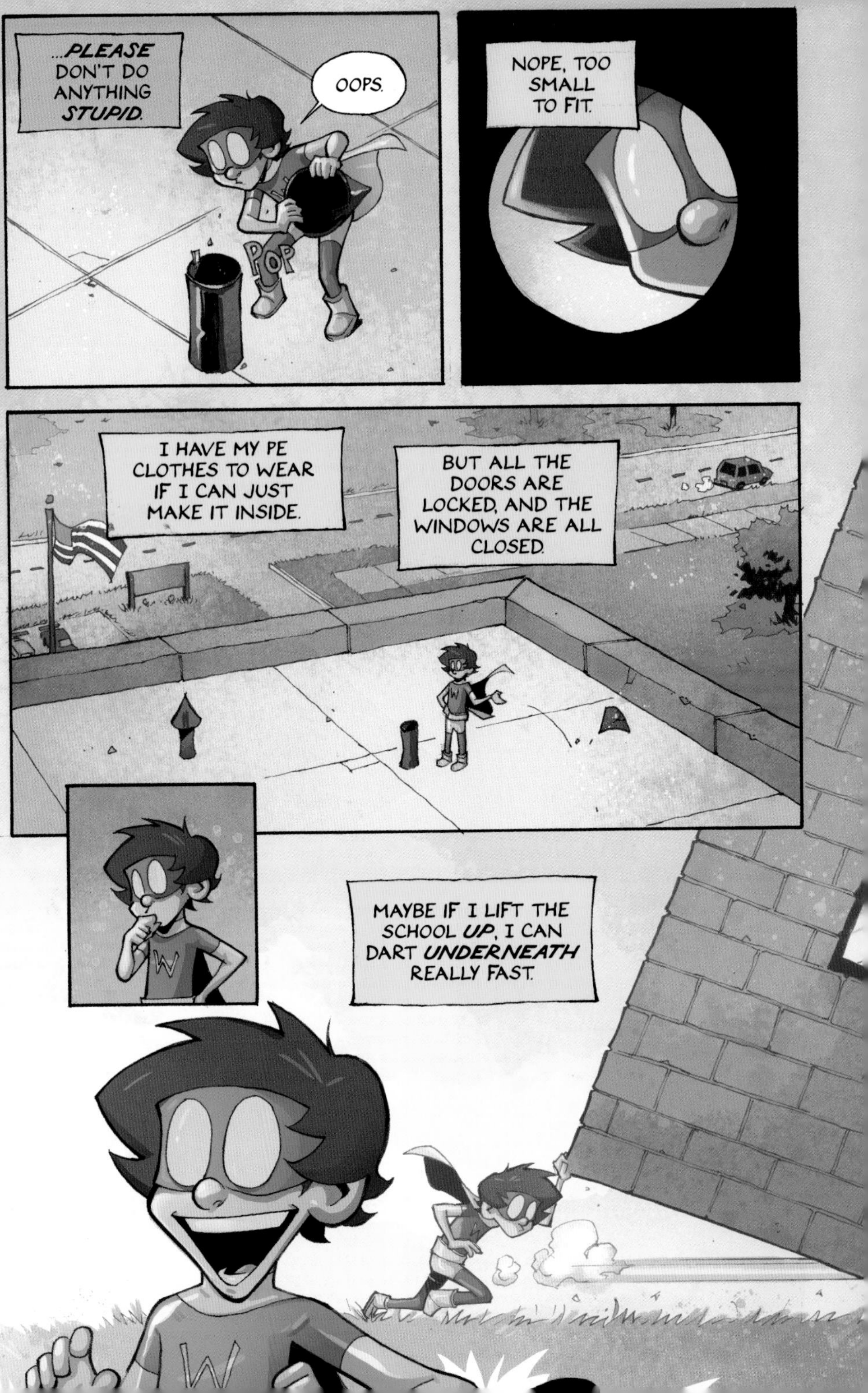
...*PLEASE* DON'T DO ANYTHING *STUPID*.
OOPS.
POP
NOPE, TOO SMALL TO FIT.
I HAVE MY PE CLOTHES TO WEAR IF I CAN JUST MAKE IT INSIDE.
BUT ALL THE DOORS ARE LOCKED, AND THE WINDOWS ARE ALL CLOSED.
MAYBE IF I LIFT THE SCHOOL *UP*, I CAN DART *UNDERNEATH* REALLY FAST.

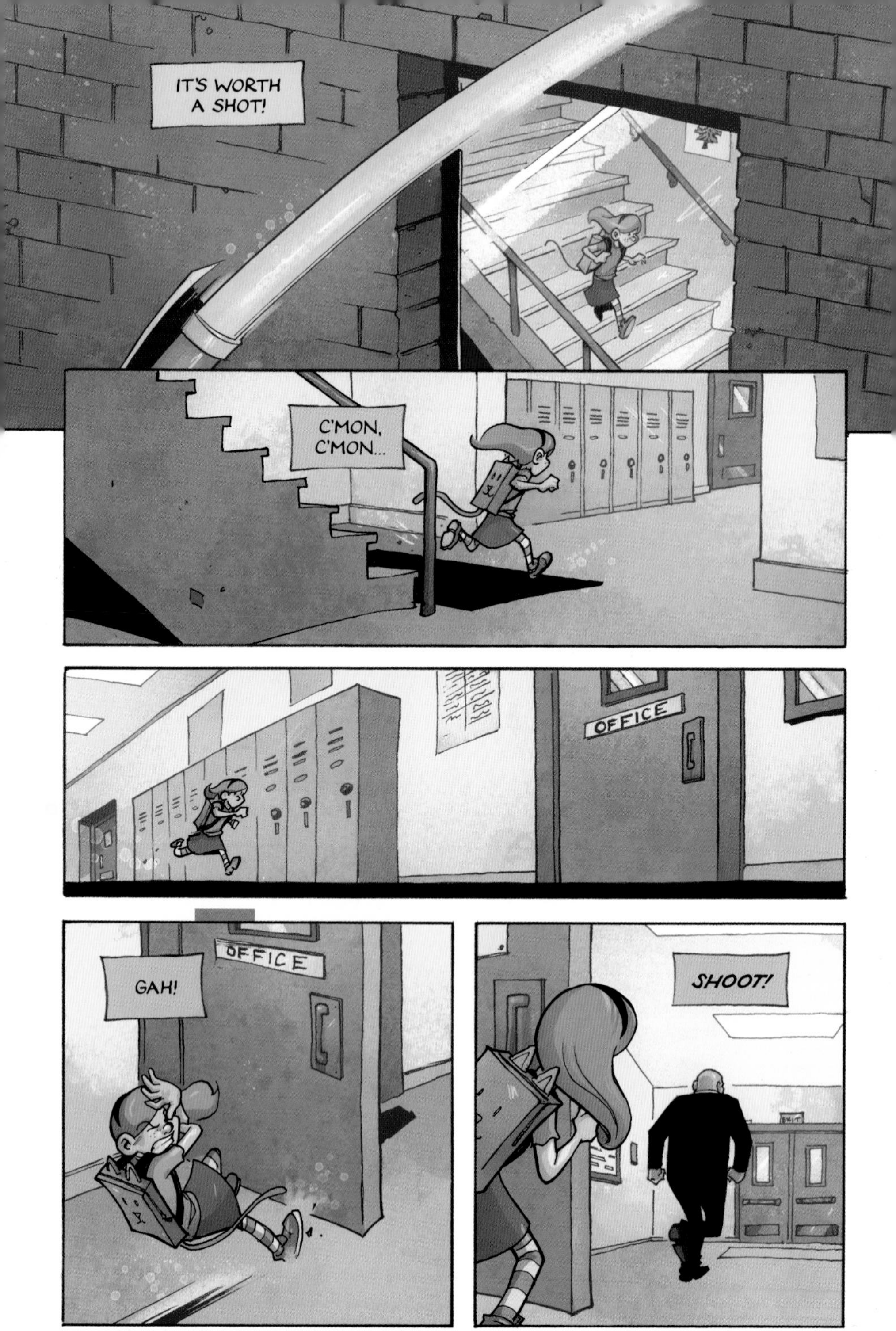
IT'S WORTH A SHOT!
C'MON, C'MON...
OFFICE
OFFICE
GAH!
SHOOT!

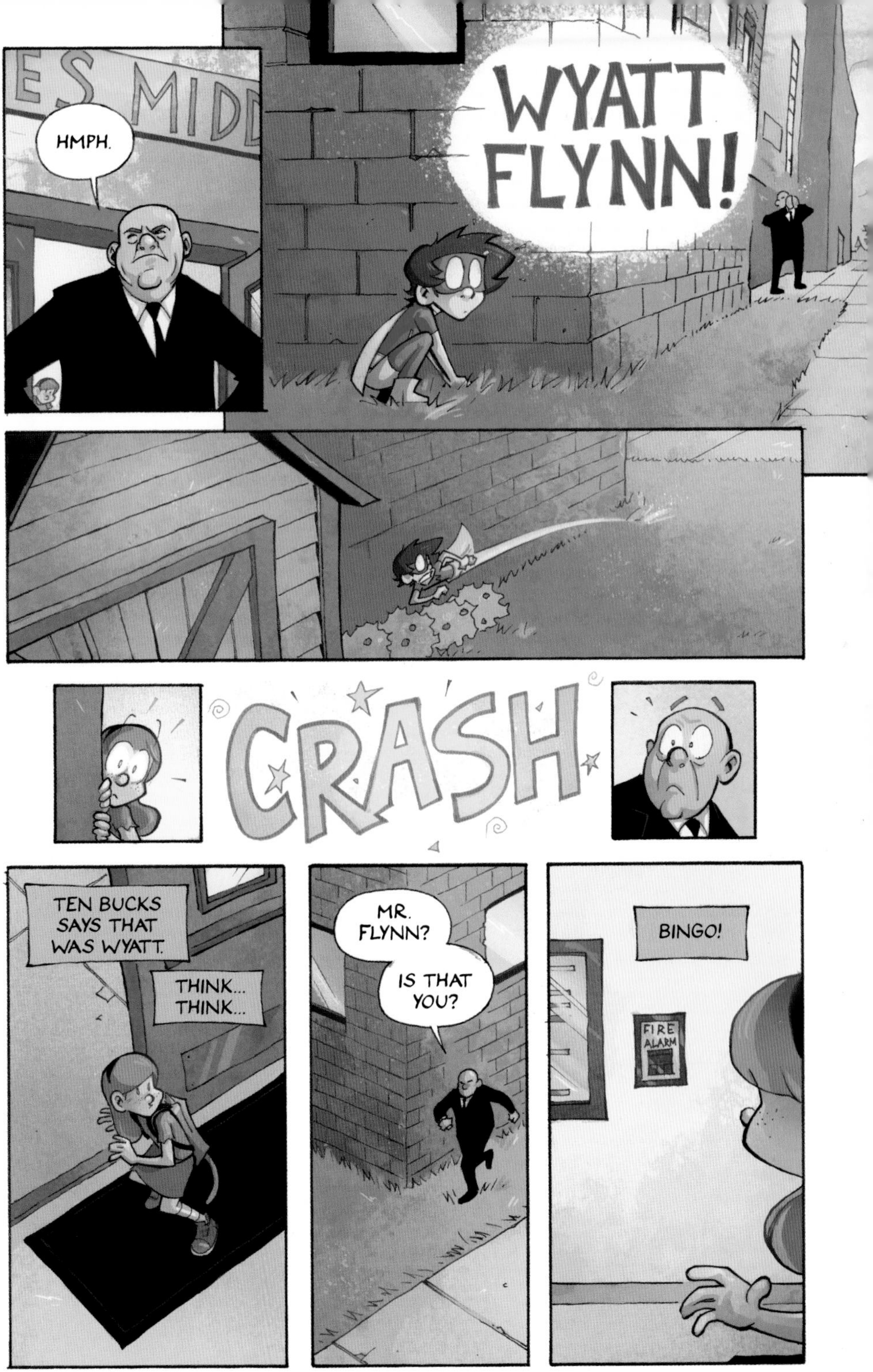

HMPH.
WYATT FLYNN!
CRASH
TEN BUCKS SAYS THAT WAS WYATT.
THINK... THINK...
MR. FLYNN?
IS THAT YOU?
BINGO!
FIRE ALARM

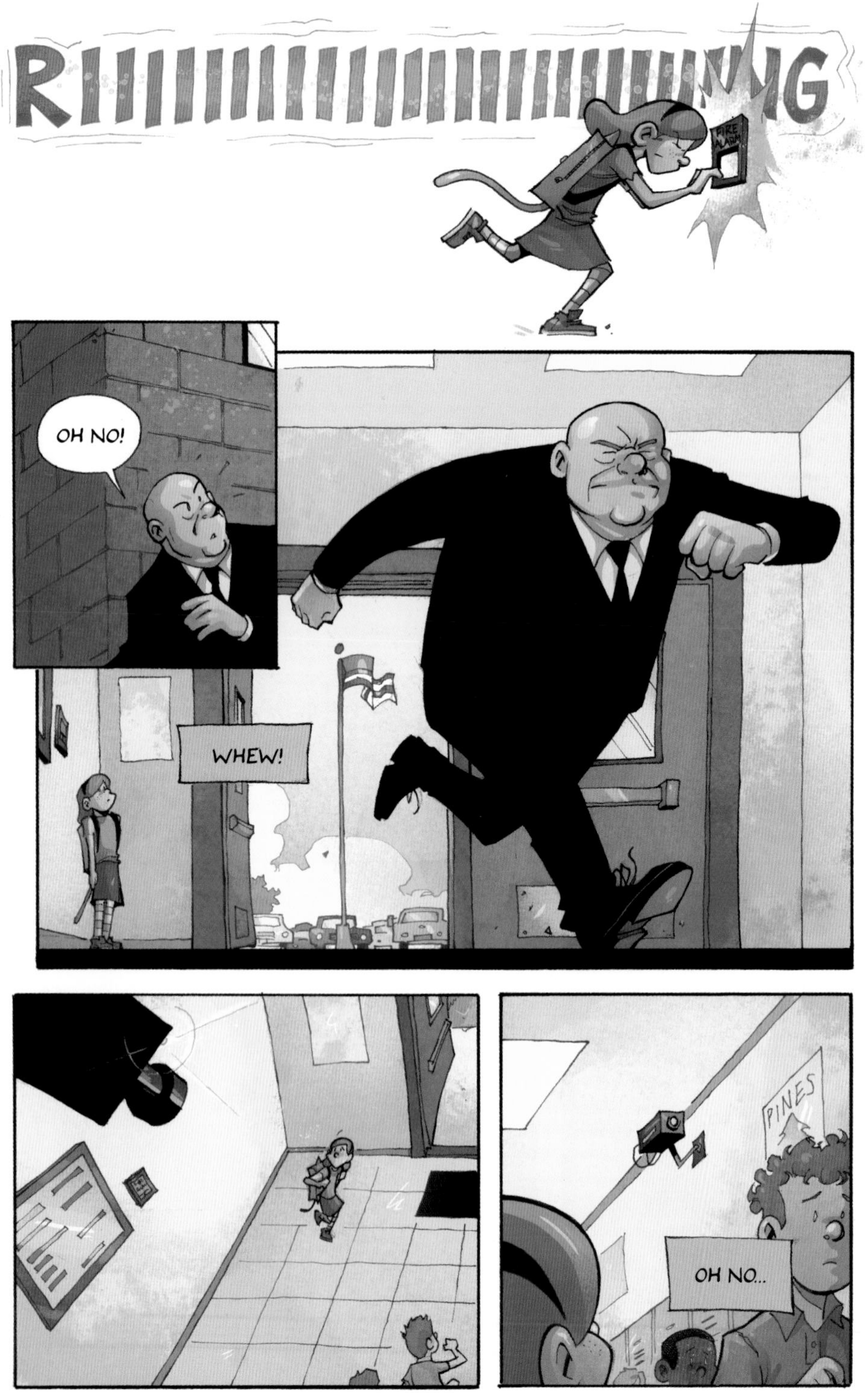
RIIIIIIIIIIIIIIIIIIIIIING
FIRE ALARM
OH NO!
WHEW!
PINES
OH NO...

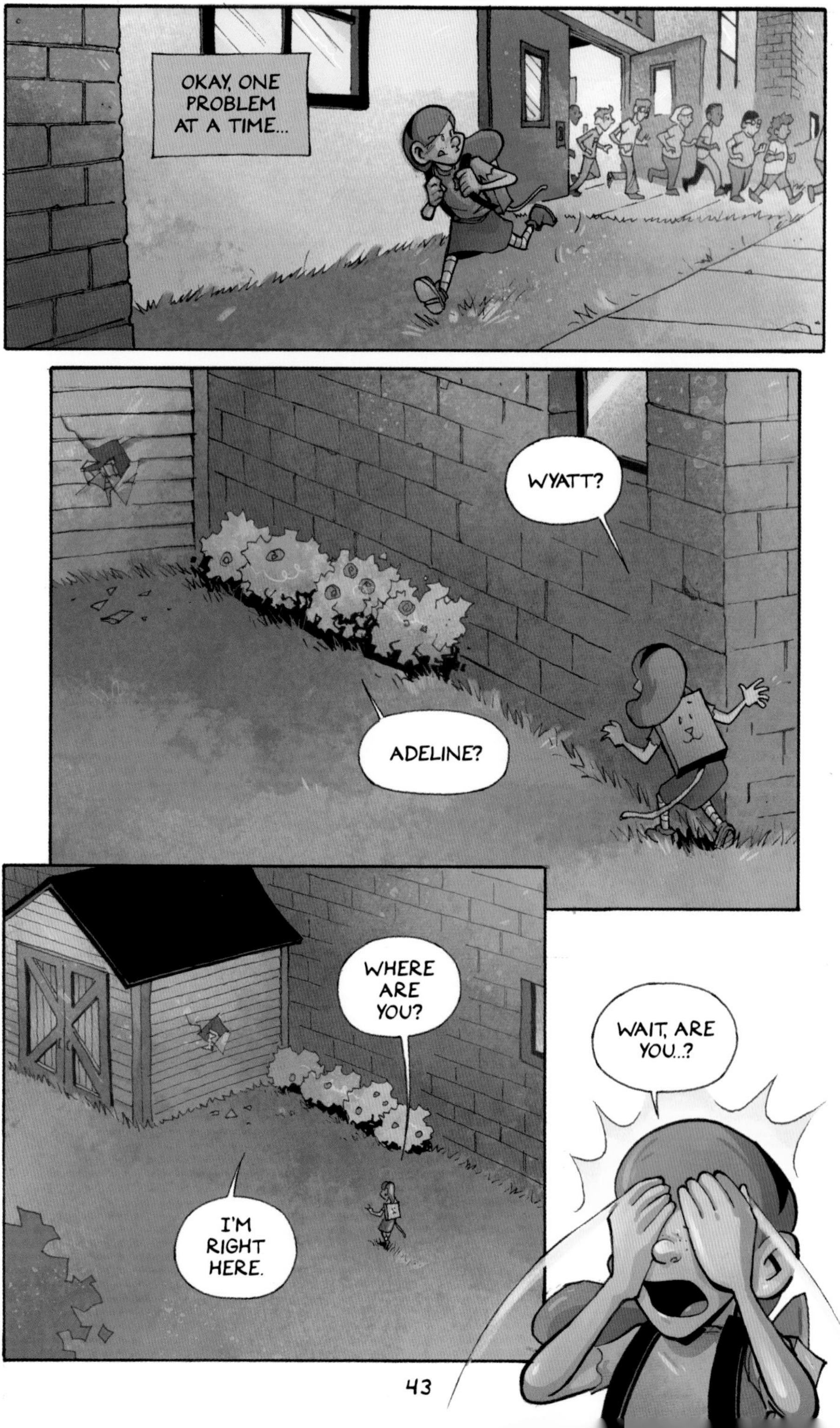
OKAY, ONE PROBLEM AT A TIME...
WYATT?
ADELINE?
WHERE ARE YOU?
I'M RIGHT HERE.
WAIT, ARE YOU..?

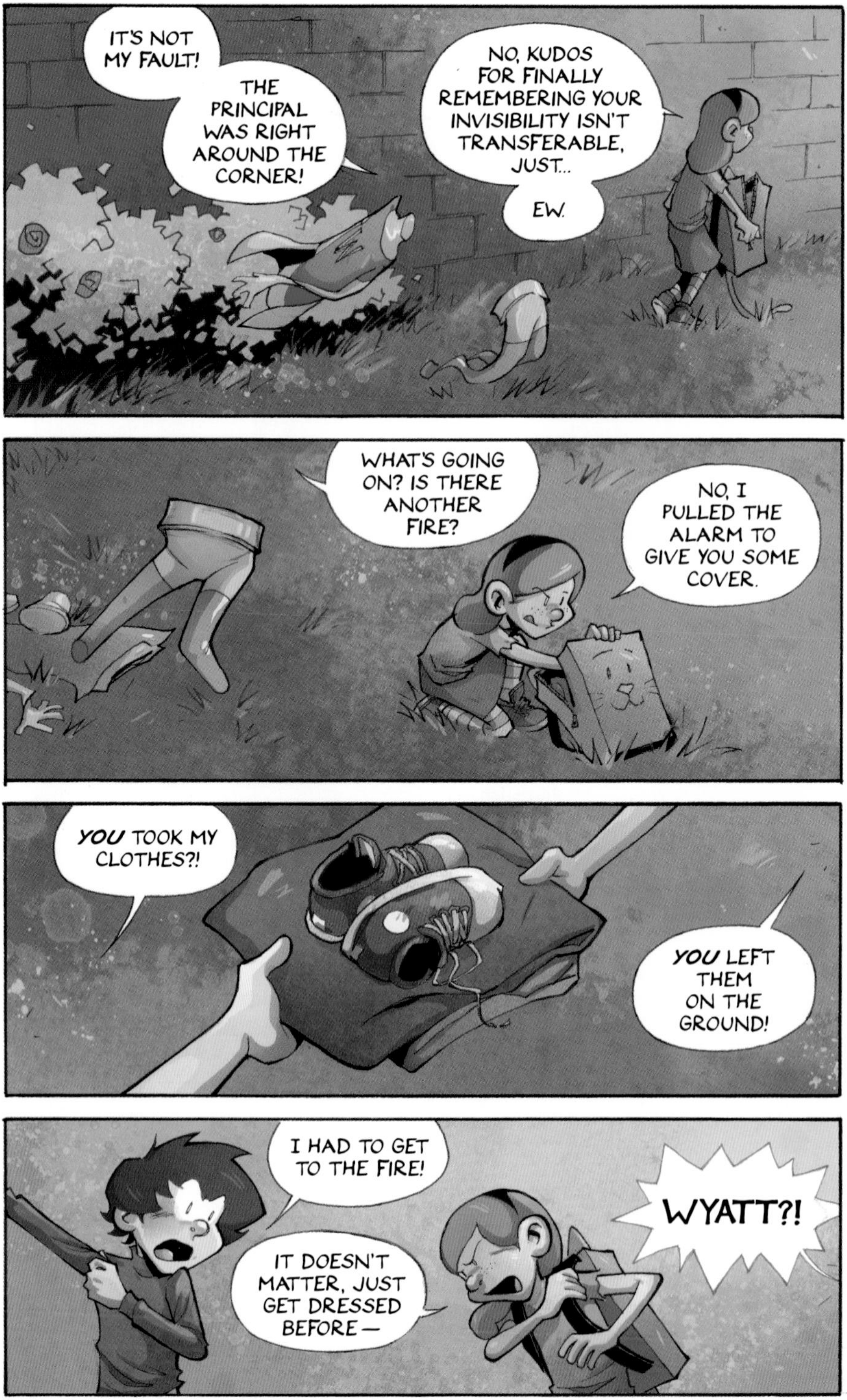
IT'S NOT MY FAULT!
THE PRINCIPAL WAS RIGHT AROUND THE CORNER!
NO, KUDOS FOR FINALLY REMEMBERING YOUR INVISIBILITY ISN'T TRANSFERABLE, JUST...
EW.
WHAT'S GOING ON? IS THERE ANOTHER FIRE?
NO, I PULLED THE ALARM TO GIVE YOU SOME COVER.
YOU TOOK MY CLOTHES?!
YOU LEFT THEM ON THE GROUND!
I HAD TO GET TO THE FIRE!
IT DOESN'T MATTER, JUST GET DRESSED BEFORE—
WYATT?!

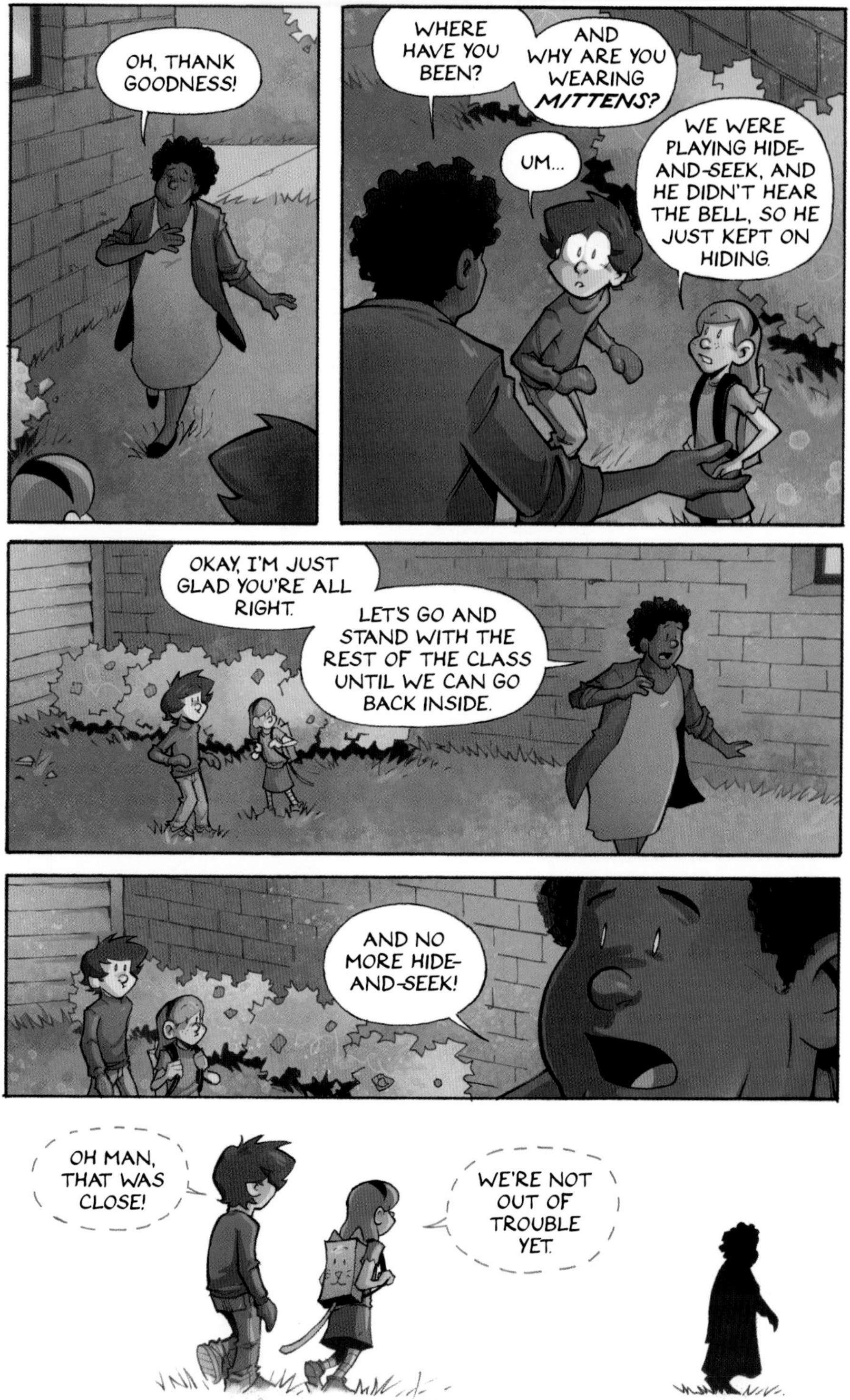
OH, THANK GOODNESS!
WHERE HAVE YOU BEEN?
AND WHY ARE YOU WEARING *MITTENS?*
UM...
WE WERE PLAYING HIDE-AND-SEEK, AND HE DIDN'T HEAR THE BELL, SO HE JUST KEPT ON HIDING.
OKAY, I'M JUST GLAD YOU'RE ALL RIGHT.
LET'S GO AND STAND WITH THE REST OF THE CLASS UNTIL WE CAN GO BACK INSIDE.
AND NO MORE HIDE-AND-SEEK!
OH MAN, THAT WAS CLOSE!
WE'RE NOT OUT OF TROUBLE YET.

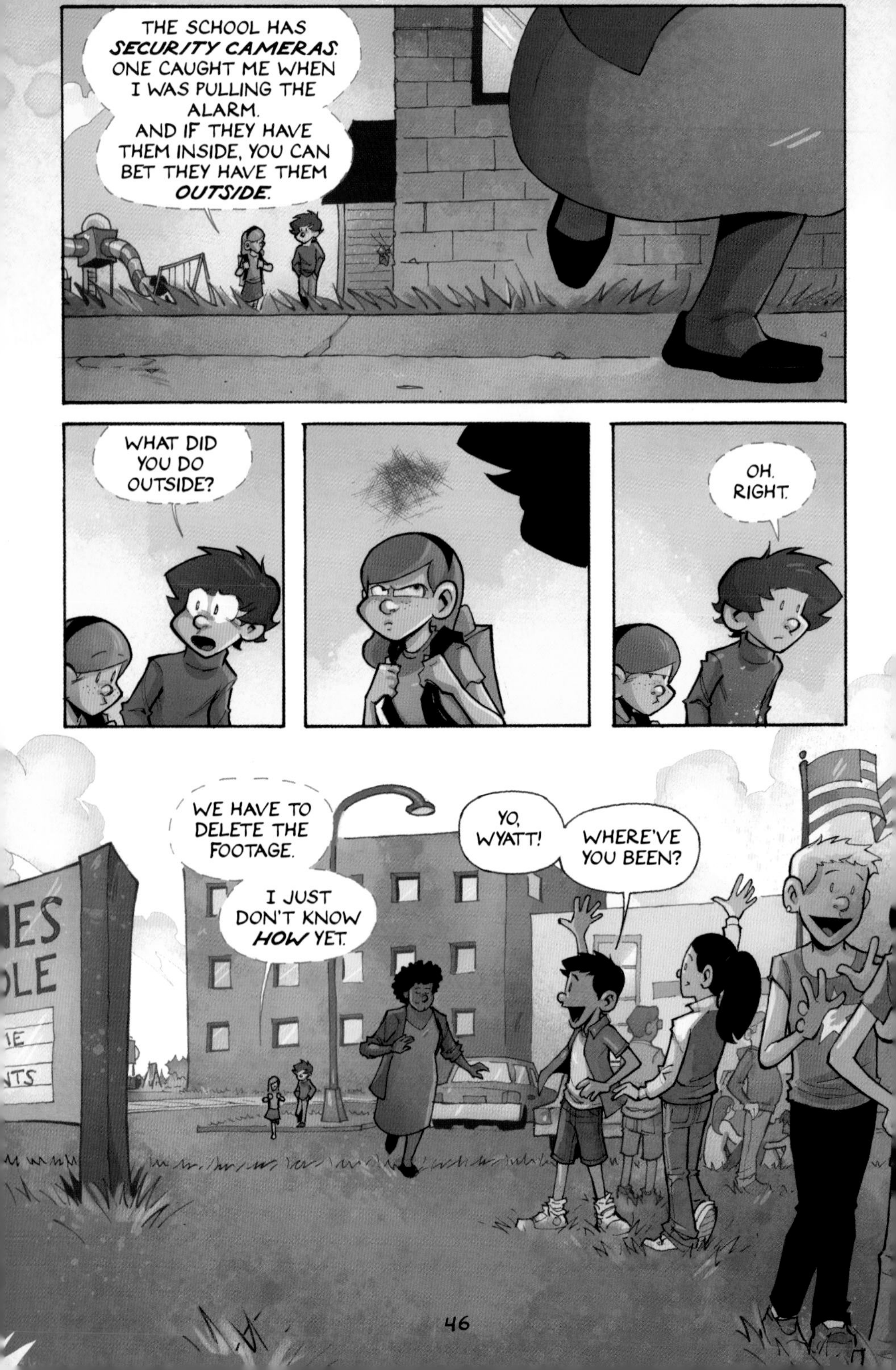
THE SCHOOL HAS SECURITY CAMERAS. ONE CAUGHT ME WHEN I WAS PULLING THE ALARM. AND IF THEY HAVE THEM INSIDE, YOU CAN BET THEY HAVE THEM OUTSIDE.
WHAT DID YOU DO OUTSIDE?
OH. RIGHT.
WE HAVE TO DELETE THE FOOTAGE.
I JUST DON'T KNOW HOW YET.
YO, WYATT!
WHERE'VE YOU BEEN?

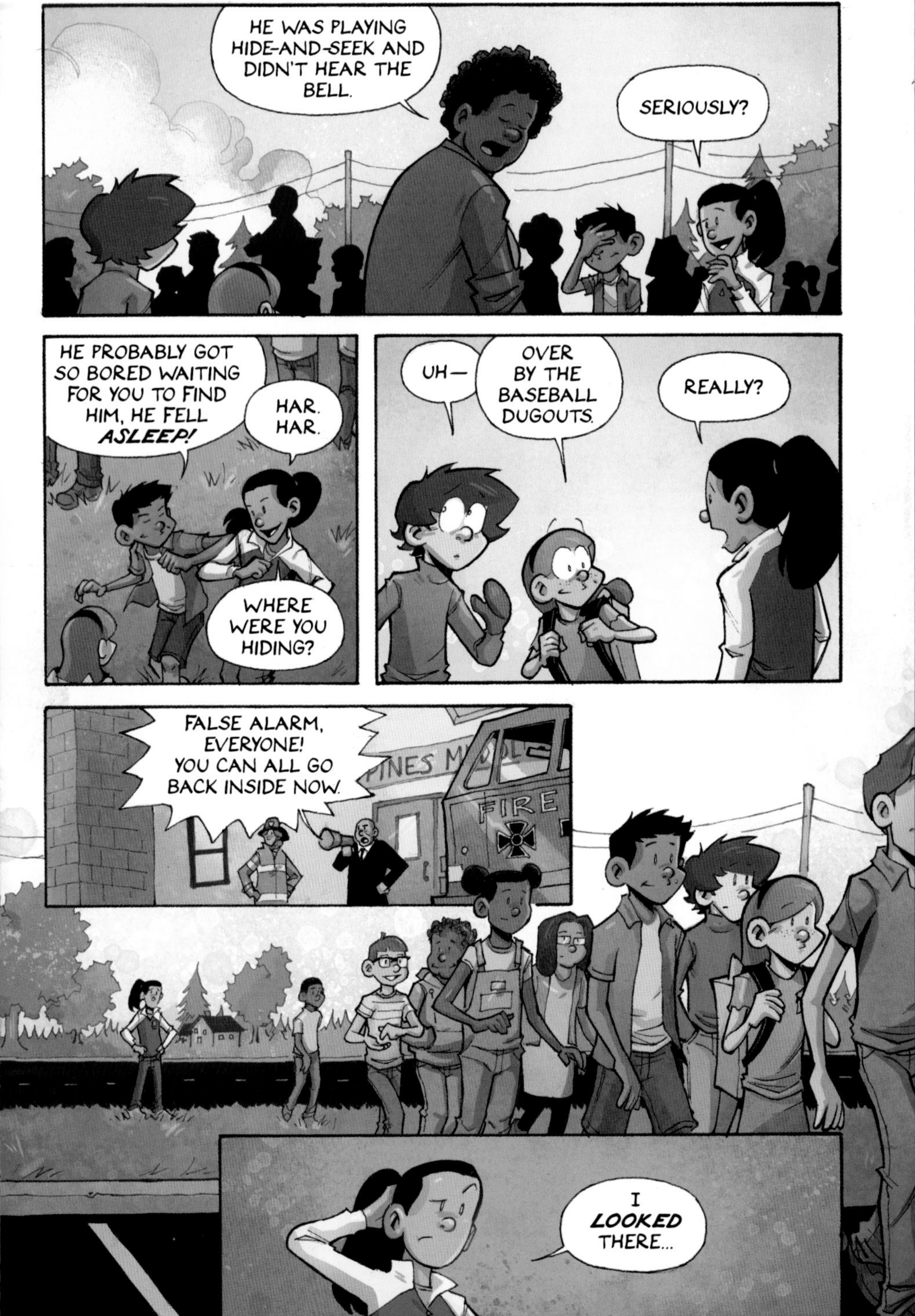
HE WAS PLAYING HIDE-AND-SEEK AND DIDN'T HEAR THE BELL.
SERIOUSLY?
HE PROBABLY GOT SO BORED WAITING FOR YOU TO FIND HIM, HE FELL ASLEEP!
HAR. HAR.
WHERE WERE YOU HIDING?
UH—
OVER BY THE BASEBALL DUGOUTS.
REALLY?
FALSE ALARM, EVERYONE! YOU CAN ALL GO BACK INSIDE NOW.
PINES M
FIRE
I LOOKED THERE...

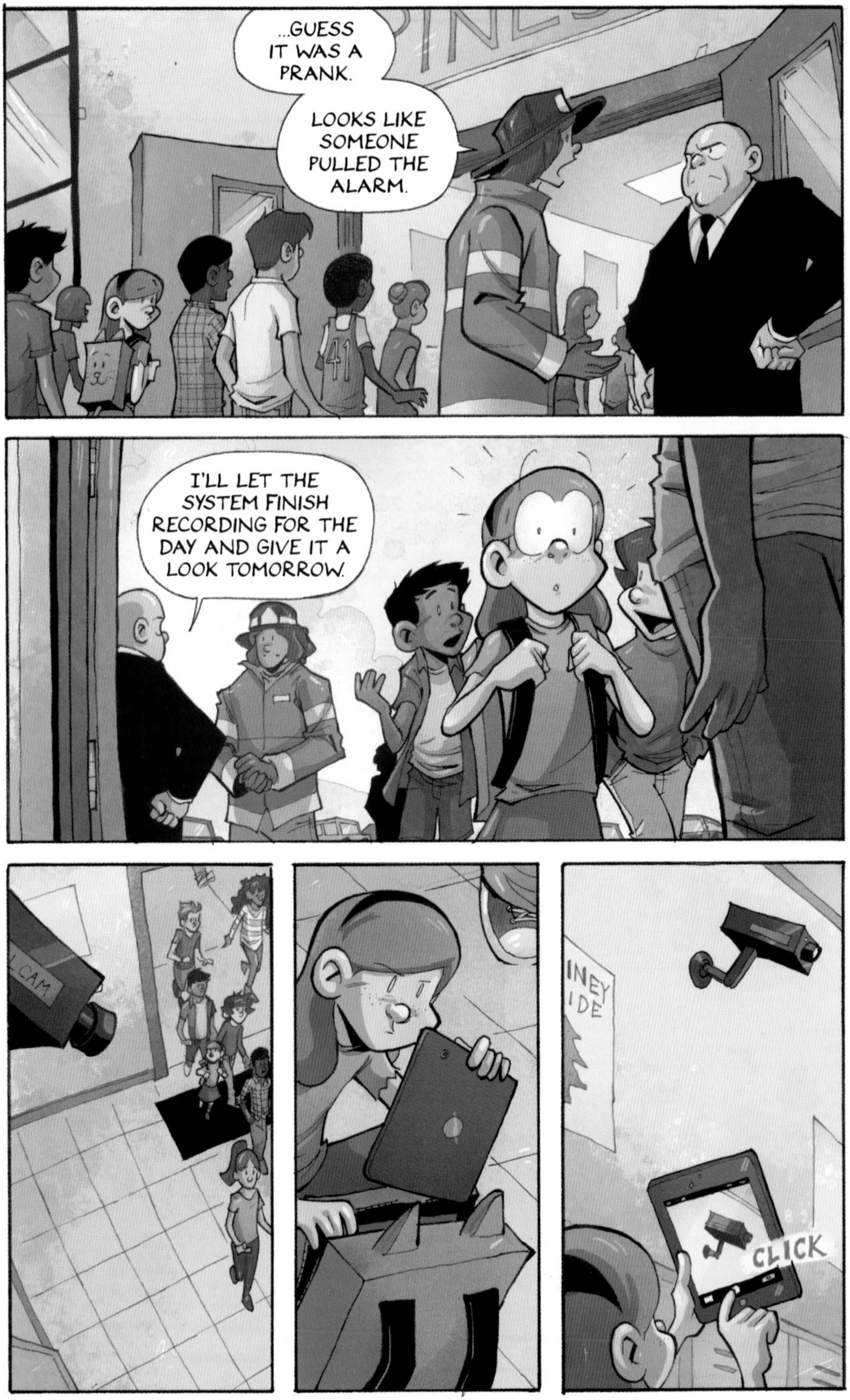
...GUESS IT WAS A PRANK.
LOOKS LIKE SOMEONE PULLED THE ALARM.
I'LL LET THE SYSTEM FINISH RECORDING FOR THE DAY AND GIVE IT A LOOK TOMORROW.
CLICK

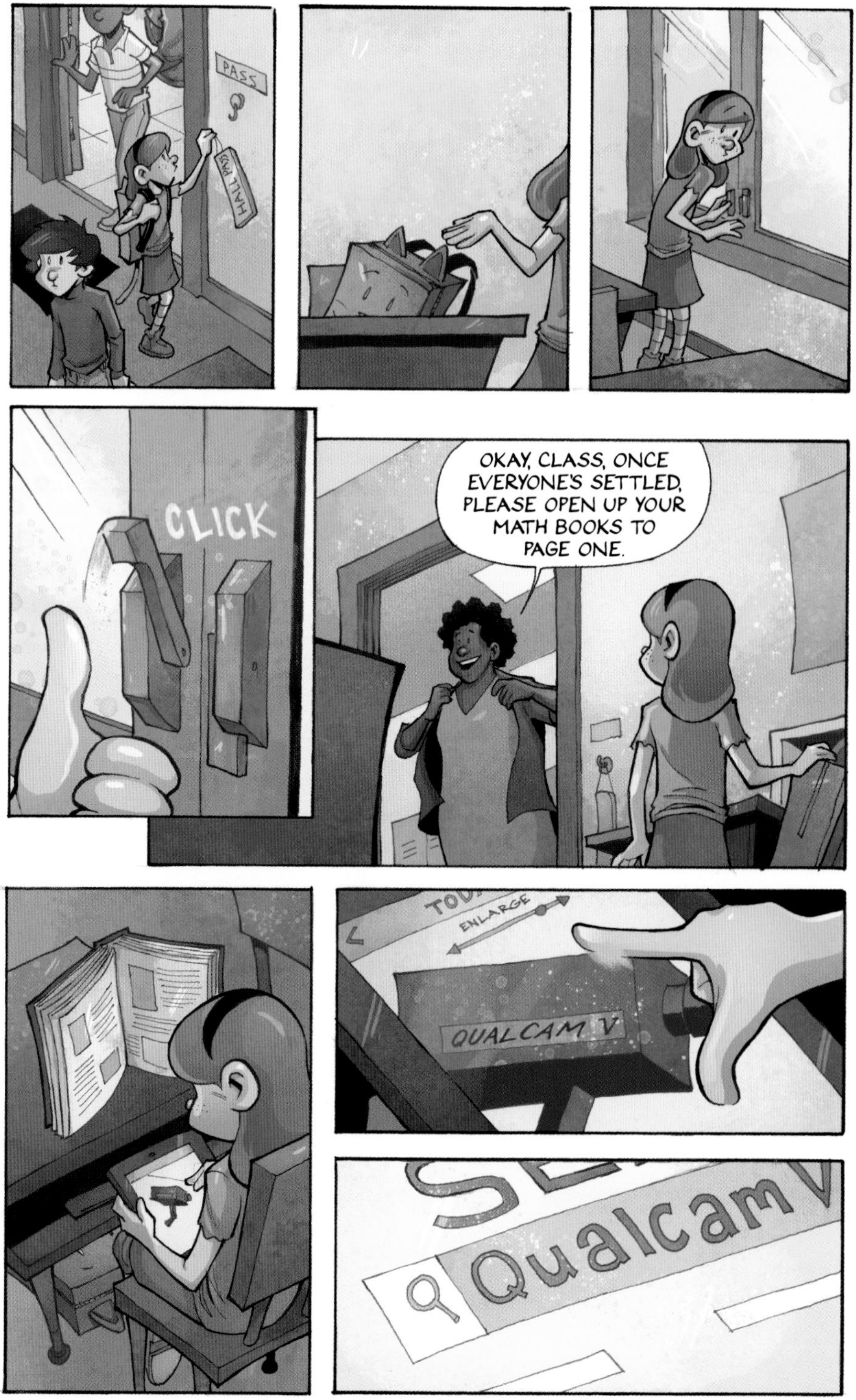
PASS
HALL PASS
CLICK
OKAY, CLASS, ONCE EVERYONE'S SETTLED, PLEASE OPEN UP YOUR MATH BOOKS TO PAGE ONE.
ENLARGE
QUALCAM V
Qualcam V

CHAPTER FOUR

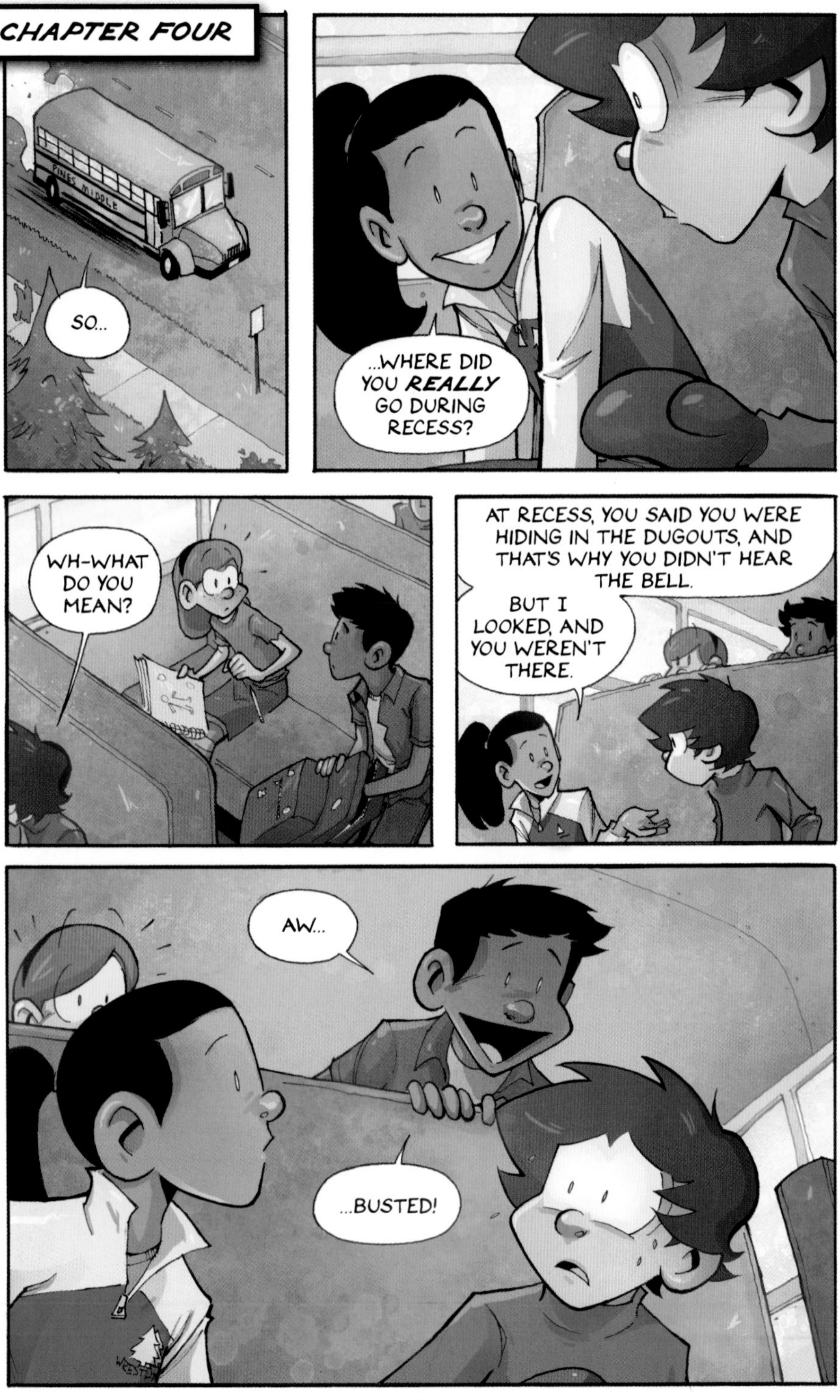

SO...
...WHERE DID YOU ***REALLY*** GO DURING RECESS?
WH-WHAT DO YOU MEAN?
AT RECESS, YOU SAID YOU WERE HIDING IN THE DUGOUTS, AND THAT'S WHY YOU DIDN'T HEAR THE BELL.
BUT I LOOKED, AND YOU WEREN'T THERE.
AW...
...BUSTED!

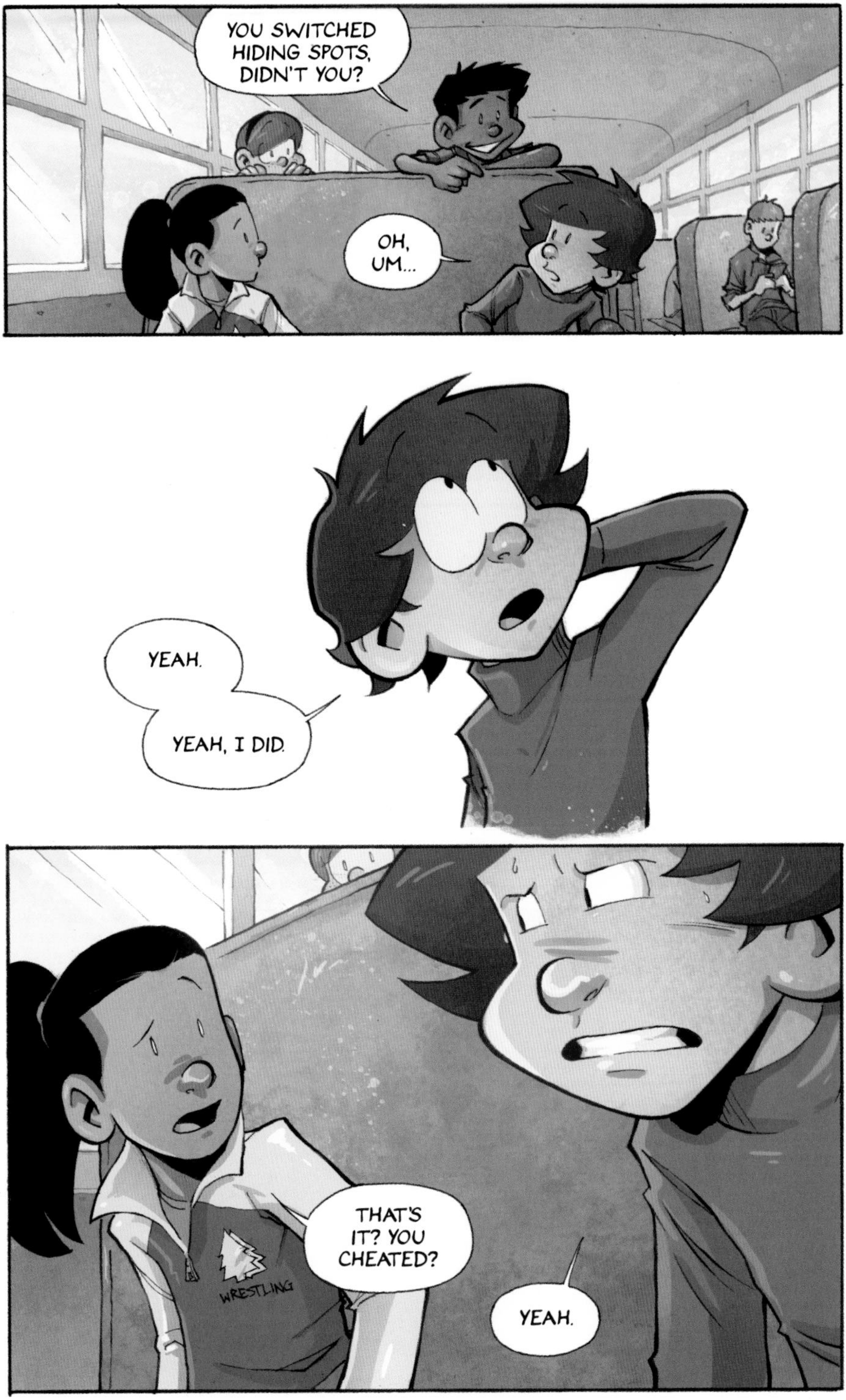
YOU SWITCHED HIDING SPOTS, DIDN'T YOU?
OH, UM...
YEAH.
YEAH, I DID.
THAT'S IT? YOU CHEATED?
YEAH.
WRESTLING

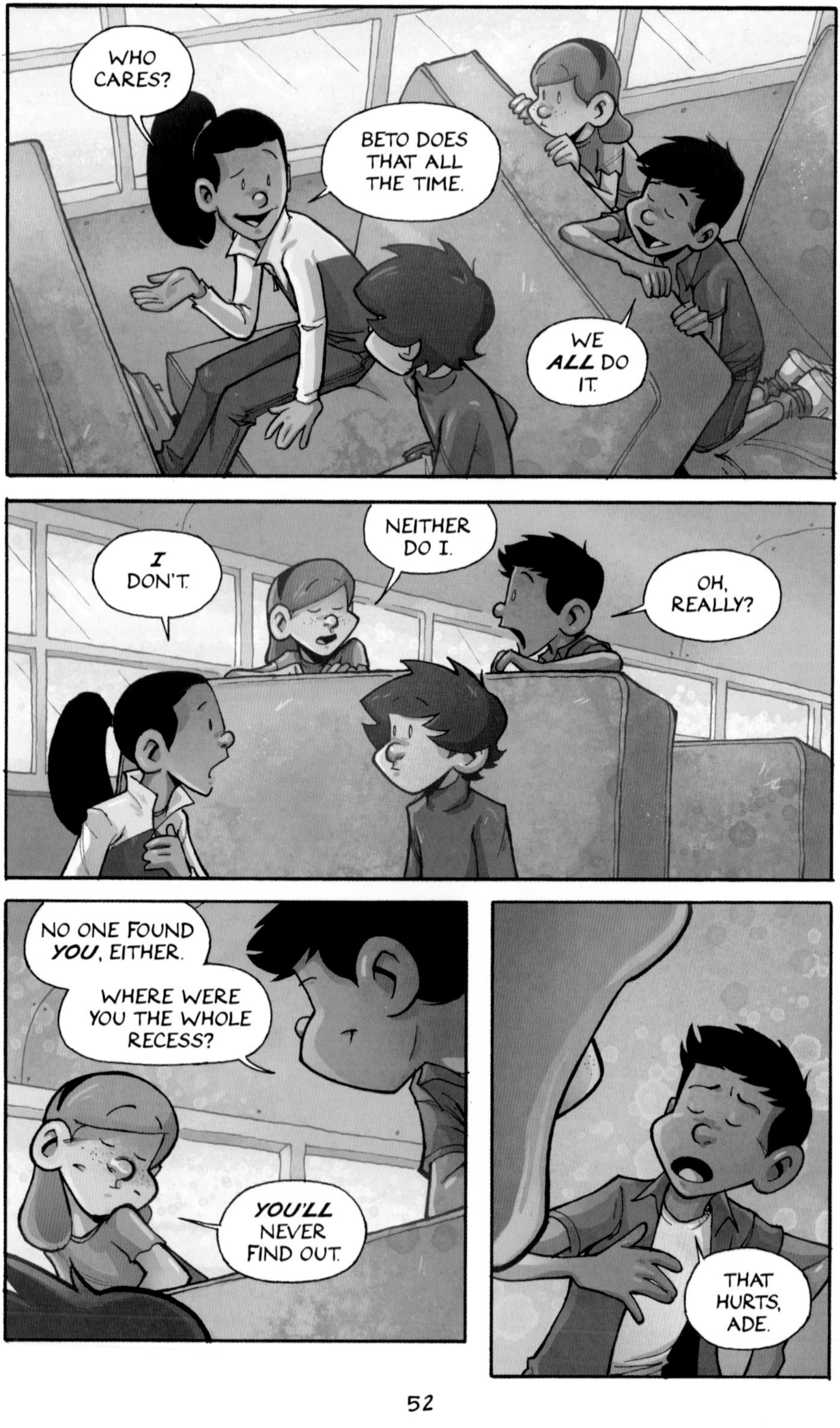
WHO CARES?
BETO DOES THAT ALL THE TIME.
WE *ALL* DO IT.
I DON'T.
NEITHER DO I.
OH, REALLY?
NO ONE FOUND *YOU*, EITHER.
WHERE WERE YOU THE WHOLE RECESS?
YOU'LL NEVER FIND OUT.
THAT HURTS, ADE.

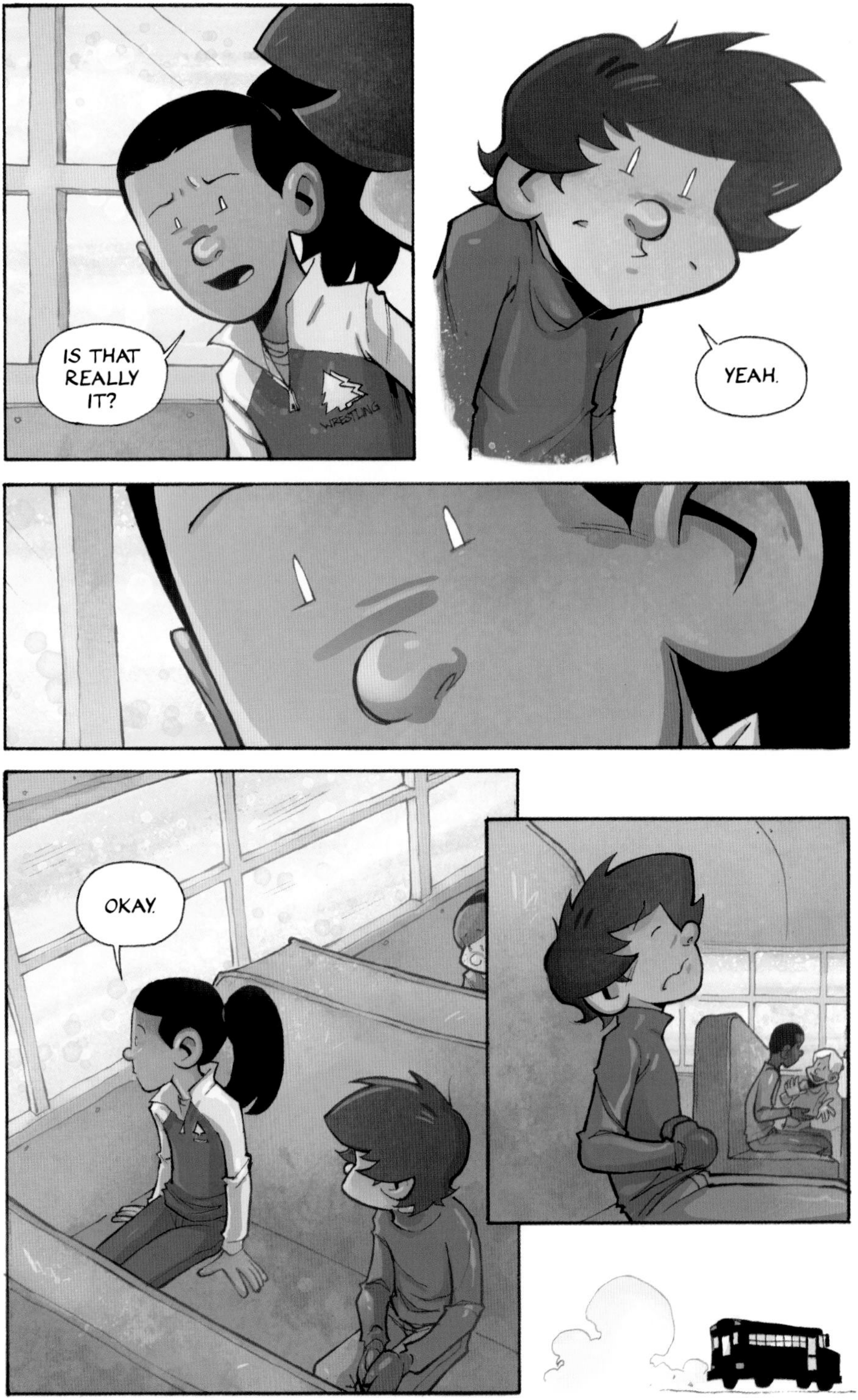
IS THAT REALLY IT?
YEAH.
WRESTLING
OKAY.

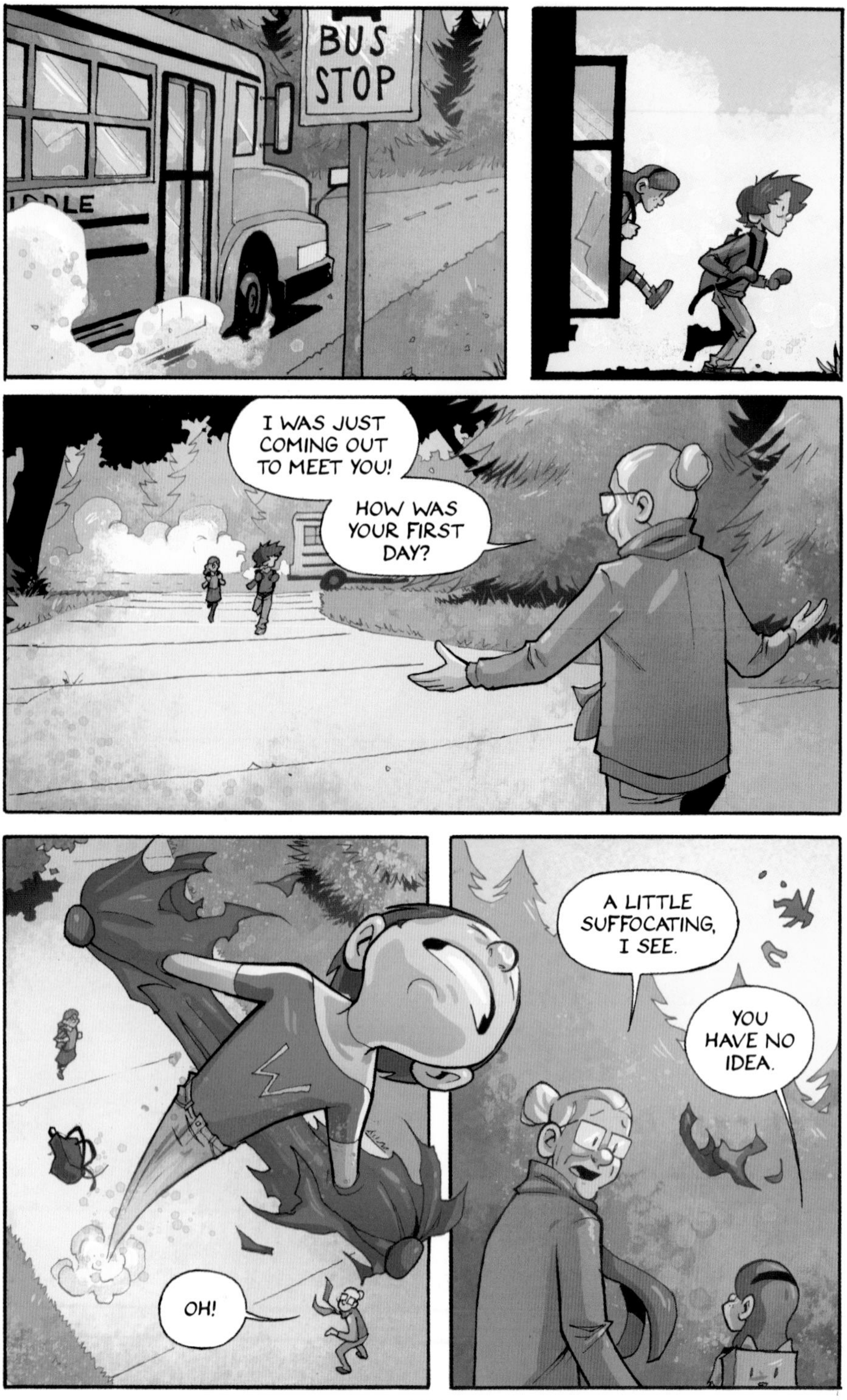
BUS STOP
IDDLE
I WAS JUST COMING OUT TO MEET YOU!
HOW WAS YOUR FIRST DAY?
OH!
A LITTLE SUFFOCATING, I SEE.
YOU HAVE NO IDEA.

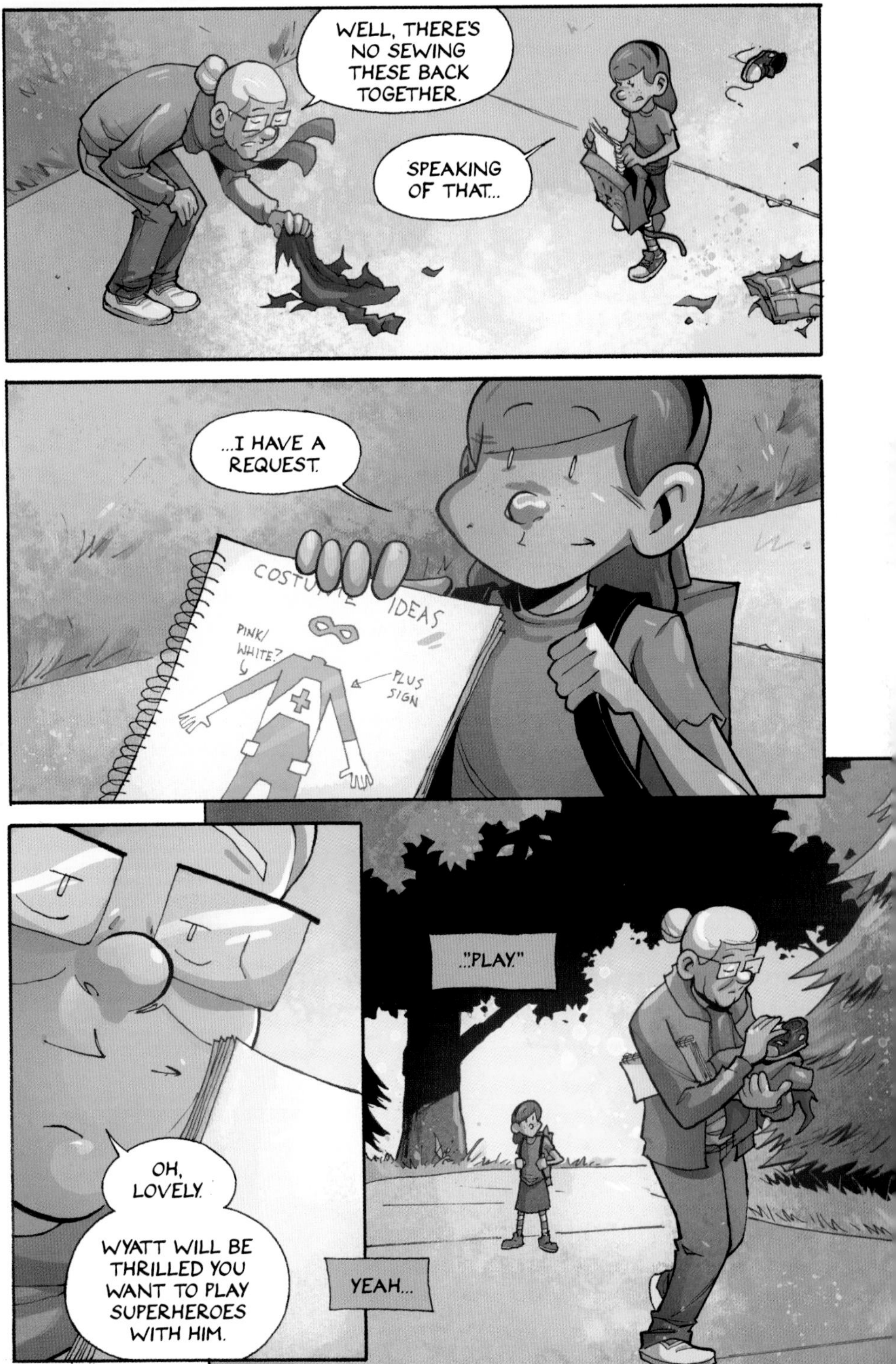
WELL, THERE'S NO SEWING THESE BACK TOGETHER.
SPEAKING OF THAT...
...I HAVE A REQUEST.
COSTUME IDEAS
PINK/ WHITE?
PLUS SIGN
OH, LOVELY.
WYATT WILL BE THRILLED YOU WANT TO PLAY SUPERHEROES WITH HIM.
..."PLAY."
YEAH...

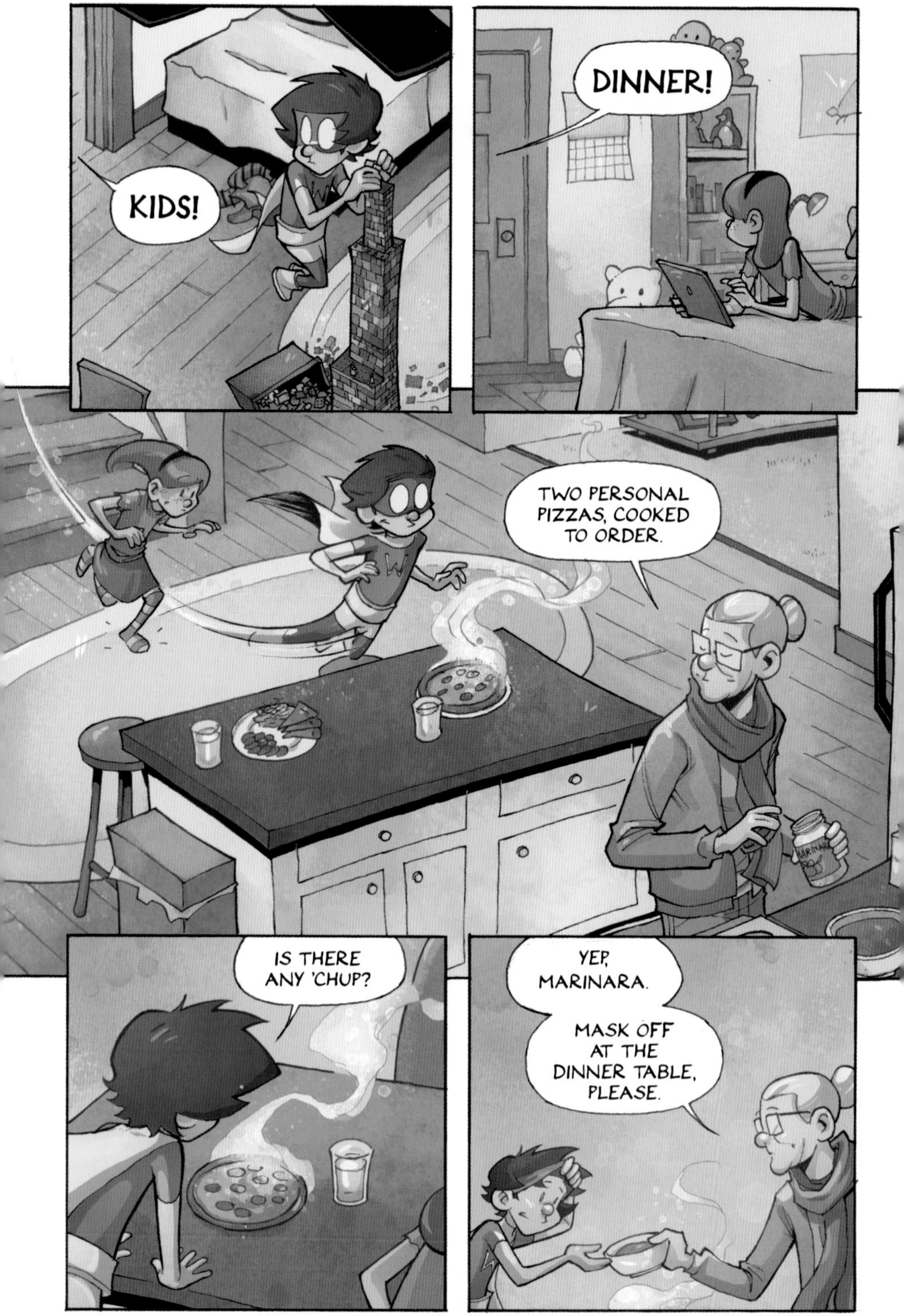
KIDS!
DINNER!
TWO PERSONAL PIZZAS, COOKED TO ORDER.
IS THERE ANY 'CHUP?
YEP, MARINARA.
MASK OFF AT THE DINNER TABLE, PLEASE.

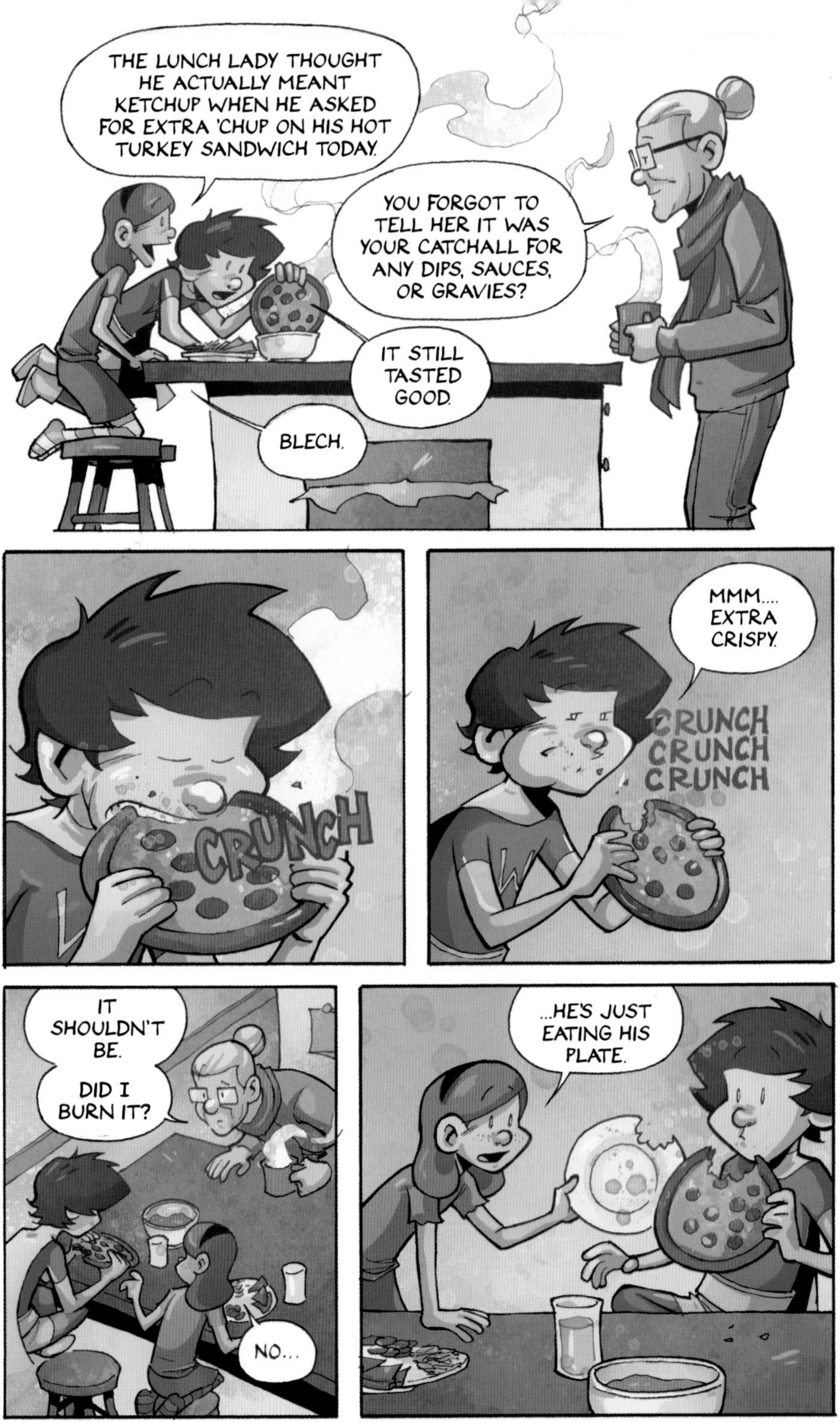
THE LUNCH LADY THOUGHT HE ACTUALLY MEANT KETCHUP WHEN HE ASKED FOR EXTRA 'CHUP ON HIS HOT TURKEY SANDWICH TODAY.
YOU FORGOT TO TELL HER IT WAS YOUR CATCHALL FOR ANY DIPS, SAUCES, OR GRAVIES?
IT STILL TASTED GOOD.
BLECH.
CRUNCH
MMM.... EXTRA CRISPY.
CRUNCH CRUNCH CRUNCH
IT SHOULDN'T BE.
DID I BURN IT?
NO...
...HE'S JUST EATING HIS PLATE.

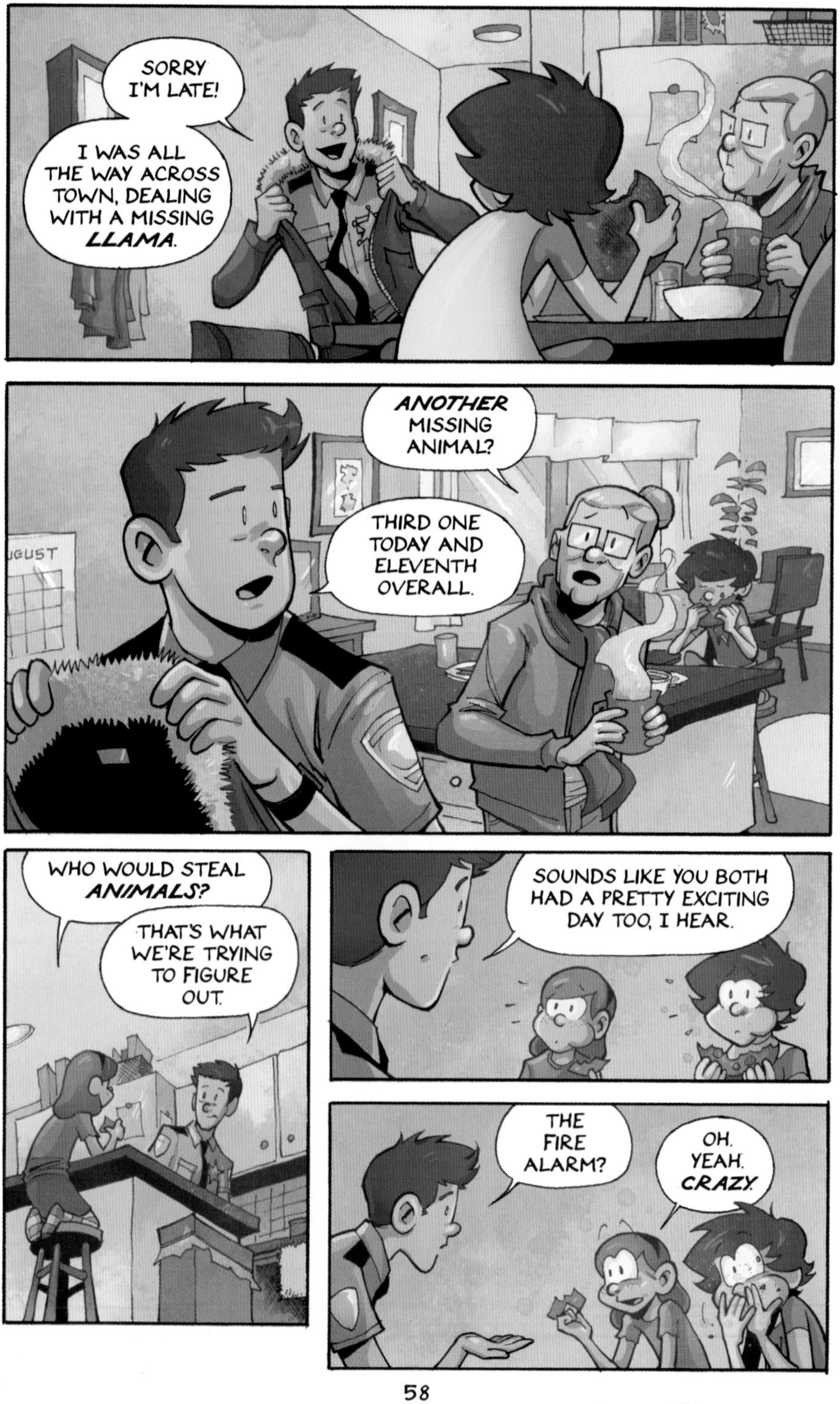
SORRY I'M LATE!
I WAS ALL THE WAY ACROSS TOWN, DEALING WITH A MISSING LLAMA.
ANOTHER MISSING ANIMAL?
THIRD ONE TODAY AND ELEVENTH OVERALL.
WHO WOULD STEAL ANIMALS?
THAT'S WHAT WE'RE TRYING TO FIGURE OUT.
SOUNDS LIKE YOU BOTH HAD A PRETTY EXCITING DAY TOO, I HEAR.
THE FIRE ALARM?
OH. YEAH. CRAZY.

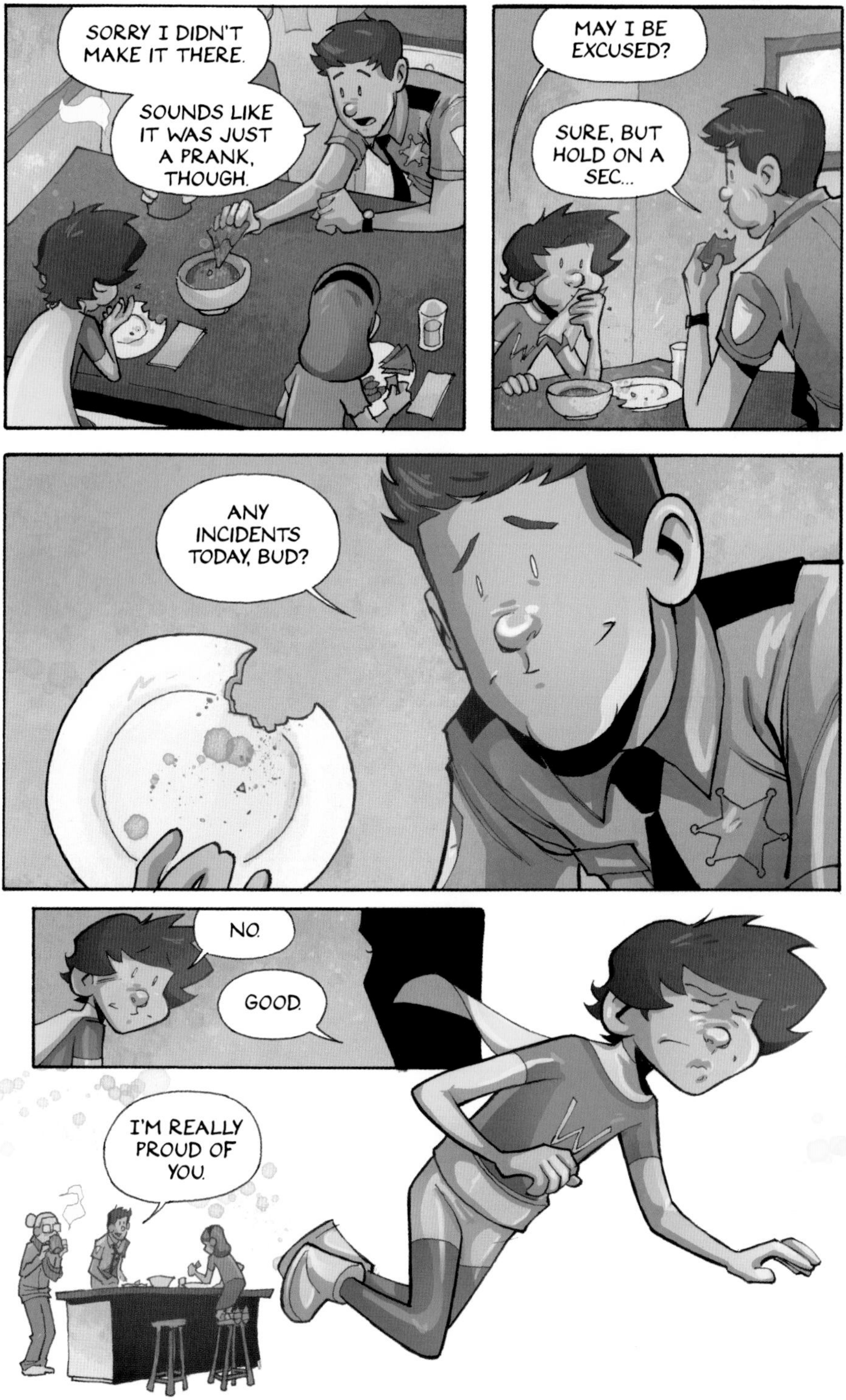
SORRY I DIDN'T MAKE IT THERE.
SOUNDS LIKE IT WAS JUST A PRANK, THOUGH.
MAY I BE EXCUSED?
SURE, BUT HOLD ON A SEC...
ANY INCIDENTS TODAY, BUD?
NO.
GOOD.
I'M REALLY PROUD OF YOU.

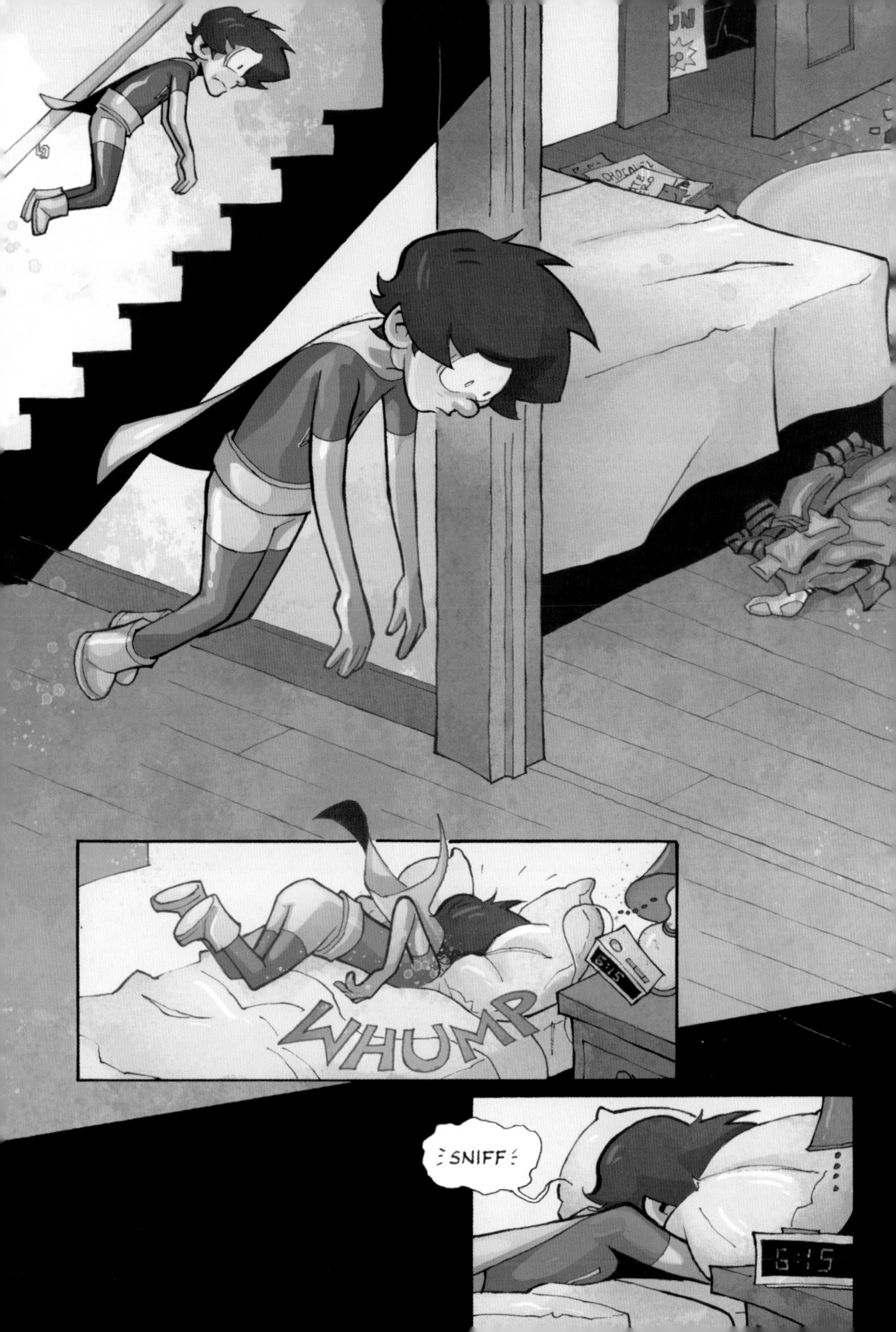
WHUMP
6:15
SNIFF
6:15

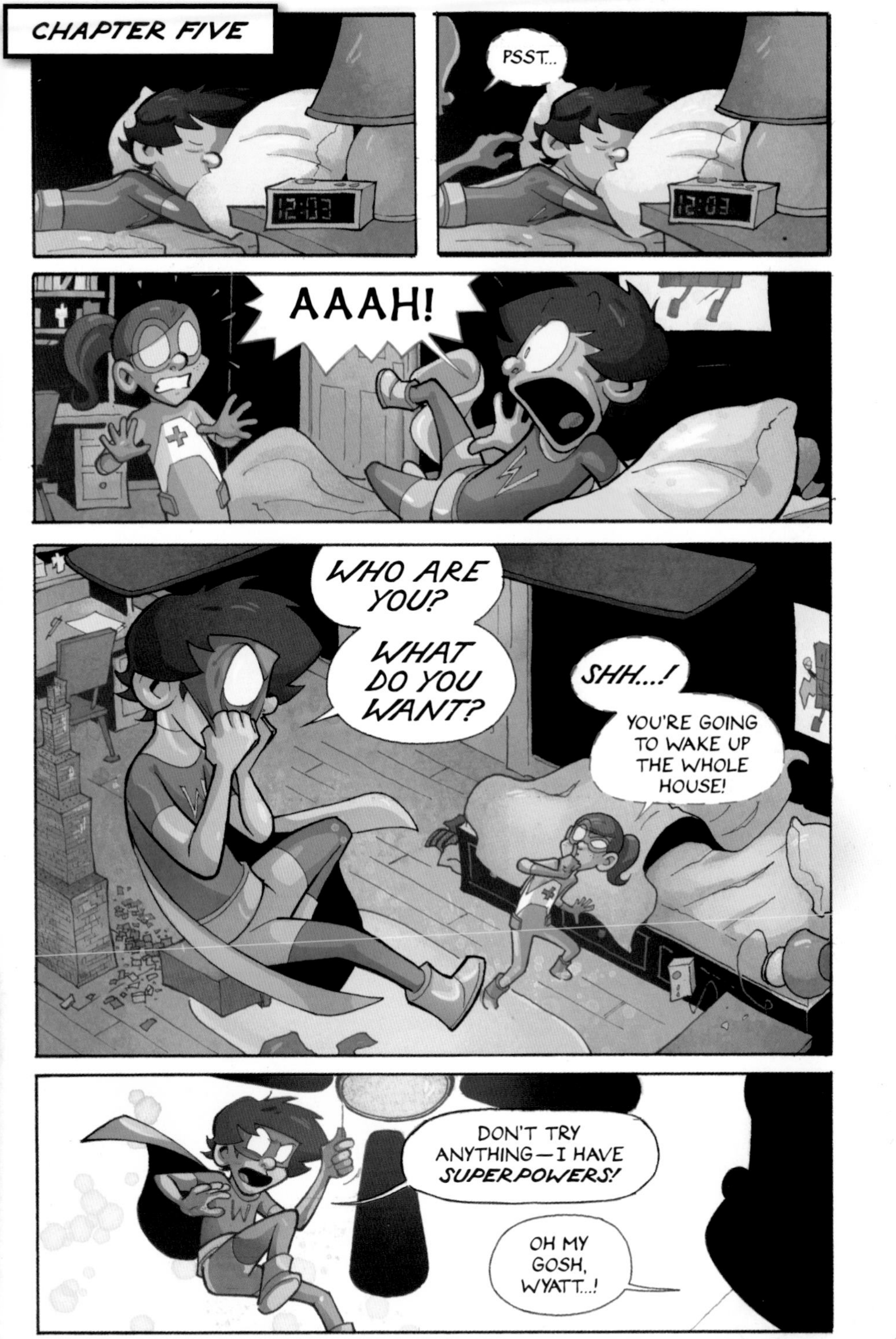
CHAPTER FIVE
12:03
PSST...
12:03
AAAH!
WHO ARE YOU?
WHAT DO YOU WANT?
SHH...!
YOU'RE GOING TO WAKE UP THE WHOLE HOUSE!
DON'T TRY ANYTHING—I HAVE SUPERPOWERS!
OH MY GOSH, WYATT...!

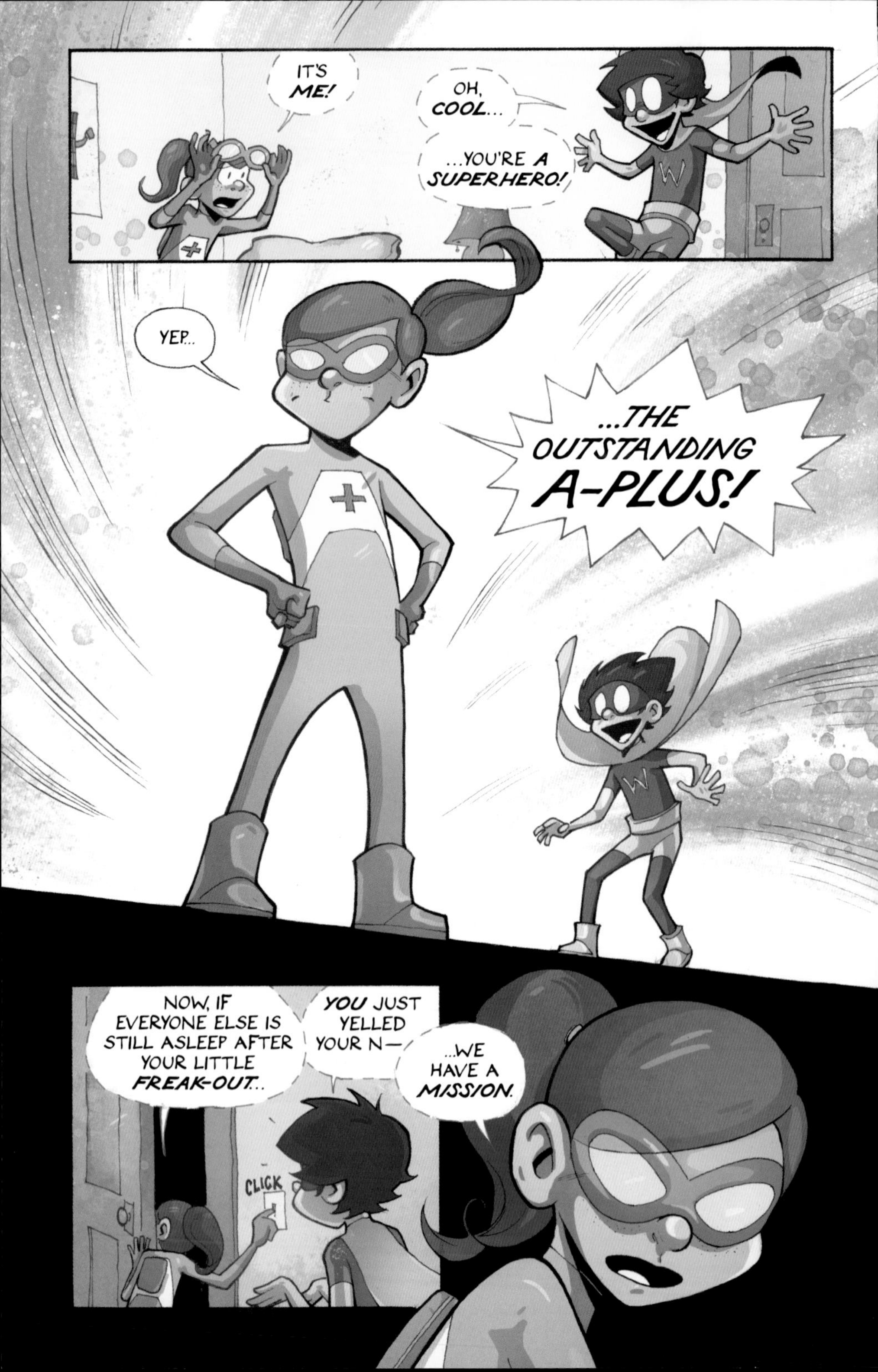
IT'S ME!
OH, COOL...
...YOU'RE A SUPERHERO!
YEP...
...THE OUTSTANDING A-PLUS!
NOW, IF EVERYONE ELSE IS STILL ASLEEP AFTER YOUR LITTLE FREAK-OUT...
YOU JUST YELLED YOUR N—
...WE HAVE A MISSION.
CLICK

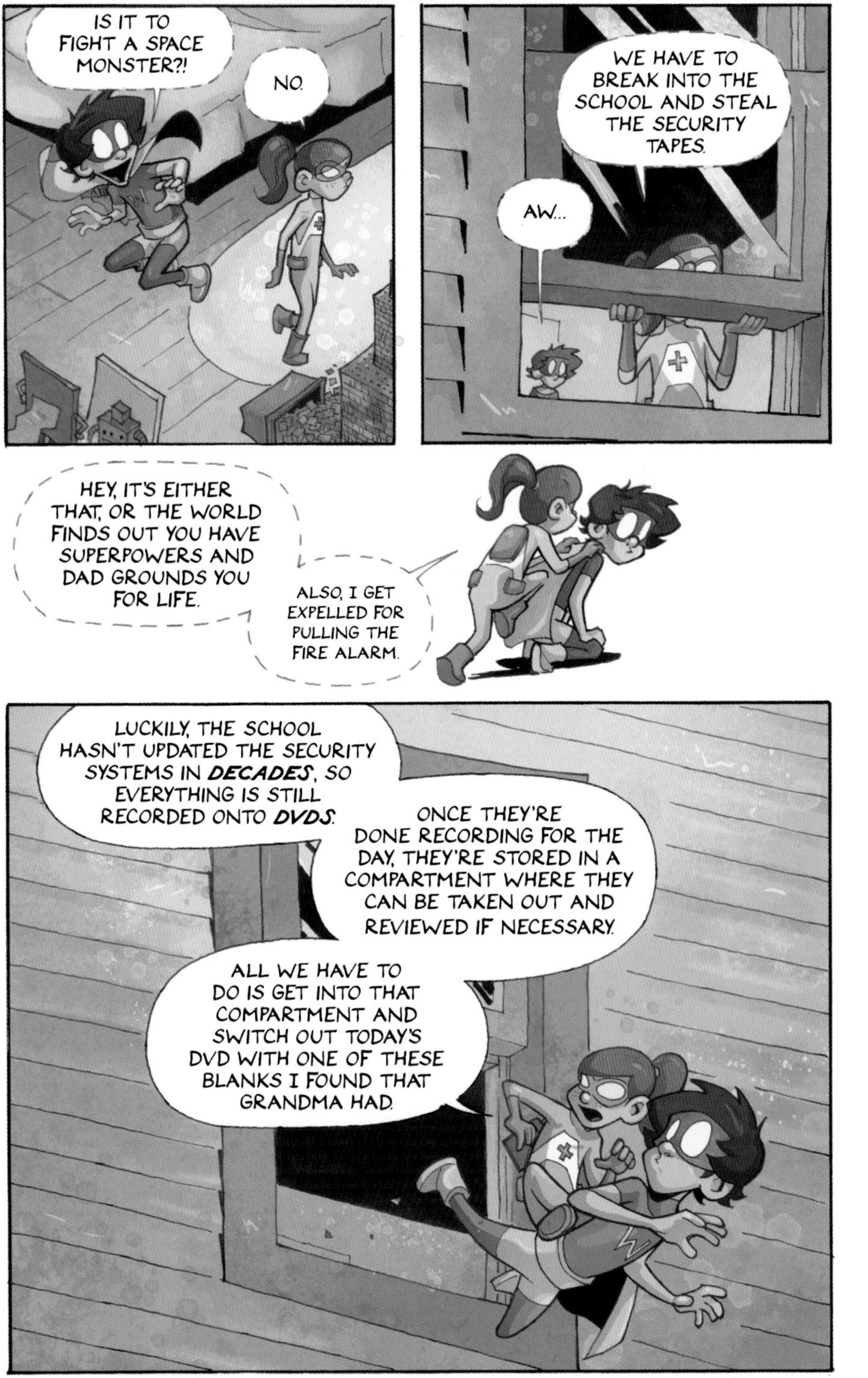
IS IT TO FIGHT A SPACE MONSTER?!
NO.
WE HAVE TO BREAK INTO THE SCHOOL AND STEAL THE SECURITY TAPES.
AW...
HEY, IT'S EITHER THAT, OR THE WORLD FINDS OUT YOU HAVE SUPERPOWERS AND DAD GROUNDS YOU FOR LIFE.
ALSO, I GET EXPELLED FOR PULLING THE FIRE ALARM.
LUCKILY, THE SCHOOL HASN'T UPDATED THE SECURITY SYSTEMS IN *DECADES*, SO EVERYTHING IS STILL RECORDED ONTO *DVDS*.
ONCE THEY'RE DONE RECORDING FOR THE DAY, THEY'RE STORED IN A COMPARTMENT WHERE THEY CAN BE TAKEN OUT AND REVIEWED IF NECESSARY.
ALL WE HAVE TO DO IS GET INTO THAT COMPARTMENT AND SWITCH OUT TODAY'S DVD WITH ONE OF THESE BLANKS I FOUND THAT GRANDMA HAD.

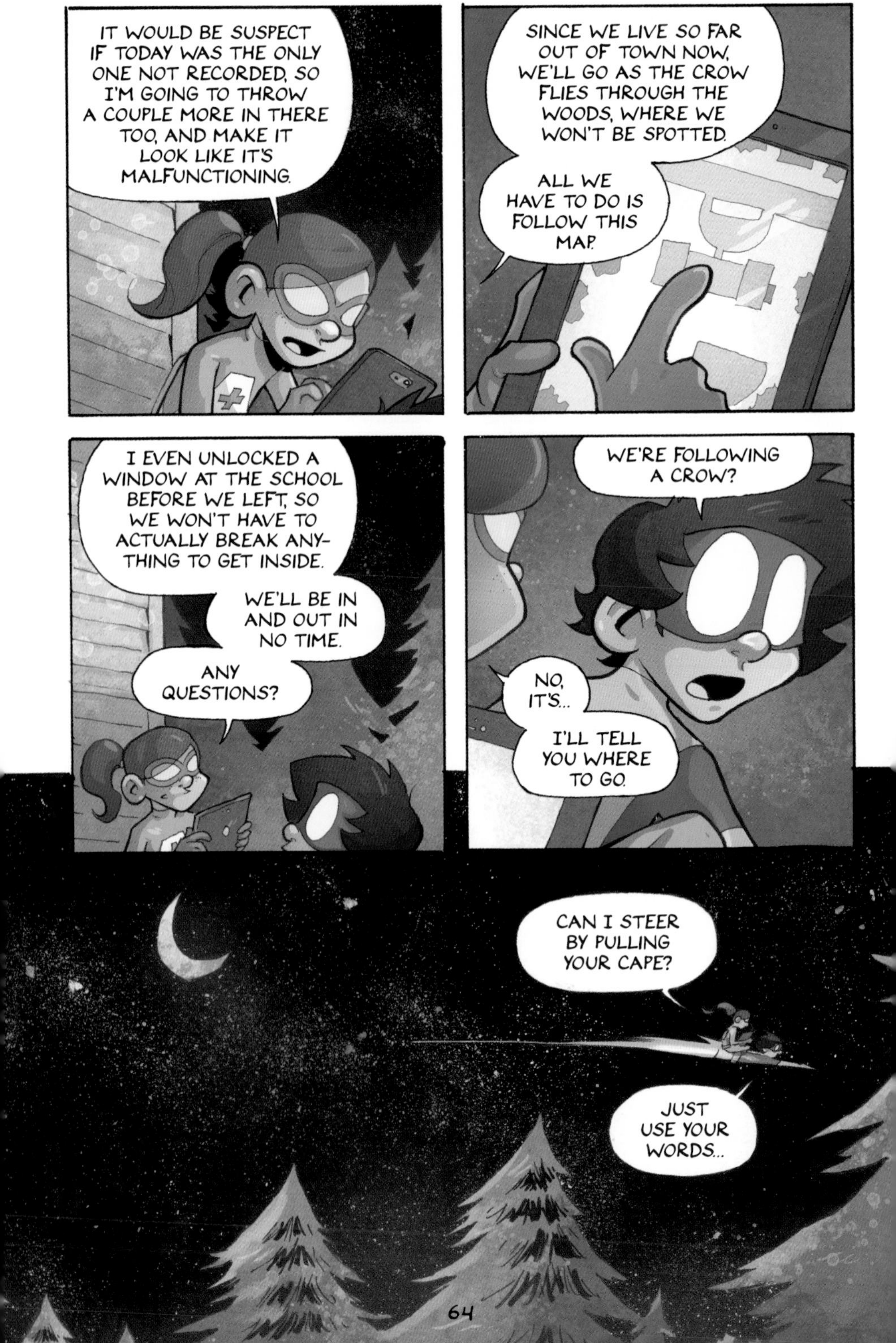
IT WOULD BE SUSPECT IF TODAY WAS THE ONLY ONE NOT RECORDED, SO I'M GOING TO THROW A COUPLE MORE IN THERE TOO, AND MAKE IT LOOK LIKE IT'S MALFUNCTIONING.
SINCE WE LIVE SO FAR OUT OF TOWN NOW, WE'LL GO AS THE CROW FLIES THROUGH THE WOODS, WHERE WE WON'T BE SPOTTED.
ALL WE HAVE TO DO IS FOLLOW THIS MAP.
I EVEN UNLOCKED A WINDOW AT THE SCHOOL BEFORE WE LEFT, SO WE WON'T HAVE TO ACTUALLY BREAK ANY-THING TO GET INSIDE.
WE'LL BE IN AND OUT IN NO TIME.
ANY QUESTIONS?
WE'RE FOLLOWING A CROW?
NO, IT'S...
I'LL TELL YOU WHERE TO GO.
CAN I STEER BY PULLING YOUR CAPE?
JUST USE YOUR WORDS...

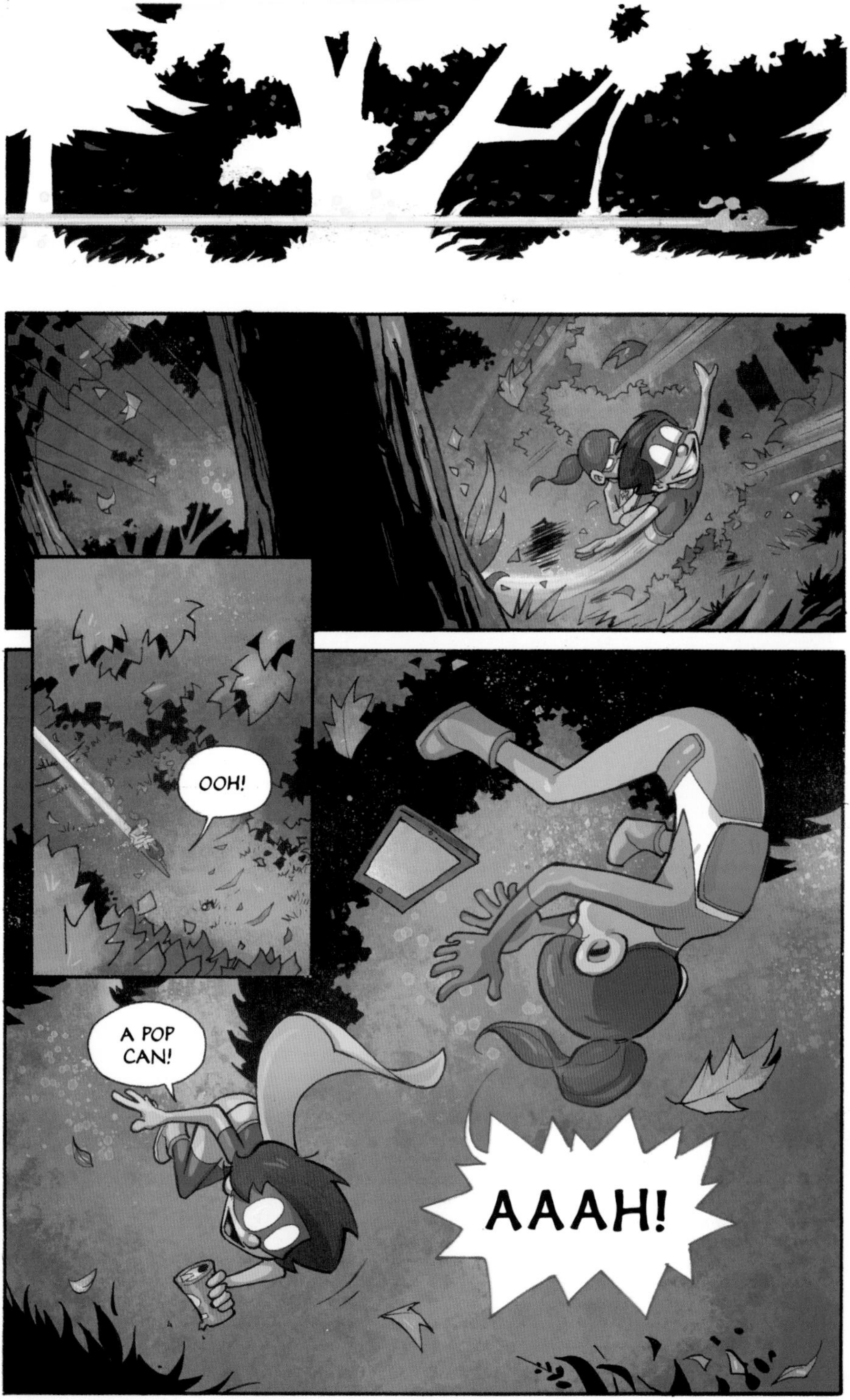
OOH!
A POP CAN!
AAAH!

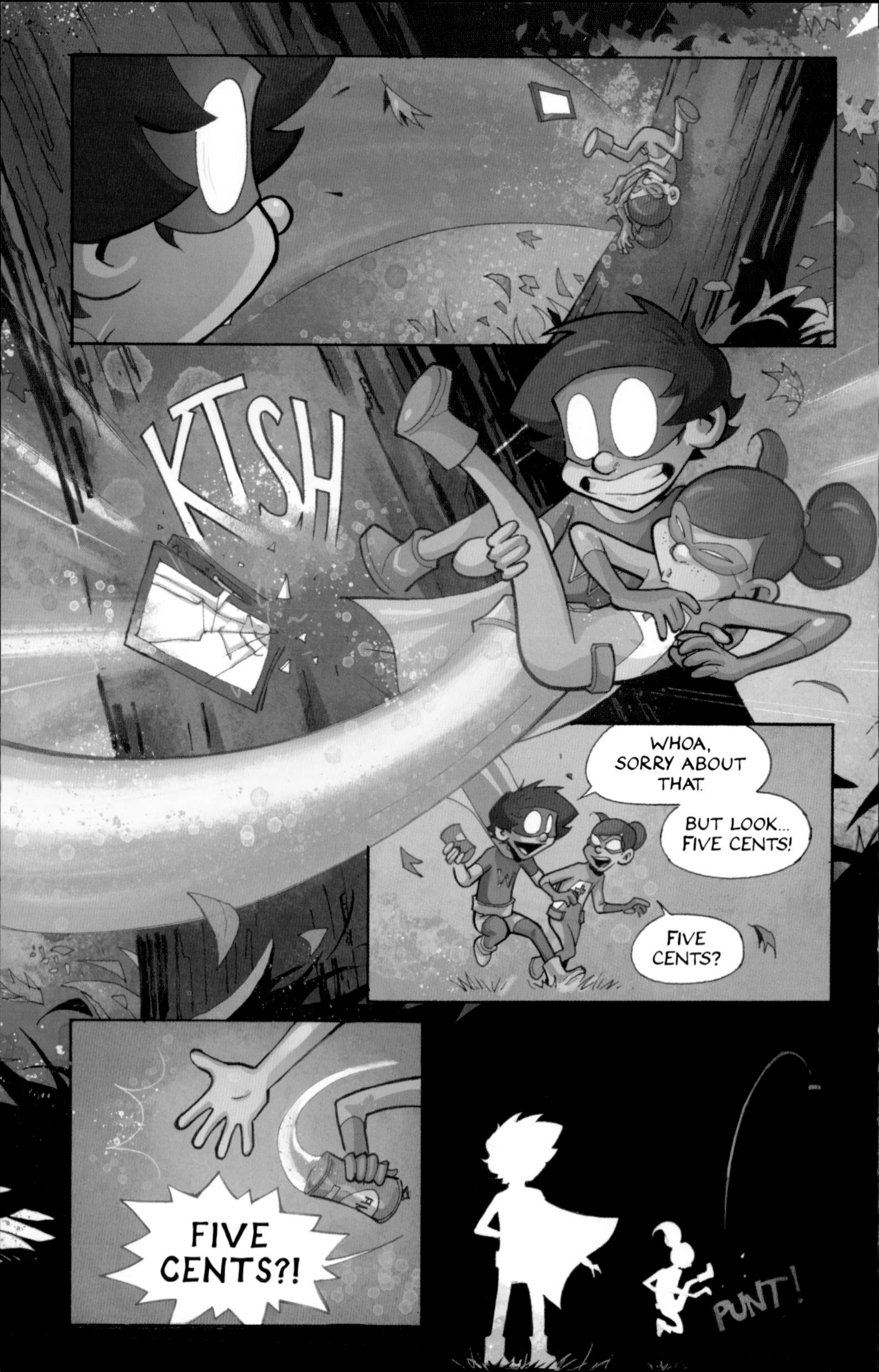
KTSH
WHOA, SORRY ABOUT THAT.
BUT LOOK... FIVE CENTS!
FIVE CENTS?
FIVE CENTS?!
PUNT!

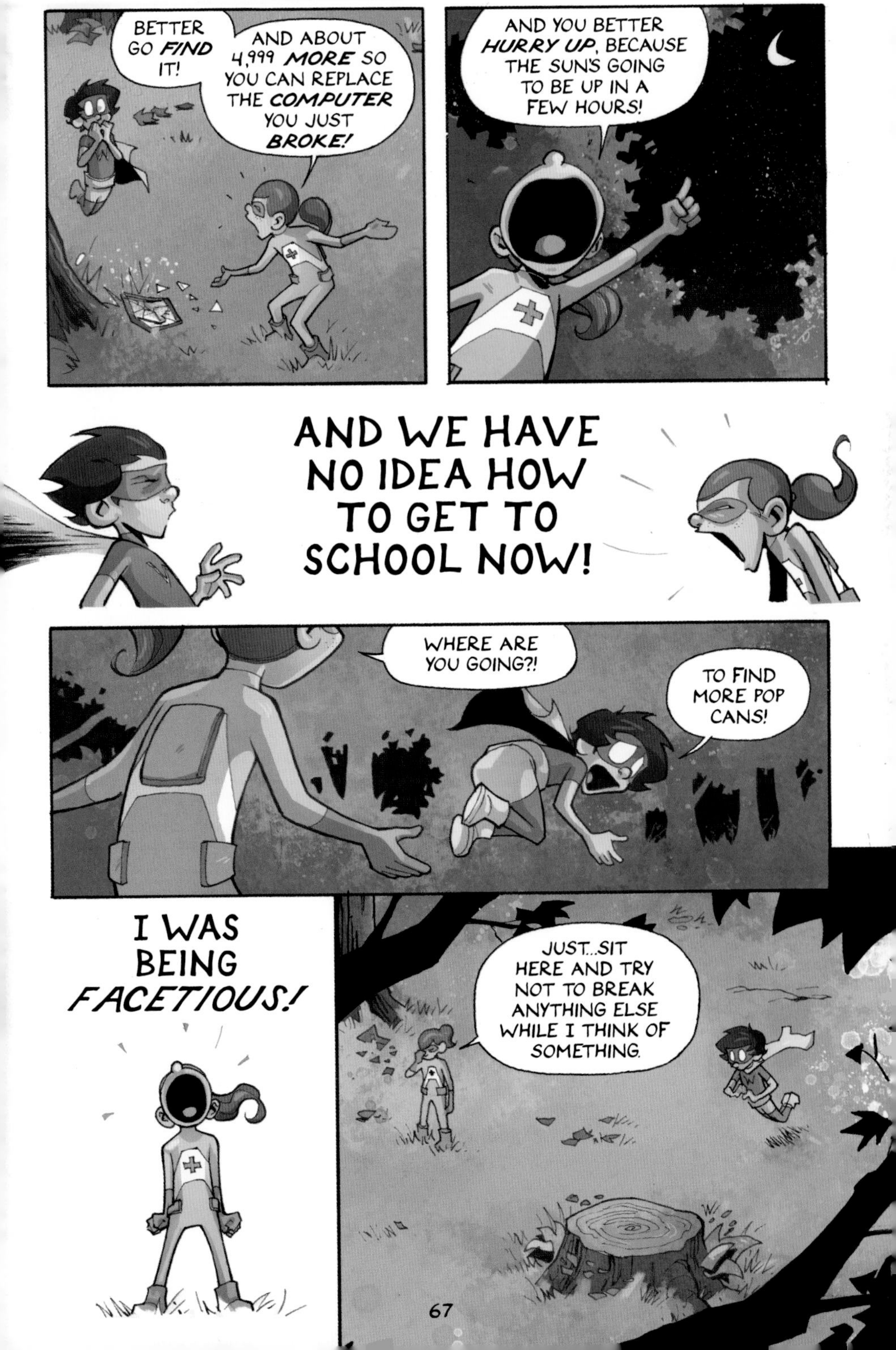
BETTER GO FIND IT!
AND ABOUT 4,999 MORE SO YOU CAN REPLACE THE COMPUTER YOU JUST BROKE!
AND YOU BETTER HURRY UP, BECAUSE THE SUN'S GOING TO BE UP IN A FEW HOURS!
AND WE HAVE NO IDEA HOW TO GET TO SCHOOL NOW!
WHERE ARE YOU GOING?!
TO FIND MORE POP CANS!
I WAS BEING FACETIOUS!
JUST...SIT HERE AND TRY NOT TO BREAK ANYTHING ELSE WHILE I THINK OF SOMETHING.

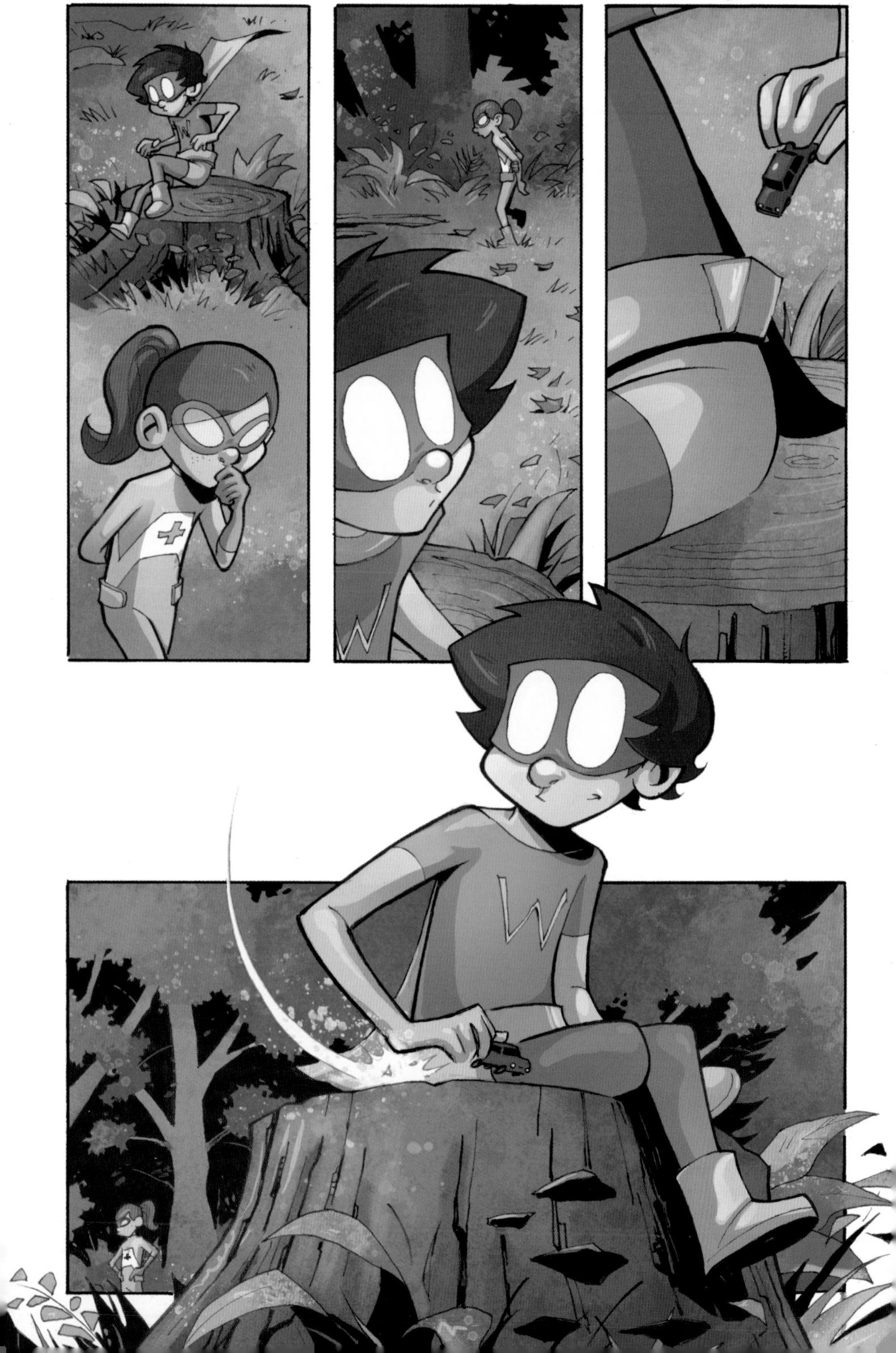

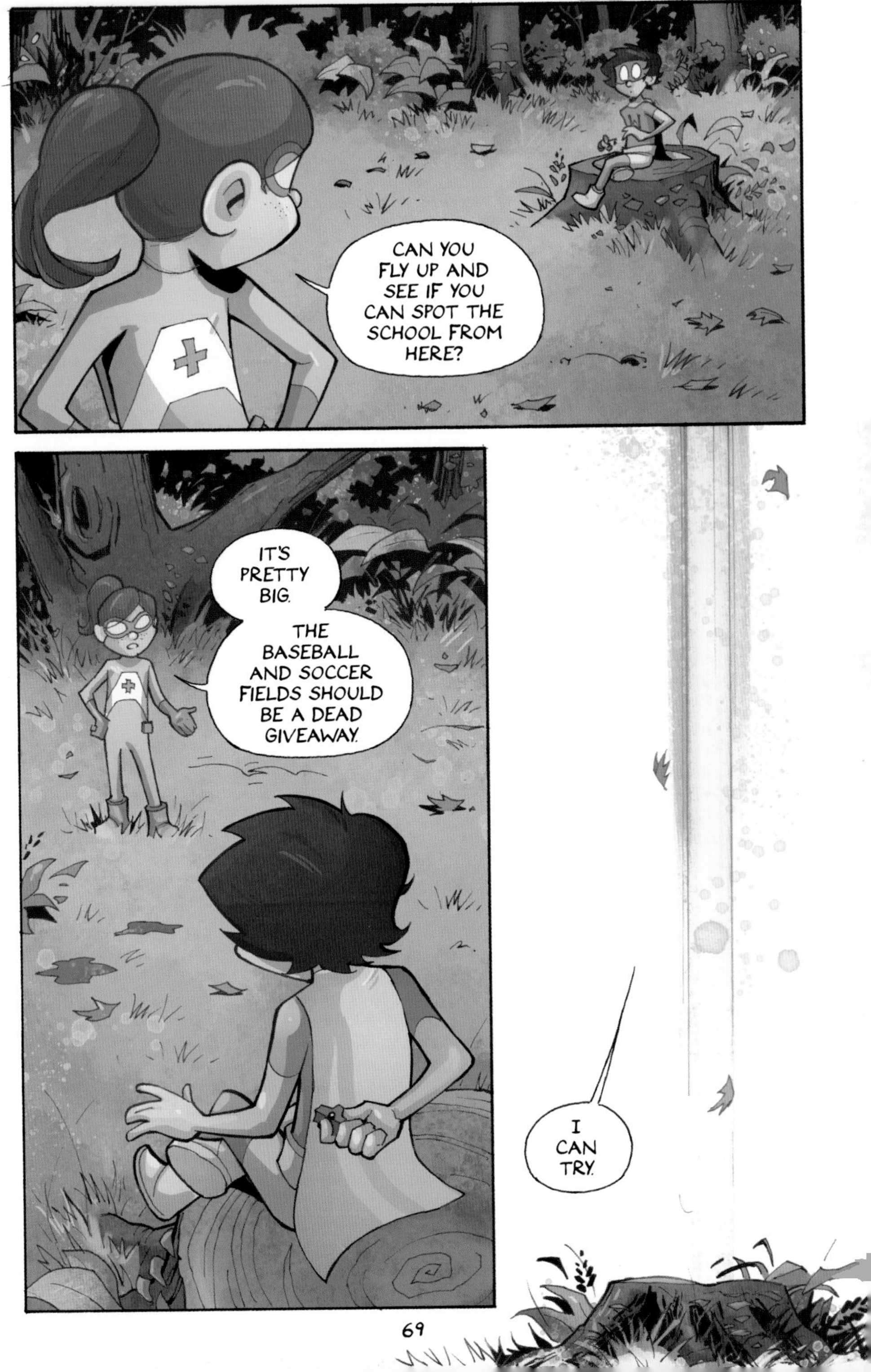
CAN YOU FLY UP AND SEE IF YOU CAN SPOT THE SCHOOL FROM HERE?
IT'S PRETTY BIG.
THE BASEBALL AND SOCCER FIELDS SHOULD BE A DEAD GIVEAWAY.
I CAN TRY.

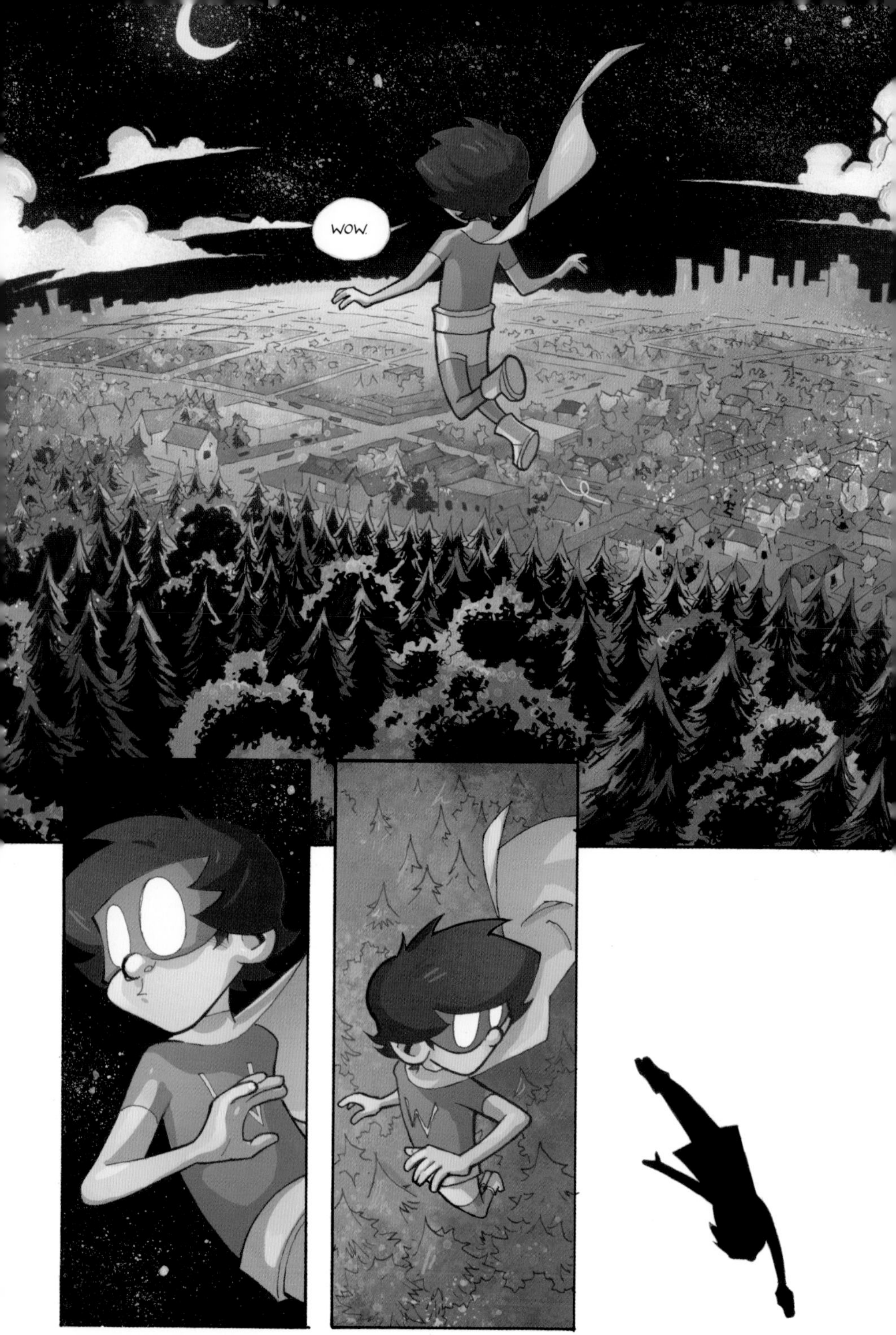
WOW.

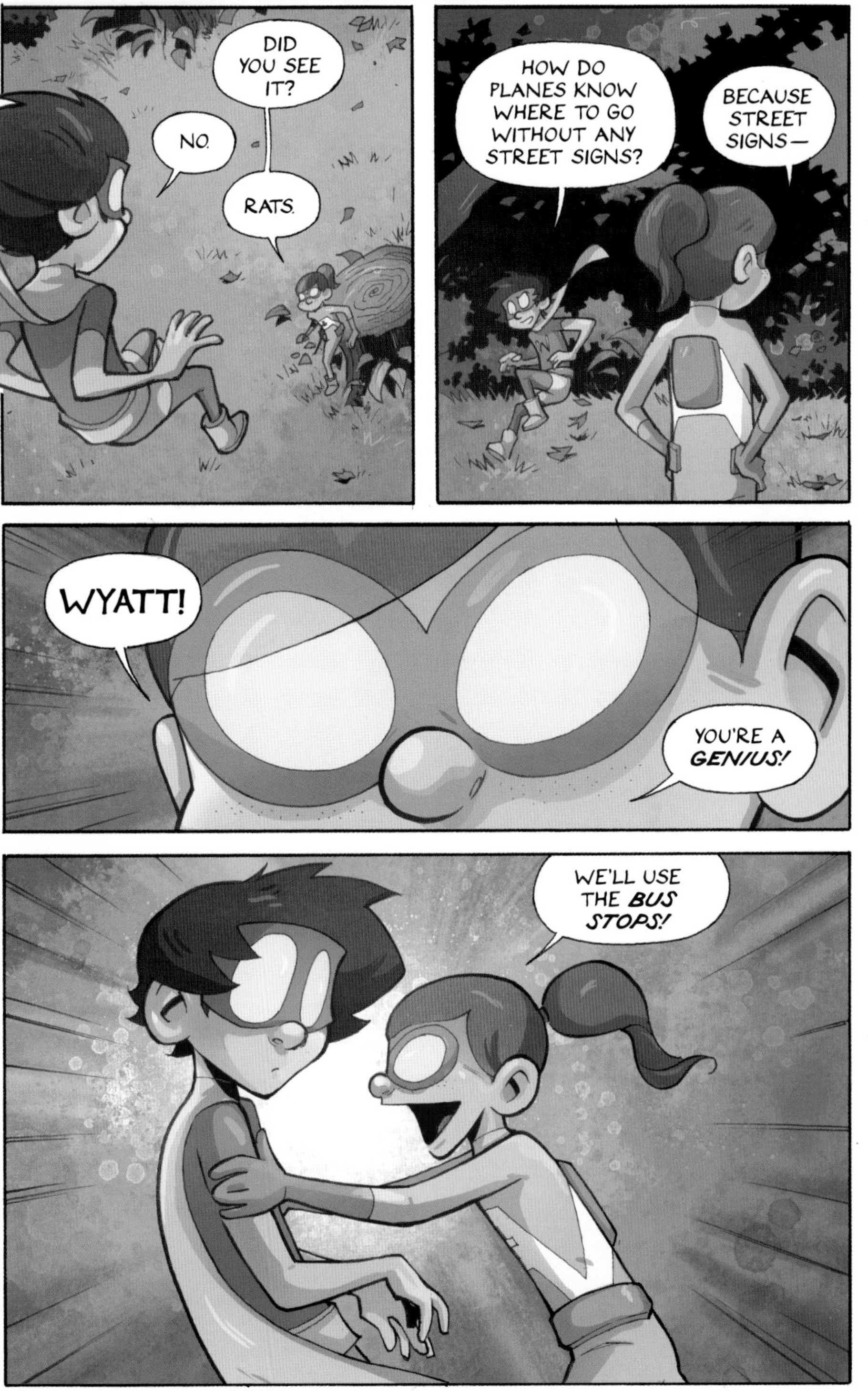
DID YOU SEE IT?
NO.
RATS.
HOW DO PLANES KNOW WHERE TO GO WITHOUT ANY STREET SIGNS?
BECAUSE STREET SIGNS—
WYATT!
YOU'RE A *GENIUS!*
WE'LL USE THE *BUS STOPS!*

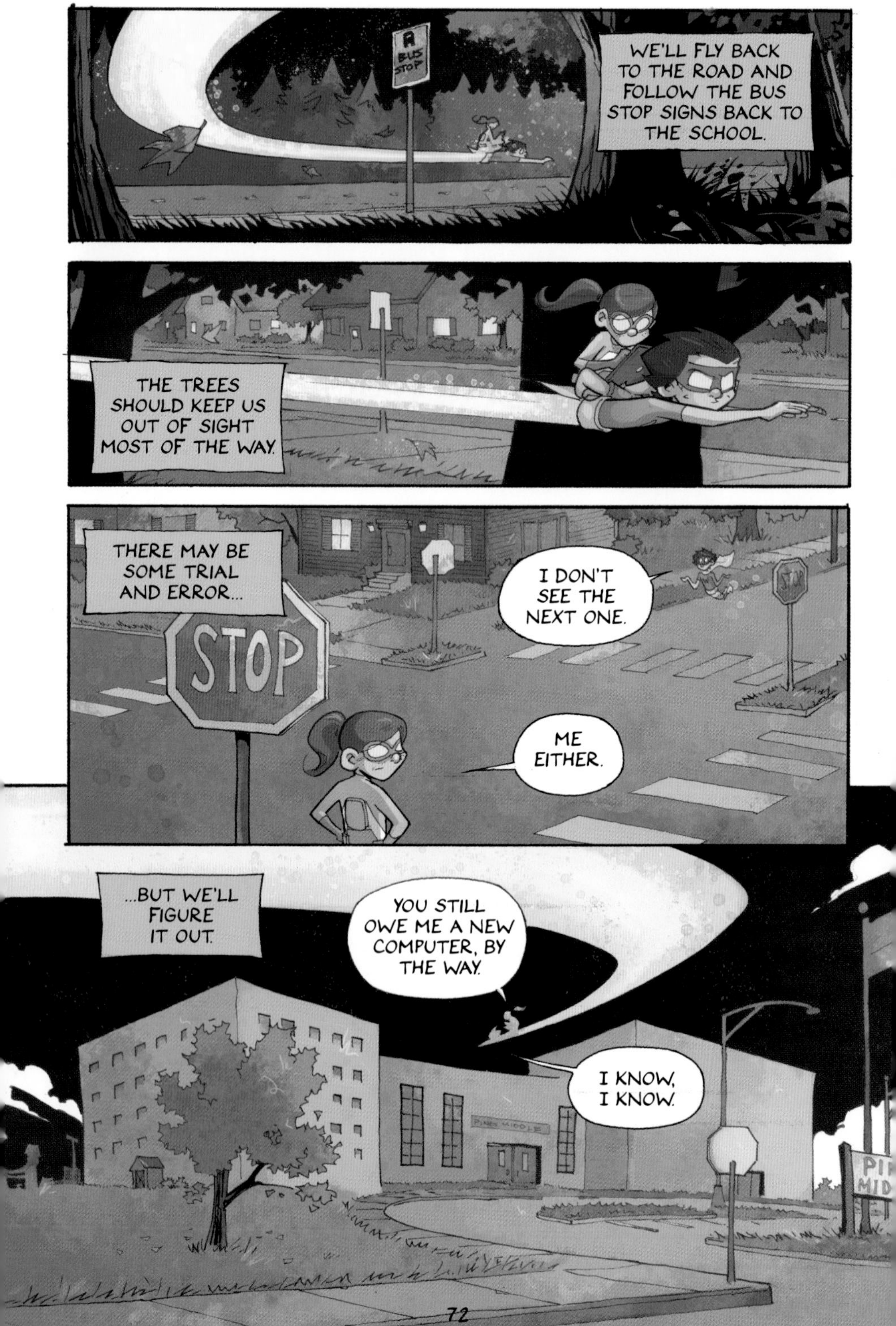

BUS STOP
WE'LL FLY BACK TO THE ROAD AND FOLLOW THE BUS STOP SIGNS BACK TO THE SCHOOL.
THE TREES SHOULD KEEP US OUT OF SIGHT MOST OF THE WAY.
THERE MAY BE SOME TRIAL AND ERROR...
STOP
I DON'T SEE THE NEXT ONE.
ME EITHER.
...BUT WE'LL FIGURE IT OUT.
YOU STILL OWE ME A NEW COMPUTER, BY THE WAY.
I KNOW, I KNOW.

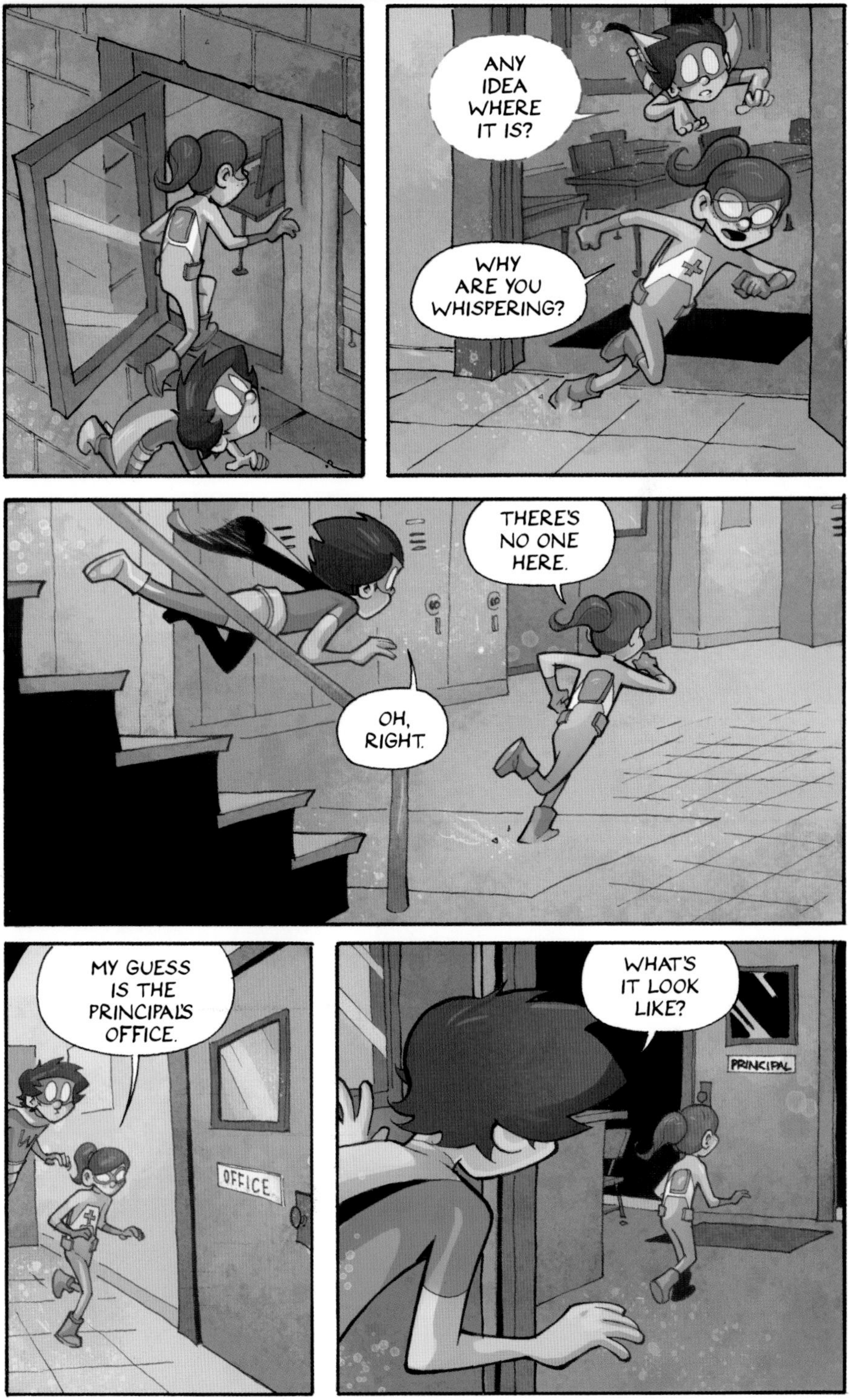
ANY IDEA WHERE IT IS?
WHY ARE YOU WHISPERING?
THERE'S NO ONE HERE.
OH, RIGHT.
MY GUESS IS THE PRINCIPAL'S OFFICE.
OFFICE
WHAT'S IT LOOK LIKE?
PRINCIPAL

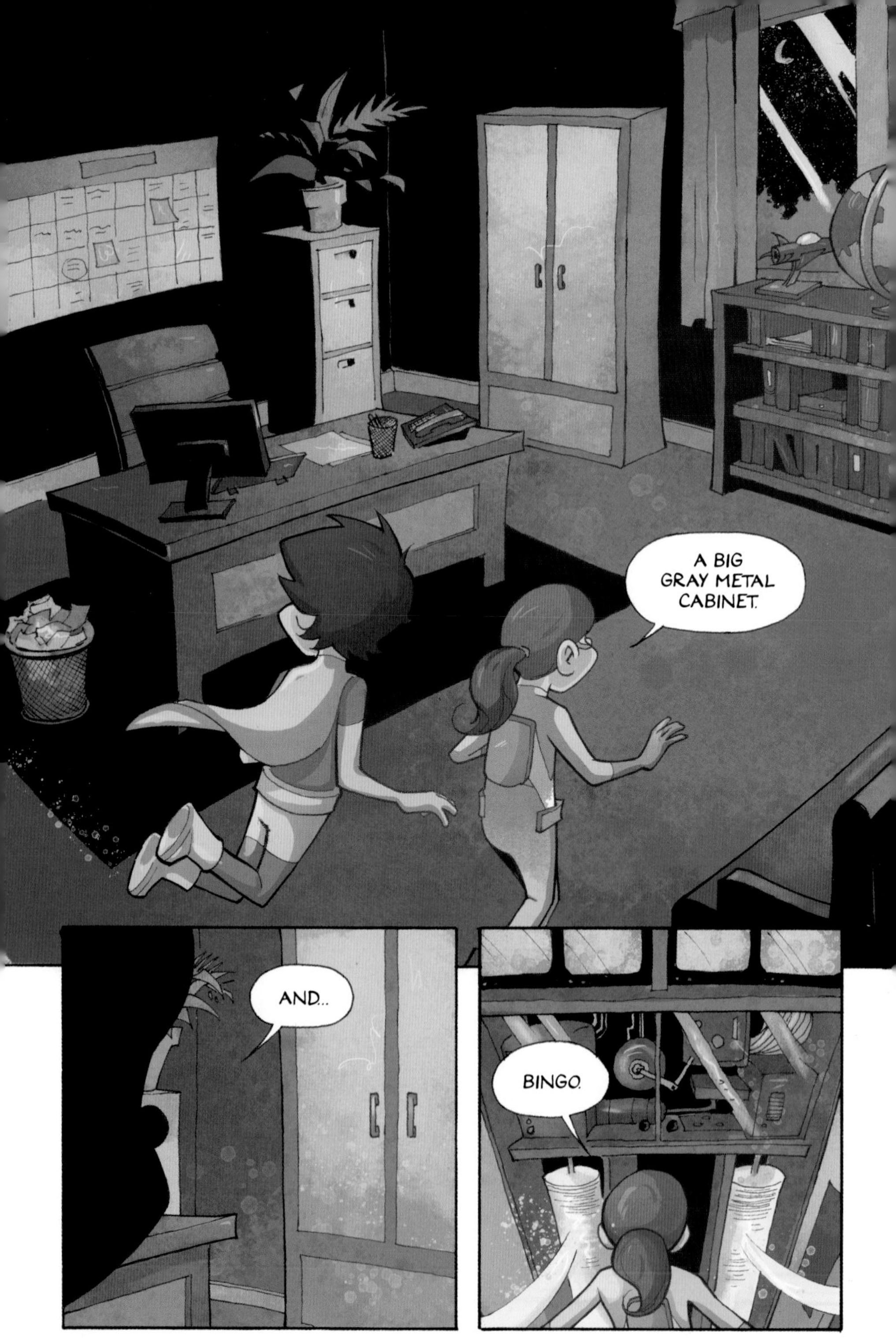
A BIG GRAY METAL CABINET.
AND...
BINGO.

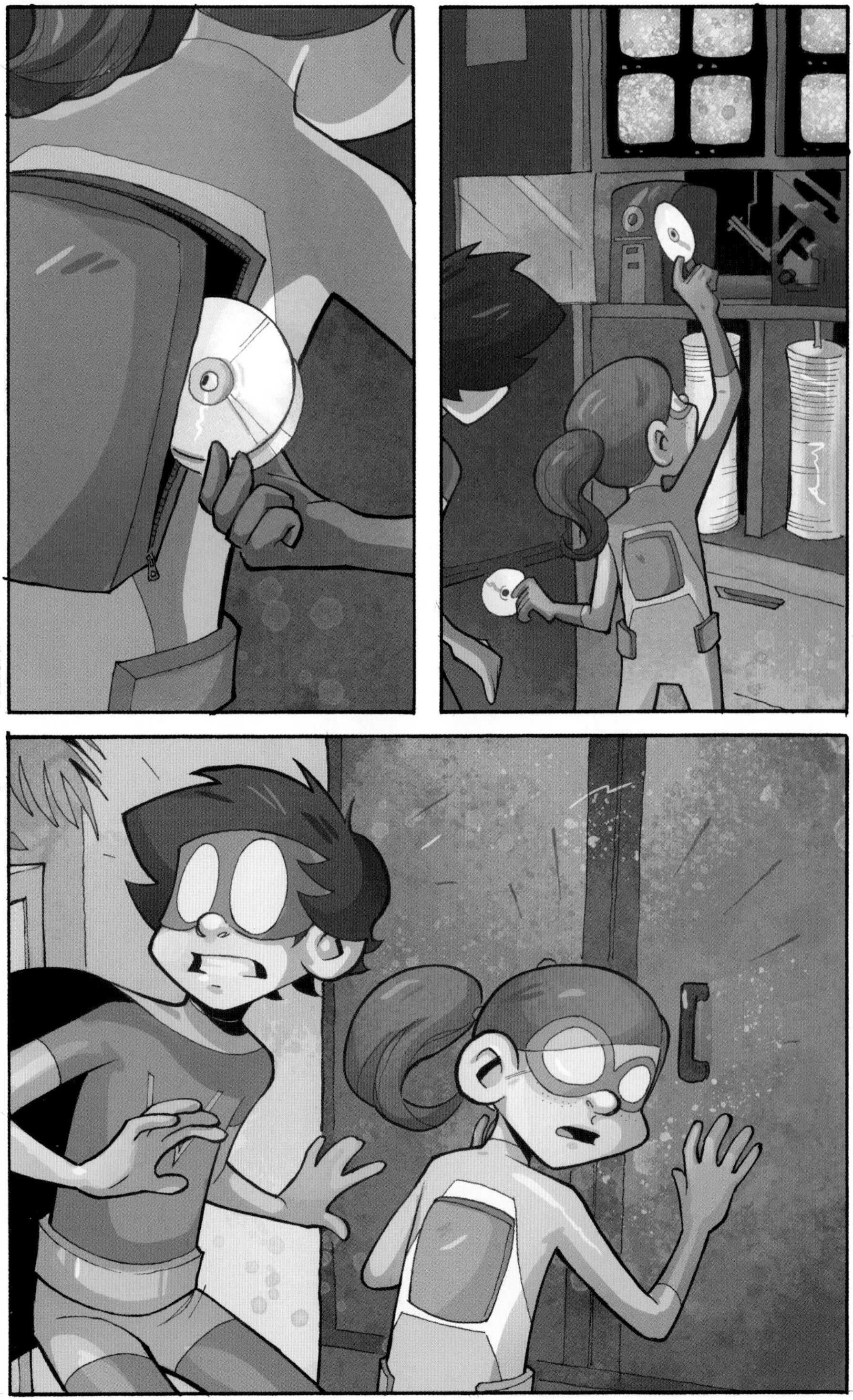

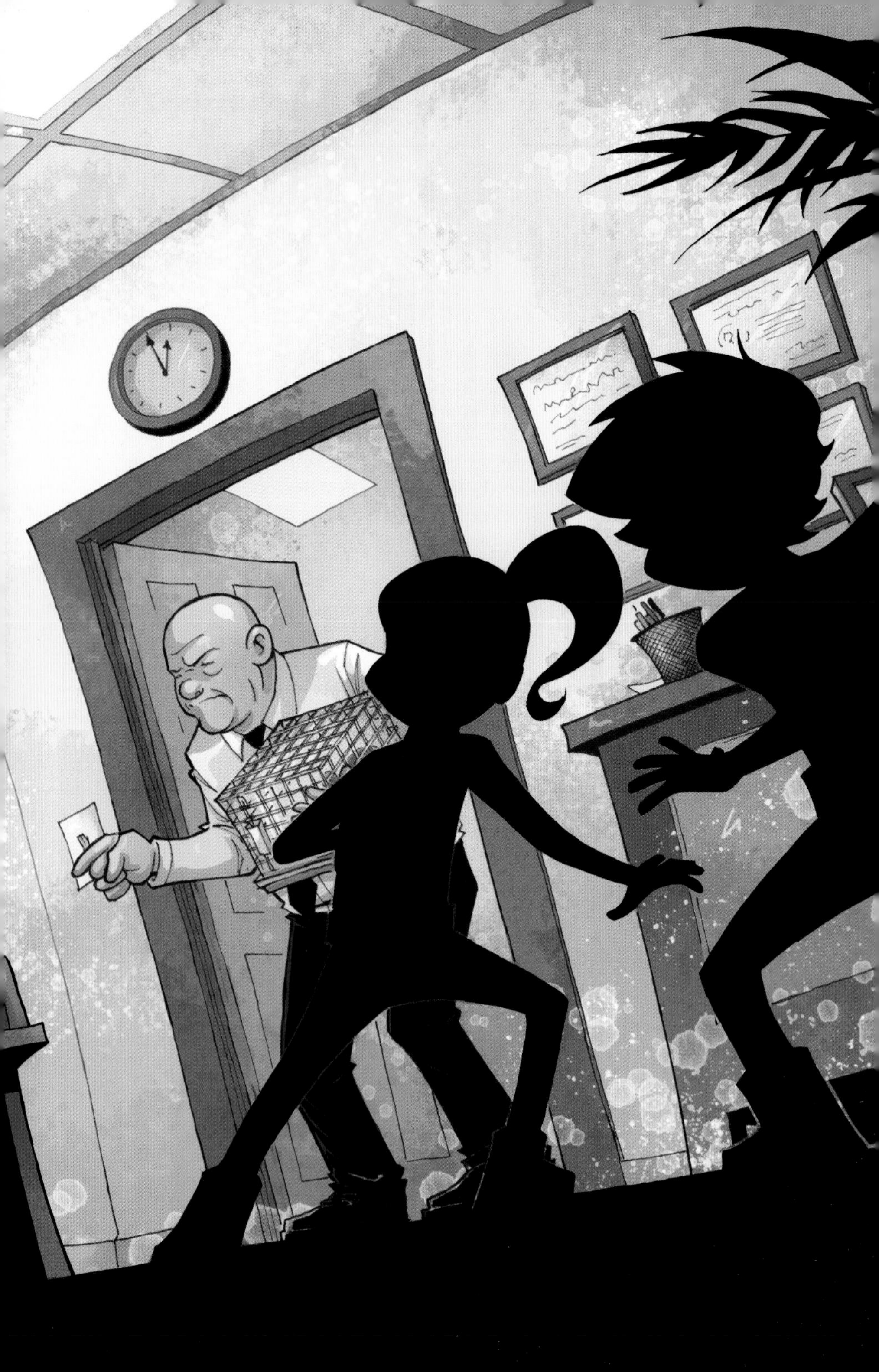

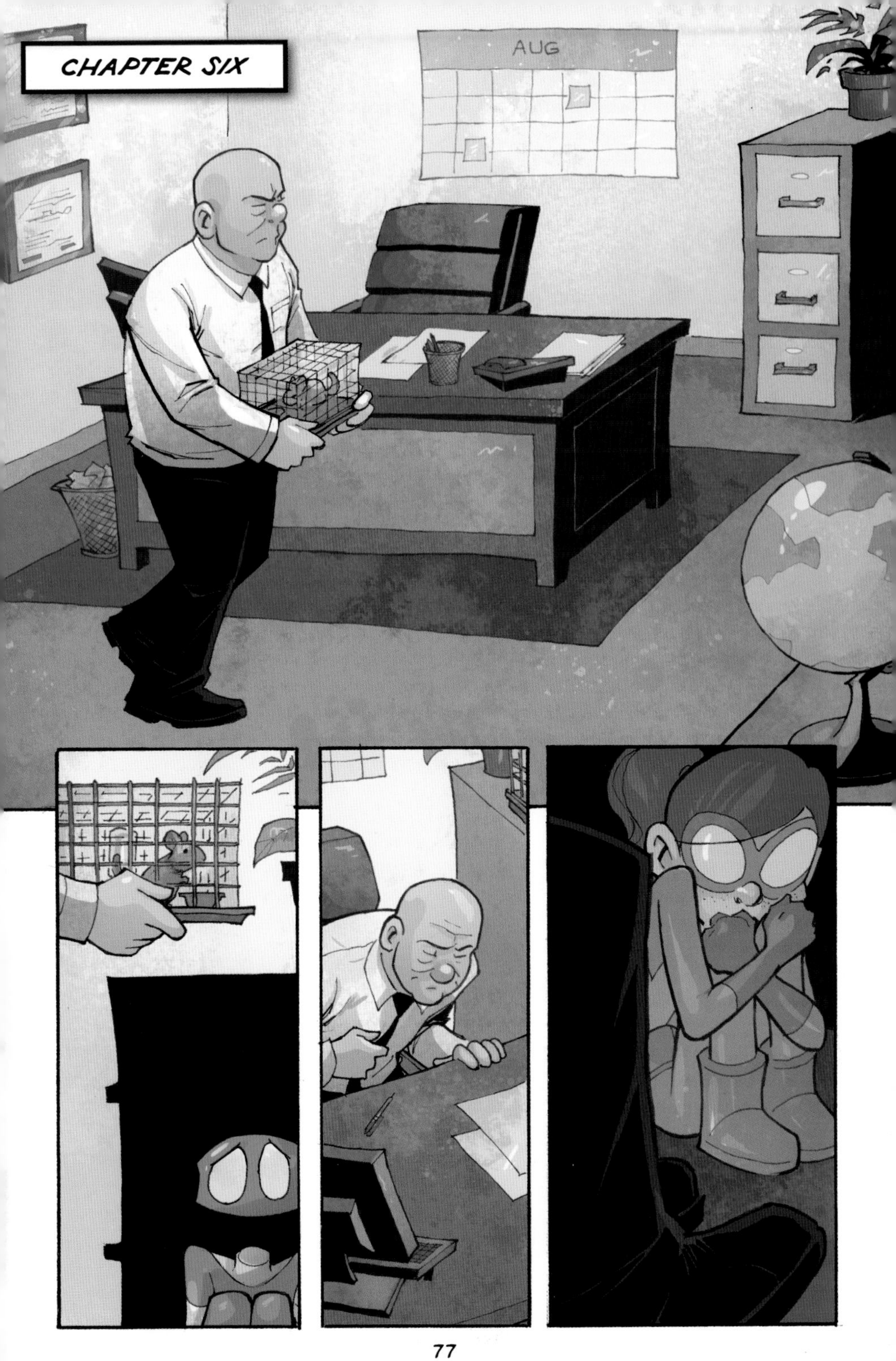
CHAPTER SIX
AUG

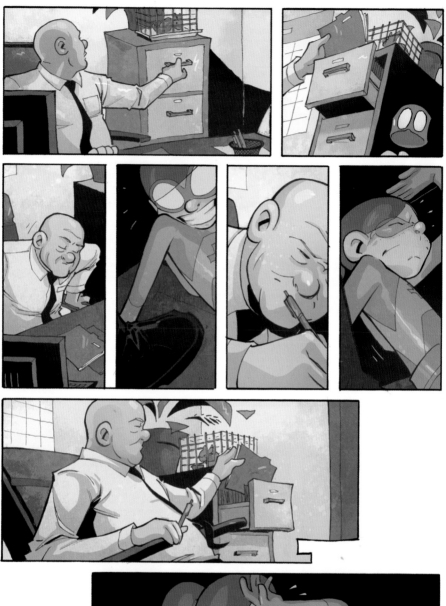

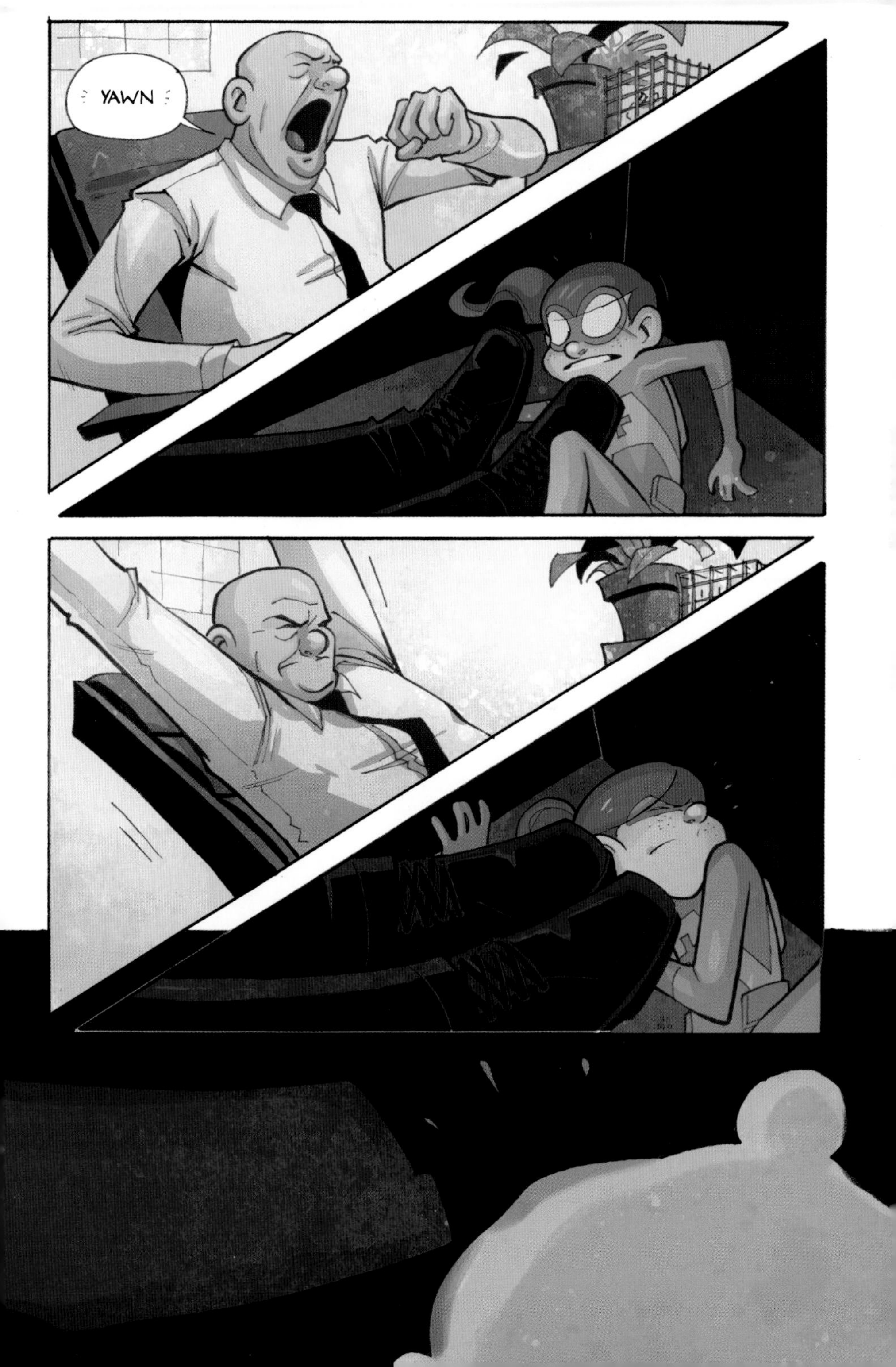
YAWN

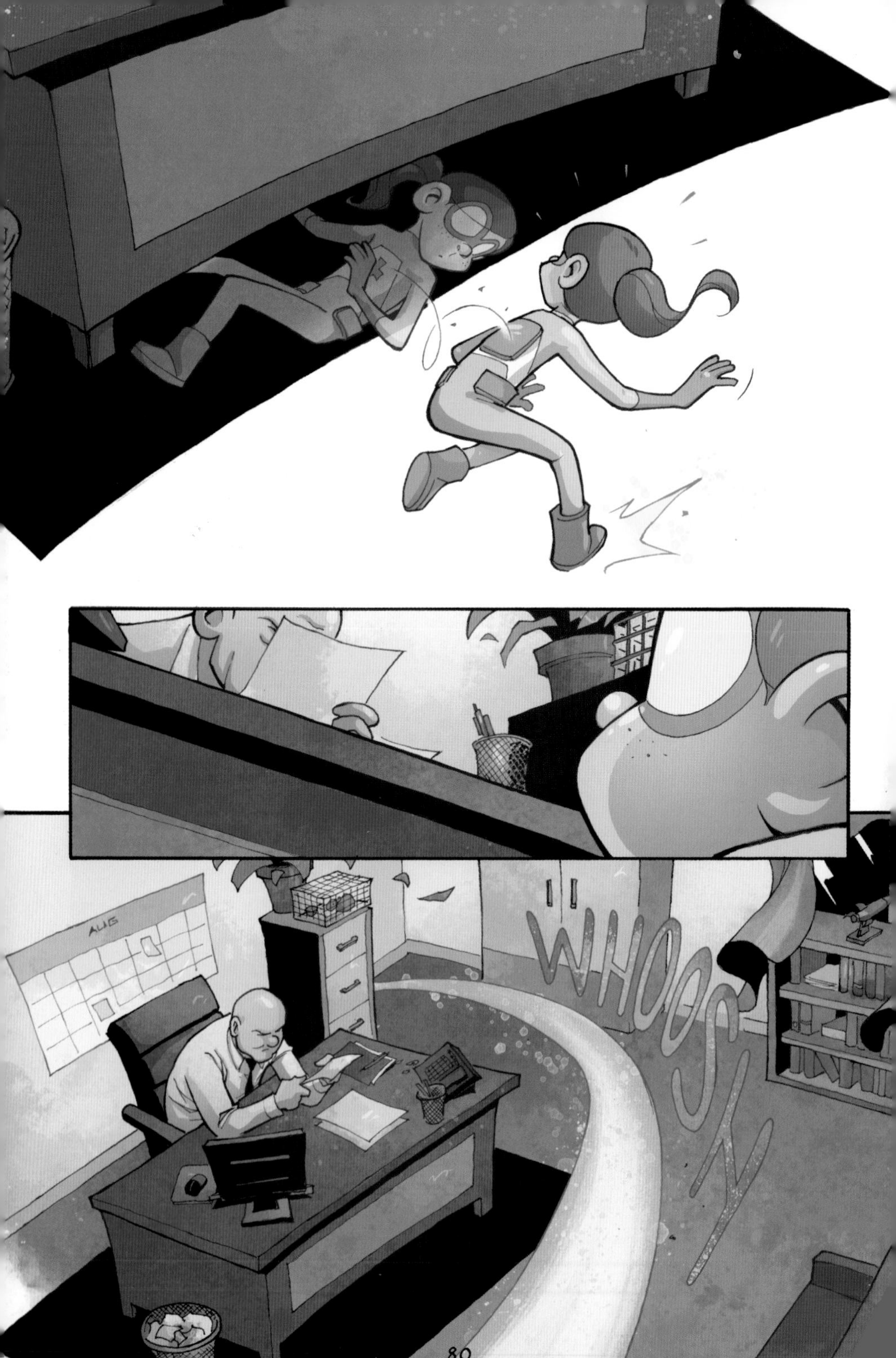
AUG
WHOOSH

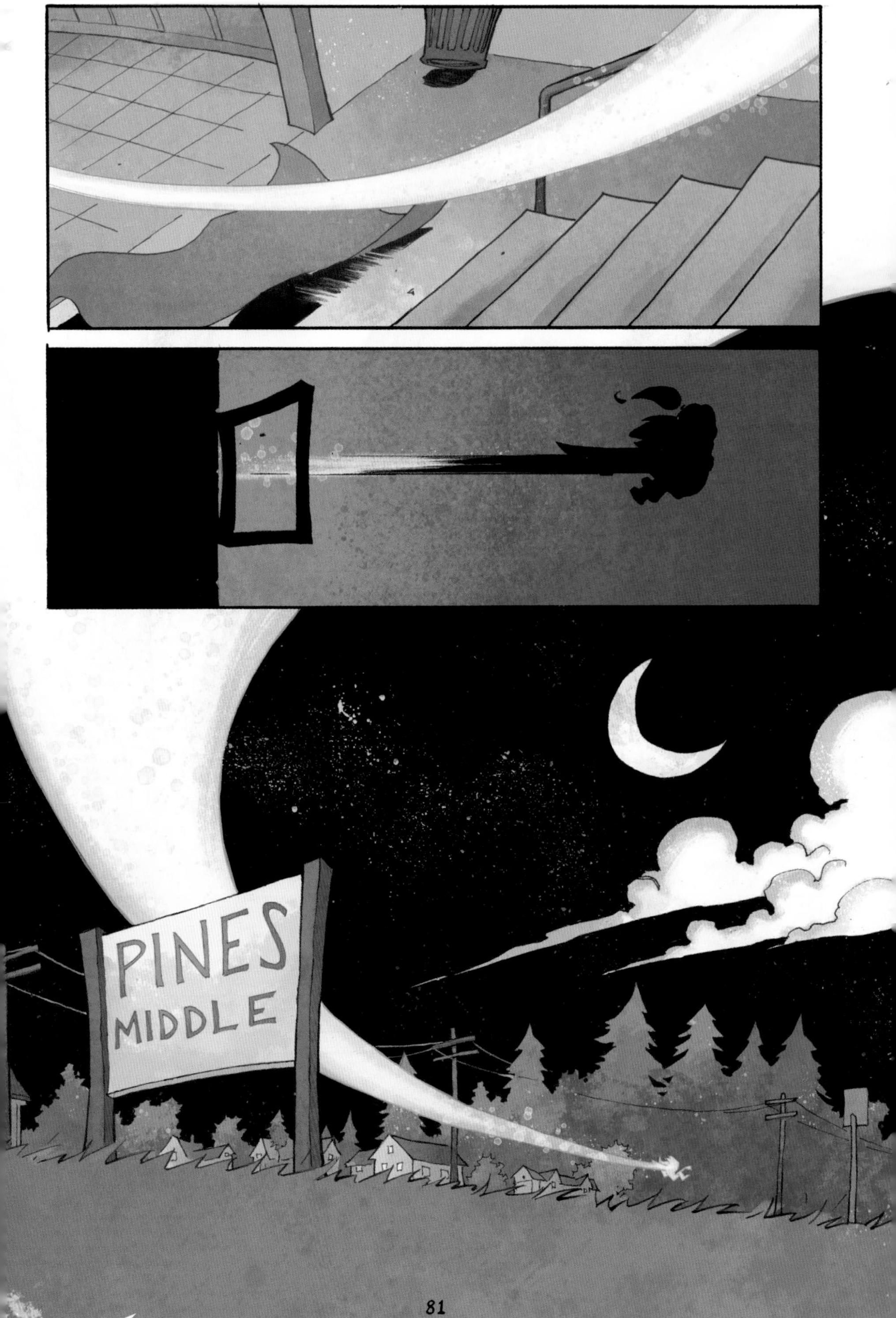
PINES
MIDDLE

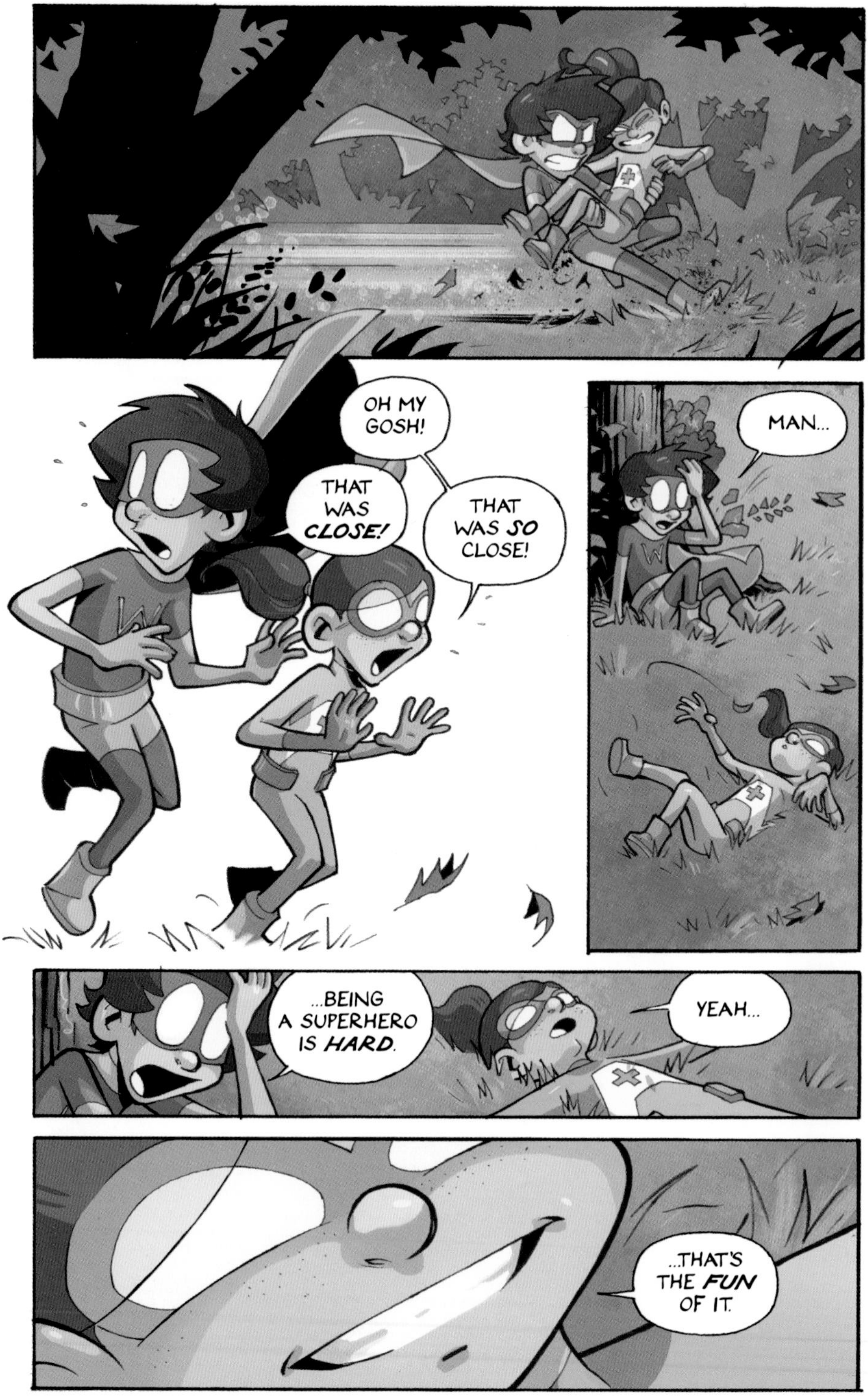

THAT WAS *CLOSE!*
OH MY GOSH!
THAT WAS *SO* CLOSE!
MAN...
...BEING A SUPERHERO IS *HARD*.
YEAH...
...THAT'S THE *FUN* OF IT.

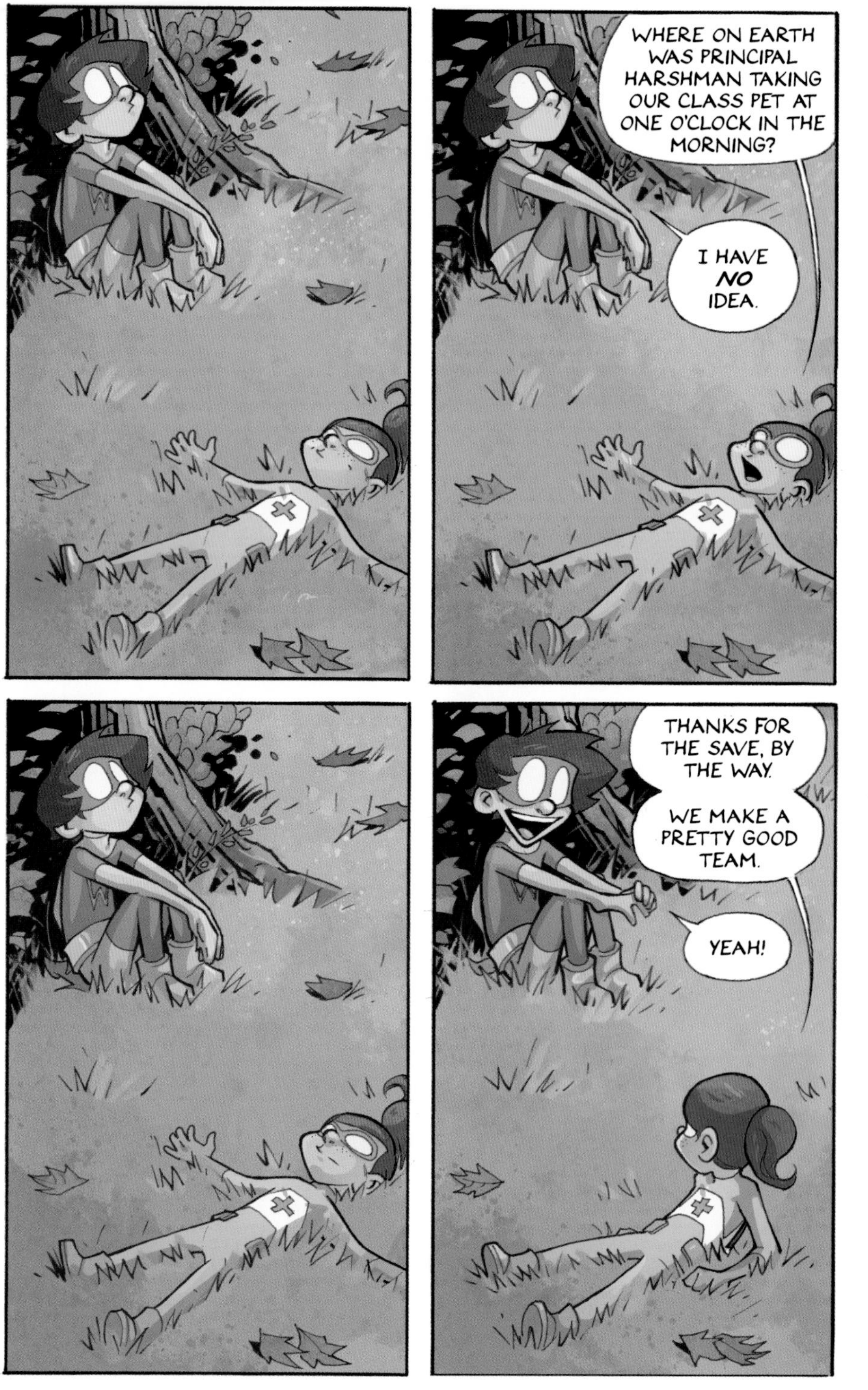
WHERE ON EARTH WAS PRINCIPAL HARSHMAN TAKING OUR CLASS PET AT ONE O'CLOCK IN THE MORNING?
I HAVE *NO* IDEA.
THANKS FOR THE SAVE, BY THE WAY.
WE MAKE A PRETTY GOOD TEAM.
YEAH!

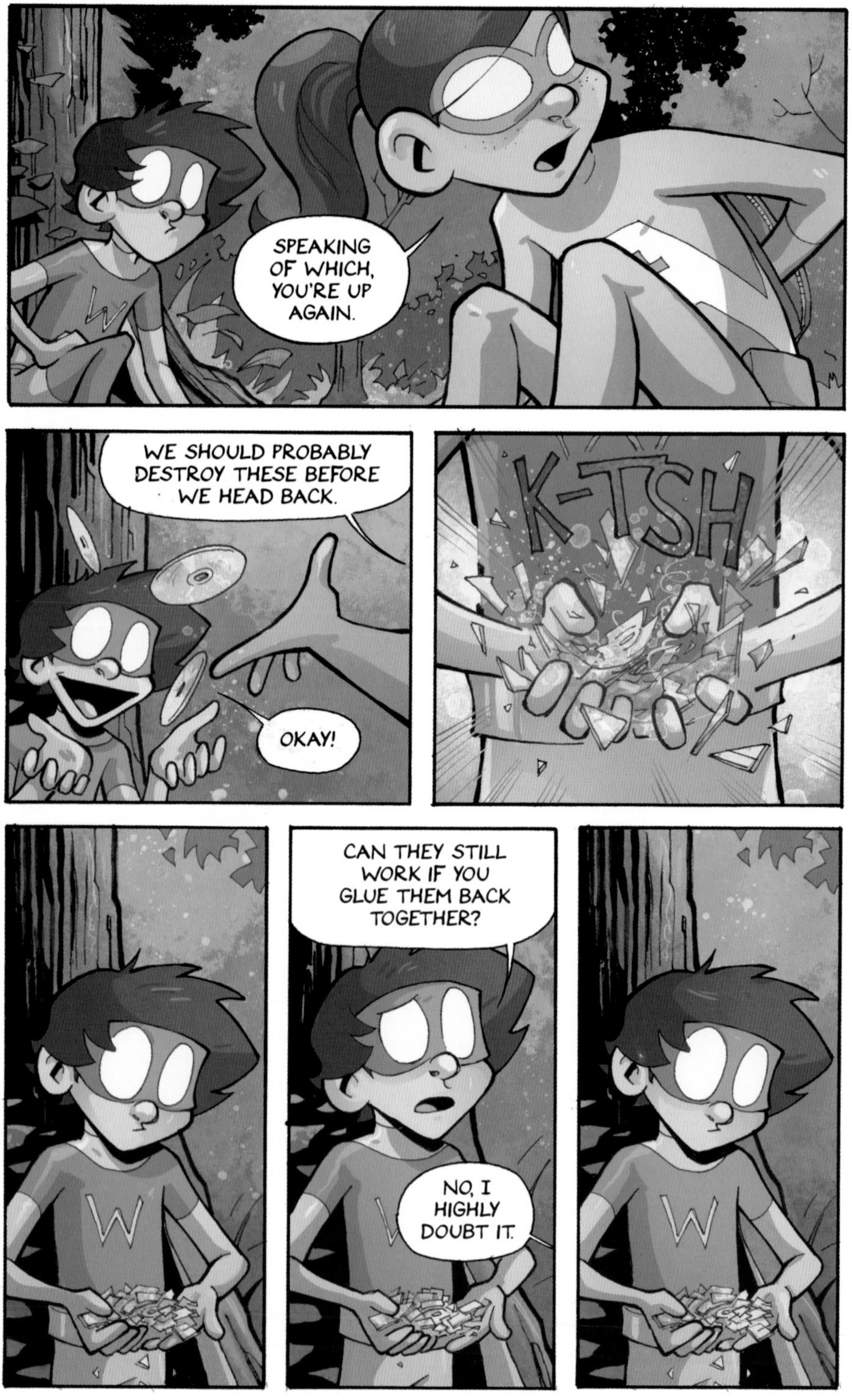
SPEAKING OF WHICH, YOU'RE UP AGAIN.
WE SHOULD PROBABLY DESTROY THESE BEFORE WE HEAD BACK.
OKAY!
K-TSH
CAN THEY STILL WORK IF YOU GLUE THEM BACK TOGETHER?
NO, I HIGHLY DOUBT IT.

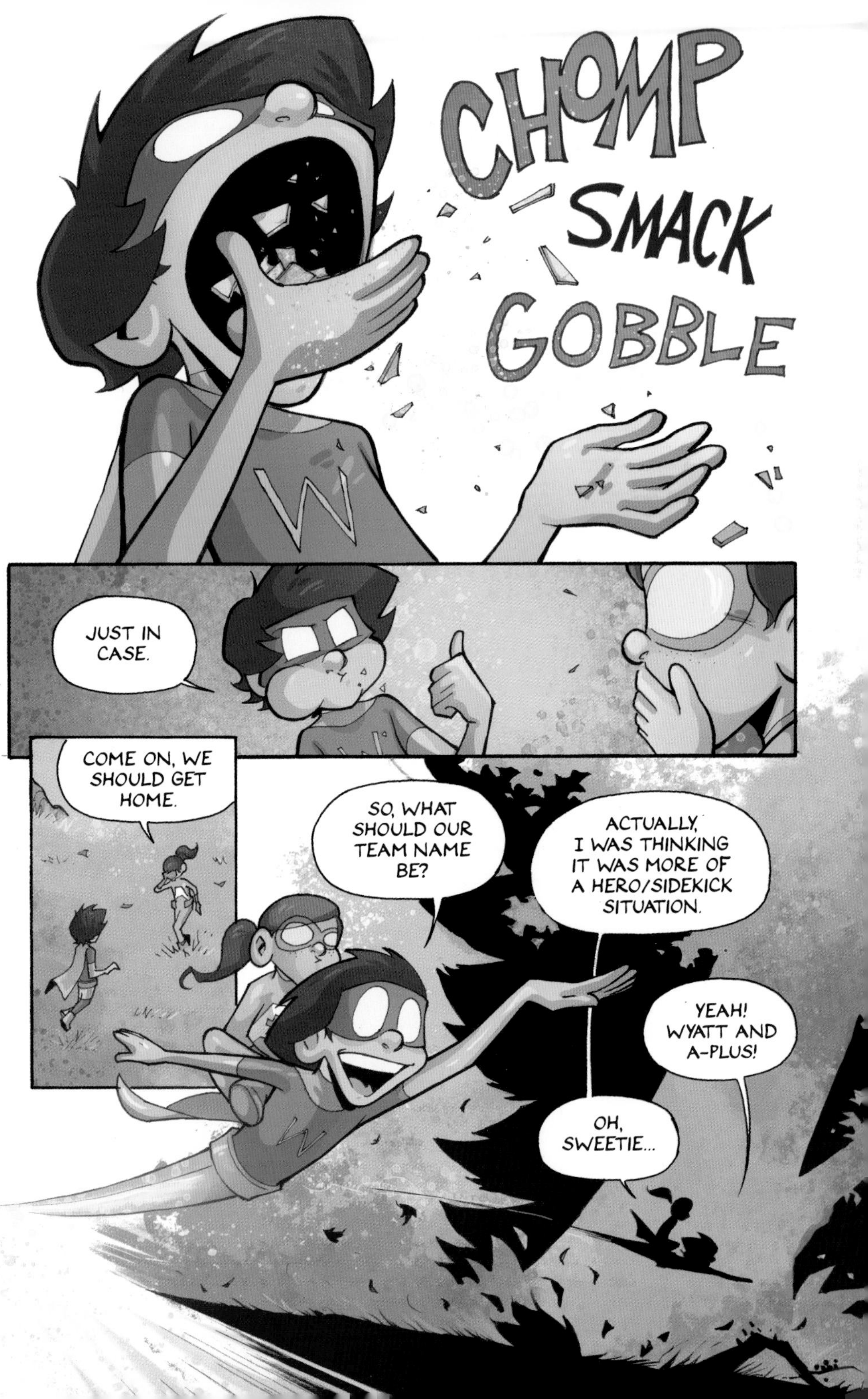
CHOMP
SMACK
GOBBLE
JUST IN CASE.
COME ON, WE SHOULD GET HOME.
SO, WHAT SHOULD OUR TEAM NAME BE?
ACTUALLY, I WAS THINKING IT WAS MORE OF A HERO/SIDEKICK SITUATION.
YEAH! WYATT AND A-PLUS!
OH, SWEETIE...

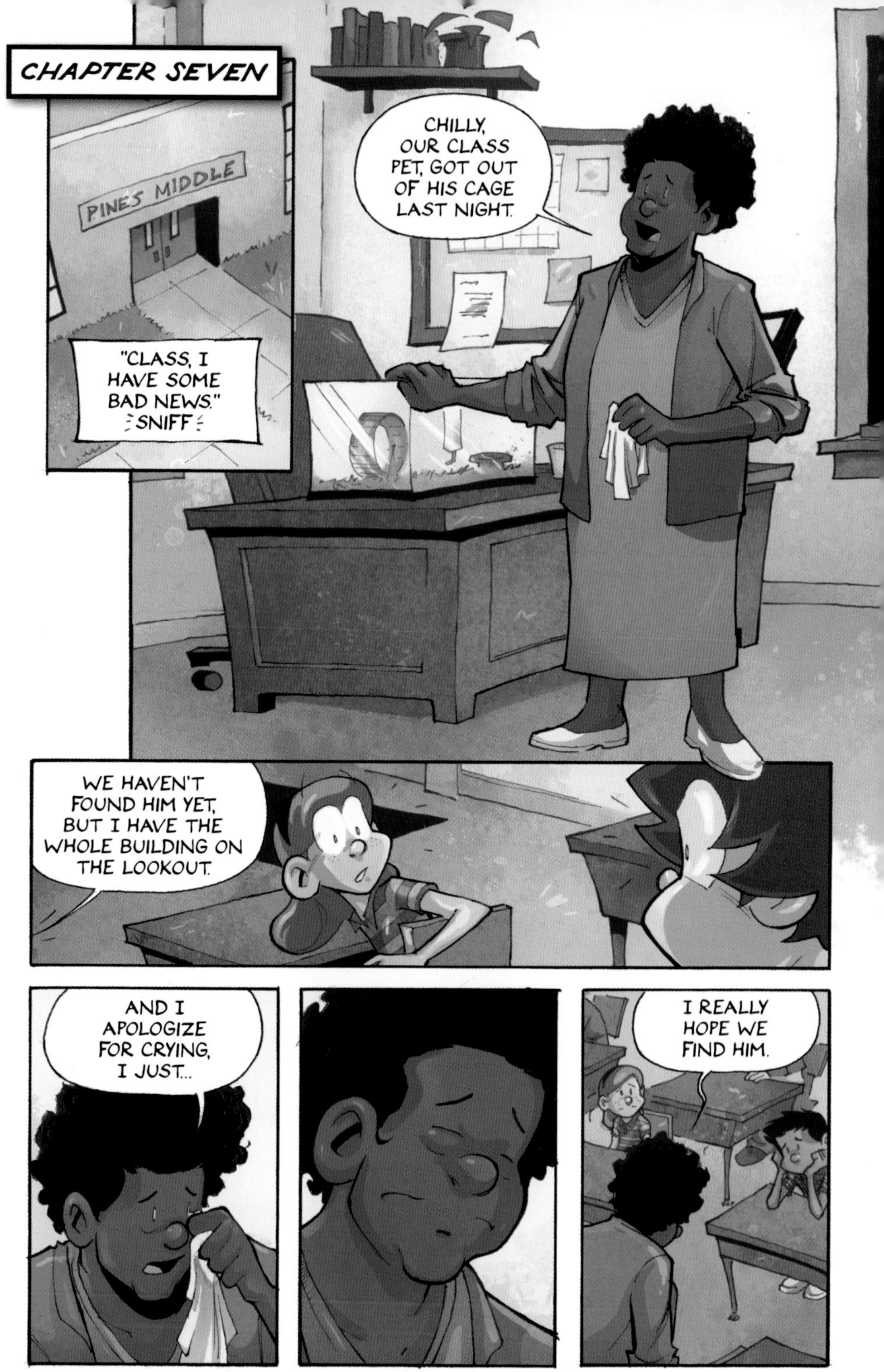
CHAPTER SEVEN
PINES MIDDLE
"CLASS, I HAVE SOME BAD NEWS."
SNIFF
CHILLY, OUR CLASS PET, GOT OUT OF HIS CAGE LAST NIGHT.
WE HAVEN'T FOUND HIM YET, BUT I HAVE THE WHOLE BUILDING ON THE LOOKOUT.
AND I APOLOGIZE FOR CRYING, I JUST...
I REALLY HOPE WE FIND HIM.

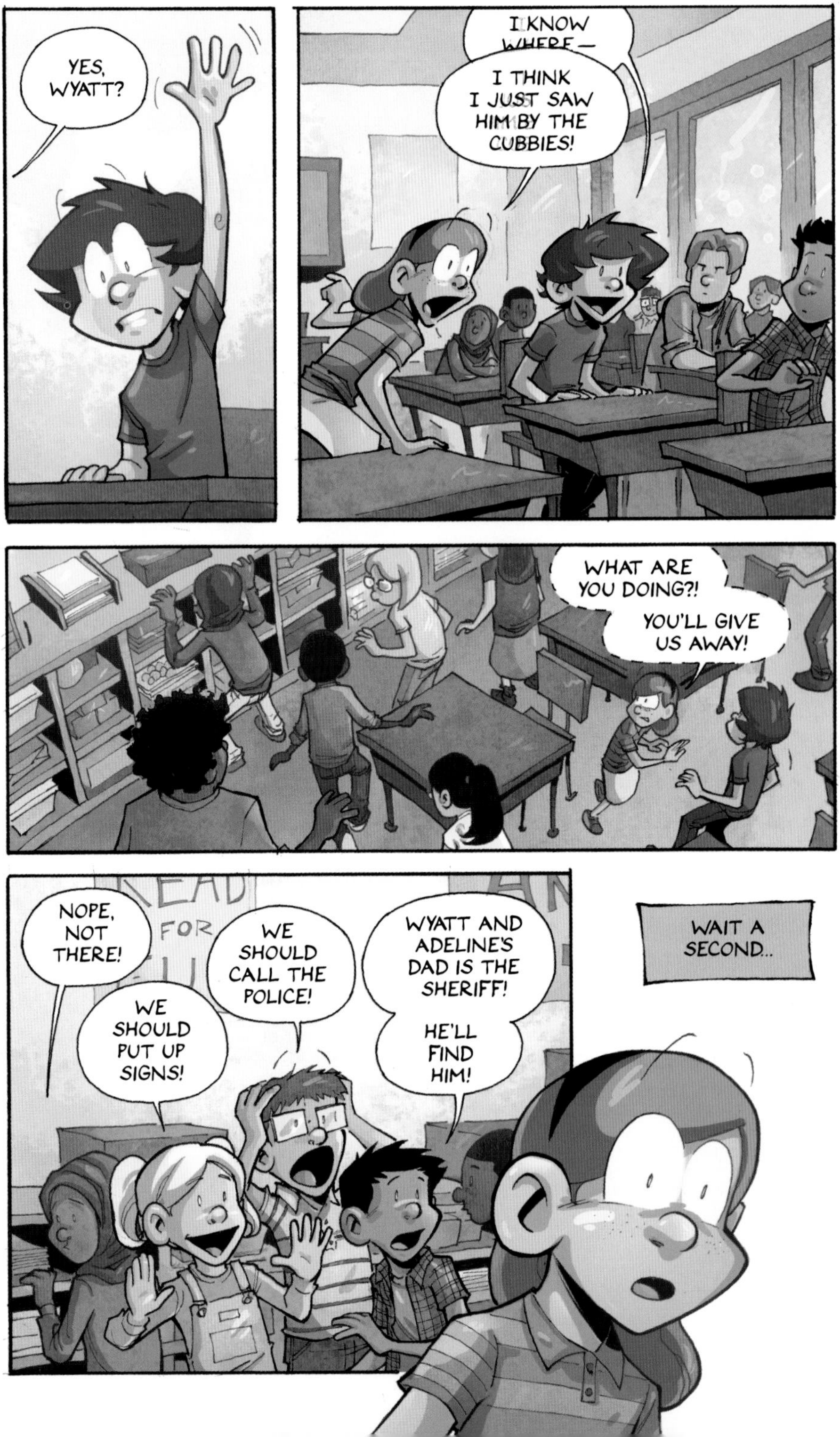
YES, WYATT?
I KNOW WHERE—
I THINK I JUST SAW HIM BY THE CUBBIES!
WHAT ARE YOU DOING?!
YOU'LL GIVE US AWAY!
NOPE, NOT THERE!
WE SHOULD PUT UP SIGNS!
WE SHOULD CALL THE POLICE!
WYATT AND ADELINE'S DAD IS THE SHERIFF!
HE'LL FIND HIM!
WAIT A SECOND...

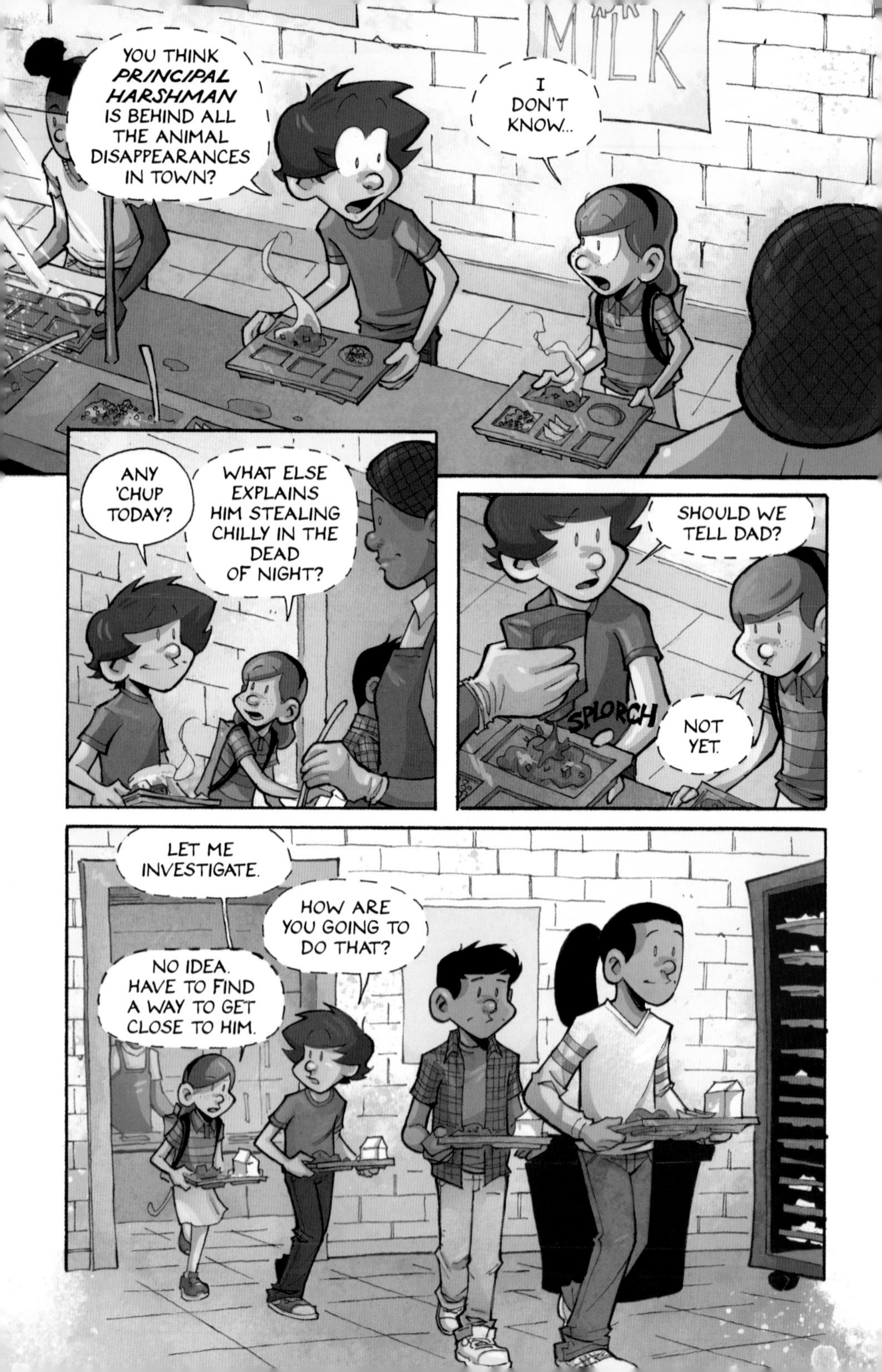
MILK
YOU THINK *PRINCIPAL HARSHMAN* IS BEHIND ALL THE ANIMAL DISAPPEARANCES IN TOWN?
I DON'T KNOW...
ANY 'CHUP TODAY?
WHAT ELSE EXPLAINS HIM STEALING CHILLY IN THE DEAD OF NIGHT?
SHOULD WE TELL DAD?
SPLORCH
NOT YET.
LET ME INVESTIGATE.
HOW ARE YOU GOING TO DO THAT?
NO IDEA. HAVE TO FIND A WAY TO GET CLOSE TO HIM.

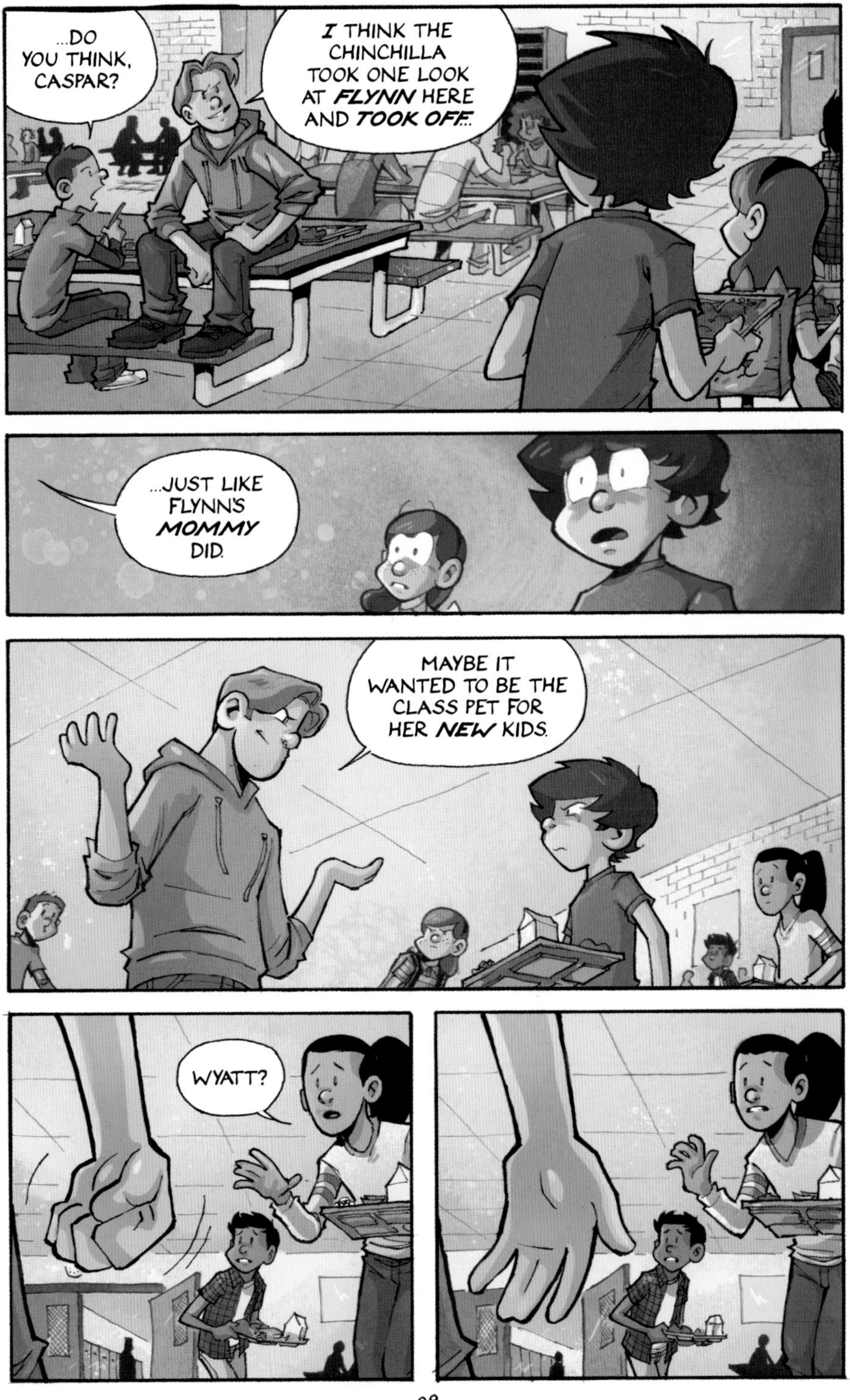
...DO YOU THINK, CASPAR?
I THINK THE CHINCHILLA TOOK ONE LOOK AT FLYNN HERE AND TOOK OFF...
...JUST LIKE FLYNN'S MOMMY DID.
MAYBE IT WANTED TO BE THE CLASS PET FOR HER NEW KIDS.
WYATT?

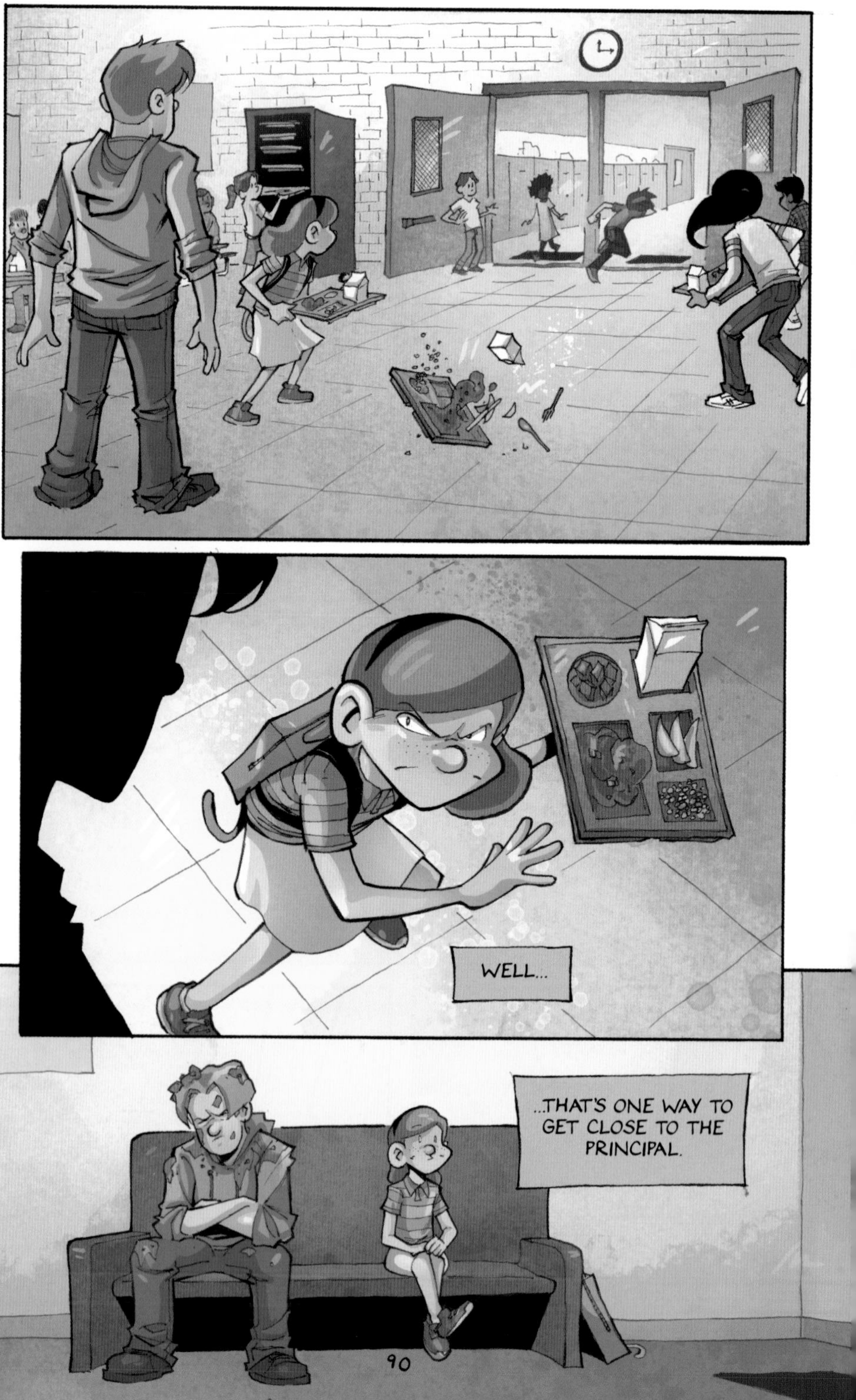
WELL...
...THAT'S ONE WAY TO GET CLOSE TO THE PRINCIPAL.

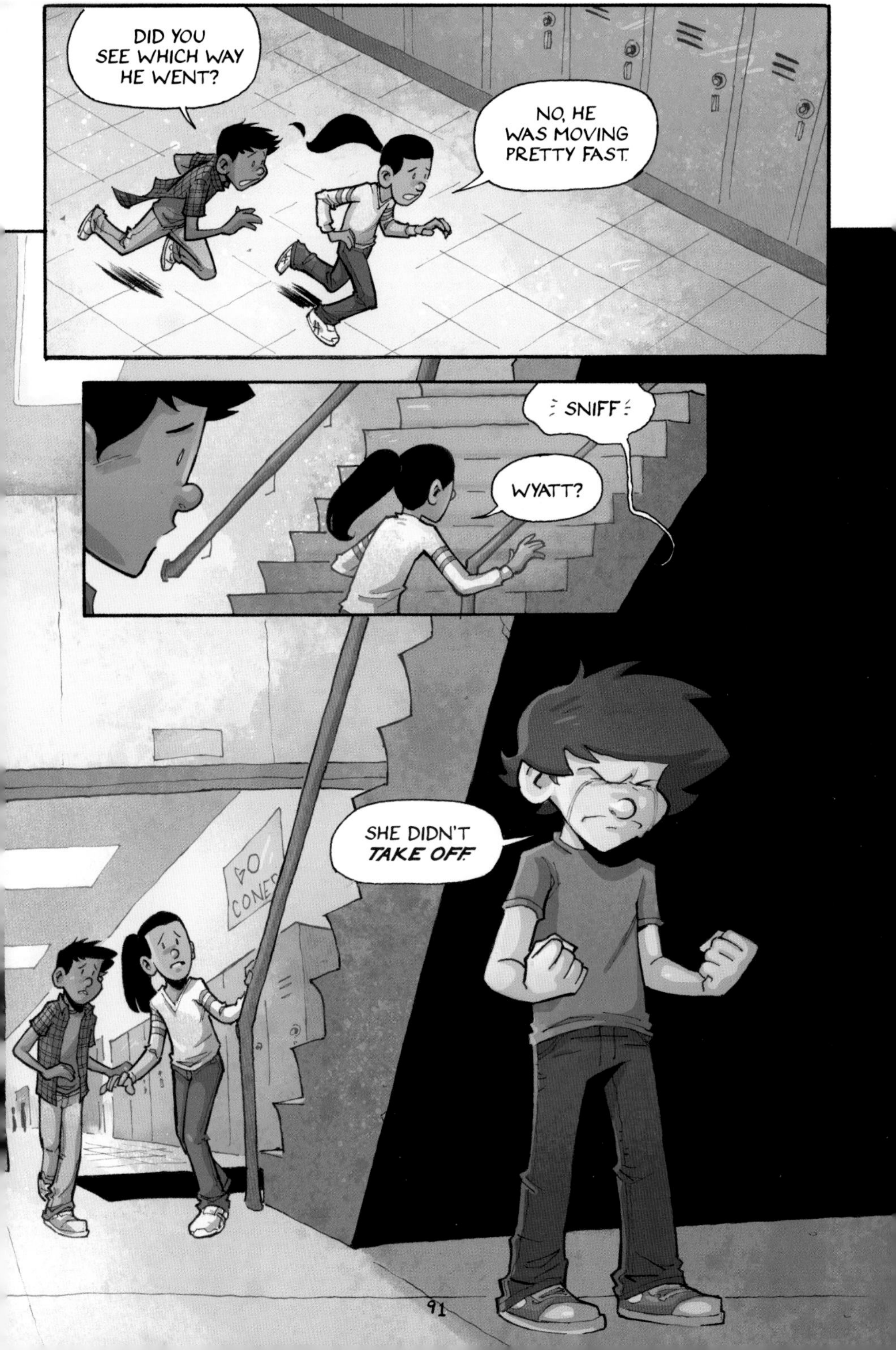
DID YOU SEE WHICH WAY HE WENT?
NO, HE WAS MOVING PRETTY FAST.
SNIFF
WYATT?
SHE DIDN'T *TAKE OFF.*

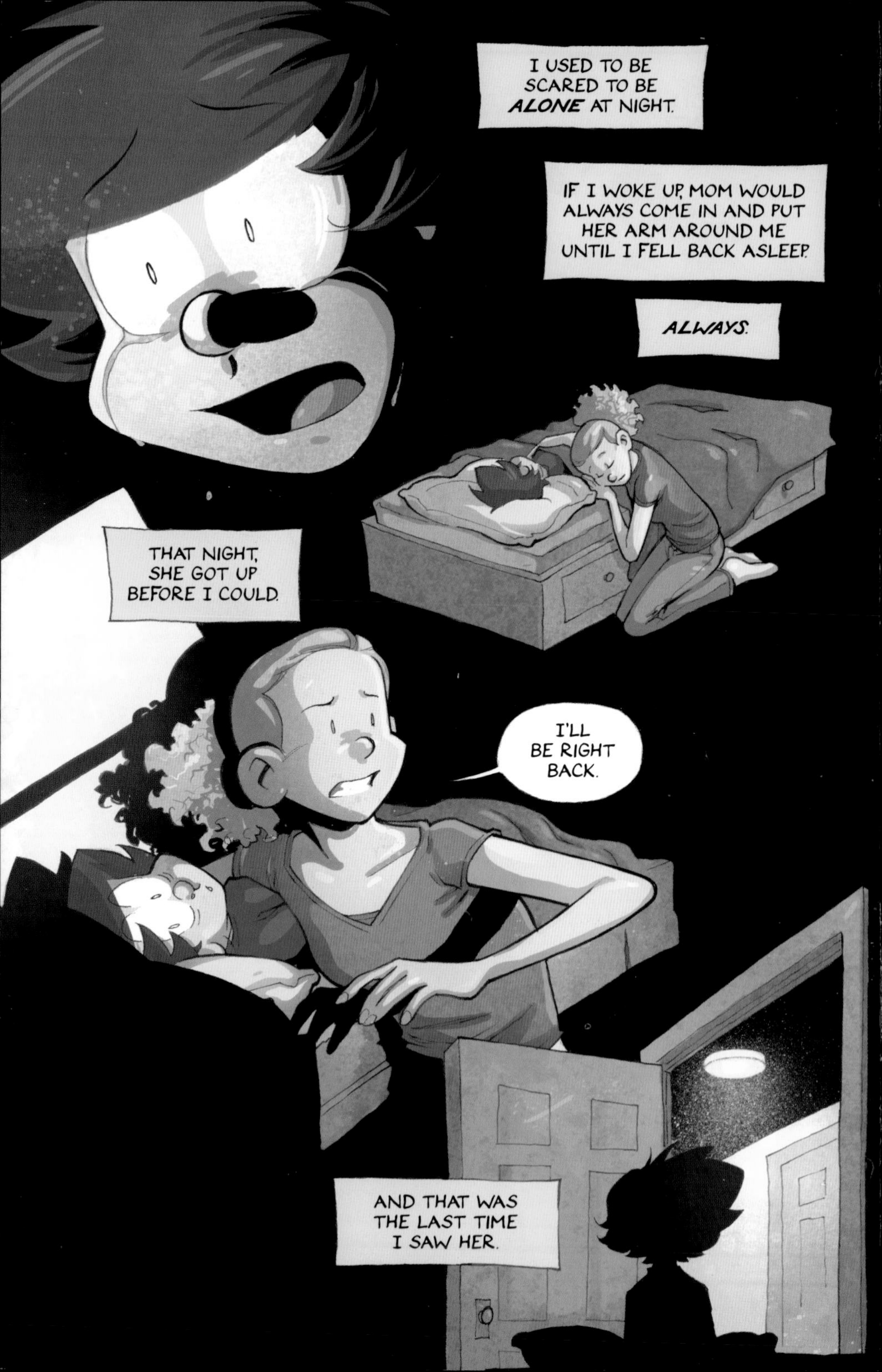
I USED TO BE SCARED TO BE *ALONE* AT NIGHT.
IF I WOKE UP, MOM WOULD ALWAYS COME IN AND PUT HER ARM AROUND ME UNTIL I FELL BACK ASLEEP.
ALWAYS.
THAT NIGHT, SHE GOT UP BEFORE I COULD.
I'LL BE RIGHT BACK.
AND THAT WAS THE LAST TIME I SAW HER.

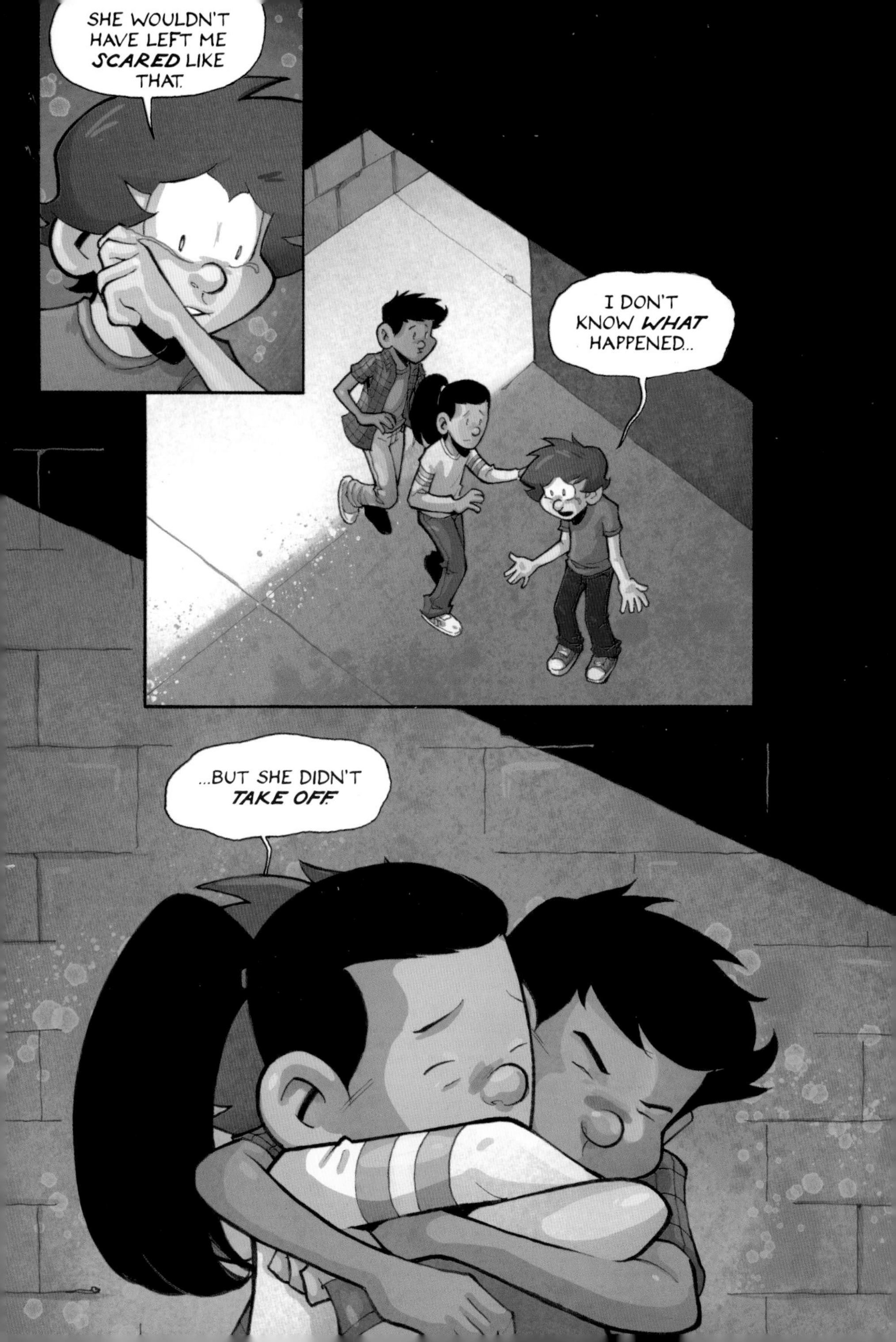
SHE WOULDN'T HAVE LEFT ME ***SCARED*** LIKE THAT.
I DON'T KNOW ***WHAT*** HAPPENED...
...BUT SHE DIDN'T ***TAKE OFF.***

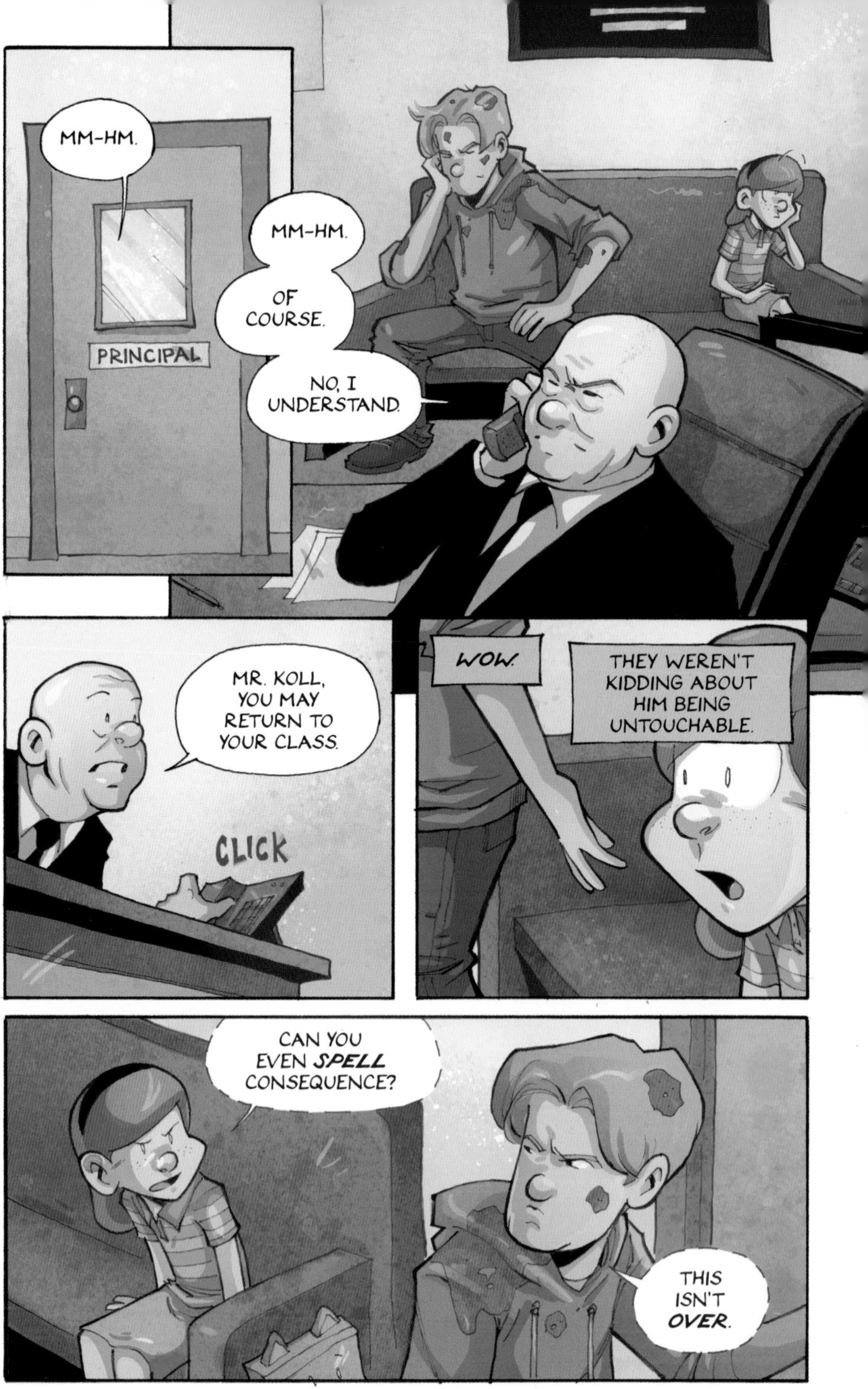
MM-HM.
PRINCIPAL
MM-HM.
OF COURSE.
NO, I UNDERSTAND.
MR. KOLL, YOU MAY RETURN TO YOUR CLASS.
CLICK
WOW.
THEY WEREN'T KIDDING ABOUT HIM BEING UNTOUCHABLE.
CAN YOU EVEN *SPELL* CONSEQUENCE?
THIS ISN'T *OVER*.

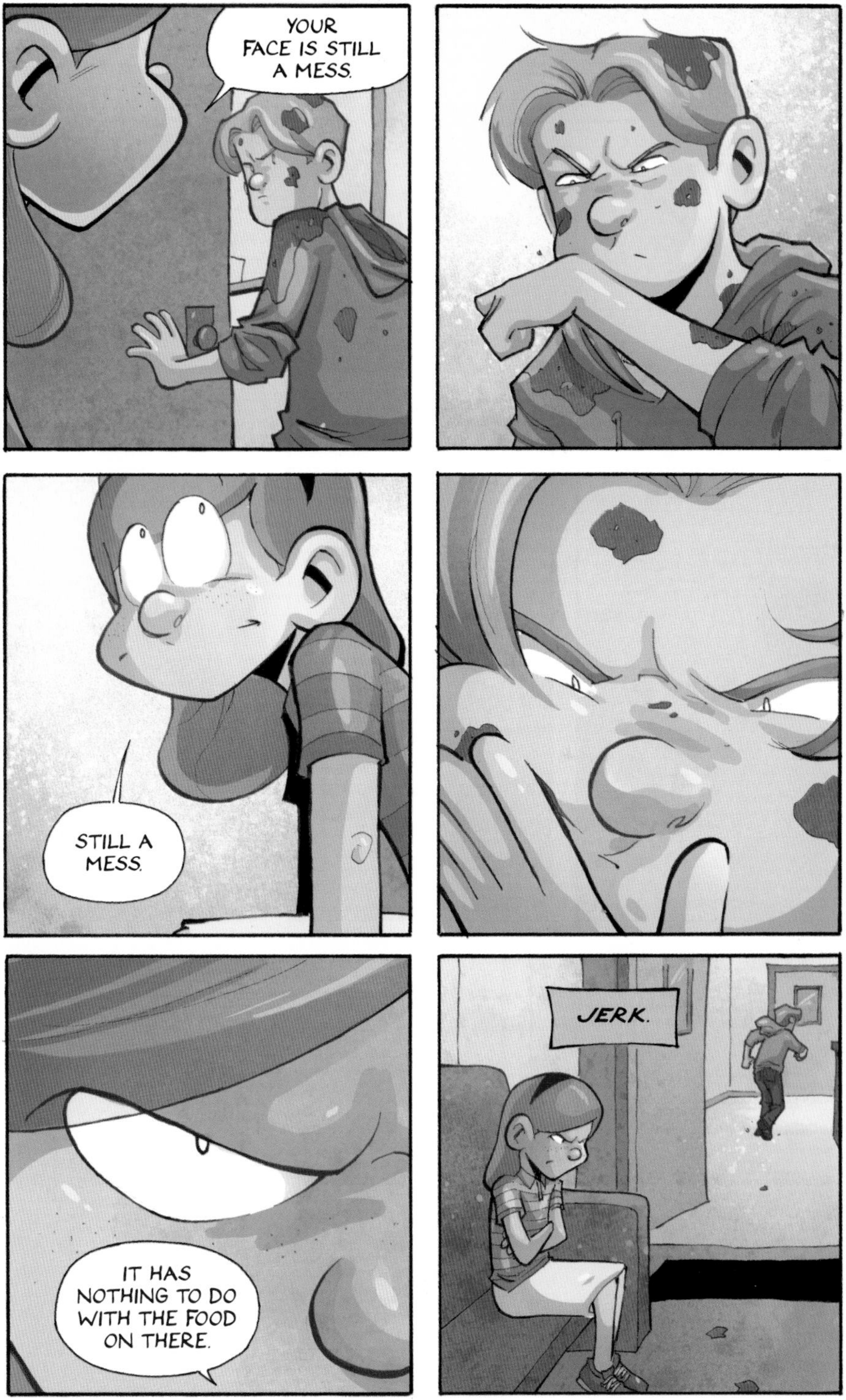
YOUR FACE IS STILL A MESS.
STILL A MESS.
IT HAS NOTHING TO DO WITH THE FOOD ON THERE.
JERK.

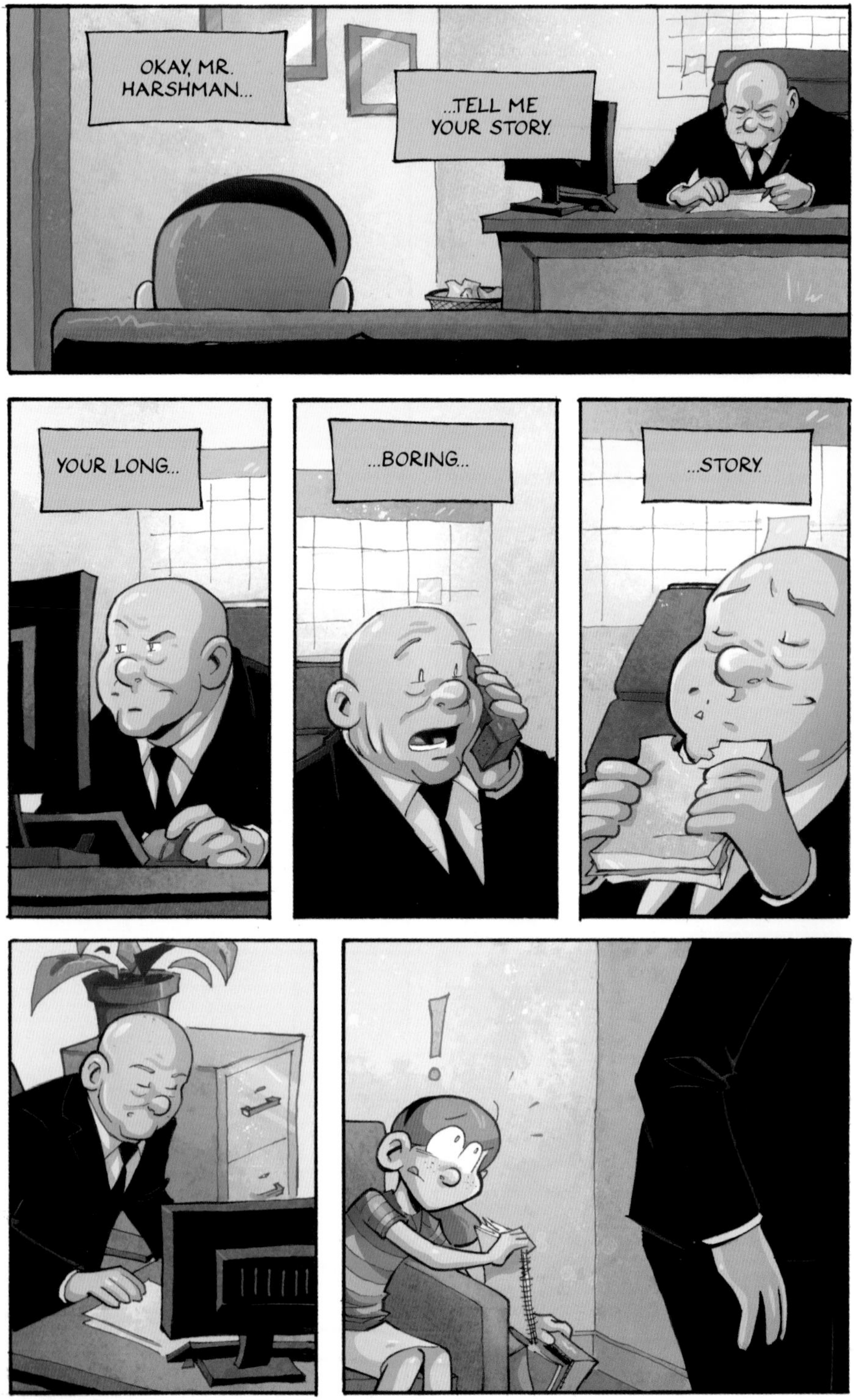
OKAY, MR. HARSHMAN...
...TELL ME YOUR STORY.
YOUR LONG...
...BORING...
...STORY.
!

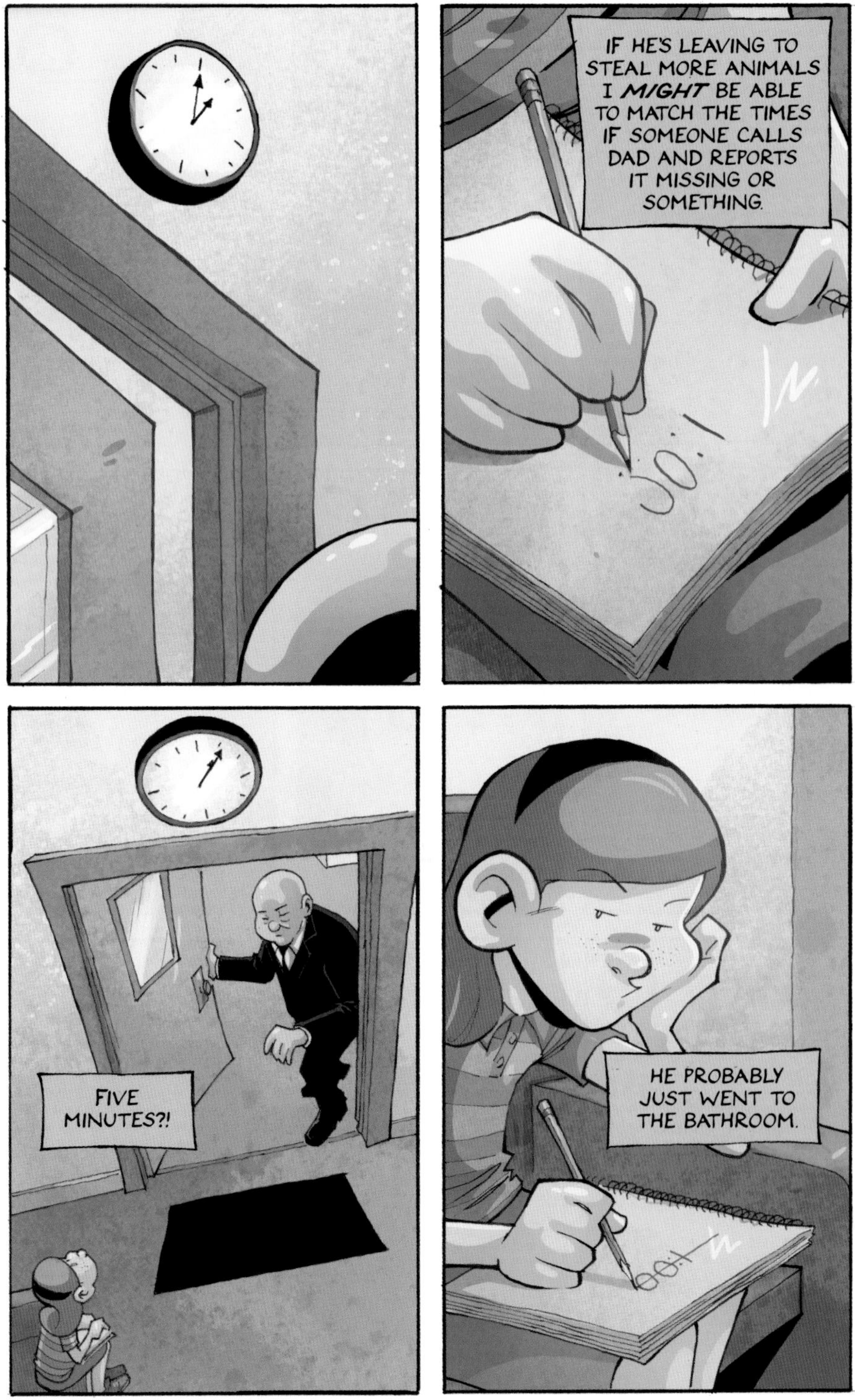
IF HE'S LEAVING TO STEAL MORE ANIMALS I *MIGHT* BE ABLE TO MATCH THE TIMES IF SOMEONE CALLS DAD AND REPORTS IT MISSING OR SOMETHING.
FIVE MINUTES?!
HE PROBABLY JUST WENT TO THE BATHROOM.

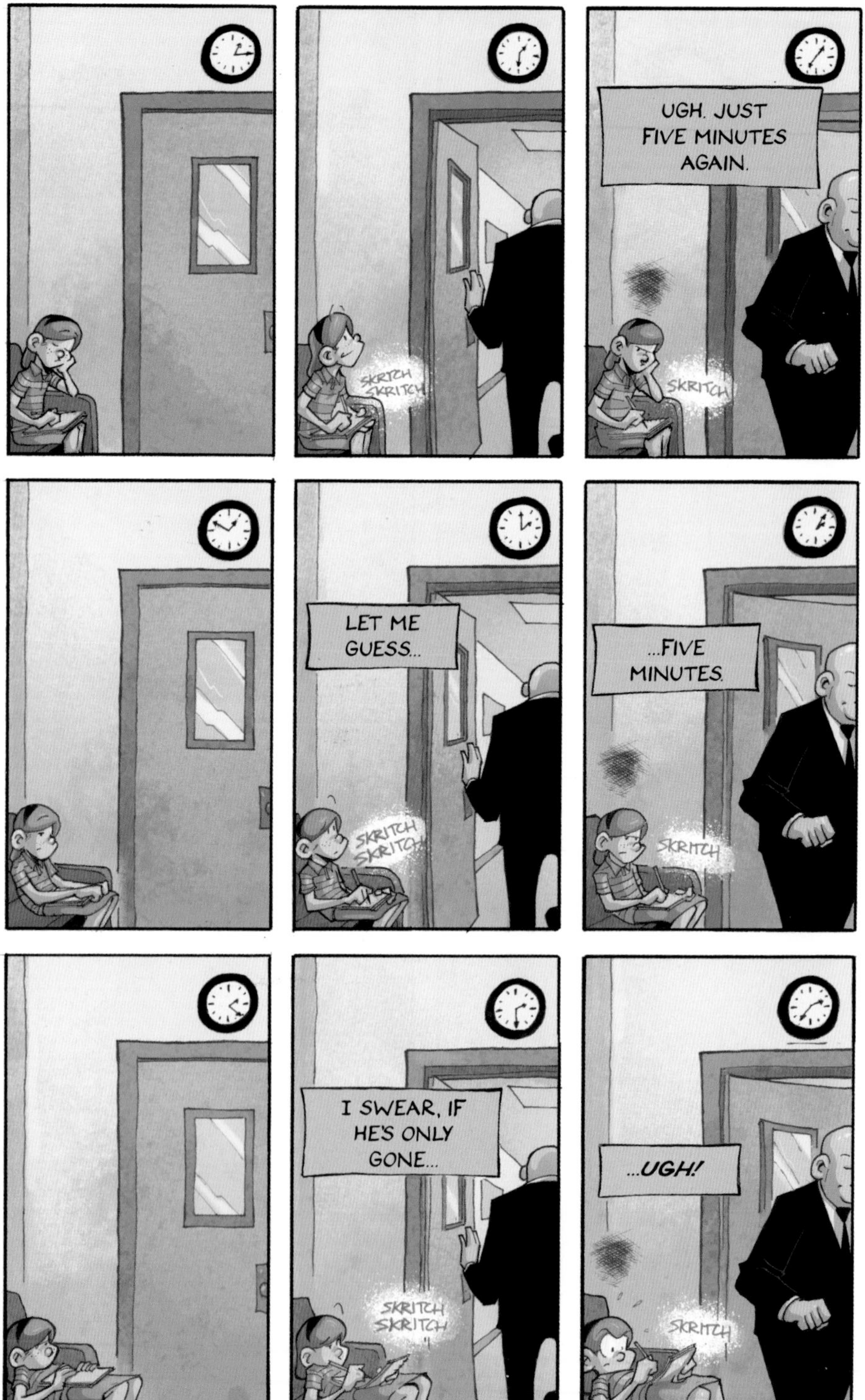
SKRITCH
SKRITCH
UGH. JUST FIVE MINUTES AGAIN.
SKRITCH
LET ME GUESS...
SKRITCH
SKRITCH
...FIVE MINUTES.
SKRITCH
I SWEAR, IF HE'S ONLY GONE...
SKRITCH
SKRITCH
...UGH!
SKRITCH

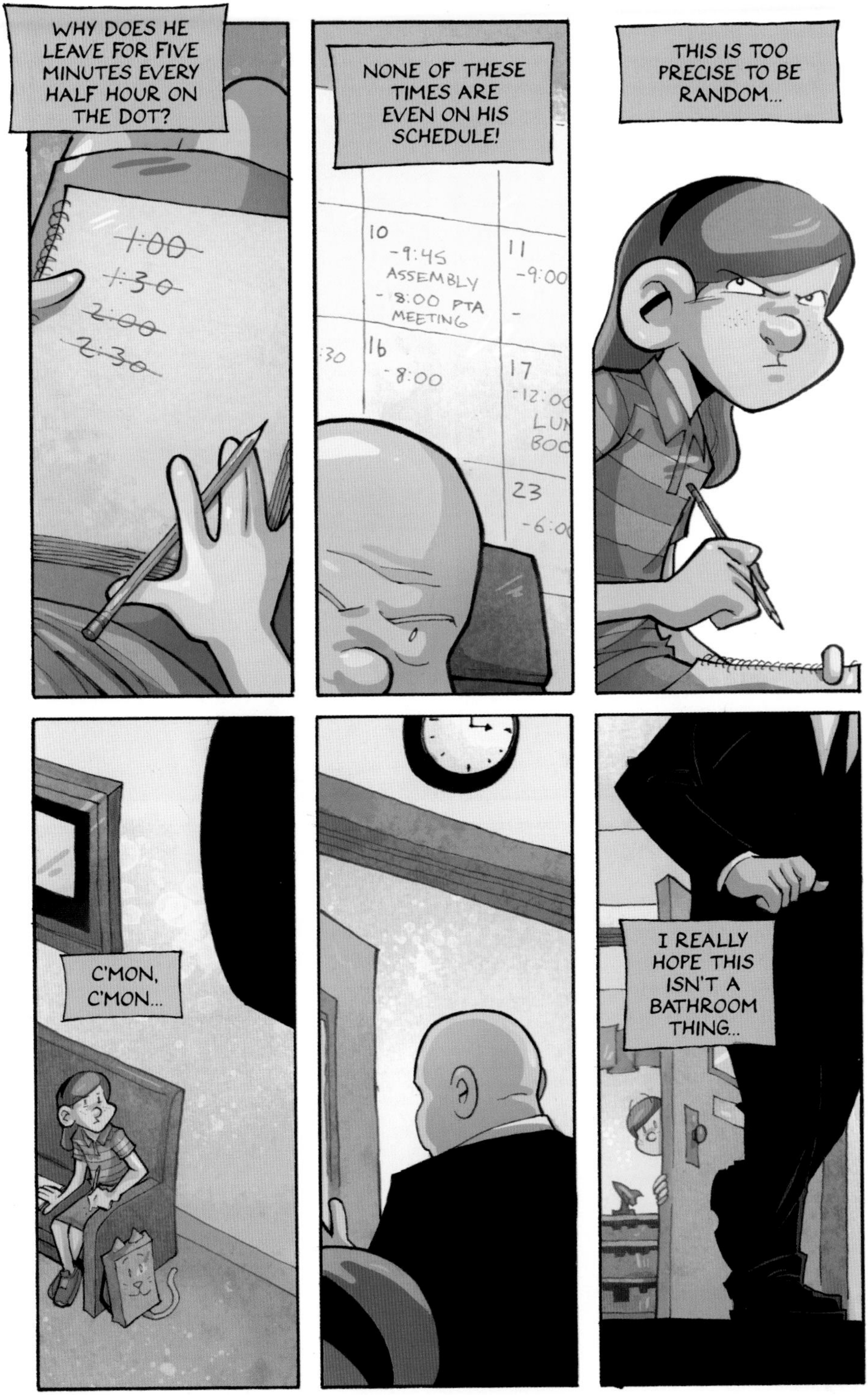
WHY DOES HE LEAVE FOR FIVE MINUTES EVERY HALF HOUR ON THE DOT?
1:00
1:30
2:00
2:30
NONE OF THESE TIMES ARE EVEN ON HIS SCHEDULE!
10
-9:45 ASSEMBLY
-8:00 PTA MEETING
11
-9:00
16
-8:00
17
-12:00
23
-6:00
THIS IS TOO PRECISE TO BE RANDOM...
C'MON, C'MON...
I REALLY HOPE THIS ISN'T A BATHROOM THING...

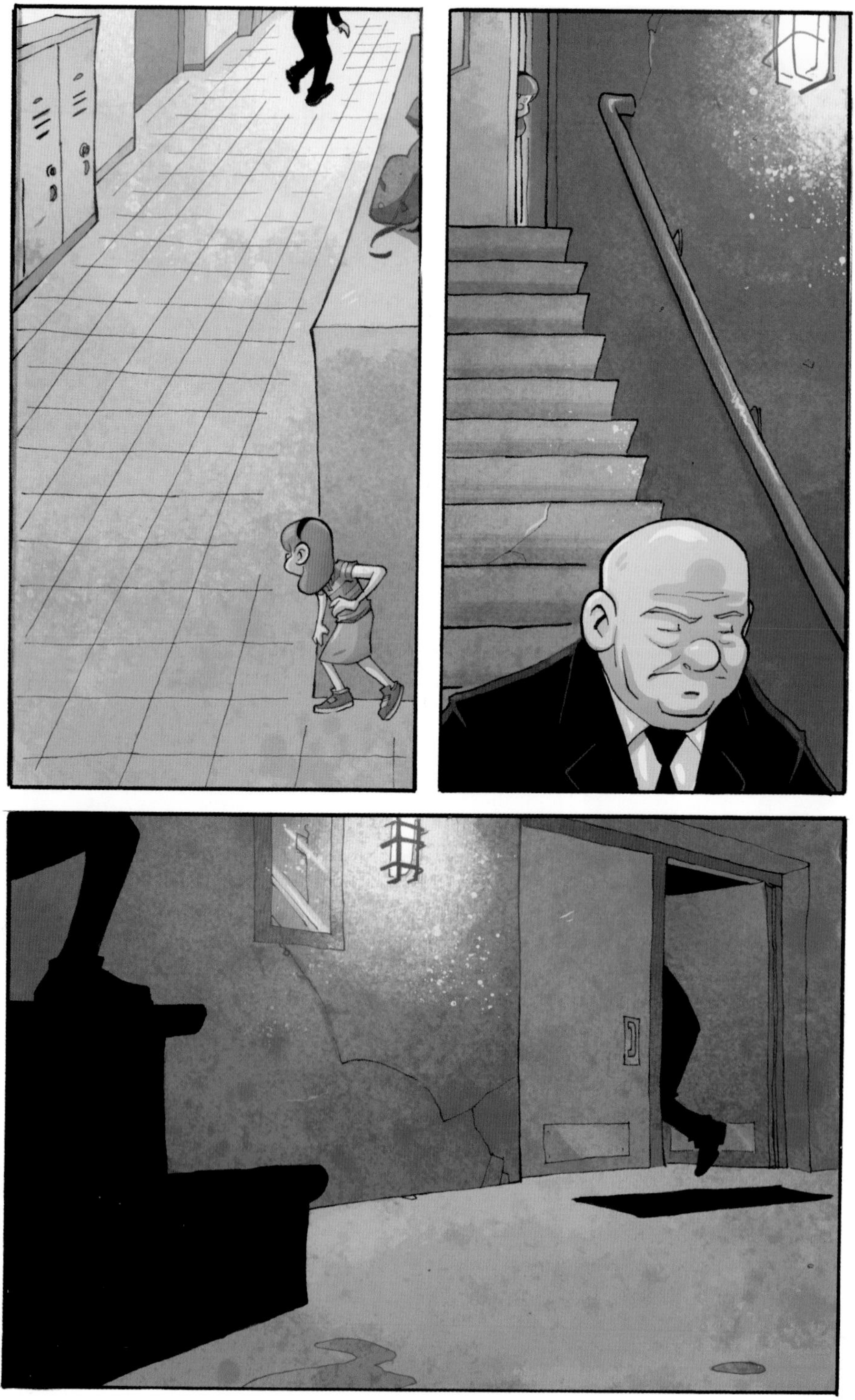

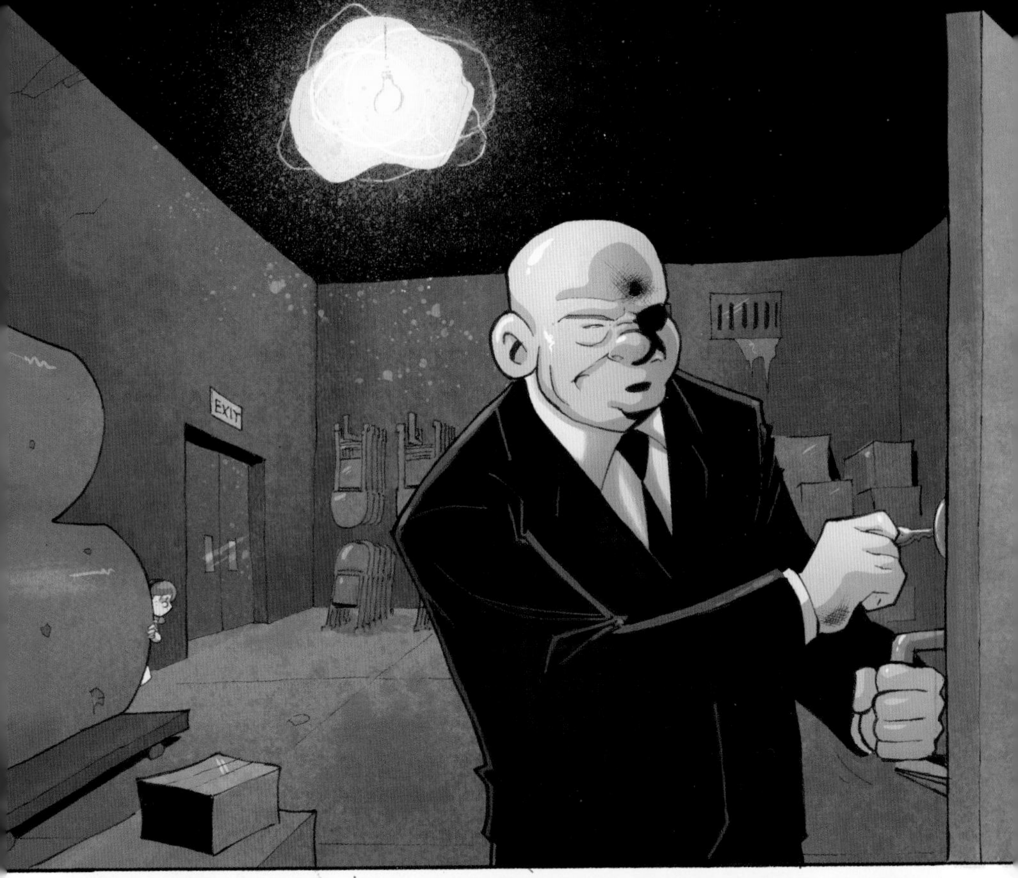
EXIT

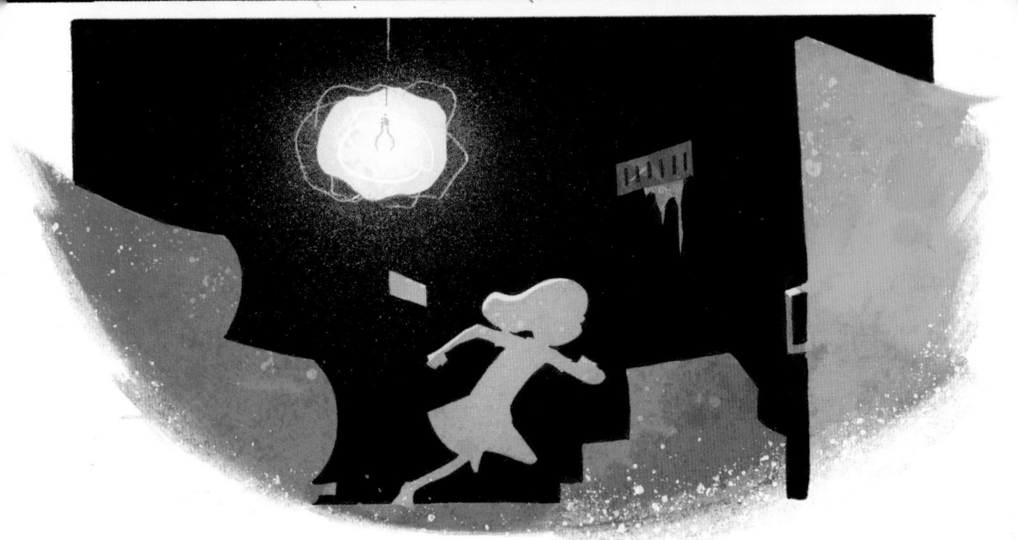

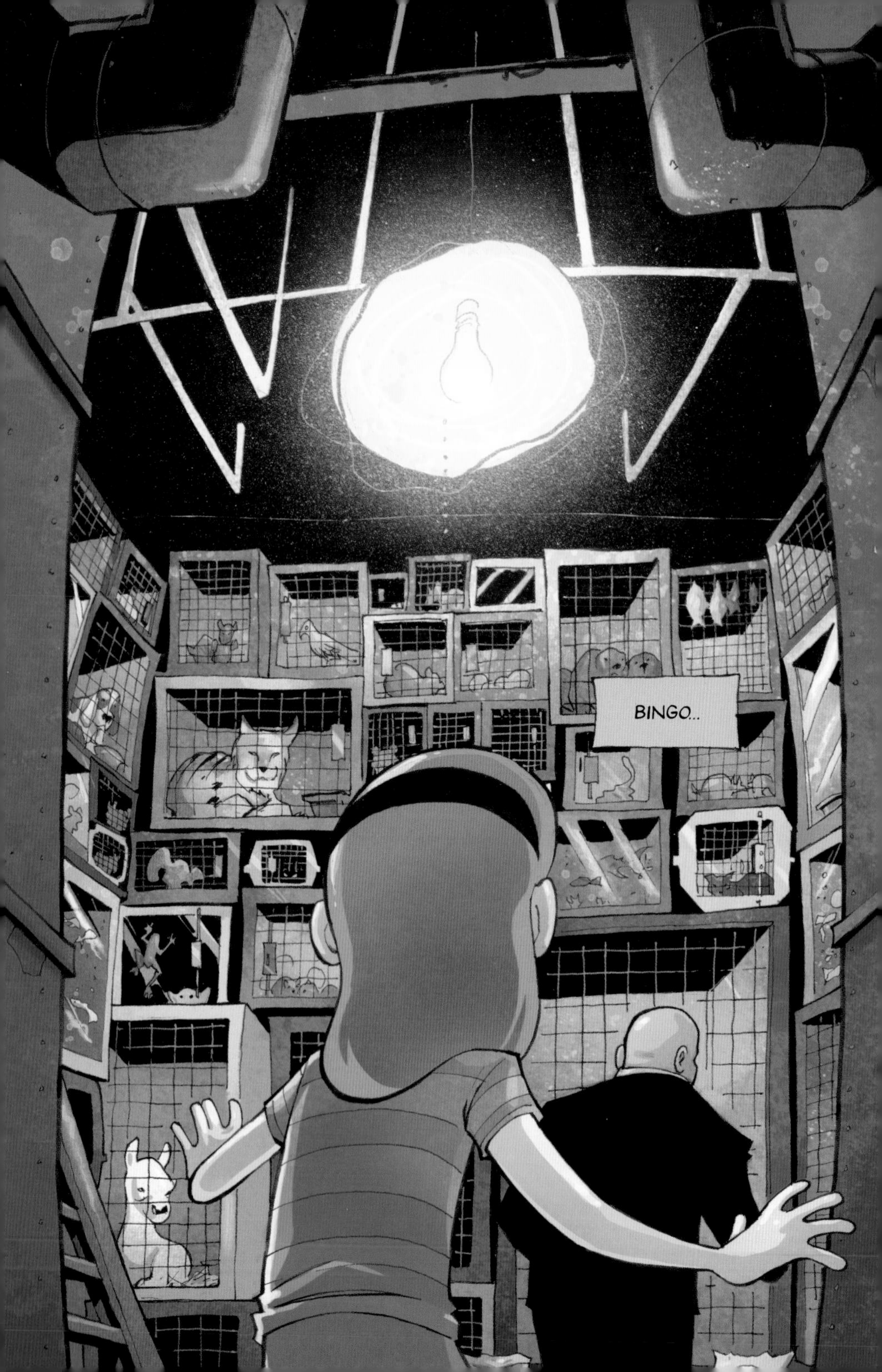
BINGO...

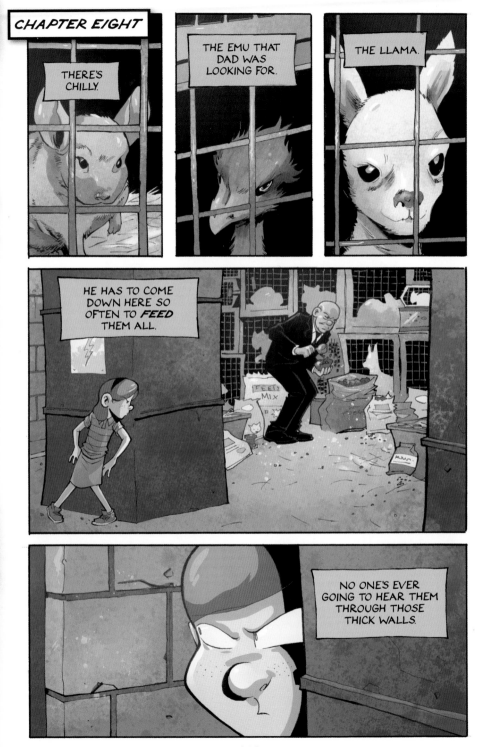

CHAPTER EIGHT

THERE'S CHILLY.

THE EMU THAT DAD WAS LOOKING FOR.

THE LLAMA.

HE HAS TO COME DOWN HERE SO OFTEN TO *FEED* THEM ALL.

NO ONE'S EVER GOING TO HEAR THEM THROUGH THOSE THICK WALLS.

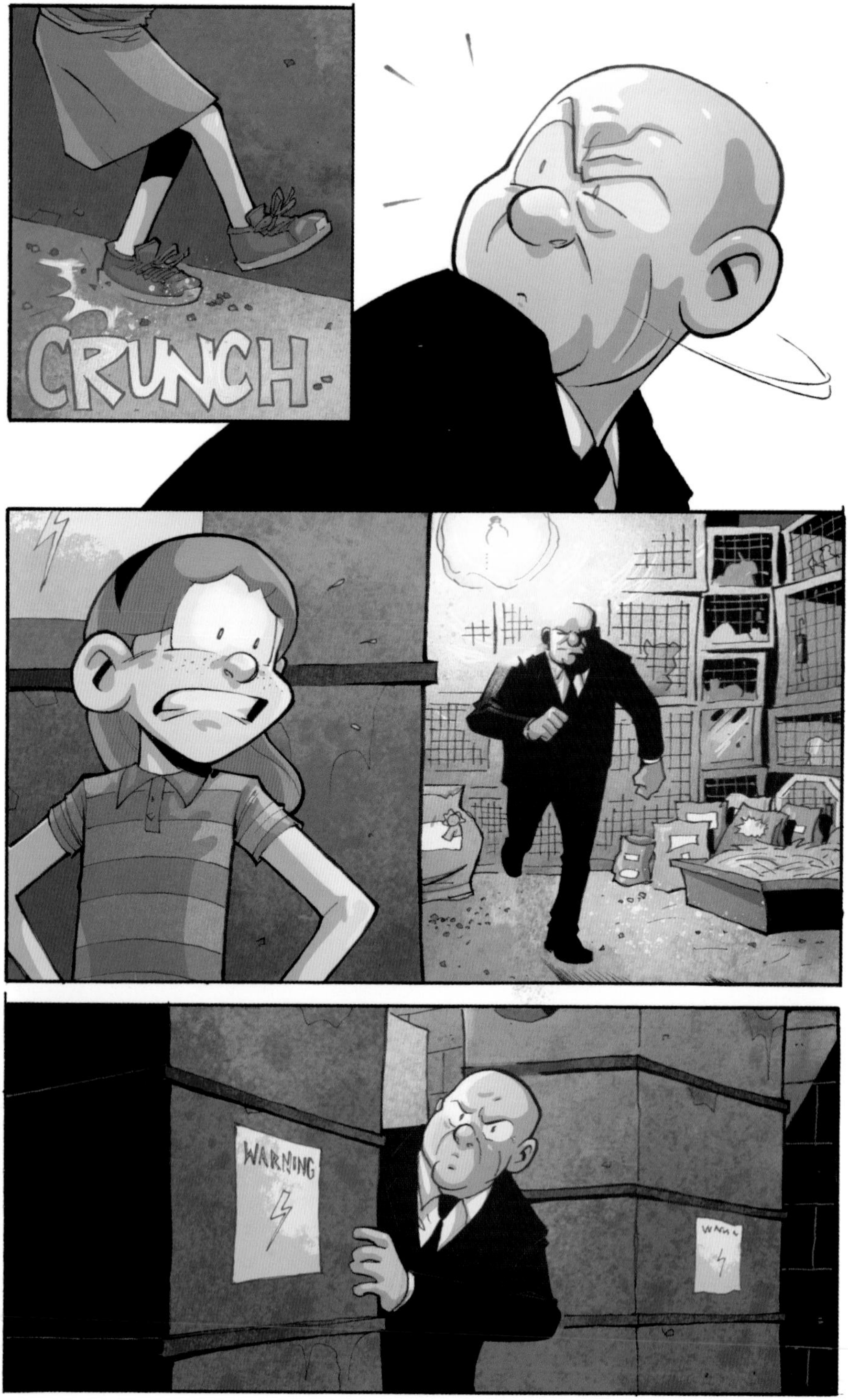
CRUNCH
WARNING

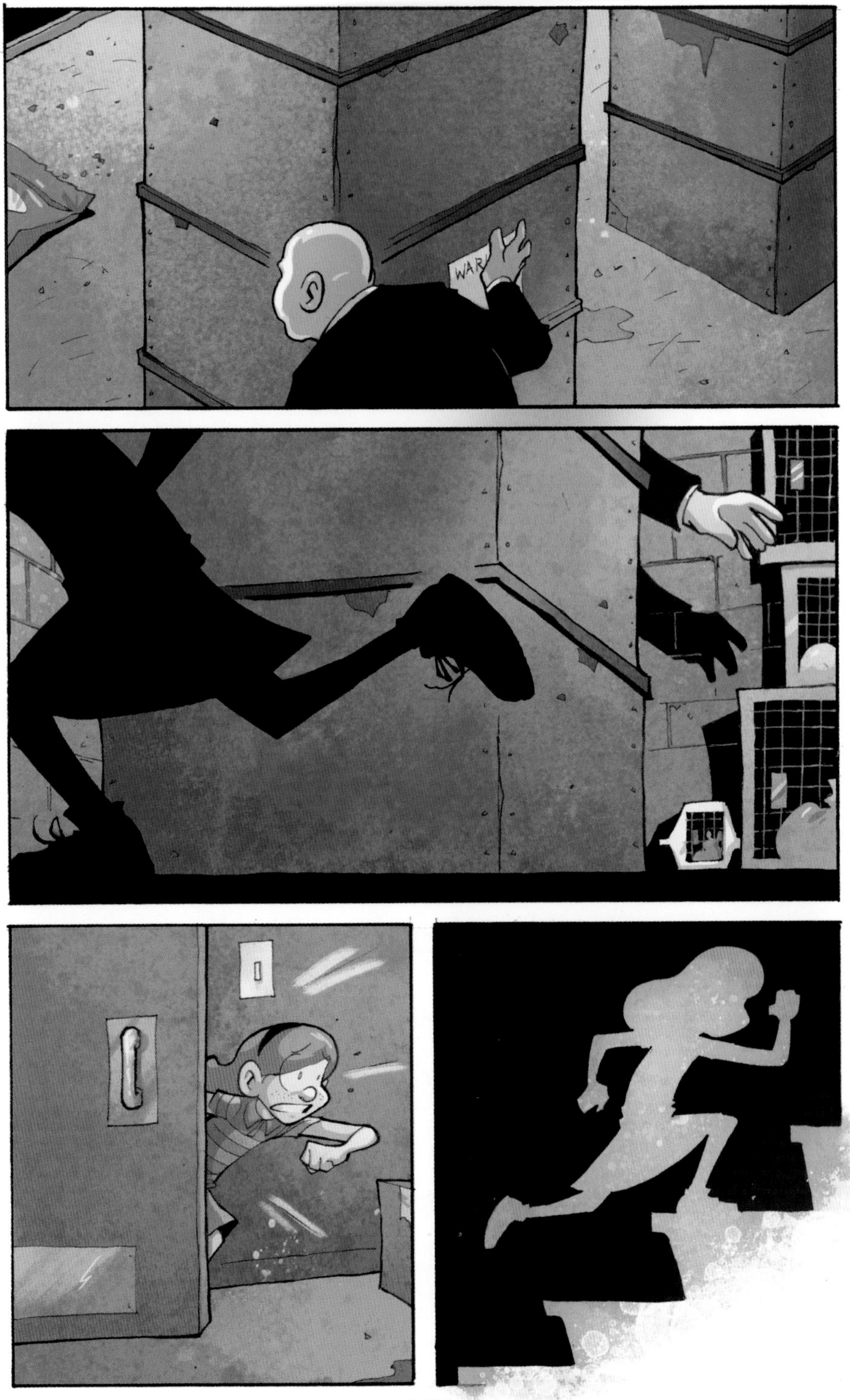

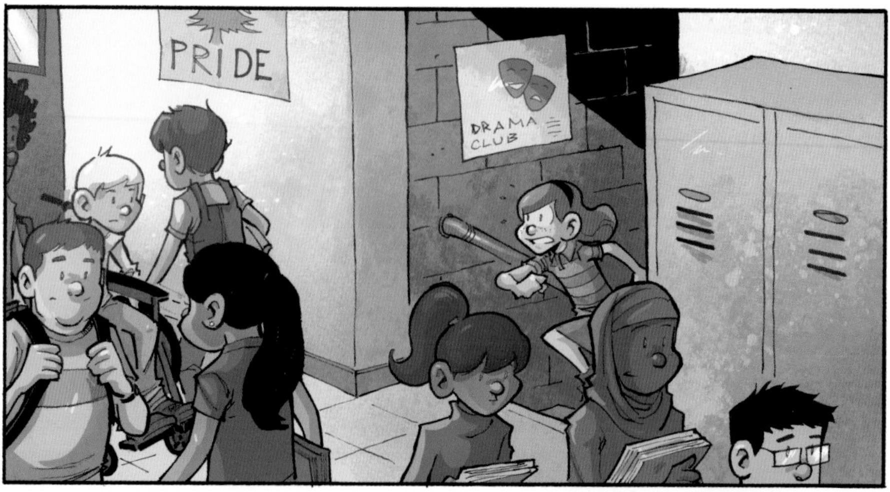
PRIDE
DRAMA CLUB

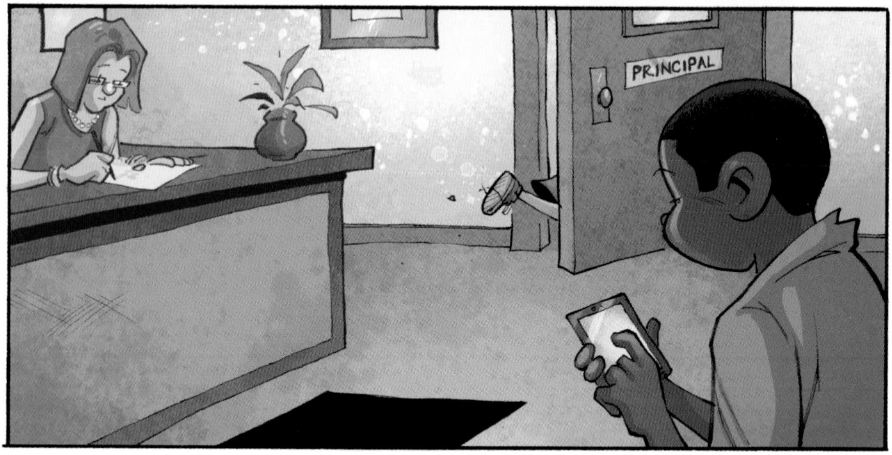
PRINCIPAL

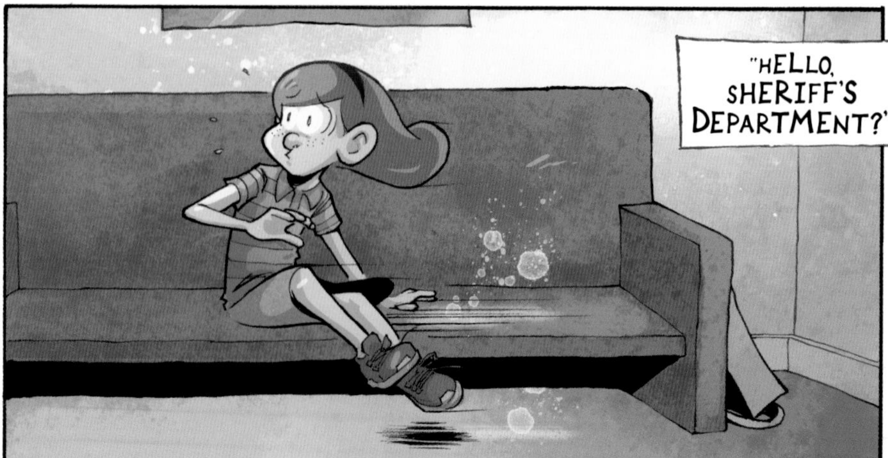
"HELLO, SHERIFF'S DEPARTMENT?"

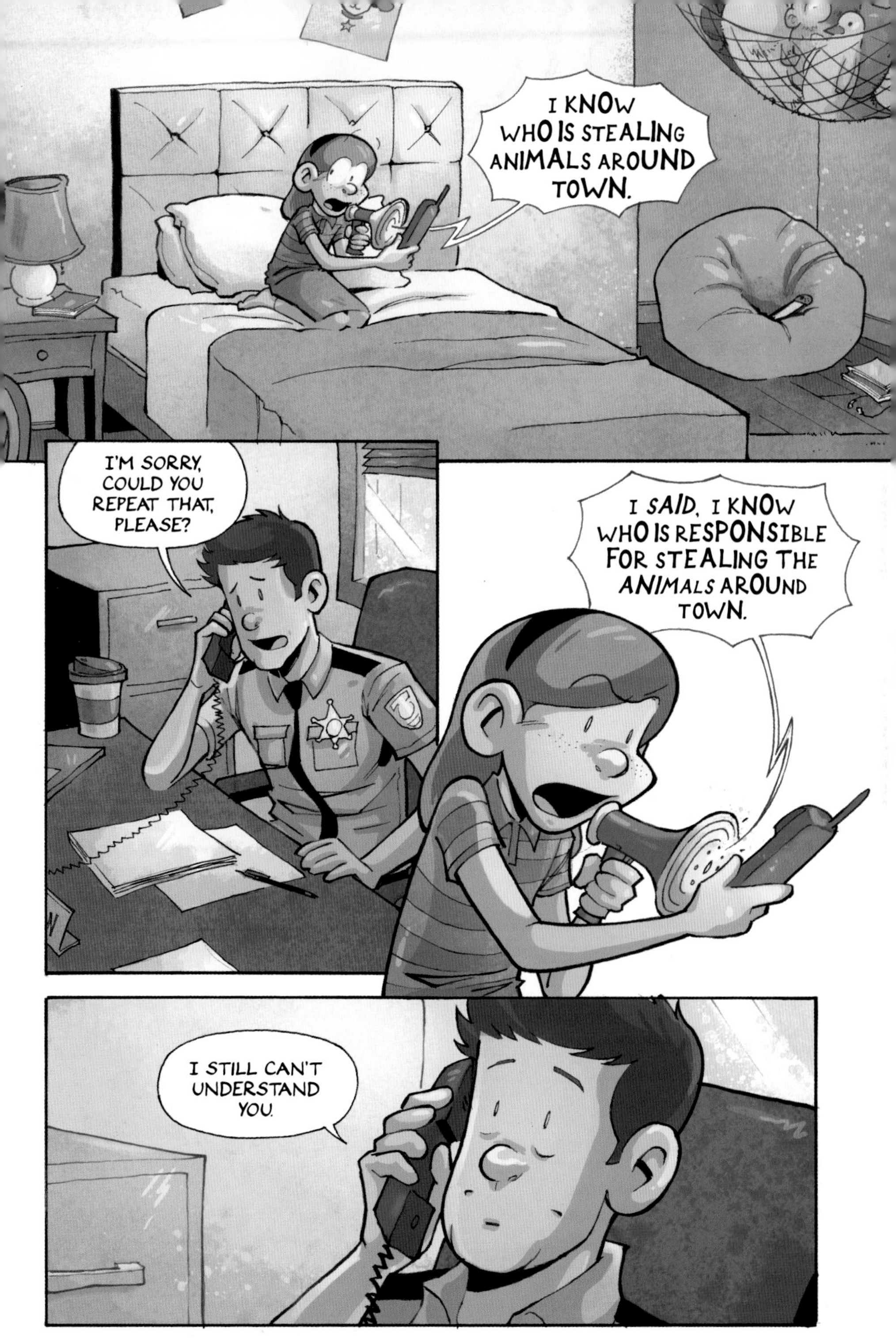
I KNOW WHO IS STEALING ANIMALS AROUND TOWN.
I'M SORRY, COULD YOU REPEAT THAT, PLEASE?
I SAID, I KNOW WHO IS RESPONSIBLE FOR STEALING THE ANIMALS AROUND TOWN.
I STILL CAN'T UNDERSTAND YOU.

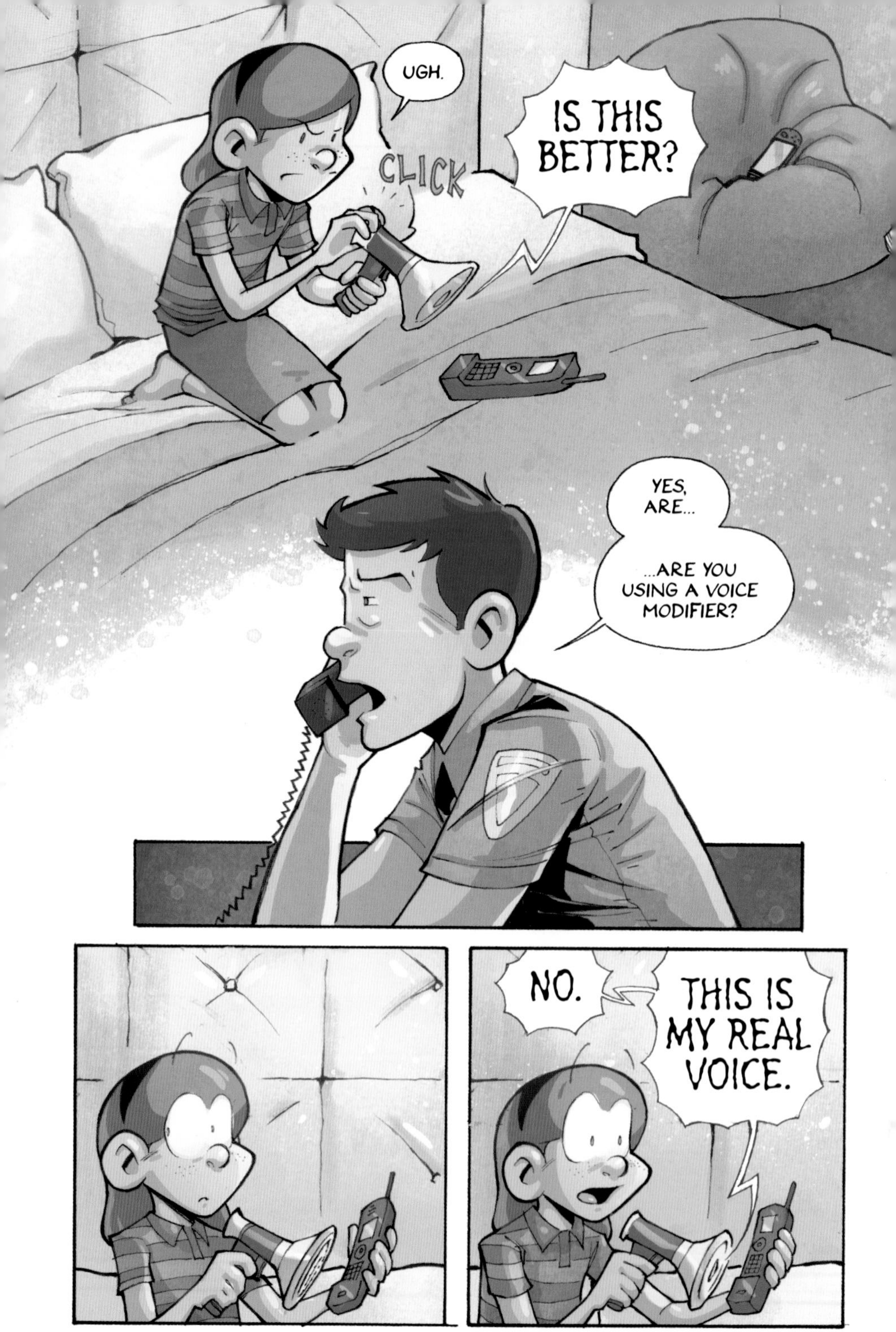
UGH.
CLICK
IS THIS BETTER?
YES, ARE...
...ARE YOU USING A VOICE MODIFIER?
NO.
THIS IS MY REAL VOICE.

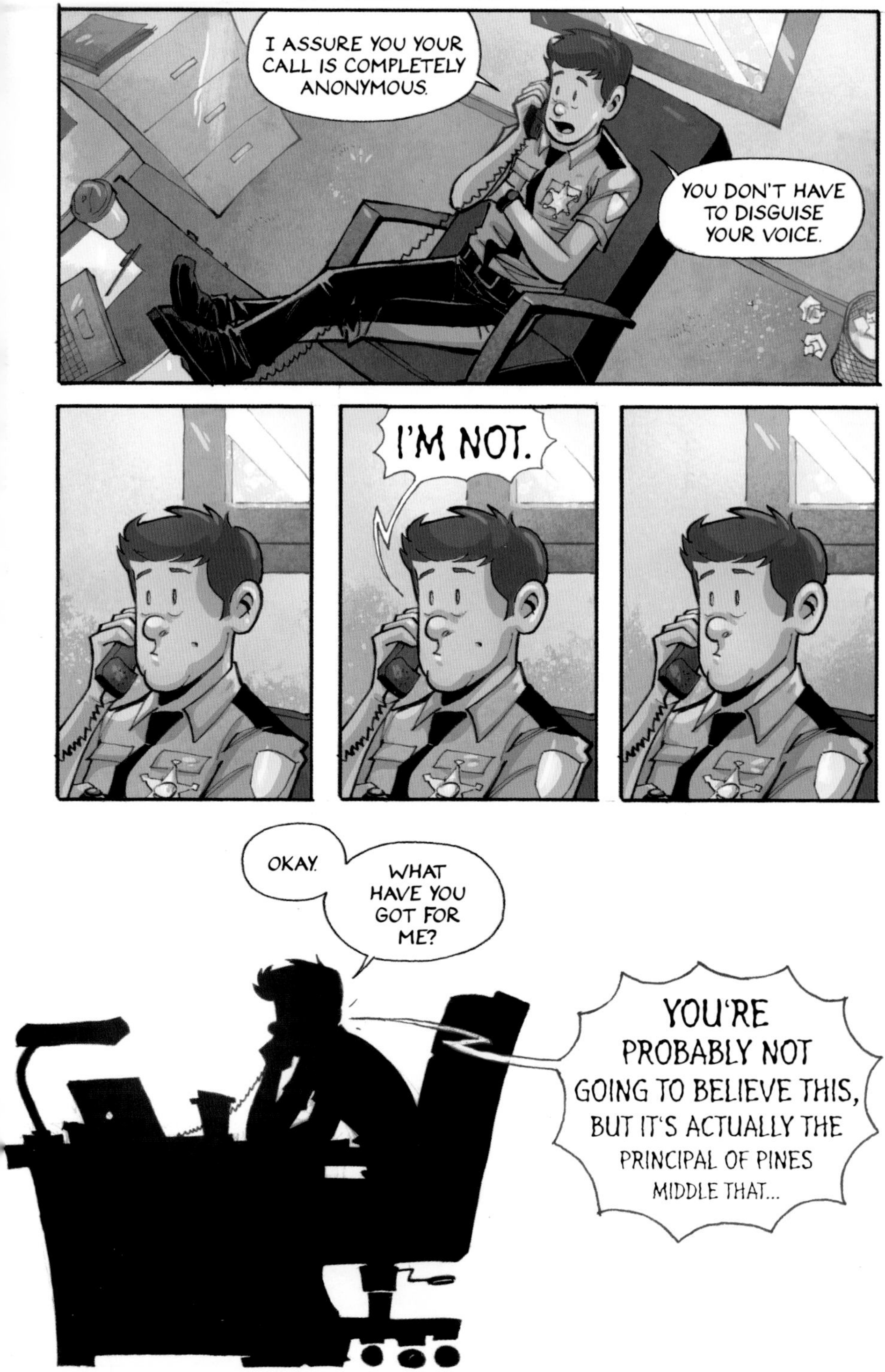
I ASSURE YOU YOUR CALL IS COMPLETELY ANONYMOUS.
YOU DON'T HAVE TO DISGUISE YOUR VOICE.
I'M NOT.
OKAY.
WHAT HAVE YOU GOT FOR ME?
YOU'RE PROBABLY NOT GOING TO BELIEVE THIS, BUT IT'S ACTUALLY THE PRINCIPAL OF PINES MIDDLE THAT...

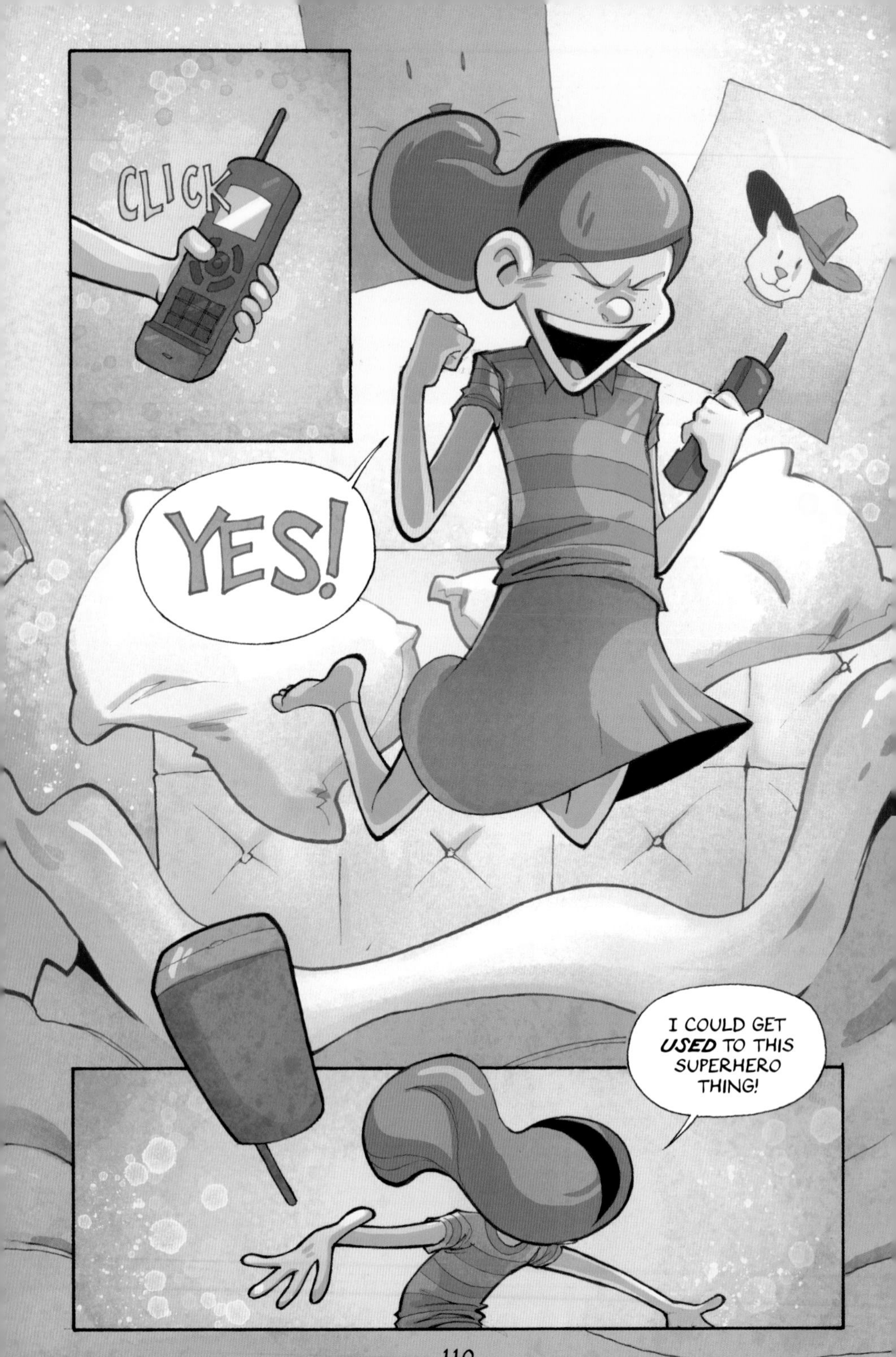
CLICK
YES!
I COULD GET USED TO THIS SUPERHERO THING!

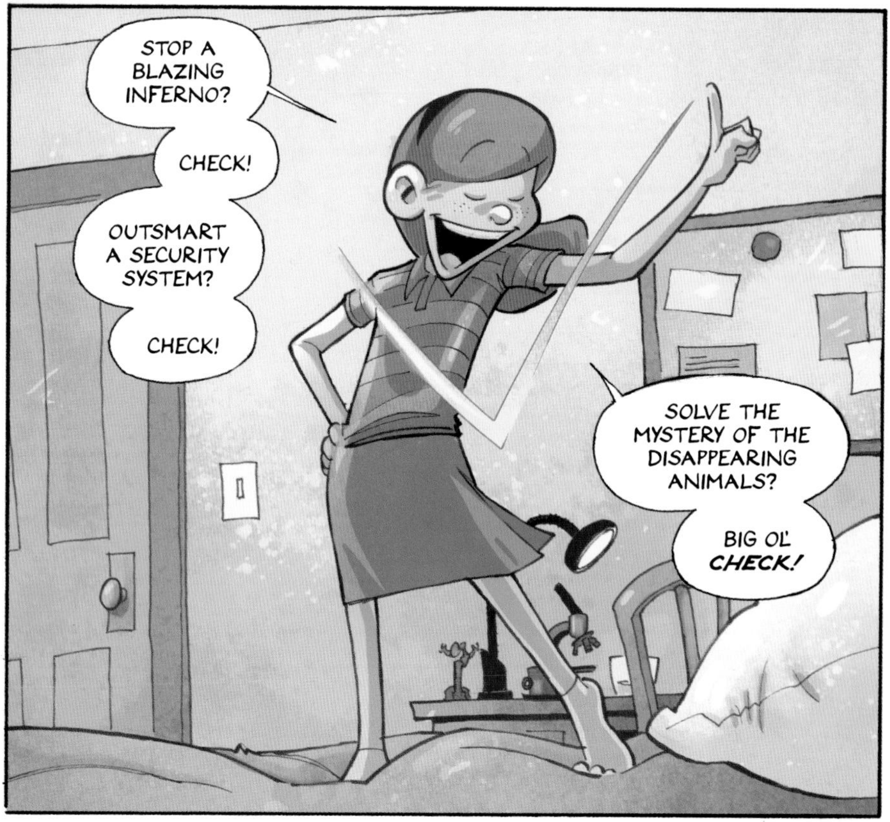
STOP A BLAZING INFERNO?
CHECK!
OUTSMART A SECURITY SYSTEM?
CHECK!
SOLVE THE MYSTERY OF THE DISAPPEARING ANIMALS?
BIG OL' *CHECK!*

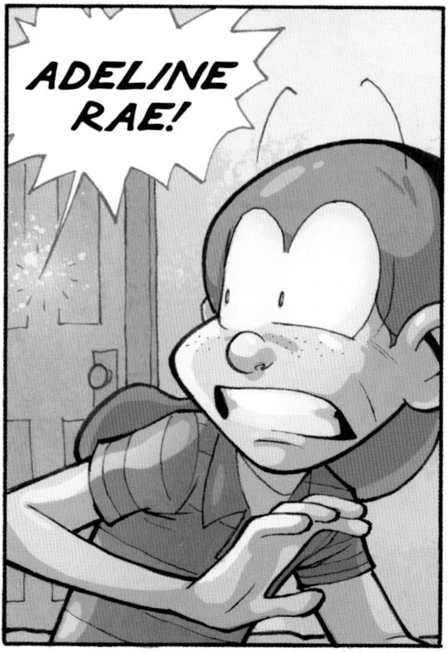
ADELINE RAE!

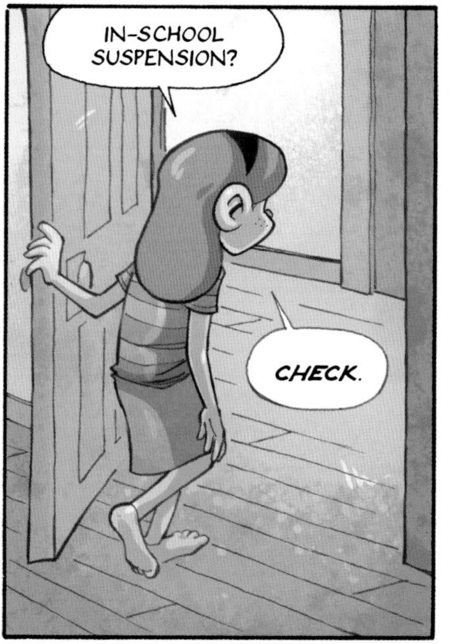
IN-SCHOOL SUSPENSION?
CHECK.

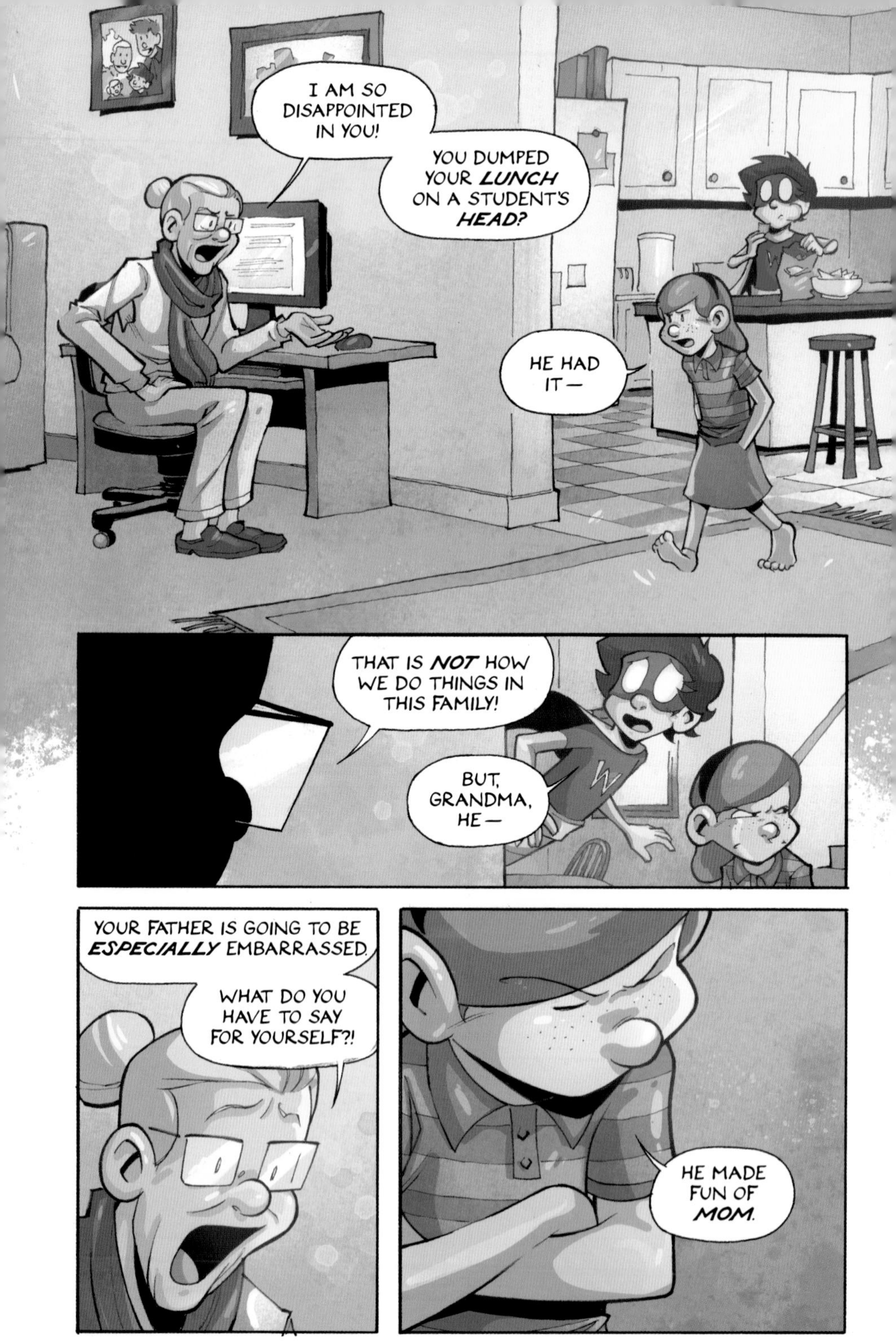
I AM SO DISAPPOINTED IN YOU!
YOU DUMPED YOUR ***LUNCH*** ON A STUDENT'S ***HEAD?***
HE HAD IT—
THAT IS ***NOT*** HOW WE DO THINGS IN THIS FAMILY!
BUT, GRANDMA, HE—
YOUR FATHER IS GOING TO BE ***ESPECIALLY*** EMBARRASSED.
WHAT DO YOU HAVE TO SAY FOR YOURSELF?!
HE MADE FUN OF ***MOM***.

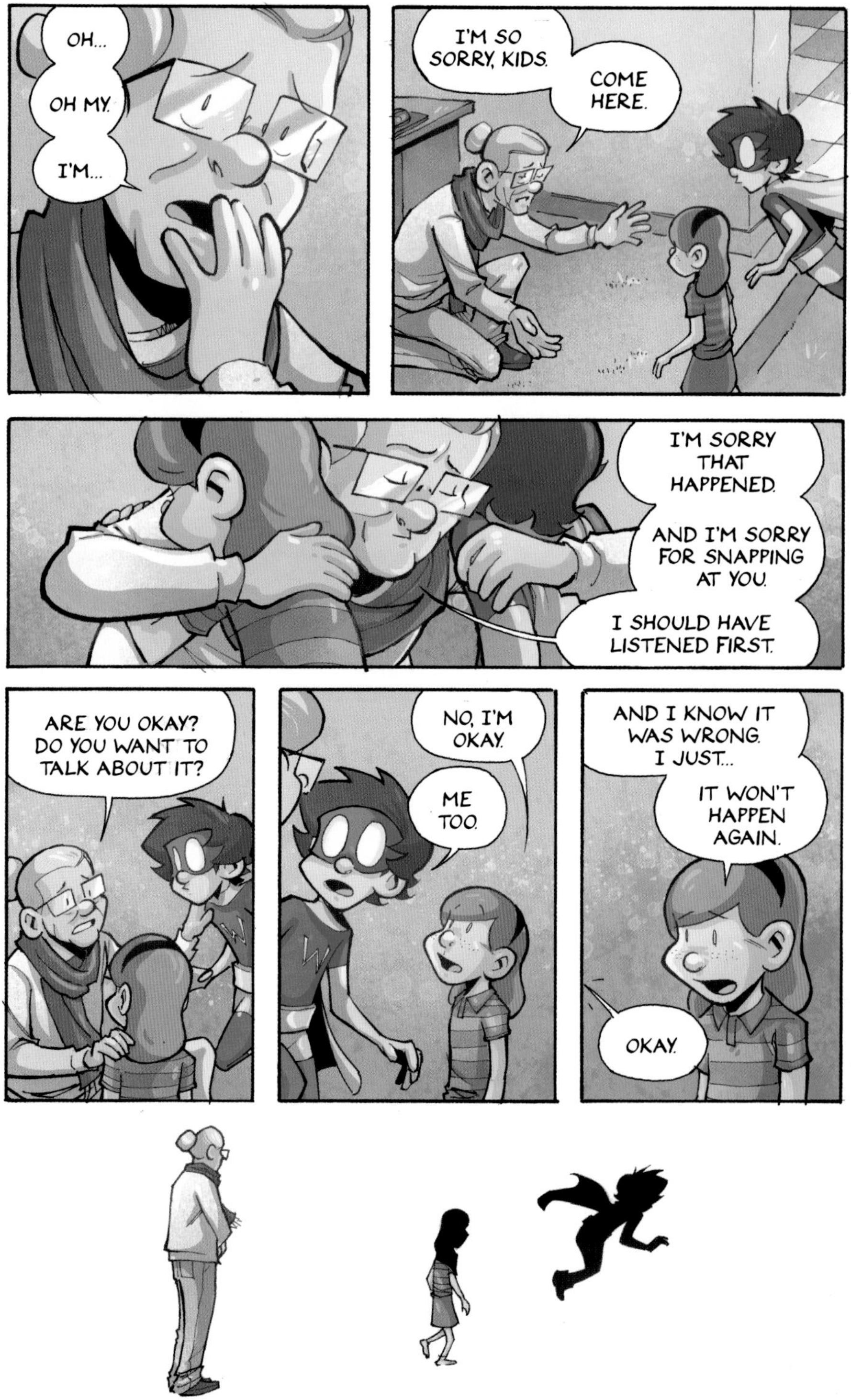
OH...
OH MY.
I'M...
I'M SO SORRY, KIDS.
COME HERE.
I'M SORRY THAT HAPPENED.
AND I'M SORRY FOR SNAPPING AT YOU.
I SHOULD HAVE LISTENED FIRST.
ARE YOU OKAY? DO YOU WANT TO TALK ABOUT IT?
NO, I'M OKAY.
ME TOO.
AND I KNOW IT WAS WRONG. I JUST...
IT WON'T HAPPEN AGAIN.
OKAY.

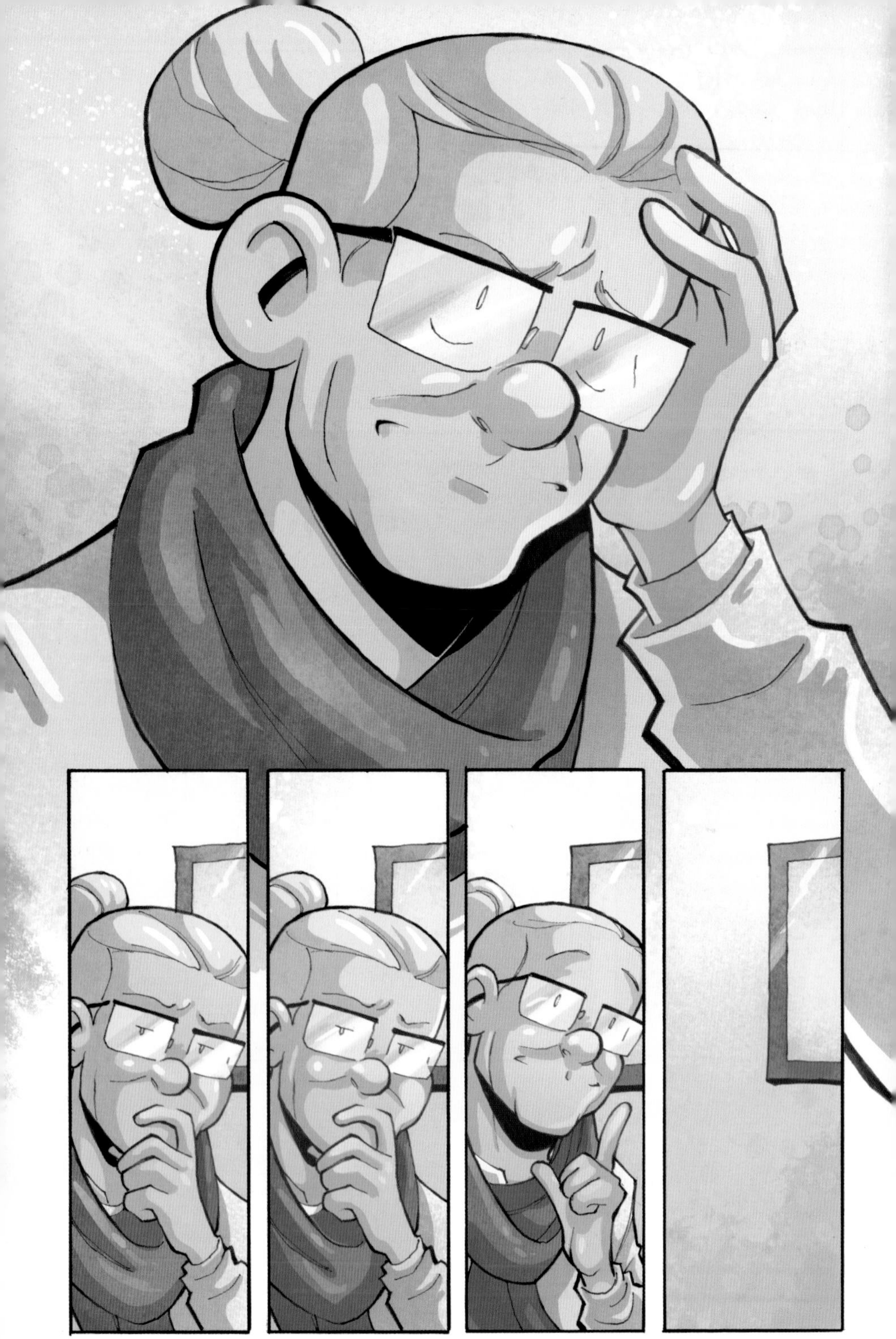

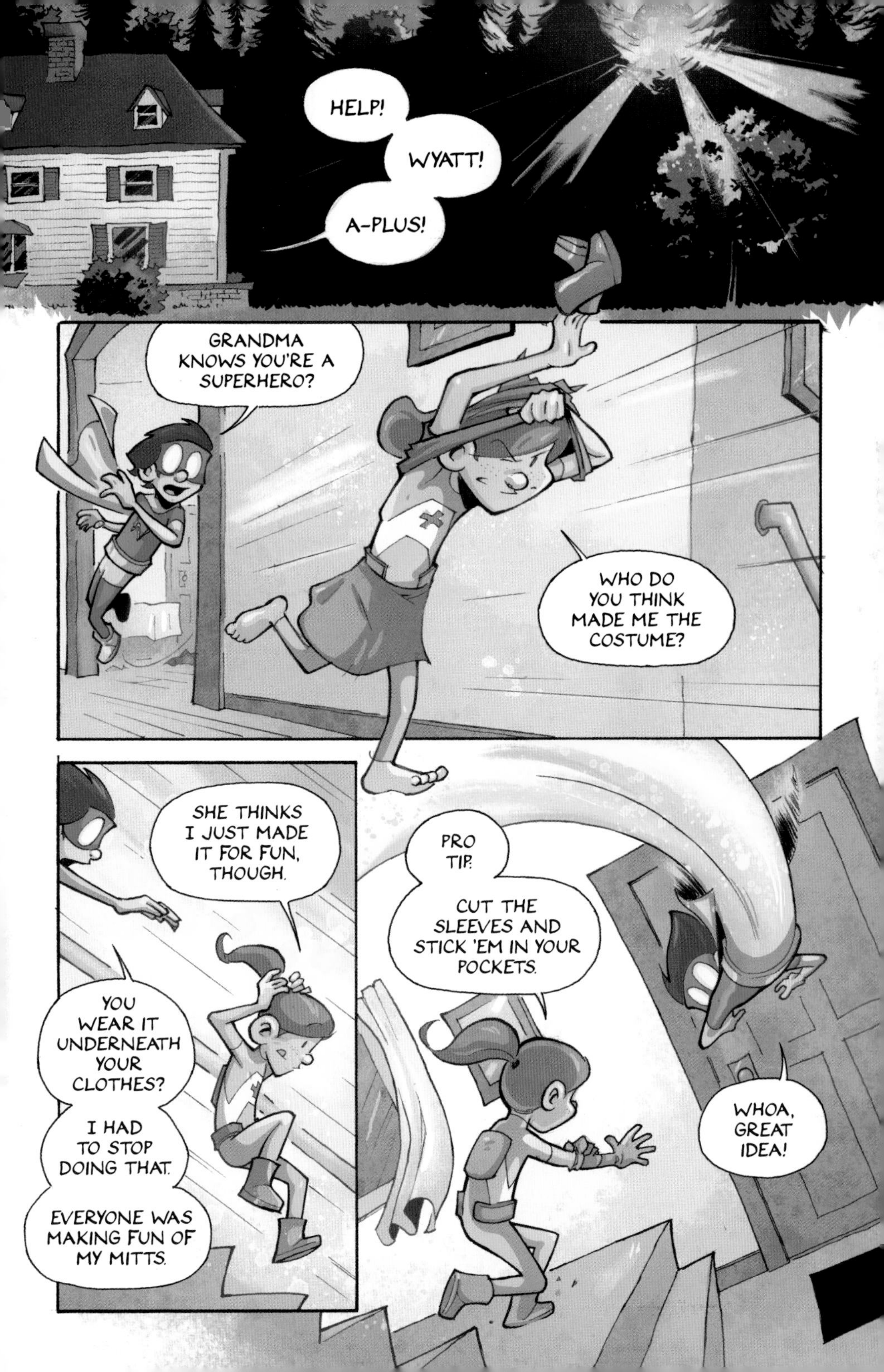
HELP!
WYATT!
A-PLUS!
GRANDMA KNOWS YOU'RE A SUPERHERO?
WHO DO YOU THINK MADE ME THE COSTUME?
SHE THINKS I JUST MADE IT FOR FUN, THOUGH.
YOU WEAR IT UNDERNEATH YOUR CLOTHES?
I HAD TO STOP DOING THAT.
EVERYONE WAS MAKING FUN OF MY MITTS.
PRO TIP.
CUT THE SLEEVES AND STICK 'EM IN YOUR POCKETS.
WHOA, GREAT IDEA!

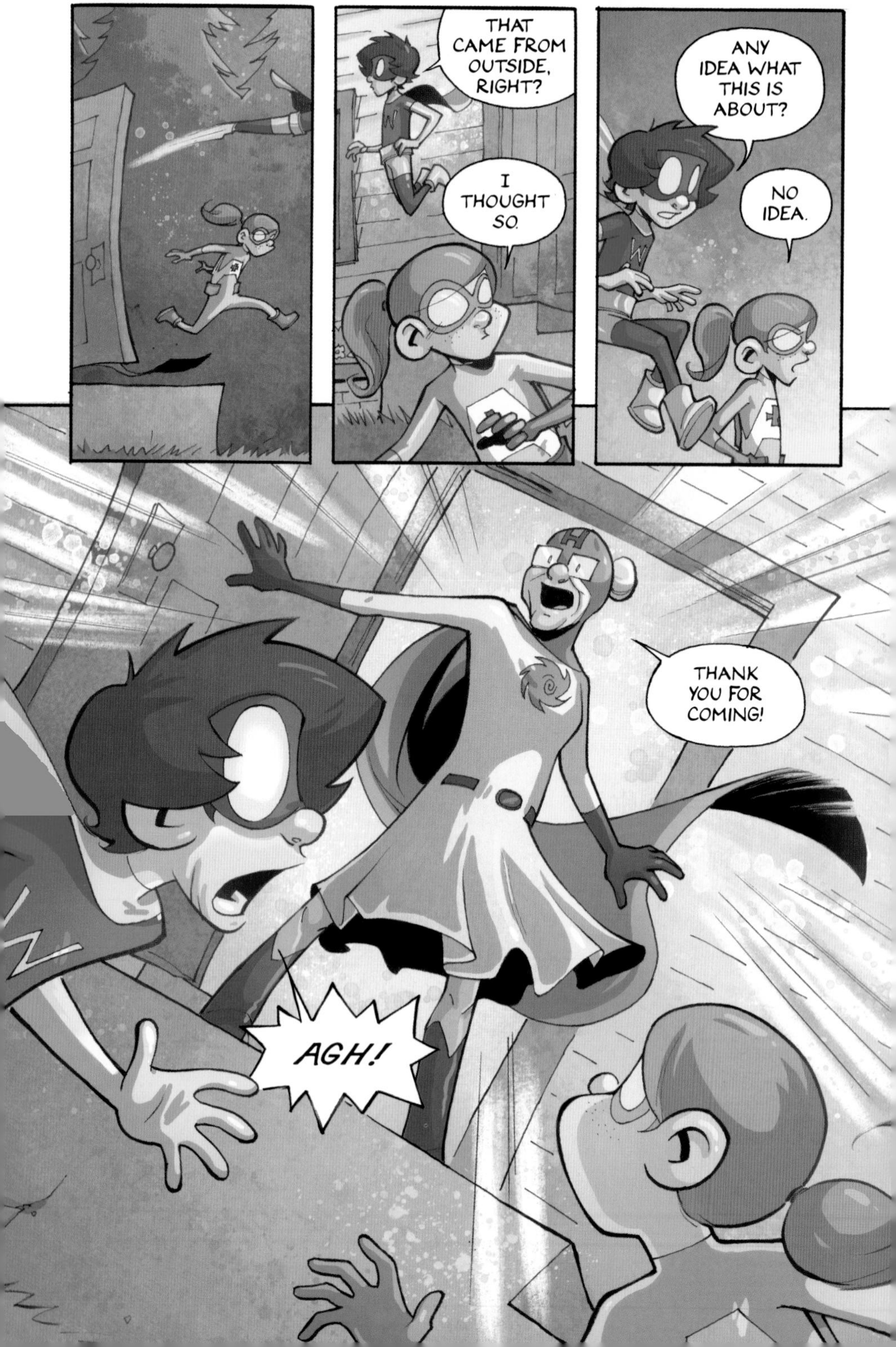
THAT CAME FROM OUTSIDE, RIGHT?
I THOUGHT SO.
ANY IDEA WHAT THIS IS ABOUT?
NO IDEA.
THANK YOU FOR COMING!
AGH!

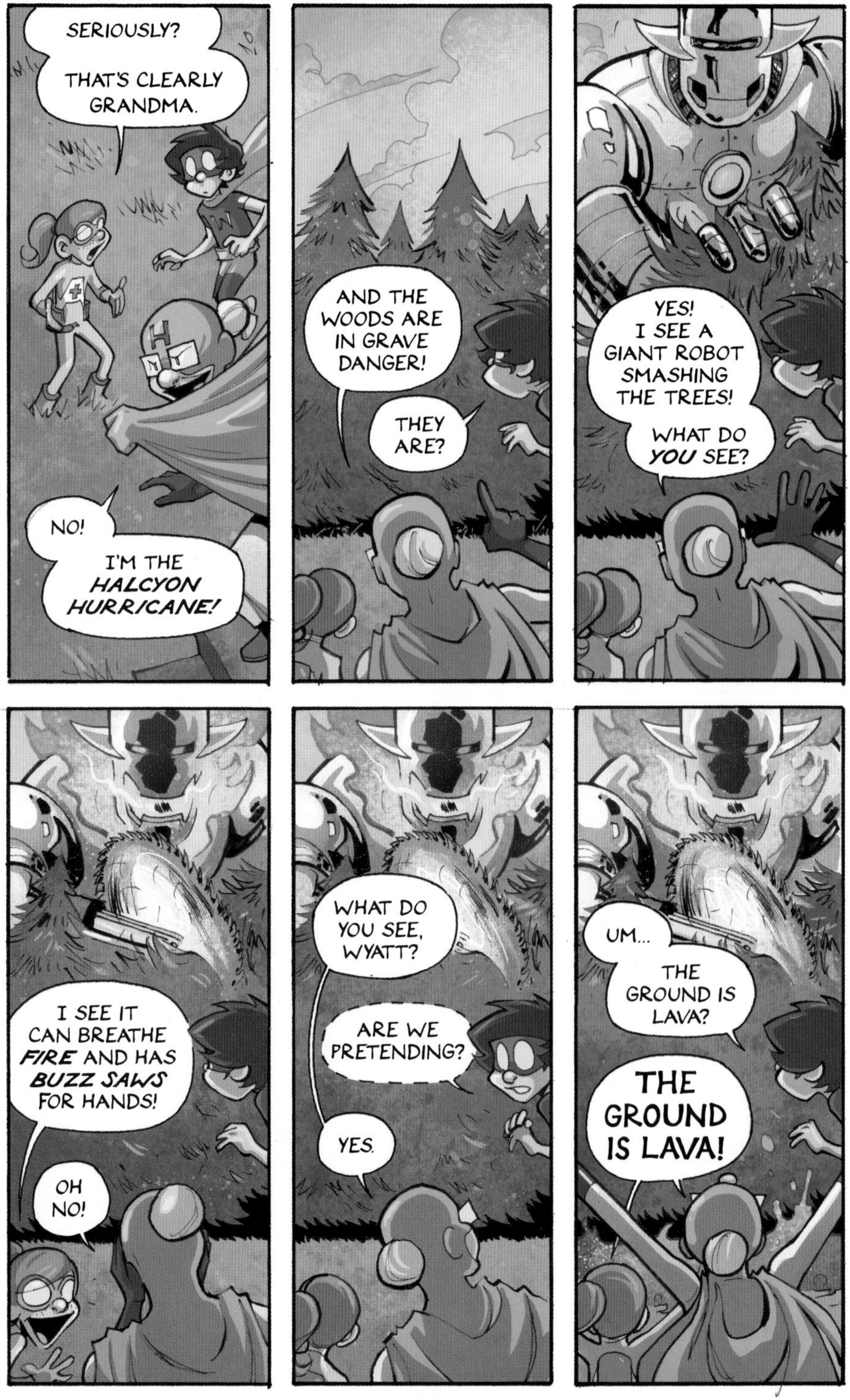
SERIOUSLY?
THAT'S CLEARLY GRANDMA.
NO!
I'M THE HALCYON HURRICANE!
AND THE WOODS ARE IN GRAVE DANGER!
THEY ARE?
YES! I SEE A GIANT ROBOT SMASHING THE TREES!
WHAT DO YOU SEE?
I SEE IT CAN BREATHE FIRE AND HAS BUZZ SAWS FOR HANDS!
OH NO!
WHAT DO YOU SEE, WYATT?
ARE WE PRETENDING?
YES.
UM...
THE GROUND IS LAVA?
THE GROUND IS LAVA!

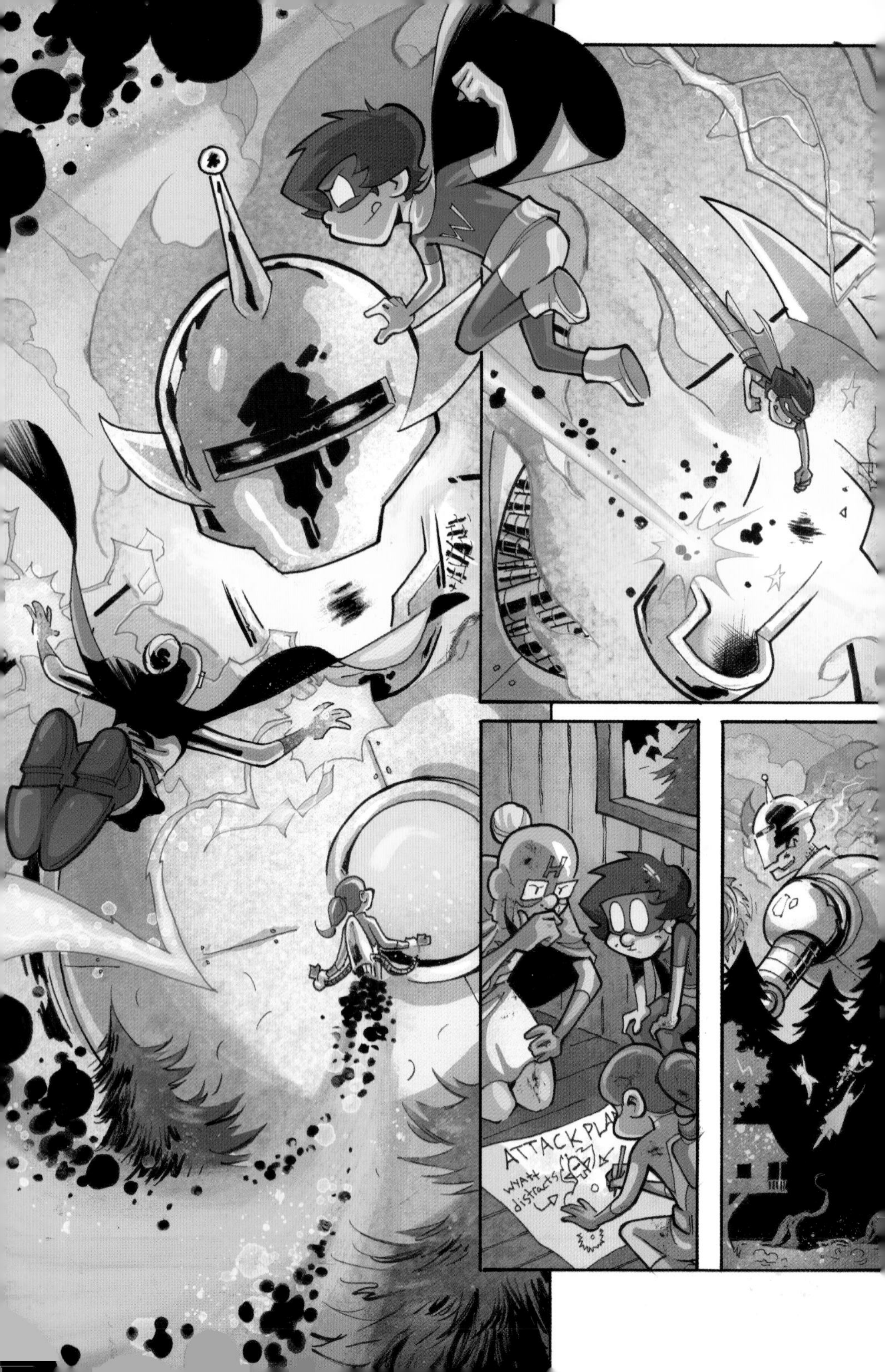
ATTACK PLA
wyatt distracts

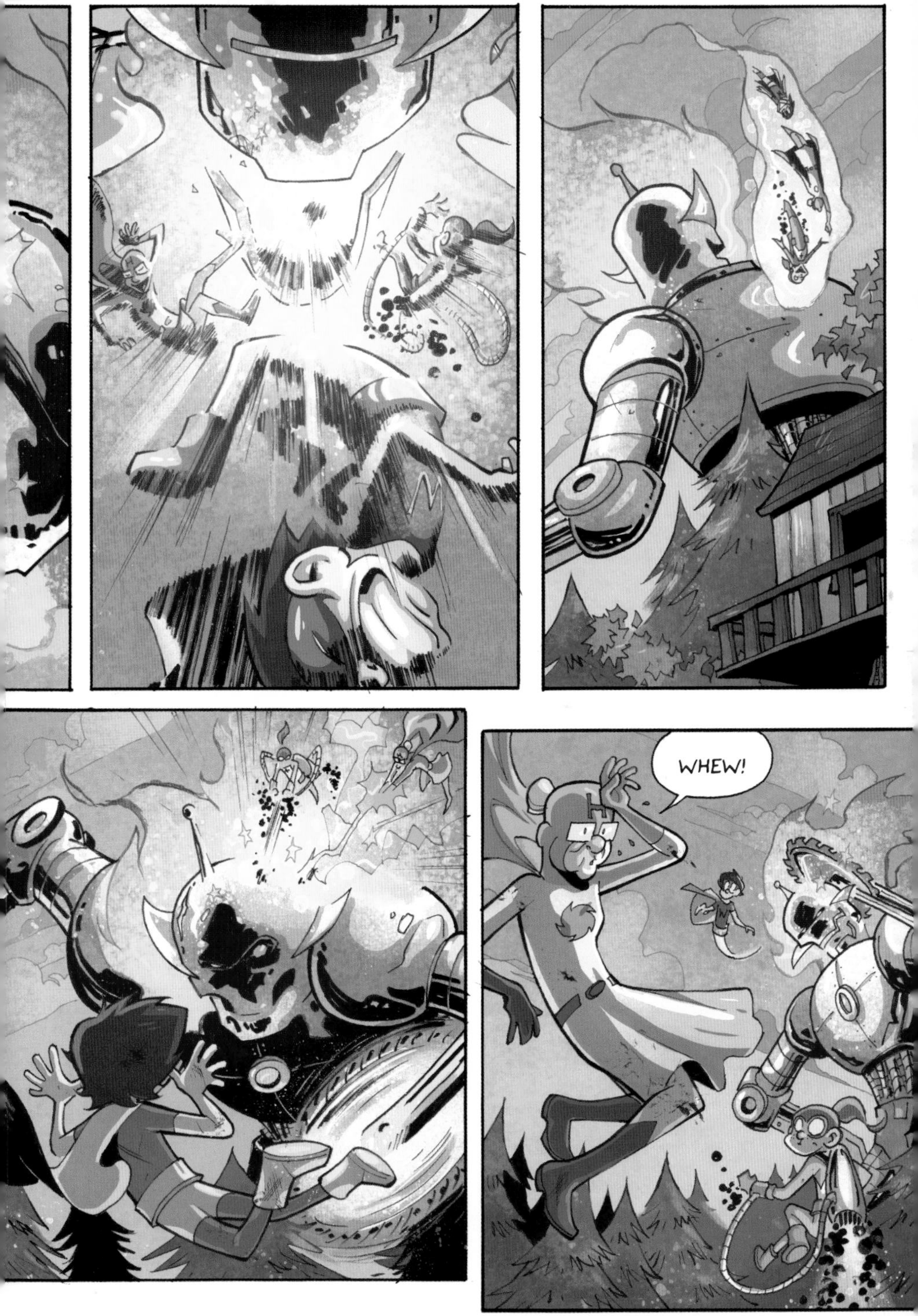
WHEW!

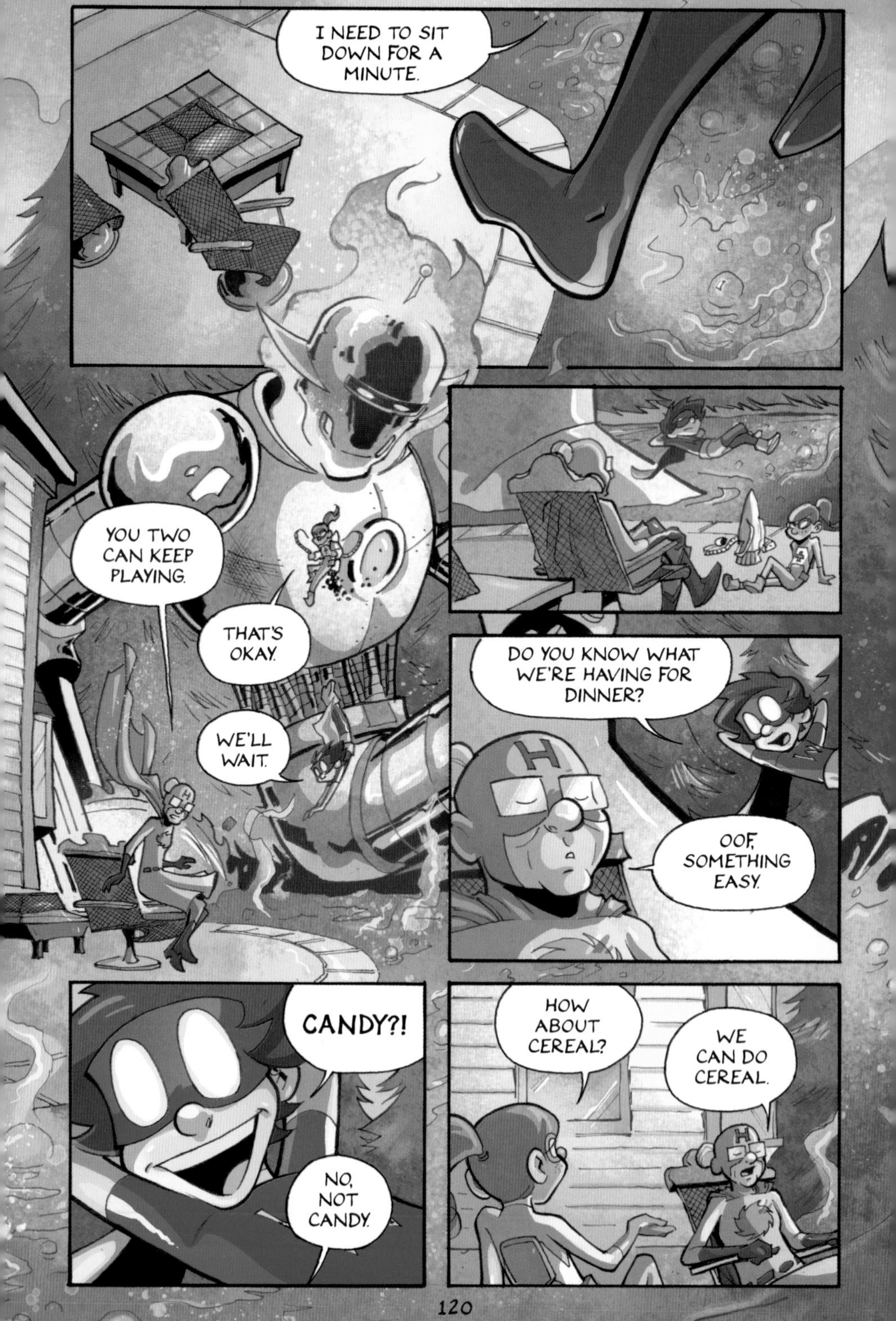
I NEED TO SIT DOWN FOR A MINUTE.
YOU TWO CAN KEEP PLAYING.
THAT'S OKAY.
WE'LL WAIT.
DO YOU KNOW WHAT WE'RE HAVING FOR DINNER?
OOF, SOMETHING EASY.
CANDY?!
NO, NOT CANDY.
HOW ABOUT CEREAL?
WE CAN DO CEREAL.

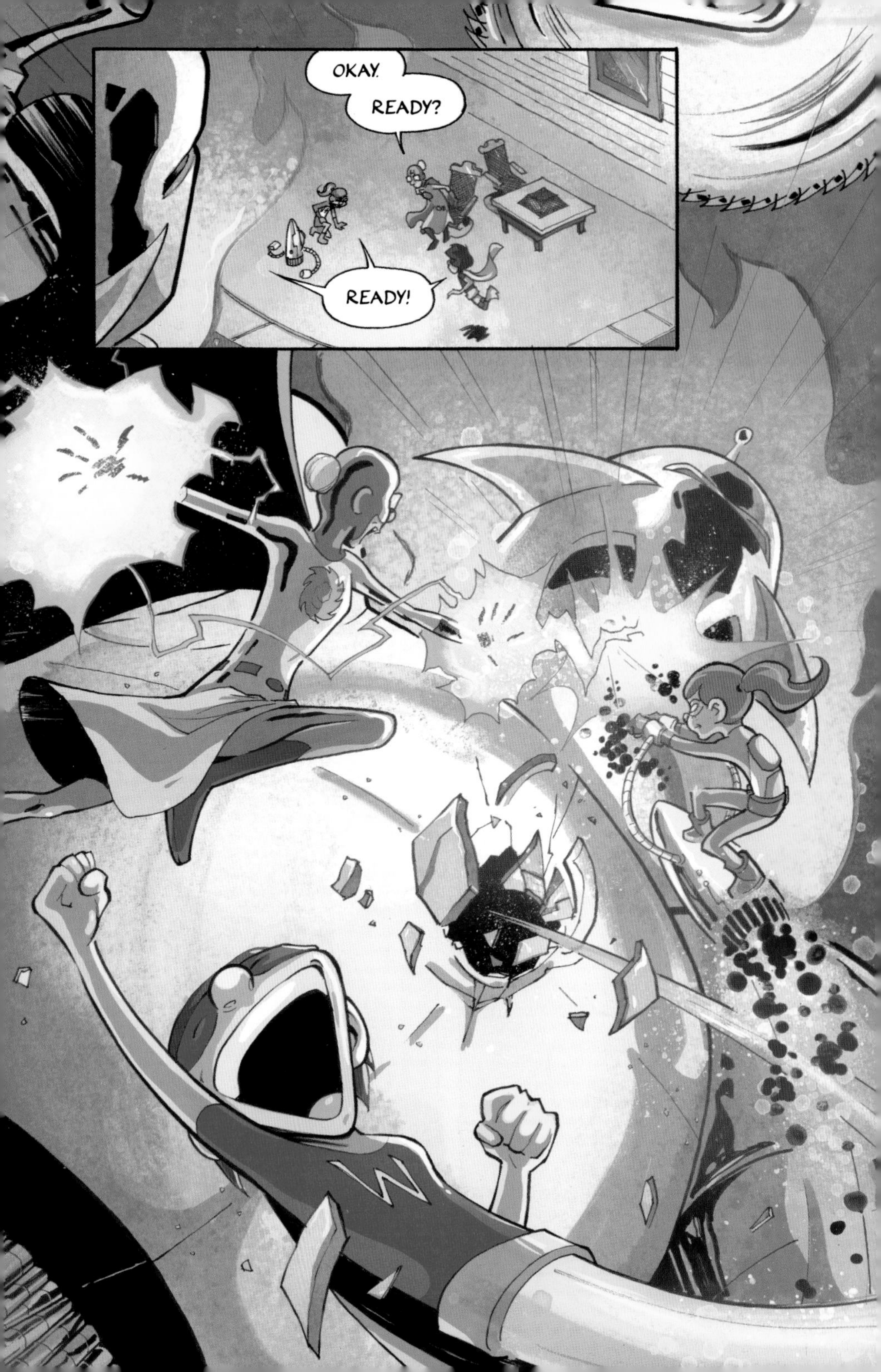
OKAY.
READY?
READY!

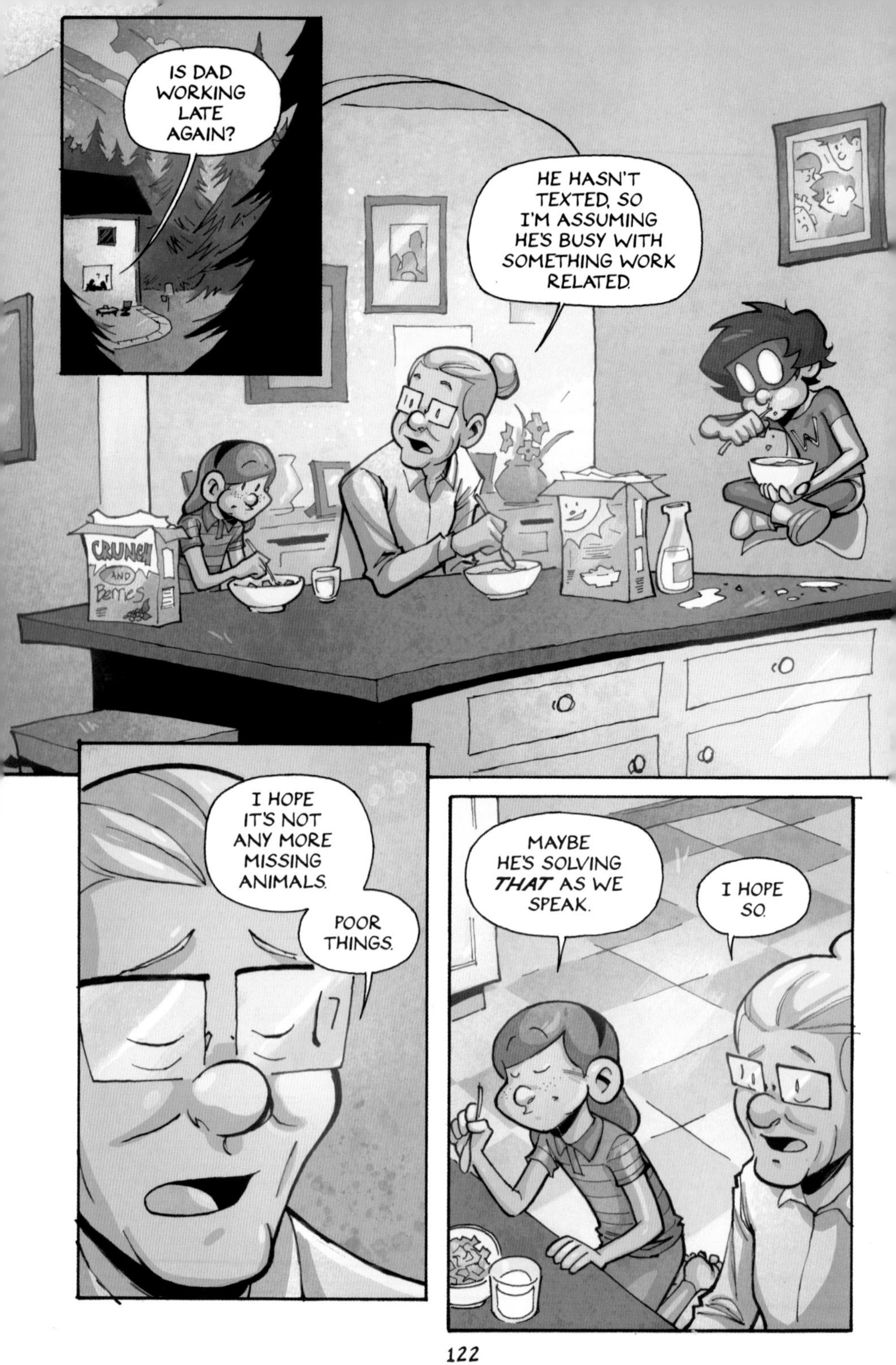
IS DAD WORKING LATE AGAIN?
HE HASN'T TEXTED, SO I'M ASSUMING HE'S BUSY WITH SOMETHING WORK RELATED.
CRUNCH AND Berries
I HOPE IT'S NOT ANY MORE MISSING ANIMALS.
POOR THINGS.
MAYBE HE'S SOLVING *THAT* AS WE SPEAK.
I HOPE SO.

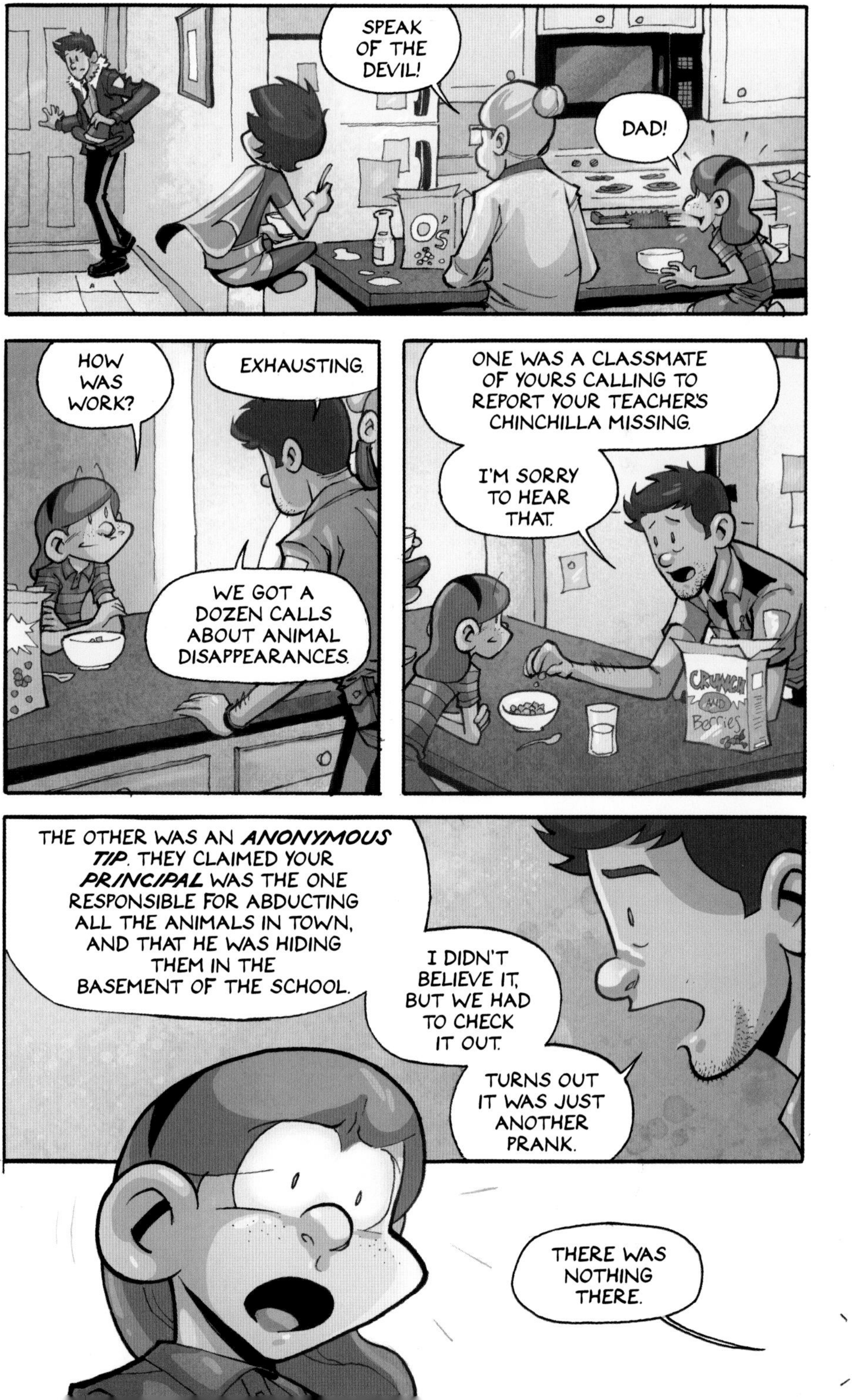
SPEAK OF THE DEVIL!
DAD!
HOW WAS WORK?
EXHAUSTING.
WE GOT A DOZEN CALLS ABOUT ANIMAL DISAPPEARANCES.
ONE WAS A CLASSMATE OF YOURS CALLING TO REPORT YOUR TEACHER'S CHINCHILLA MISSING.
I'M SORRY TO HEAR THAT.
O's
CRUNCH AND Berries
THE OTHER WAS AN *ANONYMOUS TIP*. THEY CLAIMED YOUR *PRINCIPAL* WAS THE ONE RESPONSIBLE FOR ABDUCTING ALL THE ANIMALS IN TOWN, AND THAT HE WAS HIDING THEM IN THE BASEMENT OF THE SCHOOL.
I DIDN'T BELIEVE IT, BUT WE HAD TO CHECK IT OUT.
TURNS OUT IT WAS JUST ANOTHER PRANK.
THERE WAS NOTHING THERE.

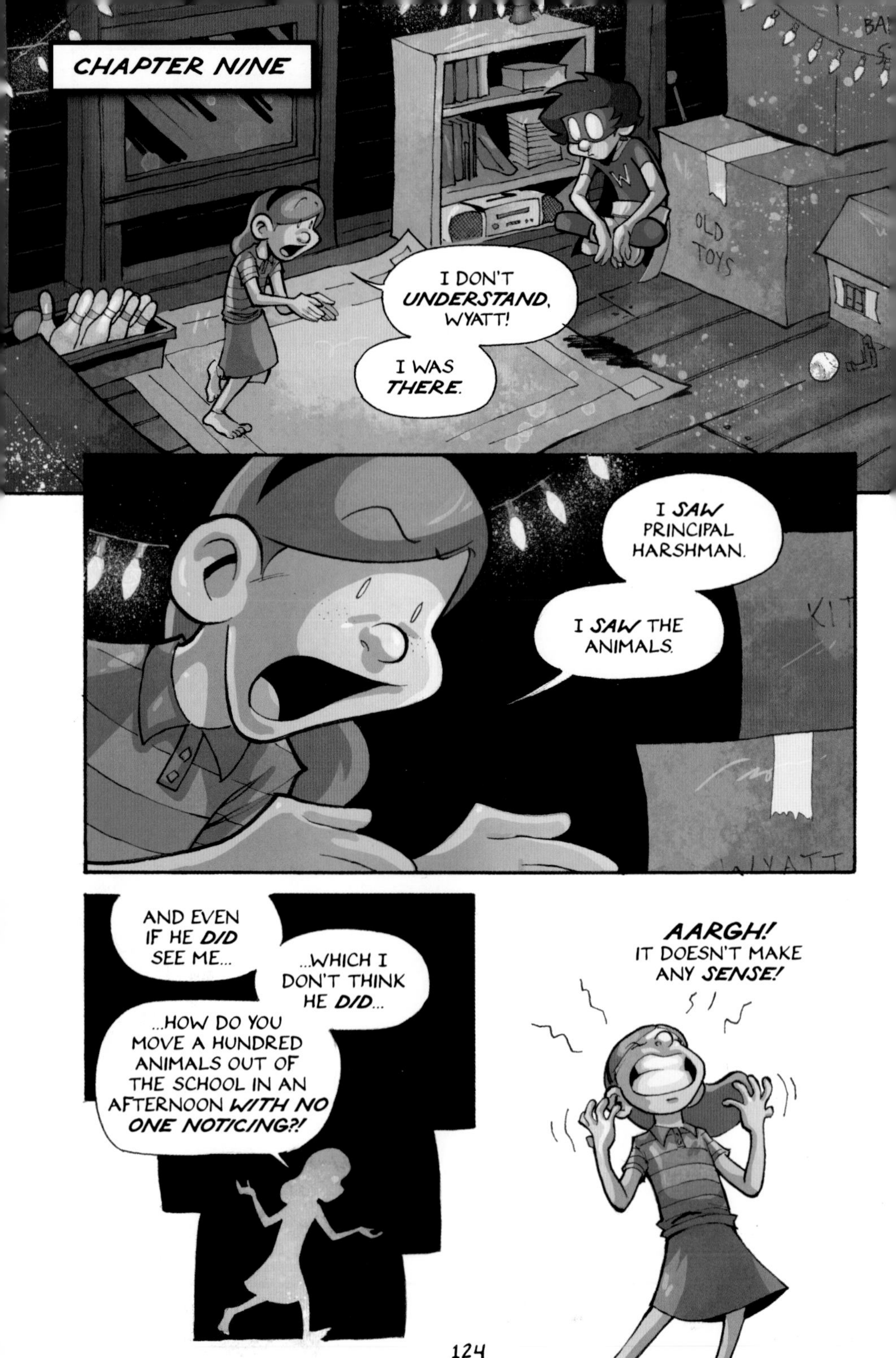
CHAPTER NINE
I DON'T UNDERSTAND, WYATT!
I WAS THERE.
OLD TOYS
I SAW PRINCIPAL HARSHMAN.
I SAW THE ANIMALS.
AND EVEN IF HE DID SEE ME...
...WHICH I DON'T THINK HE DID...
...HOW DO YOU MOVE A HUNDRED ANIMALS OUT OF THE SCHOOL IN AN AFTERNOON WITH NO ONE NOTICING?!
AARGH! IT DOESN'T MAKE ANY SENSE!

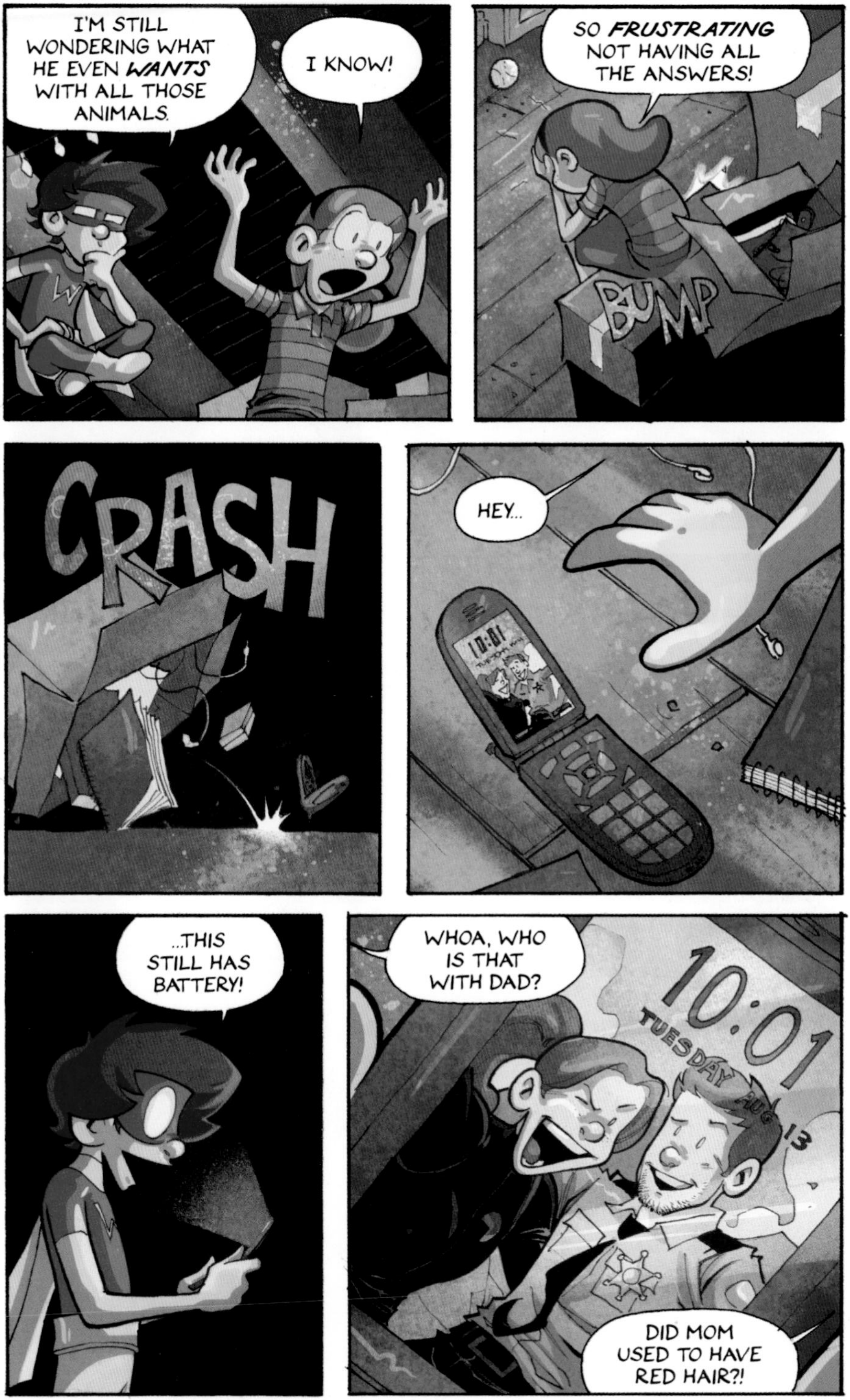
I'M STILL WONDERING WHAT HE EVEN WANTS WITH ALL THOSE ANIMALS.
I KNOW!
SO FRUSTRATING NOT HAVING ALL THE ANSWERS!
BUMP
CRASH
HEY...
...THIS STILL HAS BATTERY!
WHOA, WHO IS THAT WITH DAD?
10:01
TUESDAY AUG 13
DID MOM USED TO HAVE RED HAIR?!

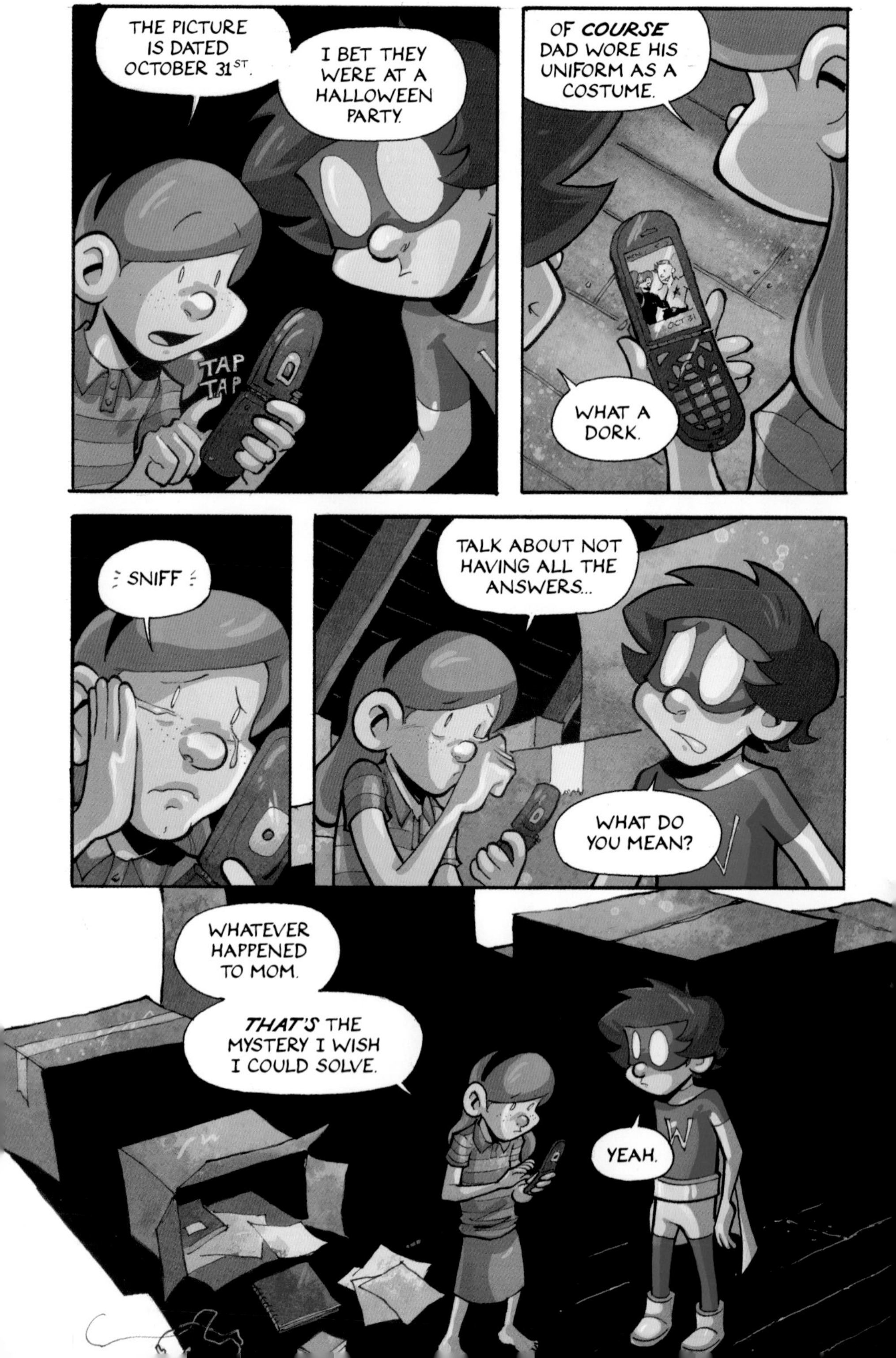
THE PICTURE IS DATED OCTOBER 31ST.
I BET THEY WERE AT A HALLOWEEN PARTY.
TAP TAP
OF COURSE DAD WORE HIS UNIFORM AS A COSTUME.
OCT 31
WHAT A DORK.
SNIFF
TALK ABOUT NOT HAVING ALL THE ANSWERS...
WHAT DO YOU MEAN?
WHATEVER HAPPENED TO MOM.
THAT'S THE MYSTERY I WISH I COULD SOLVE.
YEAH.

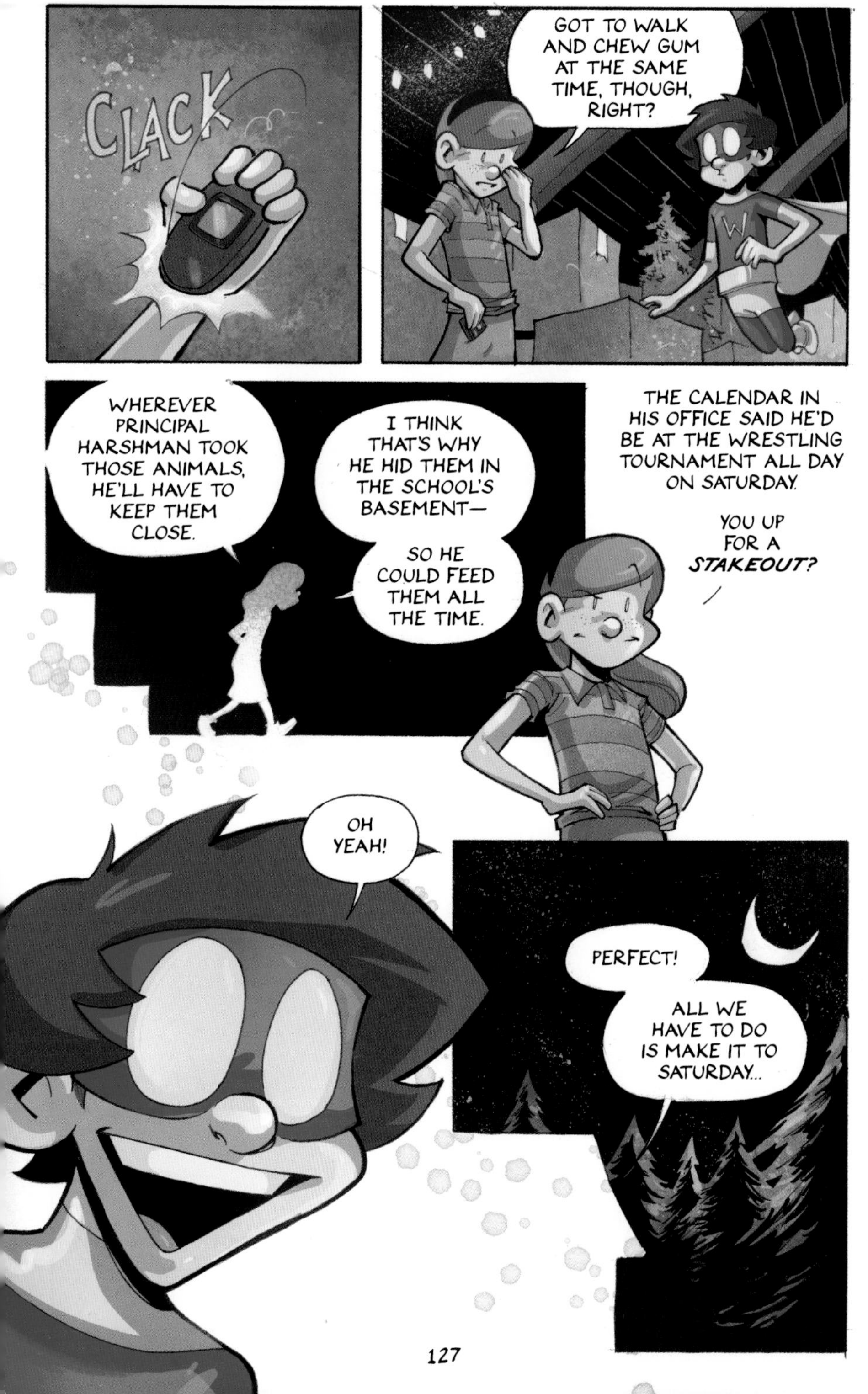
CLACK
GOT TO WALK AND CHEW GUM AT THE SAME TIME, THOUGH, RIGHT?
WHEREVER PRINCIPAL HARSHMAN TOOK THOSE ANIMALS, HE'LL HAVE TO KEEP THEM CLOSE.
I THINK THAT'S WHY HE HID THEM IN THE SCHOOL'S BASEMENT—
SO HE COULD FEED THEM ALL THE TIME.
THE CALENDAR IN HIS OFFICE SAID HE'D BE AT THE WRESTLING TOURNAMENT ALL DAY ON SATURDAY.
YOU UP FOR A *STAKEOUT?*
OH YEAH!
PERFECT!
ALL WE HAVE TO DO IS MAKE IT TO SATURDAY...

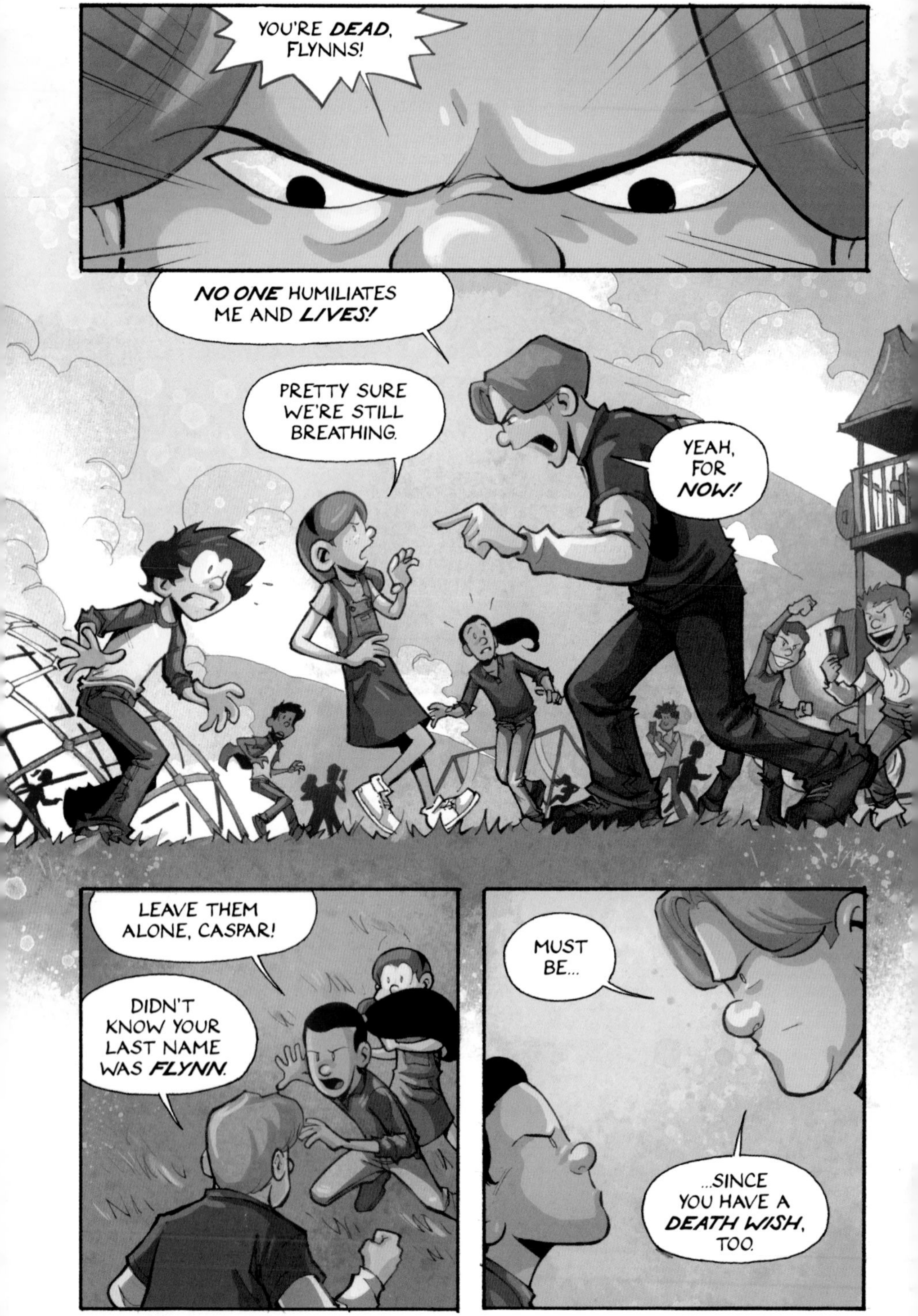
YOU'RE DEAD, FLYNNS!
NO ONE HUMILIATES ME AND LIVES!
PRETTY SURE WE'RE STILL BREATHING.
YEAH, FOR NOW!
LEAVE THEM ALONE, CASPAR!
DIDN'T KNOW YOUR LAST NAME WAS FLYNN.
MUST BE...
...SINCE YOU HAVE A DEATH WISH, TOO.

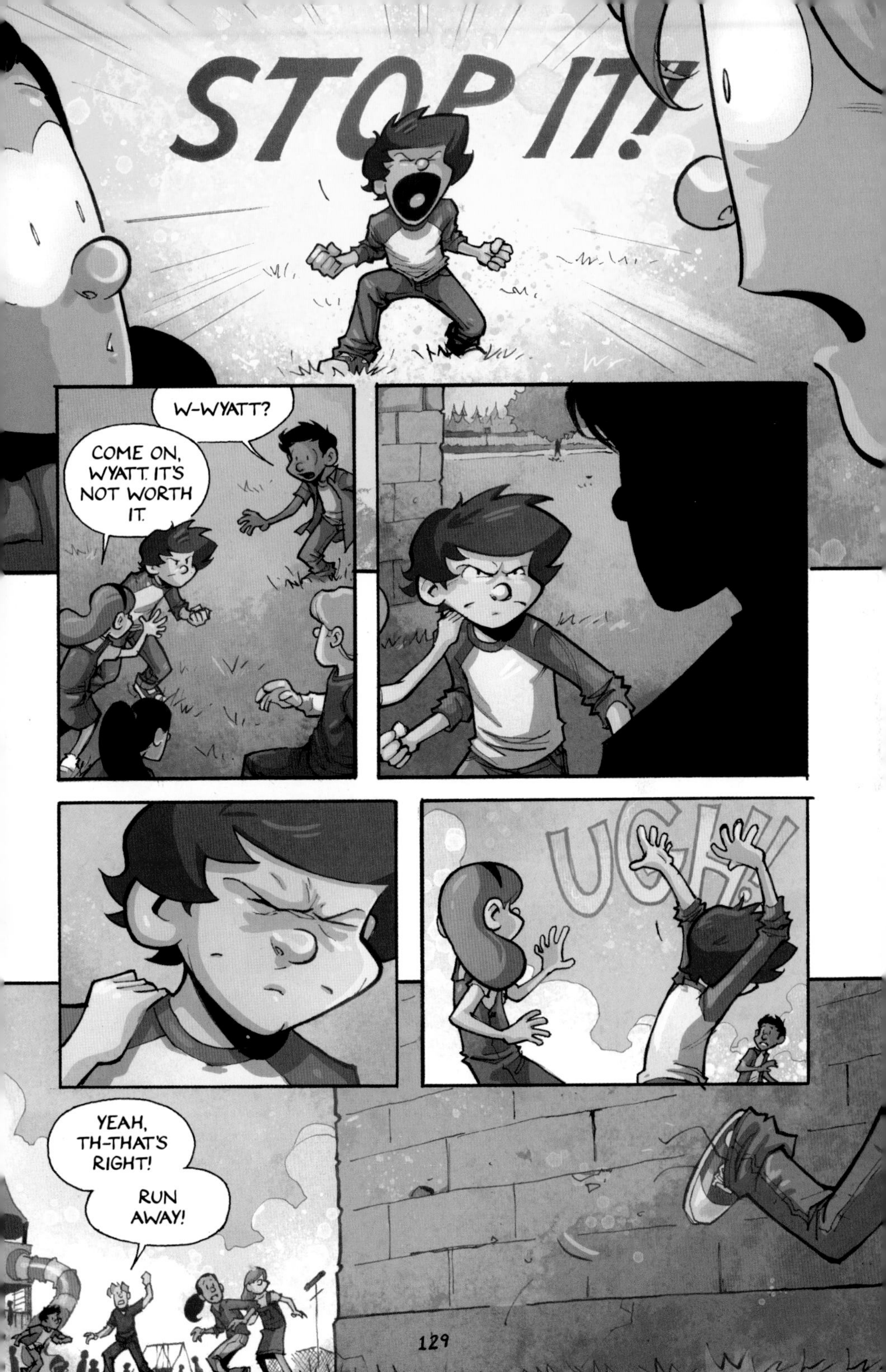
STOP IT!
W-WYATT?
COME ON, WYATT. IT'S NOT WORTH IT.
UGH!
YEAH, TH-THAT'S RIGHT!
RUN AWAY!

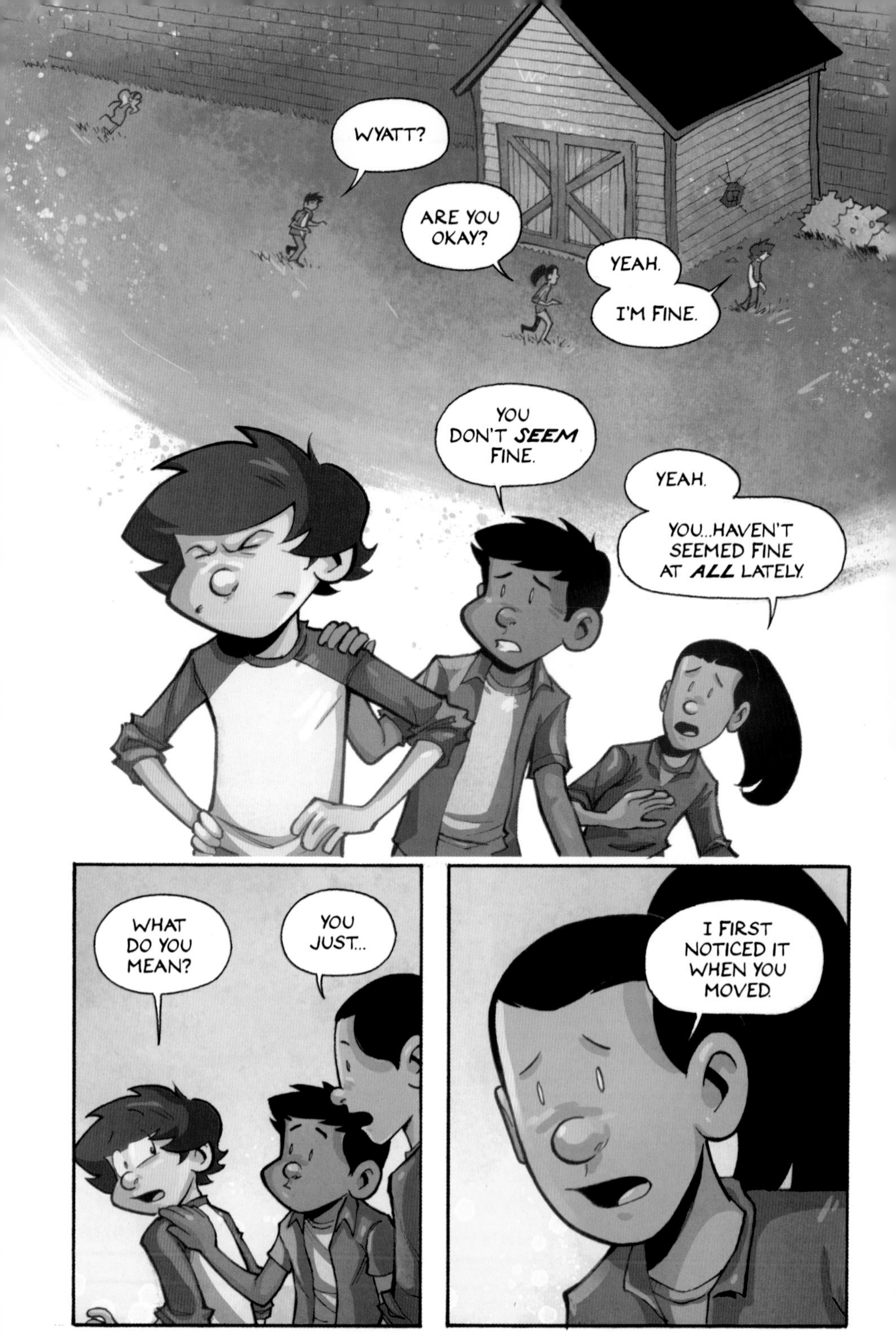
WYATT?
ARE YOU OKAY?
YEAH.
I'M FINE.
YOU DON'T *SEEM* FINE.
YEAH.
YOU...HAVEN'T SEEMED FINE AT *ALL* LATELY.
WHAT DO YOU MEAN?
YOU JUST...
I FIRST NOTICED IT WHEN YOU MOVED.

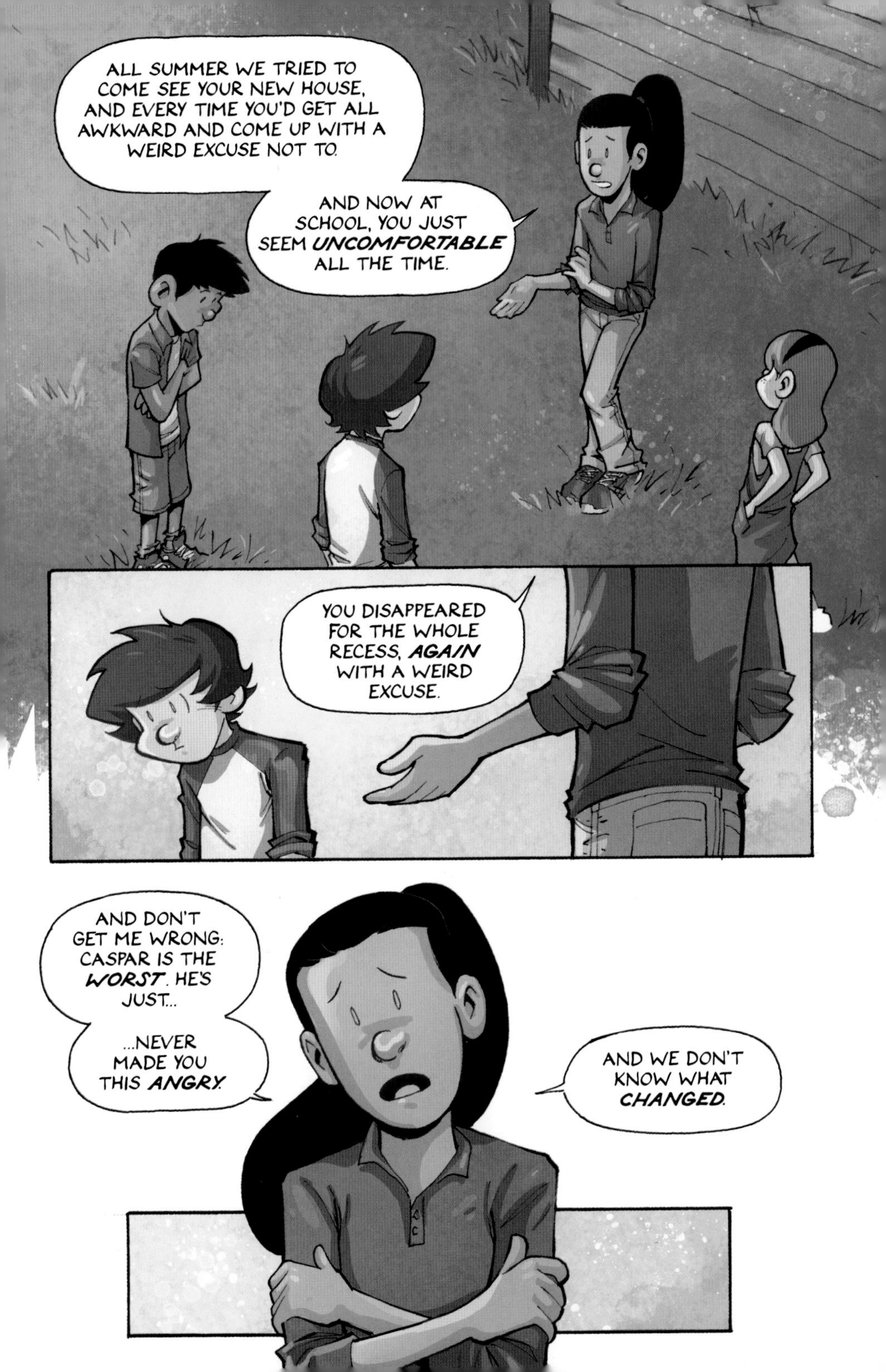
ALL SUMMER WE TRIED TO COME SEE YOUR NEW HOUSE, AND EVERY TIME YOU'D GET ALL AWKWARD AND COME UP WITH A WEIRD EXCUSE NOT TO.
AND NOW AT SCHOOL, YOU JUST SEEM *UNCOMFORTABLE* ALL THE TIME.
YOU DISAPPEARED FOR THE WHOLE RECESS, *AGAIN* WITH A WEIRD EXCUSE.
AND DON'T GET ME WRONG: CASPAR IS THE *WORST*. HE'S JUST...
...NEVER MADE YOU THIS *ANGRY*.
AND WE DON'T KNOW WHAT *CHANGED*.

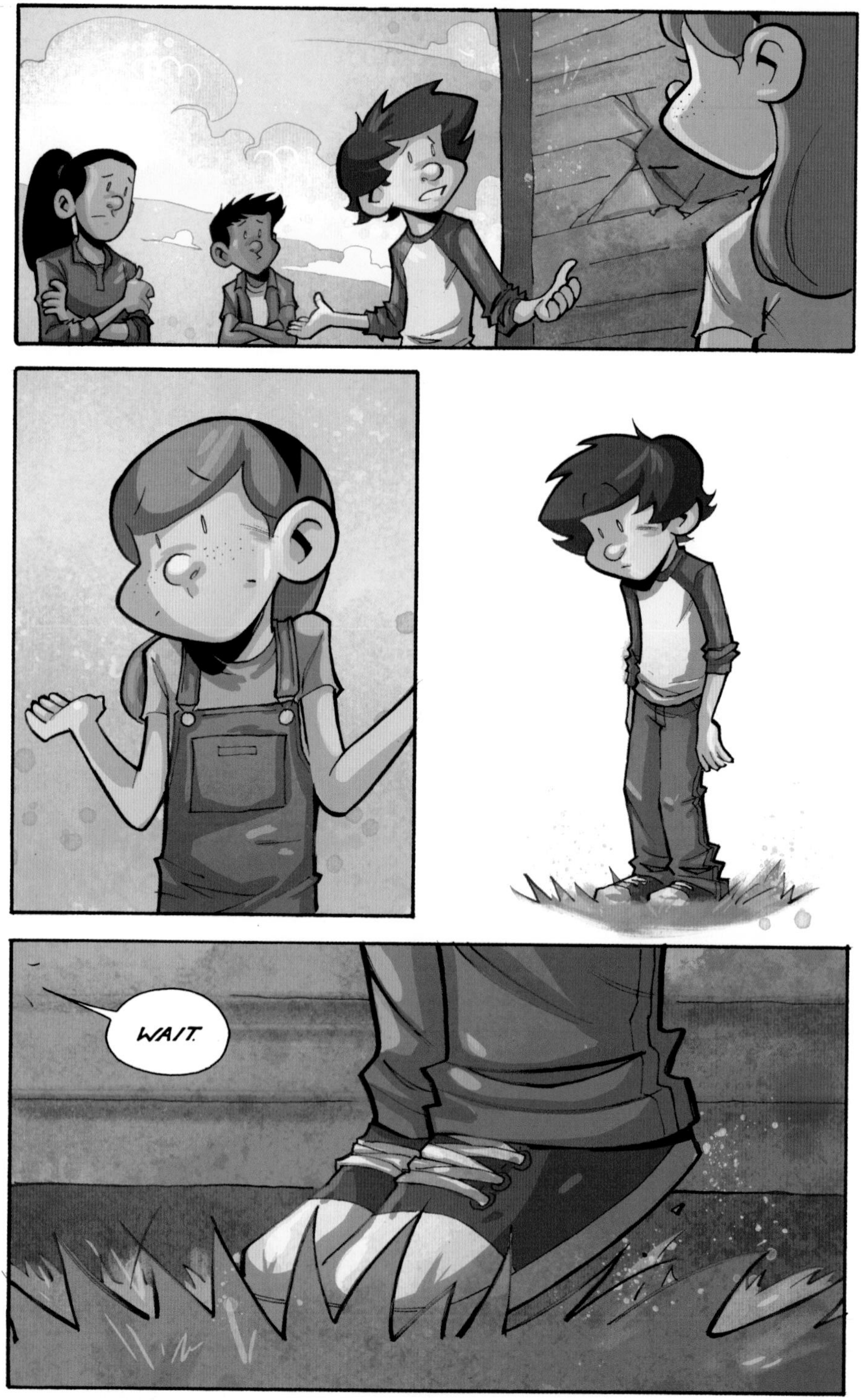
WAIT.

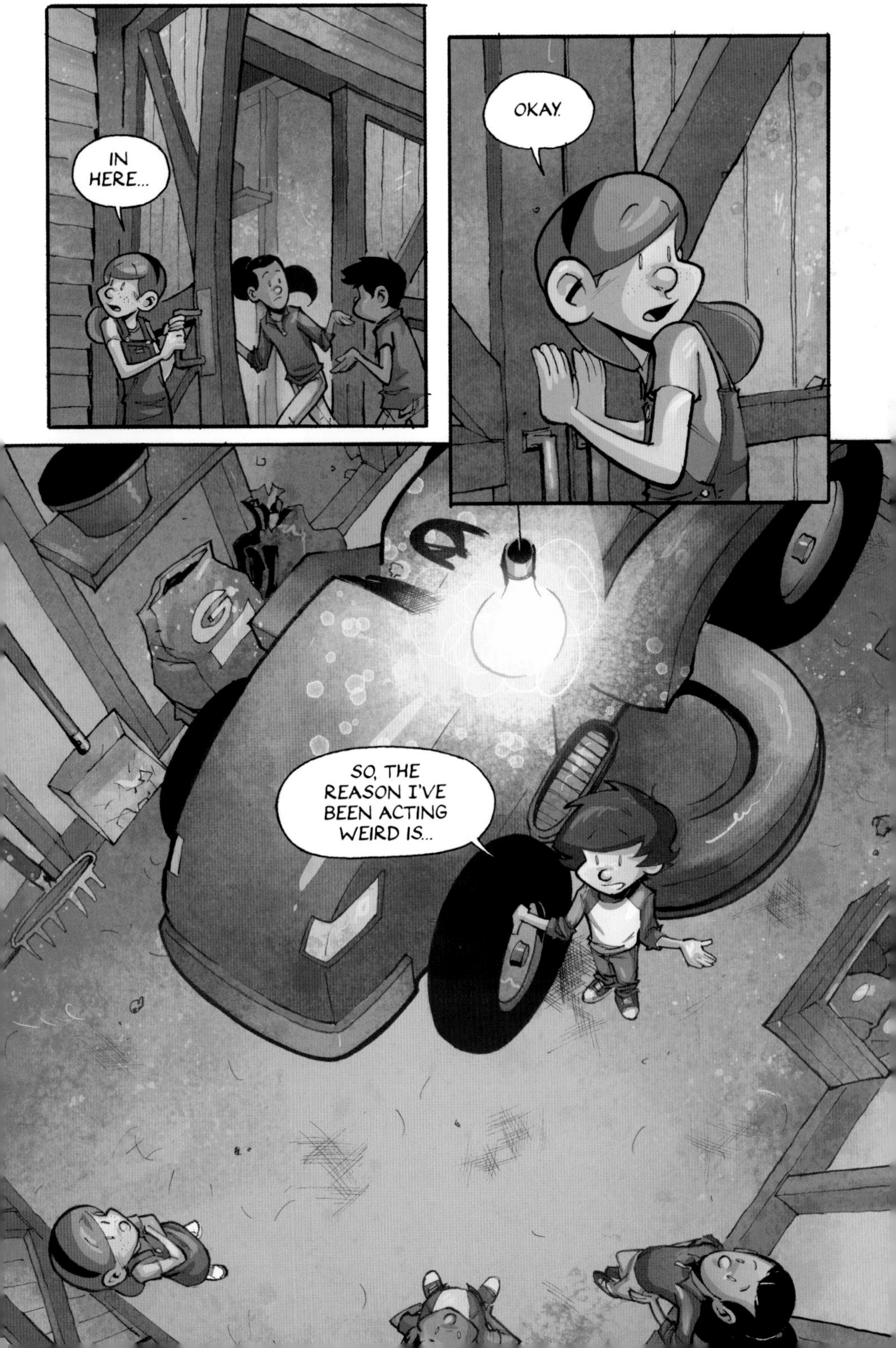
IN HERE...
OKAY.
SO, THE REASON I'VE BEEN ACTING WEIRD IS...

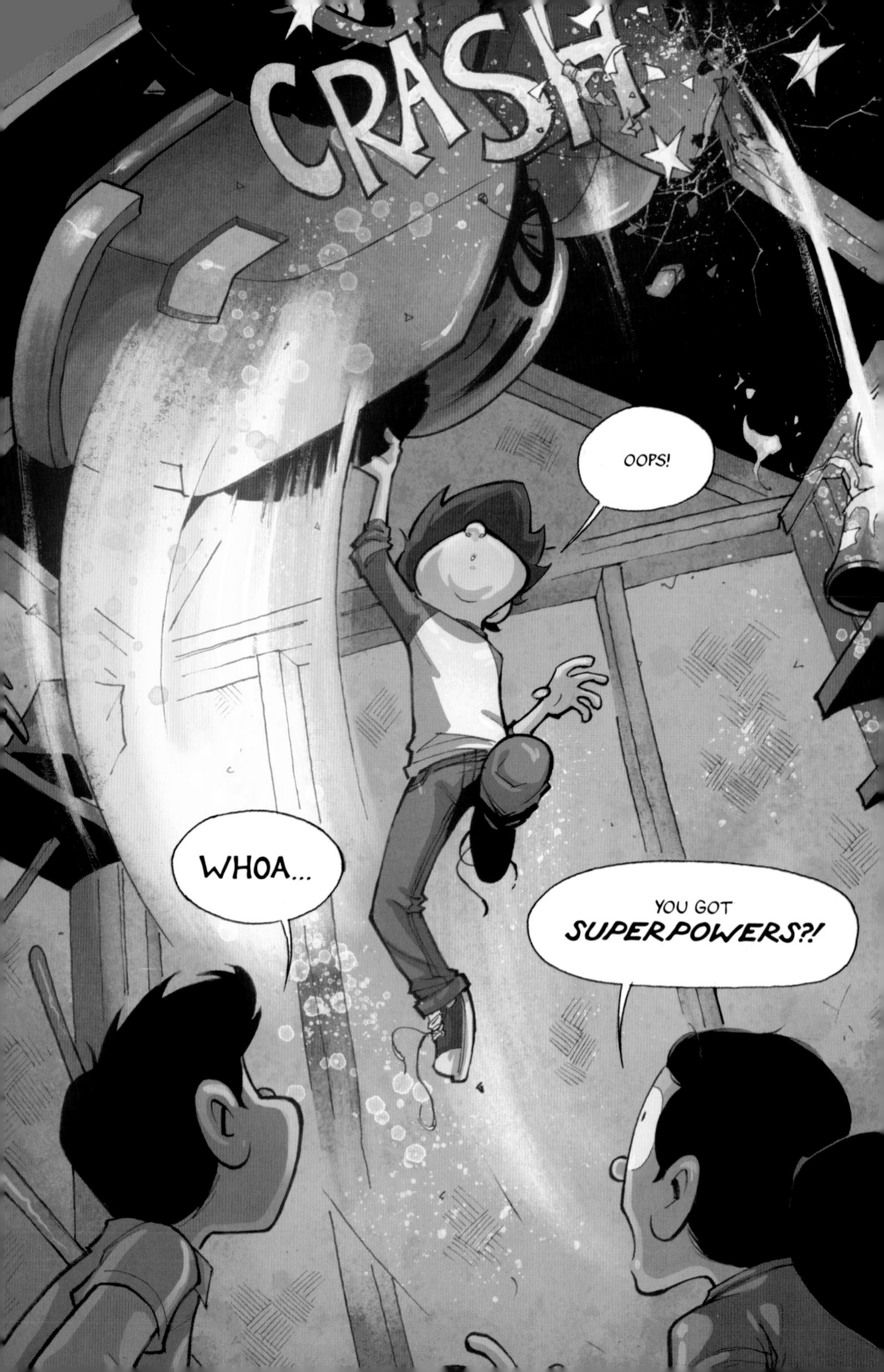
CRASH
OOPS!
WHOA...
YOU GOT SUPERPOWERS?!

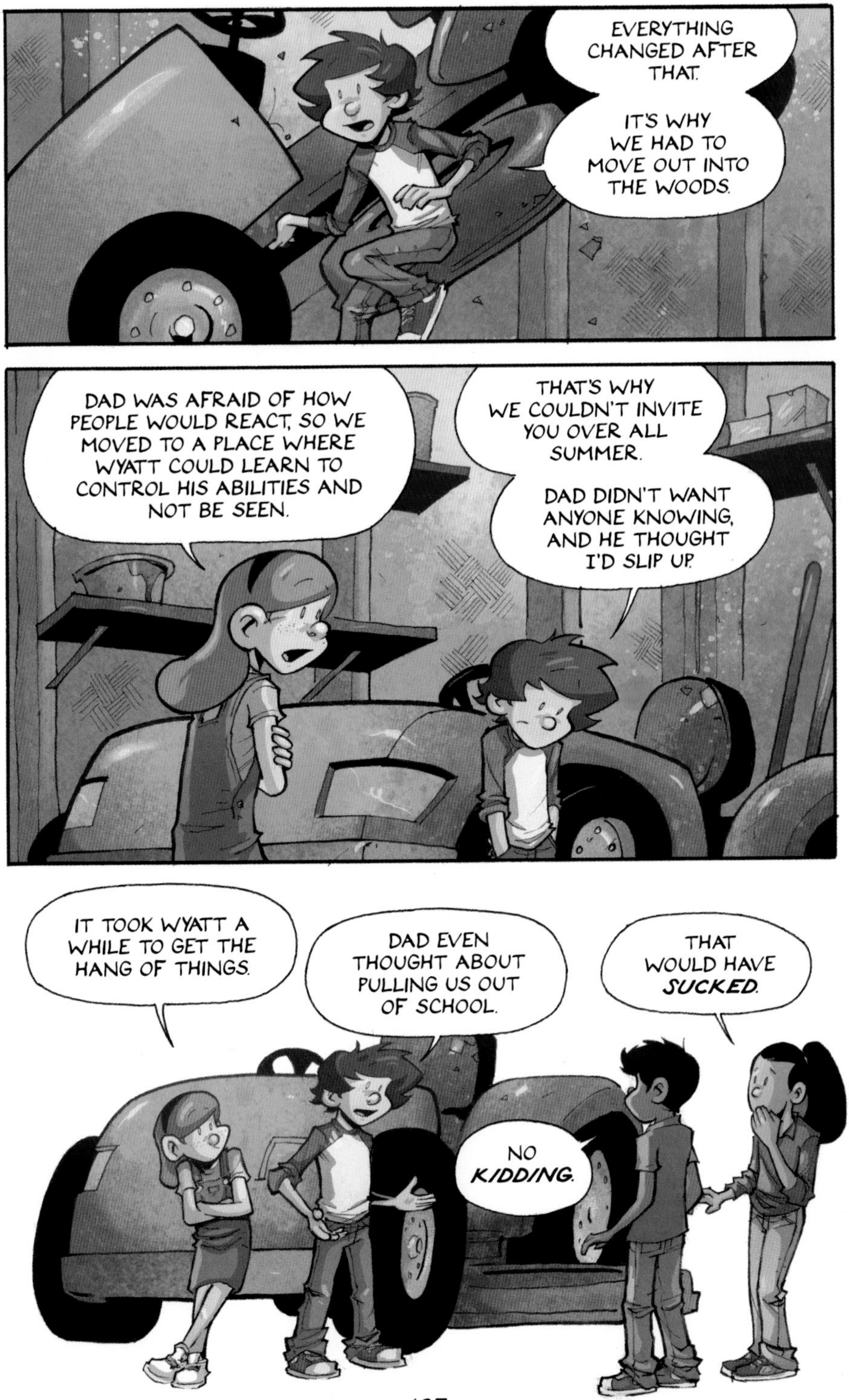
EVERYTHING CHANGED AFTER THAT.
IT'S WHY WE HAD TO MOVE OUT INTO THE WOODS.
DAD WAS AFRAID OF HOW PEOPLE WOULD REACT, SO WE MOVED TO A PLACE WHERE WYATT COULD LEARN TO CONTROL HIS ABILITIES AND NOT BE SEEN.
THAT'S WHY WE COULDN'T INVITE YOU OVER ALL SUMMER.
DAD DIDN'T WANT ANYONE KNOWING, AND HE THOUGHT I'D SLIP UP.
IT TOOK WYATT A WHILE TO GET THE HANG OF THINGS.
DAD EVEN THOUGHT ABOUT PULLING US OUT OF SCHOOL.
THAT WOULD HAVE *SUCKED*.
NO *KIDDING*.

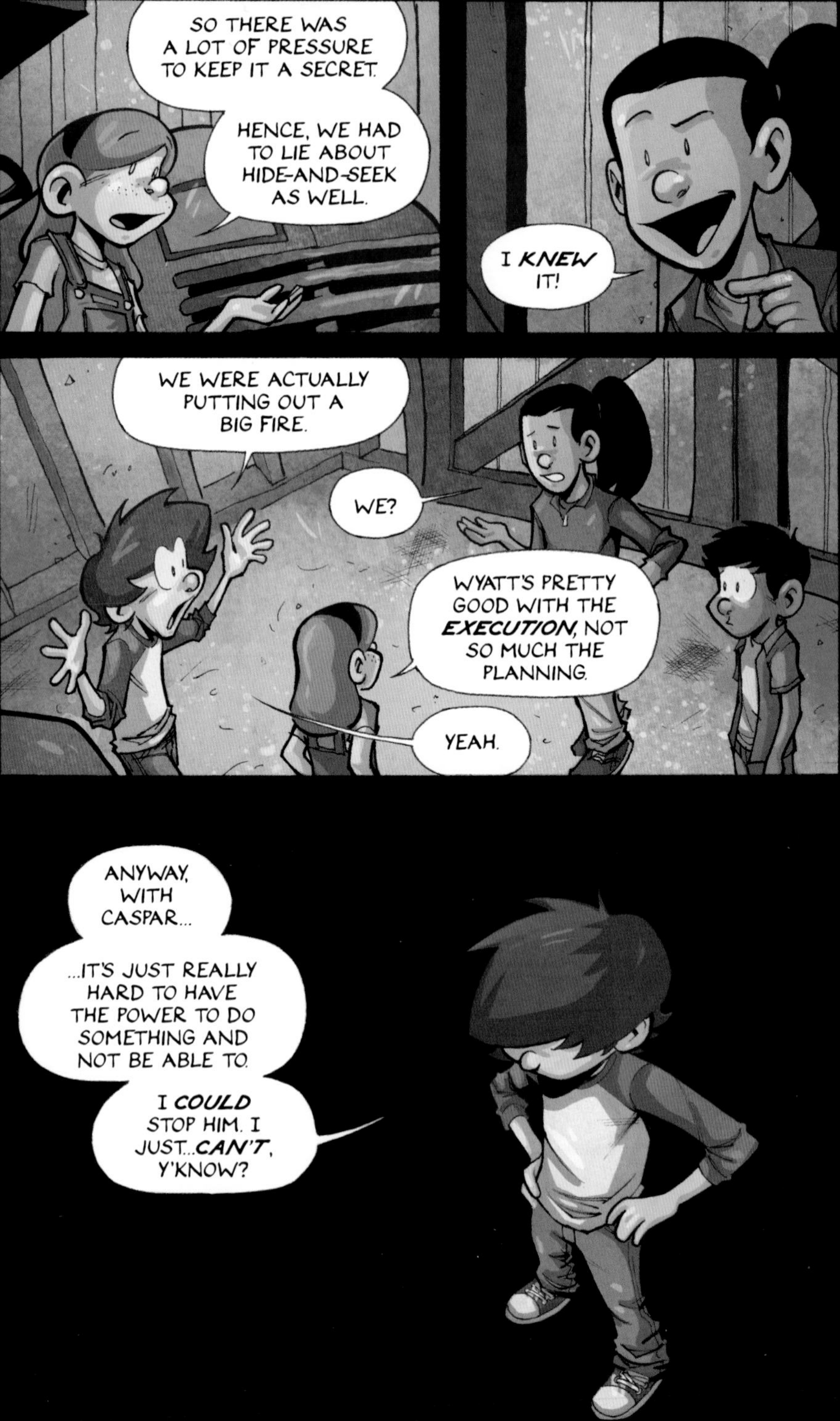
SO THERE WAS A LOT OF PRESSURE TO KEEP IT A SECRET.
HENCE, WE HAD TO LIE ABOUT HIDE-AND-SEEK AS WELL.
I KNEW IT!
WE WERE ACTUALLY PUTTING OUT A BIG FIRE.
WE?
WYATT'S PRETTY GOOD WITH THE EXECUTION, NOT SO MUCH THE PLANNING.
YEAH.
ANYWAY, WITH CASPAR...
...IT'S JUST REALLY HARD TO HAVE THE POWER TO DO SOMETHING AND NOT BE ABLE TO.
I COULD STOP HIM. I JUST...CAN'T, Y'KNOW?

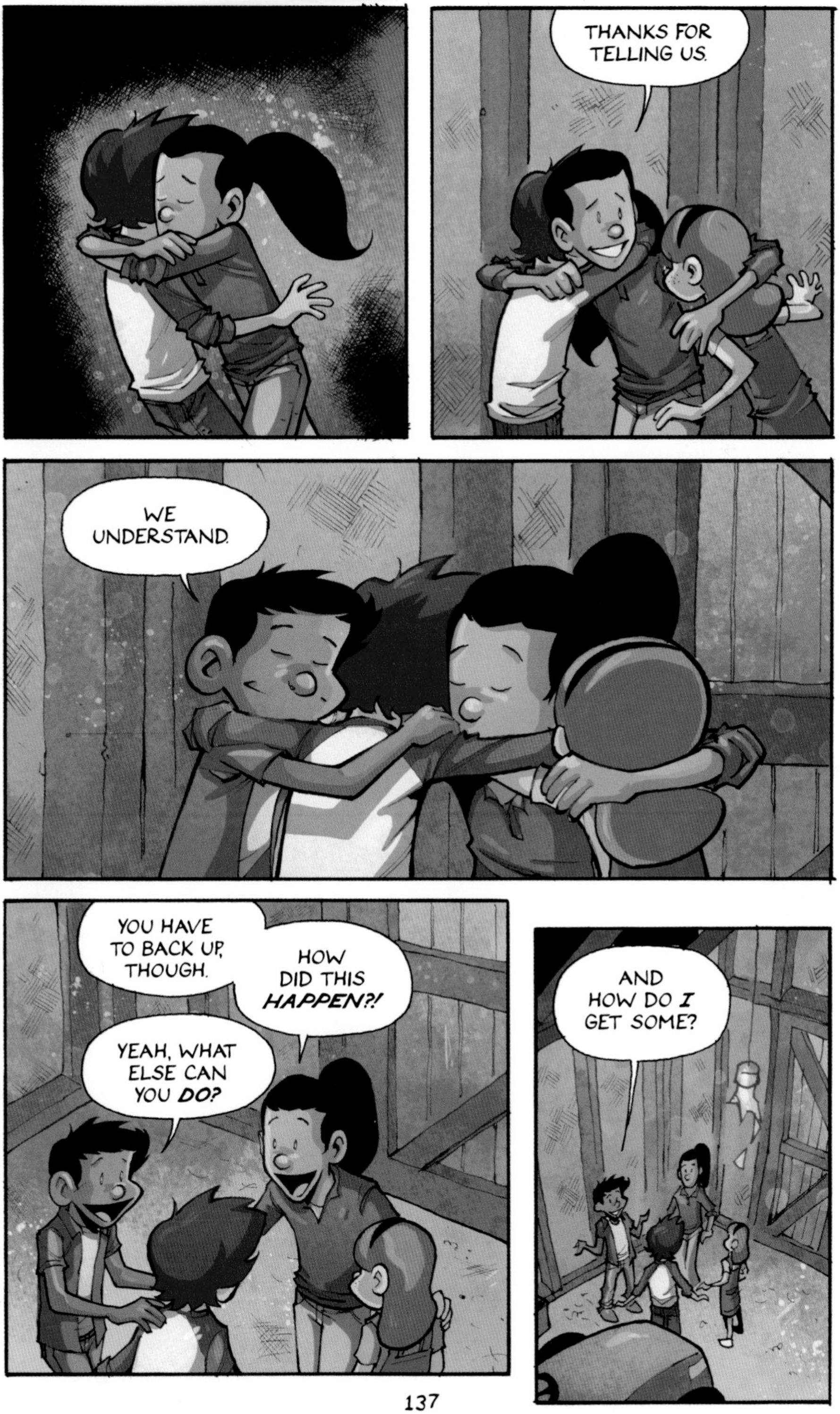
THANKS FOR TELLING US.
WE UNDERSTAND.
YOU HAVE TO BACK UP, THOUGH.
HOW DID THIS *HAPPEN?!*
YEAH, WHAT ELSE CAN YOU *DO?*
AND HOW DO *I* GET SOME?

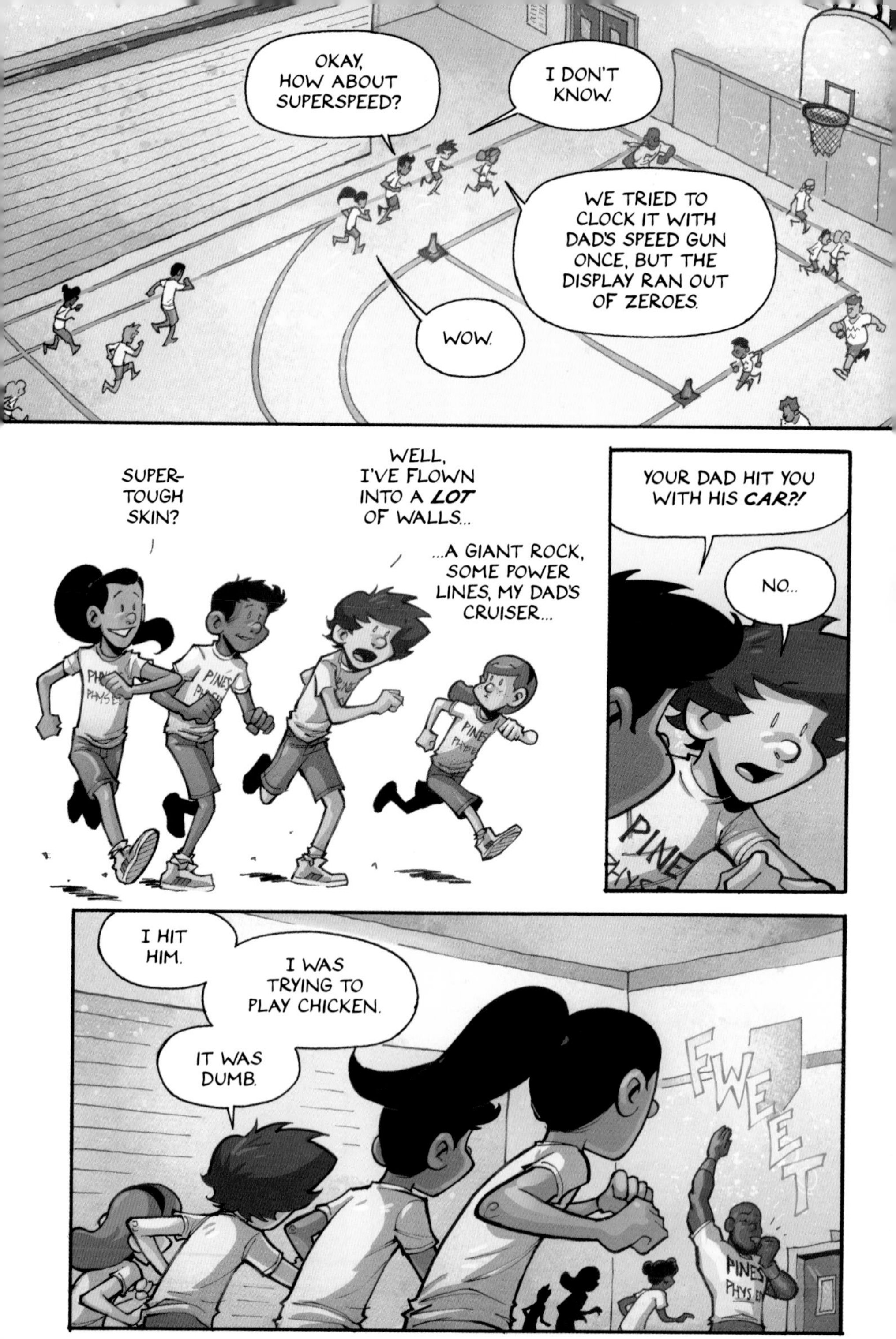
OKAY, HOW ABOUT SUPERSPEED?
I DON'T KNOW.
WE TRIED TO CLOCK IT WITH DAD'S SPEED GUN ONCE, BUT THE DISPLAY RAN OUT OF ZEROES.
WOW.
SUPER-TOUGH SKIN?
WELL, I'VE FLOWN INTO A *LOT* OF WALLS...
...A GIANT ROCK, SOME POWER LINES, MY DAD'S CRUISER...
YOUR DAD HIT YOU WITH HIS *CAR?!*
NO...
I HIT HIM.
I WAS TRYING TO PLAY CHICKEN.
IT WAS DUMB.
FWEEET

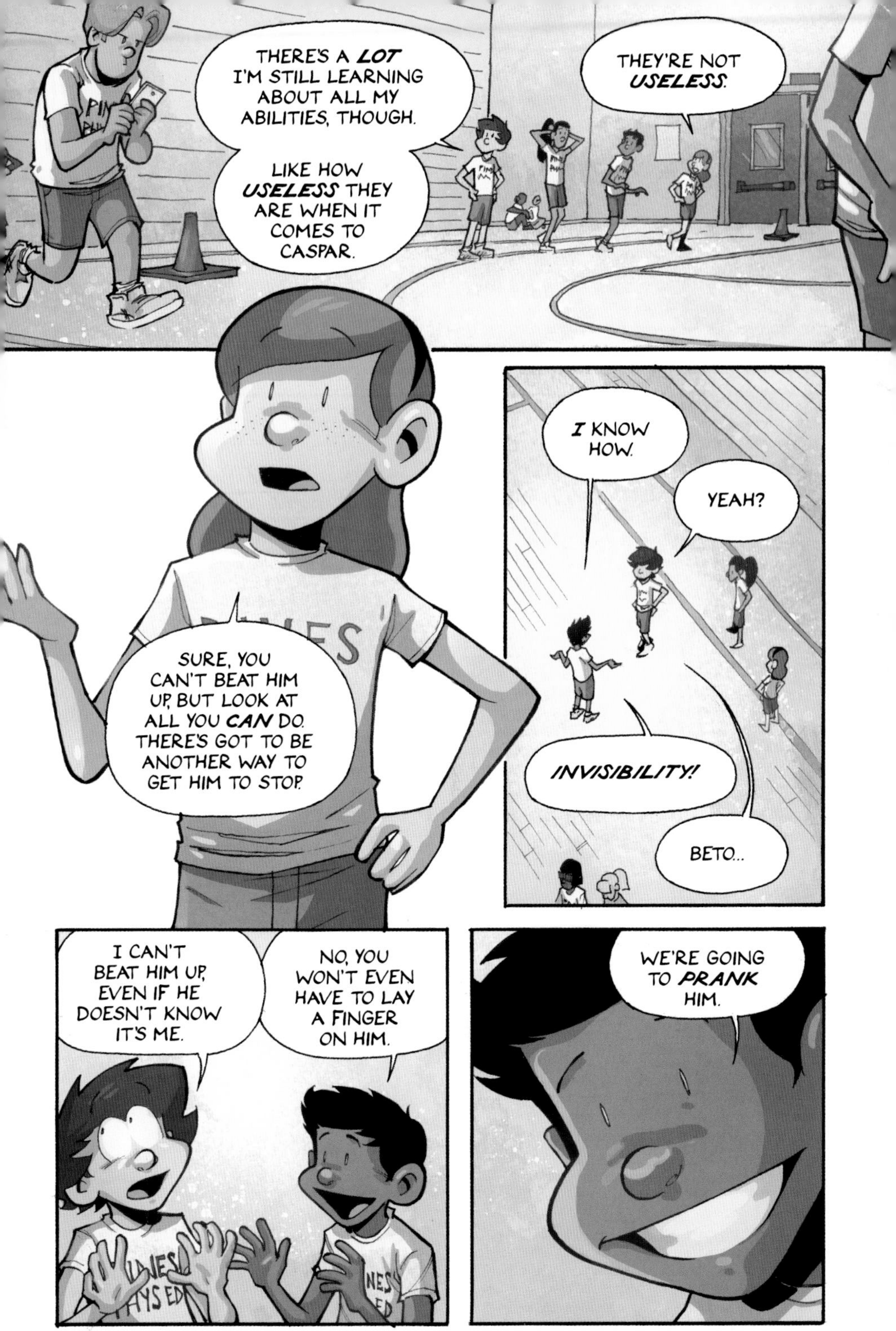
THERE'S A *LOT* I'M STILL LEARNING ABOUT ALL MY ABILITIES, THOUGH.
LIKE HOW *USELESS* THEY ARE WHEN IT COMES TO CASPAR.
THEY'RE NOT *USELESS*.
SURE, YOU CAN'T BEAT HIM UP, BUT LOOK AT ALL YOU *CAN* DO. THERE'S GOT TO BE ANOTHER WAY TO GET HIM TO STOP.
I KNOW HOW.
YEAH?
INVISIBILITY!
BETO...
I CAN'T BEAT HIM UP, EVEN IF HE DOESN'T KNOW IT'S ME.
NO, YOU WON'T EVEN HAVE TO LAY A FINGER ON HIM.
WE'RE GOING TO *PRANK* HIM.

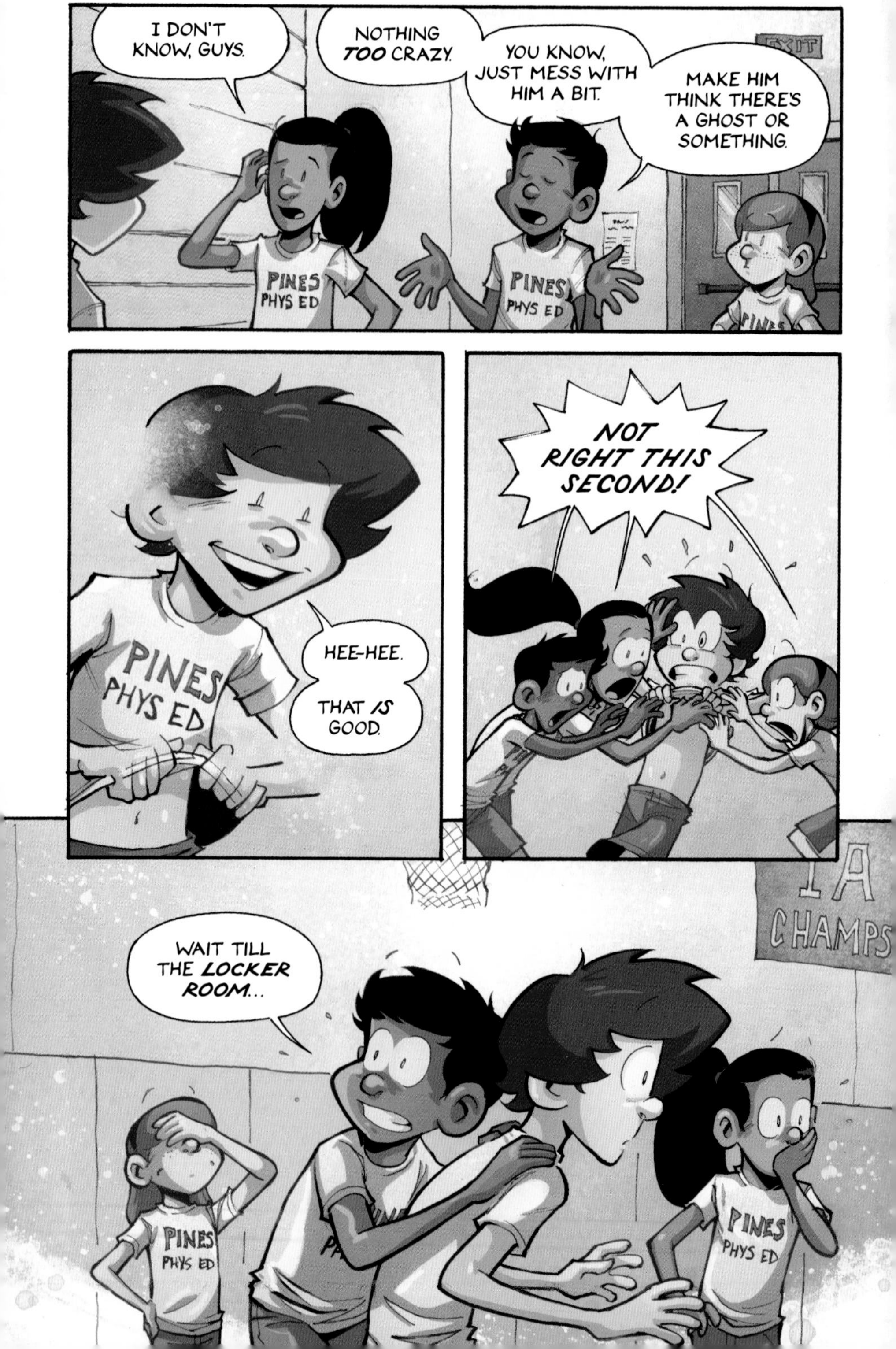
I DON'T KNOW, GUYS.
NOTHING *TOO* CRAZY.
YOU KNOW, JUST MESS WITH HIM A BIT.
MAKE HIM THINK THERE'S A GHOST OR SOMETHING.
EXIT
PINES PHYS ED
HEE-HEE.
THAT *IS* GOOD.
NOT RIGHT THIS SECOND!
WAIT TILL THE *LOCKER ROOM*...
CHAMPS

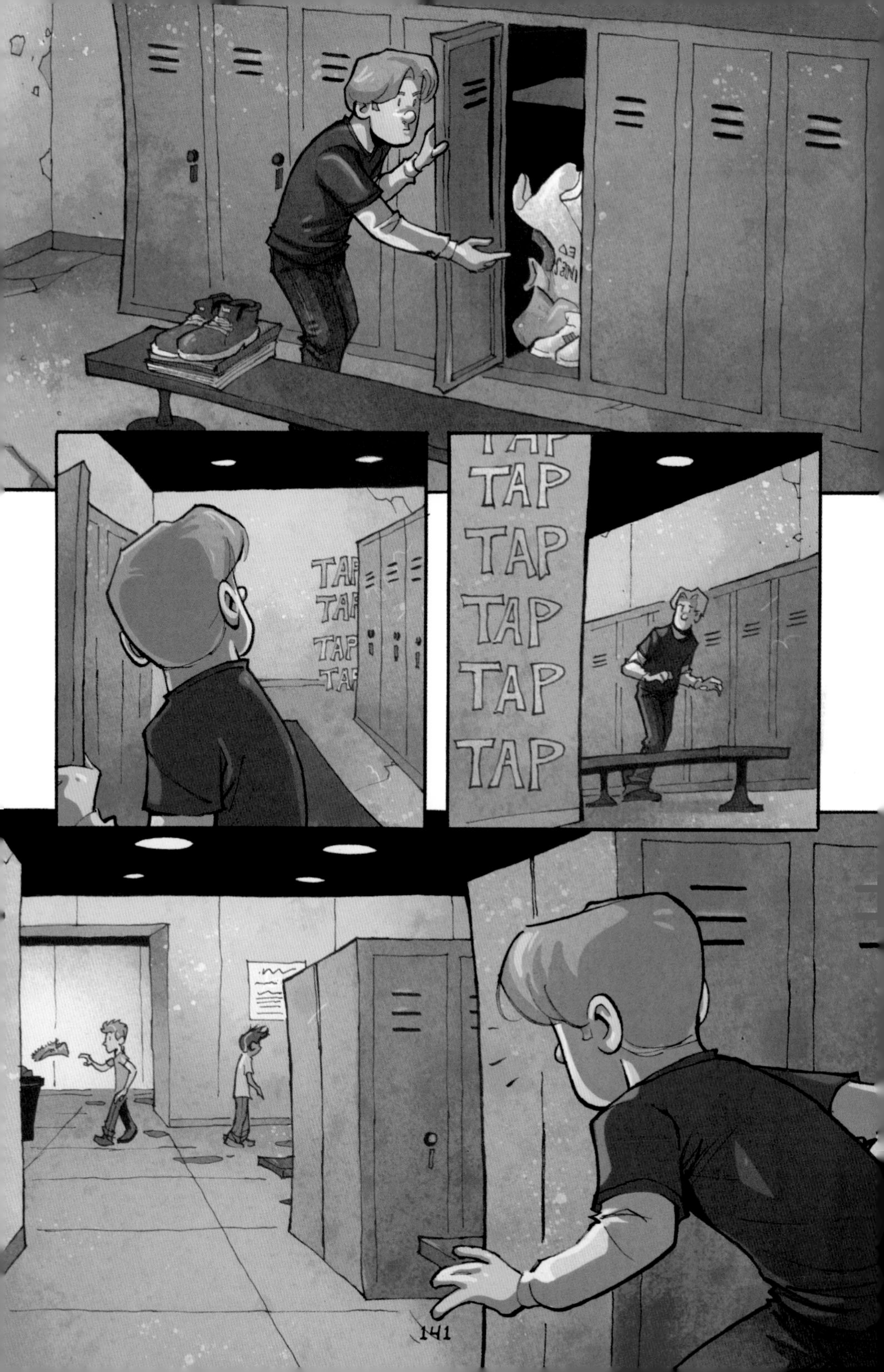
TAP
TAP
TAP
TAP
TAP
TAP
TAP
TAP
TAP
TAP
TAP

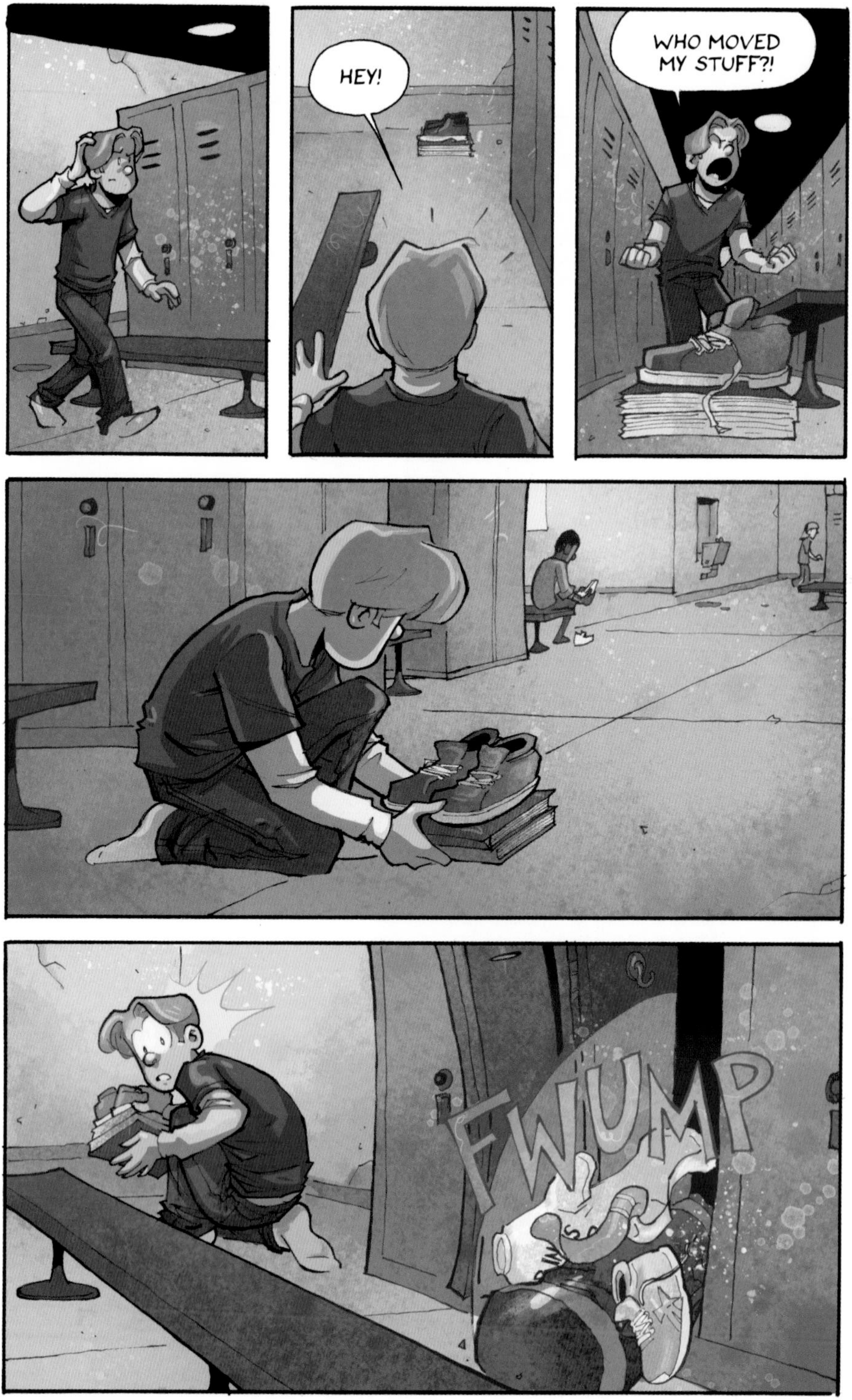
HEY!
WHO MOVED MY STUFF?!
FWUMP

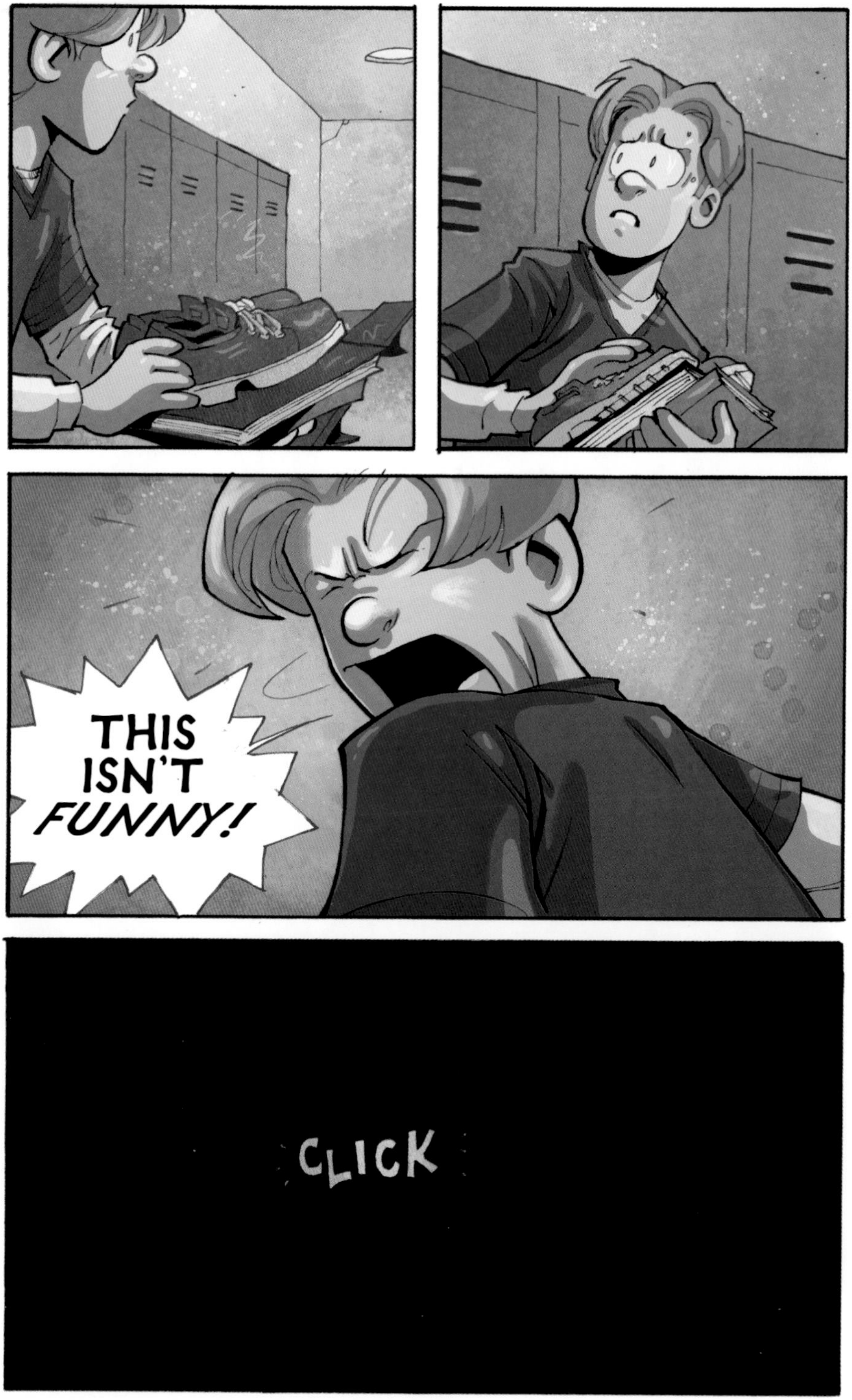
THIS ISN'T *FUNNY!*
CLICK

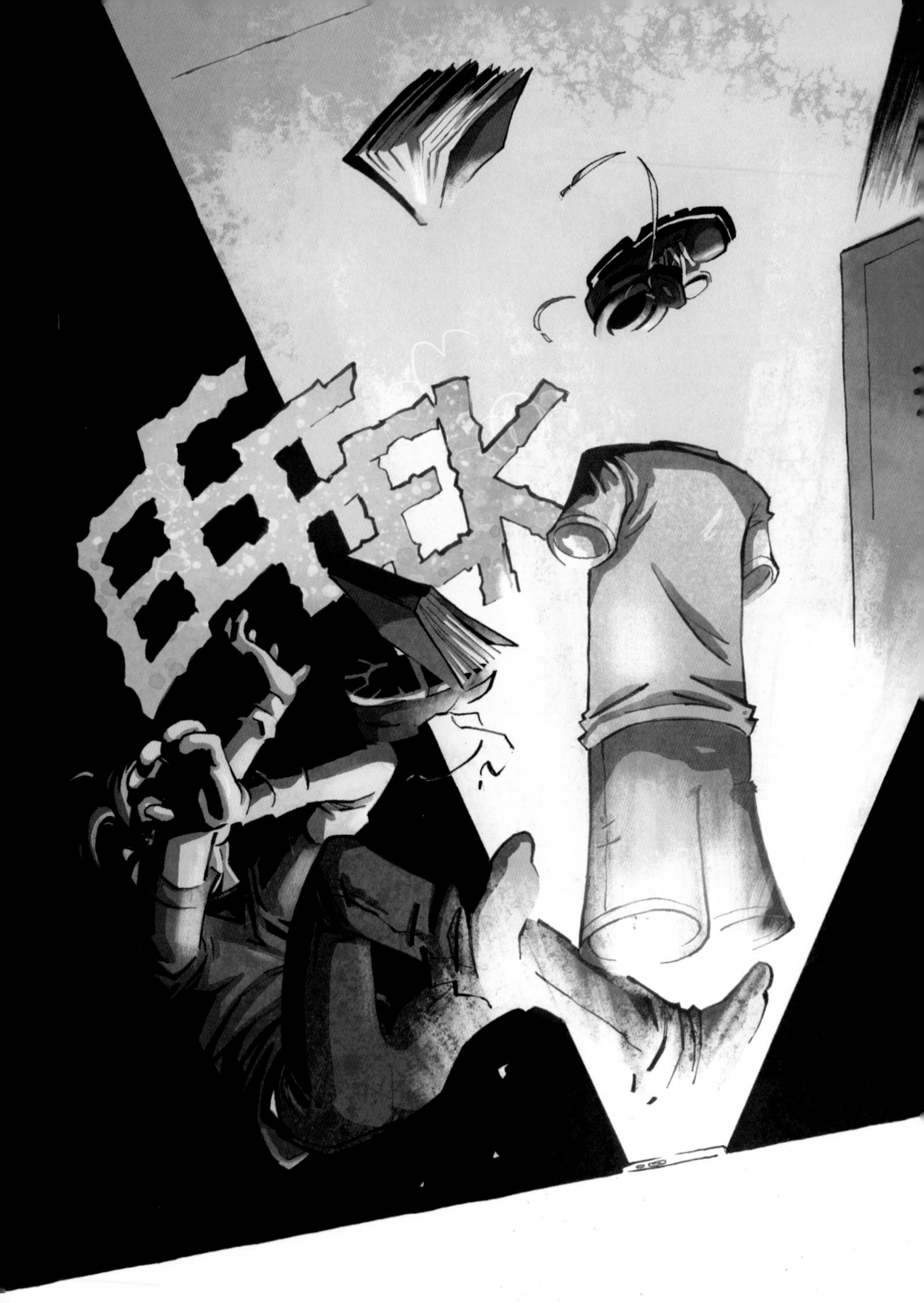

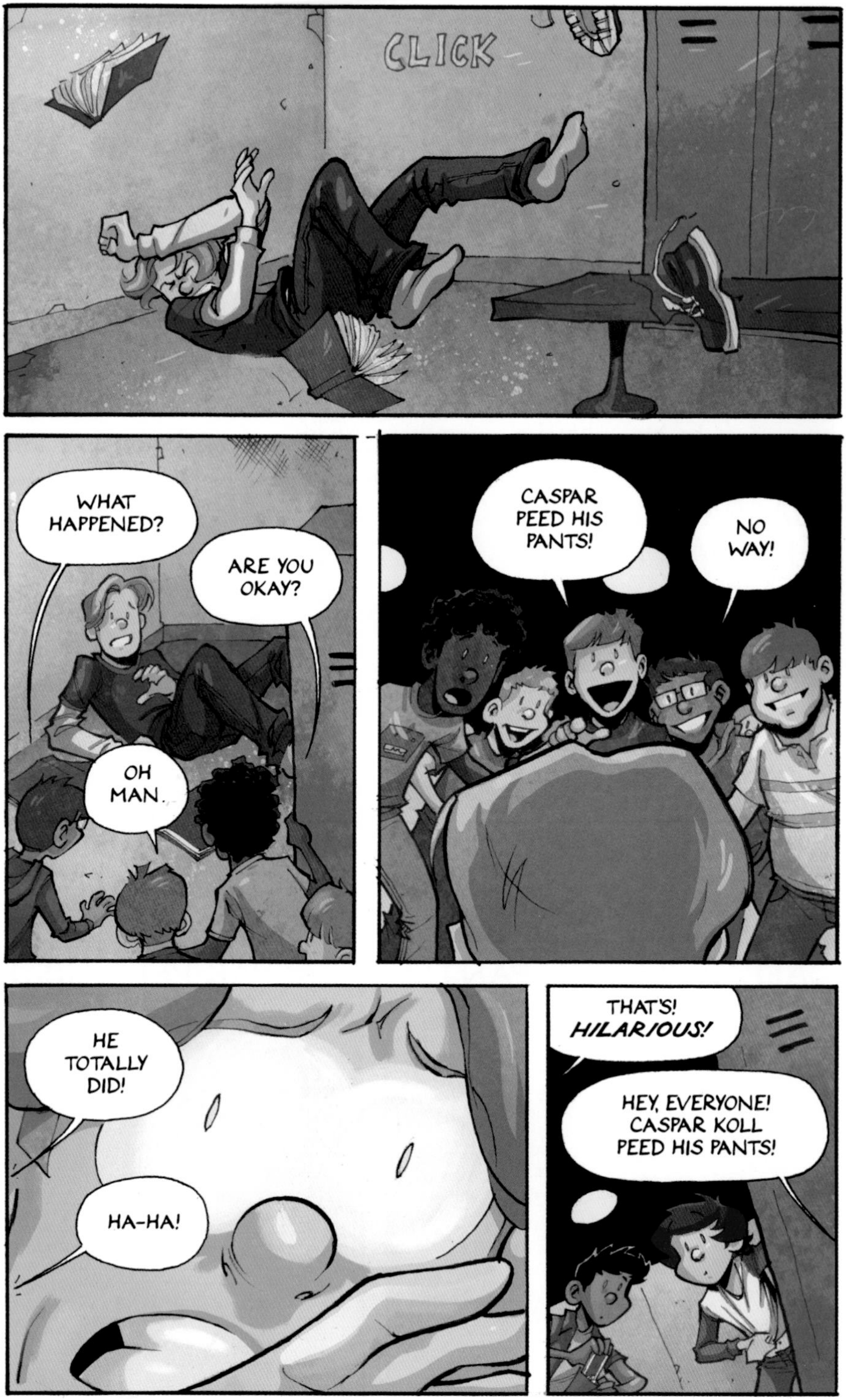
CLICK
WHAT HAPPENED?
ARE YOU OKAY?
OH MAN.
CASPAR PEED HIS PANTS!
NO WAY!
HE TOTALLY DID!
HA-HA!
THAT'S! *HILARIOUS!*
HEY, EVERYONE! CASPAR KOLL PEED HIS PANTS!

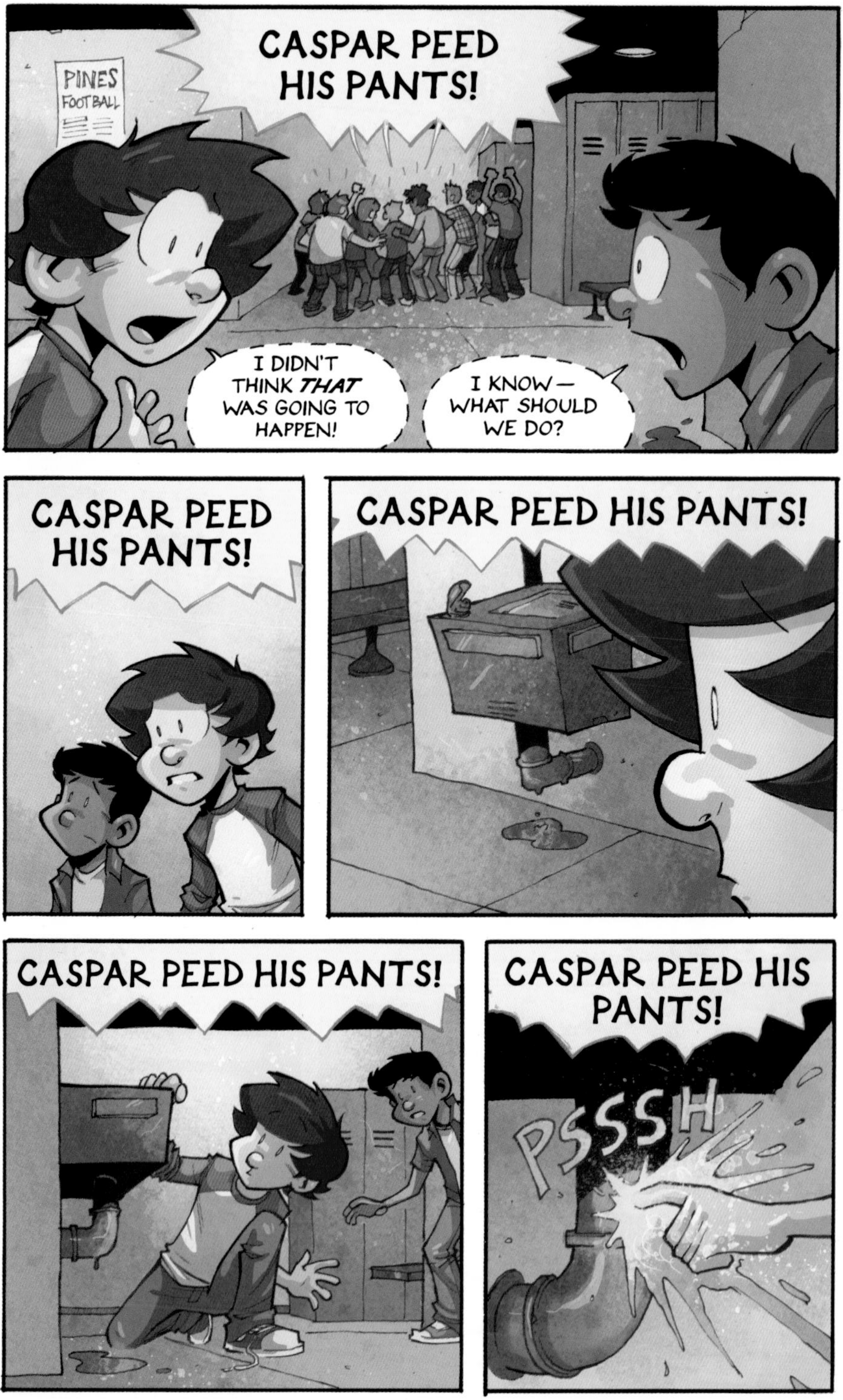
CASPAR PEED HIS PANTS!
PINES FOOTBALL
I DIDN'T THINK *THAT* WAS GOING TO HAPPEN!
I KNOW— WHAT SHOULD WE DO?
CASPAR PEED HIS PANTS!
CASPAR PEED HIS PANTS!
CASPAR PEED HIS PANTS!
CASPAR PEED HIS PANTS!
PSSSH

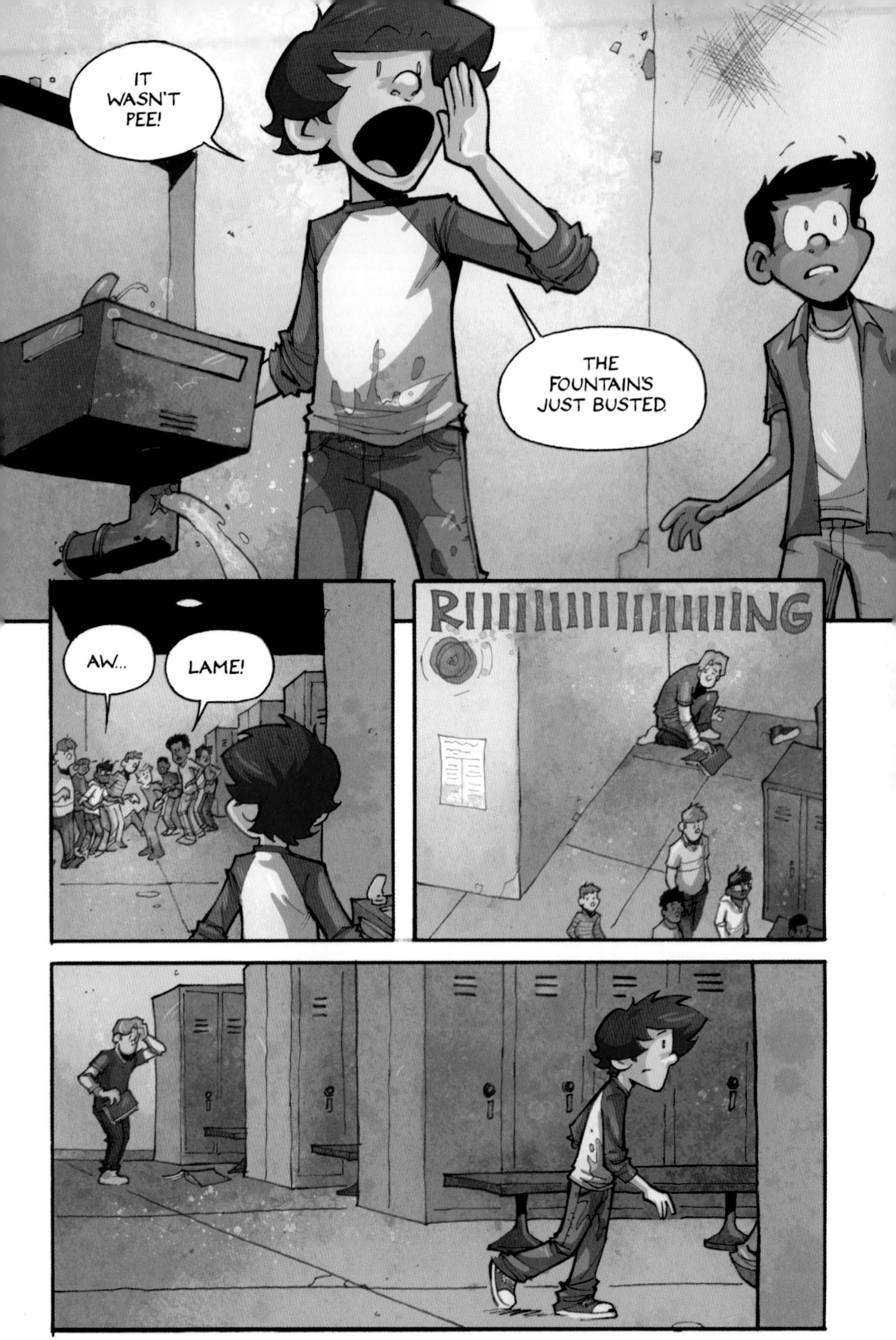
IT WASN'T PEE!
THE FOUNTAIN'S JUST BUSTED.
AW...
LAME!
RIIIIIIIIIIIIIIIING

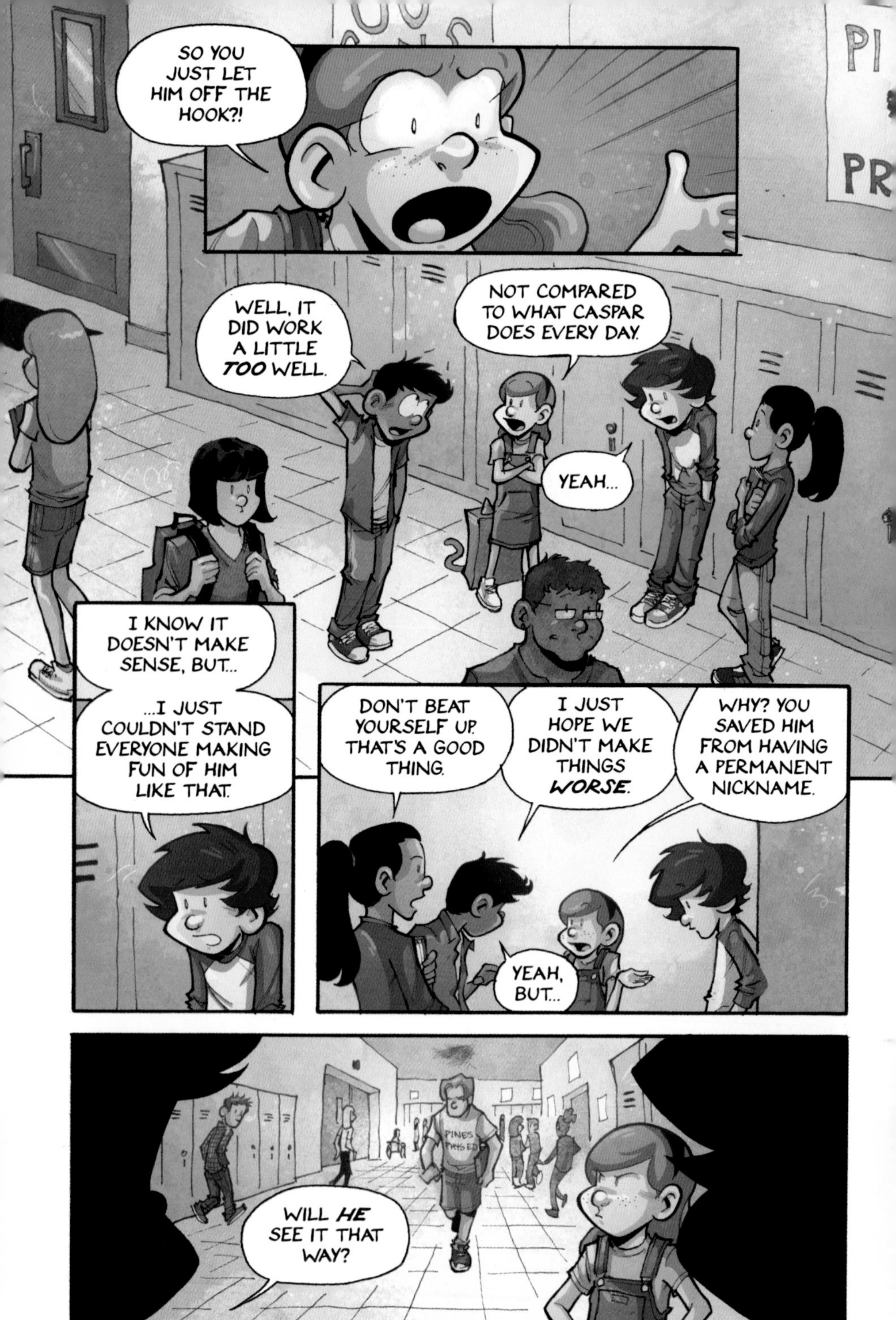
SO YOU JUST LET HIM OFF THE HOOK?!
WELL, IT DID WORK A LITTLE *TOO* WELL.
NOT COMPARED TO WHAT CASPAR DOES EVERY DAY.
YEAH...
I KNOW IT DOESN'T MAKE SENSE, BUT...
...I JUST COULDN'T STAND EVERYONE MAKING FUN OF HIM LIKE THAT.
DON'T BEAT YOURSELF UP. THAT'S A GOOD THING.
I JUST HOPE WE DIDN'T MAKE THINGS *WORSE*.
WHY? YOU SAVED HIM FROM HAVING A PERMANENT NICKNAME.
YEAH, BUT...
WILL *HE* SEE IT THAT WAY?

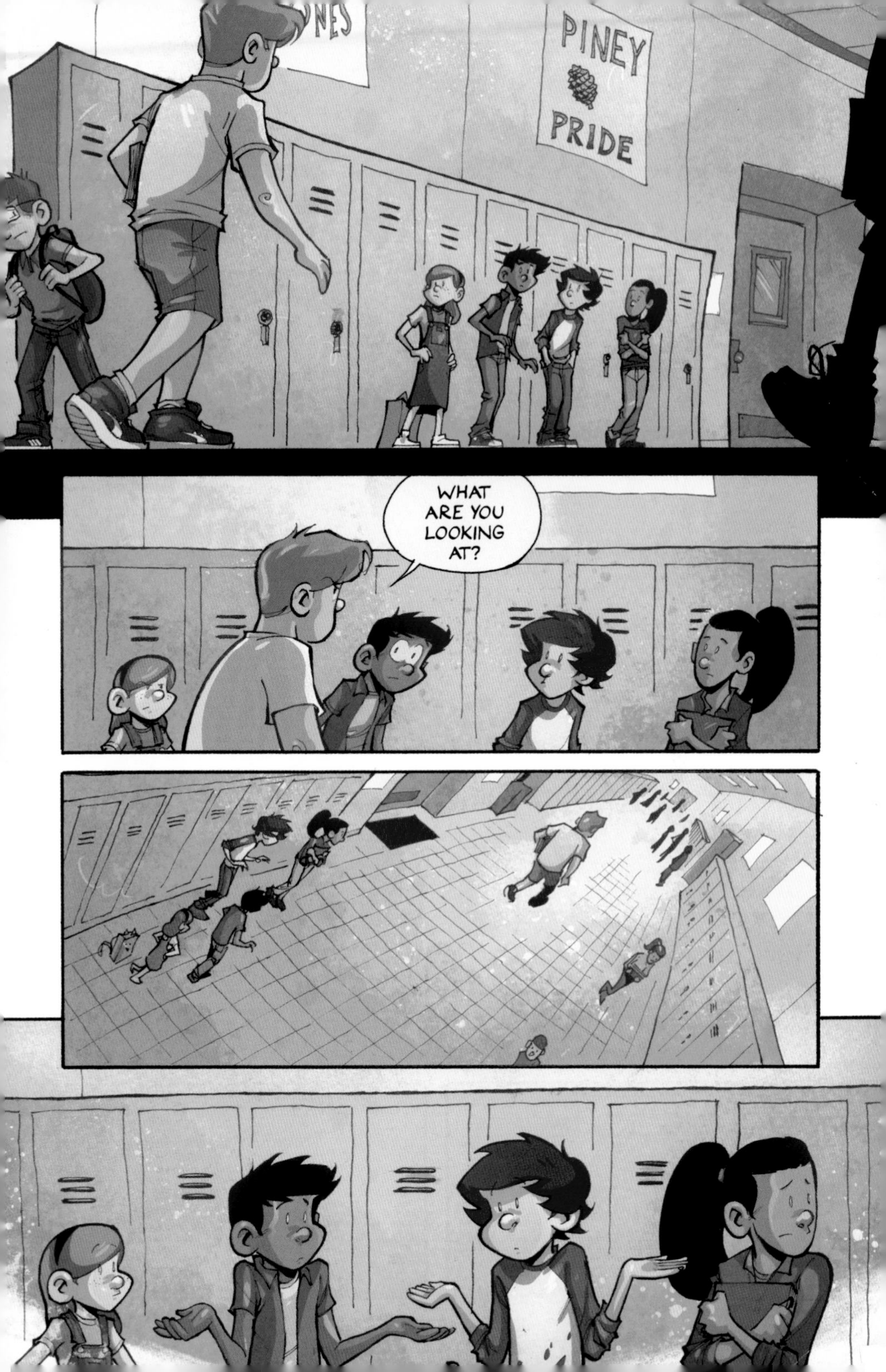
ONES
PINEY PRIDE
WHAT ARE YOU LOOKING AT?

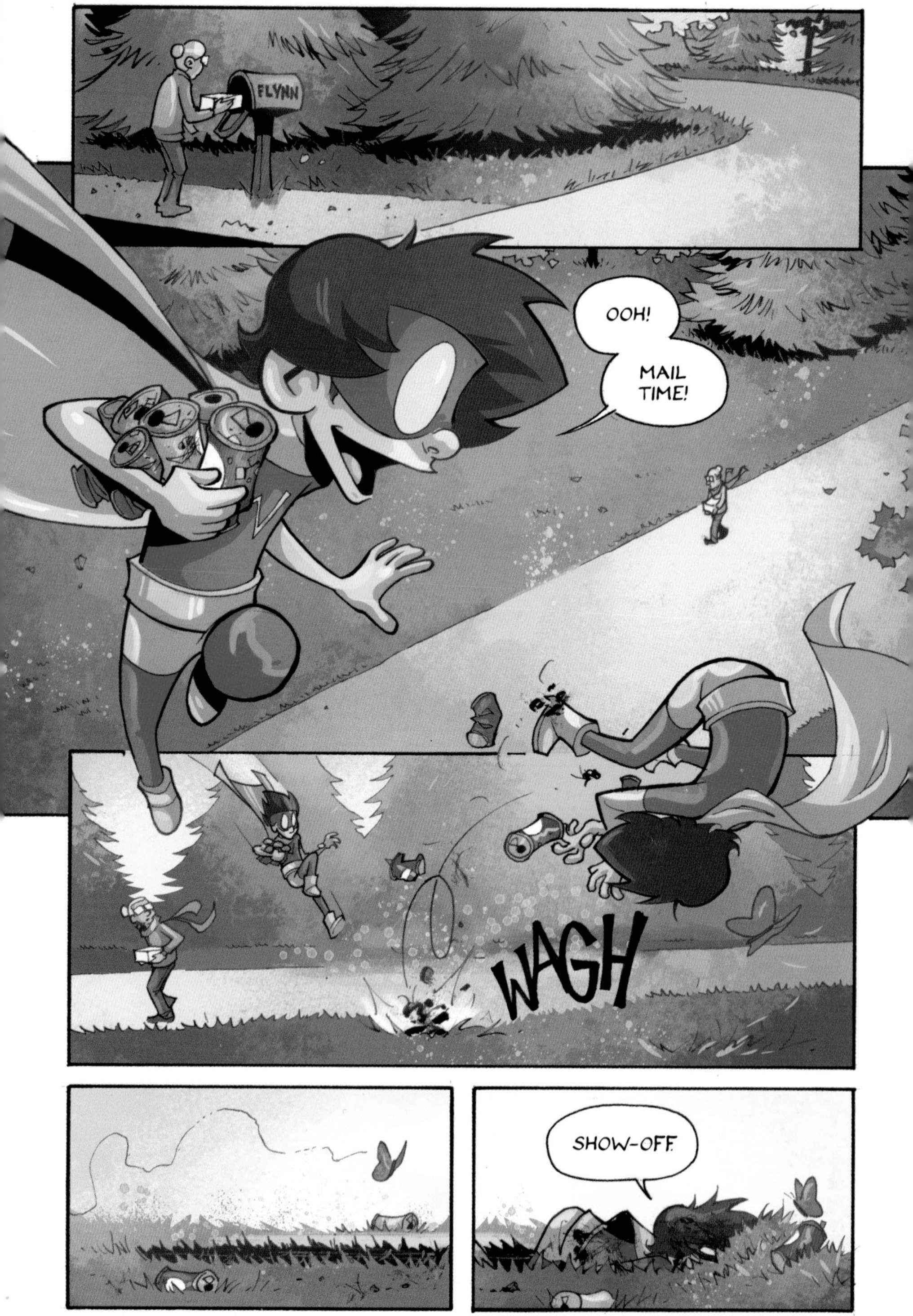
FLYNN
OOH!
MAIL TIME!
WAGH
SHOW-OFF.

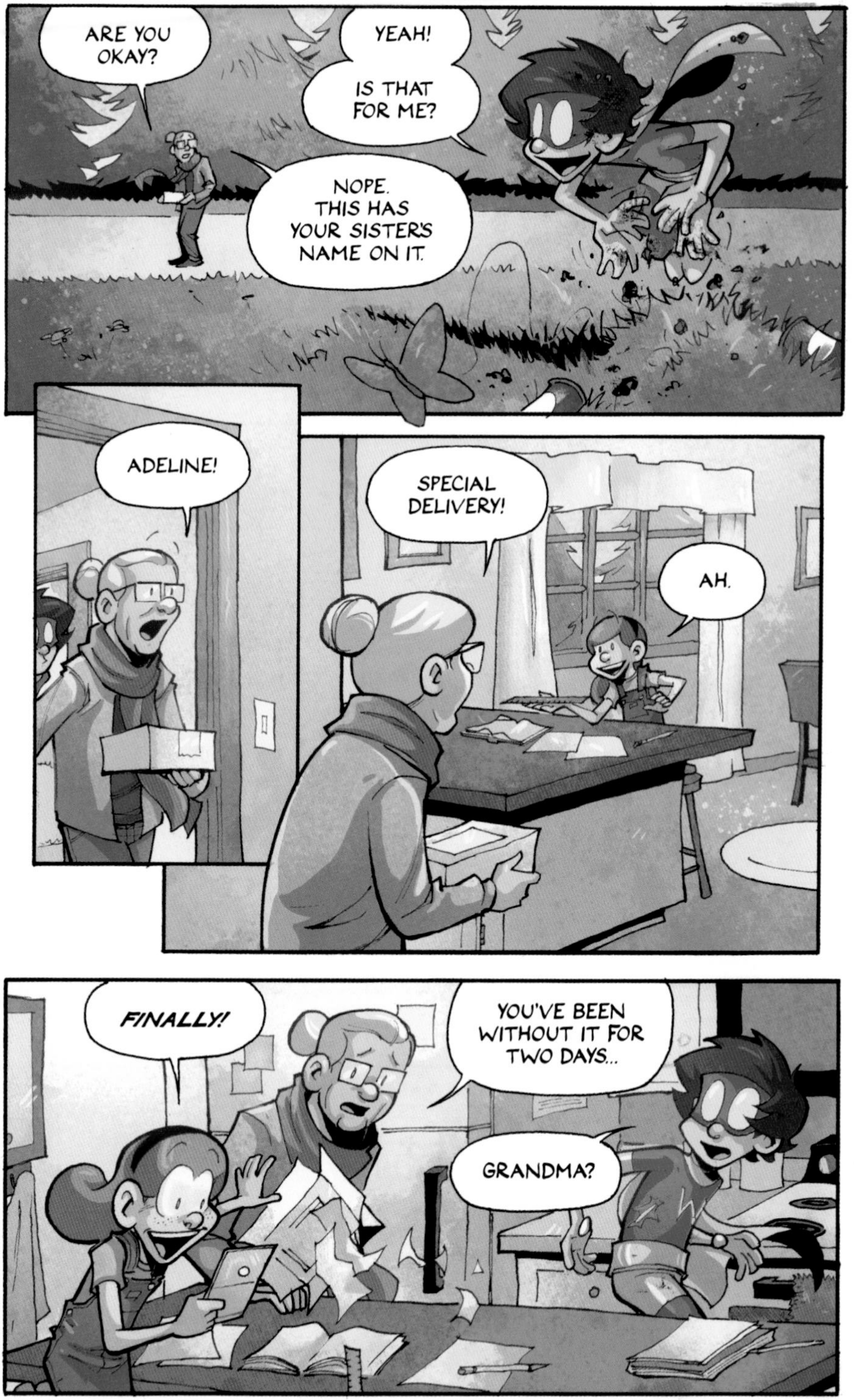
ARE YOU OKAY?
YEAH!
IS THAT FOR ME?
NOPE. THIS HAS YOUR SISTER'S NAME ON IT.
ADELINE!
SPECIAL DELIVERY!
AH.
FINALLY!
YOU'VE BEEN WITHOUT IT FOR TWO DAYS...
GRANDMA?

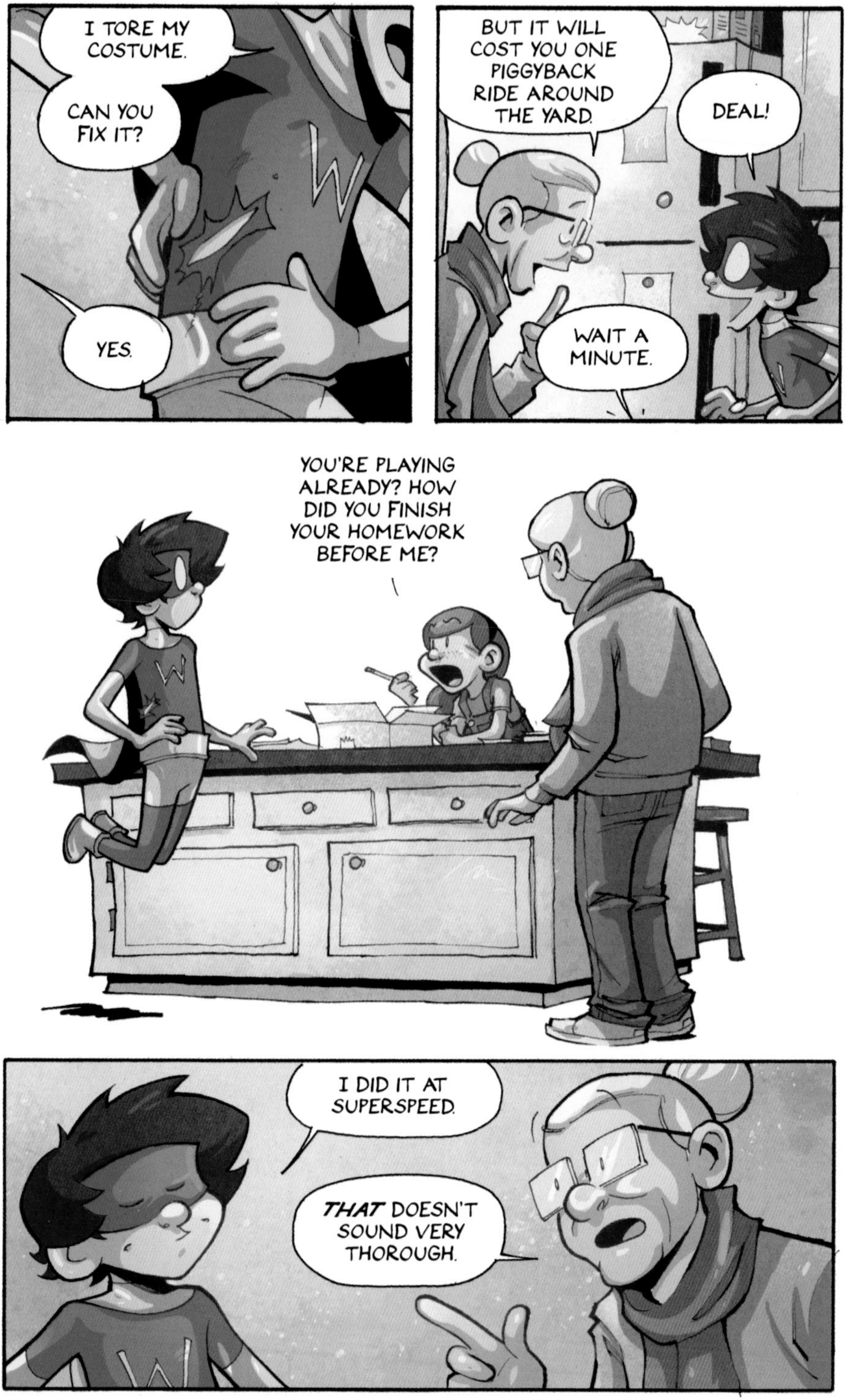
I TORE MY COSTUME.
CAN YOU FIX IT?
YES.
BUT IT WILL COST YOU ONE PIGGYBACK RIDE AROUND THE YARD.
DEAL!
WAIT A MINUTE.
YOU'RE PLAYING ALREADY? HOW DID YOU FINISH YOUR HOMEWORK BEFORE ME?
I DID IT AT SUPERSPEED.
THAT DOESN'T SOUND VERY THOROUGH.

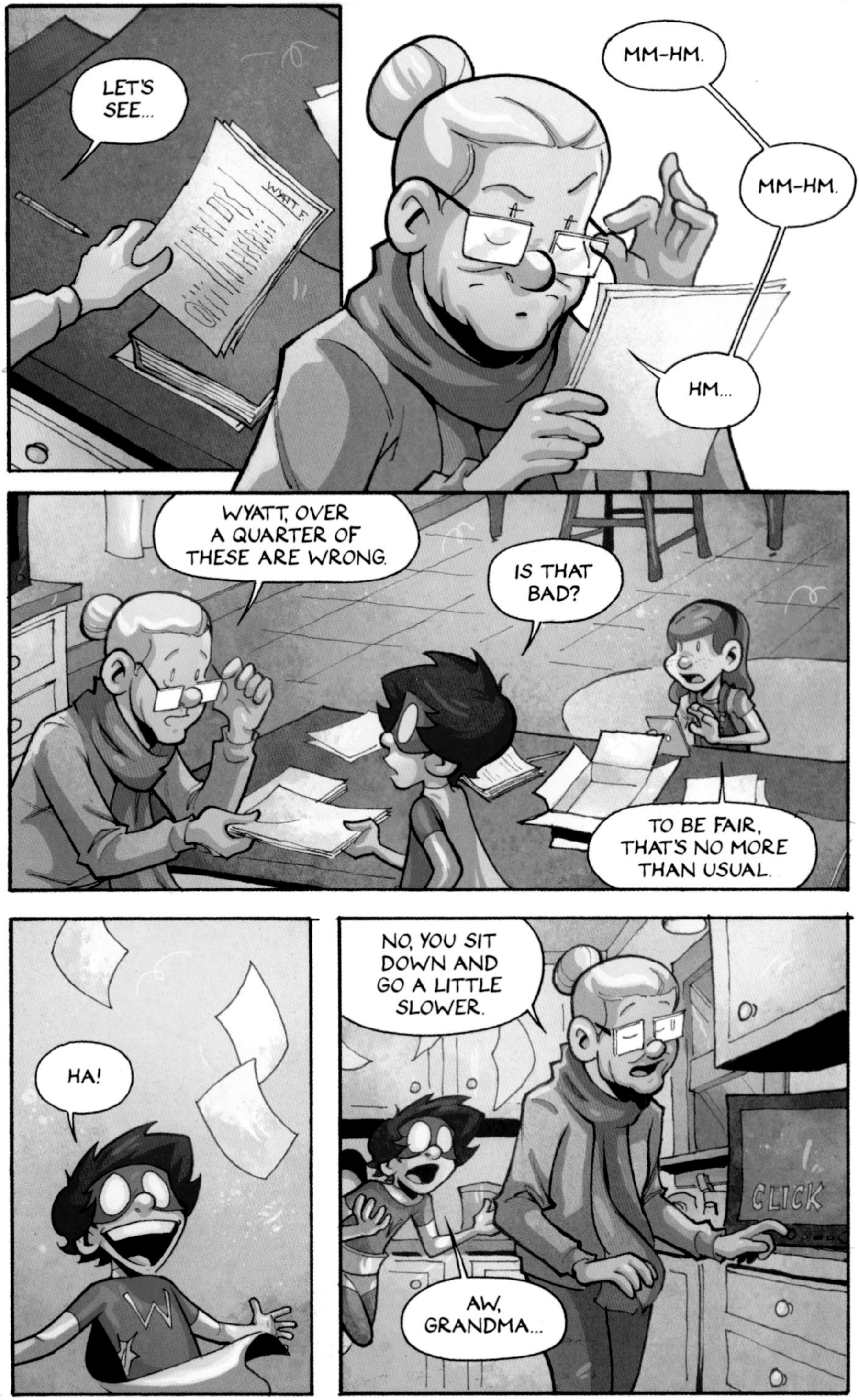
LET'S SEE...
MM-HM.
MM-HM.
HM...
WYATT, OVER A QUARTER OF THESE ARE WRONG.
IS THAT BAD?
TO BE FAIR, THAT'S NO MORE THAN USUAL.
HA!
NO, YOU SIT DOWN AND GO A LITTLE SLOWER.
CLICK
AW, GRANDMA...

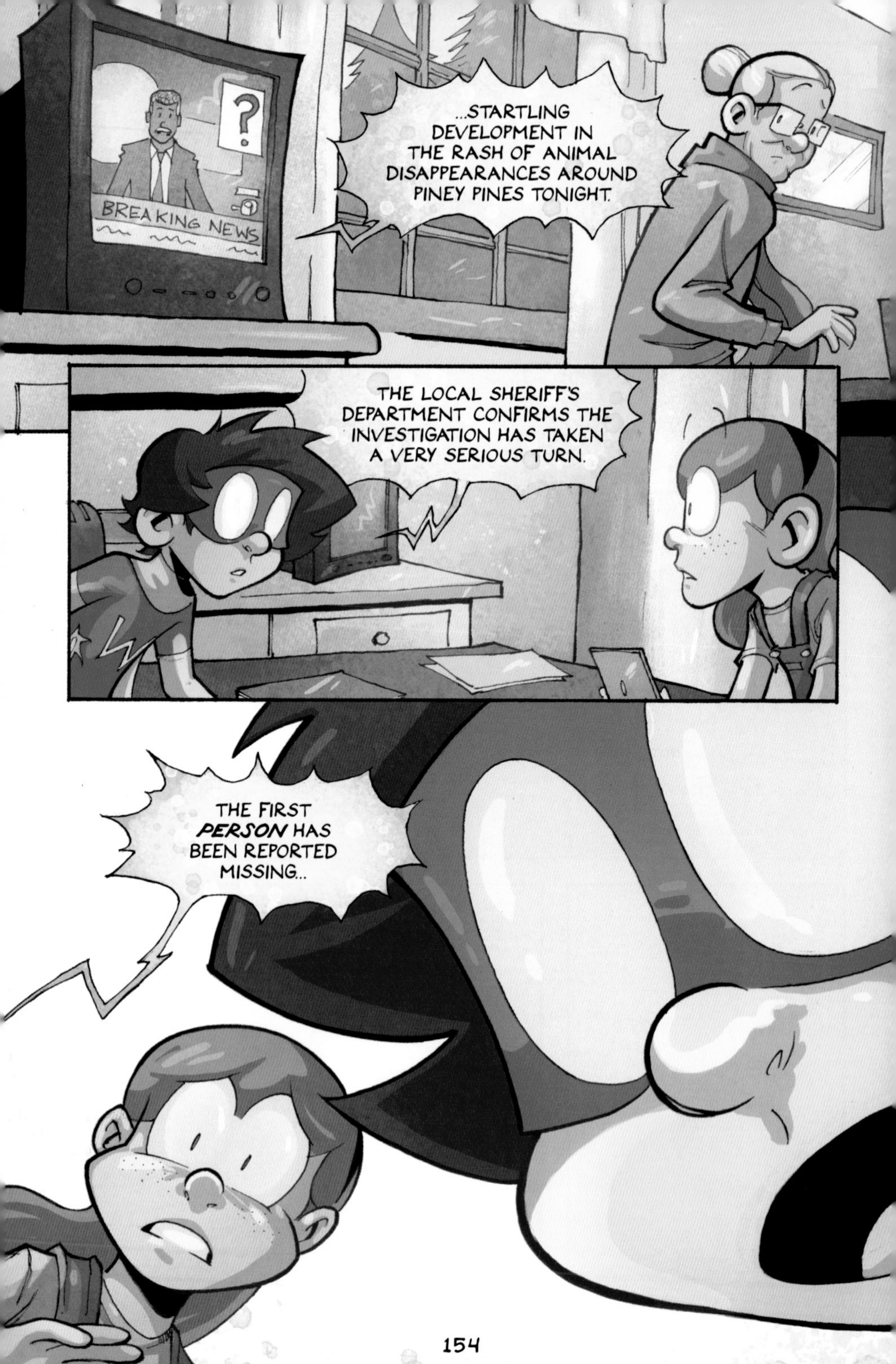
BREAKING NEWS
...STARTLING DEVELOPMENT IN THE RASH OF ANIMAL DISAPPEARANCES AROUND PINEY PINES TONIGHT.
THE LOCAL SHERIFF'S DEPARTMENT CONFIRMS THE INVESTIGATION HAS TAKEN A VERY SERIOUS TURN.
THE FIRST *PERSON* HAS BEEN REPORTED MISSING...

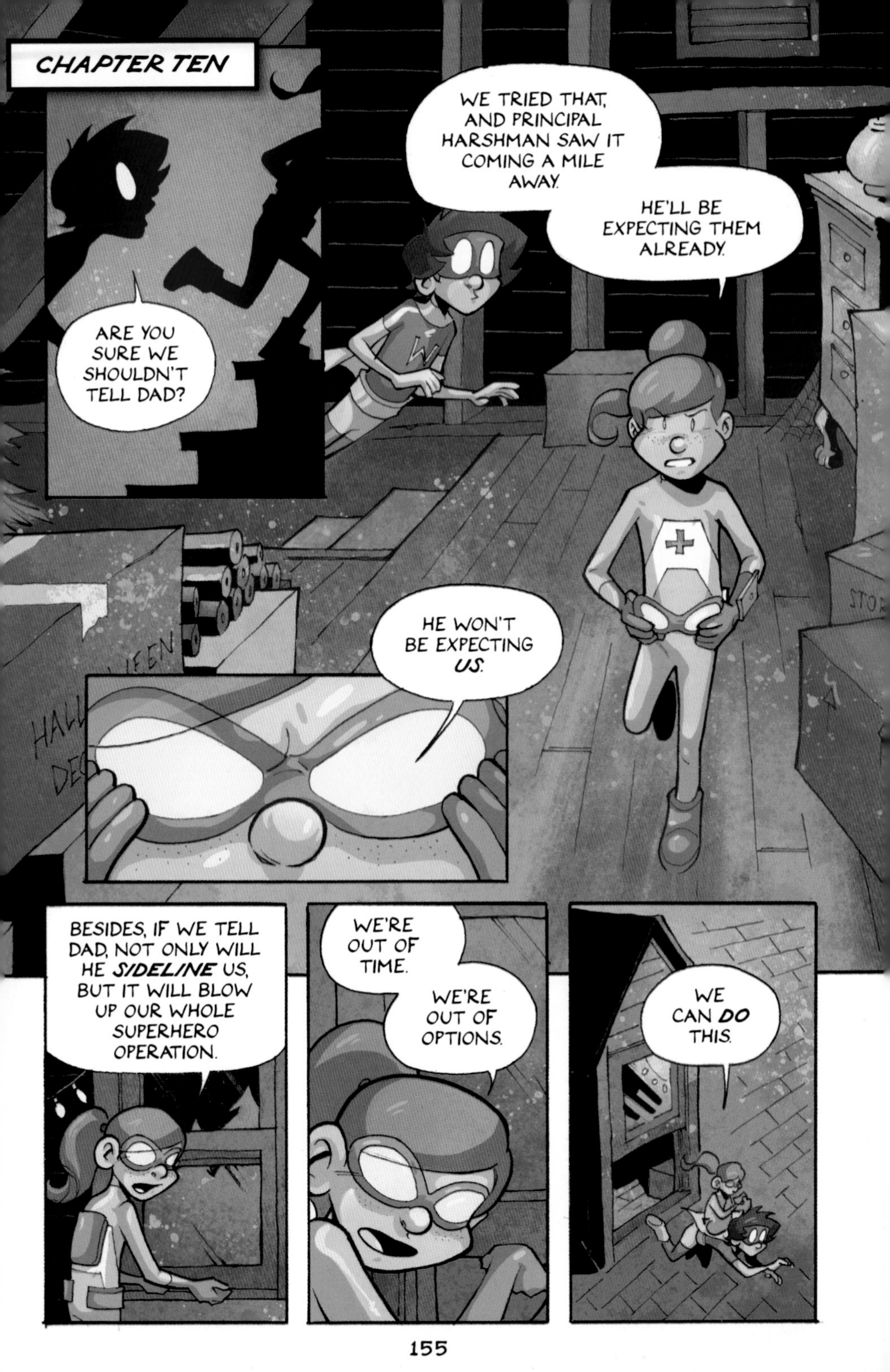
CHAPTER TEN
ARE YOU SURE WE SHOULDN'T TELL DAD?
WE TRIED THAT, AND PRINCIPAL HARSHMAN SAW IT COMING A MILE AWAY.
HE'LL BE EXPECTING THEM ALREADY.
HE WON'T BE EXPECTING *US*.
BESIDES, IF WE TELL DAD, NOT ONLY WILL HE *SIDELINE* US, BUT IT WILL BLOW UP OUR WHOLE SUPERHERO OPERATION.
WE'RE OUT OF TIME.
WE'RE OUT OF OPTIONS.
WE CAN *DO* THIS.

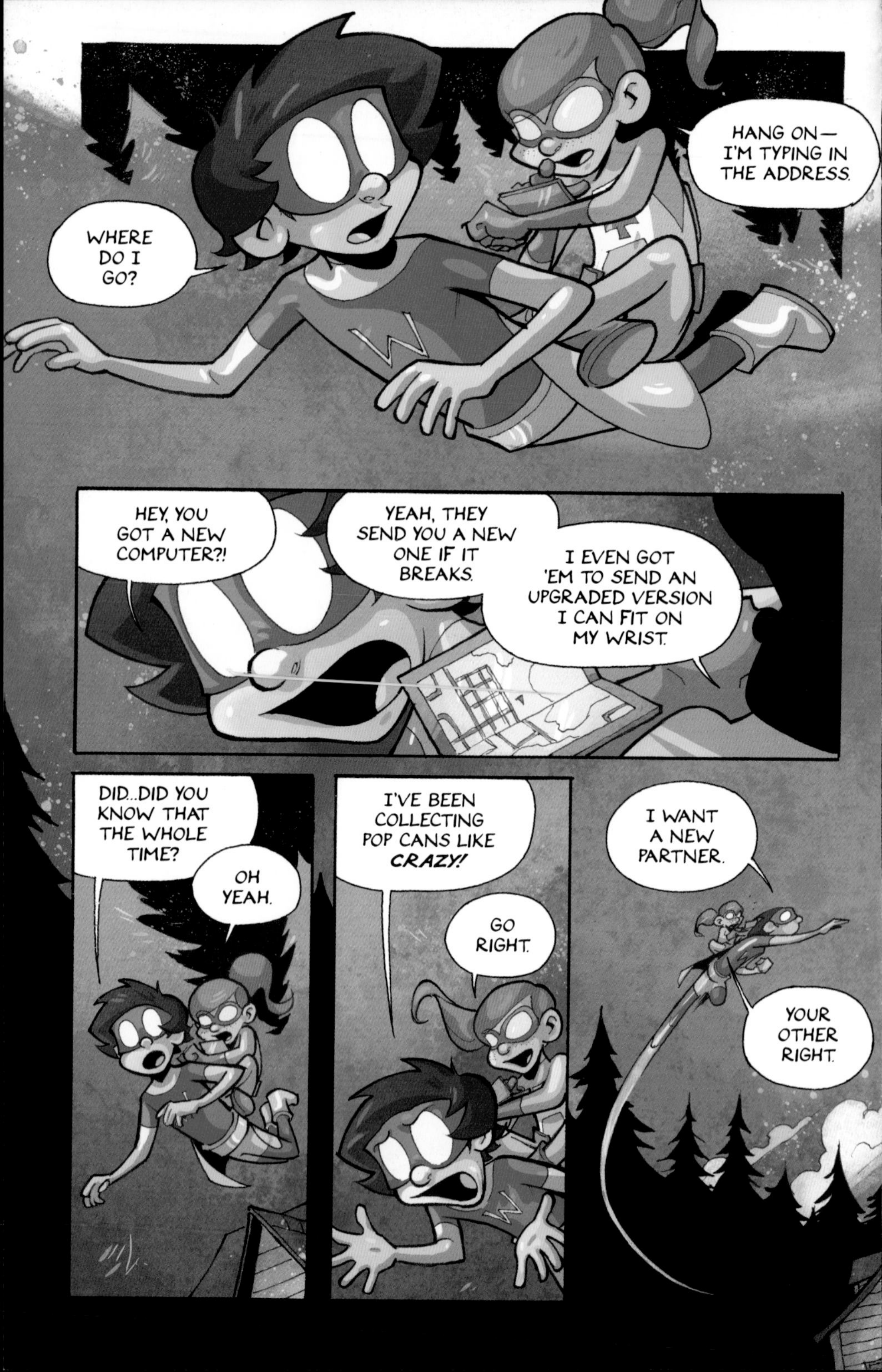
HANG ON— I'M TYPING IN THE ADDRESS.
WHERE DO I GO?
HEY, YOU GOT A NEW COMPUTER?!
YEAH, THEY SEND YOU A NEW ONE IF IT BREAKS.
I EVEN GOT 'EM TO SEND AN UPGRADED VERSION I CAN FIT ON MY WRIST.
DID...DID YOU KNOW THAT THE WHOLE TIME?
OH YEAH.
I'VE BEEN COLLECTING POP CANS LIKE *CRAZY!*
GO RIGHT.
I WANT A NEW PARTNER.
YOUR OTHER RIGHT.

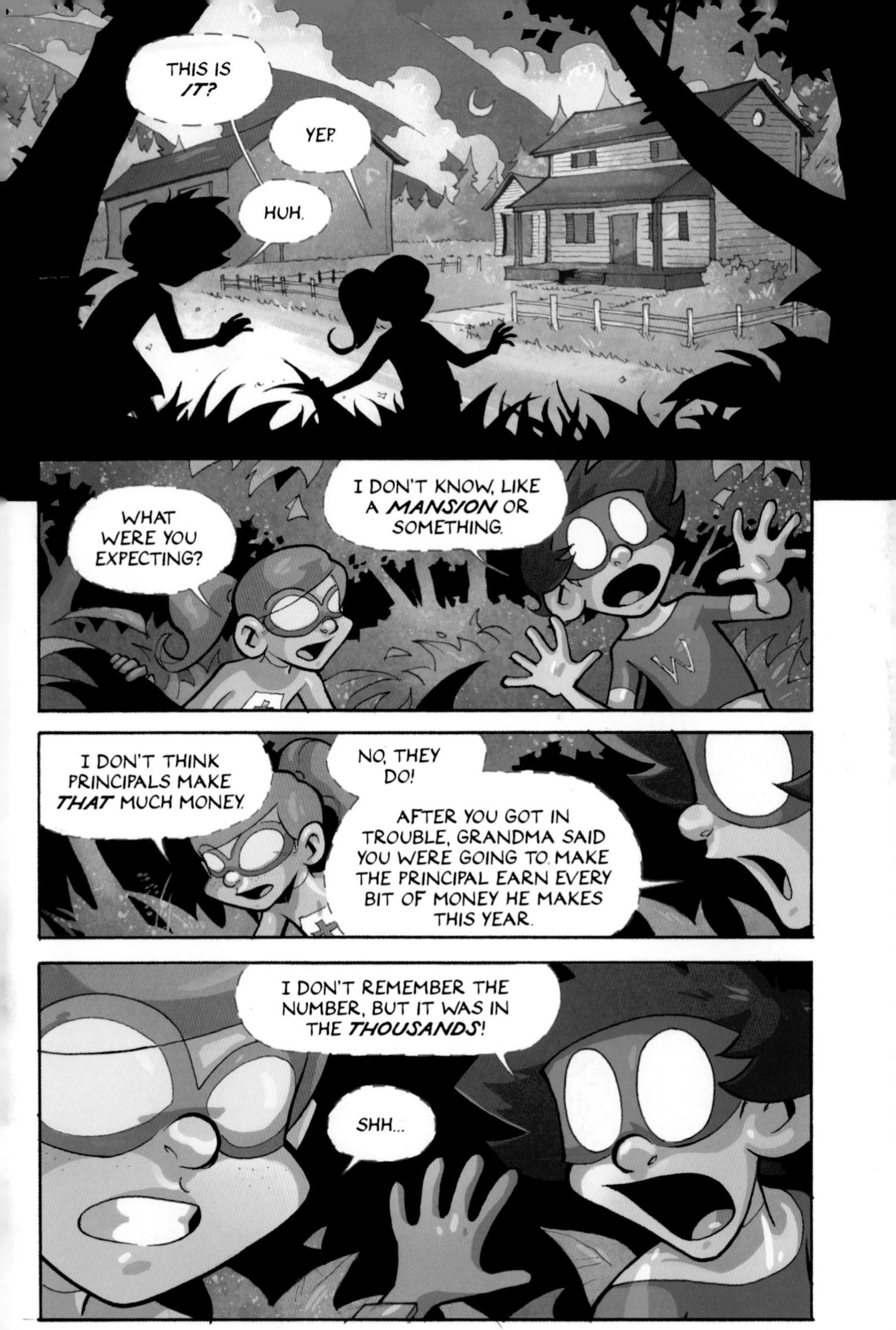
THIS IS *IT?*
YEP.
HUH.
WHAT WERE YOU EXPECTING?
I DON'T KNOW, LIKE A *MANSION* OR SOMETHING.
I DON'T THINK PRINCIPALS MAKE *THAT* MUCH MONEY.
NO, THEY DO!
AFTER YOU GOT IN TROUBLE, GRANDMA SAID YOU WERE GOING TO MAKE THE PRINCIPAL EARN EVERY BIT OF MONEY HE MAKES THIS YEAR.
I DON'T REMEMBER THE NUMBER, BUT IT WAS IN THE *THOUSANDS*!
SHH...

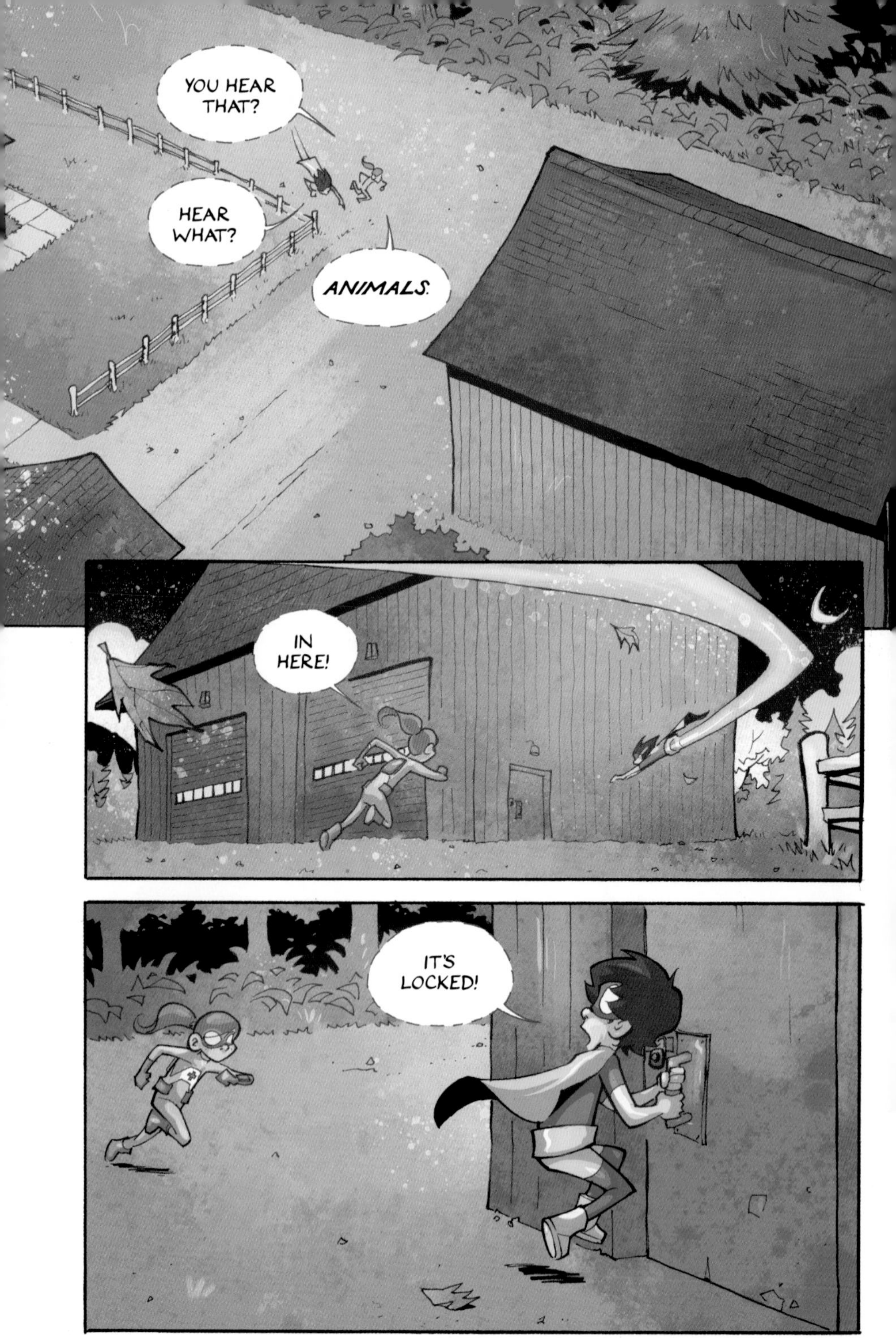
YOU HEAR THAT?
HEAR WHAT?
ANIMALS.
IN HERE!
IT'S LOCKED!

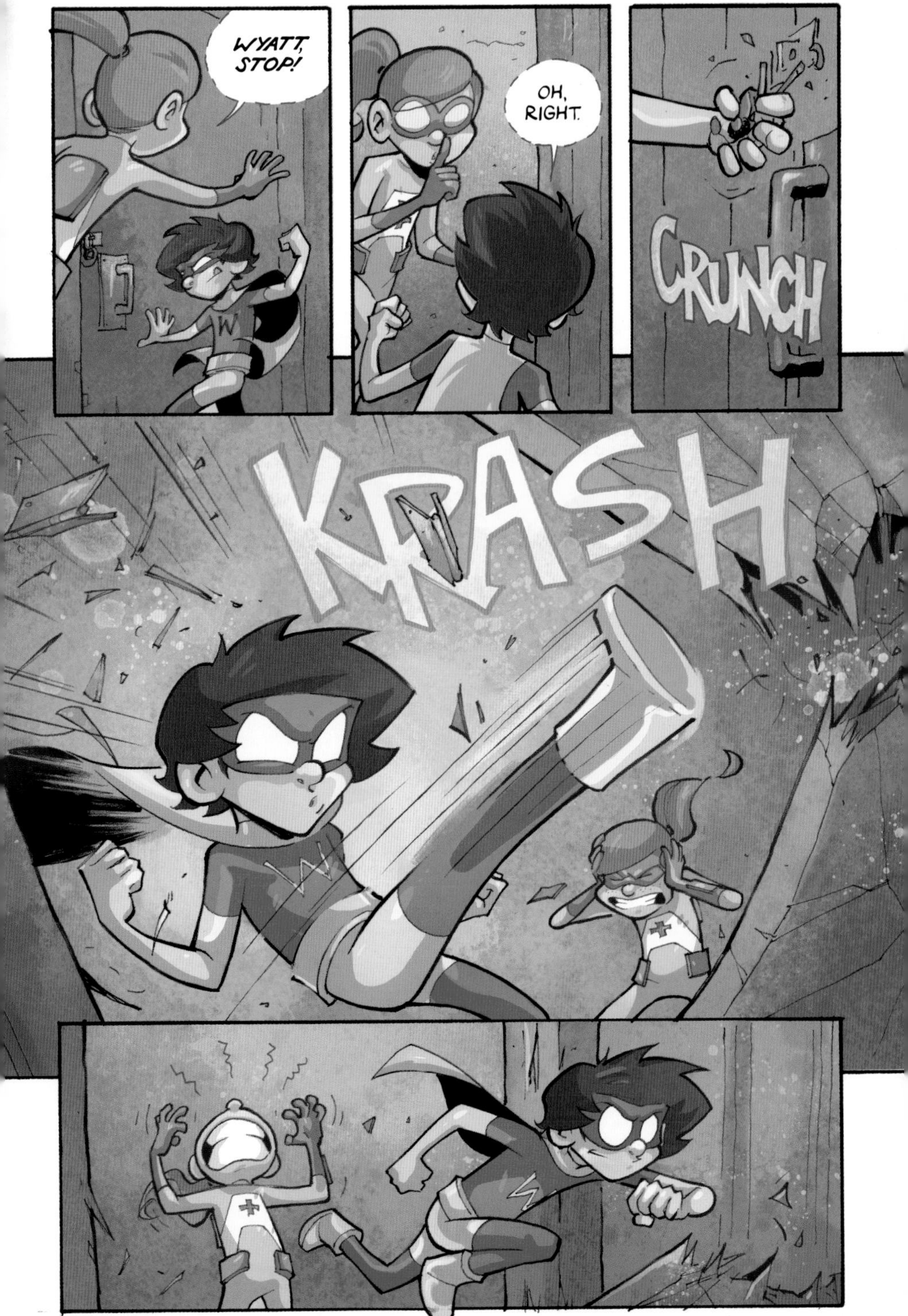
WYATT, STOP!
OH, RIGHT.
CRUNCH
KRASH

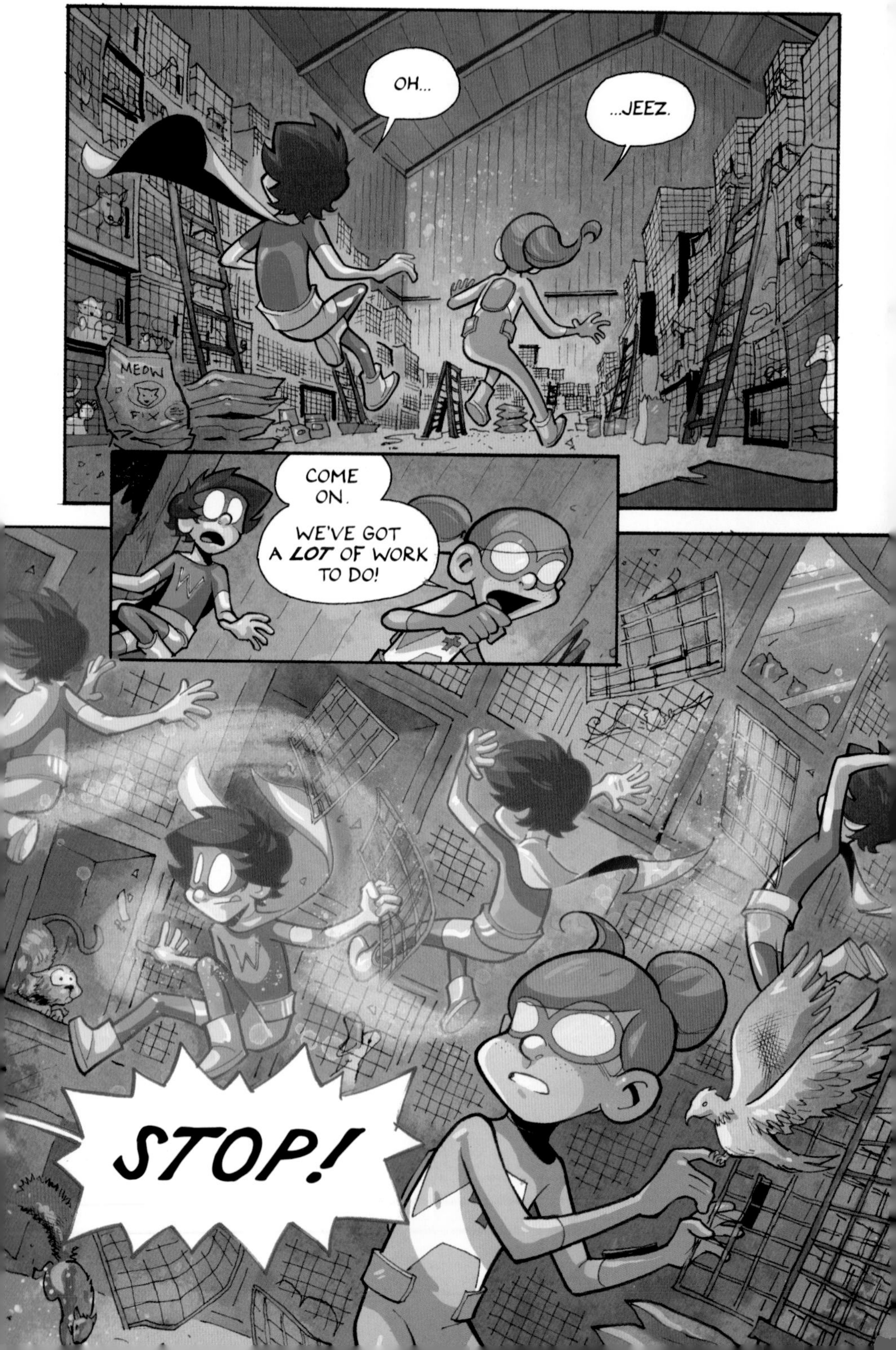
OH...
...JEEZ.
COME ON.
WE'VE GOT A *LOT* OF WORK TO DO!
STOP!
MEOW FIX

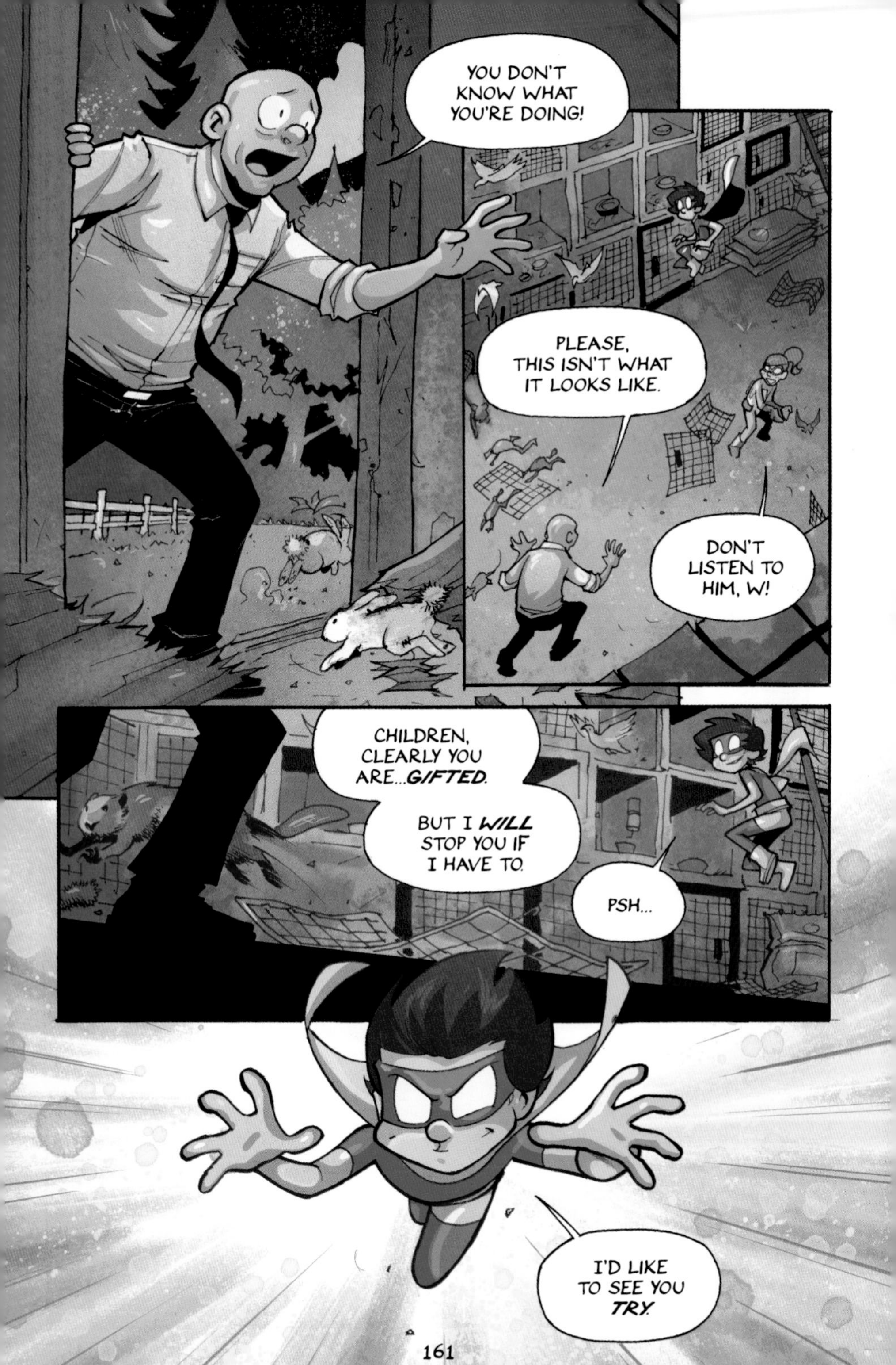
YOU DON'T KNOW WHAT YOU'RE DOING!
PLEASE, THIS ISN'T WHAT IT LOOKS LIKE.
DON'T LISTEN TO HIM, W!
CHILDREN, CLEARLY YOU ARE...GIFTED.
BUT I WILL STOP YOU IF I HAVE TO.
PSH...
I'D LIKE TO SEE YOU TRY.

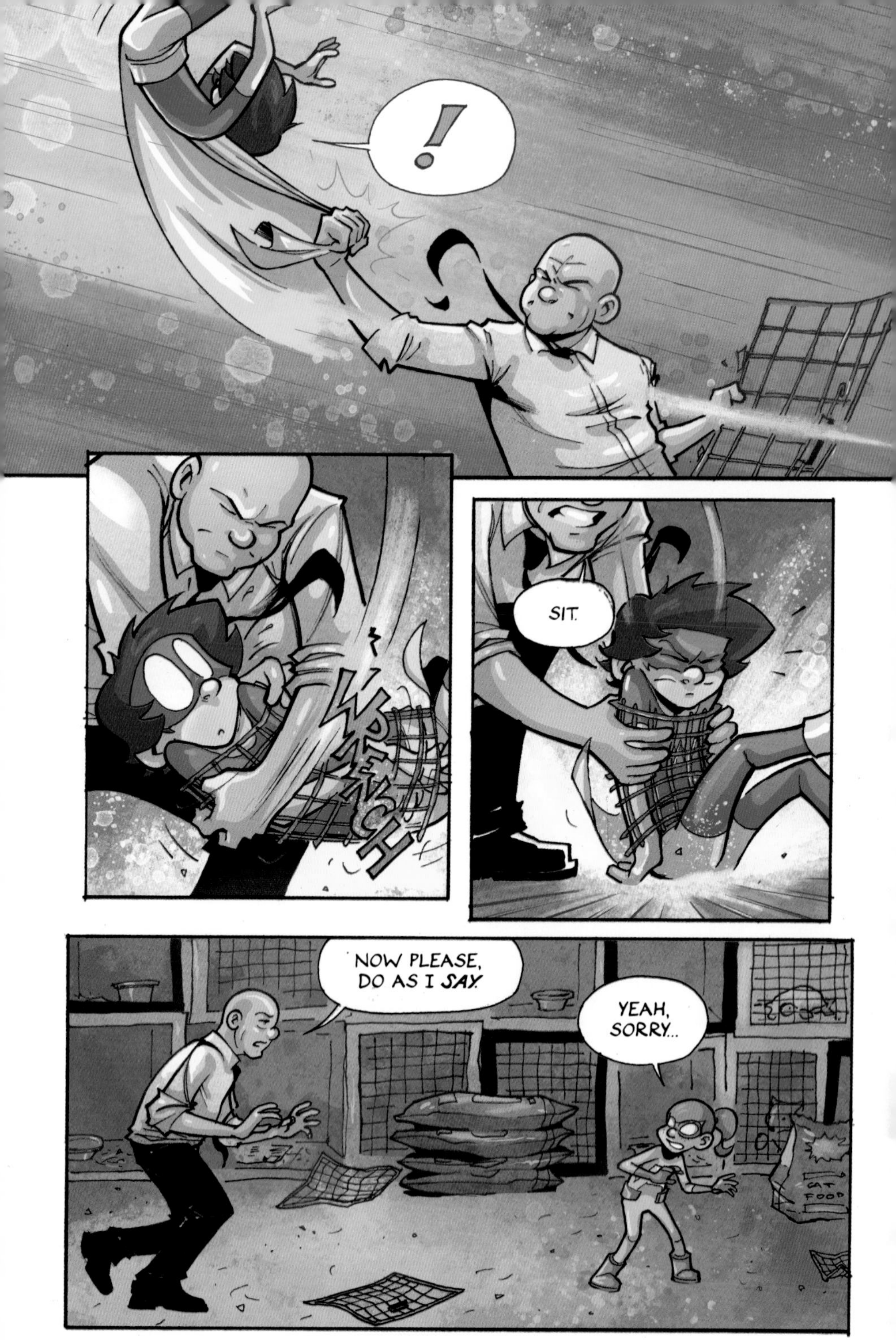

!
WRENCH
SIT.
NOW PLEASE, DO AS I SAY.
YEAH, SORRY...
CAT FOOD

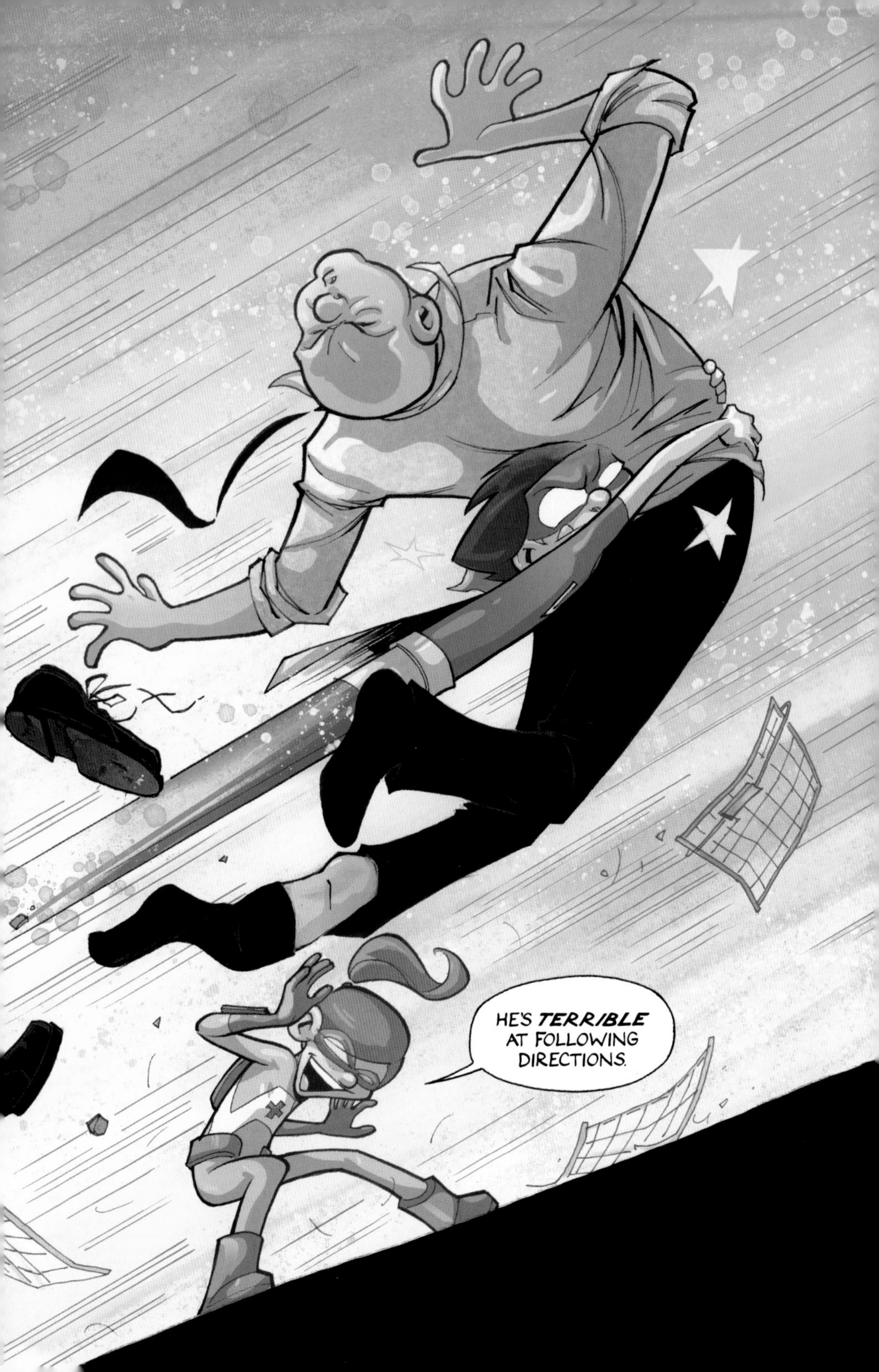
HE'S *TERRIBLE* AT FOLLOWING DIRECTIONS.

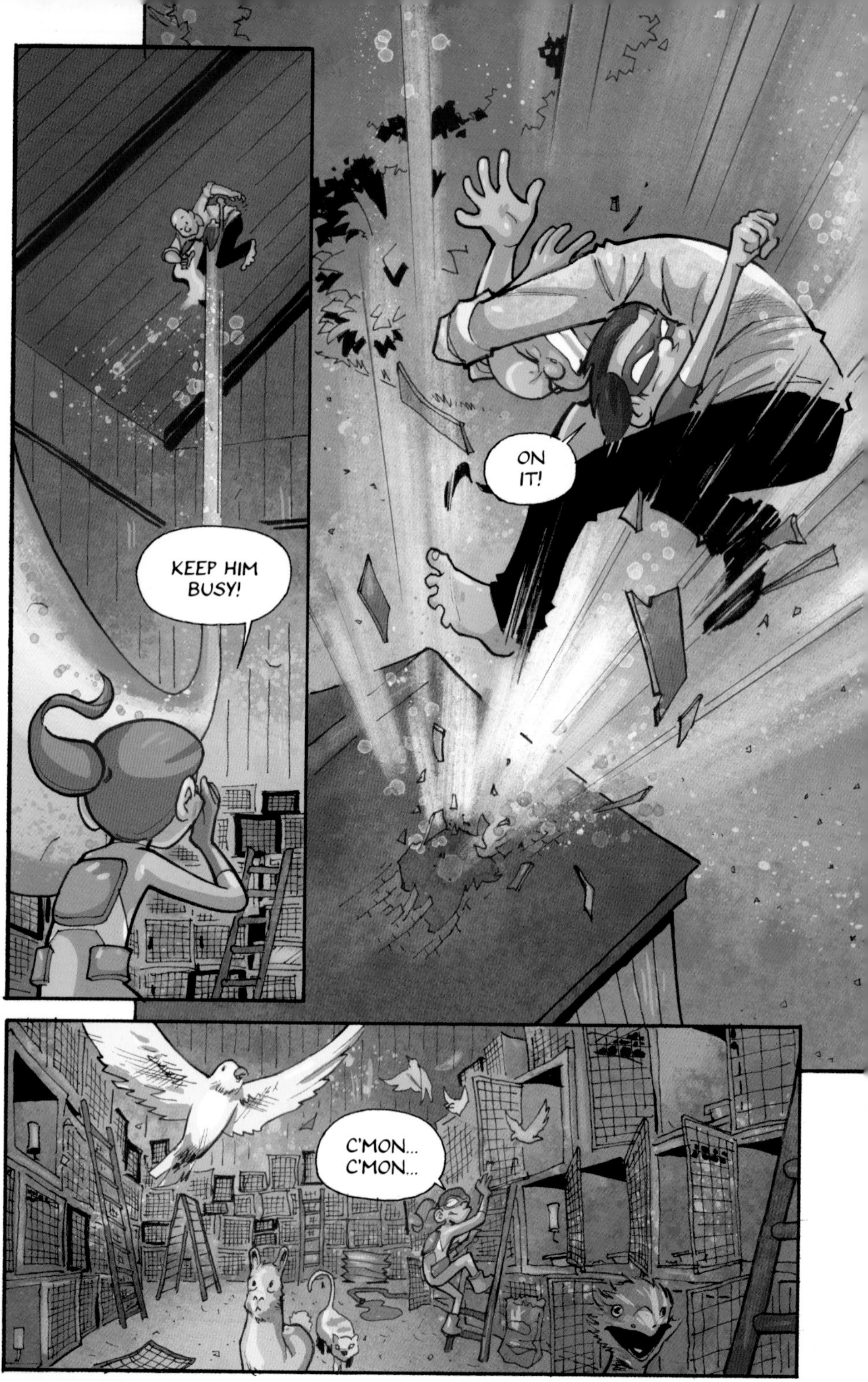
ON IT!
KEEP HIM BUSY!
C'MON... C'MON...

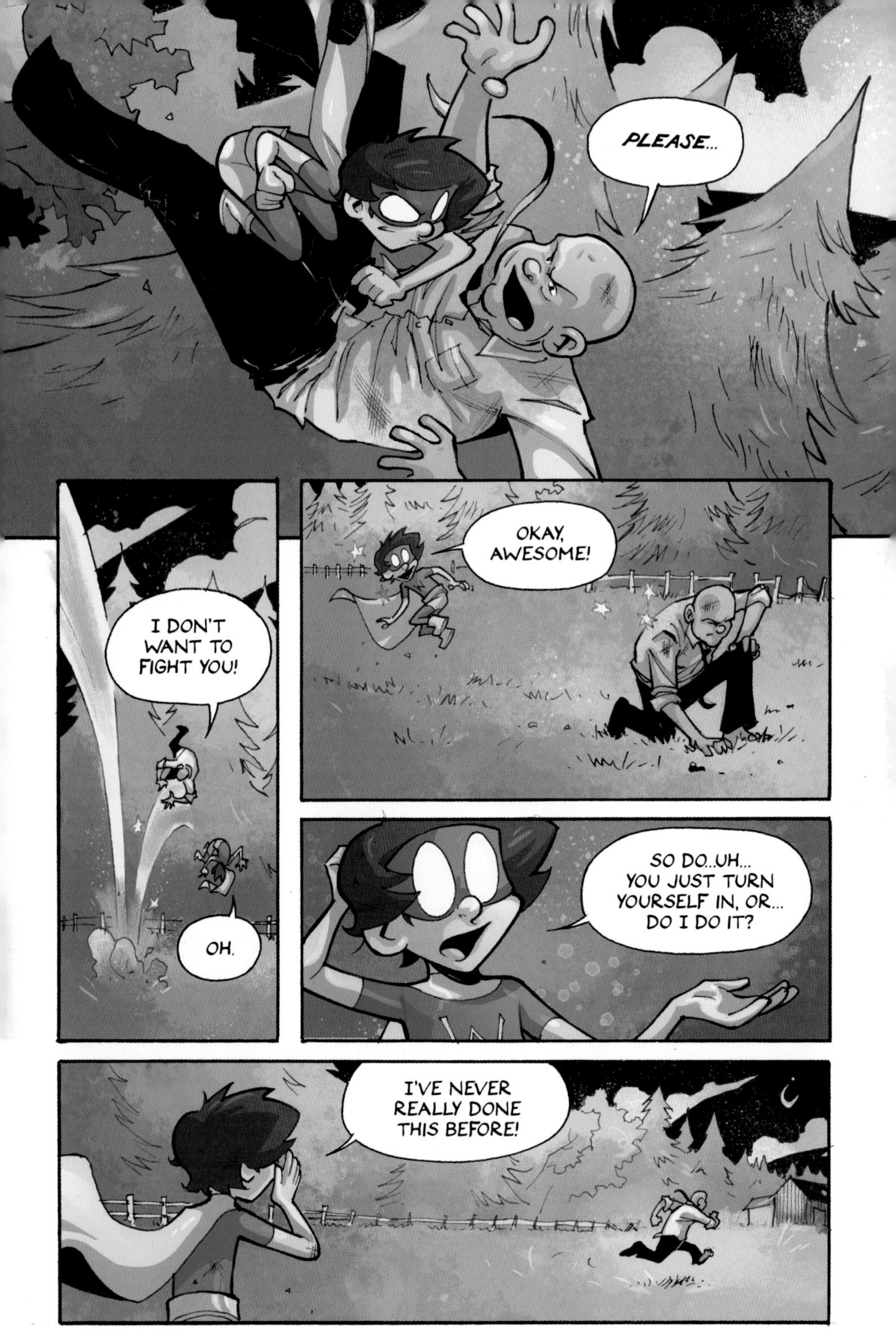
PLEASE...
I DON'T WANT TO FIGHT YOU!
OH.
OKAY, AWESOME!
SO DO...UH... YOU JUST TURN YOURSELF IN, OR... DO I DO IT?
I'VE NEVER REALLY DONE THIS BEFORE!

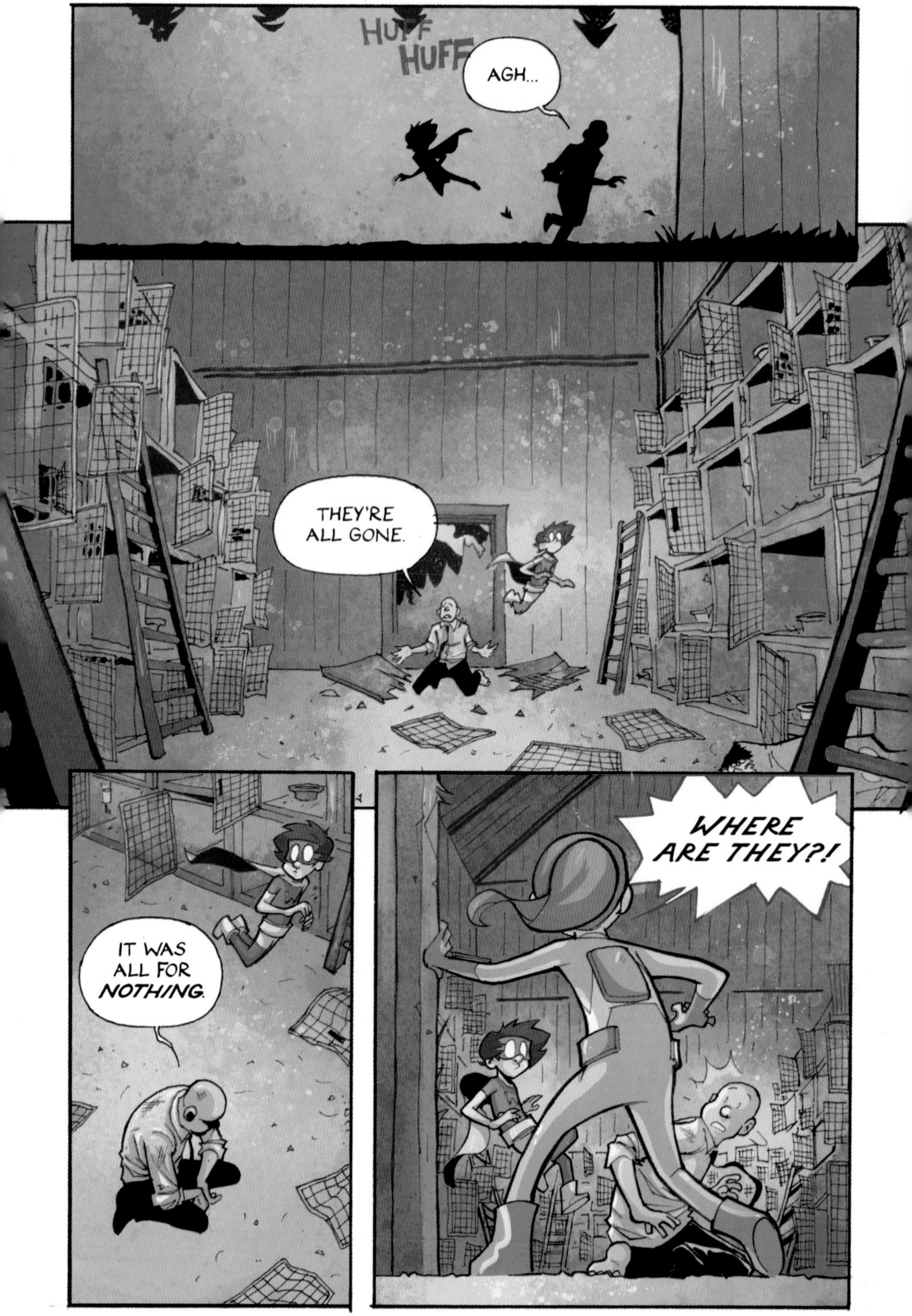
HUFF
HUFF
AGH...
THEY'RE ALL GONE.
IT WAS ALL FOR *NOTHING*.
WHERE ARE THEY?!

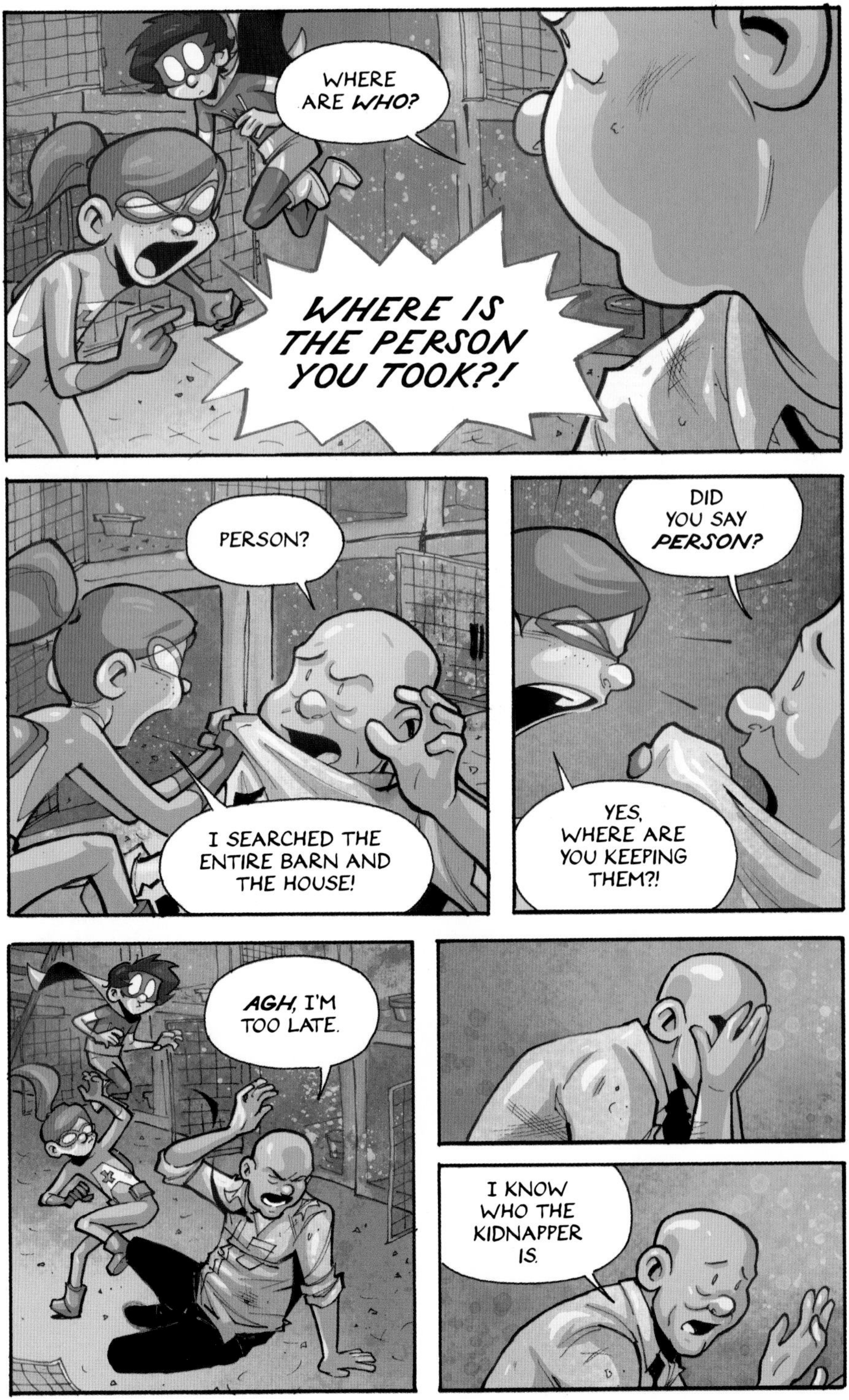
WHERE ARE *WHO?*
WHERE IS THE PERSON YOU TOOK?!
PERSON?
I SEARCHED THE ENTIRE BARN AND THE HOUSE!
DID YOU SAY *PERSON?*
YES, WHERE ARE YOU KEEPING THEM?!
AGH, I'M TOO LATE.
I KNOW WHO THE KIDNAPPER IS.

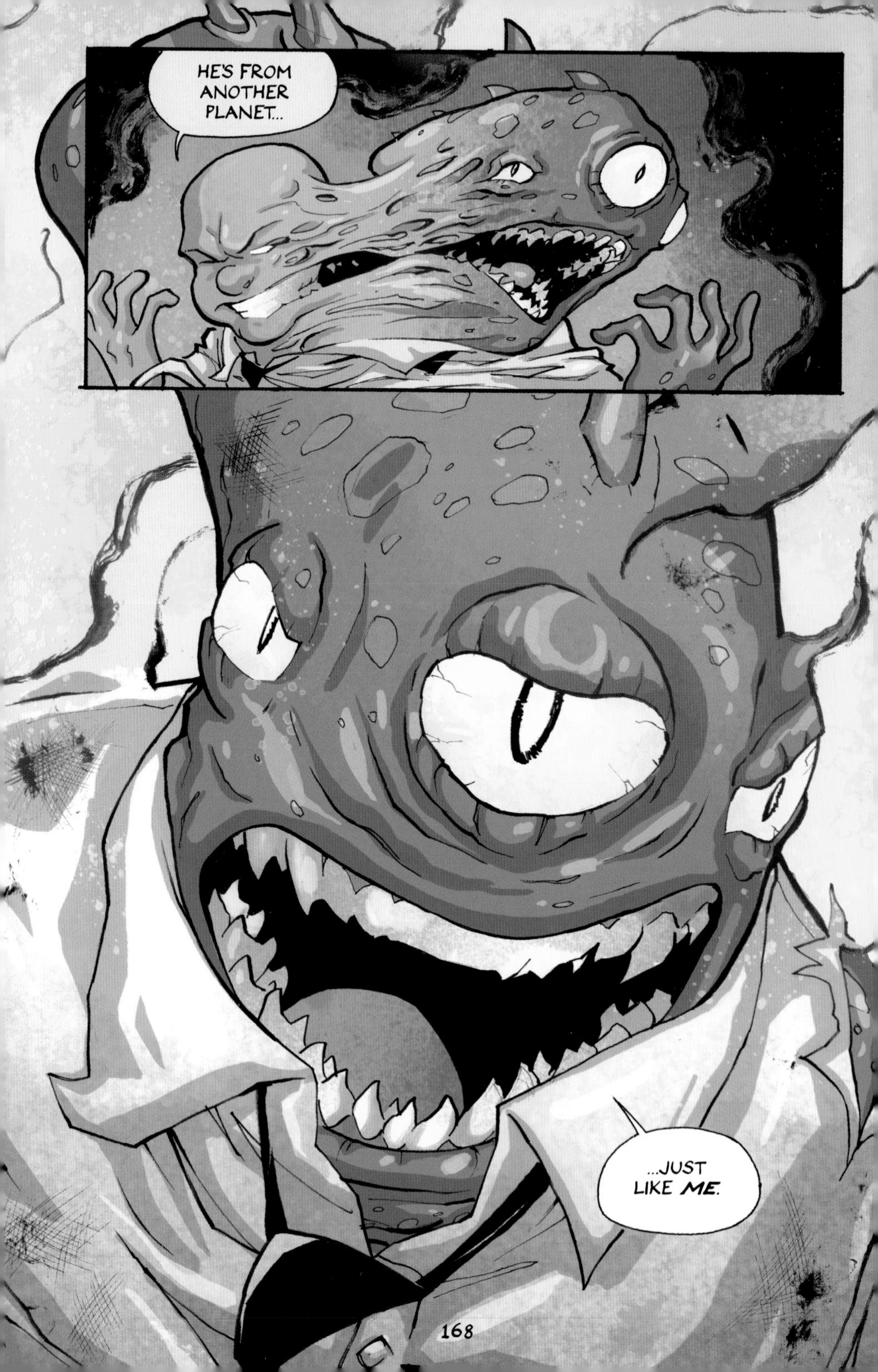
HE'S FROM ANOTHER PLANET...
...JUST LIKE *ME*.

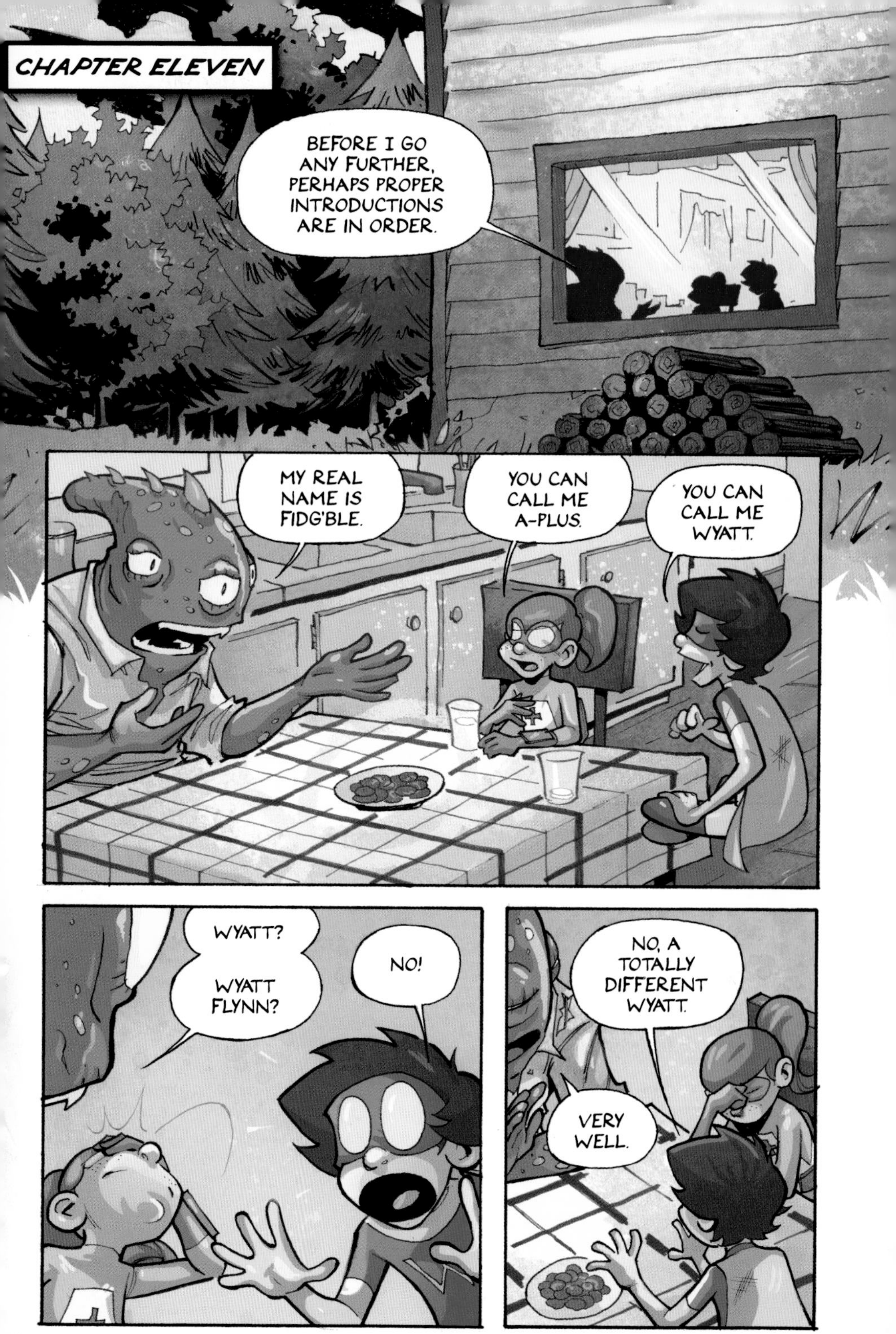
CHAPTER ELEVEN
BEFORE I GO ANY FURTHER, PERHAPS PROPER INTRODUCTIONS ARE IN ORDER.
MY REAL NAME IS FIDG'BLE.
YOU CAN CALL ME A-PLUS.
YOU CAN CALL ME WYATT.
WYATT?
WYATT FLYNN?
NO!
NO, A TOTALLY DIFFERENT WYATT.
VERY WELL.

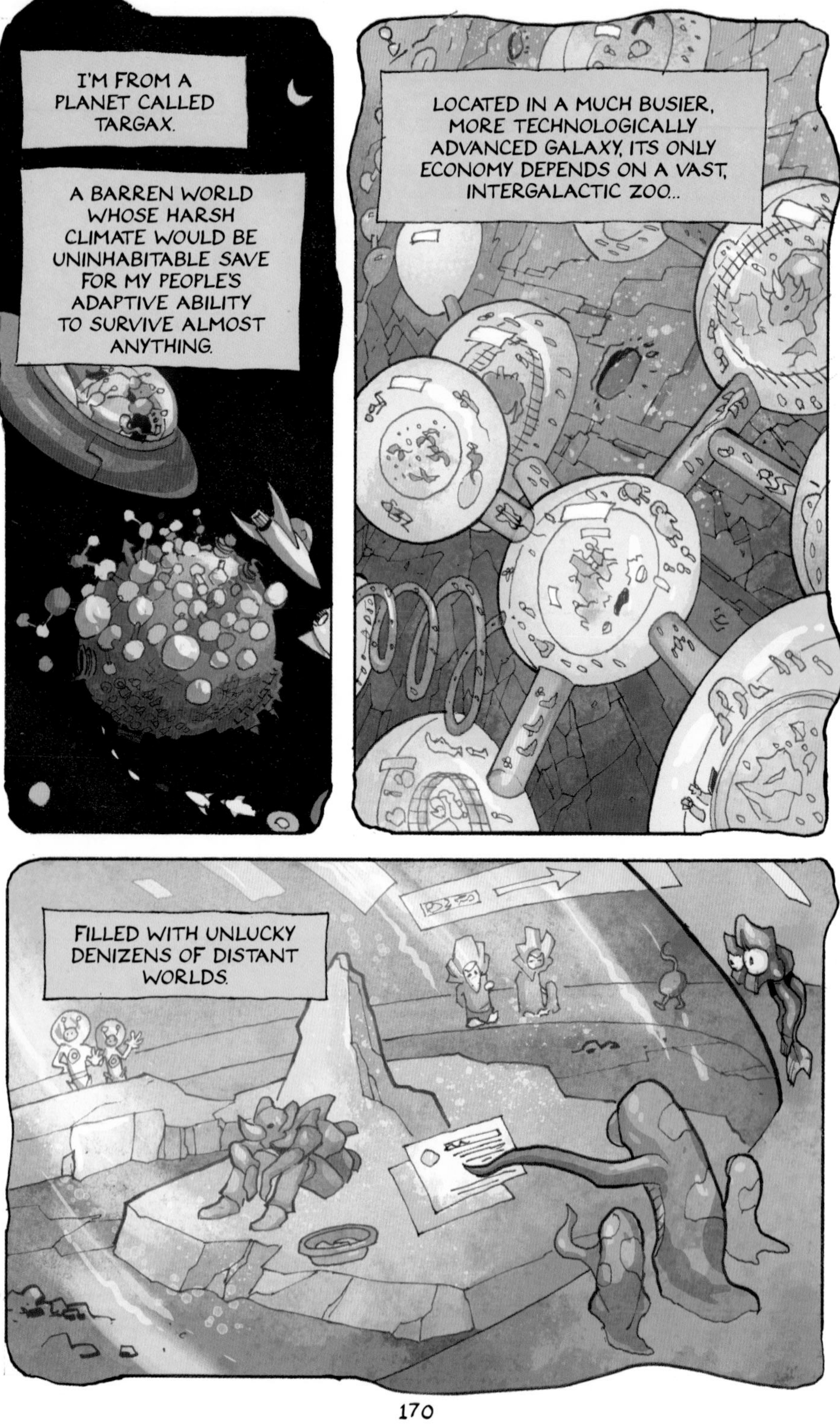
I'M FROM A PLANET CALLED TARGAX.
A BARREN WORLD WHOSE HARSH CLIMATE WOULD BE UNINHABITABLE SAVE FOR MY PEOPLE'S ADAPTIVE ABILITY TO SURVIVE ALMOST ANYTHING.
LOCATED IN A MUCH BUSIER, MORE TECHNOLOGICALLY ADVANCED GALAXY, ITS ONLY ECONOMY DEPENDS ON A VAST, INTERGALACTIC ZOO...
FILLED WITH UNLUCKY DENIZENS OF DISTANT WORLDS.

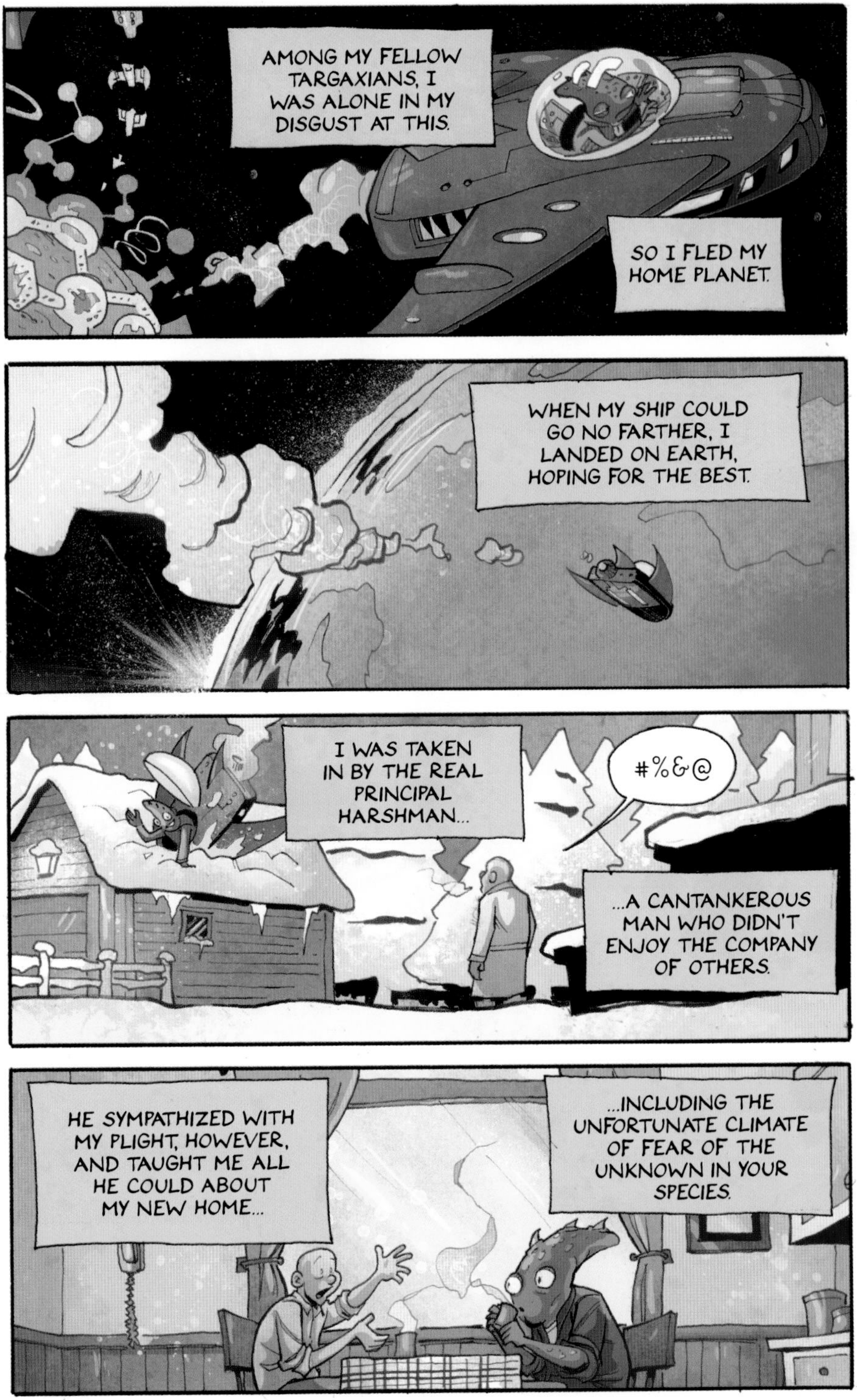
AMONG MY FELLOW TARGAXIANS, I WAS ALONE IN MY DISGUST AT THIS.
SO I FLED MY HOME PLANET.
WHEN MY SHIP COULD GO NO FARTHER, I LANDED ON EARTH, HOPING FOR THE BEST.
I WAS TAKEN IN BY THE REAL PRINCIPAL HARSHMAN...
#%&@
...A CANTANKEROUS MAN WHO DIDN'T ENJOY THE COMPANY OF OTHERS.
HE SYMPATHIZED WITH MY PLIGHT, HOWEVER, AND TAUGHT ME ALL HE COULD ABOUT MY NEW HOME...
...INCLUDING THE UNFORTUNATE CLIMATE OF FEAR OF THE UNKNOWN IN YOUR SPECIES.

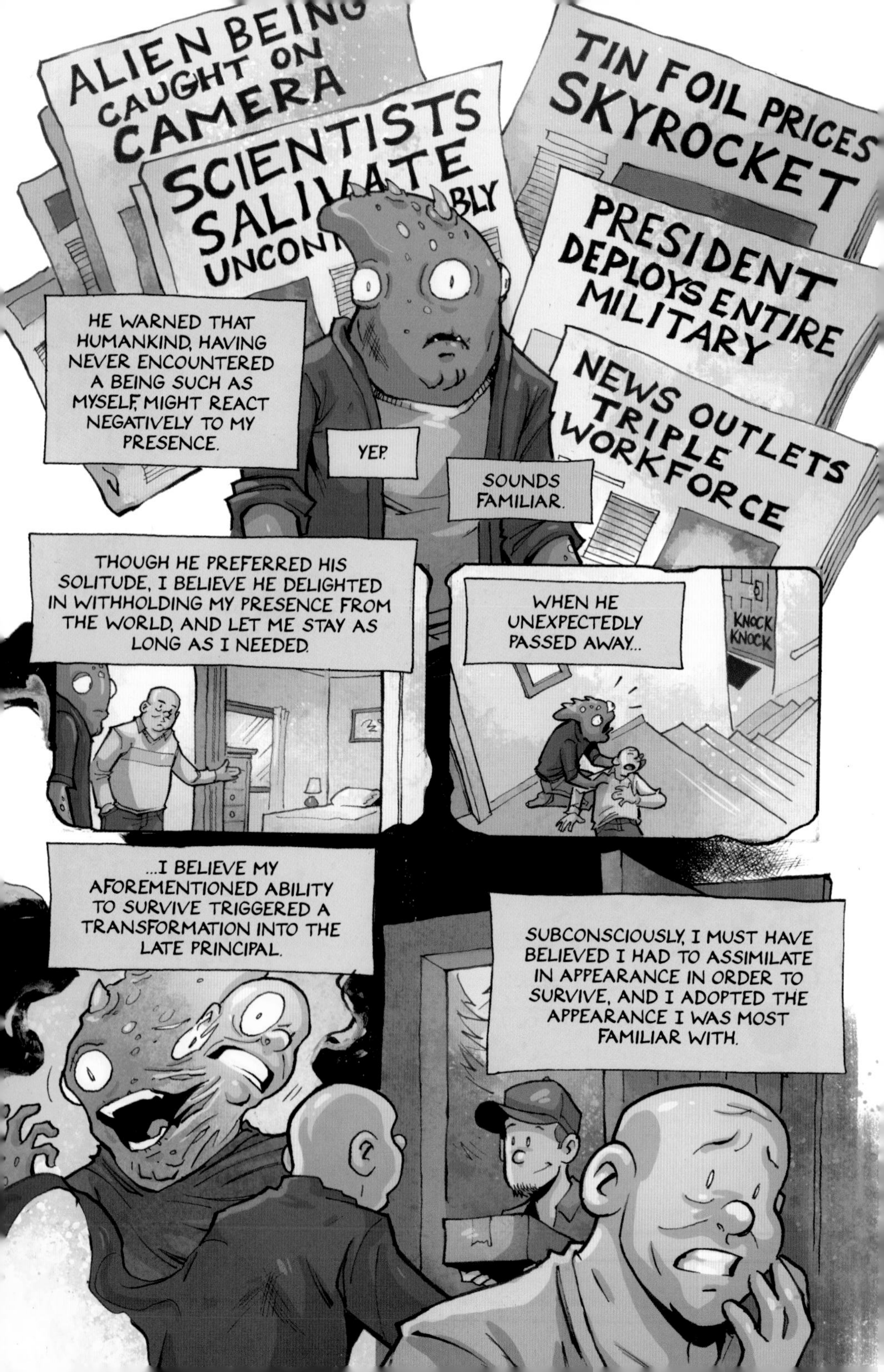
ALIEN BEING CAUGHT ON CAMERA
SCIENTISTS SALIVATE UNCON... BLY
TIN FOIL PRICES SKYROCKET
PRESIDENT DEPLOYS ENTIRE MILITARY
NEWS OUTLETS TRIPLE WORKFORCE
HE WARNED THAT HUMANKIND, HAVING NEVER ENCOUNTERED A BEING SUCH AS MYSELF, MIGHT REACT NEGATIVELY TO MY PRESENCE.
YEP.
SOUNDS FAMILIAR.
THOUGH HE PREFERRED HIS SOLITUDE, I BELIEVE HE DELIGHTED IN WITHHOLDING MY PRESENCE FROM THE WORLD, AND LET ME STAY AS LONG AS I NEEDED.
WHEN HE UNEXPECTEDLY PASSED AWAY...
KNOCK KNOCK
...I BELIEVE MY AFOREMENTIONED ABILITY TO SURVIVE TRIGGERED A TRANSFORMATION INTO THE LATE PRINCIPAL.
SUBCONSCIOUSLY, I MUST HAVE BELIEVED I HAD TO ASSIMILATE IN APPEARANCE IN ORDER TO SURVIVE, AND I ADOPTED THE APPEARANCE I WAS MOST FAMILIAR WITH.

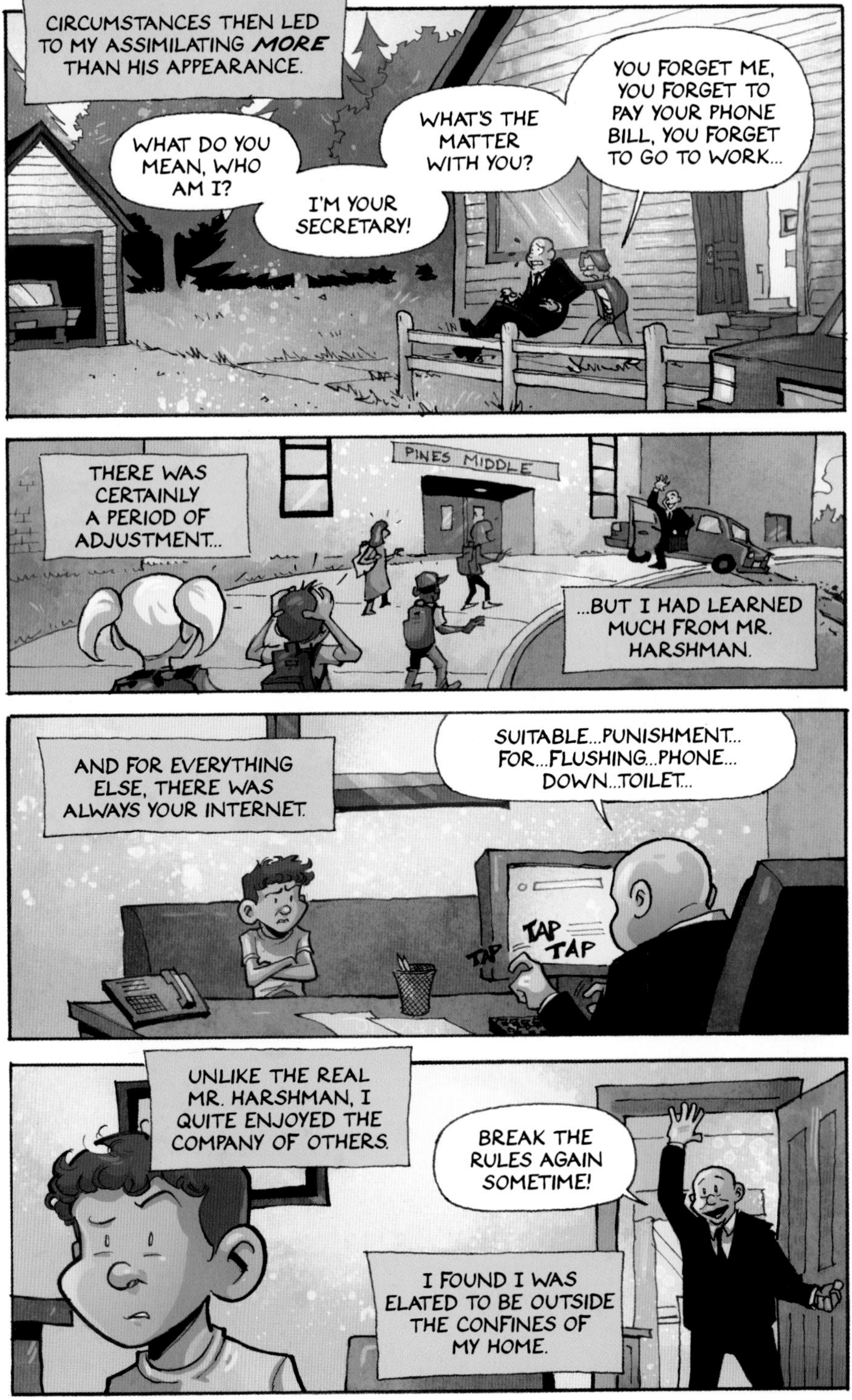
CIRCUMSTANCES THEN LED TO MY ASSIMILATING *MORE* THAN HIS APPEARANCE.
WHAT DO YOU MEAN, WHO AM I?
I'M YOUR SECRETARY!
WHAT'S THE MATTER WITH YOU?
YOU FORGET ME, YOU FORGET TO PAY YOUR PHONE BILL, YOU FORGET TO GO TO WORK...
PINES MIDDLE
THERE WAS CERTAINLY A PERIOD OF ADJUSTMENT...
...BUT I HAD LEARNED MUCH FROM MR. HARSHMAN.
AND FOR EVERYTHING ELSE, THERE WAS ALWAYS YOUR INTERNET.
SUITABLE...PUNISHMENT... FOR...FLUSHING...PHONE... DOWN...TOILET...
TAP
TAP
TAP
UNLIKE THE REAL MR. HARSHMAN, I QUITE ENJOYED THE COMPANY OF OTHERS.
BREAK THE RULES AGAIN SOMETIME!
I FOUND I WAS ELATED TO BE OUTSIDE THE CONFINES OF MY HOME.

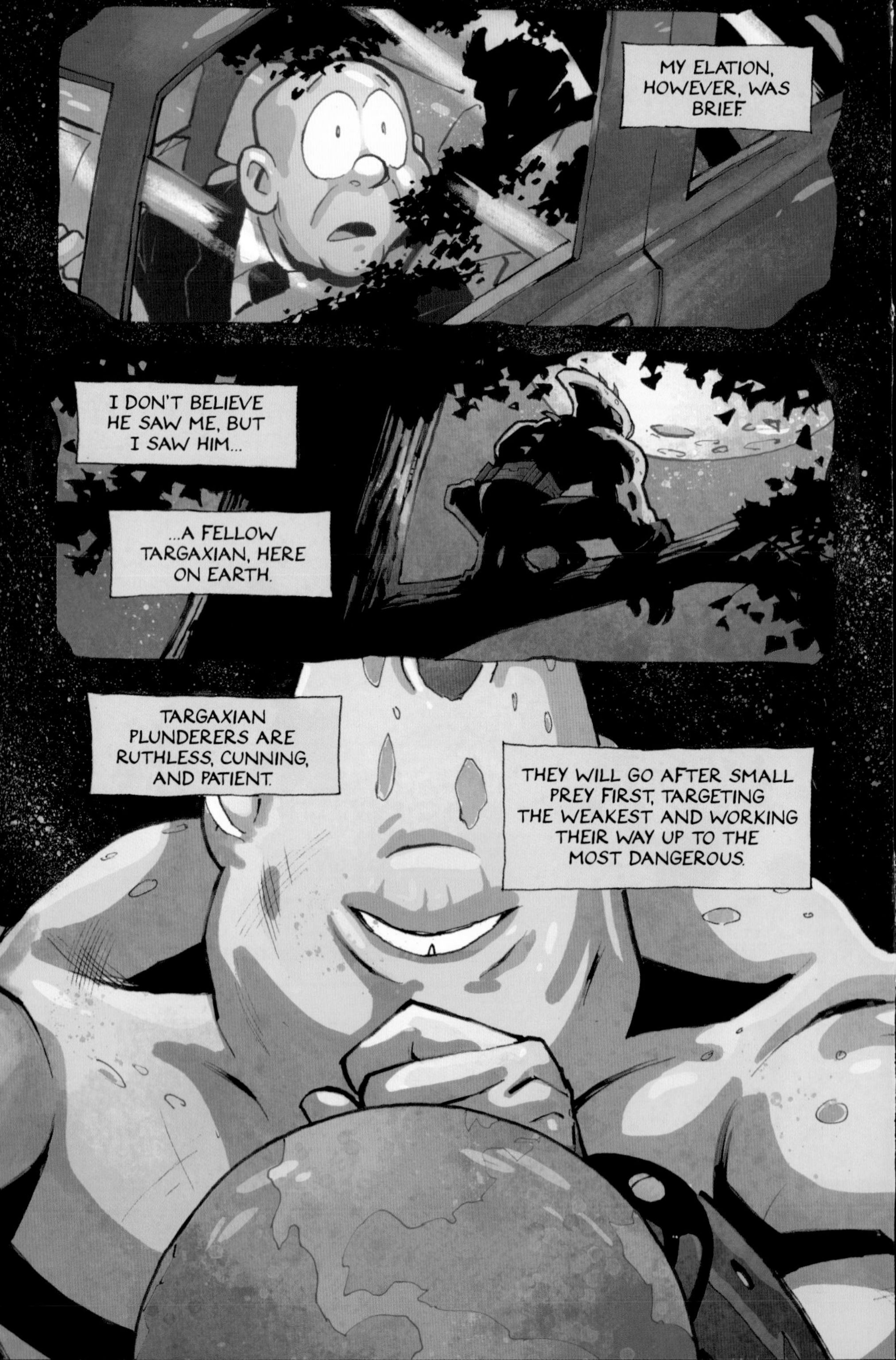
MY ELATION, HOWEVER, WAS BRIEF.
I DON'T BELIEVE HE SAW ME, BUT I SAW HIM...
...A FELLOW TARGAXIAN, HERE ON EARTH.
TARGAXIAN PLUNDERERS ARE RUTHLESS, CUNNING, AND PATIENT.
THEY WILL GO AFTER SMALL PREY FIRST, TARGETING THE WEAKEST AND WORKING THEIR WAY UP TO THE MOST DANGEROUS.

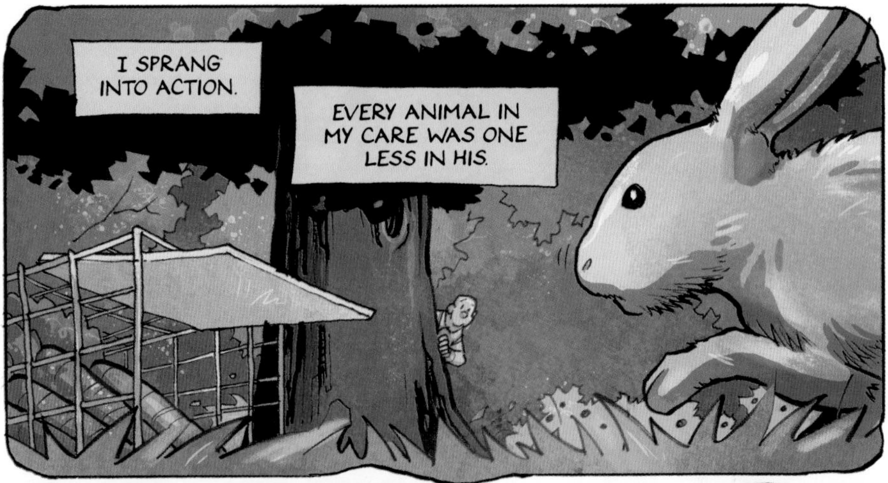
I SPRANG INTO ACTION.
EVERY ANIMAL IN MY CARE WAS ONE LESS IN HIS.

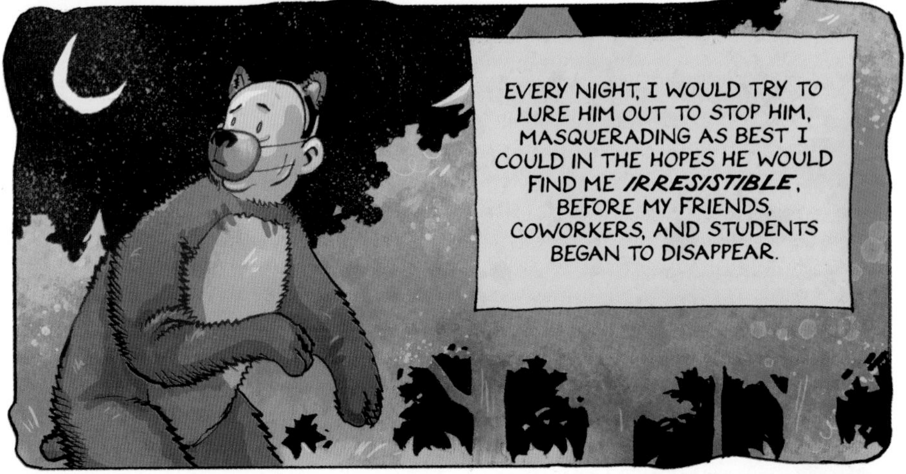
EVERY NIGHT, I WOULD TRY TO LURE HIM OUT TO STOP HIM, MASQUERADING AS BEST I COULD IN THE HOPES HE WOULD FIND ME ***IRRESISTIBLE***, BEFORE MY FRIENDS, COWORKERS, AND STUDENTS BEGAN TO DISAPPEAR.

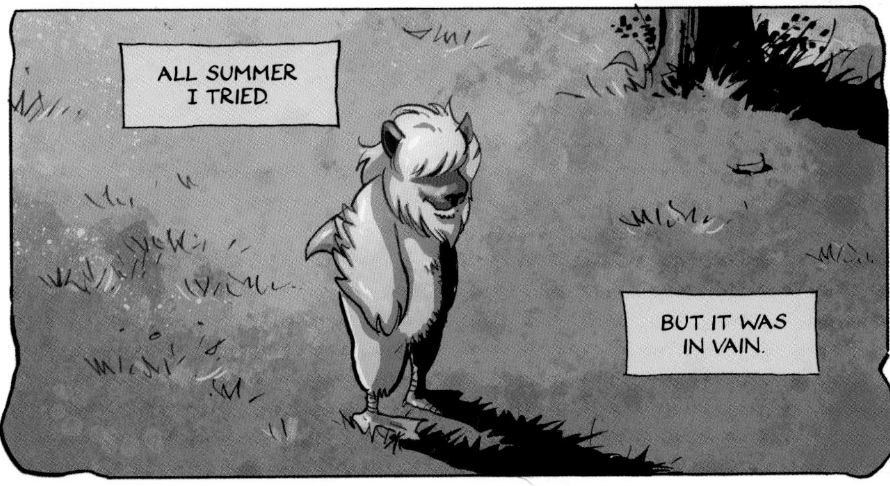
ALL SUMMER I TRIED.
BUT IT WAS IN VAIN.

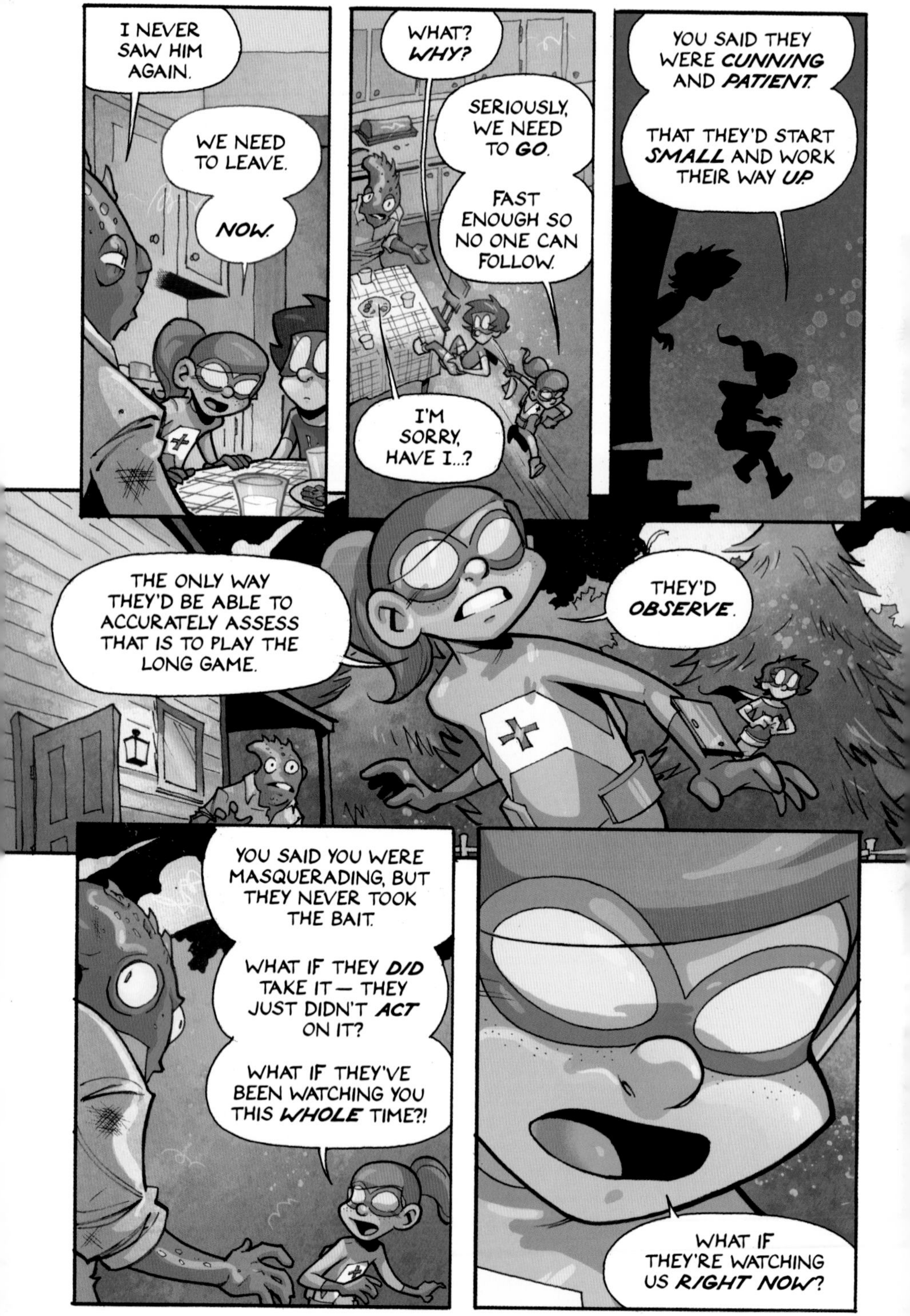
I NEVER SAW HIM AGAIN.
WE NEED TO LEAVE.
NOW.
WHAT? WHY?
SERIOUSLY, WE NEED TO GO.
FAST ENOUGH SO NO ONE CAN FOLLOW.
I'M SORRY, HAVE I...?
YOU SAID THEY WERE CUNNING AND PATIENT.
THAT THEY'D START SMALL AND WORK THEIR WAY UP.
THE ONLY WAY THEY'D BE ABLE TO ACCURATELY ASSESS THAT IS TO PLAY THE LONG GAME.
THEY'D OBSERVE.
YOU SAID YOU WERE MASQUERADING, BUT THEY NEVER TOOK THE BAIT.
WHAT IF THEY DID TAKE IT— THEY JUST DIDN'T ACT ON IT?
WHAT IF THEY'VE BEEN WATCHING YOU THIS WHOLE TIME?!
WHAT IF THEY'RE WATCHING US RIGHT NOW?

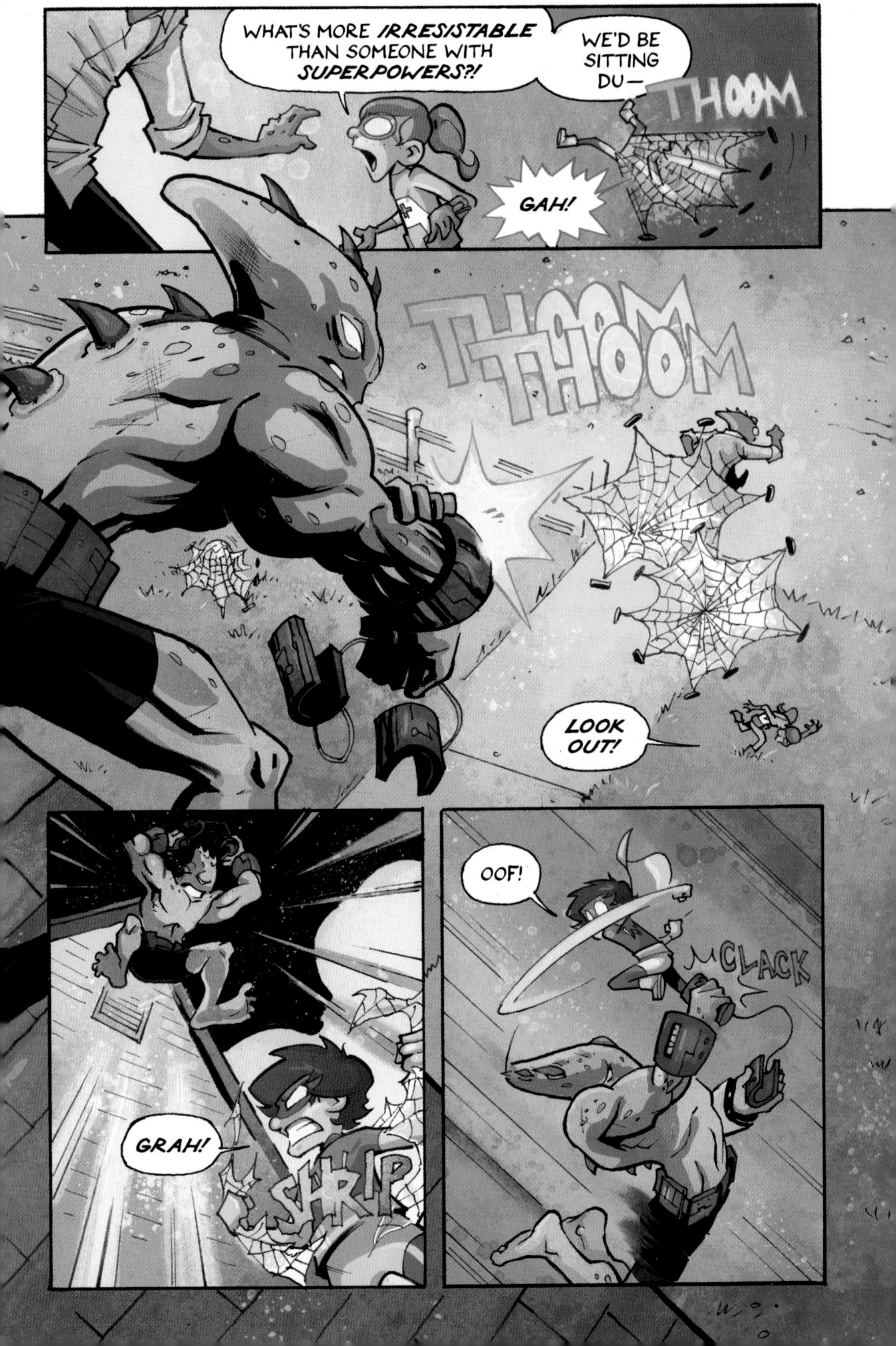
WHAT'S MORE *IRRESISTABLE* THAN SOMEONE WITH *SUPERPOWERS?!*
WE'D BE SITTING DU—
THOOM
GAH!
THOOM
THOOM
LOOK OUT!
GRAH!
SHRIP
OOF!
CLACK

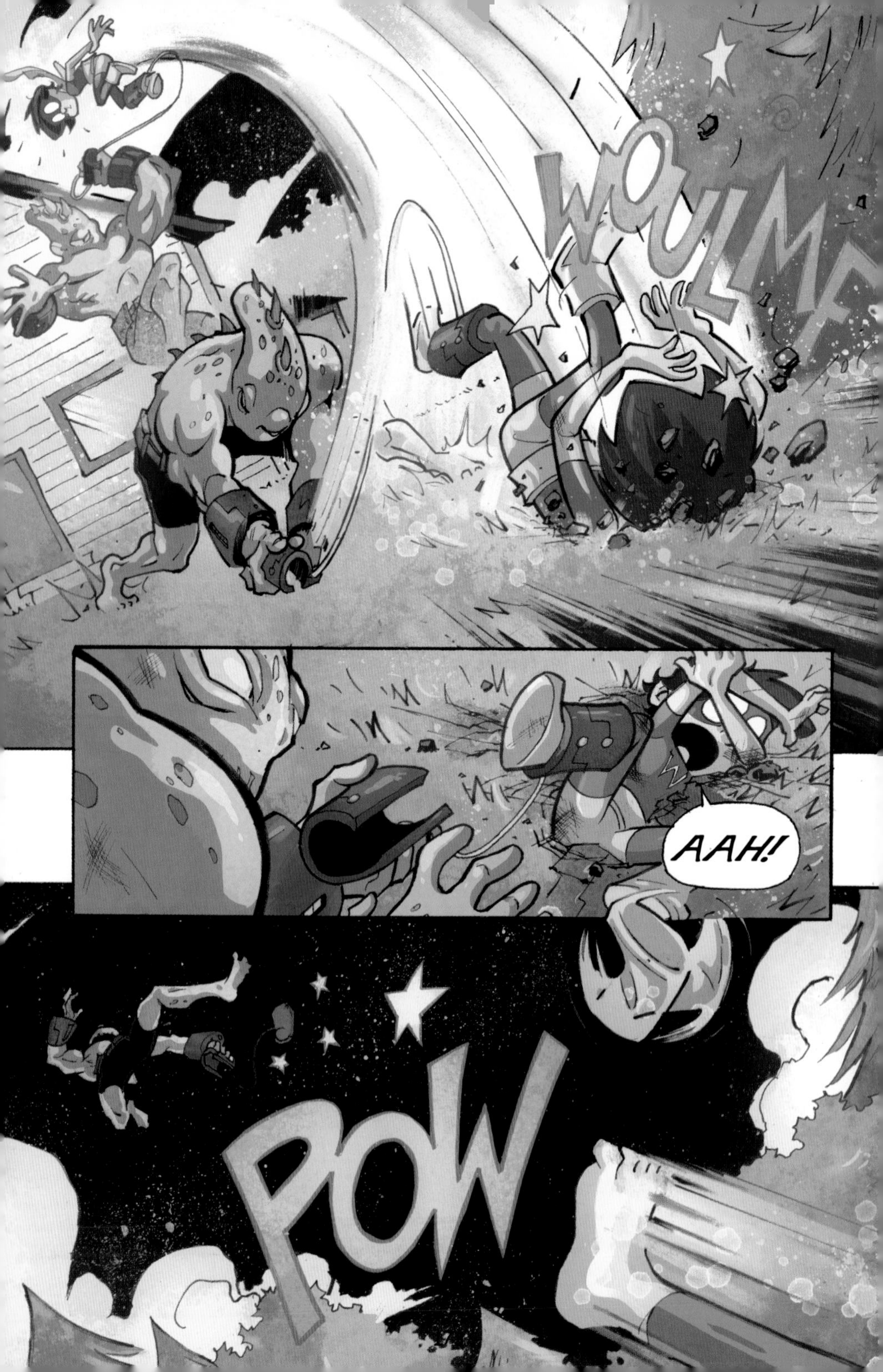
WOUMF
AAH!
POW

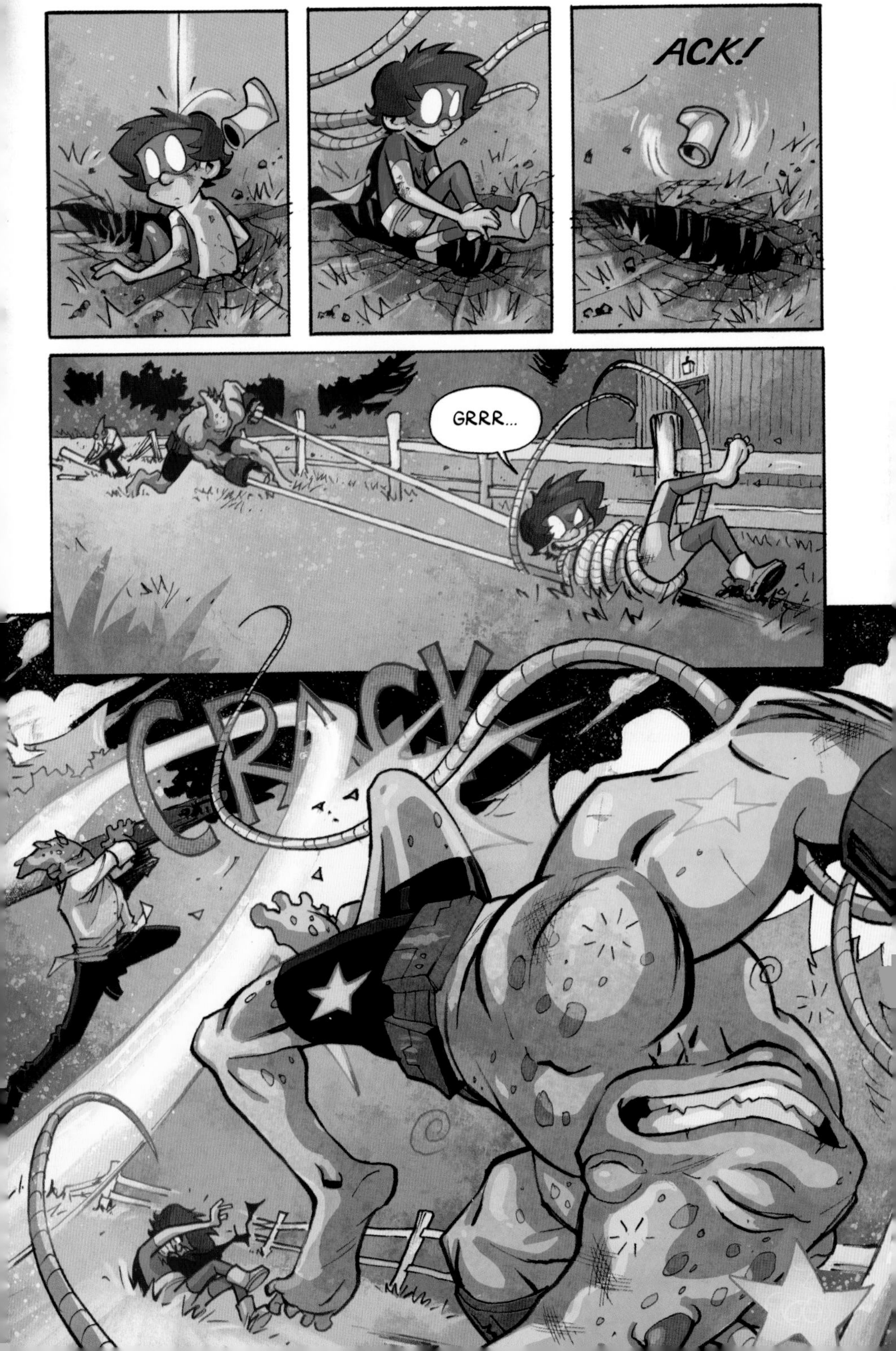
ACK!
GRRR...
CRACK

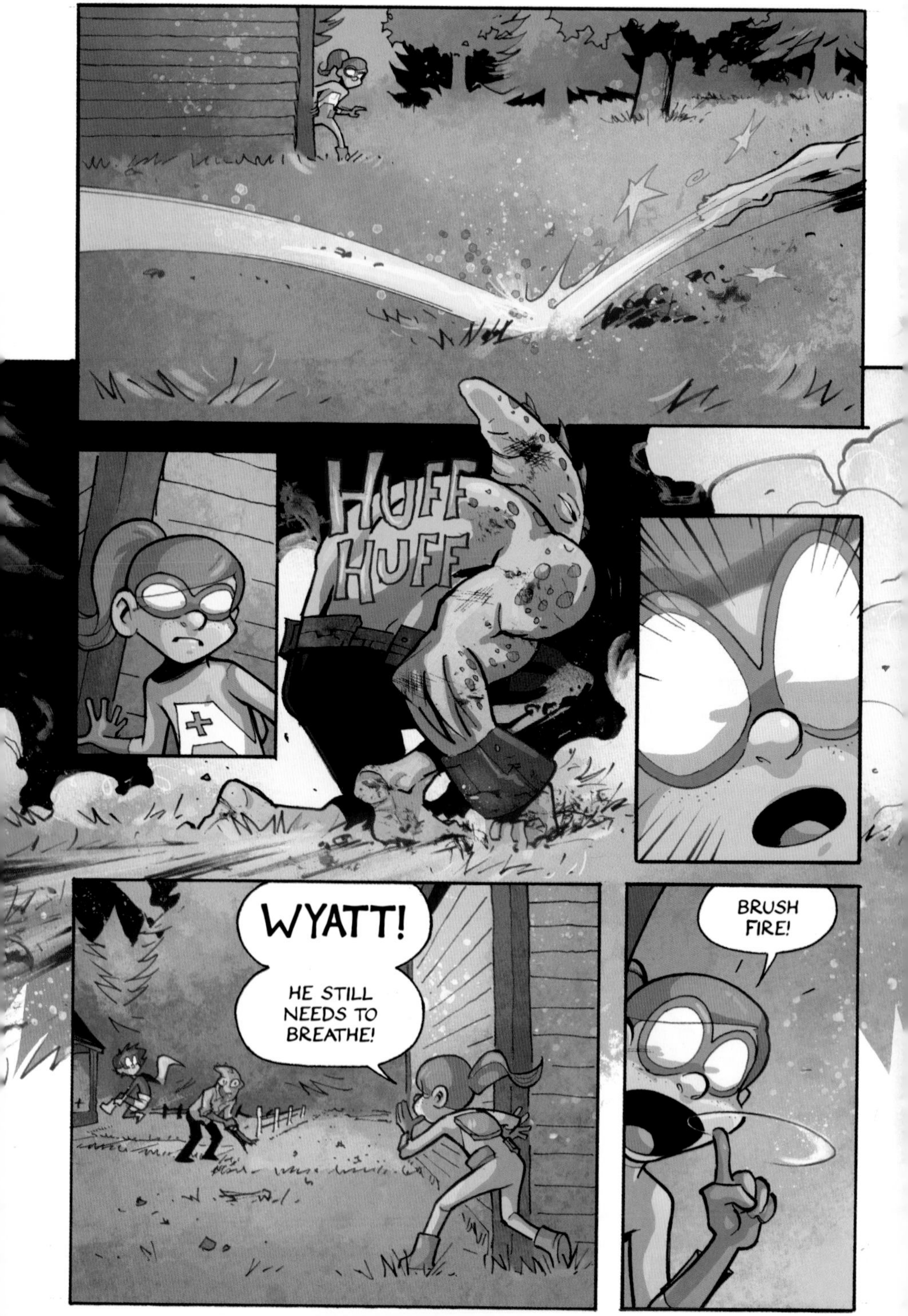
HUFF HUFF
WYATT!
HE STILL NEEDS TO BREATHE!
BRUSH FIRE!

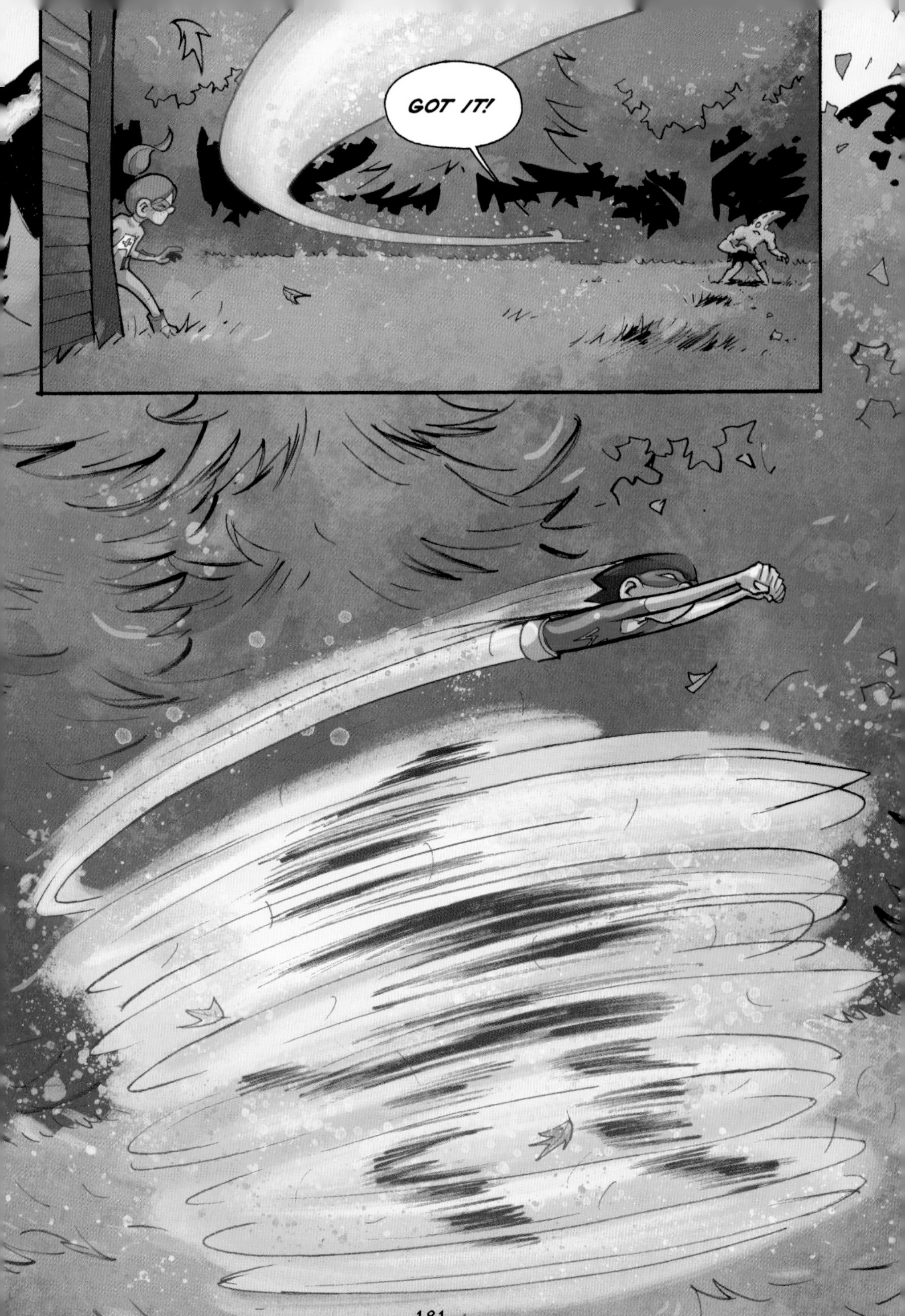
GOT IT!

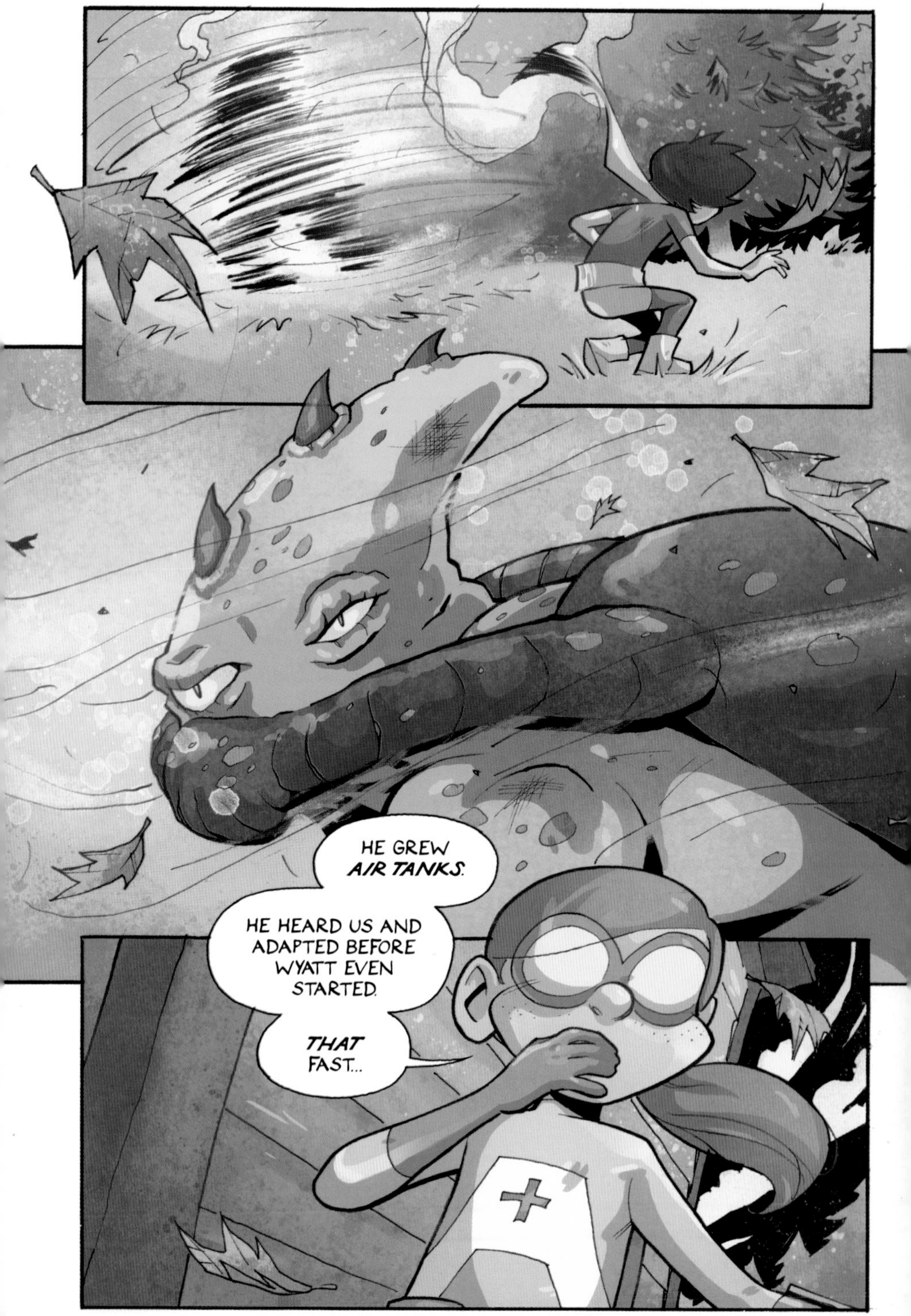
HE GREW AIR TANKS.
HE HEARD US AND ADAPTED BEFORE WYATT EVEN STARTED.
THAT FAST...

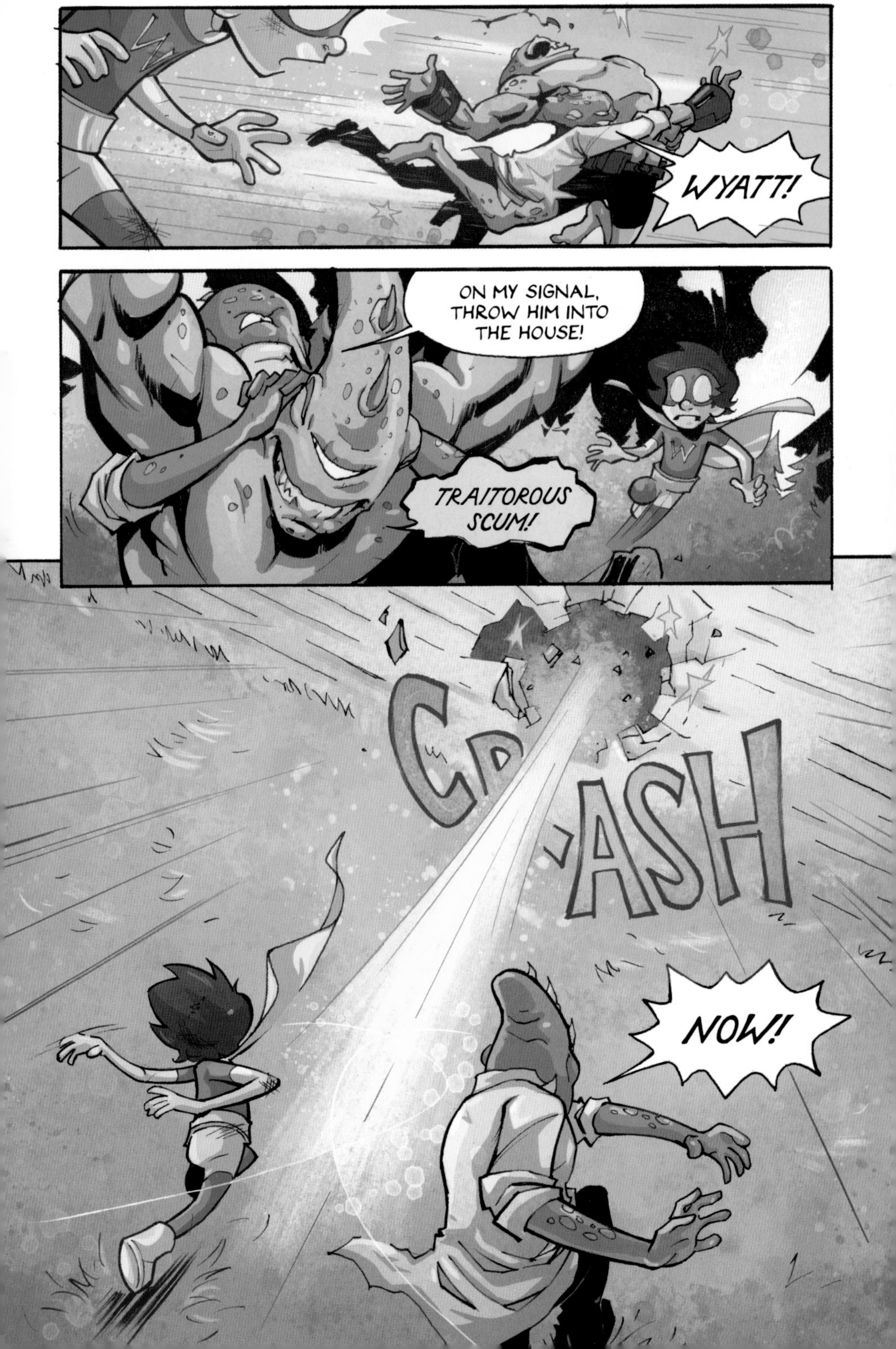
WYATT!
ON MY SIGNAL, THROW HIM INTO THE HOUSE!
TRAITOROUS SCUM!
CRASH
NOW!

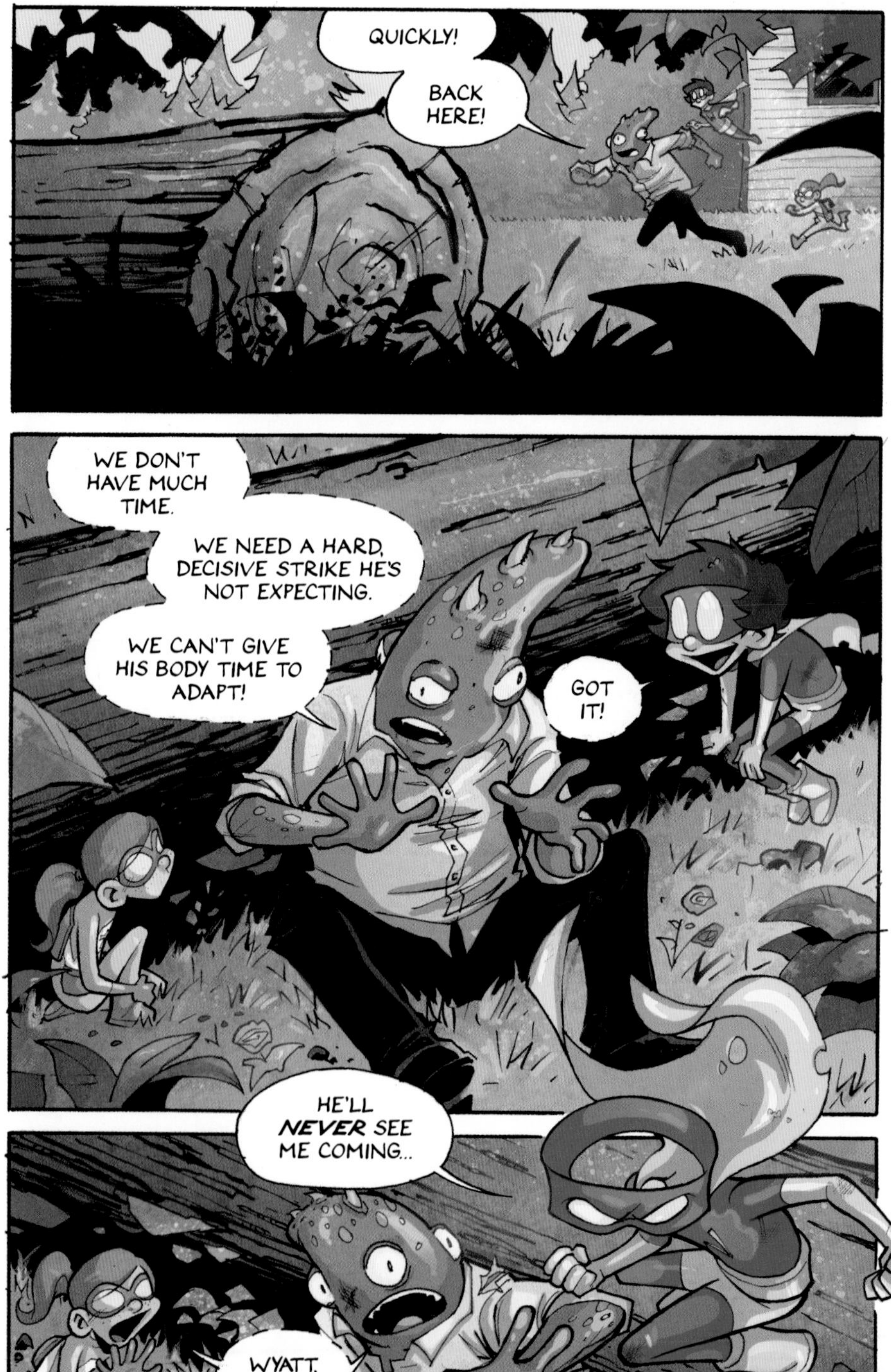
QUICKLY!
BACK HERE!
WE DON'T HAVE MUCH TIME.
WE NEED A HARD, DECISIVE STRIKE HE'S NOT EXPECTING.
WE CAN'T GIVE HIS BODY TIME TO ADAPT!
GOT IT!
HE'LL *NEVER* SEE ME COMING...
WYATT, WAIT...

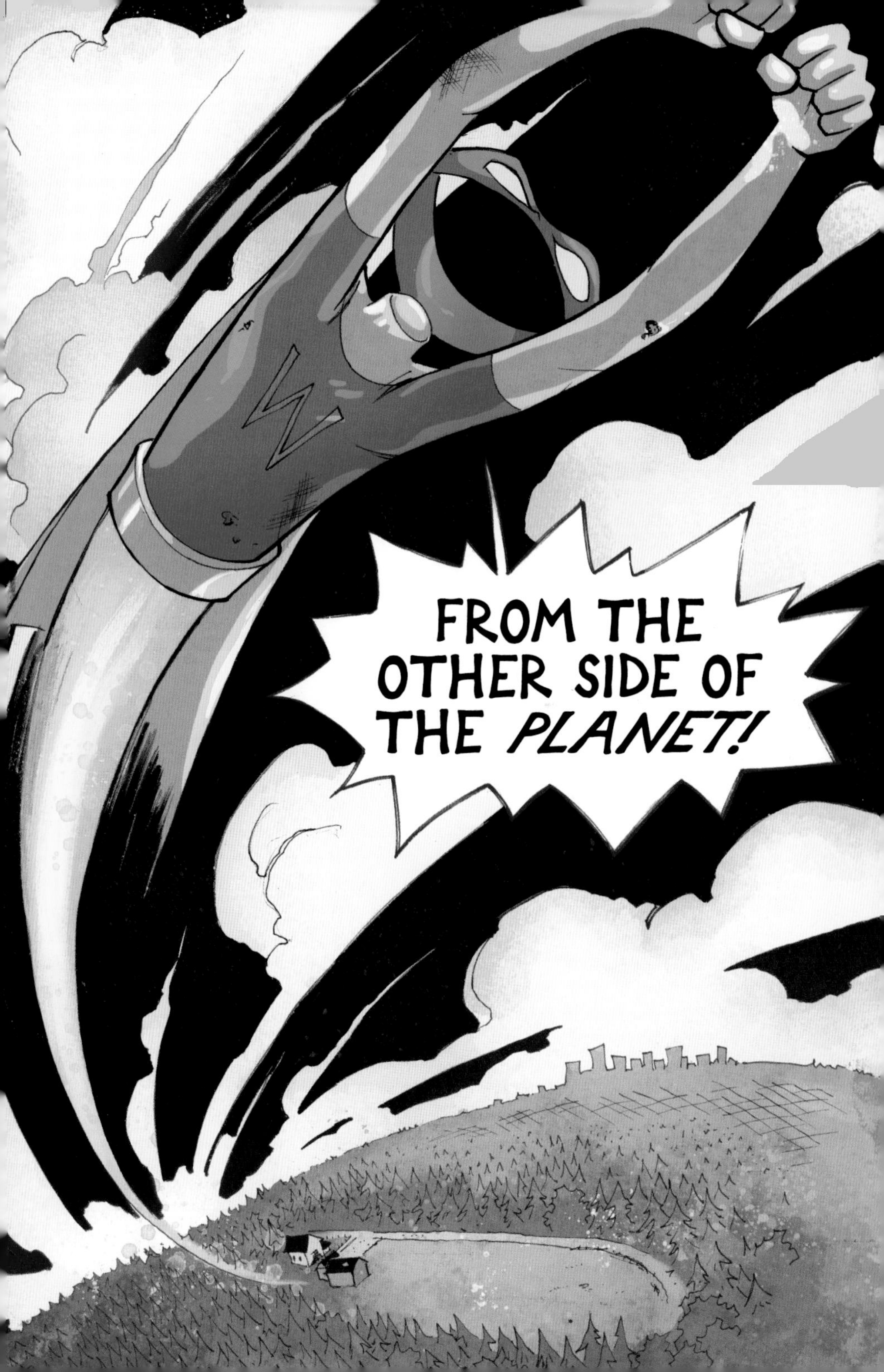
FROM THE OTHER SIDE OF THE *PLANET!*

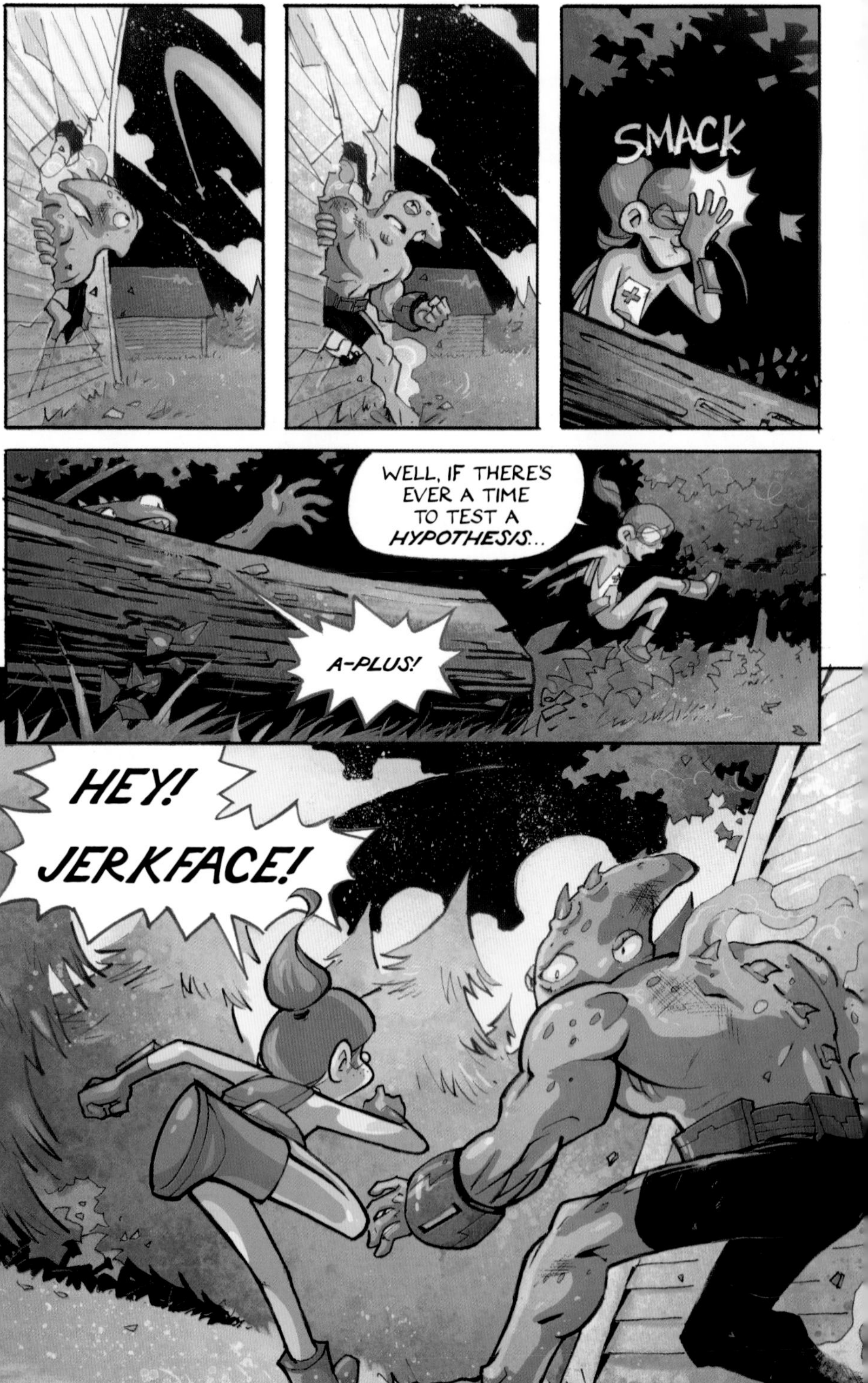
SMACK
WELL, IF THERE'S EVER A TIME TO TEST A HYPOTHESIS...
A-PLUS!
HEY! JERKFACE!

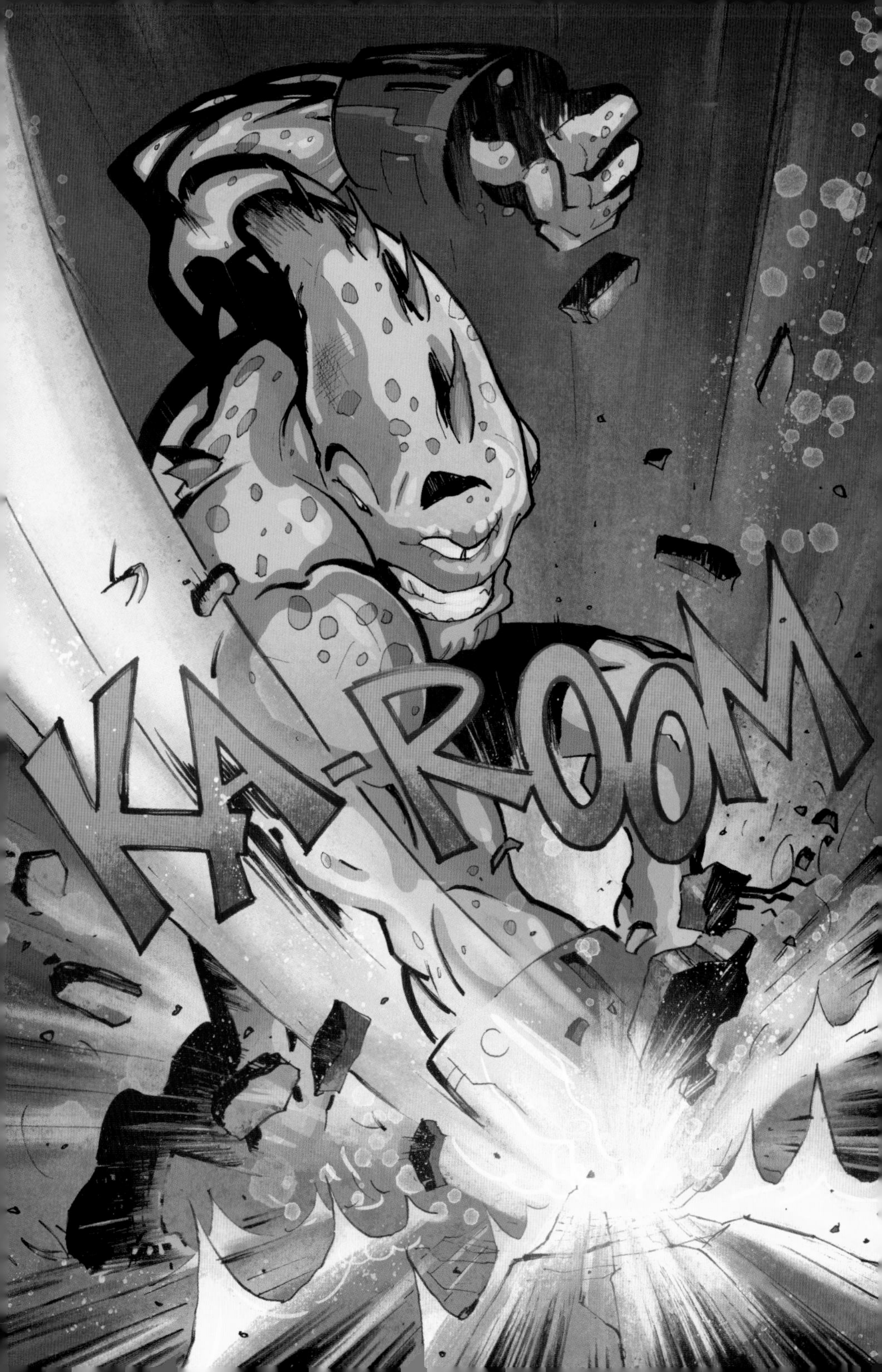
KA-ROOM

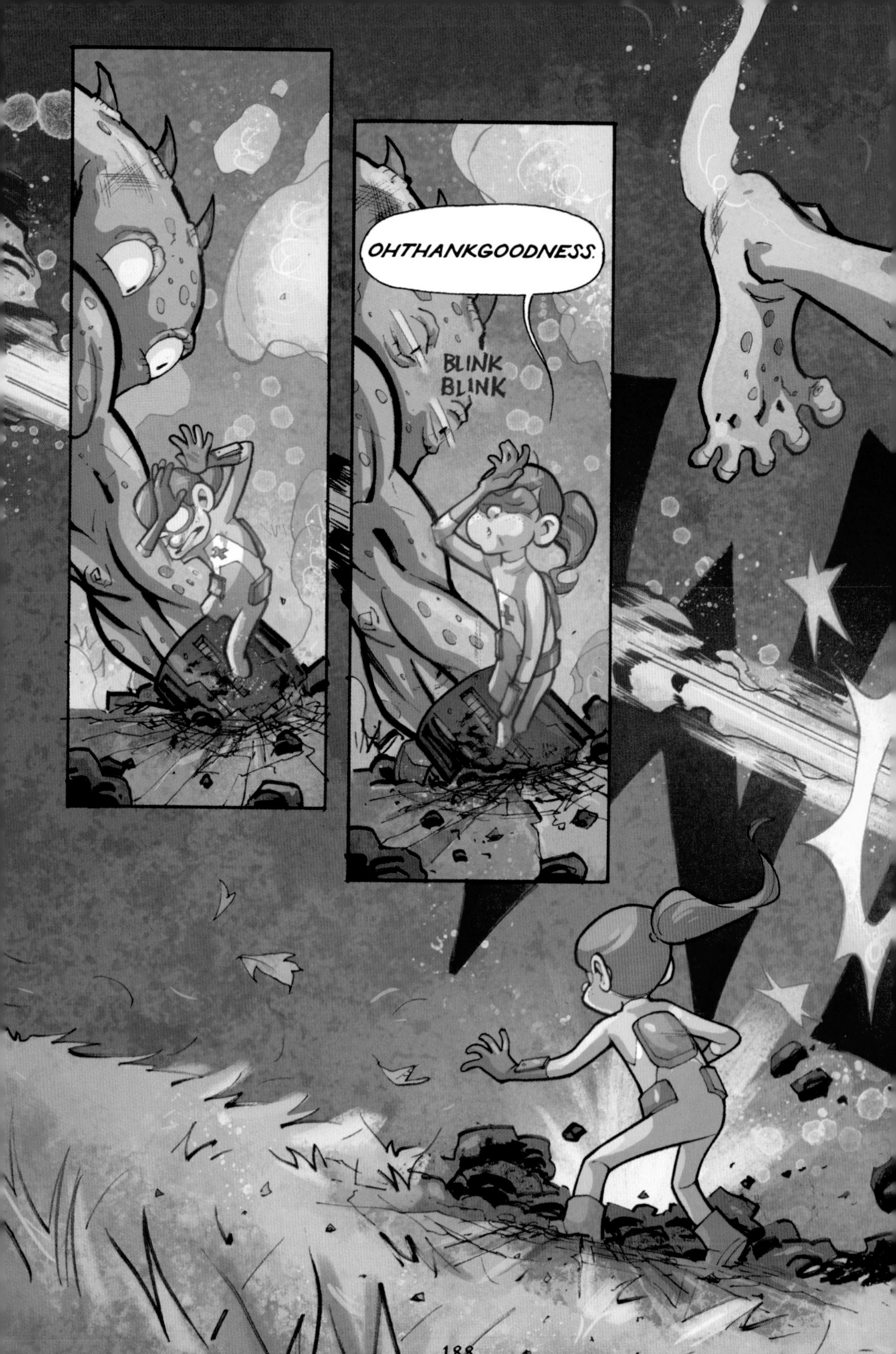
OHTHANKGOODNESS.
BLINK
BLINK

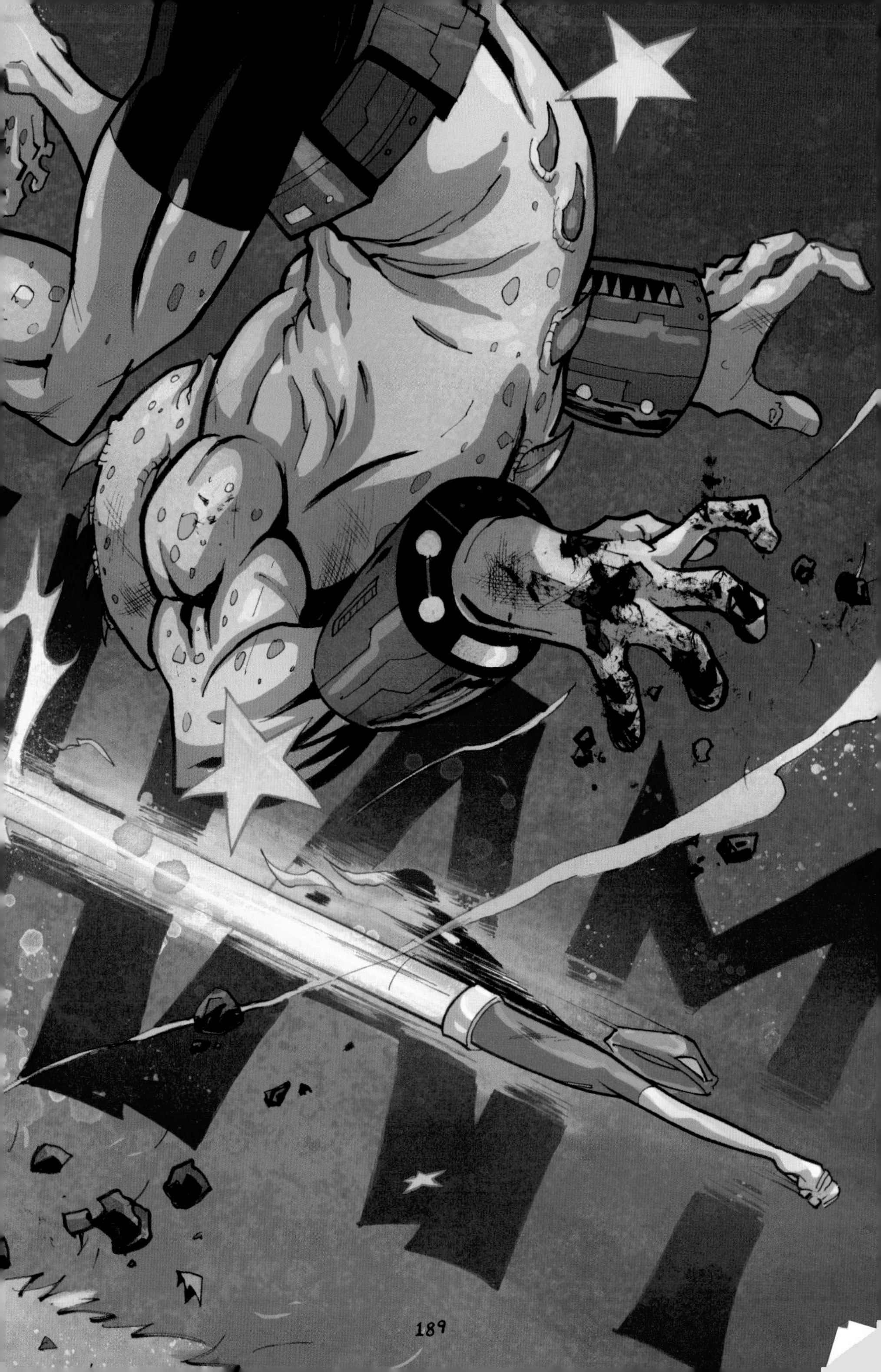

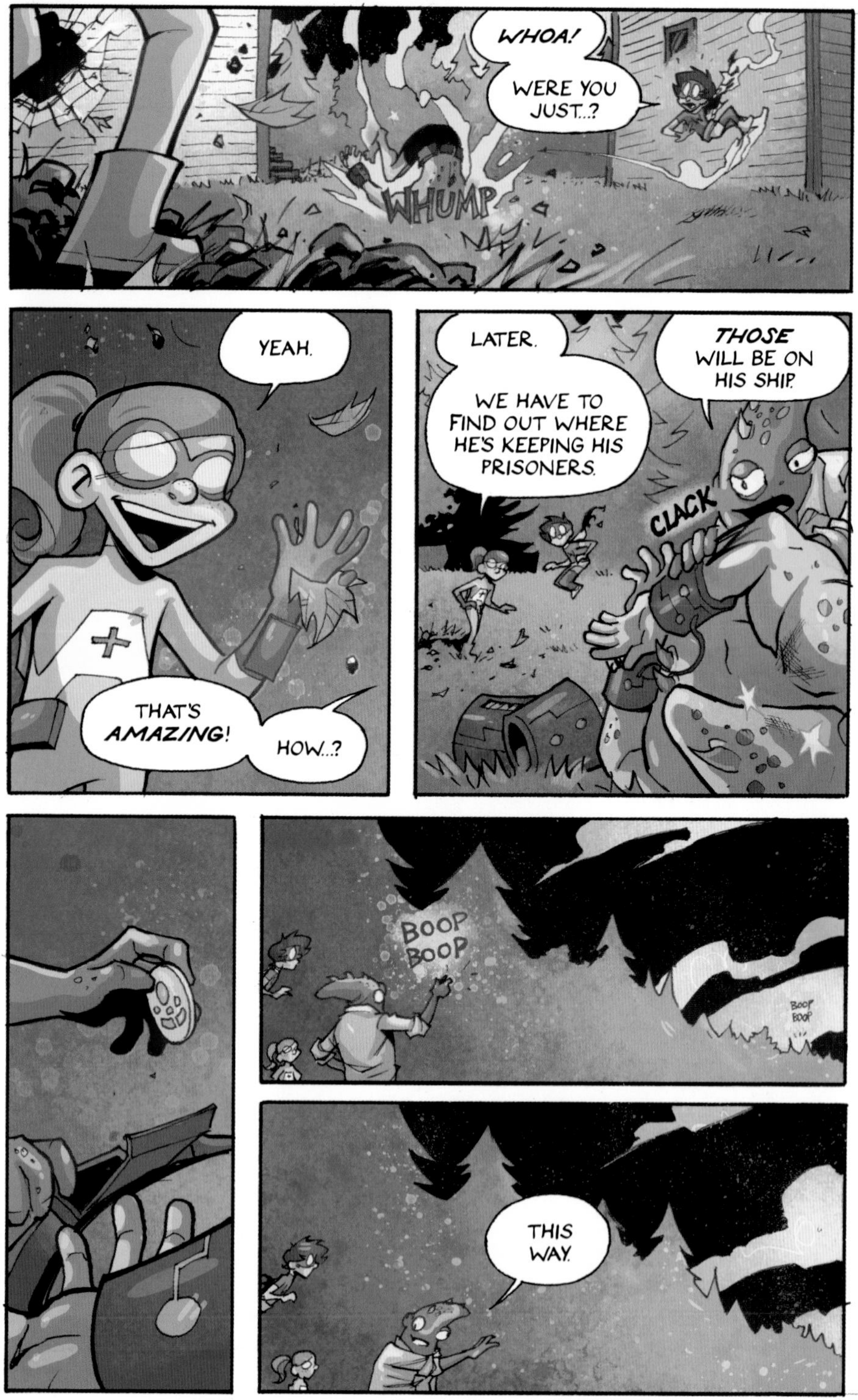
WHOA!
WERE YOU JUST...?
WHUMP
YEAH.
THAT'S AMAZING!
HOW...?
LATER.
WE HAVE TO FIND OUT WHERE HE'S KEEPING HIS PRISONERS.
THOSE WILL BE ON HIS SHIP.
CLACK
BOOP BOOP
BOOP BOOP
THIS WAY.

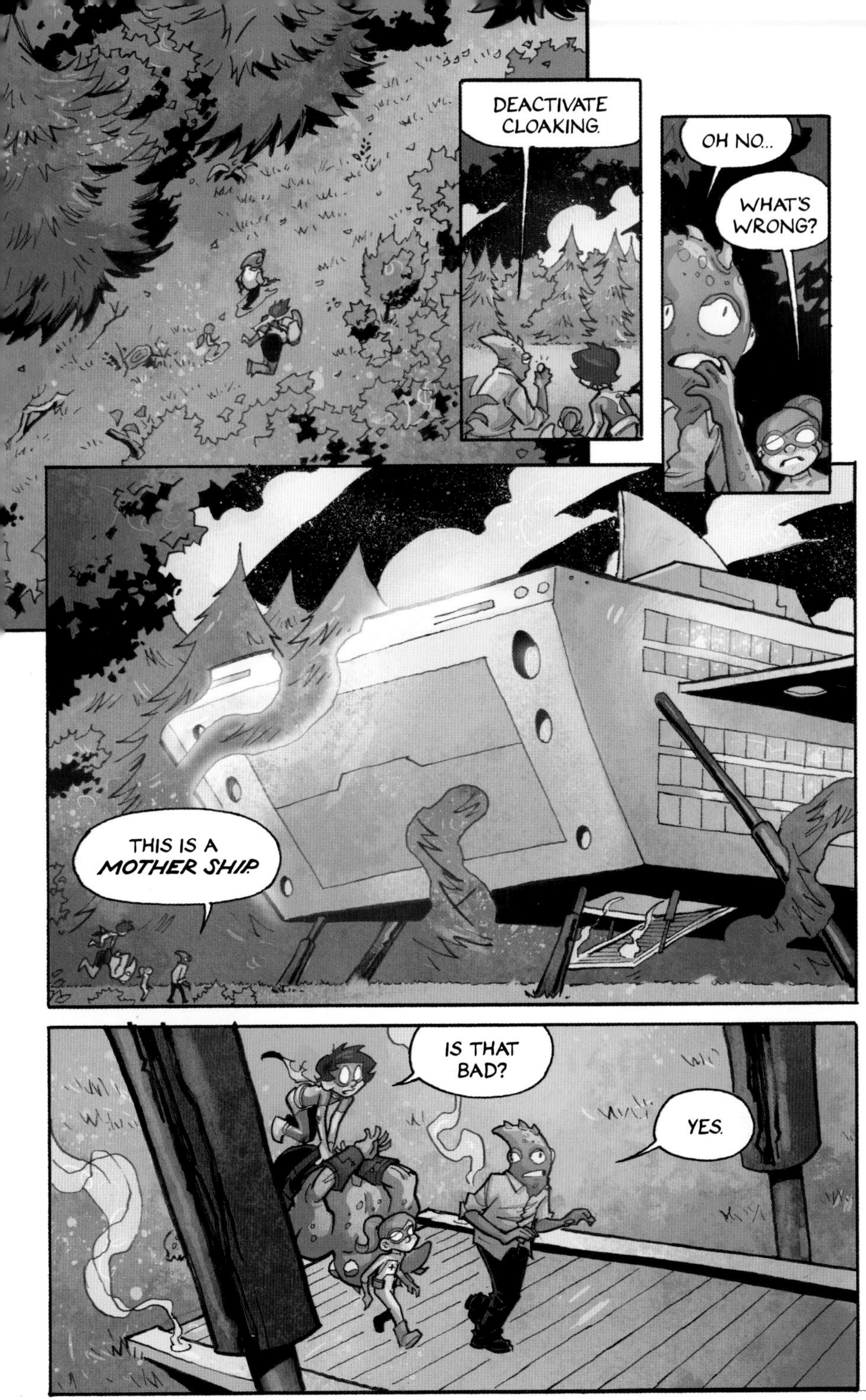
DEACTIVATE CLOAKING.
OH NO...
WHAT'S WRONG?
THIS IS A *MOTHER SHIP.*
IS THAT BAD?
YES.

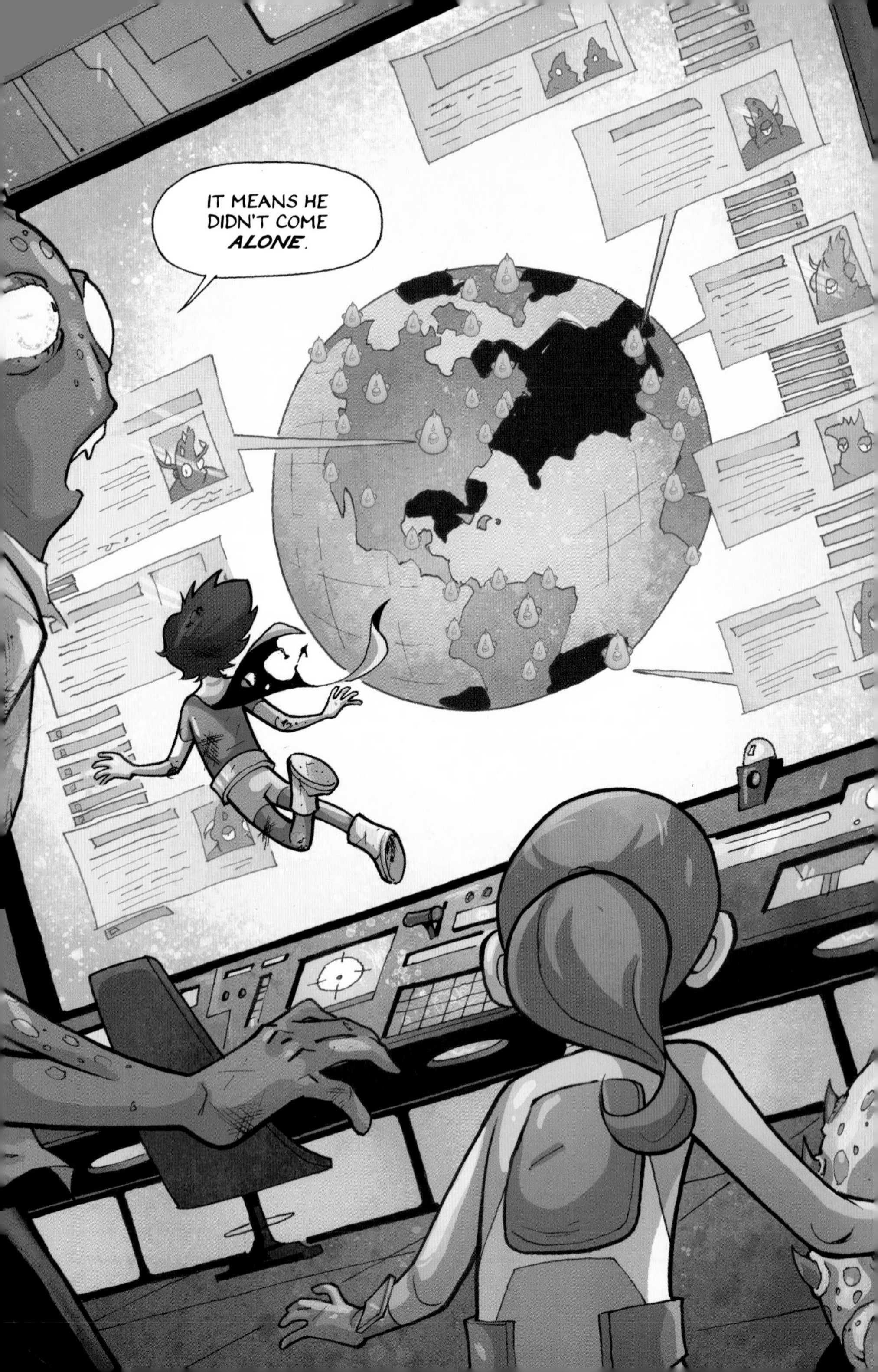
IT MEANS HE DIDN'T COME *ALONE*.

CHAPTER TWELVE

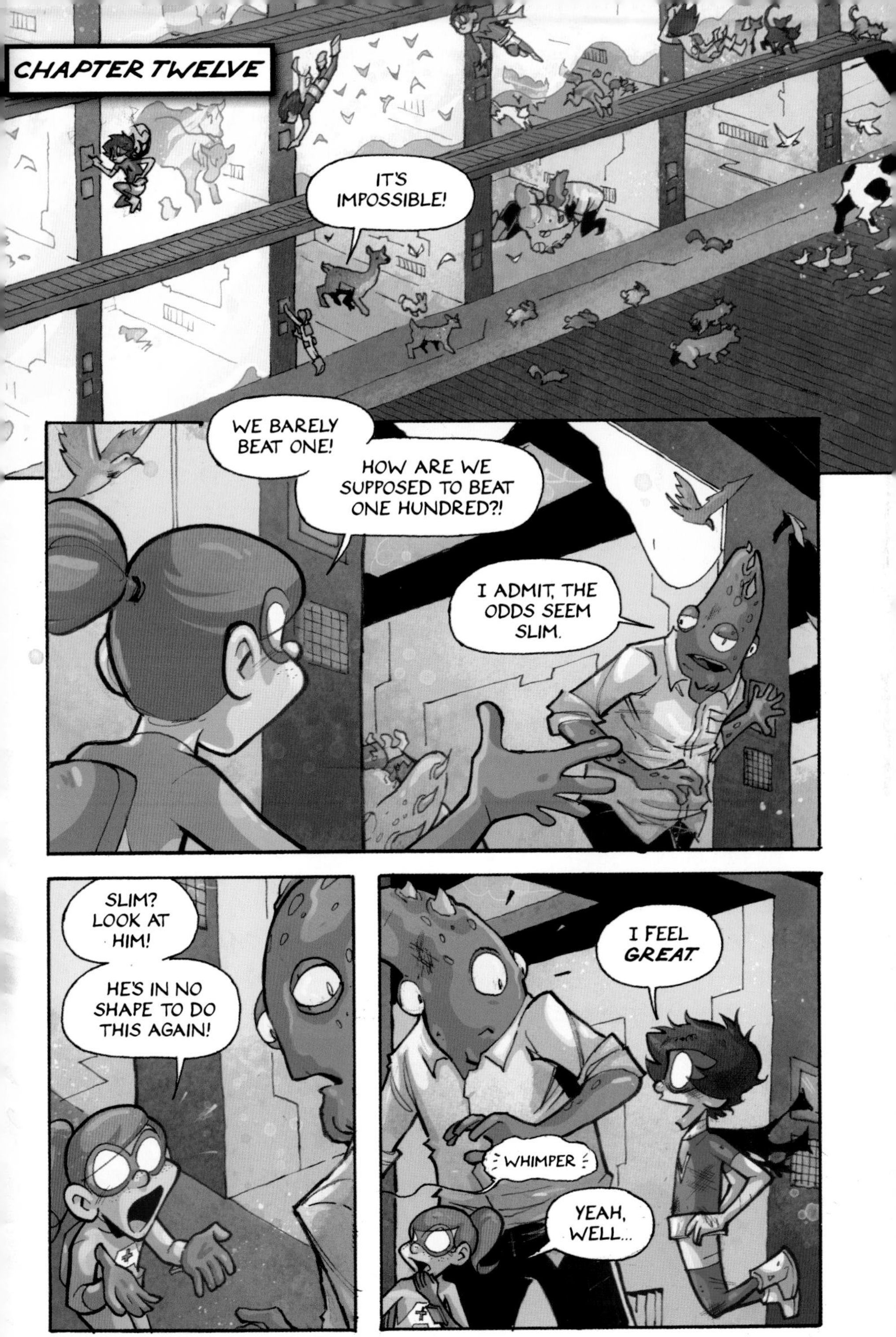
IT'S IMPOSSIBLE!
WE BARELY BEAT ONE!
HOW ARE WE SUPPOSED TO BEAT ONE HUNDRED?!
I ADMIT, THE ODDS SEEM SLIM.
SLIM? LOOK AT HIM!
HE'S IN NO SHAPE TO DO THIS AGAIN!
I FEEL GREAT.
WHIMPER
YEAH, WELL...

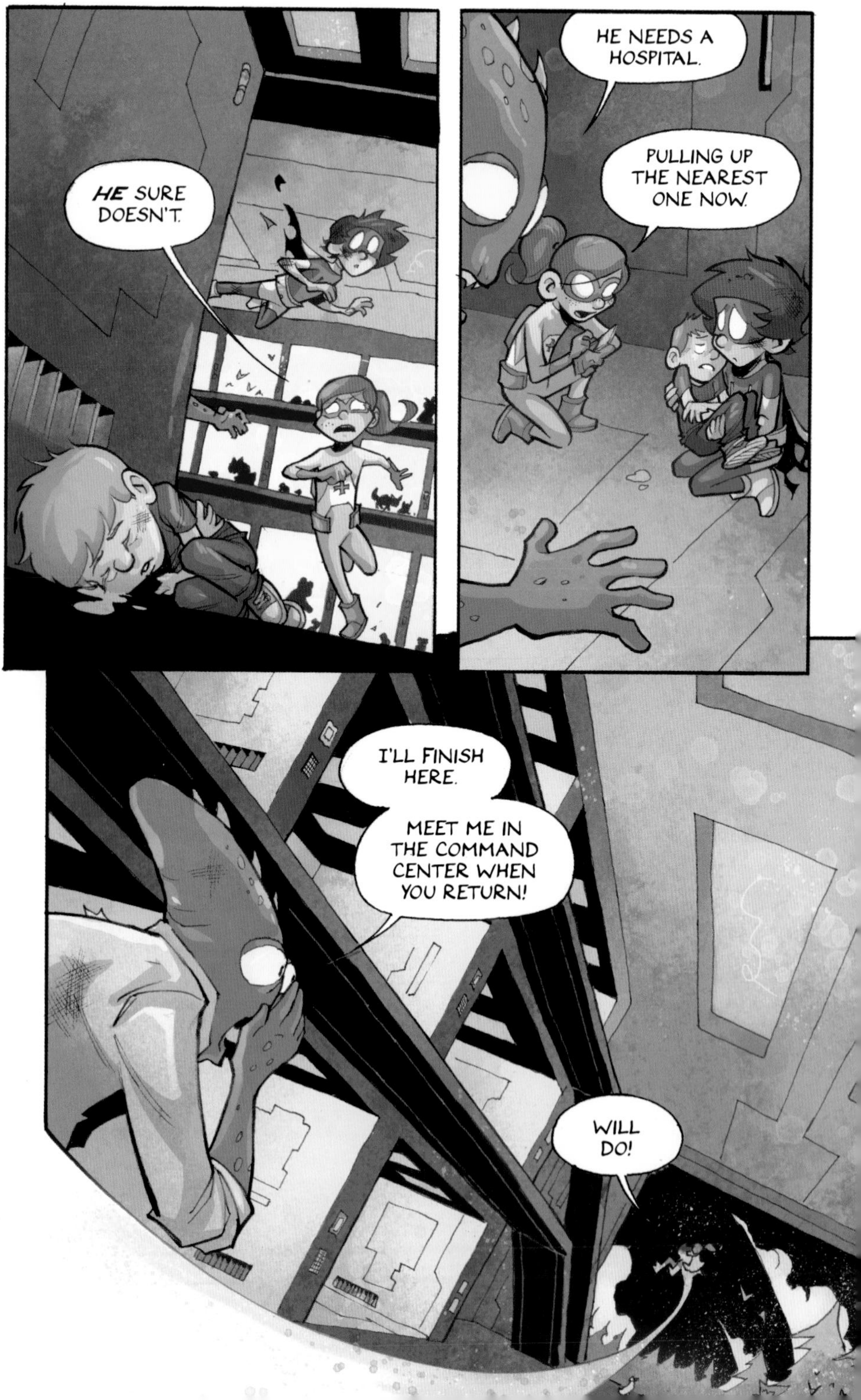
HE SURE DOESN'T.
HE NEEDS A HOSPITAL.
PULLING UP THE NEAREST ONE NOW.
I'LL FINISH HERE.
MEET ME IN THE COMMAND CENTER WHEN YOU RETURN!
WILL DO!

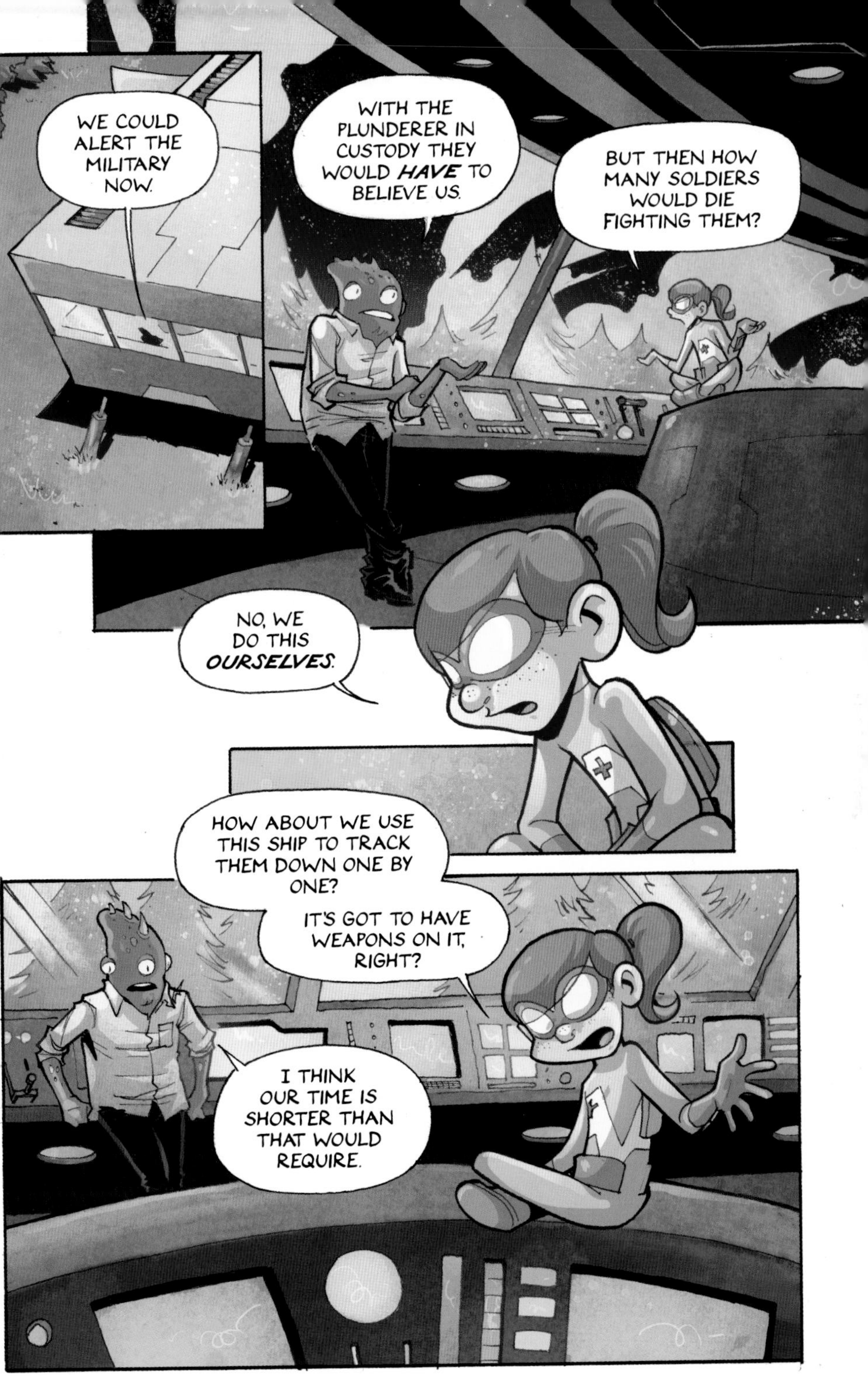
WE COULD ALERT THE MILITARY NOW.
WITH THE PLUNDERER IN CUSTODY THEY WOULD *HAVE* TO BELIEVE US.
BUT THEN HOW MANY SOLDIERS WOULD DIE FIGHTING THEM?
NO, WE DO THIS *OURSELVES*.
HOW ABOUT WE USE THIS SHIP TO TRACK THEM DOWN ONE BY ONE?
IT'S GOT TO HAVE WEAPONS ON IT, RIGHT?
I THINK OUR TIME IS SHORTER THAN THAT WOULD REQUIRE.

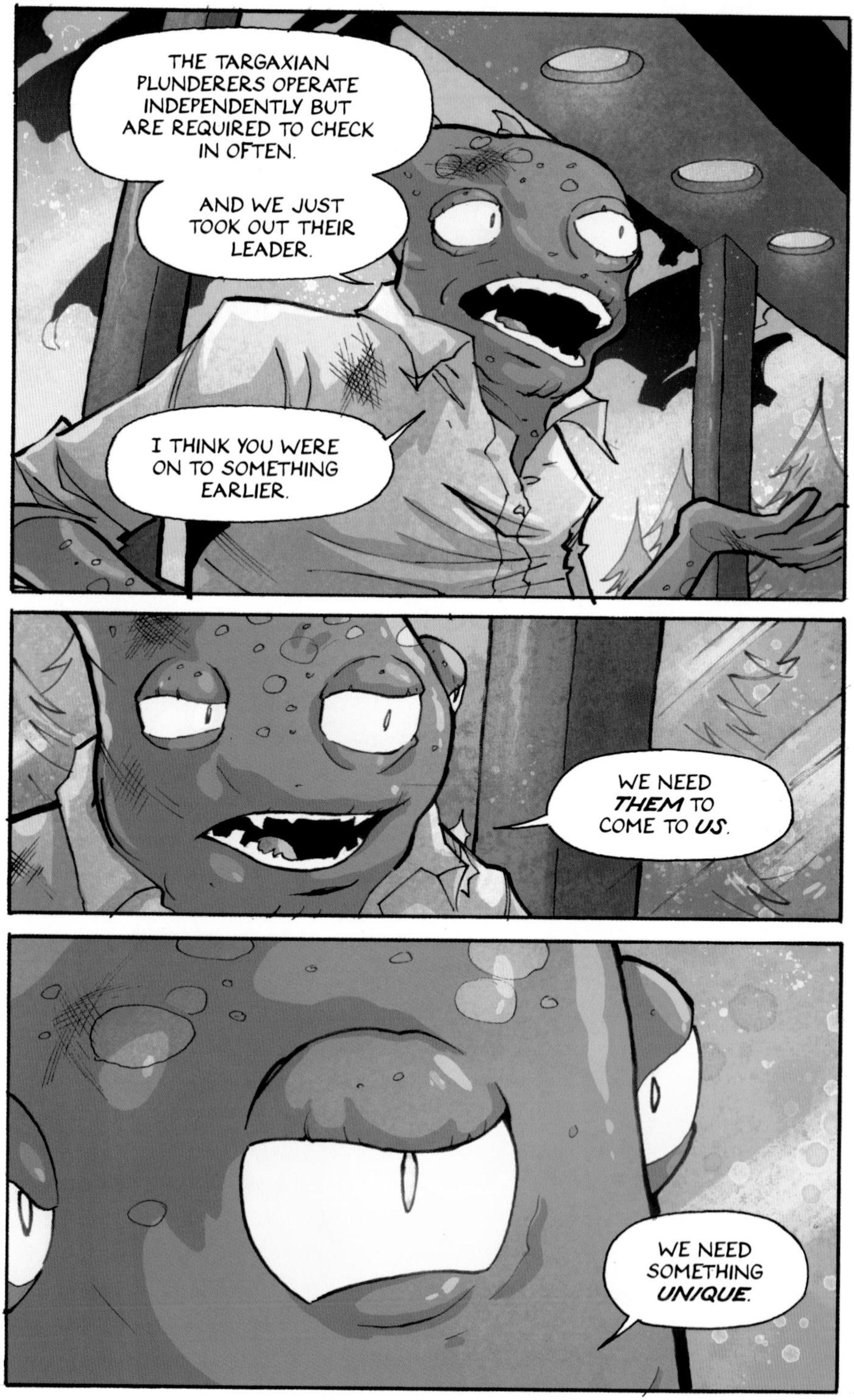
THE TARGAXIAN PLUNDERERS OPERATE INDEPENDENTLY BUT ARE REQUIRED TO CHECK IN OFTEN.
AND WE JUST TOOK OUT THEIR LEADER.
I THINK YOU WERE ON TO SOMETHING EARLIER.
WE NEED *THEM* TO COME TO *US*.
WE NEED SOMETHING *UNIQUE*.

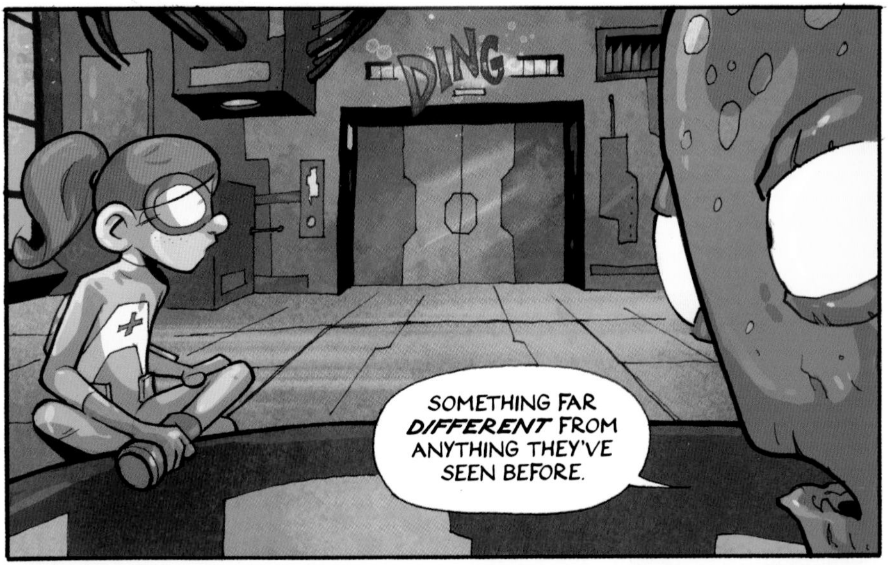
DING
SOMETHING FAR *DIFFERENT* FROM ANYTHING THEY'VE SEEN BEFORE.

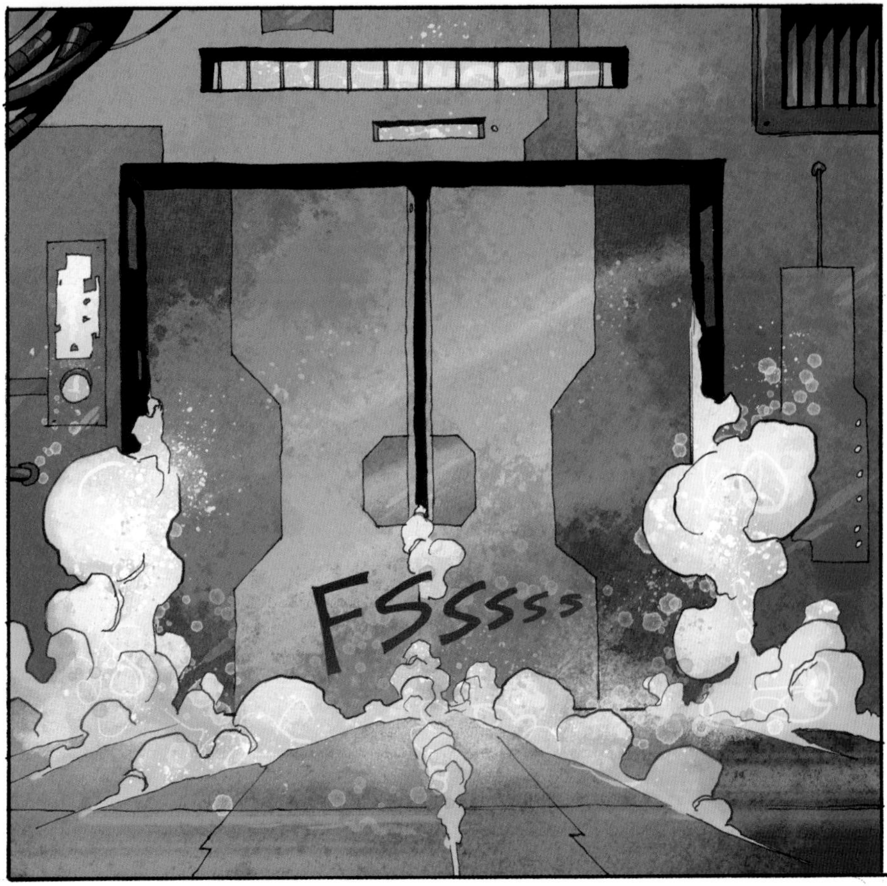
FSSSSS

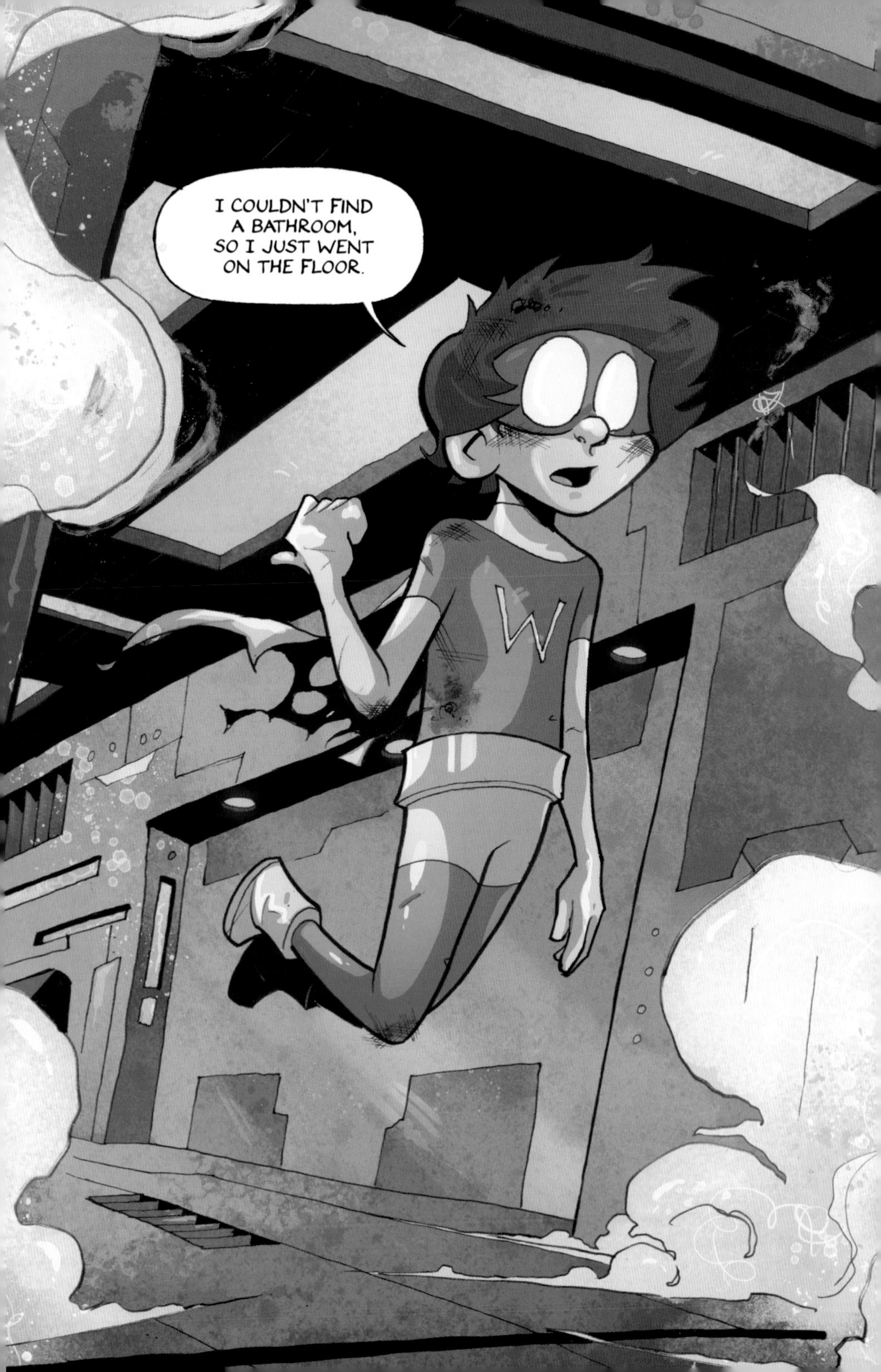
I COULDN'T FIND A BATHROOM, SO I JUST WENT ON THE FLOOR.

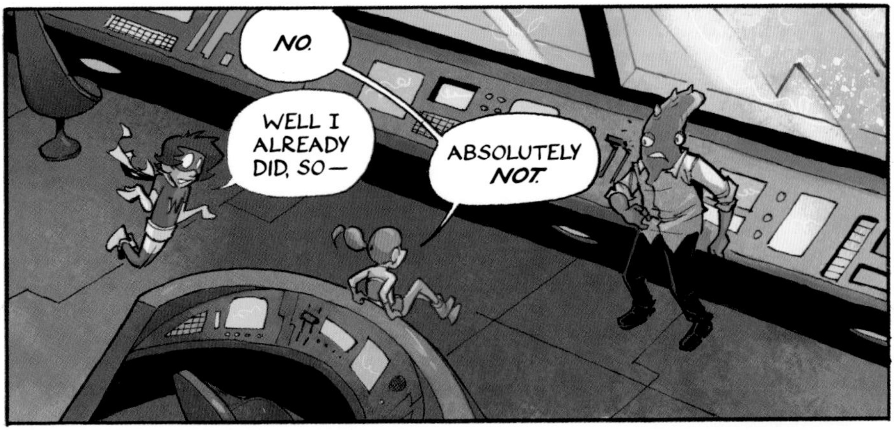
NO.
WELL I ALREADY DID, SO—
ABSOLUTELY NOT.

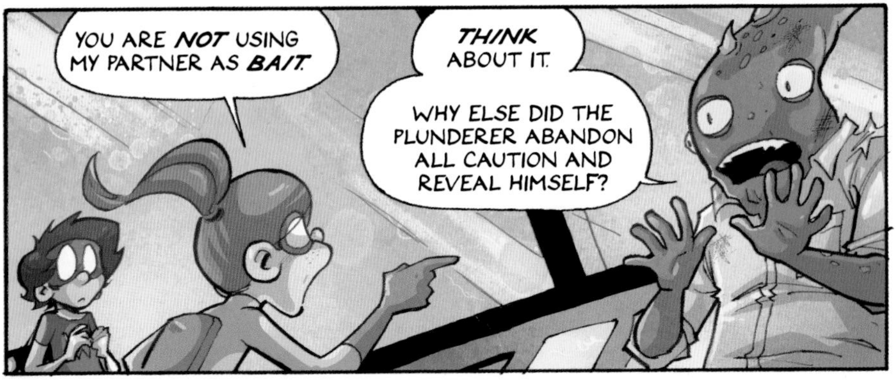
YOU ARE NOT USING MY PARTNER AS BAIT.
THINK ABOUT IT.
WHY ELSE DID THE PLUNDERER ABANDON ALL CAUTION AND REVEAL HIMSELF?

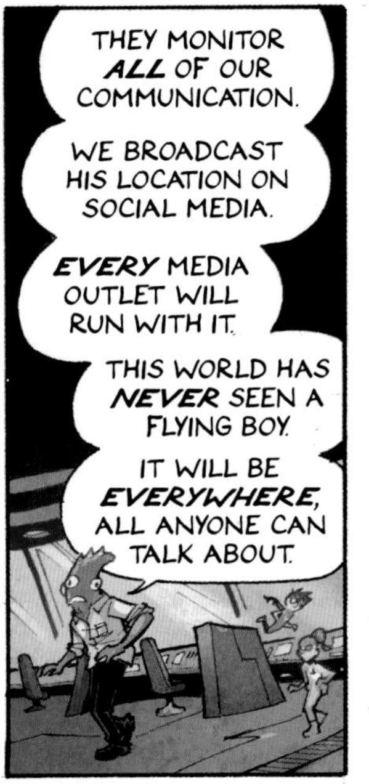
THEY MONITOR ALL OF OUR COMMUNICATION.
WE BROADCAST HIS LOCATION ON SOCIAL MEDIA.
EVERY MEDIA OUTLET WILL RUN WITH IT.
THIS WORLD HAS NEVER SEEN A FLYING BOY.
IT WILL BE EVERYWHERE, ALL ANYONE CAN TALK ABOUT.

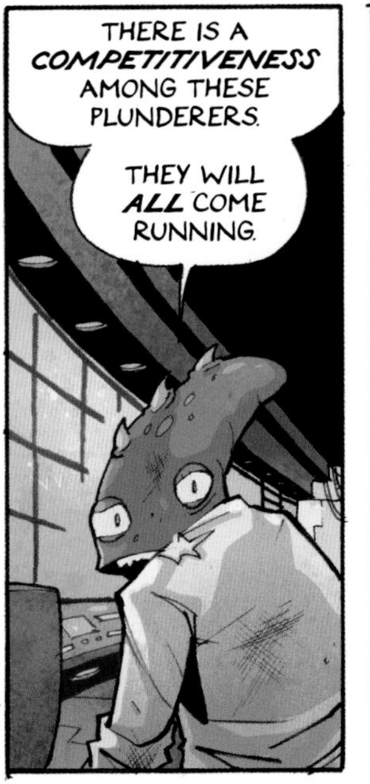
THERE IS A COMPETITIVENESS AMONG THESE PLUNDERERS.
THEY WILL ALL COME RUNNING.

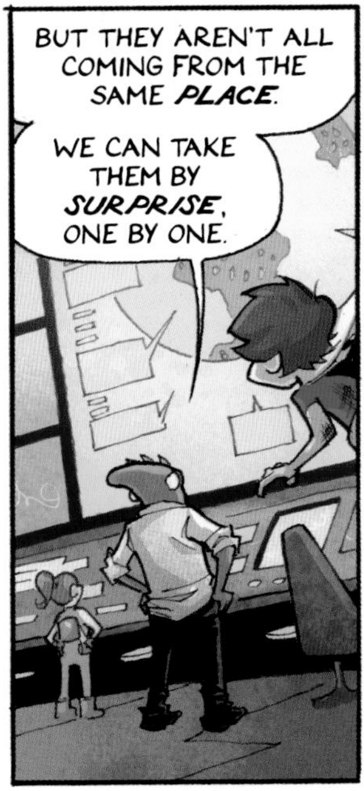
BUT THEY AREN'T ALL COMING FROM THE SAME PLACE.
WE CAN TAKE THEM BY SURPRISE, ONE BY ONE.

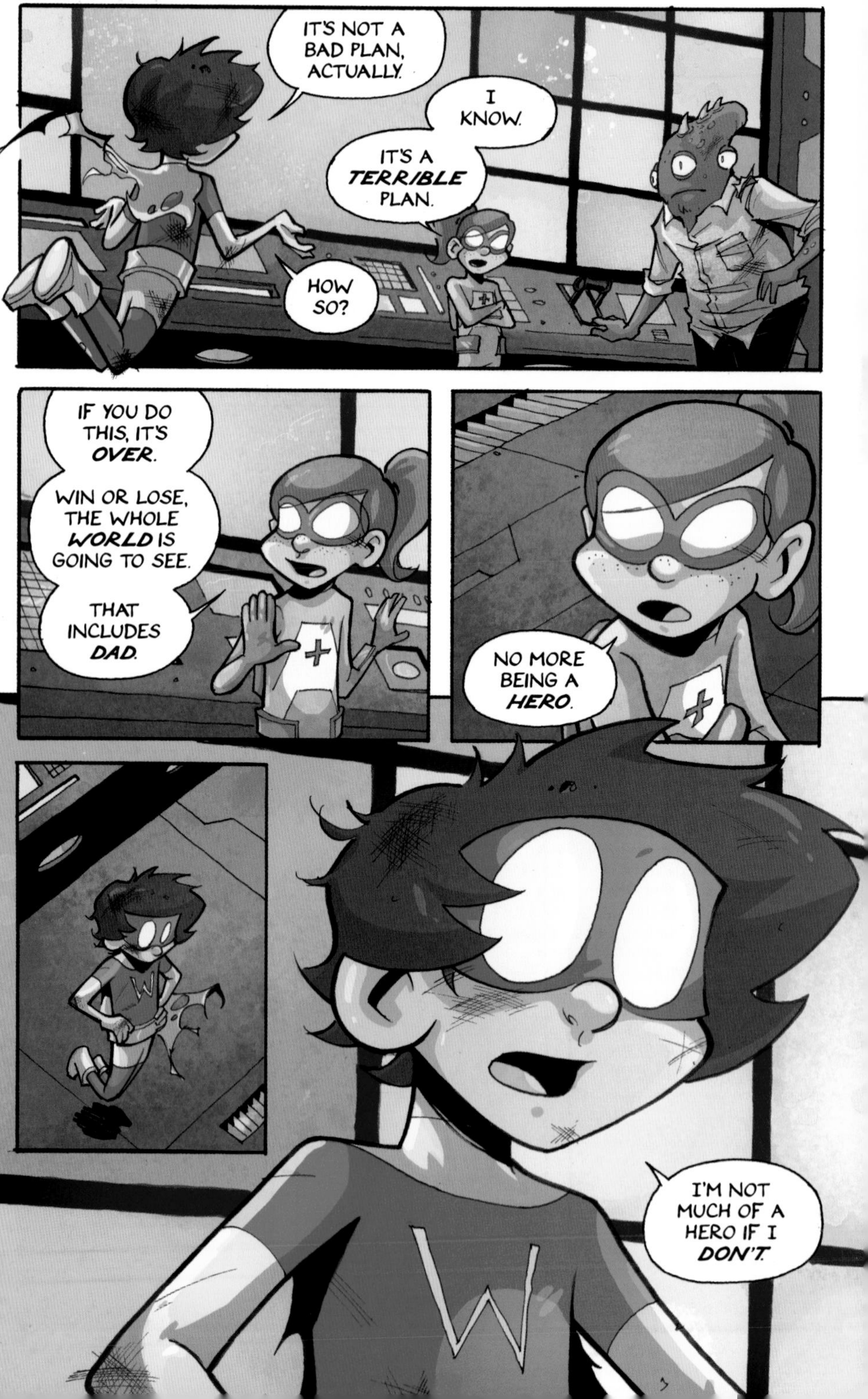
IT'S NOT A BAD PLAN, ACTUALLY.
I KNOW.
IT'S A TERRIBLE PLAN.
HOW SO?
IF YOU DO THIS, IT'S OVER.
WIN OR LOSE, THE WHOLE WORLD IS GOING TO SEE.
THAT INCLUDES DAD.
NO MORE BEING A HERO.
I'M NOT MUCH OF A HERO IF I DON'T.

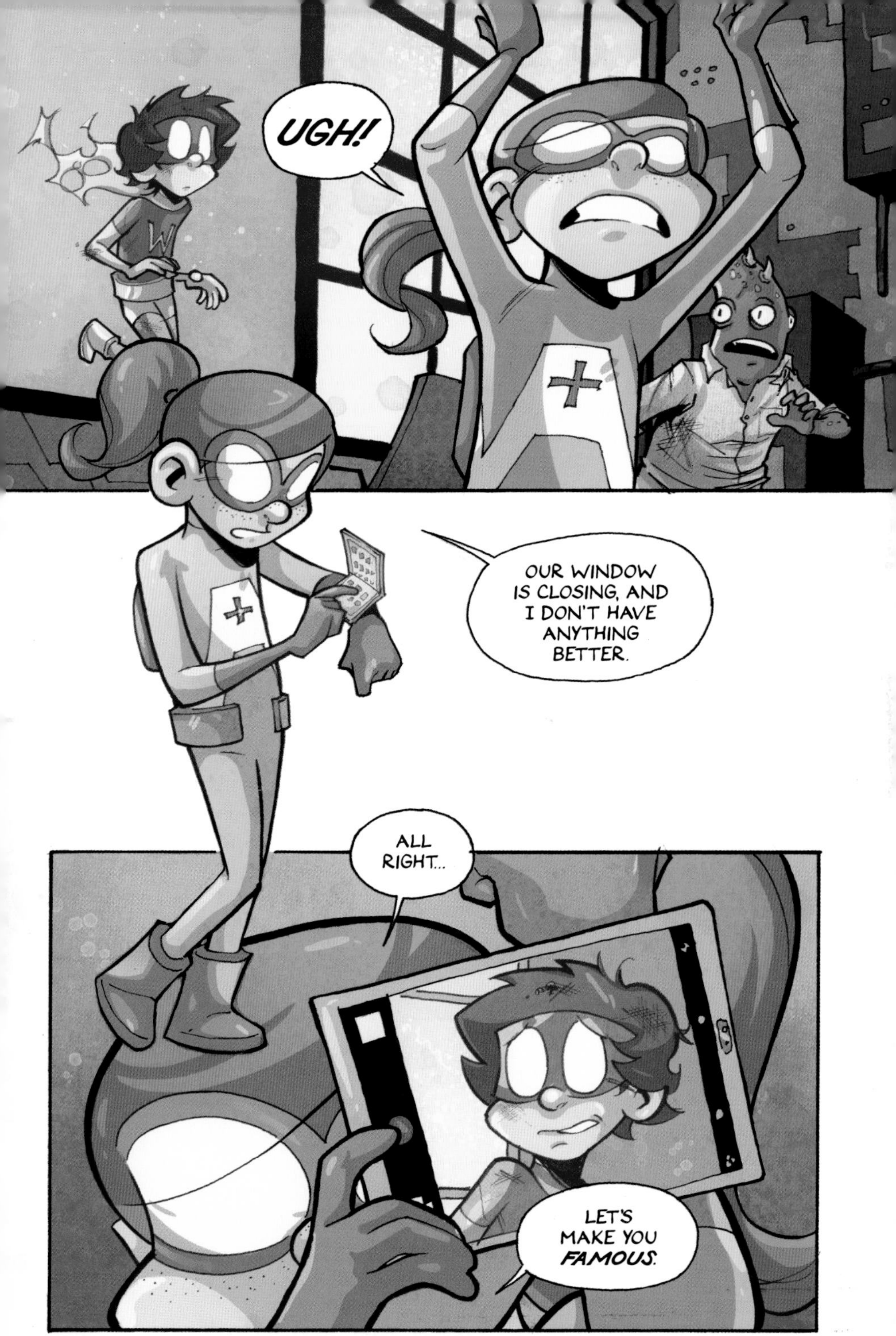
UGH!
OUR WINDOW IS CLOSING, AND I DON'T HAVE ANYTHING BETTER.
ALL RIGHT...
LET'S MAKE YOU *FAMOUS*.

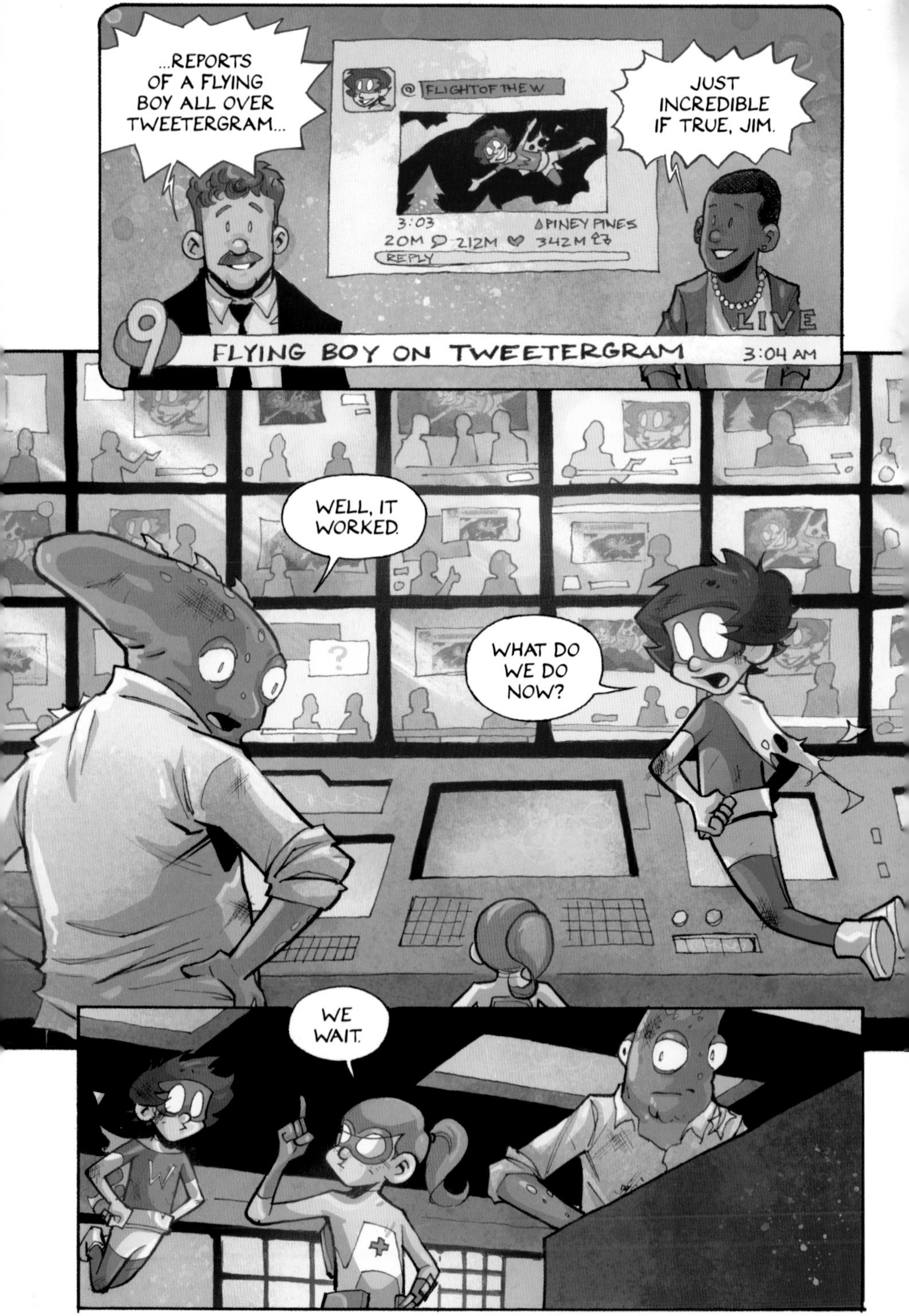
...REPORTS OF A FLYING BOY ALL OVER TWEETERGRAM...
@FLIGHTOFTHEW
3:03
PINEY PINES
20M 212M 342M
REPLY
JUST INCREDIBLE IF TRUE, JIM.
9
FLYING BOY ON TWEETERGRAM
3:04 AM
LIVE
WELL, IT WORKED.
WHAT DO WE DO NOW?
WE WAIT.

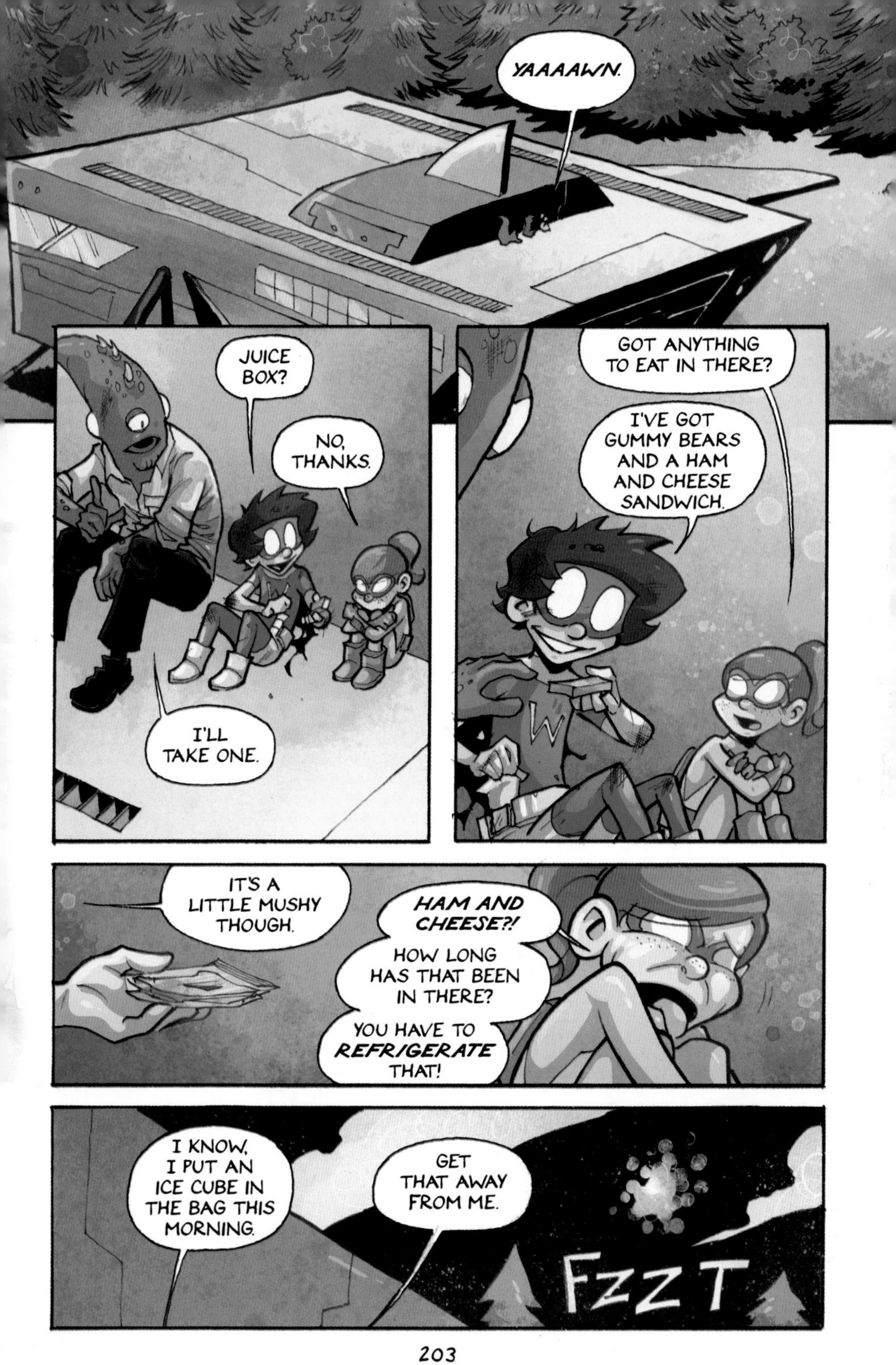
YAAAAWN.
JUICE BOX?
NO, THANKS.
I'LL TAKE ONE.
GOT ANYTHING TO EAT IN THERE?
I'VE GOT GUMMY BEARS AND A HAM AND CHEESE SANDWICH.
IT'S A LITTLE MUSHY THOUGH.
HAM AND CHEESE?!
HOW LONG HAS THAT BEEN IN THERE?
YOU HAVE TO REFRIGERATE THAT!
I KNOW, I PUT AN ICE CUBE IN THE BAG THIS MORNING.
GET THAT AWAY FROM ME.
FZZT

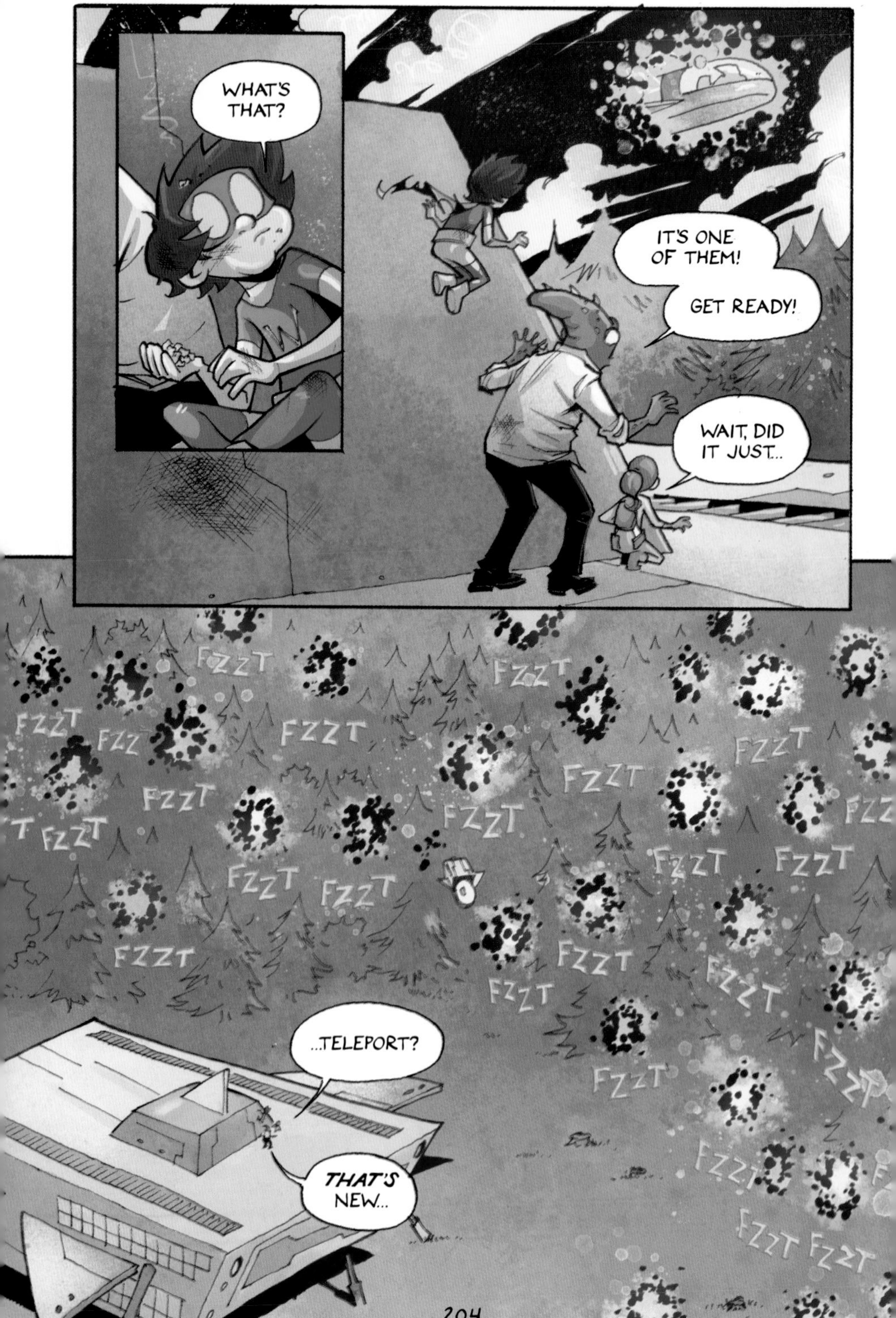
WHAT'S THAT?
IT'S ONE OF THEM!
GET READY!
WAIT, DID IT JUST...
FZZT
...TELEPORT?
THAT'S NEW...

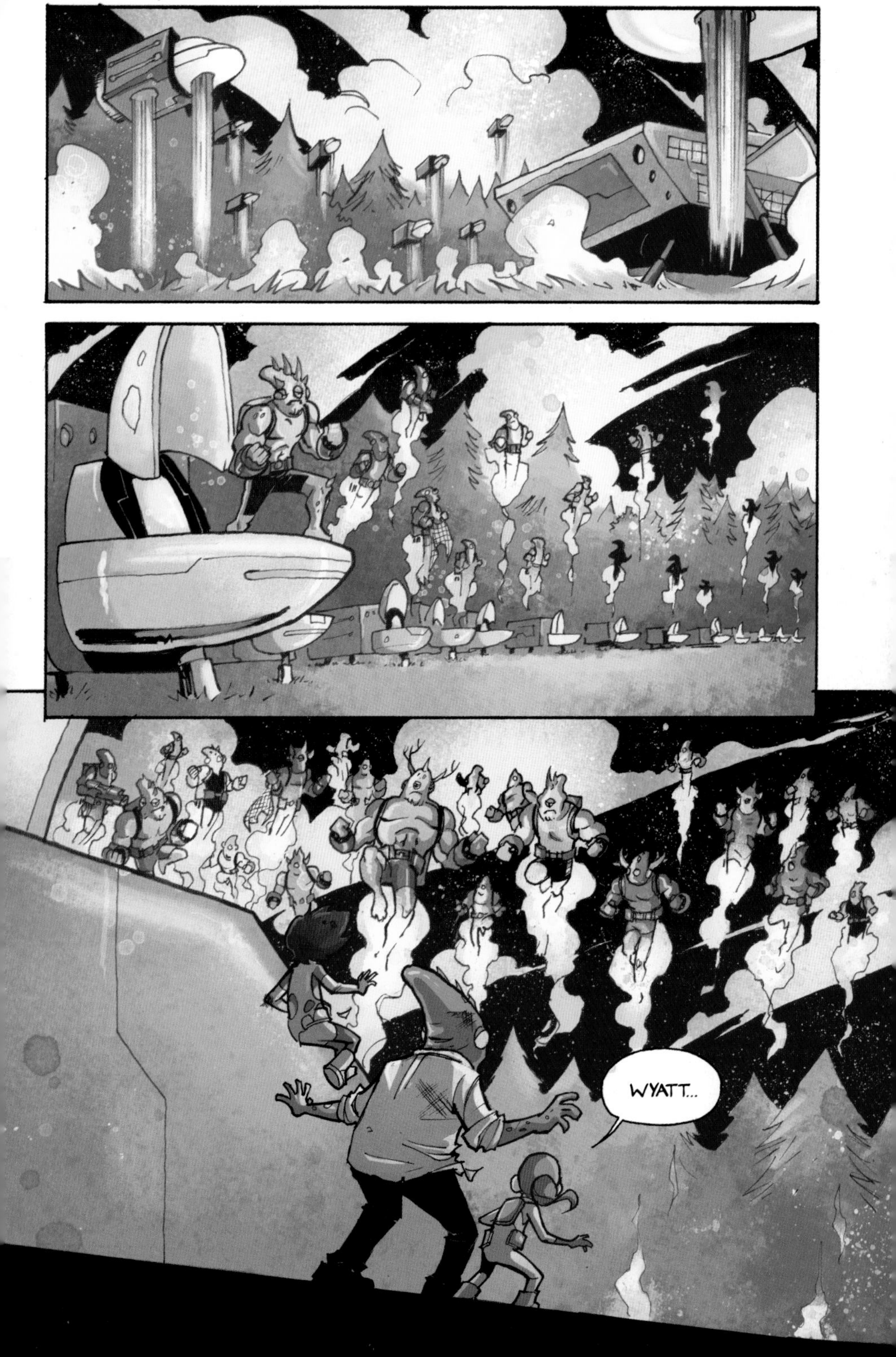
WYATT...

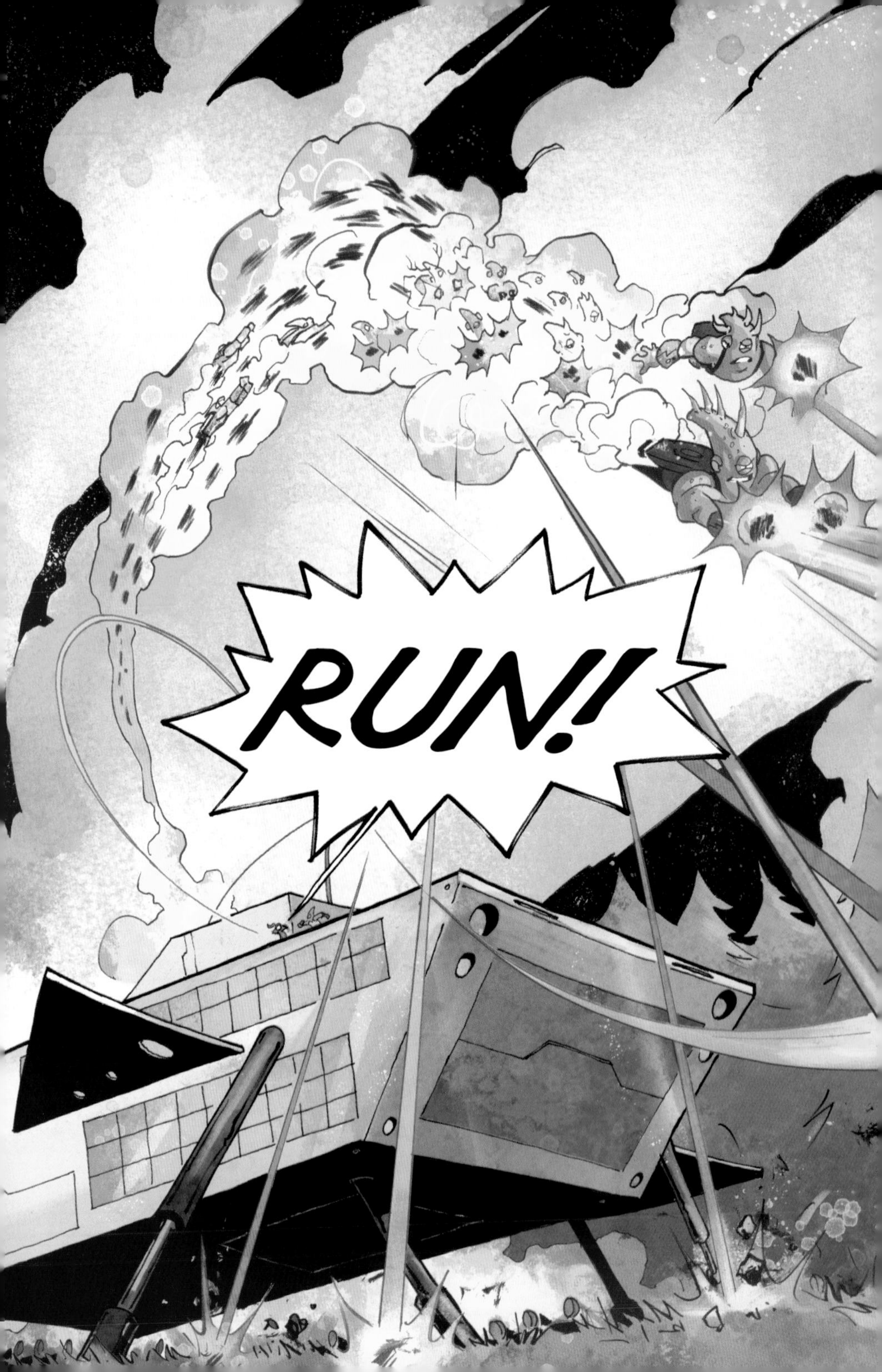
RUN!

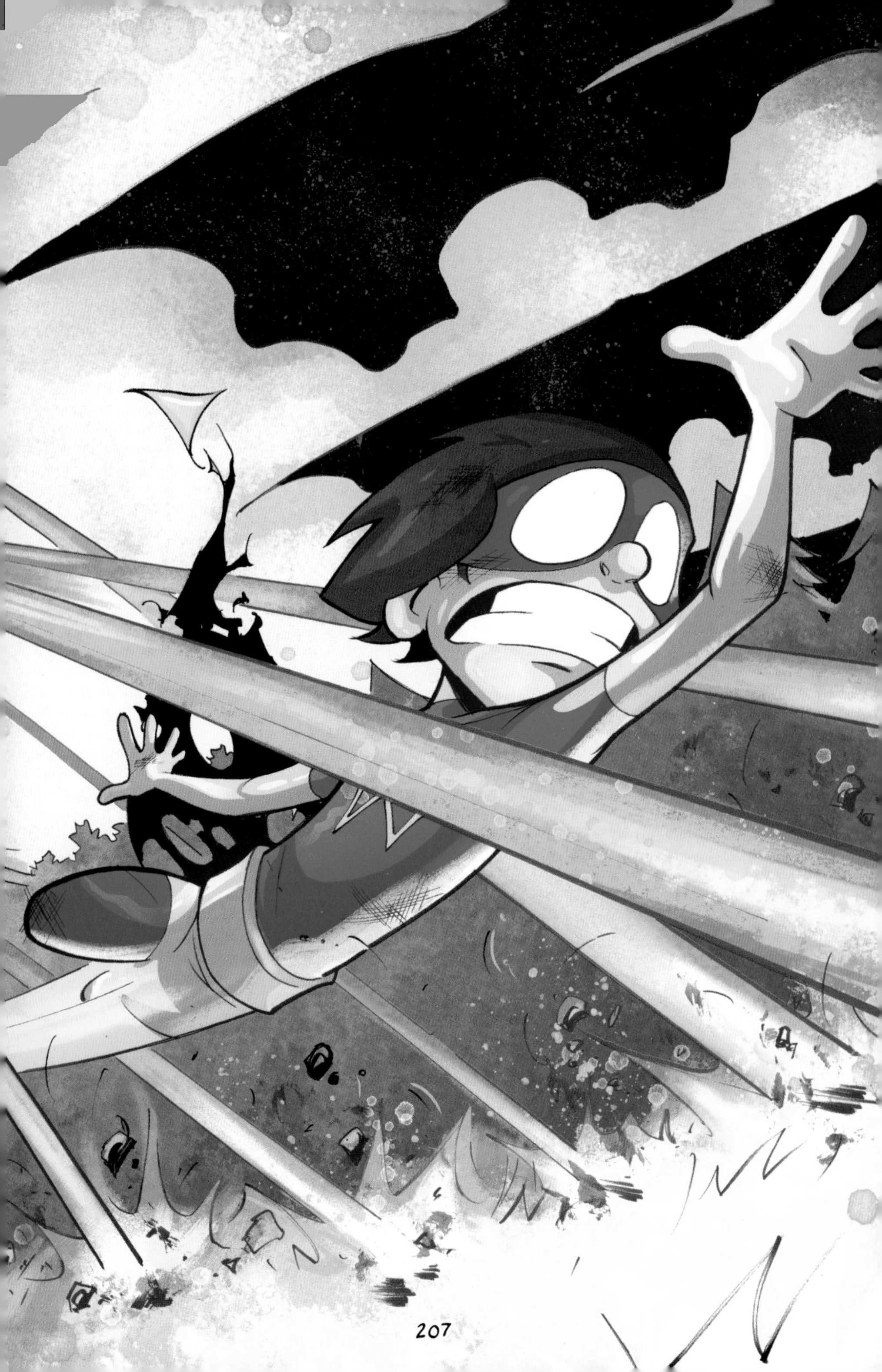

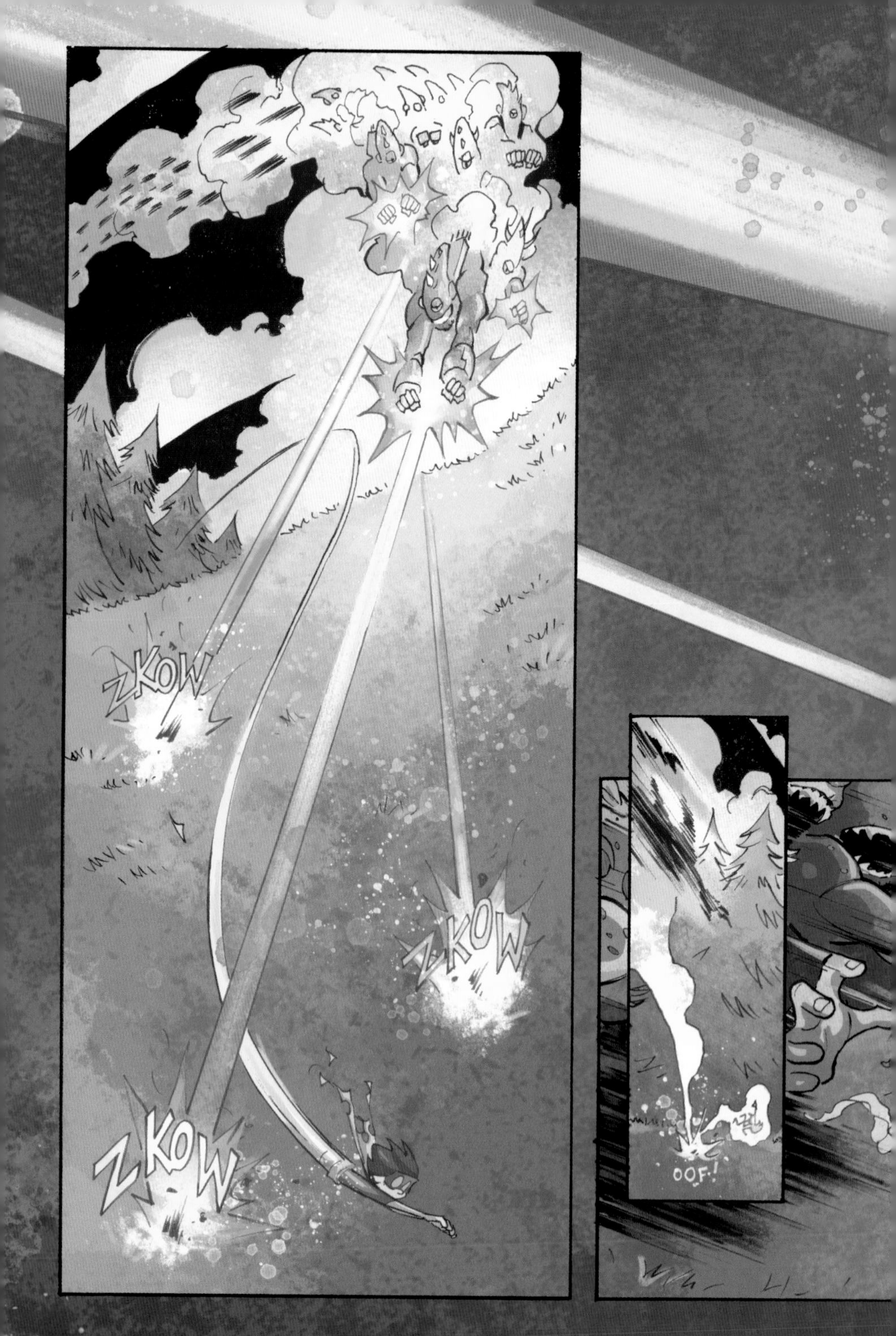
ZKOW
ZKOW
ZKOW
OOF!

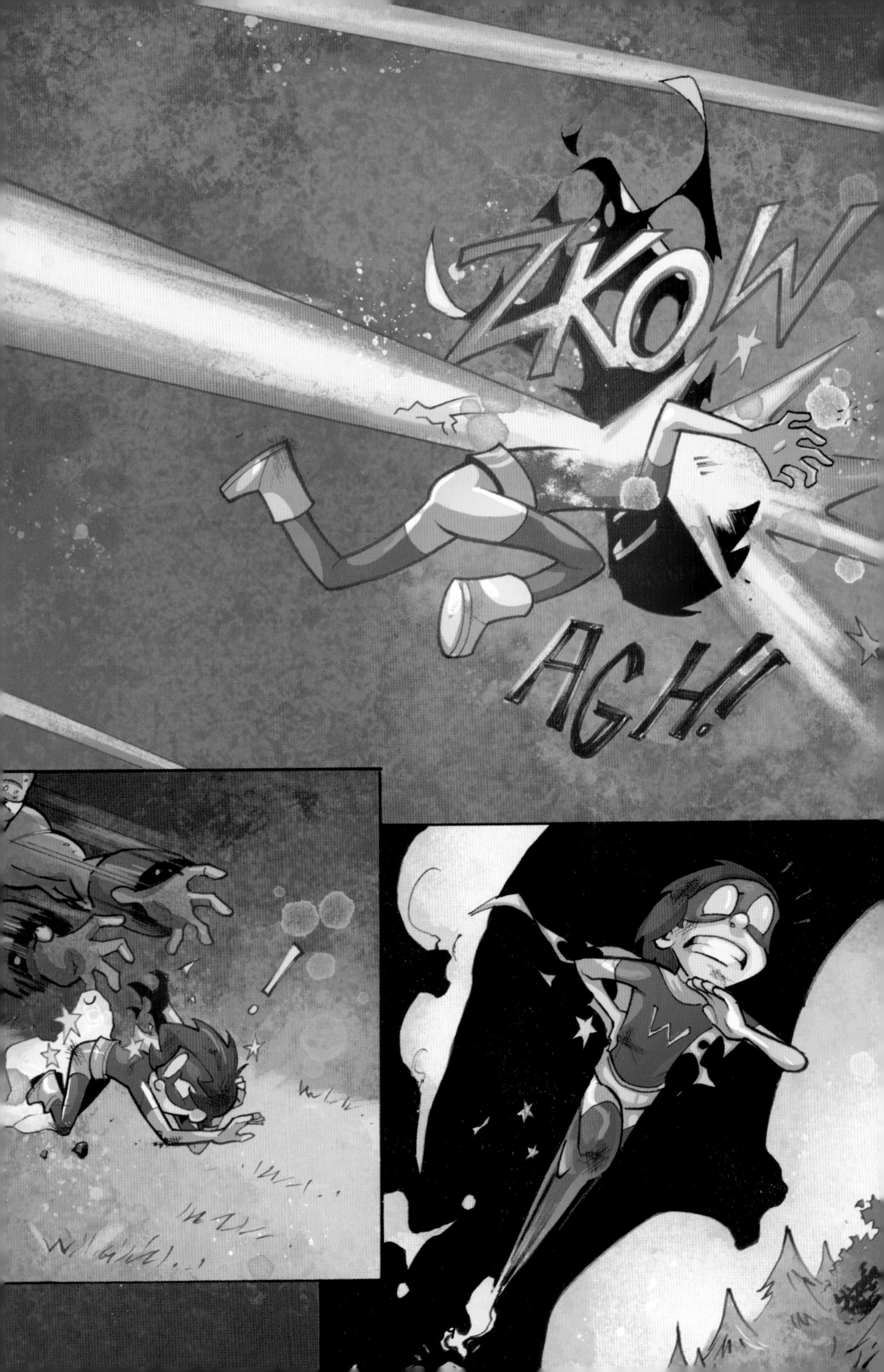

ZKOW
AGH!
!

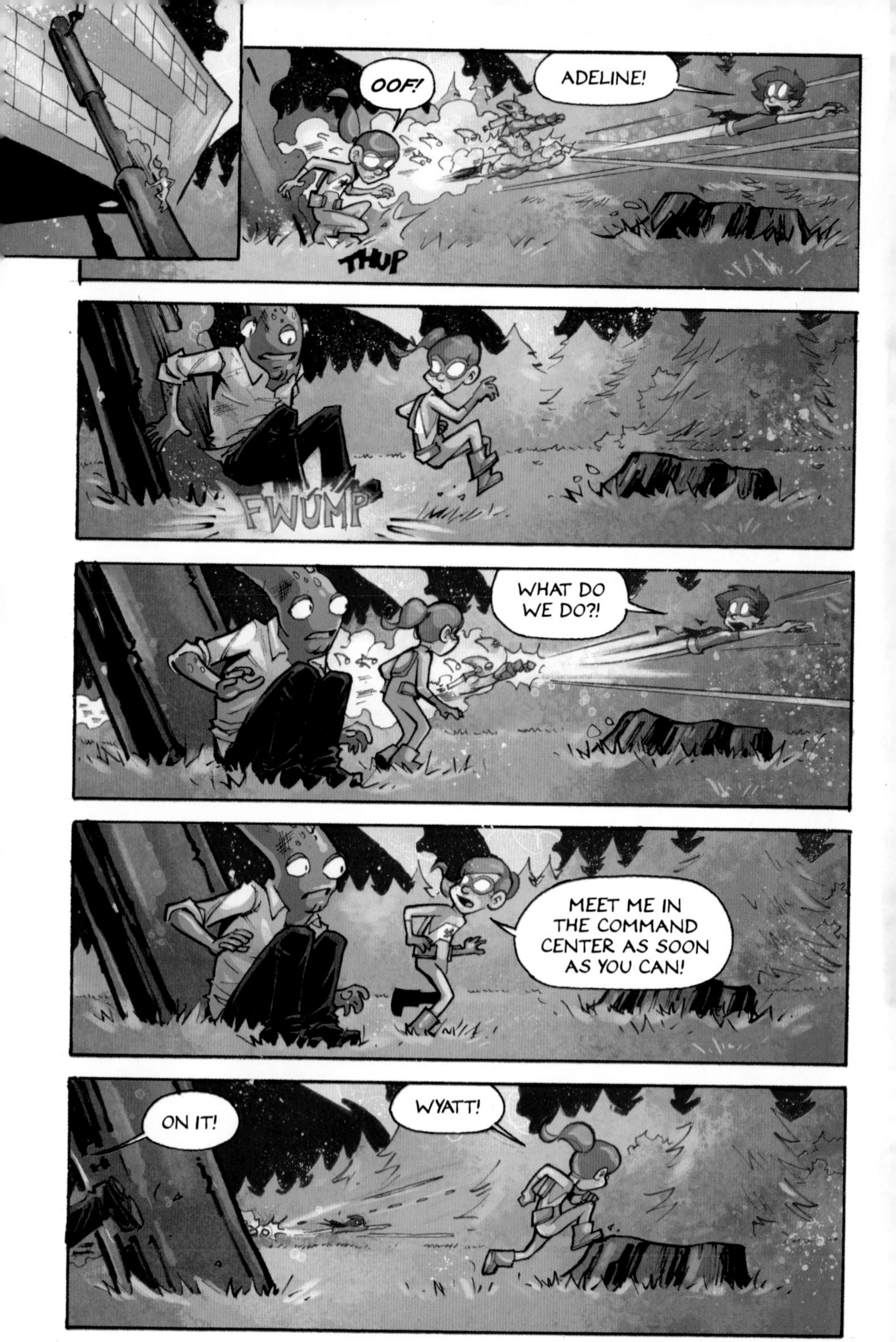
OOF!
ADELINE!
THUP
FWUMP
WHAT DO WE DO?!
MEET ME IN THE COMMAND CENTER AS SOON AS YOU CAN!
ON IT!
WYATT!

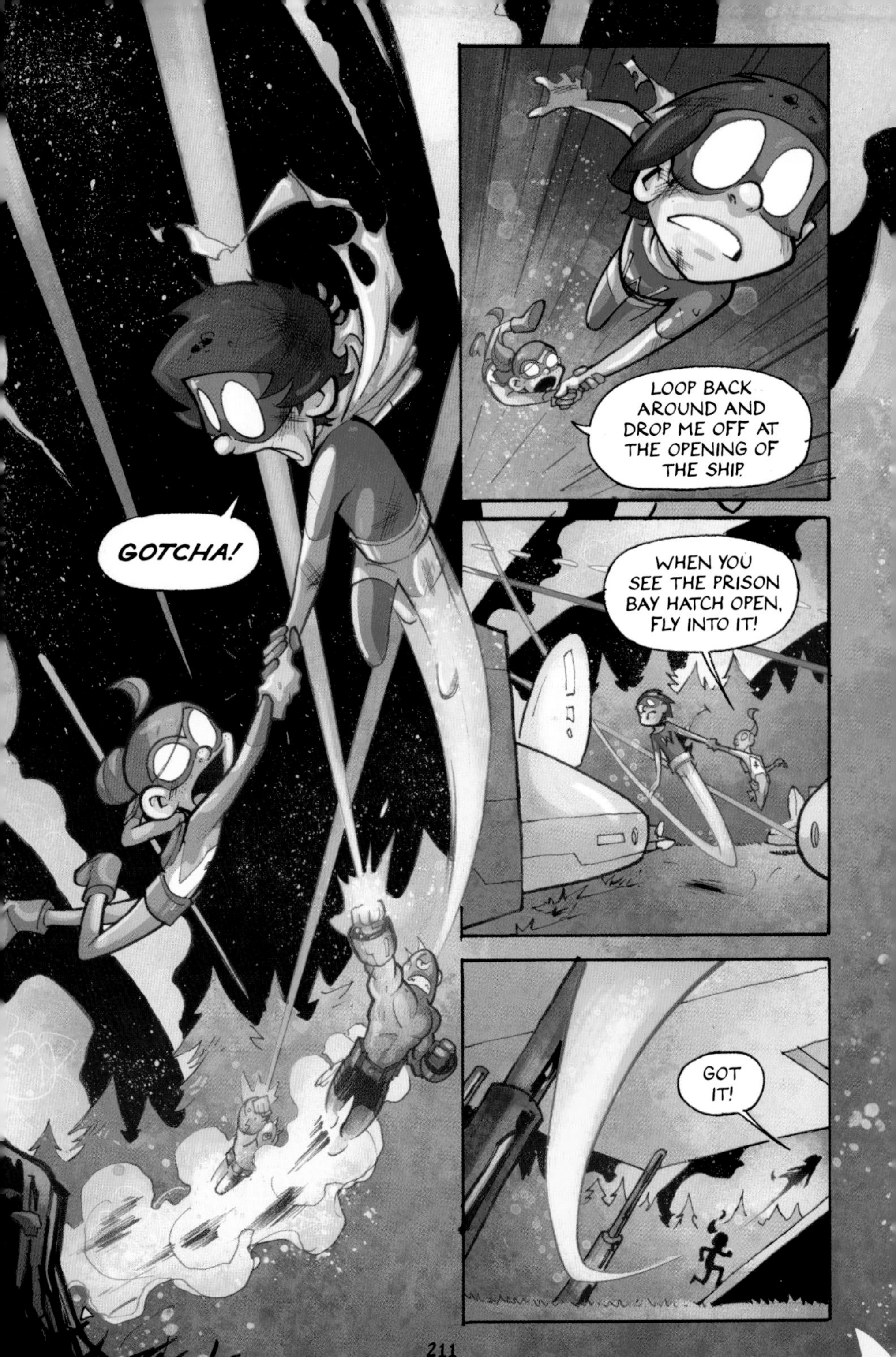
GOTCHA!
LOOP BACK AROUND AND DROP ME OFF AT THE OPENING OF THE SHIP.
WHEN YOU SEE THE PRISON BAY HATCH OPEN, FLY INTO IT!
GOT IT!

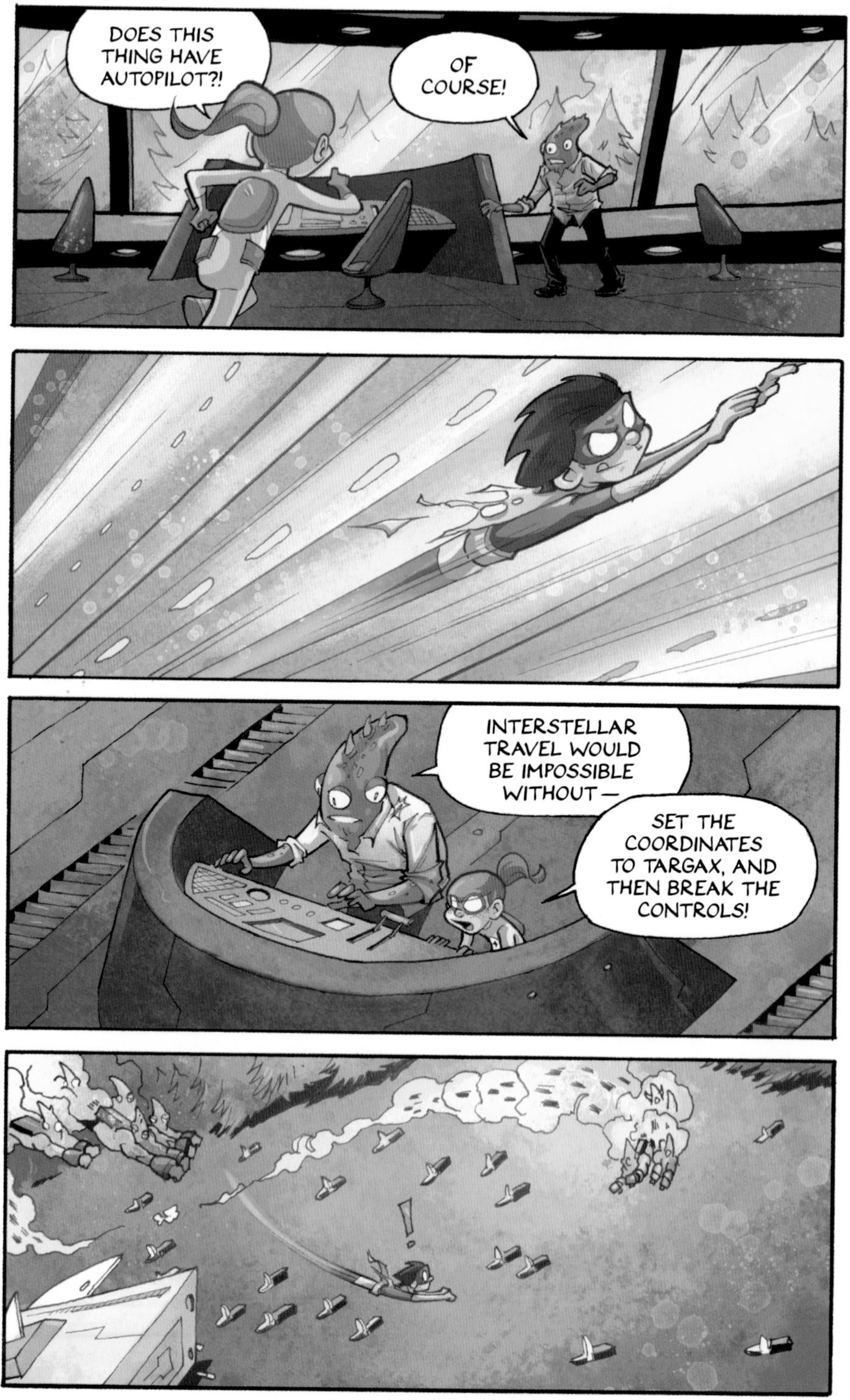
DOES THIS THING HAVE AUTOPILOT?!
OF COURSE!
INTERSTELLAR TRAVEL WOULD BE IMPOSSIBLE WITHOUT—
SET THE COORDINATES TO TARGAX, AND THEN BREAK THE CONTROLS!
!

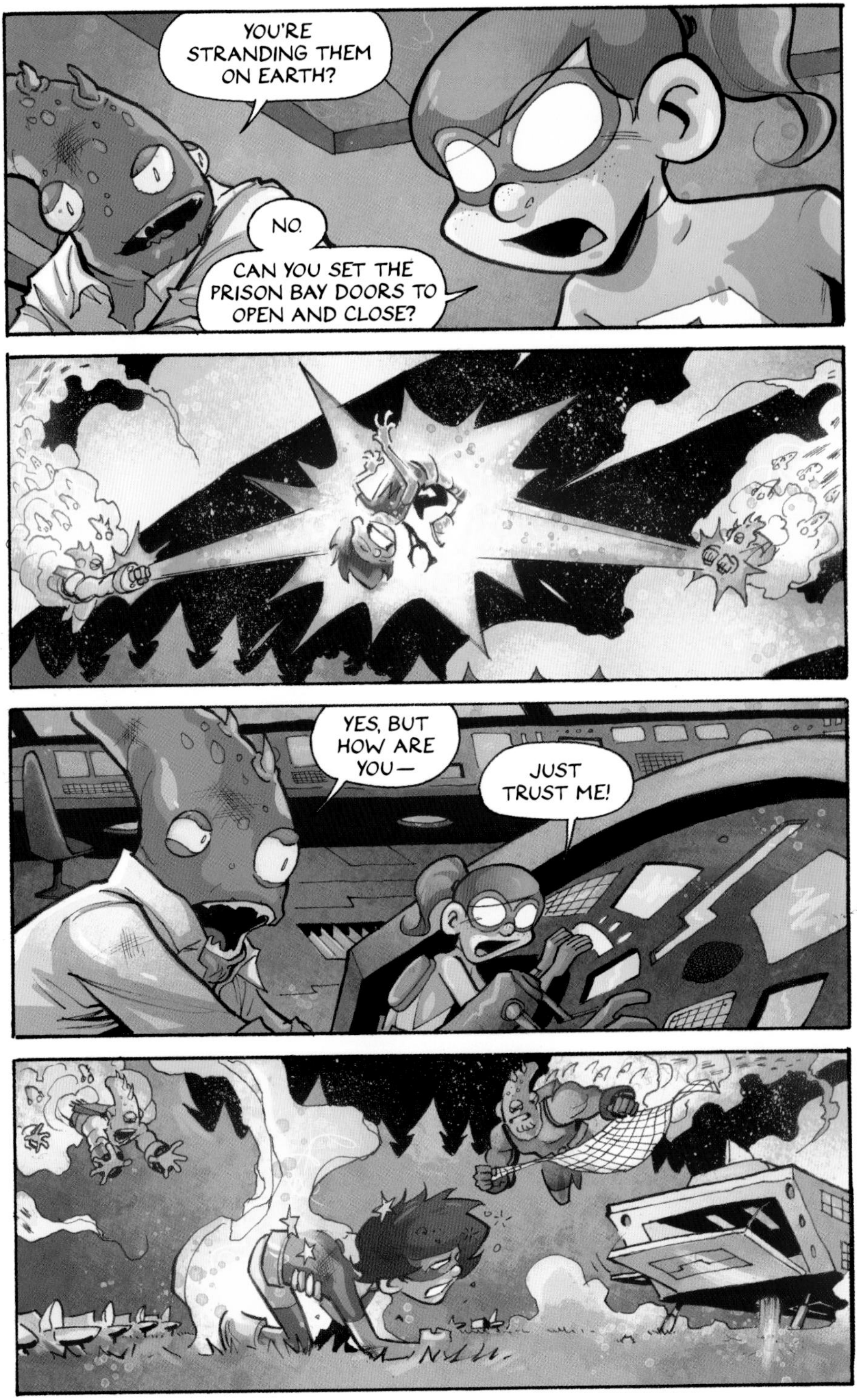
YOU'RE STRANDING THEM ON EARTH?
NO.
CAN YOU SET THE PRISON BAY DOORS TO OPEN AND CLOSE?
YES, BUT HOW ARE YOU—
JUST TRUST ME!

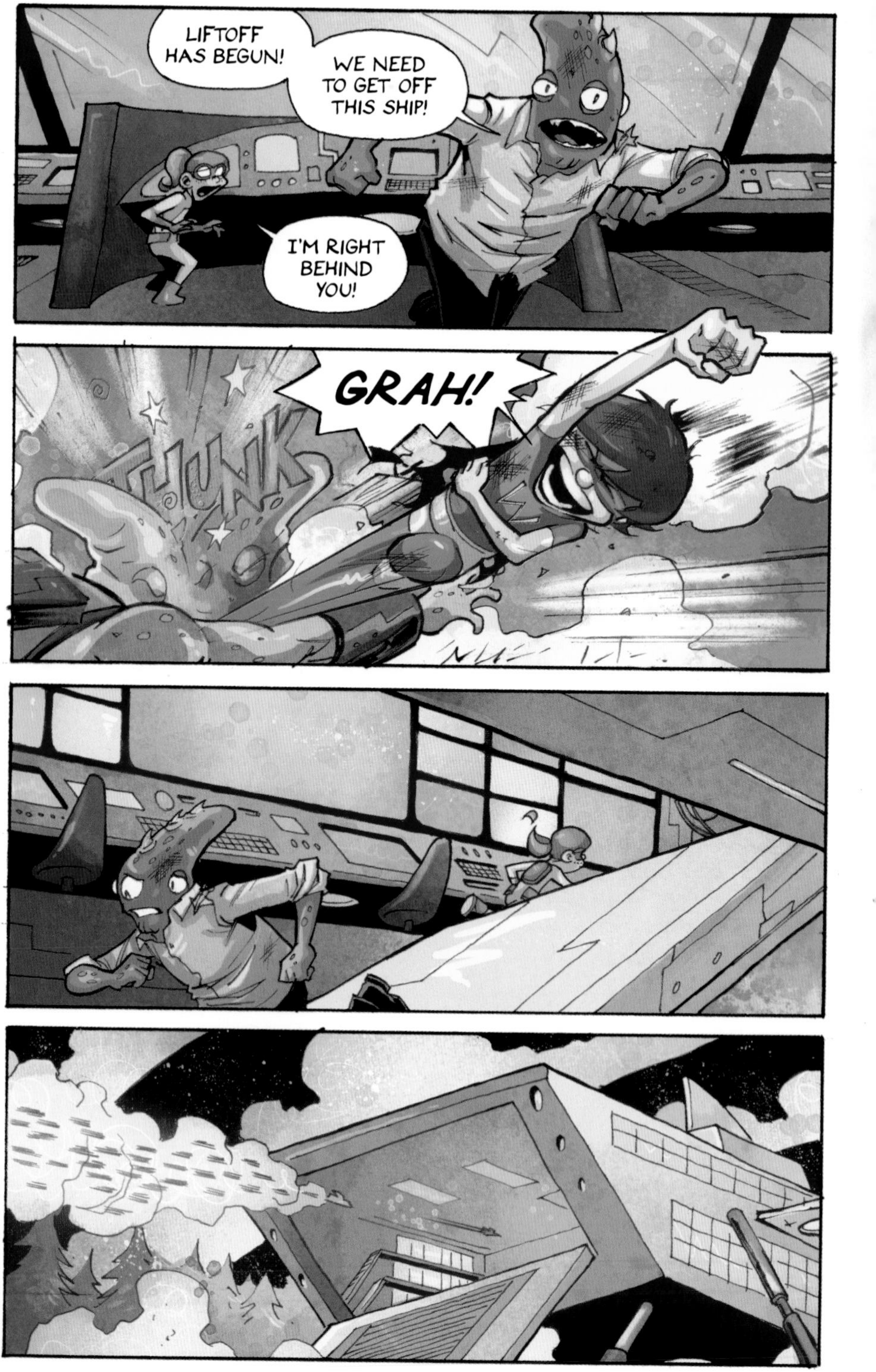
LIFTOFF HAS BEGUN!
WE NEED TO GET OFF THIS SHIP!
I'M RIGHT BEHIND YOU!
GRAH!
THUNK

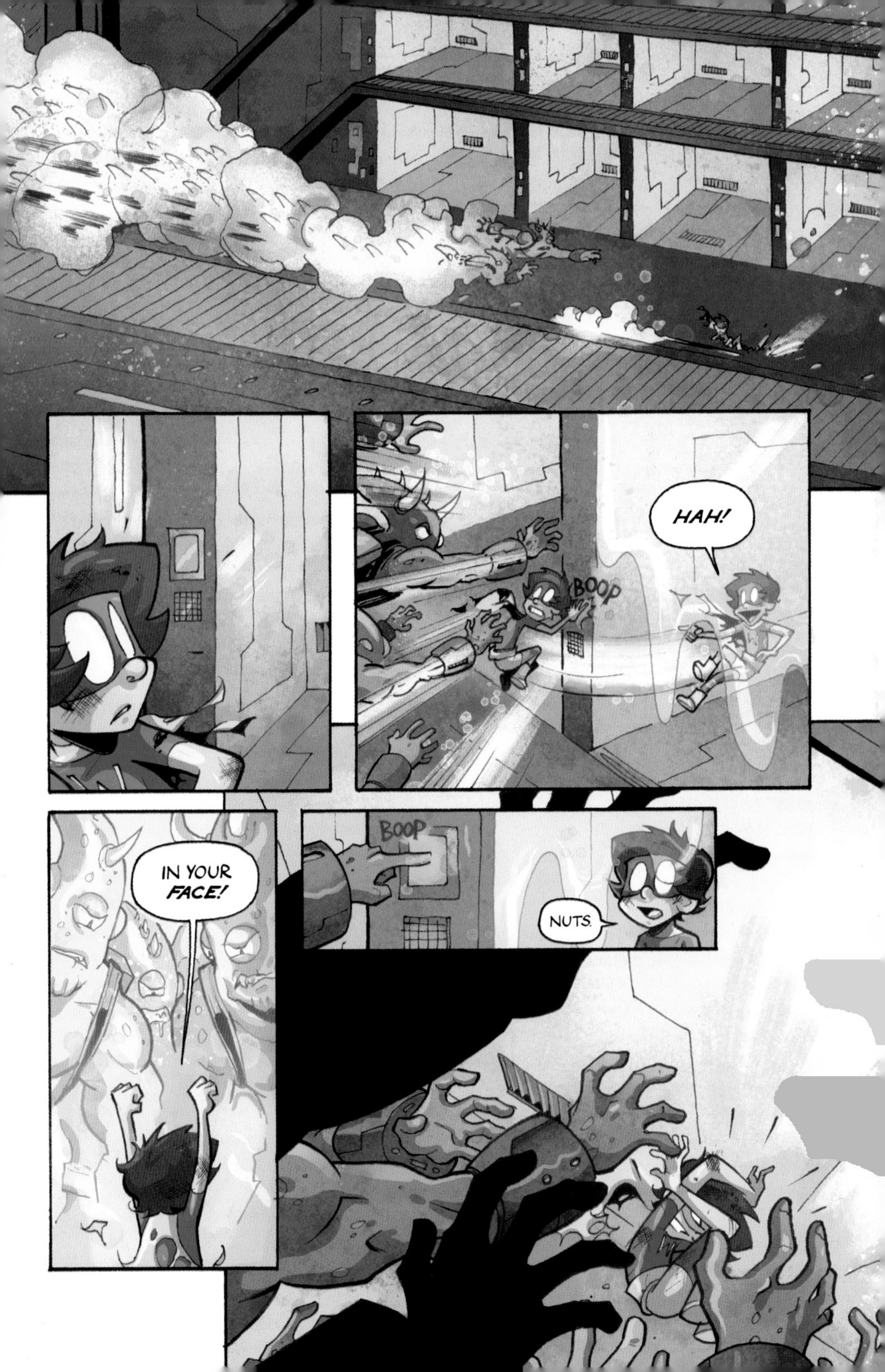

HAH!
BOOP
BOOP
NUTS.
IN YOUR *FACE!*

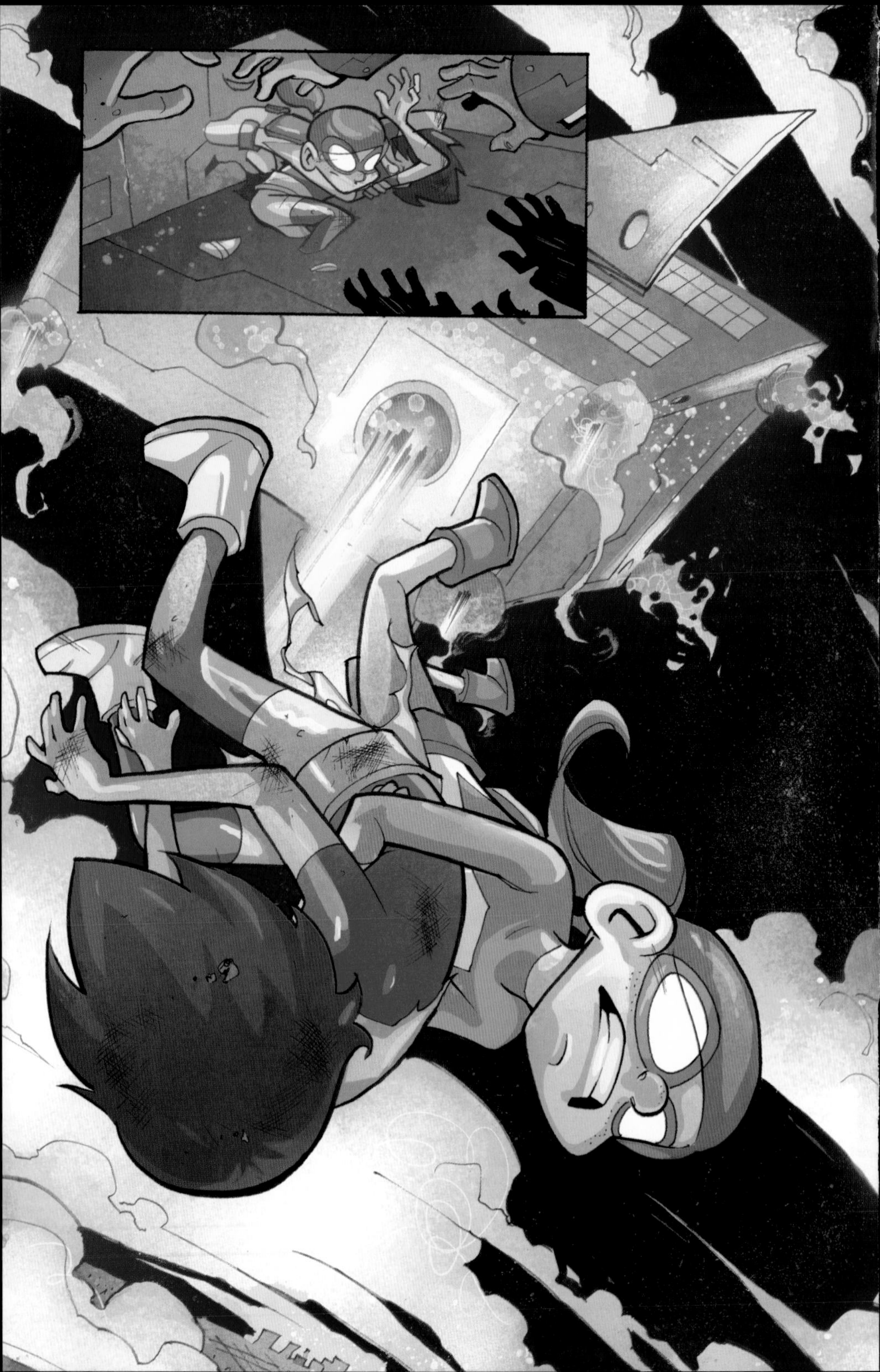

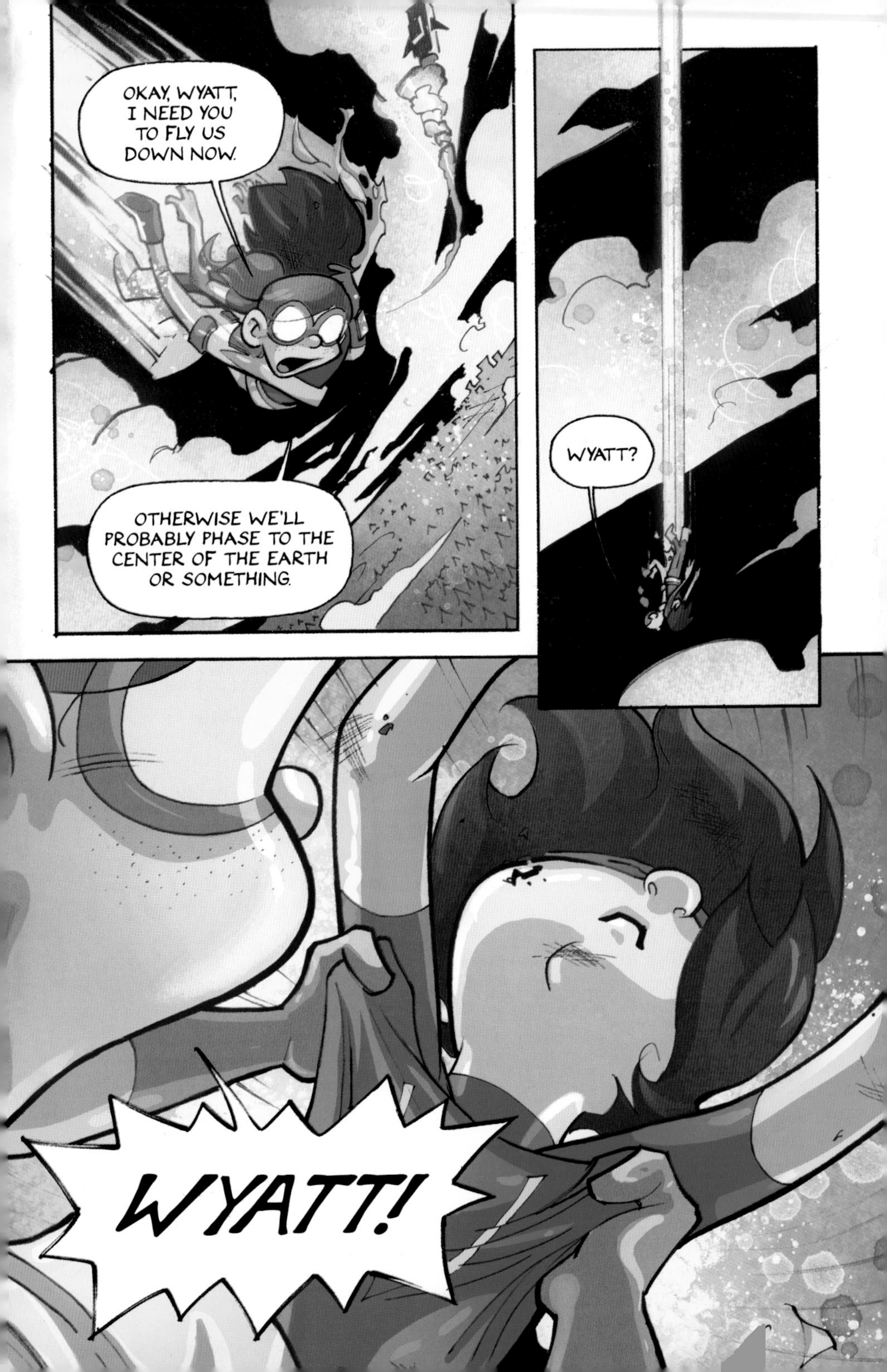
OKAY, WYATT, I NEED YOU TO FLY US DOWN NOW.
OTHERWISE WE'LL PROBABLY PHASE TO THE CENTER OF THE EARTH OR SOMETHING.
WYATT?
WYATT!

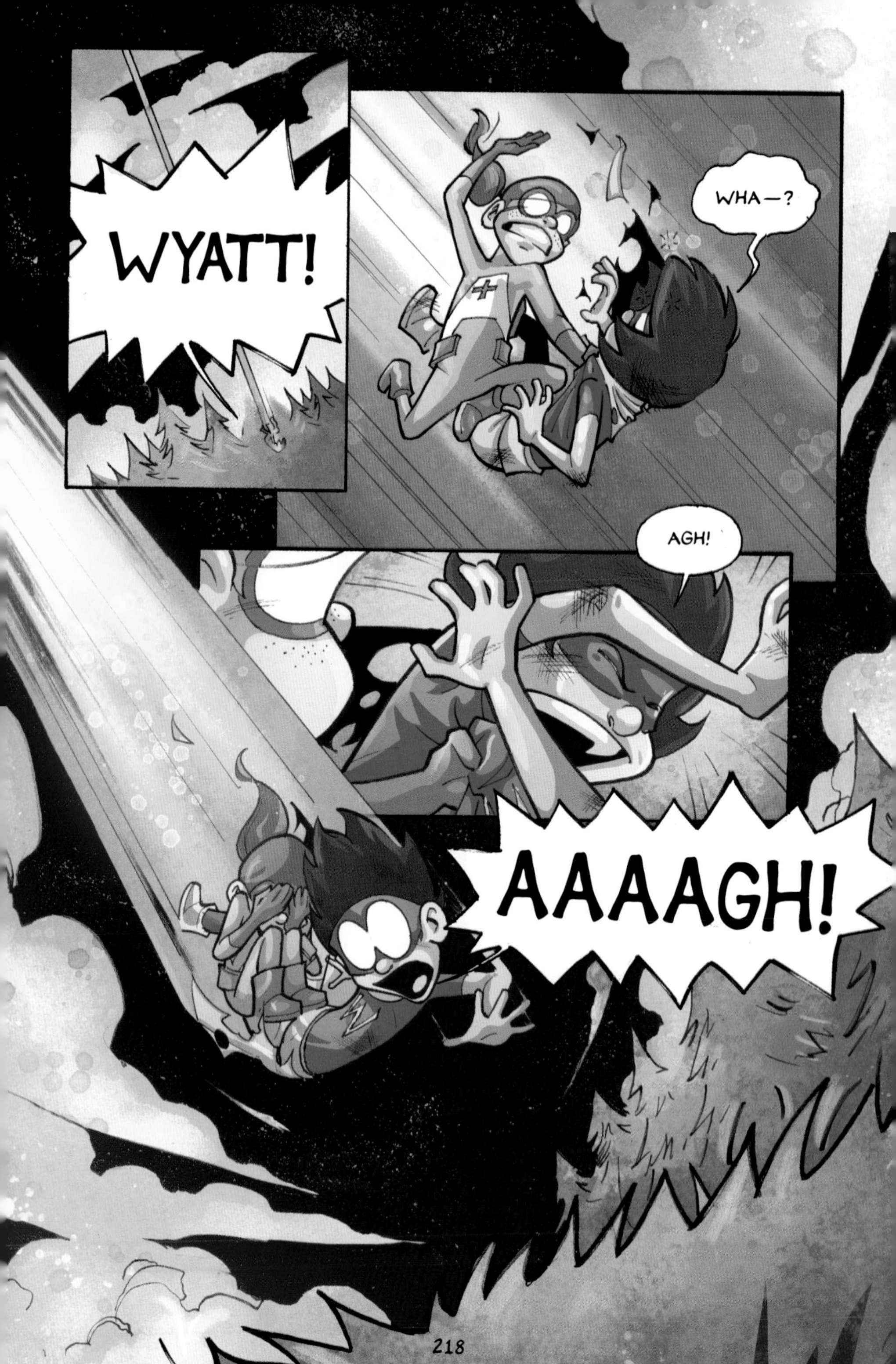
WYATT!
WHA—?
AGH!
AAAAGH!

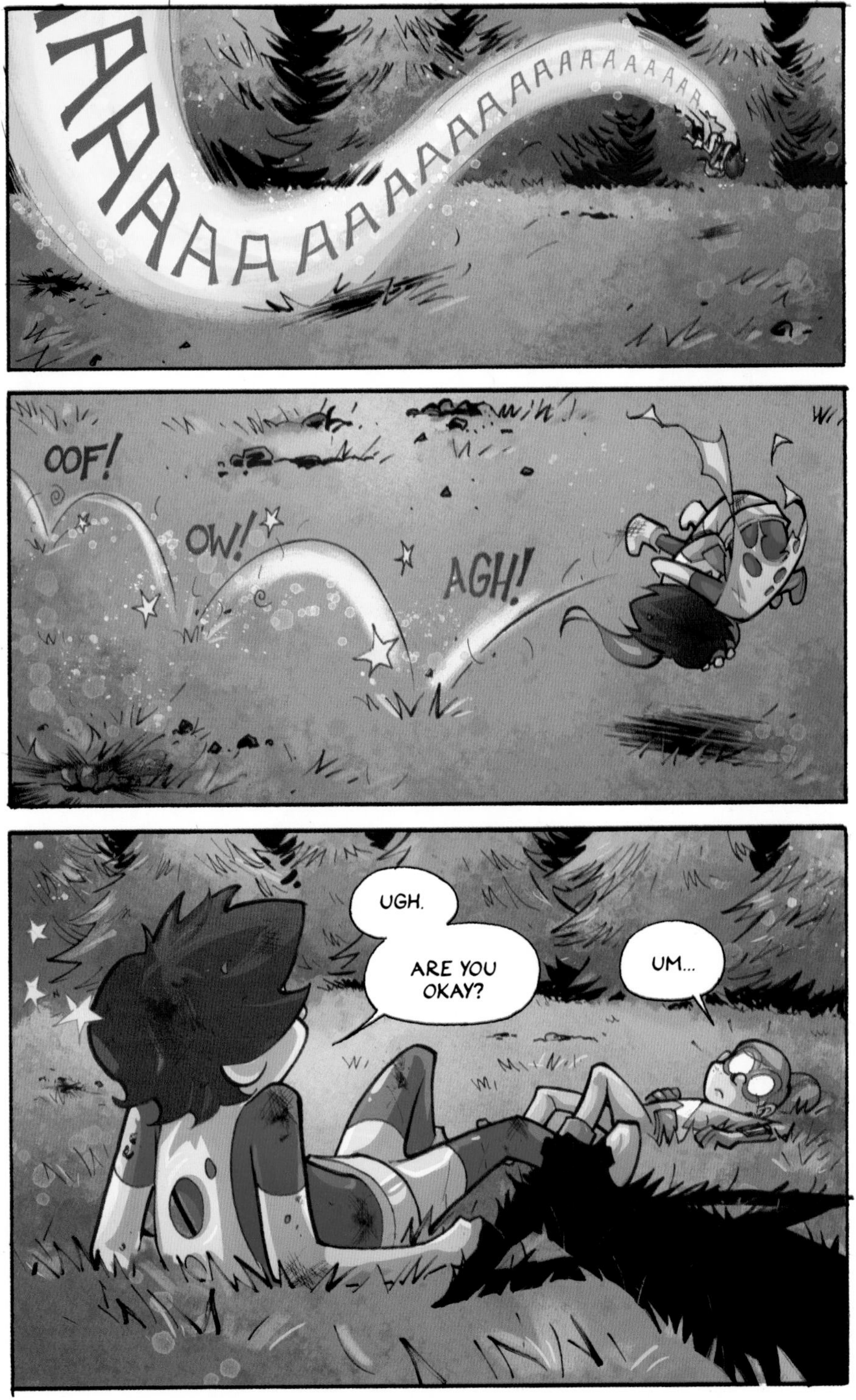
AAAAAAAAAAAAAAAAAAAAAAA
OOF!
OW!
AGH!
UGH.
ARE YOU OKAY?
UM...

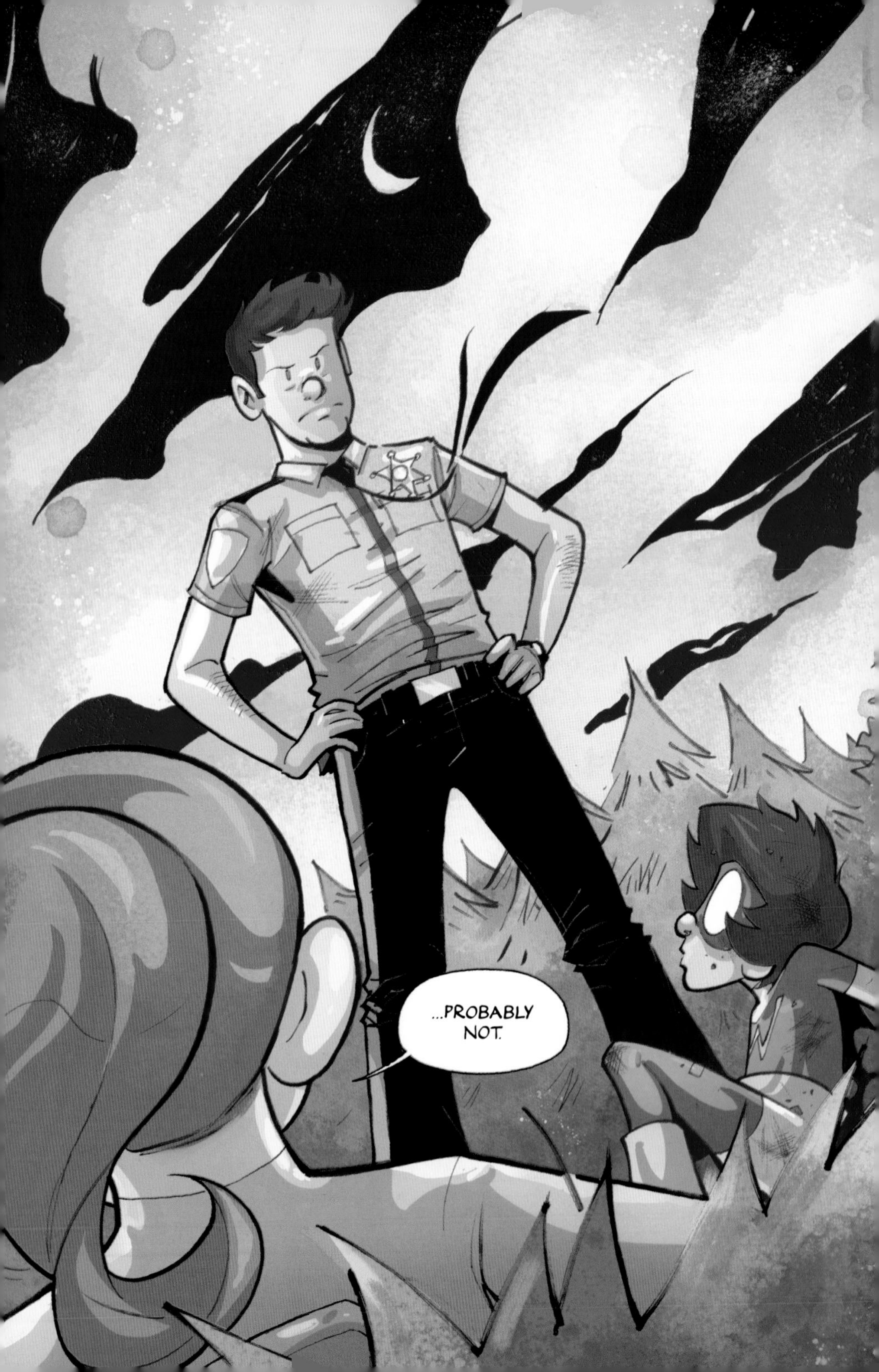
...PROBABLY NOT.

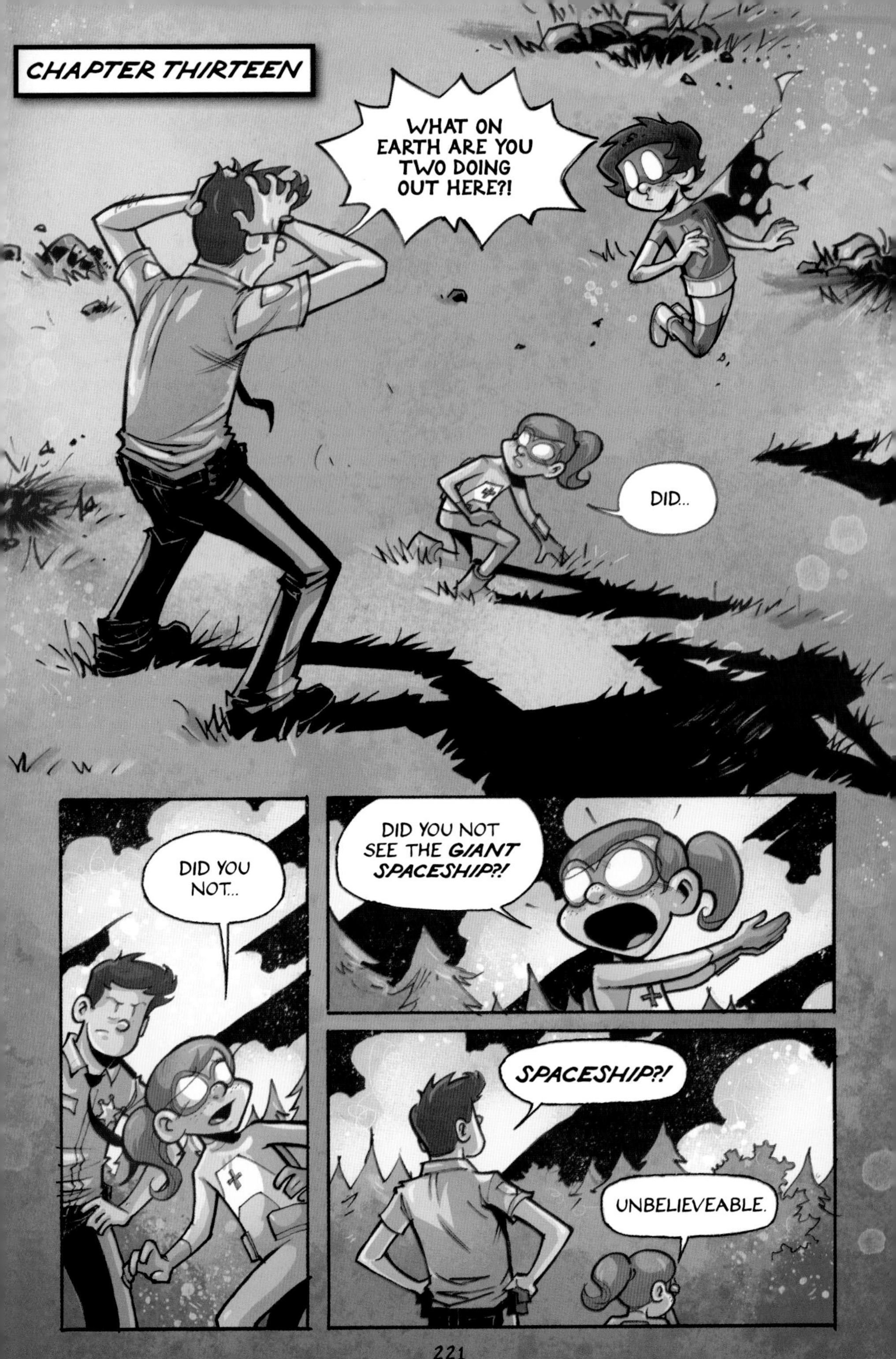
CHAPTER THIRTEEN
WHAT ON EARTH ARE YOU TWO DOING OUT HERE?!
DID...
DID YOU NOT...
DID YOU NOT SEE THE *GIANT SPACESHIP?!*
SPACESHIP?!
UNBELIEVEABLE.

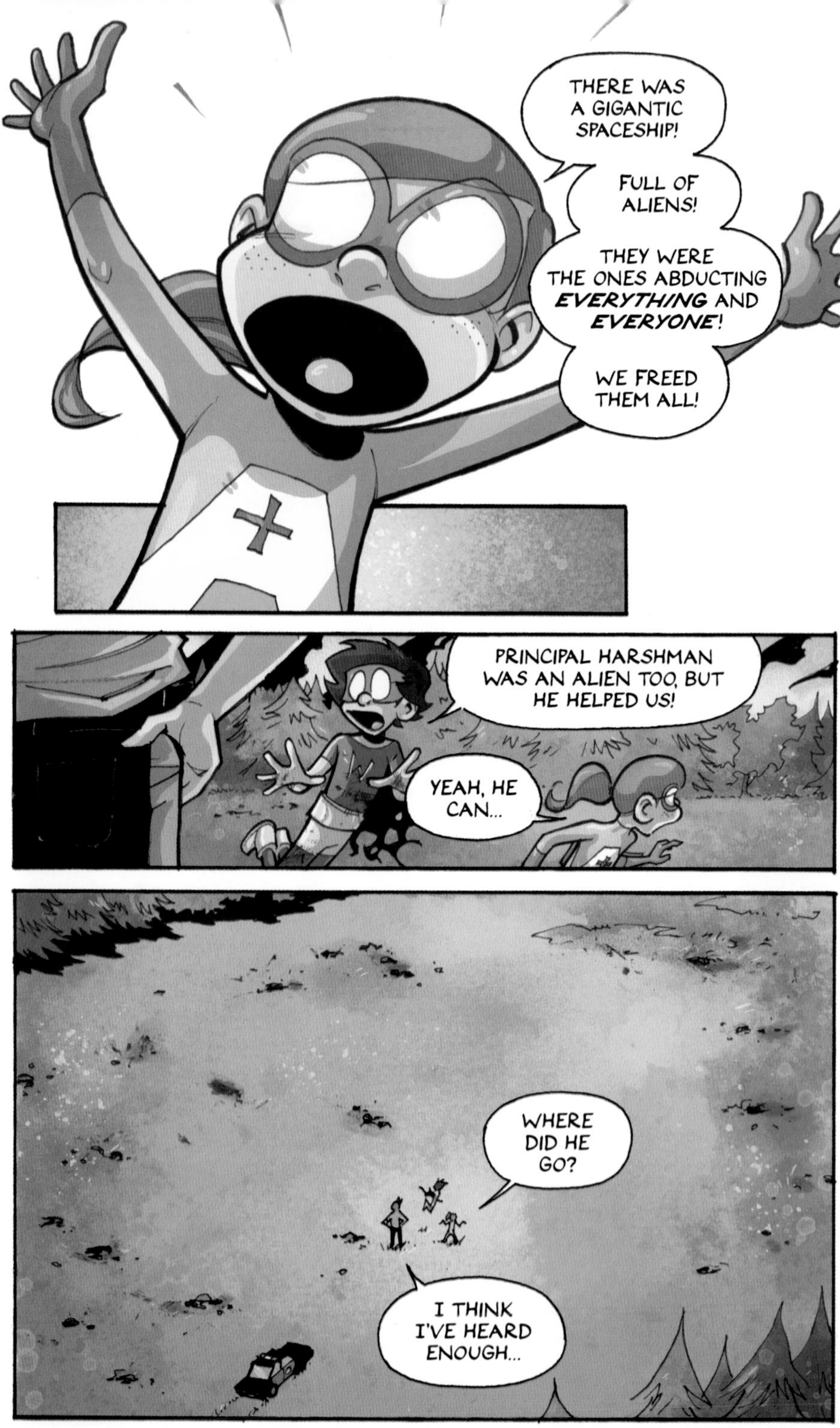
THERE WAS A GIGANTIC SPACESHIP!
FULL OF ALIENS!
THEY WERE THE ONES ABDUCTING ***EVERYTHING*** AND ***EVERYONE***!
WE FREED THEM ALL!
PRINCIPAL HARSHMAN WAS AN ALIEN TOO, BUT HE HELPED US!
YEAH, HE CAN...
WHERE DID HE GO?
I THINK I'VE HEARD ENOUGH...

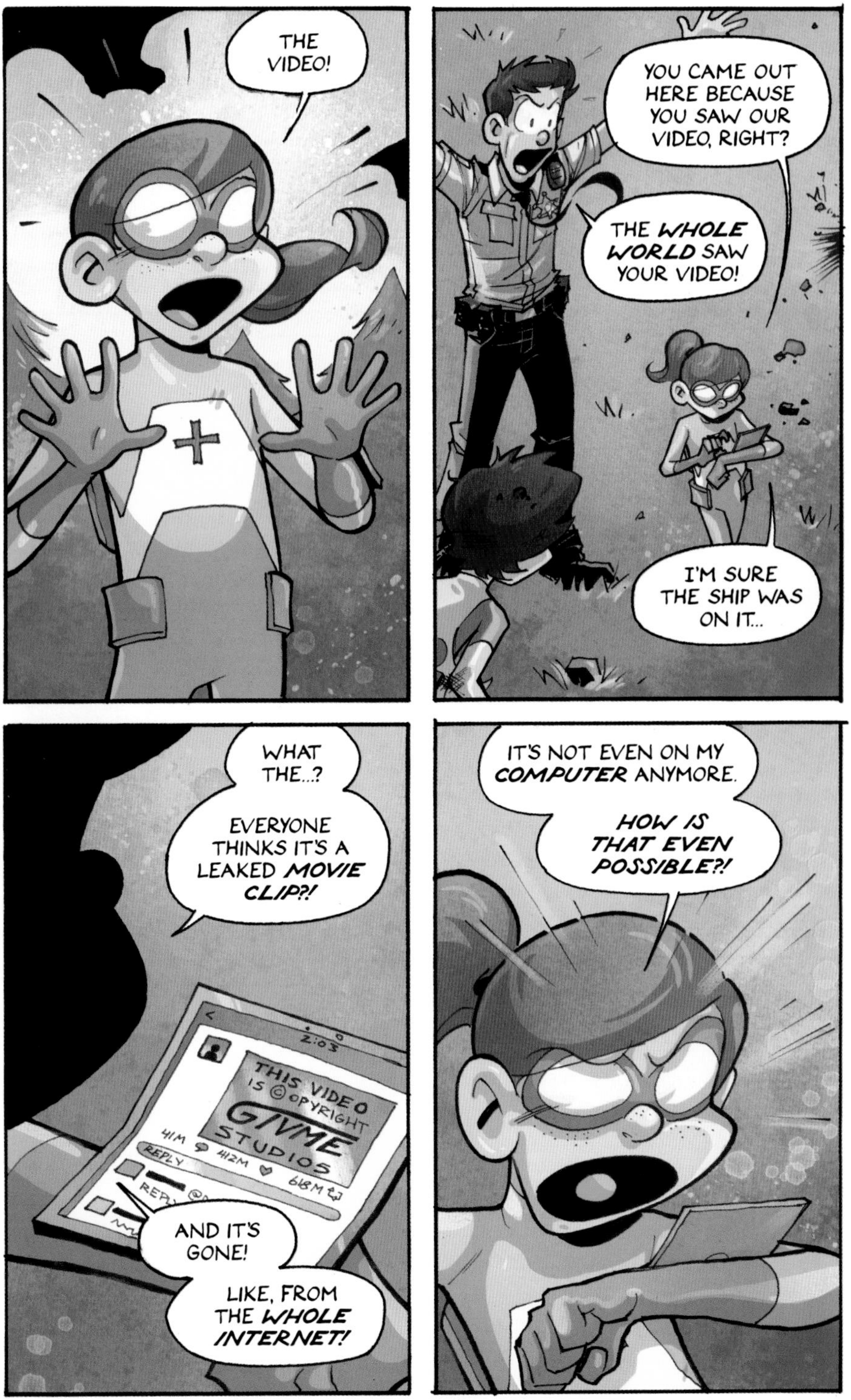
THE VIDEO!
YOU CAME OUT HERE BECAUSE YOU SAW OUR VIDEO, RIGHT?
THE WHOLE WORLD SAW YOUR VIDEO!
I'M SURE THE SHIP WAS ON IT...
WHAT THE...?
EVERYONE THINKS IT'S A LEAKED MOVIE CLIP?!
2:03
THIS VIDEO IS © OPYRIGHT GIVME STUDIOS
41M
412M
618M
REPLY
AND IT'S GONE!
LIKE, FROM THE WHOLE INTERNET!
IT'S NOT EVEN ON MY COMPUTER ANYMORE.
HOW IS THAT EVEN POSSIBLE?!

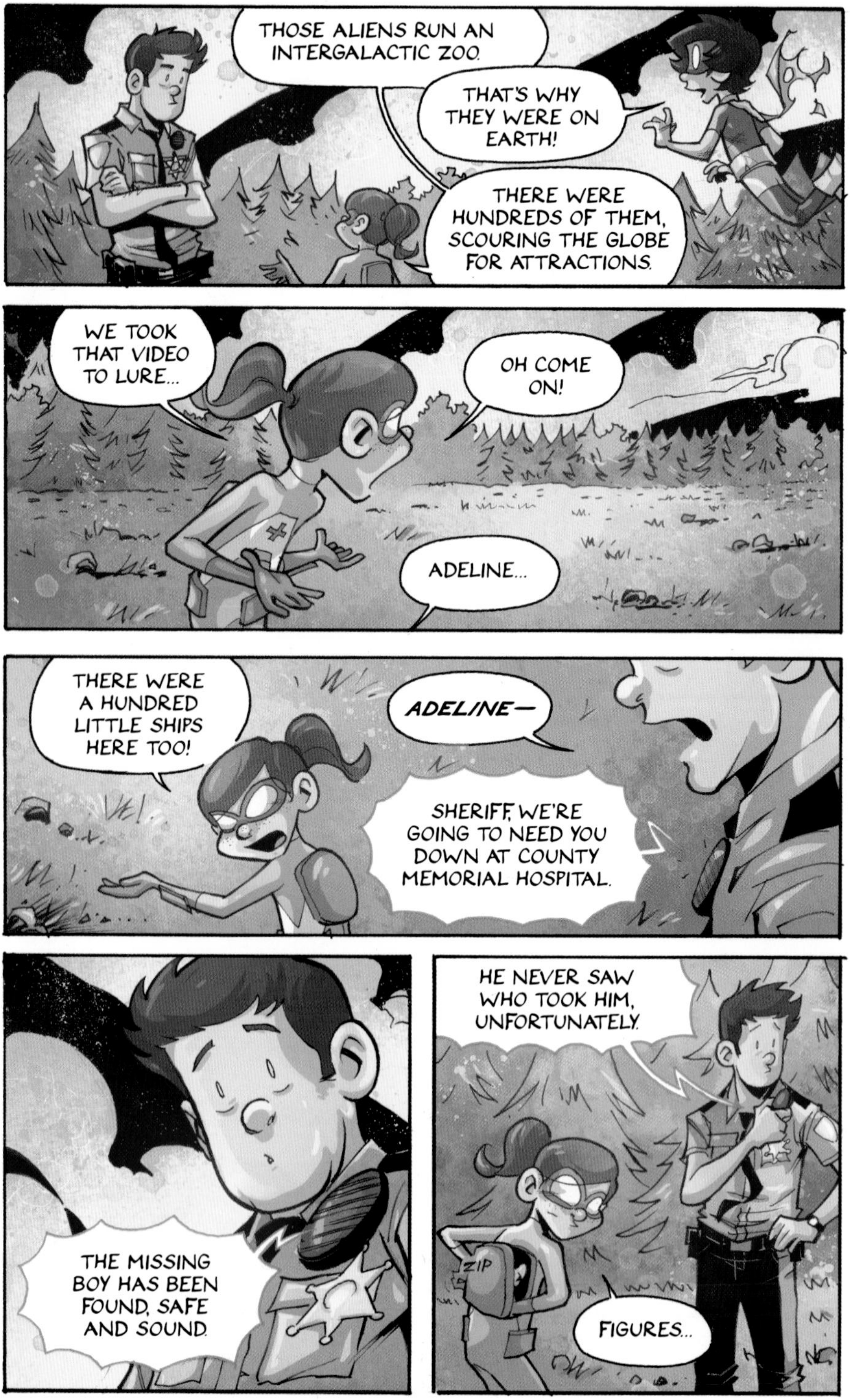

THOSE ALIENS RUN AN INTERGALACTIC ZOO.
THAT'S WHY THEY WERE ON EARTH!
THERE WERE HUNDREDS OF THEM, SCOURING THE GLOBE FOR ATTRACTIONS.
WE TOOK THAT VIDEO TO LURE...
OH COME ON!
ADELINE...
THERE WERE A HUNDRED LITTLE SHIPS HERE TOO!
ADELINE—
SHERIFF, WE'RE GOING TO NEED YOU DOWN AT COUNTY MEMORIAL HOSPITAL.
THE MISSING BOY HAS BEEN FOUND, SAFE AND SOUND.
HE NEVER SAW WHO TOOK HIM, UNFORTUNATELY.
ZIP
FIGURES...

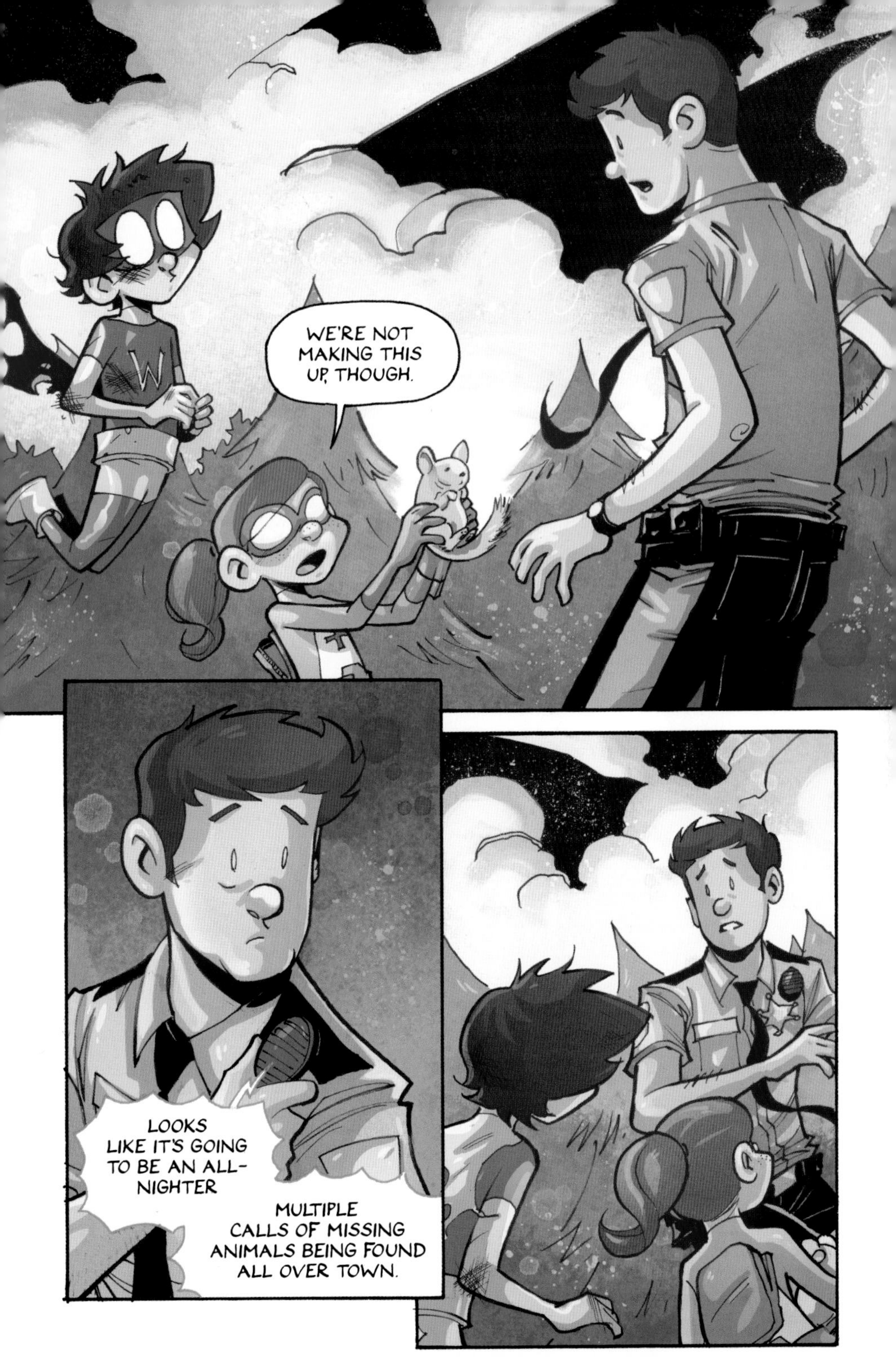
WE'RE NOT MAKING THIS UP, THOUGH.
LOOKS LIKE IT'S GOING TO BE AN ALL-NIGHTER
MULTIPLE CALLS OF MISSING ANIMALS BEING FOUND ALL OVER TOWN.

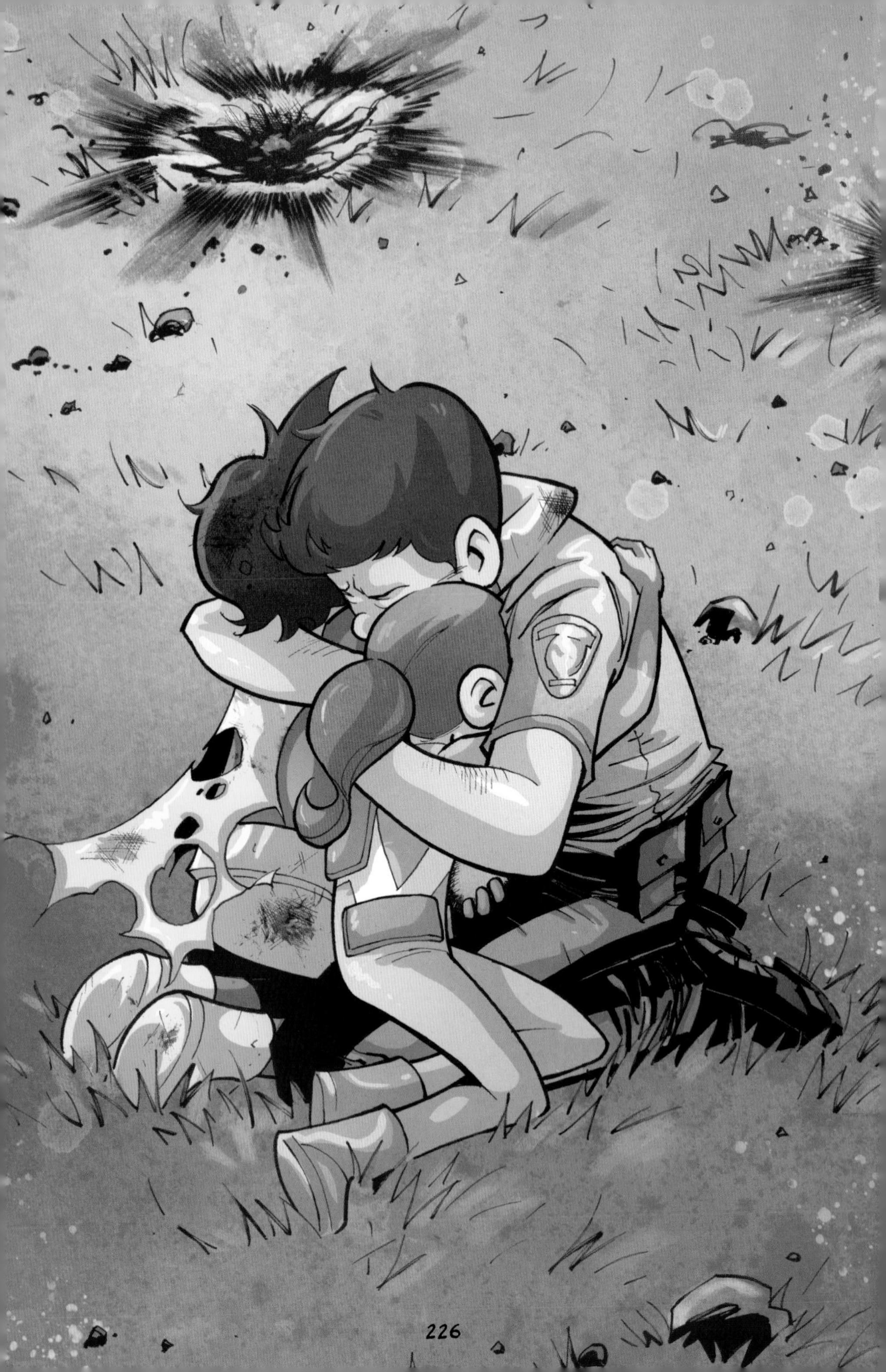

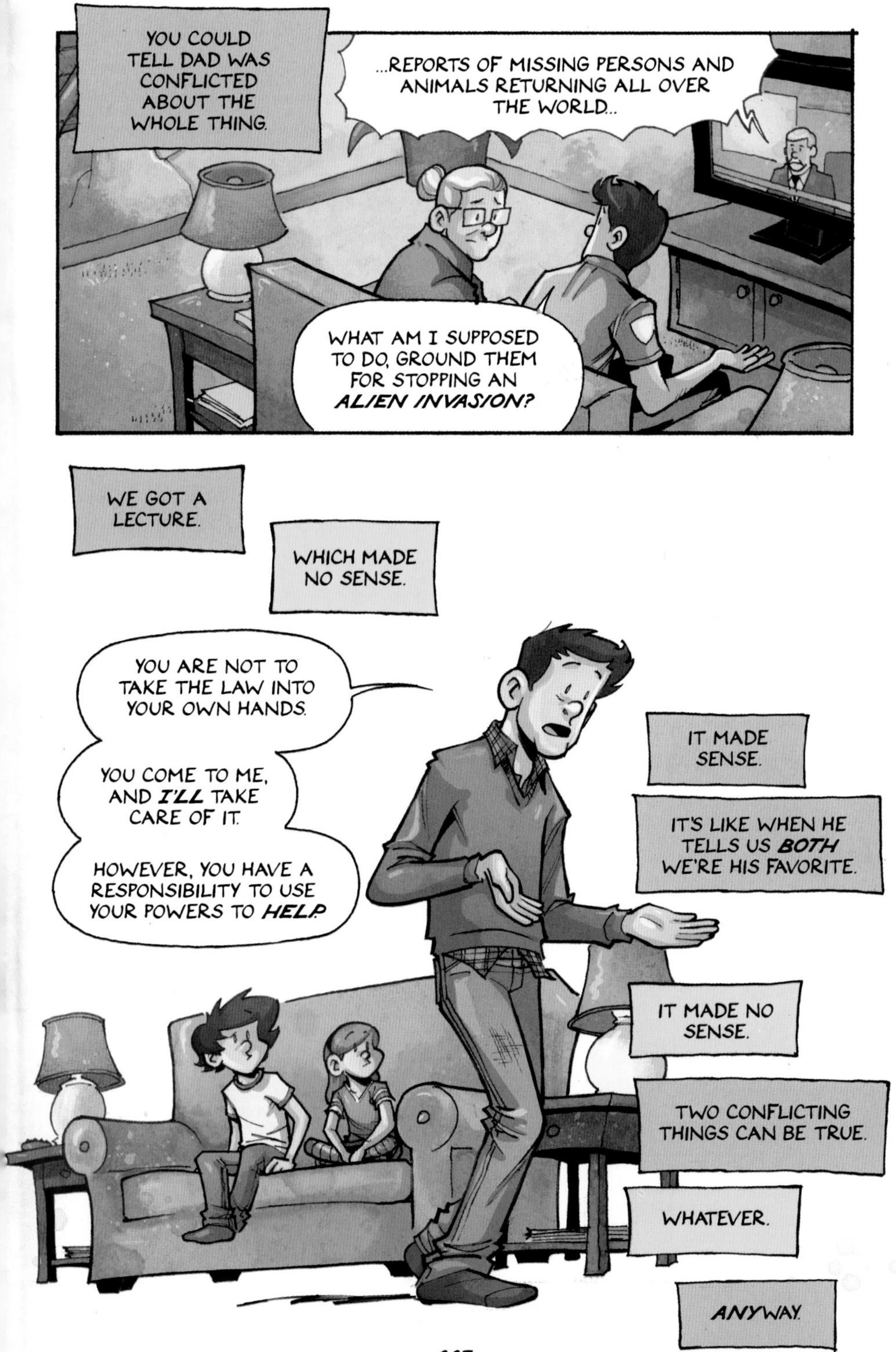
YOU COULD TELL DAD WAS CONFLICTED ABOUT THE WHOLE THING.
...REPORTS OF MISSING PERSONS AND ANIMALS RETURNING ALL OVER THE WORLD...
WHAT AM I SUPPOSED TO DO, GROUND THEM FOR STOPPING AN *ALIEN INVASION?*
WE GOT A LECTURE.
WHICH MADE NO SENSE.
YOU ARE NOT TO TAKE THE LAW INTO YOUR OWN HANDS.
YOU COME TO ME, AND *I'LL* TAKE CARE OF IT.
HOWEVER, YOU HAVE A RESPONSIBILITY TO USE YOUR POWERS TO *HELP.*
IT MADE SENSE.
IT'S LIKE WHEN HE TELLS US *BOTH* WE'RE HIS FAVORITE.
IT MADE NO SENSE.
TWO CONFLICTING THINGS CAN BE TRUE.
WHATEVER.
*ANY*WAY.

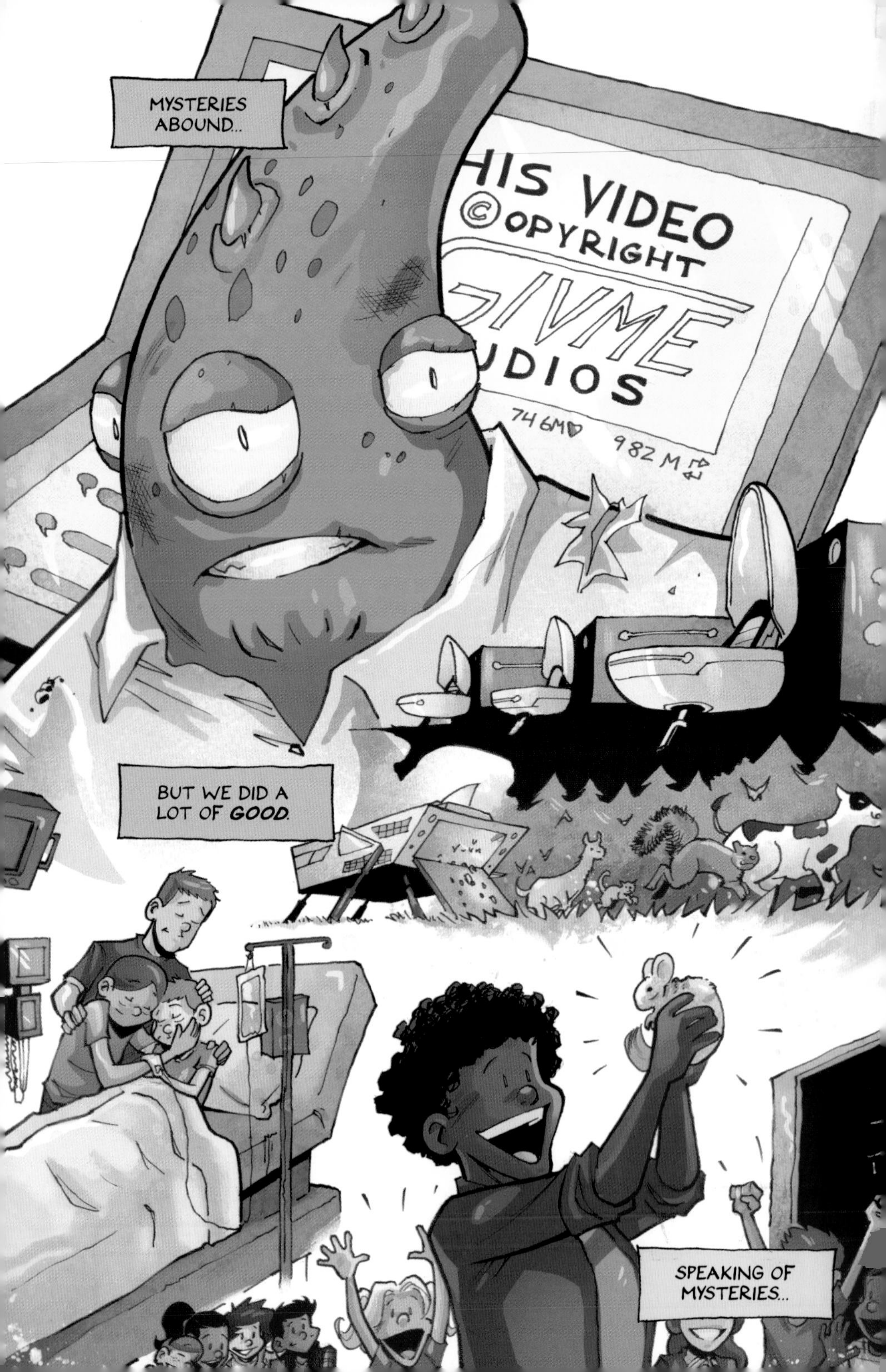
MYSTERIES ABOUND...
HIS VIDEO
©OPYRIGHT
UDIOS
BUT WE DID A LOT OF **GOOD**.
SPEAKING OF MYSTERIES...

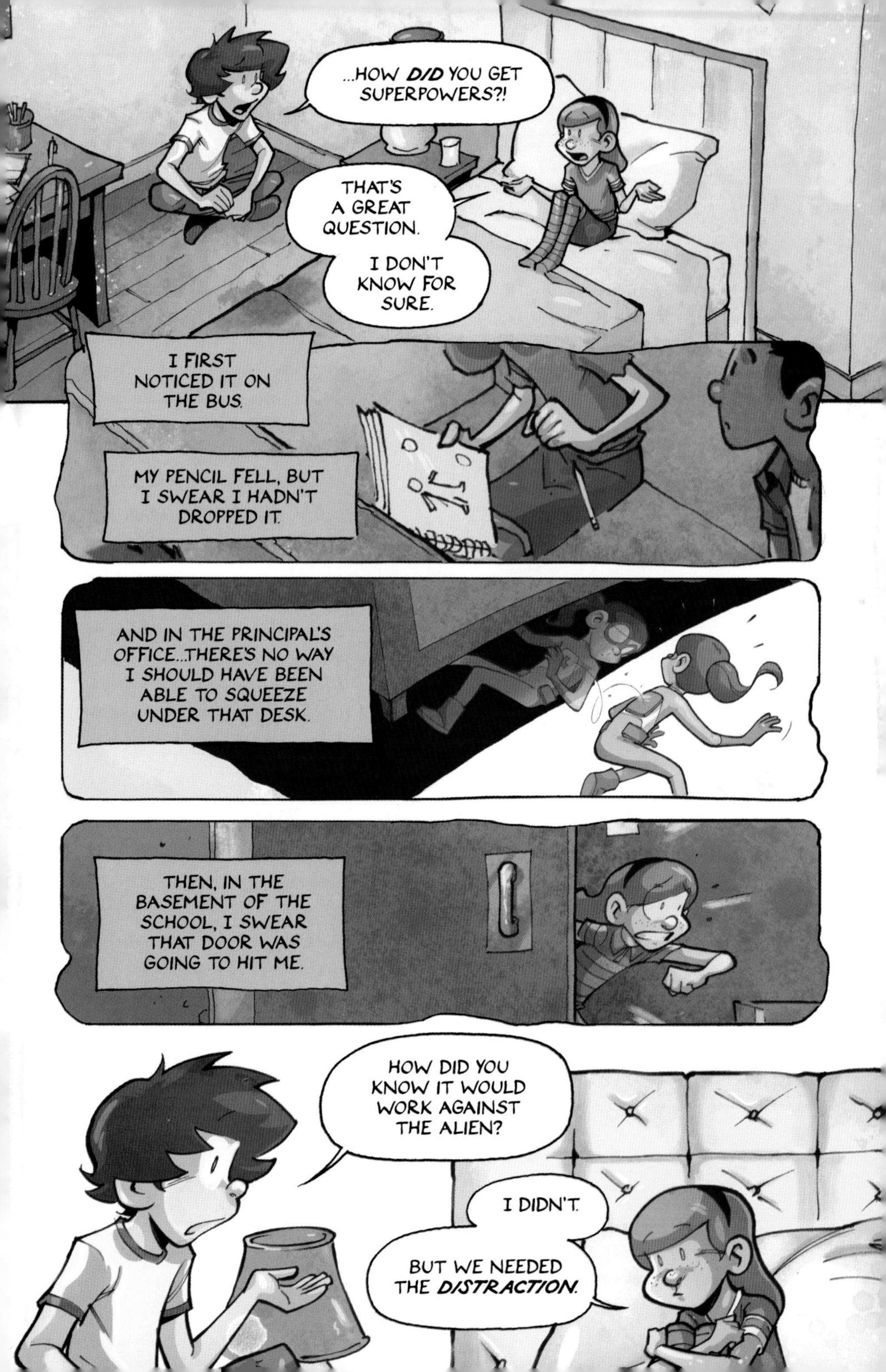
...HOW *DID* YOU GET SUPERPOWERS?!
THAT'S A GREAT QUESTION.
I DON'T KNOW FOR SURE.
I FIRST NOTICED IT ON THE BUS.
MY PENCIL FELL, BUT I SWEAR I HADN'T DROPPED IT.
AND IN THE PRINCIPAL'S OFFICE...THERE'S NO WAY I SHOULD HAVE BEEN ABLE TO SQUEEZE UNDER THAT DESK.
THEN, IN THE BASEMENT OF THE SCHOOL, I SWEAR THAT DOOR WAS GOING TO HIT ME.
HOW DID YOU KNOW IT WOULD WORK AGAINST THE ALIEN?
I DIDN'T.
BUT WE NEEDED THE *DISTRACTION*.

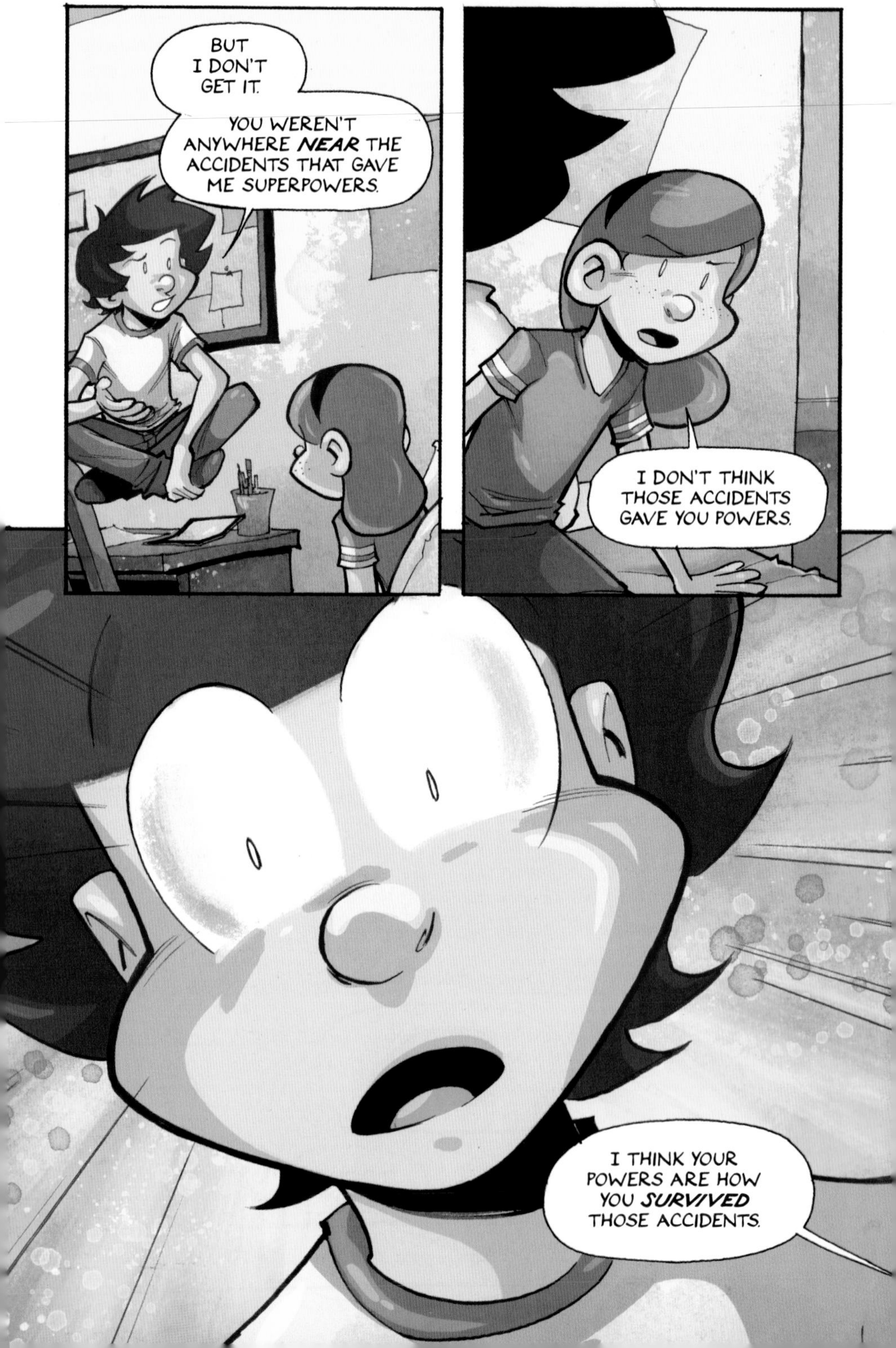
BUT I DON'T GET IT.
YOU WEREN'T ANYWHERE ***NEAR*** THE ACCIDENTS THAT GAVE ME SUPERPOWERS.
I DON'T THINK THOSE ACCIDENTS GAVE YOU POWERS.
I THINK YOUR POWERS ARE HOW YOU ***SURVIVED*** THOSE ACCIDENTS.

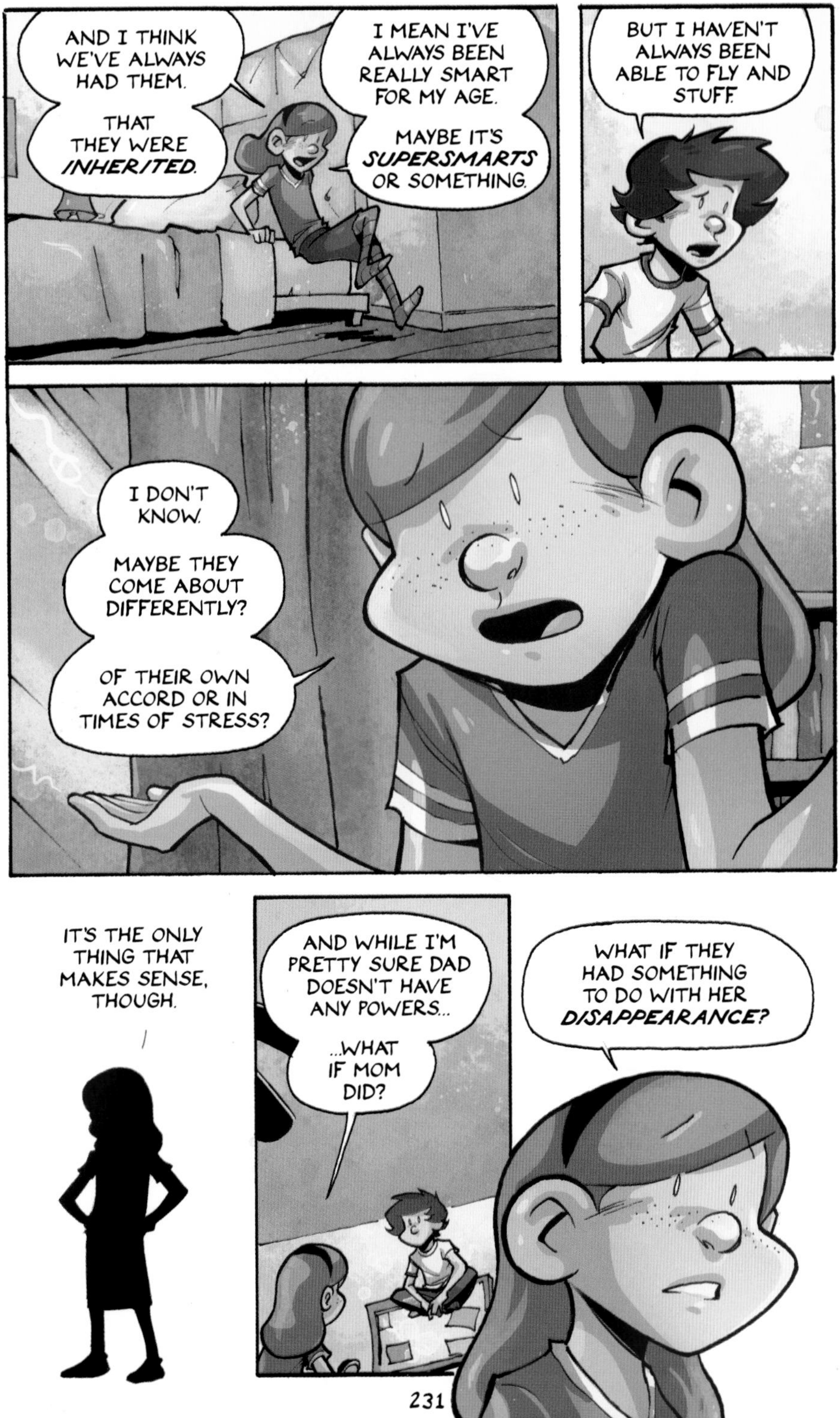
AND I THINK WE'VE ALWAYS HAD THEM.
THAT THEY WERE *INHERITED*.
I MEAN I'VE ALWAYS BEEN REALLY SMART FOR MY AGE.
MAYBE IT'S *SUPERSMARTS* OR SOMETHING.
BUT I HAVEN'T ALWAYS BEEN ABLE TO FLY AND STUFF.
I DON'T KNOW.
MAYBE THEY COME ABOUT DIFFERENTLY?
OF THEIR OWN ACCORD OR IN TIMES OF STRESS?
IT'S THE ONLY THING THAT MAKES SENSE, THOUGH.
AND WHILE I'M PRETTY SURE DAD DOESN'T HAVE ANY POWERS...
...WHAT IF MOM DID?
WHAT IF THEY HAD SOMETHING TO DO WITH HER *DISAPPEARANCE?*

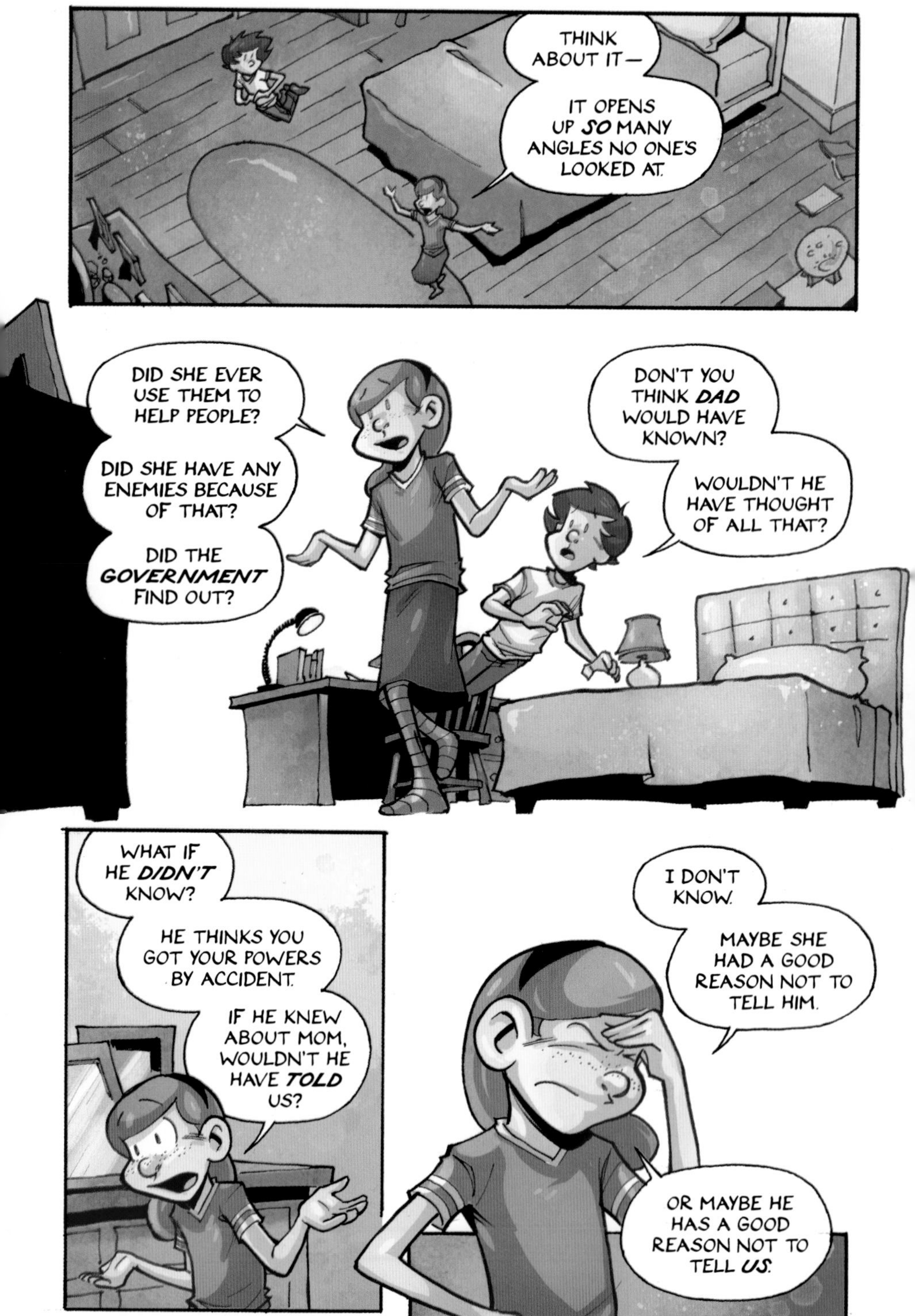
THINK ABOUT IT—
IT OPENS UP SO MANY ANGLES NO ONE'S LOOKED AT.
DID SHE EVER USE THEM TO HELP PEOPLE?
DID SHE HAVE ANY ENEMIES BECAUSE OF THAT?
DID THE GOVERNMENT FIND OUT?
DON'T YOU THINK DAD WOULD HAVE KNOWN?
WOULDN'T HE HAVE THOUGHT OF ALL THAT?
WHAT IF HE DIDN'T KNOW?
HE THINKS YOU GOT YOUR POWERS BY ACCIDENT.
IF HE KNEW ABOUT MOM, WOULDN'T HE HAVE TOLD US?
I DON'T KNOW.
MAYBE SHE HAD A GOOD REASON NOT TO TELL HIM.
OR MAYBE HE HAS A GOOD REASON NOT TO TELL US.

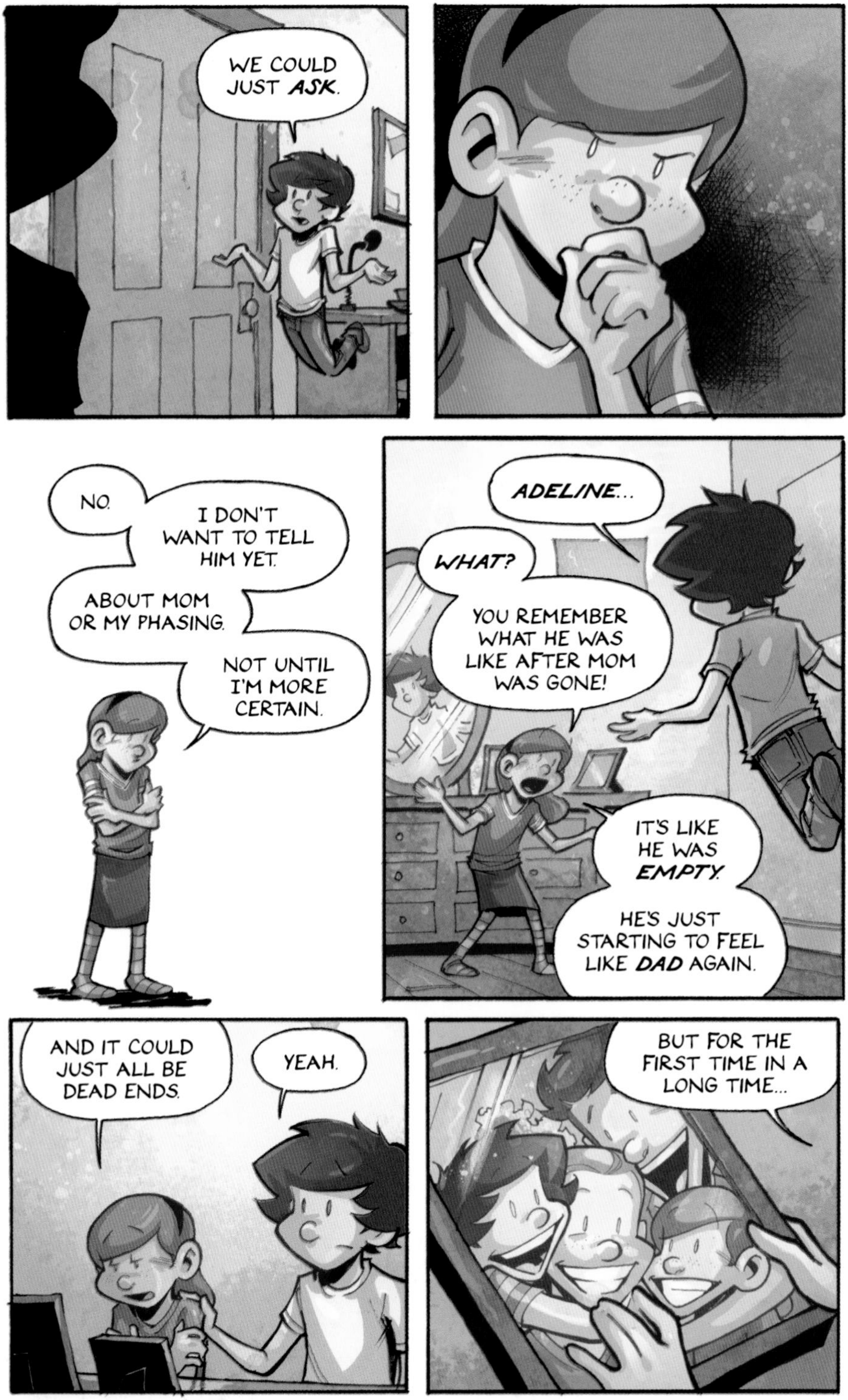
WE COULD JUST ASK.
NO.
I DON'T WANT TO TELL HIM YET.
ABOUT MOM OR MY PHASING.
NOT UNTIL I'M MORE CERTAIN.
ADELINE...
WHAT?
YOU REMEMBER WHAT HE WAS LIKE AFTER MOM WAS GONE!
IT'S LIKE HE WAS EMPTY.
HE'S JUST STARTING TO FEEL LIKE DAD AGAIN.
AND IT COULD JUST ALL BE DEAD ENDS.
YEAH.
BUT FOR THE FIRST TIME IN A LONG TIME...

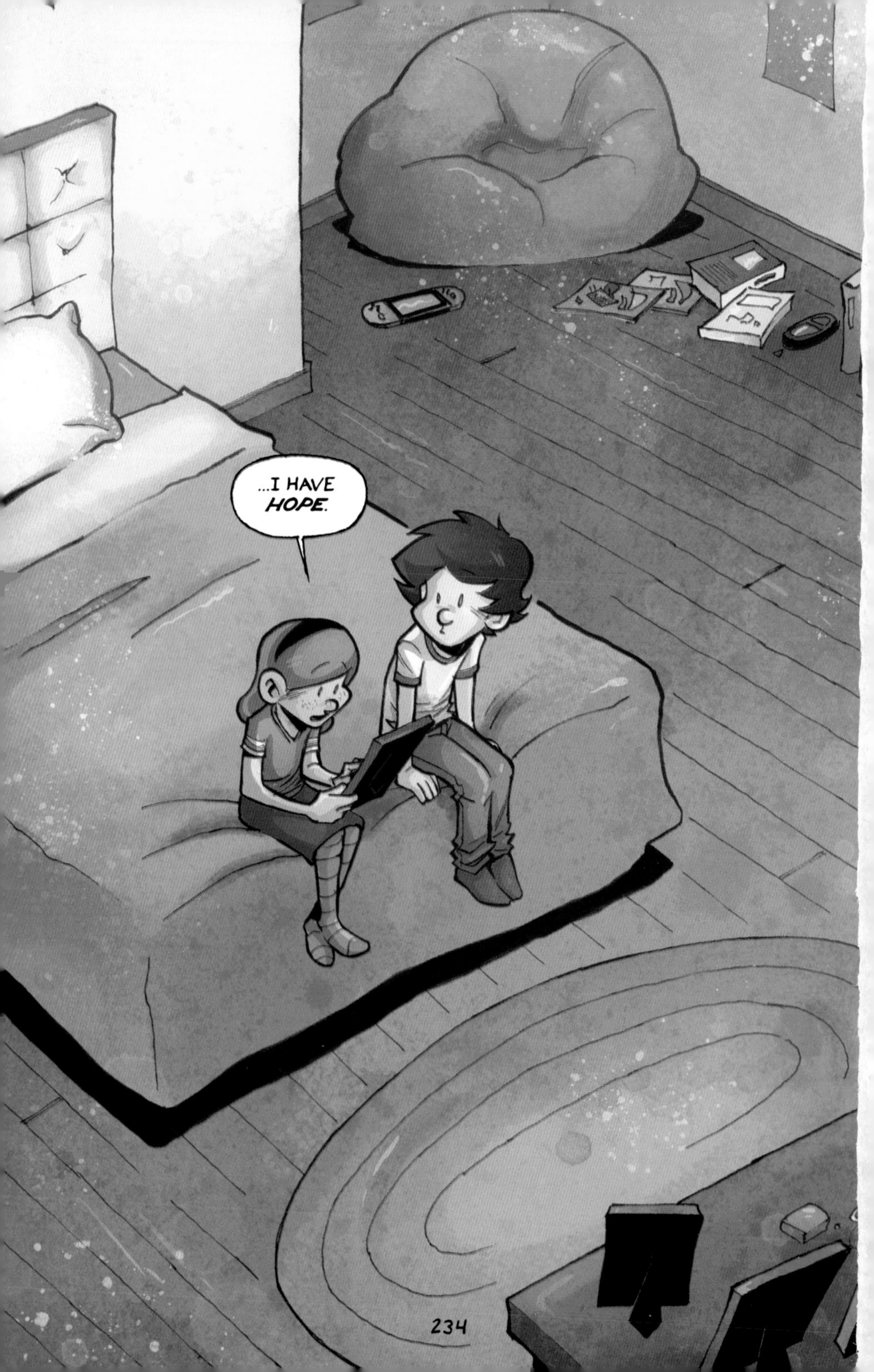
...I HAVE HOPE.